Two Classic Novels
by
Jude Deveraux

Twin of Ice
Twin of Fire

POCKET BOOKS

New York London Toronto Sydney Tokyo Singapore

This book is a work of fiction. Names, characters, places and incidents are products of the author's imagination or are used fictitiously. Any resemblance to actual events or locales or persons, living or dead, is entirely coincidental.

POCKET BOOKS, a division of Simon & Schuster Inc.
1230 Avenue of the Americas, New York, NY 10020

ISBN: 0-671-01689-X

First Pocket Books hardcover printing December 1997

10 9 8 7 6 5 4 3 2 1

POCKET and colophon are registered trademarks of
Simon & Schuster Inc.

Printed in the U.S.A.

Contents

Twin of Ice   1

Twin of Ice   1

Twin of Fire   295

Twin of Ice

❦

Prologue

The fat old woman, gray hair scraggling from beneath a battered hat, teeth blackened, was surprisingly agile as she hoisted herself onto the seat of the big wagon. Behind her lay a variety of fresh vegetables covered with a dampened canvas.

"Sadie."

She looked to her left to see Reverend Thomas, tall, handsome, his brow furrowed in concern.

"You'll be careful? You won't try anything foolish? Or call attention to yourself?"

"I promise," Sadie said in a soft, young-sounding voice. "I'll be back in no time." With that, she clucked to the horses and set off at a lumbering pace.

The road out of the town of Chandler, Colorado, and into the coal mine that was Sadie's domain was long and rutted. Once, she had to wait for a train to pass on one of the spur lines of the Colorado and Southern Railroad. Each of the seventeen coal camps outside Chandler had its own train line into the camp.

Outside the turnoff to the Fenton mine Sadie passed another huckster wagon with another old woman sitting on the seat. Sadie halted her four horses, scanning the landscape as far as she could see.

"Any trouble?" Sadie quietly asked the other old woman.

"None, but the union talk is stronger. You?"

Sadie gave a curt nod. "There was a rumble in tunnel number six last week. The men won't take the time to shore up as they dig. Do you have any peppermint?"

"Gave it all away. Sadie," the woman said, leaning closer, "be careful. The Little Pamela is the worst one. Rafe Taggert scares me."

"He scares a lot of people. Here comes another wagon." Her voice deepened as she hijahed to the horses. "See you next week, Aggie. Don't take no wooden nickels."

Sadie drove past the men on the approaching wagon and raised her hand in greeting. Moments later, she was turning down the long road into the Little Pamela mine camp.

The road was steep as she travelled up into the canyon and she didn't see the guard post until she was in front of it. In spite of herself, her heart began pounding.

"Mornin', Sadie. You got any turnips?"

"Big, fat ones." She grinned, showing her wrinkles and rotted teeth.

"Save me a sackful, will ya?" he said, as he unlocked the gate. There was no question of payment. Opening the gate to allow an outsider into the closed camp was payment enough.

The guards were posted there to make sure no union organizers got inside. If they suspected anyone of trying to organize the miners, the guards shot first and asked questions later. With that kind of power, all the guards had to do was say whomever they'd killed was a unionist and both the local and state courts freed them. The mine owners had a right to protect their property.

Sadie had to work to maneuver the big four-horse wagon through the narrow, coal-littered streets. On each side of her were frame boxes that the mine owners called houses, four or five tiny rooms, with a privy and coal shed out back. Water was drawn by buckets from a coal-infested community well.

Sadie moved the horses past the company store and coolly greeted the store owner. They were natural enemies. The miners were illegally paid in scrip so a family could purchase what it needed only from the company store. Some people said the mine owners made more money off the company store than they did from the coal.

To her right, between the railroad tracks and the steep mountainside, was Sunshine Row—a straggling line of double houses painted a ghastly yellow. There were no yards and only fifteen feet between houses and privies. Sadie knew too well the combination of train smoke and noise combined with the other smells. This was where the new mine workers lived.

Sadie halted her horses before one of the larger mine houses.

"Sadie! I thought you weren't coming," a pretty young woman said as she came out of the house, drying her wet hands and arms on a thin towel.

"You know me," Sadie said gruffly, as she laboriously dismounted. "I slept late this mornin' and my maid forgot to wake me. How you been, Jean?"

Jean Taggert gave a grin to the old woman. Sadie was one of the few outsiders allowed into the camp, and each week Jean was afraid the mine police would search her wagon.

"What did you bring?" Jean asked in a whisper.

"Cough medicine, liniment, a little morphine for Mrs. Carson, a dozen pairs of shoes. There's not much I can hide inside a head of cabbage. And lace curtains for Ezra's bride."

"Lace curtains!" Jean gasped, then laughed. "You're probably right. Lace will do more for her than anything else. Well, come on, let's get started."

It took Jean and Sadie three hours to distribute the vegetables, the townspeople paying Sadie in scrip—which Jean would later return to them in secret. The mine owners nor the camp police nor even most of the miners themselves had any idea that Sadie's vegetables and secret goods were free. The miners were proud and wouldn't have liked taking charity— but the women would take anything they could get for their children and their tired husbands.

It was late when Sadie and Jean returned with the empty wagon to Jean's house.

"How's Rafe?" Sadie asked.

"Working too hard, as is my father. And Uncle Rafe is stirring up trouble. You have to go. We can't risk your getting into trouble," she said, taking Sadie's hand. "Such a young hand."

"Trouble . . . ?" Sadie began, confused. She jerked away, making Jean laugh.

"Next week then. And Sadie, don't worry about me. I've known for a long time."

Confused into speechlessness, Sadie climbed into the wagon and clucked to the horses.

An hour later, she was parked at the back of the old rectory in Chandler. In the twilight evening, she ran through the unlocked door, down a short hall, and into the bathroom where clean clothes hung from a hook.

Quickly, she tore the wig from her head, washed the theatrical makeup from her face, scrubbed the black gum from her teeth. In another quick motion, she slipped out of the hot, padded clothes that made her look fat, and pulled on drawers and petticoats of fine lawn, a white linen corset that she laced in front, and stepped into a tailored skirt of blue serge edged with jet beads. A pale green silk blouse was covered with a jacket of blue serge trimmed with the new green looking glass velvet.

As she was fastening her dark blue leather belt, a knock sounded.

"Come in."

Reverend Thomas opened the door and stood for a moment gazing at the woman before him. Miss Houston Chandler was tall, slim and beautiful, with dark brown hair highlighted with red glints, wide-set blue-green eyes, a straight, aristocratic nose and a small, perfectly shaped mouth.

"So, Sadie has gone for another week." The reverend smiled. "Now, Houston, you must go. Your father—."

"Stepfather," she corrected.

"Yes, well, his anger is the same whatever his title."

"Did Anne and Tia make it back with their wagons?"

"Hours ago. Now get out of here."

"Yes, sir." She smiled. "See you next Wednesday," she called over her shoulder as she left by the front door of the rectory and began to walk briskly toward home.

Chapter 1

MAY 1892

Houston Chandler walked the block and a half to her house as sedately as she could manage, halting before a three-story, red brick French Victorian house that the town called the Chandler Mansion. Composing herself, smoothing her hair, she mounted the steps.

As she put her parasol in the porcelain holder in the little vestibule, she heard her stepfather bellowing at her sister.

"I'll not have language like that in my house. You may think that because you call yourself a doctor you have a right to indecent behavior, but not in my house," Duncan Gates shouted.

Blair Chandler, as like her twin sister as another person can be, glared at the man, who was a few inches shorter than she was and built as solidly as a stone building. "Since when is this *your* house? My father—."

Houston stepped into the family parlor and put herself between her sister and her stepfather. "Isn't it time for dinner? Perhaps we should go in." With her back to her stepfather, she gave a pleading look to her sister.

Blair turned away from them both, her anger obvious.

Duncan took Houston's arm and led her past the staircase

and toward the dining room. "At least I have one decent daughter."

Houston winced as she heard the often repeated remark. She hated being compared to Blair, and worse, hated being the winner.

They were barely seated at the big, mahogany table, each setting laid with crystal, porcelain and sterling, Duncan at the head, Opal Gates at the foot, the twins across from each other, when he started again.

"You'd think you'd want to do something to please your mother," Duncan said, glaring at Blair, as an eleven-pound roast was set before him. He picked up carving utensils. "Are you too selfish to care about anybody else? Doesn't your mother mean anything to you?"

Blair, her jaw clenched, looked at her mother. Opal was like a faded copy of her beautiful daughters. It was obvious that what spirit she'd ever had was either gone or deeply buried. "Mother," Blair said, "do you want me to return to Chandler, marry some fat banker, have a dozen children and give up medicine?"

Opal smiled fondly at her daughter as she took a small helping of eggplant from the platter held by a maid. "I want you to be happy, dear, and I believe it's rather noble of you to want to save people's lives."

Blair turned triumphant eyes toward her stepfather. "Houston's given up her life in order to please you. Isn't that enough for you? Do you have to see me broken too?"

"Houston!" Duncan thundered, clutching the big carving knife until his knuckles were white. "Are you going to allow your sister to say such things?"

Houston looked from her sister to her stepfather. Under no circumstances did she want to side with either one of them. When Blair returned to Pennsylvania after the wedding, Houston'd still be in the same town with her stepfather. With joy, she heard the downstairs maid announce Dr. Leander West-field.

Quickly, Houston stood. "Susan," she said to the serving maid, "set another place."

Leander walked into the room with long, confident strides.

He was tall, slim, dark, extremely good-looking—with green eyes to die for, as a friend of Houston's once said—and exuded an air of self-assurance that made women stop on the street and stare. He greeted Mr. and Mrs. Gates.

Leander leaned across the edge of the table and gave Houston a quick kiss on the cheek. Kissing a woman, even your wife, and certainly your fiancée, so publicly was outrageous, but Leander had an air about him that allowed him to get away with things other men couldn't.

"Will you have dinner with us?" Houston asked politely, indicating the place set next to her.

"I've eaten, but maybe I'll join you for a cup of coffee. Good evening, Blair," he said as he sat down across from her.

Blair only glanced at him in answer as she poked at the food on her plate.

"Blair, you'll speak to Leander properly," Duncan commanded.

"That's all right, Mr. Gates," Leander replied pleasantly, but looking at Blair in puzzlement. He smiled at Houston. "You're as pretty as a bride today."

"Bride!" Blair gasped, standing and nearly upsetting her chair before she ran from the room.

"Why, that—," Duncan began, putting down his fork and starting to rise.

But Houston stopped him. "Please don't. Something's upsetting her badly. Perhaps she misses her friends in Pennsylvania. Leander, didn't you want to talk to me about the wedding? Could we go now?"

"Of course." Leander silently escorted her to his waiting buggy, clucked to the horse and drove her up the steep end of Second Street and parked on one of the many dead ends in Chandler. It was beginning to get dark and the mountain air was growing cold. Houston moved back into the corner of the carriage.

"Now, tell me what's going on," he said as he tied the horse's reins, put on the brake, and turned to her. "It seems to me that you're as upset as Blair."

Houston had to blink back tears. It was so good to be alone with Lee. He was so familiar, so safe. He was an oasis of sanity in her life. "It's Mr. Gates. He's always antagonizing Blair, telling her she's no good, reminding her that even as a child he thought there was no hope for her, and he's always demanding that she give up medicine and remain in Chandler. And, Lee, he keeps telling Blair how perfect I am."

"Ah, sweetheart," Lee said, pulling her into his arms, "you *are* perfect. You're sweet and kind and pliable and—."

She pulled away from him. "Pliable! You mean like taffy?"

"No," Lee smiled at her, "I just meant that you're a pretty, sweet woman, and I think it's good of you to be so worried about your sister, but I also think Blair should have been prepared for some criticism when she became a doctor."

"*You* don't think she should give up medicine, do you?"

"I have no idea what your sister should do. She's not my responsibility." He reached for her again. "What are we talking about Blair for? We have our own lives to live."

As he spoke, his arms tightened around her and he began to nuzzle her ear.

This was the part of their courtship Houston always hated. Lee was so easy to be around, someone she knew so well. After all, they'd been a "couple" since she was six and he was twelve. Now, at twenty-two, she'd spent a great deal of time near Leander Westfield, had known forever that she was going to be Mrs. Westfield. All her schooling, everything she'd ever learned was in preparation for the day she'd be Lee's wife.

But a few months ago, after he'd returned from studying in Europe, he'd started this kissing, pushing her into the buggy seat, groping at her clothes, and all she'd felt was that she wished he'd stop fumbling at her. Then Lee'd get angry, once again call her an ice princess, and take her home.

Houston knew how she was supposed to react to Lee's touch. For all its appearance of staidness, Chandler, Colorado, was an enlightened town—at least its women were—but for the life of her Houston felt nothing when Lee touched her. She'd cried herself to sleep with worry many times. She couldn't imagine loving anyone more than she loved Leander, but she was just not excited by his touch.

He seemed to sense what Houston was thinking and drew away from her, his anger showing in his eyes.

"It's fewer than three weeks," she said with hope in her voice. "In a short time we'll be married and then . . ."

"And then what?" he said, looking at her sideways. "The ice princess melts?"

"I hope so," she whispered, mostly to herself. "No one hopes so more than I do."

They were silent for a moment.

"Are you ready for the governor's reception tomorrow?" Lee asked, pulling a long cheroot from his pocket and lighting it.

Houston gave him a trembling smile. These few minutes after she'd turned him down were always the worst. "My Worth gown's steamed and ready."

"The governor will love you, you know that?" He smiled at her, but she sensed he was forcing the smile. "Someday I'll have the most beautiful wife in the state at my side."

She tried to relax. A governor's reception was a place she felt confident. This was something she was trained for. Perhaps she should have taken a course in how not to be a cold, sexless wife. She knew that some men thought their wives shouldn't enjoy sex, but she also knew Leander was like no one else. He'd explained to her that he expected her to enjoy him and Houston'd told herself she would, but mostly she felt annoyed when Leander kissed her.

"I have to go to town tomorrow," he said, interrupting her thoughts. "Want to come along?"

"I'd love to. Oh! Blair wanted to stop by the newspaper office. I believe someone sent her a new medical journal from New York."

Houston leaned back in the carriage as Leander clucked to the horse and wondered what he'd say if he knew his "pliable" intended was, once a week, doing something that was quite illegal.

Blair lounged against the end of the ornate, canopied, walnut bed, one knee bent, showing the separation of her Turkish pants. Her big blue and white room was on the third floor, with a beautiful view of Ayers Peak out the west window. She'd had a room on the second floor with the rest of the family, but after she'd left Chandler when she was twelve,

Opal'd become pregnant and Mr. Gates had made her room into a bath and a nursery. Opal lost the child and the little room stood unused now, filled with dolls and toy soldiers Mr. Gates had bought.

"I really don't see why we have to go with Leander," Blair said to Houston who sat quite straight on a white brocade chair. "I haven't seen you in years and now I have to share you."

Houston gave her sister a little smile. "Leander asked us to accompany him, not the other way around. Sometimes I think you don't like him. But I can't see how that could be possible. He's kind, considerate, he has position in the community and he—."

"And he completely owns you!" Blair exploded, jumping up from the bed, startling Houston with the strength of her outburst. "Don't you realize that in school I worked with women like you, women who were so unhappy they repeatedly attempted suicide?"

"Suicide? Blair, I have no idea what you're talking about. I have no intention of killing myself." Houston couldn't help drawing away from her sister's vehemence.

"Houston," Blair said quietly, "I wish you could see how much you've changed. You used to laugh, but now you're so distant. I understand that you've had to adjust to Gates, but why would you choose to marry a man just like him?"

Houston stood, putting her hand on the walnut dresser and idly touching Blair's silver-backed hairbrush. "Leander isn't like Mr. Gates. He's really very different. Blair"—she looked at her sister in the big mirror—"I love Leander," she said softly. "I have for years, and all I've ever wanted to do is get married, have children and raise my family. I never wanted to do anything great or noble like you seem to want to do. Can't you see that I'm happy?"

"I wish I could believe you," Blair said sincerely. "But something keeps me from it. I guess I hate the way Leander treats you, as if you were already his. I see the two of you together and you're like a couple who've lived together for twenty years."

"We have been together a long time." Houston turned back

to face her sister. "What should I look for in a husband if it isn't compatibility?"

"It seems to me that the best marriages are between people who find each other interesting. You and Leander are too much alike. If he were a woman, he'd be a perfect lady."

"Like me," Houston whispered. "But I'm not *always* a lady. There are things I do—."

"Like Sadie?"

"How did you know about that?" Houston asked.

"Meredith told me. Now, what do you think your darling Leander is going to say when he finds out that you're putting yourself in danger every Wednesday? And how will it look for a surgeon of his stature to be married to a practicing criminal?"

"I'm not a criminal. I'm doing something that's good for the whole town," Houston said with fire, then quieted. She slipped another hairpin invisibly into the neat chignon at the back of her head. Carefully arranged curls framed her forehead beneath a hat decorated with a spray of iridescent blue feathers. "I don't know what Leander will say. Perhaps he won't find out."

"Hah! That pompous, spoiled man will forbid you to participate in anything dealing with the coal miners and, Houston, you're so used to obeying that you'll do exactly what he says."

"Perhaps I should give up being Sadie after I'm married," she said with a sigh.

Suddenly, Blair dropped to her knees on the carpet and took Houston's hands. "I'm worried about you. You're not the sister I grew up with. Gates and Westfield are eating away at your spirit. When we were children, you used to throw snowballs with the best of them but now it's as if you're afraid of the world. Even when you do something wonderful like drive a huckster wagon, you do it in secret. Oh, Houston—."

She broke off at a knock on the door. "Miss Houston, Dr. Leander is here."

"Yes, Susan, I'll be right down." Houston smoothed her skirt. "I'm sorry you find me so much to your distaste," she said primly, "but I *do* know my own mind. I want to marry

Leander because I love him." With that, she swept out of the room, and went downstairs.

Houston tried her best to push Blair's words from her mind but she couldn't. She greeted Leander absently and was vaguely aware of a quarrel going on between Lee and Blair, but she really heard nothing except her own thoughts.

Blair was her twin, they were closer than ordinary sisters and Blair's concern was genuine. Yet, how could Houston even think of not marrying Leander? When Leander was eight years old, he'd decided he was going to be a doctor, a surgeon who saved people's lives, and by the time Houston met him, when he was twelve, Lee was already studying textbooks borrowed from a distant cousin. Houston decided to find out how to be a doctor's wife.

Neither wavered from his decision. Lee went to Harvard to study medicine, then to Vienna for further study, and Houston went to finishing schools in Virginia and Switzerland.

Houston still winced whenever she thought of the argument she and Blair'd had about her choice of schools. "You're going to give up an education just so you can learn to set a table, so you can learn how to walk into a room wearing fifty yards of heavy satin and not fall on your face?"

Blair went to Vassar, then medical school, while Houston went to Miss Jones's School for Young Ladies where she was put through years of rigorous training in everything from how to arrange flowers to how to stop men from arguing at the dinner table.

Now, Lee took her arm as he helped her into the buggy. "You look as good as always," he said close to her ear.

"Lee," Houston said, "do you think we find each other . . . interesting?"

With a smile, his eyes raked down her body, over the dress that glued itself to her tightly corseted, exaggerated hourglass figure. "Houston, I find you fascinating."

"No, I mean, do we have enough to talk about?"

He raised one eyebrow. "It's a wonder I can remember how to talk when I'm around you," he answered as he helped her into his buggy, and drove them the six blocks into the heart of Chandler.

Chapter 2

Chandler, Colorado, was a small place, only eight thousand inhabitants, but its industries of coal, cattle, sheep, and Mr. Gates's brewery made it a rich little town. It already had a telephone system and electricity, and, with three train lines through town, it was easy to reach the larger cities of Colorado Springs and Denver.

The eleven blocks comprising downtown Chandler were covered with buildings that were almost all new and built of stone from the Chandler Stone Works. The greenish gray stone was often carved into intricate patterns for use as cornices for the Western Victorian style buildings.

Scattered outside the town were houses in varied styles of Queen Anne and High Victorian. At the north end of town, on a small rise, was Jacob Fenton's house, a large brick Victorian structure that until a few years ago had been Chandler's largest house.

At the west end of town, just a short distance from the Fenton house, on the flattened top of what most citizens had once considered part of the mountains, was Kane Taggert's house. Fenton's house would have fit into the wine cellar of the Taggert house.

"The whole town still trying to get inside the place?" Blair asked Houston as she nodded toward the house barely visible behind the trees. That "barely visible" part was large enough to be seen from almost anywhere in town.

"Everyone," Houston smiled. "But when Mr. Taggert ignored all invitations and extended none of his own, I'm afraid people began spreading awful rumors about him."

"I'm not so sure all the things people say about him are rumors," Leander said. "Jacob Fenton said—."

"Fenton!" Blair exploded. "Fenton is a conniving, thieving—."

Houston didn't bother to listen but leaned back in the carriage and gazed at the house through the window at the back of the buggy. Lee and Blair continued arguing while he halted the carriage to wait for one of the new horse-drawn trolley cars to pass.

She had no idea whether what was said about Mr. Taggert was true or not, but it was her own opinion that the house he'd built was the most beautiful thing she'd ever seen.

No one in Chandler knew much about Kane Taggert, but five years ago over a hundred construction workers had arrived from the East with an entire train loaded with materials. Within hours, they'd started what was soon to become the house.

Of course everyone was curious—actually, a good deal more than curious. Someone said that none of the construction workers ever had to pay for a meal because all the women of Chandler fed them in an attempt to get information. It didn't do any good. No one knew who was building the house or why anyone'd want such a place in Nowhere, Colorado.

It took three years to complete, a beautiful, white U-shaped building, two stories, with a red tile roof. The size of it was what boggled people's minds. One local store owner liked to say that every hotel in Chandler could be put on the first floor, and considering that Chandler was a crossroads between north and south Colorado, and the number of hotels in town, that was saying a great deal.

For a year after the house was completed, trainloads of wooden boxes were delivered to the house. They had labels on them from France, England, Spain, Portugal, all over the world.

Still, there was no sign of an owner.

Then one day, two men stepped off the train, both tall, big men, one blond and pleasant looking, the other dark, bearded, angry. They both wore the usual miner's garb of canvas pants, blue chambray shirt, and suspenders. As they walked down the street, women pulled their skirts aside.

The dark one went up to Jacob Fenton, and everyone

assumed he was going to ask for a job in one of the mines Fenton owned. But instead, he'd said, "Well, Fenton, I'm back. You like my house?"

It wasn't until he had walked through town and onto the land of the new house and then through its locked front door that anyone had had any idea he mean *that* house.

For the next six months, according to Duncan Gates, Chandler was the site of a full-fledged war. Widows, single women and mothers of young women made an all-out attack for the hand in marriage of the man they'd swept their skirts aside for. Dressmakers by the dozen came down from Denver.

Within a week, the women'd found out his name and Mr. Taggert was besieged. Some of the attempts to get his attention were quite ordinary; for instance, it was amazing how many women fainted when near him, but some attempts were ingenious. Everyone agreed that the prize went to Carrie Johnson, a pregnant widow who climbed down a rope and into Mr. Taggert's bedroom while she was having labor pains. She thought he'd deliver her baby and of course fall passionately in love with her and beg her to marry him. But Taggert was away at the moment, and all the assistance she got was from a passing laundress.

After six months, nearly every woman in town'd made a fool of herself with no success, so they began to talk sour grapes. Who wanted a rich man who didn't know how to dress properly? And his grammar was that of the lowest cowboy. They started asking questions about him. What had he meant when he'd said, "I'm *back*"?

Someone located an old servant of Jacob Fenton's who remembered that Kane Taggert had been the stable lad until he started dallying with Pamela Fenton, Jacob's young daughter. Jacob kicked him off his property—and rightly so.

This gave the town something new to talk about. Who did Taggert think he was, anyway? What right did he have to build that outlandish, garish house overlooking the peaceful, pretty little town of Chandler? And was he planning revenge on dear Jacob Fenton?

Once again, women started sweeping their skirts aside when he passed.

But Taggert never seemed to notice any of it. He stayed in his house most of the time, drove his old wagon into town once a week and bought groceries. Sometimes, men would arrive on the train and ask directions to his house, then leave town before sundown. Other than these men, the only people to enter or leave the big house were Taggert and the man he called Edan, who was always with him.

"That's Houston's dream house," Leander said when the trolley car had passed, bringing Houston back to the present. He'd finished—or stopped—his argument with Blair. "If Houston didn't have me, I think she'd have joined the line of women fighting for Taggert and that house of his."

"I *would* like to see the inside," she said with more wistfulness than she meant to reveal, then, to cover herself, she said, "You can drop me here, at Wilson's, Lee. I'll meet you at Farrell's in an hour."

Once out of the buggy, she realized she was glad to get away from their constant bickering.

Wilson's Mercantile was one of four large, all-purpose dry-goods stores in Chandler. Most people shopped at the newer, more modern store, The Famous, but Mr. Wilson had known Houston's father.

The walls were lined with tall, walnut, glass-doored cases, interspersed with marble-topped counters covered with goods.

Behind one counter sat Davey Wilson, Mr. Wilson's son, a ledger open before him, but his fountain pen was unmoving.

In fact, neither the three customers nor the four clerks seemed to be moving. Everything was unnaturally quiet. Instantly, Houston saw the reason why: Kane Taggert stood at one counter, his back to the few people in the store.

Silently, Houston went to a counter to look at a selection of patent medicines, which she had no intention of buying, but she sensed something was happening.

"Oh, Mamma," Mary Alice Pendergast wailed in her high voice, "I *couldn't* wear that, I'd look like a coal miner's bride. People would think I was a no-'count . . . servant, a scullery maid, who thought she was a big cheese. No, no, Mamma, I couldn't wear that."

Houston gritted her teeth. Those two women were baiting

Mr. Taggert. Since he'd turned all the women in town down, they seemed to think it was open season for their nasty games. She glanced toward him and, when she did, she saw his face in an advertising mirror behind the counter. There was so much hair surrounding his face that his features could barely be seen, but Houston could see his eyes. He most certainly was hearing Mary Alice's nasty little comments and, what's more, they were bothering him. There was a furrow between his eyes.

Mary Alice's father was a gentle rabbit of a man who never raised his voice. But Houston knew, from living with Mr. Gates, what an angered man could say and do. She didn't know Mr. Taggert, but she thought she saw anger in those dark eyes.

"Mary Alice," Houston said, "how do you feel today? You look a little pale."

Mary Alice looked up in surprise, as if she'd just seen Houston. "Why, Blair-Houston, I feel fine. Nothing's wrong with me."

Houston examined a bottle of liver activator. "I was just hoping you wouldn't faint—again," she said pointedly, her eyes boring into Mary Alice's. Mary Alice had fainted in front of Taggert twice when he'd first come to town.

"Why you—! How dare—!" Mary Alice sputtered.

"Come along, dear," her mother said, pushing her daughter toward the door. "We know who our friends are."

Houston felt quite annoyed with herself after Mary Alice and her mother had left. She'd have to apologize later. Impatiently, she tugged at her kid gloves, preparing to leave the store, when she again glanced toward Mr. Taggert and saw, in the mirror, that he was watching her.

He turned to face her. "You're Houston Chandler, ain't you?"

"I am," she said coolly. She had no intention of having a conversation with a man she didn't know. What in the world had made her take this stranger's side against someone she'd known all her life?

"How come that woman called you Blair? Ain't that your sister?"

From a few feet away, Davey Wilson gave a little snort. There were only the four clerks in the store now besides Houston and Kane, and each one was nailed to his place.

"My sister and I are identical twins and, since no one can tell us apart, the townspeople call us Blair-Houston. Now if you'll excuse me, sir." She turned to leave.

"You don't look like your sister. I seen her and you're prettier."

For a moment, Houston paused to gape at him. *No* one had *ever* been able to tell them apart. When her momentary shock was over, she again turned to leave.

But as her hand touched the doorknob, Taggert bounded across the room and grabbed her arm.

All her life, Houston had lived in a town filled with coal miners, cowboys and inhabitants of a part of town she wasn't supposed to know existed. Many women carried a good strong parasol which they found useful for cracking over men's heads. But Houston could give looks that could freeze a man.

She gave one to Mr. Taggert now.

He withdrew his hand from her arm but he stayed close to her, the size of him making her feel small.

"I wanted to ask you a question," he said, his voice low. "If you don't mind, that is," he added, with laughter in his voice.

She gave him a curt nod, but she wasn't going to encourage his speaking to her.

"I was wonderin' about somethin'. If you, bein' a lady an' all, was gonna make curtains for my house, you know, the white one on the hill, which one of these here materials would you pick?"

She didn't bother to look at the shelves of bolts of fabric to which he was pointing. "Sir," she said with some haughtiness in her voice, "if I had your house, I'd order the fabric specially woven in Lyons, France. Now, good day." As quickly as possible, she left the store to emerge under the striped awnings which covered the southern side of the street, her heels clicking on the wide boardwalk. The town was busy today and she nodded and spoke to several people.

As she turned the corner of Third and Lead, she opened her parasol against the brilliant mountain sun and started toward

Farrell's Hardware Store. She could see Lee's buggy parked in front.

Just past Freyer's Drugs, she began to relax and to muse on her encounter with the elusive Mr. Taggert.

She could hardly wait to tell her friends about the meeting, and how he'd asked if she knew which house was his. Perhaps she should have volunteered to measure his windows and order his curtains. That way she'd get to see the inside of his house.

She was smiling to herself when a hand suddenly caught her upper arm and roughly pulled her into the shadowy alleyway behind the Chandler Opera House. Before she could scream, a hand clamped down on her mouth, and she was pushed against the stone wall. With frightened eyes, she looked up at Kane Taggert.

"I ain't gonna hurt you. I just wanted to talk to you, and I could see you wasn't gonna say nothin' in front of them others. You ain't gonna scream?"

Houston shook her head, and he dropped his hand but he stayed close to her. She wanted to be calm, but she was breathing quite hard.

"You're prettier up close." He didn't move but glanced down over her snug green wool suit. "And you look like a lady."

"Mr. Taggert," she said with all the calmness she could muster, "I very much resent being pulled into an alley and held against a wall. If you have something to say to me, please do so."

He didn't move away from her but put one hand on the wall beside her head. There were little lines beside his eyes, his nose was small, and the lower lip visible under his mass of beard was full.

"How come you stood up for me in that store? How come you reminded that woman about when she fainted in front of me?"

"I . . ." Houston hesitated. "I guess I don't like anyone hurting another person. Mary Alice was embarrassed because she'd made a fool of herself in front of you and you hadn't noticed."

"I noticed all right," he said, and Houston saw that lower lip stretch into a smile. "Me and Edan laughed at all of 'em."

Houston stiffened. "That wasn't very polite of you. A gentleman should not laugh at a lady."

He gave a little snort into her face and Houston found herself thinking that he had especially sweet-smelling breath, and wondered what he looked like when he wasn't under so much hair.

"The way I figure it, all them women was carryin' on so because I'm rich. In other words, they was makin' whores of themselves, so they wasn't ladies, so I didn't have to act like no gentleman and pick 'em up."

Houston blinked at his vocabulary. No man had ever used such a word in front of her.

"How come you didn't try to get my attention? Ain't you wantin' my money?"

That snapped Houston out of her lethargy. She came to attention and realized she'd been almost lounging against the wall. "No, sir, I do *not* want your money. Now, I have places to go. Do not ever accost me like this again." With that she turned on her heel and, as she left him in the alley, she heard him chuckling behind her.

She realized she was angry when she crossed the wide, dusty street and narrowly missed being run down by a smelly wagon loaded with hides. No doubt Mr. Taggert thought her action this morning was another play for his money.

Lee said something to her as a greeting but she was too distracted to hear him.

"I beg your pardon," Houston said.

Lee took her elbow and escorted her to the carriage. "I said that you'd better get home now so you can start getting ready for the governor's reception tonight."

"Yes, of course," she said absently as he led her to his waiting buggy.

Houston was almost glad when Blair and Lee started arguing again because it gave her time to think about her encounter this morning. It sometimes seemed that all her life she'd been Miss Blair-Houston. Even when Blair was away, out of habit, the name stayed. Yet today someone'd told her she wasn't at all like her sister. Of course, surely, he was just bragging. He couldn't actually tell them apart.

As they were driving west, out of town, she found herself straightening her spine as she saw Mr. Taggert and Edan about to pass them in their dilapidated old wagon.

Kane pulled the horses to a halt and shouted, "Westfield!" at the same time.

Startled, Lee halted his horse.

"I wanted to say good mornin' to the ladies. Miss Blair," he said to Blair on the far side. "And Miss Houston," he said, his voice softening as he looked at her directly. "Mornin' to you," he said, then cracked a whip over the heads of his four horses to set them into motion.

"What in the world was that about?" Leander asked. "I didn't know you knew Taggert."

Before Houston could answer, Blair said, "*That* was the man who built that house? No wonder he doesn't ask anyone to it. He knows they'd turn him down. By the way, how could he tell us apart?"

"Our clothes," Houston answered too quickly. "I saw him in the mercantile store."

Blair and Leander continued talking, but Houston didn't hear a word that was said. She was thinking about her encounter that morning.

Chapter 3

The Chandler house was set on one-half acre of land, with a brick carriage house in back and a latticed grape arbor just off the deep porch that surrounded three sides of the house. Over the years, Opal'd turned the land into a jewel of a garden. Elm trees that she'd planted when the house was new were now mature and shaded the lush lawns and flowers from the moisture-stealing Colorado sun. There were narrow brick pathways, stone statues and birdbaths hidden in the orderly tangle of flowers. Between the house and coach house was a cutting garden, and Opal always kept every room in her house filled with fresh, lovely flowers.

"All right," Blair said as Houston bent over a rosebush in the garden at the northwest corner of their property. "I want to know what's going on."

"I have no idea what you're talking about."

"Kane Taggert."

Houston paused for a moment, her hand on a rose. "I saw him in Wilson's Mercantile and later he said good morning to us."

"You're not telling me everything."

Houston turned to her sister. "I probably shouldn't have involved myself, but Mr. Taggert looked as if he were getting angry and I wanted to prevent a quarrel. Unfortunately, it was at Mary Alice's expense." She told Blair about Miss Pendergast's nasty remarks.

"I don't like your getting mixed up with him."

"You sound like Leander."

"For once, he's right!"

Houston laughed. "Perhaps we should mark this day in the family Bible. Blair, after tonight I swear I'll never even mention Mr. Taggert's name."

"Tonight?"

Houston pulled a piece of paper from inside her sleeve. "Look at this," she said eagerly. "A messenger brought it. He's invited me to dinner at his house."

"So? You're supposed to go somewhere with Leander tonight, aren't you?"

Houston ignored the remark. "Blair, you don't seem to realize what a stir that house has caused in this town. *Everyone* has tried to get an invitation to see the inside of it. People have come from all over the state to see it, but no one has been invited in. Once, it was even put to Mr. Taggert that an English duke who was passing through should be allowed to stay in the house, but Mr. Taggert wouldn't even listen to the committee. And now *I've* been invited."

"But you have to go somewhere else. The governor will be there. Surely he's more important than the inside of any old house."

"You couldn't understand what it was like," Houston said with a faraway look in her eyes. "Year after year we watched the train unload its goods. Mr. Gates said the owner didn't build a spur line to the house site because he wanted everyone to see everything going all the way through town. There were crates of goods from all over the world. Oh, Blair, I know they must have been filled with furniture. And tapestries! Tapestries from Brussels."

"Houston, you cannot be in two places at once. You promised to go to the reception and you must go."

Idly, Houston toyed with a rose. "When we were children, we could be in two places at once."

It took Blair a minute to understand. "You want us to trade places?" she gasped. "You want *me* to spend an evening with Leander, pretending I like him, while you go see some lecherous man's house?"

"What do you know about Kane to call him lecherous?"

"Kane, is it? I thought you didn't know him?"

"Don't change the subject. Blair, please trade places with me. Just for one night. I'd go another night but I'm afraid Mr. Gates would forbid it, and I'm not sure Leander would want me to go either, and I'll never get another opportunity like this. Just one last fling before I get married."

"You make marriage sound like death. Besides, Leander would know I wasn't you in a minute."

"Not if you behaved yourself. You know that we're both good actresses. Look at how I pretend to be an old woman every Wednesday. All you have to do is be quiet and not start an argument with Lee, and refrain from talking about medicine and walk like a lady instead of looking like you're running to a fire."

Blair took a long time before she answered, but Houston could see she was weakening. "Please, please, Blair. I hardly ever ask you for anything."

"Except to spend months in the house of our stepfather whom you know I detest. To spend weeks in the company of that self-congratulating man I think you intend to marry. To—."

"Oh, Blair, please," Houston whispered. "I really do want to see his house."

"It's just his house you're interested in, not Taggert?"

Houston knew she'd won. Blair was trying to act reluctant, but for some reason of her own, she was going to agree. She hoped Blair wouldn't try to get Lee to take her to the Infirmary.

"For Heaven's sake!" Houston said, "I've been to hundreds of dinner parties and I haven't yet been swept off my feet by the host. Besides, there'll be other people there." At least, she hoped there would be. She didn't want to be held against a wall again.

Blair suddenly smiled. "After the wedding, would you mind if I told Leander he spent an evening with me? Just to see the look on his face would be worth everything."

"Of course you may. Lee has a very good sense of humor, and I'm sure he'll enjoy the joke."

"I somehow doubt that, but at least I'll enjoy it."

Houston threw her arms about her sister. "Let's go get ready. I want to wear something befitting that house, and you'll get to wear the blue satin Worth gown," she said enticingly.

"I should wear my knickerbockers, but that would give it away, wouldn't it?" Blair said as she followed her sister into the house, a light dancing in her eyes.

What followed was an orgy of indecision. Houston went through her entire extensive trousseau that had been made for her wedding, in an attempt to find just the right dress.

At last she settled on a gown of mauve and silver brocade, the low square neck and hem edged with ermine, the short, puffed sleeves made of mauve chiffon. She would hide the dress in a leather valise—Blair was always carrying bags full of oddly-shaped medical instruments—and change at Tia's.

She didn't want to use the telephone for fear someone'd hear her, so she paid a penny to one of the Randolph boys to deliver a message to her friend Tia Mankin, whose house was near the foot of Kane's drive, that asked her to say Blair was there, should anyone ask.

Blair started complaining again, acting as if Houston were sending her on an impossible quest. And she wailed for twenty minutes about the tightness of the corset that forced her waist small enough to wear the Worth gown. But when Blair looked in the mirror, Houston saw the sparkle in her eyes and knew she was pleased with how she looked.

The few minutes they spent in the parlor with their mother and Mr. Gates were a joy to Houston. Blair's comfortable clothes made her feel quite the tomboy, and she antagonized Mr. Gates to no end.

And when Leander came, she enjoyed baiting him too. Lee's reserved coolness, the way nothing she said to him penetrated his superior attitude, began to make her angry and, by the time they reached Tia's, she was glad to get away from both Lee and Blair.

She met Tia in the dense shadow of a cottonwood tree and followed her up the back stairs to her room.

"Blair," Tia whispered, as she helped Houston to dress, "I had no idea you knew our mysterious Mr. Taggert. I wish I could go with you tonight, and I bet Houston wanted to go too. She loves that house. Did she ever tell you about the time she . . . ? Maybe I'd better not tell."

"Maybe you shouldn't," Houston said. "Now, I must go. Wish me luck."

"Tell me about it tomorrow. I want to hear about every stick of furniture, every floor, every ceiling," Tia said, following her friend down the stairs.

"I will," Houston called as she ran up the drive leading to the Taggert house. She hated arriving without a carriage, on foot, like a runaway or a beggar, but she couldn't risk being denied this opportunity.

The circular drive led to the front of the house, tall white wings radiating out like arms on each side of her. Around the roof was a railing and she wondered if there were terraces above.

The front door was white, with two long glass panels in it, and as she peered inside and smoothed her dress, she tried to calm her pounding heart and knocked. Within minutes, she heard heavy footsteps echoing through the house.

Kane Taggert, still wearing his coarse clothing, grinned as he opened the door for her.

"I hope I'm not early," Houston said, keeping her eyes on his face and forcing herself not to gawk at her surroundings.

"Just in time. Supper's ready." He stepped back and Houston had her first look at the interior of the house.

Directly in front of her, sweeping from both sides, was a magnificent double staircase, a black iron, brass-railed bannister gracefully curving along it. Supporting it, white columns topped with intricately carved headers rose to the high, panelled ceiling. It was a study in white and gold, with the soft electric lights drenching everything in their golden haze.

"You like it?" Kane asked and was obviously laughing at her expression.

Houston recovered herself enough to close her gaping mouth. "It's the most beautiful thing I've ever seen," she managed to whisper.

Kane puffed up his big chest in pride. "You wanta look around some or eat?"

"Look," she said, even as her eyes tried to devour every corner of the hall and stairwell.

"Come on, then," Kane said, setting off quickly.

"This little room is my office," he said, throwing open the door to a room as large as the downstairs of the Chandler house. It was beautifully panelled in walnut, a marble fireplace along one wall. But in the center of the room was a cheap oak desk, two old kitchen chairs beside it. Papers littered the top of the desk, fell onto the parqueted floor.

"And this is the library."

He didn't give her time to look longer but led her to a vast, empty room, with golden colored panelled walls inset with empty bookcases. Three large bare areas of plastered wall interrupted the panelling.

"Some rugs go there but I ain't hung 'em up yet," he said as he left the room.

"And this is what's called the large drawing room."

Houston only had time to look into a large white room, completely empty of furniture, before he showed her a small drawing room, a dining room painted the palest green, then led the way down a hallway to the service area.

"This is the kitchen," he said unnecessarily. "Have a seat." He nodded toward a big oak table and chairs that must have come from the same place as the desk in his office.

As she took a seat, she saw that there was grease on the table edge. "Your table and desk seem to match," she said cautiously.

"Yeah, I ordered 'em all from Sears, Roebuck," he said as he filled bowls from a huge pot on the cast-iron stove. "I got some more stuff upstairs. Real pretty, too. One of the chairs is red velvet with yellow tassels on it."

"It sounds like an interesting piece."

He put before her a bowl of stew with enormous pieces of meat swimming in grease, and sat down. "Eat it before it gets cold."

Houston picked up her big spoon and toyed with the stew. "Mr. Taggert, who designed your house?"

"A man back East, why? You like it, don't you?"

"Very much. I was just curious, though."

" 'Bout what?" he asked, mouth full of stew.

"Why it's so bare. Why is there no furniture in the rooms? We, the people of Chandler that is, saw crates delivered after the house was finished. We all assumed they contained furniture."

He was watching her as she moved the meat around in her bowl. "I bought lots of furniture, and rugs, and statues. Actually, I paid a couple of men to buy it for me and it's all in the attics now."

"Stored? But why? Your house is so lovely, yet you live here, I believe, alone, with only one employee, and not even a chair to sit on. Except what you bought from Sears, Roebuck, of course."

"Well, little lady, that's why I invited you here. You gonna eat that?" He took her bowl away and began to eat the stew himself.

Houston had her elbows on the table, leaning forward in fascination. "Why did you invite me, Mr. Taggert?"

"I guess you know that I'm rich, real rich, and I'm good at

makin' money—after the first five million the rest is easy—but the truth is, I don't know how to spend money."

"Don't know how . . . ?" Houston murmured.

"Oh, I can make an order from Sears all right but when it comes to spendin' millions, I have to hire other people. The way I got this house was I asked some man's wife who I should get to build me a house. She gave me a man's name, I called him to my office and told him I wanted somethin' that'd be beautiful and he built me this place. He hired those two men I told you about to buy furniture for it. I ain't even seen what they bought."

"Why didn't you have the men arrange the furniture?"

"Because my wife might not like what they did and she'd want it rearranged, and I didn't see no reason to do it twice."

Houston leaned back in her chair. "I didn't know you were married."

"I ain't, yet. But I got her all picked out."

"Congratulations."

Kane smiled at her through his beard. "I can't have just any woman in this house. She has to be a real, true, deep-down lady. Somebody once told me that a *real* lady was a leader, that she'd fight for causes and stand up for the underdog and still keep her hat on straight. And a real lady could freeze a man with a look. That's what you done today, Houston."

"I beg your pardon."

He pushed the second empty bowl out of the way and leaned toward her. "When I first come back to this town, all them women made fools of themselves over me, and when I ignored 'em they started actin' like the bitches they was. The men all stood back and laughed, or some of 'em got mad, but they never said nothin' to me. And not one of 'em was ever just plain nice to me. Except you."

"Surely, Mr. Taggert, other women—."

"None of 'em defended me like you done today, and the way you looked at me when I touched you! Near froze me to death."

"Mr. Taggert, I believe I should go." She didn't like the turn this conversation was taking. She was alone with this huge, half-civilized man; no one even knew where she was.

"You can't leave yet. I got somethin' to say."

"Perhaps you could send me a letter. I really must go."

"Come outside with me. I got lots of plants outside," he said in a little-boy pleading way.

She hoped she wouldn't regret this, but then maybe his "lots of plants" was a garden.

It was a garden: acres of fragrant, flowering shrubs and perennials, roses and trees.

"It's as beautiful as the house," she said, wishing she could explore the pathways she saw outlined in the moonlight. "What else did you have to say to me, Mr. Taggert? I really must leave soon."

"You know, I used to see you when you was a little girl. You used to play with Marc Fenton. Course you never noticed me. I was just the stable boy," he said tightly, then relaxed. "I always wondered what you'd turn out like, what with bein' a Chandler and playin' with the Fentons, but you turned out real good."

"Thank you." She was puzzled by this talk and wondered where it was leading.

"What I got to say is that I'm thirty-four years old, I got more money 'n I know what to do with, I got a big empty house and an attic full of furniture that needs movin' downstairs, and I wish somebody'd hire me a cook so me and Edan don't have to eat our own food. What I need, Miss Houston Chandler, is a wife and I decided I want you." He said the last triumphantly.

It took Houston a moment before she could speak. "Me?" she whispered.

"Yes, you. I think it's fittin' that a Chandler should live in this, the biggest house Chandler, Colorado, will ever see and, too, I had somebody do a search on you. You been to some real fine schools and you know how to buy things. And you know how to give parties, like the ones Jay Gould's wife used to give. I'll even buy you some real gold plates if you want 'em."

Houston was recovering herself, and the first thing she did was turn on her heel and start walking.

"Wait a minute," he said, walking beside her. "What about a date for the weddin'?"

She stopped and glared at him. "Mr. Taggert, let me make

myself perfectly clear. First of all, I am already engaged to be married. Second, even if I weren't engaged, I know nothing about you. No, I will *not* marry you, even if you ask me properly instead of making a lordly decree." She turned away again.

"Is that what you want? Courtin'? I'll send you roses every day until the weddin'."

She stopped again, took a deep breath, and faced him. "I do *not* want you to court me. In fact, I'm not sure I ever want to see you again. I came to see your house and I thank you for showing me. Now, Mr. Taggert, I want to go home, and if you want a wife perhaps you should look at one of the many unattached women in this town. I'm sure you can find another so-called true, deep-down lady." With that, Houston turned, and if she didn't quite run toward the front of the house, she certainly didn't collect any dust.

"Damn!" Kane said when she was gone, and he made his way upstairs.

Edan stood in the upstairs hallway. "Well?"

"She told me no," Kane said in disgust. "She wants that penniless Westfield. And don't you say nothin' about I-told-you-so. I ain't done yet. Before I'm through, I'm gonna have 'Lady' Chandler as my wife. I'm hungry. Let's go find somethin' to eat."

Chapter 4

Houston crept quietly into the Chandler house, making sure the stairs didn't creak as she tiptoed up them. Mr. Gates trusted Leander completely and Houston was quite unsupervised when she went out with him.

As she slipped into her room, she smiled at her mother,

whose frowning face was peeping through her bedroom door. Once inside, the door closed, Houston smiled as she realized that her mother was probably frowning because Houston was supposed to be Blair yet she'd just entered Houston's room. No doubt her mother'd guessed their game and not liked it.

With a shrug, Houston dismissed her mother's disapproval. Opal Gates loved her daughters, indulged them, and wouldn't question what they'd done, or betray them to Mr. Gates.

As Houston began to undress, she thought of her evening. That beautiful house, so empty, so uncared for. And the owner had offered it to her! Of course, he was part of the package, but then every worthwhile gift had some strings attached.

Sitting down at her dressing table, wearing her corset and drawers, she absently applied cold cream to her face. No man had ever treated her as Kane Taggert had tonight. All her life she'd lived in this little town, and everyone knew she was the last of the founding family. She'd grown up being aware that she was some sort of possession to be acquired, as in "no party is complete without one of the Chandlers." When the prominent, rich Westfields came here from the East when Houston was a child, it seemed to be taken for granted that a Chandler and a Westfield would marry.

And Houston always did as she was told. Blair stood up to people but Houston never did. Over the years Houston had learned to do exactly what was expected of her. Everyone around her thought she should marry Leander Westfield so she set out to do so. Since she was a Chandler, she was expected to be a lady, so she was one.

Dressing like a fat old woman and going into the coal camps was the only unladylike thing she'd ever done, and that was in secret.

Looking into the mirror, she saw fear enter her face as she thought of what Leander would have to say if he found out about Sadie. Leander liked things his own way. He knew exactly what he wanted in a wife: one without surprises.

Standing, she began to unfasten her corset. Tonight had been an adventure, a one-time happening before she gave up all adventures and became Mrs. Leander Westfield.

Taking a few deep breaths once her corset was off, she allowed an irreverent thought to flash through her mind: what would a man like Kane Taggert do if he found out his wife was the driver of a huckster wagon every Wednesday?

"Well, honey," Houston said aloud, deepening her voice, "just make sure you keep your hat on straight. Real ladies do, you know."

Trying to cover her laughter, Houston fell back onto her bed. Wouldn't all of Chandler be surprised, she thought, if she decided to accept Mr. Taggert's offer?

She sat upright. What in the *world* would he wear to the wedding? Perhaps a red suit with gold tassels on it?

Still laughing to herself, she finished undressing and put on her nightgown. It had been quite nice to receive another marriage proposal, to find out that at least not everyone took it for granted that she was Leander's personal property. Everyone, including Houston, knew what her future was going to be. She and Lee had been together so long that she knew what he ate for breakfast, how he liked his shirts done.

The only unknown question was the wedding night. Well, perhaps after that one night Leander wouldn't expect her to do it again for a long time. It wasn't that she didn't like men, especially after what happened the night before her friend Ellie got married, but sometimes touching Leander seemed, well . . . incestuous. She loved Leander, knew she'd have no difficulty living with him, but the thought of lying with him . . .

She climbed into bed, pulled a quilt over her and prepared for sleep. I wonder how Blair did with Leander, she thought briefly. No doubt he'll be in a bad mood tomorrow because, of course, he and Blair must have had a quarrel. They couldn't possibly spend hours together and not be at each other's throats.

With a sigh, she drifted into sleep. Today had been an adventure; tomorrow she would be back to her humdrum everyday existence.

Houston had to ward off Leander's advances as he helped her into his carriage, and again she thought how oddly

everyone was behaving. All morning Blair had been evading
her, and she looked as if she'd been crying. Houston hoped
Blair and Lee hadn't had a serious argument last night, and
that Lee hadn't found out they'd traded places. Houston had
tried to talk to Blair about last night, but Blair had just looked
at her as if her life were over and run from the room.

At eleven, Lee had arrived to take her on a picnic, a pleasant
surprise, and Houston had heard Blair shouting at him on the
front porch. To further confuse her, Lee had been quite
forward with her physically in the middle of the street and
Houston had thought she was going to have to slap his
wayward hands.

Now, feeling as if she'd walked into the middle of a play and
understood nothing about what was going on, she sat beside
Lee in the buggy. He just drove, saying nothing, but he was
smiling. Houston began to relax. Nothing too bad could have
happened last night if he was smiling.

He drove her to a place of big rocks and tall trees that she'd
never seen before, miles out of town, secluded and enclosed.

He had barely helped her out of the carriage, in such a hurry
that she nearly fell, when he grabbed her in a smothering
embrace. She was fighting so hard to breathe that at first she
didn't hear him.

"I thought about nothing else but you last night," he said. "I
could smell your hair on my clothes, I could taste your lips on
mine, I could—."

Houston managed to pull away from him. "You what?" she
gasped.

He began disarranging her hair and looking at her strangely.
"You aren't going to be shy with me today, are you? You aren't
going to be the way you were before last night, are you?"

While he was talking, Houston was thinking, but she didn't
believe what she thought could be the only answer to his
bizarre words. Blair couldn't have . . . Couldn't have made
herself available to Lee? Could she? Impossible.

"Houston, you've proven to me that you can be different, so
there's no need to go back to being the ice princess. I know
what you're really like now, and I can tell you that if I never

see that cool woman again, I'll be even happier. Now come here and kiss me like you did last night."

Houston suddenly realized what else he was saying besides telling her how wonderful Blair was. He'd not only enjoyed Blair last night, but he never wanted the cool woman he was engaged to to return. She pushed free of him. "Are you saying that I wasn't like I usually am last night? That I was . . . better?"

He smiled in an idiotic way and continued raving about how wonderful Blair was.

"You know you were. You were like I've never seen you. I didn't know you could be like that. You'll laugh at this but I was beginning to believe that you were incapable of any real passion, that beneath your cool exterior was a heart of ice. But, if you can have a sister like Blair who starts fires at the least provocation, surely some of it had to rub off."

He grabbed her again before she could say a word and gave her an unpleasant, lip-grinding kiss, and when Houston managed to escape, she saw that he was angry.

"You're carrying this game too far," he said. "You can't be wildly passionate one minute and frigid the next. What are you, two people?"

Houston wanted to scream at him that he was lusting after the wrong sister, that he was engaged to the cold, frigid one and not the fiery one he seemed to prefer.

It was as if Lee read her thoughts, because his face changed.

"That's an impossibility, isn't it, Houston?" he said. "Tell me that what I'm thinking is wrong. No one can be two people, can she?"

Houston knew that what had been a simple game was becoming serious now. How could Blair have done this to her?

Lee walked away and sat down heavily on a rock. "Did you and your sister trade places last night?" he asked softly. "Did I spend the evening with Blair and not with you?"

Somehow, she managed to whisper, "Yes."

"I should have known from the first: how well she handled that suicide and she didn't even know it was the house I'd bought for her—you. I don't think I wanted to see. From the moment she said she wanted to go on the case with me to see if she could be of any help, I was so stupidly pleased that I never questioned anything after that. I should have known when I kissed her . . .

"Damn both of you! I hope to hell you enjoyed making a fool of me."

"Lee," Houston said, her hand on his arm. She didn't know what she could say to him, but she wanted to try.

The face he turned to her was frightening. "If you know what's good for you, you won't say a word. I don't know what possessed either of you to play such a dirty little trick, but I can tell you that I don't like being the butt of such a joke. Now that you and your sister have had a good laugh at my expense, I have to decide what to do about last night."

Leander took her home and nearly shoved her from the carriage before driving away.

Blair was standing on the porch.

"We need to talk," Houston said to her sister, but Blair only nodded, following her sister mutely into the little rose garden, away from the house.

"How could you do this to me?" Houston began. "What kind of morals do you have that you can go out with a man once and sleep with him? Or am I assuming too much? You did sleep with him?"

Mutely, Blair nodded.

"After one evening?" Houston was incredulous.

"But I was *you!*" Blair said. "I was engaged to him. I assumed you always . . . After he kissed me like that, I thought for sure that the two of you . . ."

"We what?" Houston gasped. "You mean you thought we repeatedly . . . made love? Do you think I would have asked you to trade places if that had been true?"

Blair hid her face in her hands. "I didn't think. I couldn't think. After the reception, he took me to his house, and—."

"*Our* house," Houston said. "The one I've spent months decorating, preparing for *my* marriage."

"There were candles and caviar and roast duck and cham-pagne, lots of champagne. He kissed me and I kept drinking champagne and there were the candles and his eyes and I couldn't stop myself. Oh, Houston, I'm sorry. I'll leave Chandler. You'll never have to see me again. Leander will forgive us after a while.''

"No doubt he kissed you and you saw red,'' she said in a voice heavy with sarcasm.

"With little gold and silver sparks." Blair was quite serious.

Houston was gaping at her sister. What in the world was she talking about? Champagne and candles? Had Lee tried to seduce his fiancée? Had he planned something that had backfired so that he'd spent the night with the wrong sister?

Or *was* Blair the wrong sister?

"What was his kiss like?" Houston asked softly.

Blair looked shocked. "Don't torture me. I'll try to make it up to you, Houston, I swear I will, no matter what I have to do. I'll—.''

"What was his kiss like?" she asked louder.

Blair sniffed and her sister handed her a handkerchief. "You know what they're like. I don't need to describe them.''

"I don't think I *do* know.''

Blair hiccupped. "It was . . . It was wonderful. I never thought a man as cool as Lee could have so much fire. When he touched me . . ." She looked up at her sister. "Houston, I'll go to Lee and explain that it was all my fault, that it was my idea to trade places and that you were entirely innocent. I don't see why anyone but the three of us should ever know what happened. We'll sit down together and talk and he'll understand what happened.''

Houston leaned forward. "Will he? How will you explain that I wanted to spend the evening with another man? Will you tell Lee that his mere touch enflamed you so that you couldn't control yourself? That will certainly be a contrast to the frigid Miss Houston Chandler.''

"You're not frigid!''

Houston was silent for a moment. "All Lee could talk about was how magnificent you were last night. He's not going to like someone inexperienced after you . . .''

Blair's head came up. "I'd never made love to anyone before. Lee was the first.''

Houston wasn't sure whether to laugh or be overcome with admiration. She was scared to death of her wedding night, and she was sure there wasn't enough champagne in the world to make her react as Blair had done. Lee's kisses had never made her forget anything.

"Houston, do you hate me?" Blair asked softly.

She considered this. It was odd, but she wasn't even jealous. Her main thought was that now Lee was going to want the same thing from her, and how could she live up to what Blair had done? Maybe Blair had learned how in medical school but at Miss Jones's School for Young Ladies in Virginia, they taught that a woman's place was in the parlor, and no mention was made of what went on in the bedroom.

"You're looking at me strangely."

It was on the tip of Houston's tongue to ask Blair for details of last night but she couldn't. "I'm not angry. I just need time to adjust," she said. "You're not in love with Lee, are you?"

Blair looked up in horror. "No! Never! That's the last thing I am. Did . . . did he say much about me today?"

Houston ground her teeth together, remembering how he had said Houston was usually so frigid, but last night . . . "Let's forget this if we can. I'll talk to Lee when he's over his anger and we'll keep it between the three of us. This may make things awkward for a while, but I'm sure we can work out a satisfactory solution. Let's not allow something like this to come between us. Our sisterhood is more important than this."

"Thank you," Blair said, impulsively hugging her sister. "No one ever had a sister like you. I love you."

Blair seemed to feel better, but Houston had some nagging doubts which she told herself were absurd. She loved Lee, had always loved him, had planned to marry him since she was a child. This one little thing, this one night with the wrong sister wouldn't change anything, would it?

"Of course not," she said aloud, smoothed her skirt and went toward the house. One night wasn't going to erase years together.

Chapter 5

At four o'clock, Houston, Blair and their mother were sitting in the parlor, Blair reading her medical journal, the other two women sewing, when the front door was opened, followed by a jamb-jarring slam.

"Where is she?" Duncan Gates bellowed, making the chandelier above their heads rattle. "Where is that immoral harlot? Where is the Jezebel?"

Mr. Gates burst into the room, his stout body puffed with fury. He grabbed Blair's arm, pulled her out of her chair, dragging her toward the door.

"Mr. Gates!" Opal said, on her feet at once. "What is the meaning of this?"

"This . . . this daughter of Satan has spent the night with Leander and, in spite of the fact that she's unclean, he plans to make an honest woman of her."

"What?!" the three women gasped.

"Leander is going to marry the harlot, I said." With that he half-dragged a protesting Blair out of the house.

Houston sat down heavily, not able to comprehend what was happening around her.

"Houston," her mother said. "You and Blair traded places last night, didn't you?"

Houston only nodded silently and picked up her sewing as if nothing had happened.

The sun set, the room darkened, and the maid switched on the electric lights, but still mother and daughter didn't speak.

Only one thought went through Houston's mind: It's over. Everything is over.

At midnight, the front door opened and Duncan pushed Blair into the parlor ahead of him.

"It's settled," he said in a voice hoarse with overuse. "Blair and Leander will be married in two weeks. It will be announced in church on Sunday."

Quietly, Houston stood.

"Daughter," Duncan said with feeling, "I'm sorry about this."

Houston merely nodded as she started toward the stairs.

"Houston," Blair said from the foot of the staircase. "Please," she whispered.

But at the moment, Houston had no compassion to give her sister and, even when she heard Blair at last break into weeping, she didn't look back.

In her room, she still seemed to be numb. Her whole life over, turned around in one single night. Everything lost.

On the wall hung a framed diploma from Miss Jones's School for Young Ladies. With violence, she tore the diploma from the wall and flung it across the room, feeling no relief when the glass shattered.

With steady fingers, she began to unbutton her dress. Moments later she was standing in her nightgown, just standing, not moving, not aware of when her mother entered the room.

"Houston?" Opal said, her hand on her daughter's shoulder.

"Go to her," Houston said. "Blair needs you. If she stays here and marries Leander, she's going to give up a great deal."

"But you have, too. You've lost a lot tonight."

"I lost it long before tonight. Really, go to her. I'll be all right."

Opal picked up the broken diploma. "Let me see you in bed."

Obediently, Houston climbed into bed. "Always obedient, aren't I, Mother? I always obey. If not my parents, then Leander. I've always been such a good little girl and what has it gotten me? I'm a true, deep-down lady and my sister with her knickers and her kisses is getting everything I've worked for since the first grade."

"Houston," Opal pleaded.

"Leave me alone!" Houston screamed. "Just leave me alone."

With a shocked look on her face, Opal left the room.

Sunday morning dawned bright and beautiful, the sun highlighting Ayers Peak that graced the western side of Chandler. There were many churches in town, covering every denomination, and nearly all were full of people.

But even the sun couldn't melt the coldness inside the Chandler twins, who walked on opposite sides of their stepfather. Their mother had suddenly been attacked with a mysterious ailment that kept her from witnessing her daughters' public humiliation.

Leander waited in the pew for them, his eyes looking toward Houston, and when they neared the bench, he put his hand out to her. "Houston," he whispered.

Now he can tell us apart, she thought, but said nothing as she moved aside to keep from touching him.

Duncan nearly pushed Blair toward Lee and at last they were seated, Blair beside Lee, then Duncan and Houston on the end.

The service seemed to pass in seconds because Houston knew that at the end of it *the* announcement was going to be made.

It came much too soon.

Unfortunately, Reverend Thomas wasn't conducting the service today but was replaced by Reverend Smithson who could have been more tactful.

"Now I have an announcement to make," he said with an amused tone. "It seems that our own Leander has changed his mind about which twin to marry and is now engaged to Blair. I don't believe I could make up my mind between them, either. Congratulations again, Lee."

For a moment the church was thunderstruck. Then, men began to chuckle, and women gasped in astonishment. Everyone rose to leave.

"Houston, you must listen to me," Lee said, catching her arm. "I must explain."

"You have explained," she hissed at him. "When you told

me how wonderful Blair was, and how you hoped the ice princess would never return, *that's* when you did your explaining. Good morning," she smiled at a passerby.

"Hello, Houston, or are you Blair?" someone asked.

"Congratulations, Lee." A man slapped him on the shoulder and went away laughing.

"Houston, let's go somewhere."

"You can go to . . . your bride." She glared at him in anger.

"Houston," Lee pleaded. "Please."

"If you don't take your hand off me I'll scream, for surely I can suffer no more embarrassment than you have caused me already."

"Leander!" Duncan said. "Blair is waiting for you."

Lee reluctantly turned away from Houston, clutched Blair's arm, shoved her into his buggy and drove away much too fast.

The minute Houston was alone, women descended on her, edging her away from Duncan's protection. The many faces were concerned, curious, some sympathetic. Mostly, the women seemed to be puzzled.

"Houston, what happened? I thought you and Lee were so happy."

"How could Leander want Blair? They argue constantly."

"When was the decision made?"

"Houston, is there someone else?"

"You're damned right there is, ladies," came a booming voice from behind them, and they all turned to look up at Kane Taggert. No one in town had ever heard him say much and he had certainly never seemed to be aware of what any of the townspeople were doing.

The women gaped openly at this big man in his rough clothes, with his unkempt beard, as he made his way through them. No one was more surprised than Houston.

"I'm sorry I didn't make the service today or I could a sat with you," he said as he reached her. "Don't look so surprised, sweetheart. I know I promised to keep our secret a little longer, but I couldn't keep quiet after ol' Lee told ever'body."

"Secret?" one of the women prompted.

Kane put his arm around Houston. They were an incongruous pair, him hairy, rumpled, her perfect. "Houston broke her engagement to Leander because she fell right smack in love with me. Ladies, she just couldn't help herself."

"When did this happen?" one of the women recovered herself enough to ask.

Houston was beginning to breathe again. "It started when Mr. Taggert and I had dinner together at his house," she whispered, knowing she was going to regret every word later, but now it was nice not to have to admit she'd been jilted.

"But what about Leander?"

"Leander consoled himself with the love of Houston's dear sister, Blair," Kane said sweetly. "And now, ladies, we got to be goin'. I hope all of you will come to the weddin'—a double weddin'—in two weeks." He put his hand on the small of Houston's back, and pushed her toward his old wagon.

As he drove away, Houston sat rigidly on the edge of her seat.

He halted the wagon at the edge of his own property. Before them spread his acres of garden and in the background was his house. He put up his arms to help her down. "You and me gotta talk."

Houston was too numb to do anything but obey.

"I woulda come to church to sit with you, but I had some work to do. It looks like I got there just in time. Another minute and them ol' biddies would of eaten you alive."

"I beg your pardon." Houston was only vaguely listening. Until this morning she'd hoped it was all a bad dream, that she'd wake up and Leander and she would still be engaged.

"Are you listenin' to me at all? What's wrong with you?"

"Other than public humiliation, Mr. Taggert, nothing is wrong with me." She stopped. "I apologize. I didn't mean to burden you with my problems."

"You ain't heard a word I've said, have you? Didn't you hear me tell 'em you and me was gonna get married? I invited 'em all to a double weddin'."

"And I thank you for it," Houston said, managing a smile. "It was very kind of you to come to my rescue. You would make a splendid knight. Now, I think I should leave."

"You're the damnedest woman I ever met! If you don't marry me, what else you gonna do? You think any of the so-called society men are gonna have you? They're afraid of the whole Westfield clan. You think Marc Fenton wants you?"

"Marc Fenton?" she asked, puzzled. "Why should Marc, as you put it, 'want me'?"

"I was just wonderin', that's all." He stepped closer to her. "How come you don't wanta marry me? I'm rich and I gotta big house and you just got jilted and you ain't got nothin' else to do."

She looked up at him, his size making her a little uneasy, but she wasn't really afraid of him. Suddenly, all thought of Leander and Blair was gone. "Because I don't love you," she said firmly. "And I know nothing about you. For all I know, you could have been married ten times before and have locked all your wives away in the cellar. You look like you're capable of such a trick," she said as she looked down her nose at his hairy face and heavy shirt that was torn at the shoulder.

For a full minute, Kane stared at her in open-mouthed astonishment. "Is that what you think of me? Listen, lady." He took a step closer to her. "I ain't had *time* to marry anybody. Since I was eighteen and Fenton tossed me out on my ass, I've done nothin' but make money. There was three years when I didn't even sleep. And here you're tellin' me I might of had time to marry ten women."

By the time he finished, Houston was leaning backward, Kane bending over her.

"I think perhaps I was in error," she said with a gentle smile.

Kane didn't move. "You know, you're the prettiest woman I ever seen in my life."

With that, he slipped one arm around her back, pulled her to him, as he buried his right hand in her carefully pinned coiffure, and kissed her.

Houston had kissed Leander hundreds of times. He was familiar to her, nothing unexpected—but Kane's kiss was unlike anything she'd ever experienced before. His mouth was demanding on hers, not the refined kiss of a gentleman with a lady, but more like how she'd imagine a stableman would kiss.

He released her so abruptly she nearly fell, and for a moment they looked at each other. "Lady, if you can kiss me like that when you love that Westfield, I'll manage to do without your love."

Houston could say nothing.

He took her elbow. "I'm gonna take you back now, and you can start plannin' for our weddin'. Buy yourself whatever you need. I'll put some money in the bank for you. I want lots of flowers at the weddin' so get some sent here. Have 'em sent from California if you want or come look at what I got in my glasshouse. And we'll be married in my house. There's chairs in the attic. I want ever'body in town to come."

"Wait! Please," she said, repinning her hair as he propelled her along. "I haven't agreed yet. Please, Mr. Taggert, give me some time. I haven't yet recovered from losing my fiancé." She put her hand on his arm, could feel the muscles of his forearm under his heavy shirt.

He lifted her hand and for a moment she thought he was going to kiss it.

"I'll buy you a ring. What do you like? Diamonds? Emeralds? What are those blue ones?"

"Sapphires," she said absently. "Please don't buy me a ring. Marriage is a lifetime commitment. I can't rush into this too quickly."

"You take your time. You got two whole weeks before the weddin' to get used to the idea of bein' my wife."

"Mr. Taggert," she said with exasperation, "do you *ever* listen to what other people say?"

He grinned at her from beneath his beard. "No, never. That's the way I got rich. If I saw somethin' I wanted, I went after it."

"And I'm next on your list of things you want?" she asked softly.

"At the very top. Right up there with an apartment buildin' in New York that Vanderbilt owns and I want. Now, I'll take you home so you can tell your family about me and you can put me in Westfield's place. He's gonna be sorry! He got a Chandler all right but I'm gettin' the lady one." He flipped the reins to the horses so suddenly Houston fell back into her seat before she could say a word.

At the door to her house, he jumped from the wagon and nearly pulled her to the ground. "I got to get back now. You tell your parents about me, will ya? And I'll send a ring over to you tomorrow. Anything you need, you let me or Edan know. I'll try to see you tomorrow." He gave a quick look over her shoulder toward her house, then said again, "I got to go," and bolted into the wagon.

Houston stood before the little stone fence in front of her house and watched him speed away, dust almost obscuring the buggy from view. She felt as if she'd just weathered a tornado.

Inside the house, both Duncan and Opal were waiting for her, Opal in a chair, her eyes red from crying, while Duncan, arms folded, was pacing the floor.

Houston braced herself before entering the room. "Good afternoon, Mother, Mr. Gates."

"Where have you been?" Duncan seethed.

"Oh, Houston," Opal cried, "you don't have to marry him. You'll find someone else. Just because Leander made a mistake doesn't mean you should, too."

Before Houston could speak, Duncan started on her. "Houston, you've always been the sensible one. Blair never did have any sense. Even as a little girl she'd rush off head first into trouble, but you always had as much sense as a woman is capable of. You were going to marry Leander and—."

"Leander is no longer going to marry me," Houston pointed out.

"But not Kane Taggert!" Opal wailed and buried her face in her damp handkerchief.

Houston began to feel protective of Kane. "What in the world has the man done to deserve so much hostility? I have not agreed to marry him, but I don't see why I shouldn't."

Jumping up from her seat, Opal ran to her daughter. "He's a monster. Look at him. You can't live with that great smelly bear of a man. Every friend you ever had would desert you. And there are terrible stories about him."

"Opal!" Duncan commanded and, meekly, she went back to her seat to continue sobbing. "Houston, I'm going to address you as I would a man. I couldn't care less if the man'd never had a bath in his life. That doesn't bother me. He can certainly afford a bathtub. But there are things . . ." He gave her a hard look. "There are stories, among the men, that Taggert has had a couple of men killed in order to make his fortune."

"Killed?" Houston whispered. "Where did you hear that?"

"It doesn't matter where—."

"It *does* matter!" she snapped. "Don't you see? The women of this town were angry because he ignored them, so they made up stories about him. Why would the men be any different? Leander told me of several men in town who tried to sell Mr. Taggert things such as worn-out gold mines. Perhaps one of them began the rumors."

"What I heard comes from a very reliable source," Duncan said darkly.

Houston was quiet for a moment. "Jacob Fenton," she said softly and saw by the expression on Duncan's square face that she was right. "From the gossip I've heard," Houston continued, "Mr. Taggert dared to make advances to Jacob Fenton's precious daughter Pamela. When I was a girl, I remember people whispering about the disgraceful way Mr. Fenton spoiled her. Of course he'd hate a man who'd once been his stable boy and who had the audacity to want to marry his spoiled daughter."

"Are you saying Fenton's a liar?" Duncan accused. "Are you choosing this newcomer over a family you've known all your life?"

"If I do marry Kane Taggert—and I mean *if*—yes, I will believe in him over the Fentons. Now, if you'll excuse me, I suddenly feel very tired and I think I'll lie down."

She swept out of the room with more grace than she actually felt and, once in her room, she collapsed onto the bed.

Marry Kane Taggert? she thought. Marry a man who talked and acted worse than any River Street ruffian? Marry a man who treated her without respect, one who hauled her in and out of carriages as if she were a sack of potatoes? Marry a man who kissed her as if she were a scullery maid?

She sat upright. "Marry a man who, as Blair says, when he

kisses me makes me see red with little sparks of gold and silver?" she said aloud.

"I just might," she whispered, leaned back against the bed, and for the first time began to consider becoming Mrs. Kane Taggert.

Chapter 6

By morning Houston had convinced herself that she couldn't possibly, under any circumstances, marry Mr. Taggert. Her mother'd sniffed throughout breakfast and cried repeatedly, "My beautiful daughters, what will become of them?" while Blair and Duncan'd argued about how Blair'd ruined Houston's life. Houston wasn't sure it was an argument, since they seemed to be agreeing with one another.

Houston entered the discussion when it was said that Kane Taggert was her means of punishing herself for losing Leander. But no one seemed to hear what Houston said, and nothing made any difference to Blair's misery, so Houston stopped listening to them. But being the cause of so much weeping made her decide she couldn't marry Mr. Taggert.

Immediately after breakfast, people began "dropping by."

"I was just starting to bake an apple pie and knew how much you liked them, Opal, so I baked two and brought you one. How are the twins?"

By midmorning, the house was full of food and people. Mr. Gates stayed in his brewery office, having one of the maids bring him his lunch, so Houston, Blair and Opal had to fend off the questions by themselves.

"Did you really fall in love with Mr. Taggert, Houston?"

"Have another piece of pie, Mrs. Treesdale," Houston answered.

At eleven, Blair managed to slip away, leaving Opal and Houston alone to cope, and Blair didn't return until three o'clock. "Are they *still* here?" she gasped, looking at the crowd on the lawn.

At three thirty, a man pulled up in front of the Chandler house driving a beautiful carriage such as no one in Chandler had ever seen. It was painted white, with white wheels, a cream-colored collapsible hood on top with shiny brass detailing. There was a seat in front upholstered in red leather and a smaller seat in back for an attendant.

The group of people on the lawn, on the deep porch, and spilling into the garden, stopped their questions and gawked.

A man, crudely dressed, stepped down and walked straight into the midst of the people. "Who's Miss Houston Chandler?" he asked into the silence.

"I am," Houston said, stepping forward.

The man reached into his pocket, pulled out a slip of paper and began to read. "This here carriage is from the man you're gonna marry, Mr. Kane Taggert. It's a lady's drivin' carriage, a spider phaeton, and the horse is a good 'un."

He folded the paper, put it back into his pocket and turned away. "Oh yeah." He turned back. "Mr. Taggert sent you this, too." He tossed a small parcel wrapped in brown paper toward Houston and she caught it.

The man went down the path, whistling. Everyone watched him until he was out of sight around a corner.

"Well, Houston," Tia said, "aren't you going to open your gift?"

Houston wasn't sure she should open the package because she knew what she'd find inside, and if she accepted his ring, it would mean she accepted him.

Inside the box was the biggest diamond she'd ever seen, an enormous, breathtaking chunk of brilliance surrounded by nine square-cut emeralds.

The combined intake of breath from the women around her was enough to stir the tree leaves.

With resolution, Houston snapped the blue velvet box shut, and walked straight down the path toward the carriage. She didn't hesitate or answer any questions thrown at her but snapped the reins and the lovely brown horse moved briskly.

She drove straight up Sheldon street, across the Tijeras River that separated the north and south sections of town, and up the steep drive to the Taggert house. Since pounding on the front door brought no answer, she strode inside, took a left and stopped in the doorway of Kane's office.

He sat hunched over his desk, puffing away on a vile cigar, making notes and giving quick orders to Edan, who was leaning back in a chair, his feet on the desk, smoking an equally awful cigar.

Edan saw her first and the big blond man stood at once and punched Kane on the shoulder.

Kane looked up with a frown.

"You must be Edan," Houston said, going forward, her hand outstretched. She wasn't sure if he was a servant or a friend. "I'm Houston Chandler."

"Houston," he said. He was not a servant, not with that air of confidence.

"I'd like to talk to you," Houston said, turning to Kane.

"If it's about weddin' plans, I'm real busy right now. If you need money, tell Edan, he'll write you a check."

Waving smoke away from her face, she went to a window and opened it. "You shouldn't sit in this smoke. It isn't good for you."

Kane looked up at her with cold eyes. "Who are you to give me orders? Just because you're gonna be my wife, don't—."

"As far as I can recall, I haven't yet agreed to be your wife and if you can't find time to talk to me—in private—I don't think I *will* be your wife. Good day, Mr. Taggert, and Edan."

"Good day, Houston," Edan said with a slight smile.

"Women!" she heard Kane say behind her. "I told you a woman'd take a lot of my time."

He caught up with her at the front door. "Maybe I was a little hasty," he said. "It's just that when I'm workin' I don't like no interruptions. You got to understand that."

"I wouldn't bother you if it weren't important," she said coolly.

"All right," he said. "We'll go in here an' talk." He pointed to the echoing emptiness of the library. "I'd offer you a chair, but the only ones I got are in my bedroom. You wanta go up there?" He gave her a grinning leer.

"Definitely not. What I want to talk about, Mr. Taggert, is whether or not you are quite serious about your marriage proposal to me."

"You think I got the time to waste doin' all the courtin' I been doin' if I wasn't serious?"

"Courting?" she said. "Yes, I guess you could call Sunday morning courting. What I want to ask you, sir, is, well, have you ever killed or hired someone to kill for you?"

Kane's mouth dropped open and his eyes grew angry, but then he began to look amused. "No, I ain't never killed nobody. What else you wanta know about me?"

"Anything you care to tell me," she said seriously.

"Ain't much. I grew up in Jacob Fenton's stable"—a muscle twitched in his cheek—"I got tossed out for messin' with his daughter and I been makin' money since then. I ain't killed nobody, robbed nobody, cheated nobody, never beat up no woman and only knocked out an average number of men. Anythin' else?"

"Yes. When you proposed, you said you wanted me to furnish your house. What do I get to do with you?"

"With me?" With a grin, he looped his thumbs in the empty belt loops on his trousers. "I ain't gonna hold nothin' back from you if that's what you mean."

"I do *not* mean whatever you're implying, I'm sure," she said stiffly. "Mr. Taggert," she said, as she began walking around him. "I know men who work in coal mines who are better dressed than you are. And your language is atrocious, as well as your manners. My mother is scared to death of my marrying a barbarian like you. Since I cannot spend my life frightening my own mother, you will have to agree to some instruction from me."

"Instruction?" he said, narrowing his eyes at her. "What can you teach me?"

"How to dress properly. How to eat—."

"Eat? I eat plenty."

"Mr. Taggert, you keep mentioning names like Vanderbilt and Gould. Tell me, were you ever invited to the homes of any of those families when the women were present?"

"No, but—," he began, then looked away. "I was once, but there was an accident and some dishes got broke."

"I see. I wonder how you expect me to be your wife, to run a magnificent house like this, to give dinner parties like you want while you sit at the head of the table eating peas from a knife. I assume you do eat peas with a knife."

"I don't eat peas at all. A man needs meat, and he don't need a woman to tell him—."

"Good day, sir." She turned on her heel and took two steps before he grabbed her arm.

"You ain't gonna marry me if I don't let you teach me?"

"And dress you, and shave you."

"Anxious to see my face, are you?" he grinned, but stopped when he saw how serious Houston was. "How long I got to decide this?"

"About ten minutes."

He grimaced. "Who taught you how to do business? Let me think about this then." He walked toward a window, and stood there for several long minutes.

"I got some requests of you," he said when he came back to her. "I know you're marryin' me for my money." He put up his hand when she began to speak. "Ain't no use denyin' it. You wouldn't consider marryin' me with my knife-eatin' ways if I didn't have a big house to give you. A lady like you wouldn't even talk to a stableboy like me. What I want is for you to pretend, and to tell ever'body, that you . . ." He looked down at the parqueted floor. "I want people to think you did, uh, fall in love with me and that you ain't just marryin' me 'cause your sister jumped the gun and I just happened along. I want even your sister"—he said this with emphasis—"to think you're crazy for me, just like I said in front of the church. And I want your mother to think so, too. I don't want her to be afraid of me."

Houston had expected anything but this. So this was the big, fearsome man who stood aloof from the whole town. How awful it must be to not be able to do the smallest social thing. Of course women wouldn't put up with having him in their houses when there were "accidents" and china was broken. Right now, he didn't fit into any world, neither the poor one where his manners and speech placed him, nor the rich one where his money placed him.

He needs me, she thought. He needs me as no one ever has before. To Leander, I was something extra, nice but not necessary. But to this man, the things I've learned are vital.

"I will pretend to be the most loving of wives," she said softly.

"Then you *are* gonna marry me?"

"Why, yes, I believe I am," she said with a feeling of surprise.

"Hot damn! Edan!" he bellowed as he ran out of the room. "Lady Chandler's gonna marry me."

Houston sat down on a window ledge. *He* was going to marry "Lady" Chandler. Who in the world had *she* agreed to marry?

It was evening before Houston drove back to her own home. She was exhausted, and at the moment she wished she'd never heard of Kane Taggert. He seemed to think he would be able to stay at his house and work, and his fiancée could attend all the engagement parties alone, tell everyone she was in love with him, and all would be well.

"Unless they see us together, no one will believe we even know each other," she said to him across his littered desk. "You *have* to attend the garden party the day after tomorrow, and before then we have to make you a proper suit of clothes and shave you."

"I'm tryin' to buy some land in Virginia and a man's comin' tomorrow. I got to stay here."

"You can talk business during your fittings."

"You mean, have one of them little men put his little hands all over me? I ain't havin' that. You have somebody send over some suits and I'll pick one out."

"Red or purple?" she asked quickly.

"Red. I seen some red plaid ones once—."

Houston's half scream stopped him. "You *will* have a tailor make a suit for you and *I* will choose the fabric. And you *will* attend the garden party with me, and you will also attend several other functions with me within the next few weeks before our marriage."

"You sure real ladies are this bossy? I thought real ladies never raised their voices."

"They don't raise their voices to real gentlemen, but to men who want to wear red plaid suits they are allowed to use blunt instruments."

Kane had looked sulky at that, but he'd given in. "All right then, I'll have a suit made like you want, and I'll go to your dam . . . your lovely, dainty tea party," he changed it to, making her smile, "but I don't know about them other parties."

"We'll do one day at a time," she said, suddenly feeling exhausted. "I must return home. My parents will be worried."

"Come 'ere," he said, motioning her around his desk.

Thinking he wanted to show her something, she did as he bid. Roughly, he caught her wrist and pulled her into his lap. "You get to be my teacher, I guess I'm gonna have to teach you about some things, too."

He began nuzzling her neck with his face, his lips nibbling her skin. She was about to protest his treatment of her, but then parts of her body began to melt.

"Kane," Edan said from the doorway. "Excuse me."

Without ceremony, Kane pushed her off his lap. "You'll get more of that later, honey," he said, as if she were a street trollop. "Go on home now, I got to work."

Houston swallowed what she wanted to say and, with a face red from embarrassment, murmured a good night to both men and left the house.

Now, driving home at last, tired, hungry, still suffering from an emotion that was half anger, half embarrassment, she faced telling her family that she'd agreed to marry the notorious Mr. Kane Taggert.

Why, she asked herself as she slowed the horse to the barest walk. Why in the world was she agreeing to marry a man she didn't love, who didn't love her, a man who made her furious every other minute, a man who treated her like something he'd bought and paid for?

The answer came to her quickly.

Because he made her feel alive. Because he *needed* her.

Blair had said that when they were children, Houston had thrown snowballs with the best of them, but Duncan and Leander had taken away her spirit. Long ago she'd learned that it was easier to give in to the men, to be the quiet, ladylike, spiritless woman they wanted.

But there were times, at receptions, at dinner gatherings, when she felt as if she were a painting on a wall—pretty and nice to have around, but completely unnecessary to anyone's day-to-day well-being. She'd even said something like this to Leander once and he'd talked about the quality of life changing without art objects.

But in the end, Lee had traded Houston's quiet, serene beauty for a woman who set his body on fire.

Never had a man made her feel as Kane Taggert did. Lee's taste in clothing and furniture was impeccable. Easily, he could have done the interiors of the house he'd had built for them by himself. But Mr. Taggert was at such a loss about what to do that, without her, he couldn't even arrange his furniture, much less buy it.

Houston thought of all the years of work she'd gone through at school. Blair seemed to think her sister had done little but drink tea and arrange flowers, but Houston remembered the strict discipline and Miss Jones's ruler slapping on tender palms when a girl failed.

When she was with Lee, she had to make a conscious effort to put all her schooling into effect because Lee would know when she was wrong. But with Mr. Taggert, she felt free. Today she'd screeched at him. In fourteen years of knowing Lee, never once had she raised her voice to him.

She took a breath of cool, night air. All the work ahead of her! Arranging the wedding, the surprise of exploring the attics and putting the furniture where *she* wanted it. And the challenge of trying to turn Mr. Taggert into some form of gentleman!

By the time she reached home, she was bursting with excitement. She was going to marry a man who *needed* her.

She left the horse and carriage with the groom, straightened her shoulders, and prepared herself to face the storm that was her family.

Chapter 7

Much to her surprise—and relief—the house was quiet when Houston entered through the kitchen, only the cook and Susan washing up.

"Has everyone gone to bed?" she asked, her hand on the big oak table that nearly filled the room.

"Yes, Miss Blair-Houston," Susan answered as she cleaned the coffee grinder. "More or less."

"Houston," she said automatically, ignoring the maid's last comment. "Will you bring me something on a tray and come to my room, Susan?"

As she walked through the house to the stairs, she noticed several large bouquets of freshly cut flowers, not flowers from her mother's garden. She saw a card attached:

To my wife to be, Blair, from Leander.

Leander had never sent her flowers in all the months they were engaged.

She held her head high and went upstairs.

Houston's bedroom was papered in a subtle cream and white design, the woodwork was painted white and the windows were hung with handmade Battenberg lace. The low tables and the backs of the two chairs were also adorned with the airy lace. The underside of her bed canopy was of gathered silk in a light tan and the bedspread was intricately quilted, all in white.

When Houston had undressed down to her underwear, Susan came with the tray. While eating, Houston began giving orders.

"I know it's late but I need you to send Willie on some errands. He's to take this note to Mr. Bagly, the tailor on Lead Avenue. I don't care if Willie has to drag the man out of bed, he is to make sure Mr. Bagly personally gets this. He must be at the Taggert house at eight o'clock tomorrow."

"At the Taggert house?" Susan asked, as she put away Houston's clothes. "Then it's true, Miss, you're going to marry him?"

Houston was sitting at her tiny mahogany desk and she turned around. "How'd you like to work for me? To live in the Taggert house?"

"I'm not sure, Miss. Is Mr. Taggert as bad as people say?"

Houston considered this. It was her experience that servants often knew much more about a man than his peers. Even though Kane lived alone, no doubt the servants knew things about him that no one else did. "What have you heard about him?"

"That he has a violent temper and he yells a fierce lot and nothing ever pleases him."

"I'm afraid that's all probably true," Houston sighed, turning around again, "but at least he doesn't beat women or cheat people."

"If you're not afraid to live with him, Miss Houston, then I'll do it. I don't guess this house'll be a fit place to live after you twins are gone."

"I don't imagine it will be either," Houston said absently, as she made a note to herself to call the barber, Mr. Applegate on Coal Avenue, and request that he arrive at nine o'clock. She thought how much time it'd save if everyone in town were on the telephone system.

"Susan, don't you have a couple of brothers?"

"Yes, Miss."

"I'll need six brawny men for all day tomorrow. They'll be

moving furniture downstairs. They'll be paid well and fed well and they're to arrive at eight thirty. Do you think you can find six men?"

"Yes, Miss."

Houston wrote another note. "Willie must deliver this to Mrs. Murchison. She's staying with Reverend Thomas while the Conrads are in Europe. I want her to come and cook at the Taggert house until they return. I hope she'll be glad to have something to do. Willie will have to wait for a reply because I've told her the kitchen is bare and she's to stock it with whatever she needs and to send Mr. Taggert the bill. Willie may have to meet her in the morning with a wagon. If so, I'm sure he can borrow the Oakleys' big wagon."

She leaned back in the chair. "There, that should take care of tomorrow. I have Mr. Taggert dressed and shaved, the furniture moved, and everyone fed."

Susan began to unpin Houston's hair and brush it.

"That feels lovely," she said, closing her eyes.

Minutes later she was in bed and, for the first night in days, she didn't feel like crying herself to sleep. In fact, she felt quite happy. She'd bargained with her sister so she could have one night of adventure, but it looked as if she were going to have weeks of adventure.

When Susan knocked on her door at six the next morning, Houston was already half dressed for work in a white cotton blouse, a black cord skirt that cleared the floor and a wide leather belt. A little jacket and matching hat completed the outfit.

Tiptoeing downstairs through the silent house, she placed a note on the dining table for her mother explaining where she'd be all day, then ate a hurried meal in the kitchen and went to the carriage house where she made a sleepy Willie harness the horse to the beautiful new buggy Kane had sent her.

"Did you give out all the messages, Willie?"

"All of them. Mrs. Murchison was right glad to get busy. I'm to meet her with a wagon at six thirty and meet Mr. Randolph at the grocery store. Mrs. Murchison called him late last night with a long list of things she wanted. And then we're goin' out to the Conrad place and raid their garden. She wanted to know how many she's to feed."

"There'll be about a dozen people but most of them are men so tell her to cook for thirty. That should do it. And tell her to bring pots and pans. I don't imagine Mr. Taggert has any. Come as soon as you can, Willie."

Everything was silent at the Taggert house as Houston unhitched her horse and tied it in the shade. She knocked at a side entrance but no one heard her so she tried the door, found it open and entered the kitchen. Feeling a bit like a thief, she began opening cabinets. If this house was to prepare a feast for a large number of wedding guests within two weeks, she needed to know what resources she had.

The cabinets were empty except for cases of canned peaches—no cookware except the cheapest enamelware.

"Sears again," she murmured as she decided to explore the rest of the service area. A large butler's pantry separated the dining room from the kitchen, and behind the kitchen was an L-shaped wing with pantry, scullery, quarters with a bath for three servants, the housekeeper's room and, beside it, the housekeeper's office.

In the corridor outside the kitchen was a stairway and Houston took it. Pausing at the second floor, she peeped down a hallway but could see only shadows on oak floors and panelled walls. She continued toward the attics.

As she'd already guessed, the attics were actually servants' quarters that were now being used for storage. There were two bathrooms, one male, one female, and the rest of the space was divided into small rooms. And each room was stacked to the ceiling with crates and boxes; some had furniture hidden under dust covers.

Tentatively, she lifted a dust sheet. Beneath it were two gilded chairs covered in tapestries of cherubs. A tag was attached. Holding her breath, she read the tag:

> *Mid-eighteenth century*
> *tapestries woven at Gobelin works*
> *believed to have belonged to Mme. de Pompadour*
> *one of set of twelve chairs, two settees*

"My goodness," Houston breathed, allowing the cover to fall back into place.

Against the wall was a rolled carpet. Its tag read:

Late seventeenth century
made at Savonnerie factory for Louis XIV

A crate, obviously holding a painting, was merely labelled "Gainsborough." Beside it stood one with the word "Reynolds" painted on it.

Slowly, Houston removed the cover from the Mme. de Pompadour chairs, lifted off the top chair and sat down. She needed a moment to collect her thoughts. Looking about her, she could see gold feet protruding from beneath the sheeted furniture, and without further exploring, she knew that all the furniture and works of art were museum quality. Absently, she lifted a sheet beside her. Beneath it sparkled a chandelier that looked as if it were made of diamonds. Its tag read: 1780.

She was still sitting, a bit stunned at the prospect of living daily with the treasures around her when she heard a carriage below. "Mr. Bagly!" she said as she flew down the stairs and managed to arrive at the front door just as he and his assistant were leaving their carriage.

"Good morning, Blair-Houston," he said.

Mr. Bagly was a tiny, white-faced little man who somehow managed to be a tyrant. As Chandler's premier tailor, Mr. Bagly received a great deal of respect.

"Good morning," she answered. "Do come in. I'm not sure what you've heard, Mr. Bagly, but Mr. Taggert and I are to be married within two weeks and he'll need an entire wardrobe. But right now, he needs one good afternoon suit for a reception tomorrow, something in vicuña, three buttons, gray trousers and a vest of cashmere. That should do it. Do you think you can have it ready by two o'clock tomorrow?"

"I'm not sure. I have other customers."

"I'm sure no one is in as much need as Mr. Taggert. Put as many seamstresses on it as possible. You will be paid."

"I think I can arrange it. Now, if I could begin measuring Mr. Taggert, I could start the suit."

"He is upstairs, I believe."

Mr. Bagly looked at her steadily. "Blair-Houston, I've known you all your life, and I'm willing to put aside all my other work to do a job for you, and I'm willing to come here this early in the morning in order to measure your fiancée, but I will *not* go up those stairs and search for him. Perhaps we should come back when he's awake."

"But you won't have time to make the suit! Please, Mr. Bagly."

"Not if you went on your knees to me. We will wait in here for one half-hour. If Mr. Taggert is not downstairs by then, we will leave."

Houston was almost glad there were no chairs for them in the large drawing room where they planned to wait. Courage, she told herself and started up the stairs.

The second floor was as beautiful as the first, with white painted panelling, and directly in front of her was a wide, open room with a green tiled area in back. "An aviary," she whispered with delight.

With a sigh, she knew she must get down to business. Around her were many closed doors and behind one of them was Kane.

She opened one door and, in the dim light, she saw a blond head in the midst of a rumpled bed. Quietly, she closed the door again, not wanting to wake Edan.

She went through four rooms before she found Kane's bedroom at the back of the house. Suspended from picture wires from the ceiling mold were crude curtains blocking out the morning sun. The furniture consisted of an oak bed, a little table littered with papers, an earthenware water pitcher on it, and a three-piece set of upholstered furniture covered in a ghastly red plush with bright yellow tassels at the bottom.

Houston looked toward the attics. "Forgive him, Mme. de Pompadour," she whispered.

With resolution, she pulled back the curtains, tied them in a fat knot so they'd stay in place, and let the sunlight in.

"Good morning, Mr. Taggert," she said loudly, as she stood over his bed.

Kane roused, turned over, but continued sleeping.

He was exposed from the waist up, nude, and, she suspected, nude the rest of the way down, too. For a moment she stood still, looking at him. It was few times that she'd seen a man's bare chest before and Kane was built like a prizefighter—big, muscular, his chest very hairy. His skin was dark and warm-looking.

One minute she was standing beside the bed and the next minute a great hand caught her thigh and she was pulled across him and into the bed.

"Couldn't wait for me, could you?" Kane said, as he began hungrily kissing her neck and throat as his hands energetically ran over her body. "I've always been partial to a good romp in the mornin'."

Houston struggled against him for a moment, saw it was useless and began looking for other ways to stop his attack on her. Her groping hand came in contact with the handle of the pitcher on the table, and she swiftly brought it down on his head.

The thin chalkware broke, and water and pieces of the pitcher cascaded down as Houston jumped out of the bed, moving safely to the foot of it.

"What the hell—," Kane began, sitting up, rubbing his head. "You could a killed me."

"Not likely," Houston said. "I correctly assumed your taste in quality toiletries would match your taste in furniture."

"Listen, you little bitch, I'll—."

"No, Mr. Taggert, you listen to me. If I am to be your wife, you will treat me with the respect due a woman in that position. I will not be treated as some hussy you've . . . you've hired for the evening." Her face turned red but she continued. "I did *not* come to your bedroom because, as you say, I couldn't wait to share your bed. I was in a sense blackmailed into this. Below, I have a tailor waiting to measure you for a suit, I have furniture movers arriving any minute, a cook is coming with a wagonload of food and, in less than an hour, a barber will remove that mass of hair you're sporting. If I am going to prepare both you and this house for a wedding, I will unfortunately need your presence, and therefore you cannot be allowed to loll about in bed, sleeping the day away."

Kane just looked at her while she delivered her speech. "Is my head bleedin'?" he asked.

With a sigh, Houston went to him and examined his head, until he caught her about the waist and pressed his face against her breast. "Any of that paddin'?" he asked.

Houston pushed him away in disgust. "Get up, get dressed and come downstairs as quickly as possible," she said before turning on her heel and leaving the room.

"Damned bossy female," she heard him say behind her.

Downstairs, everything was chaos. The six men Susan'd hired were strolling through the house as if they owned it, shouting comments to one another. Willie and Mrs. Murchison were waiting to ask her questions and Mr. Bagly had decided to leave.

Houston set to work.

By nine o'clock, she was wishing she knew how to use a whip. She had immediately fired two of the furniture movers for insolence and then asked who wanted to earn a day's pay.

Kane didn't like Mr. Bagly touching him and didn't like Houston deciding what he could and could not wear.

Mrs. Murchison was beside herself, trying to cook in the bare kitchen.

When the barber arrived, Houston slipped out the side door and nearly ran for the privacy of the big glasshouse that for days she'd been wanting to explore. She closed the door and gazed with pleasure down the three-hundred-foot-long expanse of flowering plants. The fragrance and the peace were what she needed.

"Noise get too much for you?"

She turned to see Edan, as he set down a big pot of azaleas. He was nearly as large as Kane, handsome, blond, and, she guessed, younger than Kane. "I guess we woke you," she said. "There seems to have been a great deal of shouting this morning."

"If Kane's around, people usually shout," he said matter-of-factly. "Could I show you my plants?"

"This is yours?"

"More or less. There's a little house past the rose garden where a Japanese family lives. They take care of the outside gardens, but in here is mine. I have plants from all over the world."

She knew she had no time, but she also knew she wanted a few minutes of quiet.

With pride, Edan showed her the many plants in the glasshouse: cyclamen, primroses, tree ferns, orchids, exotic things she'd never heard of.

"You must enjoy it in here," she said, touching a cymbidium orchid leaf. "I broke a pitcher over his head this morning."

For a moment, Edan's mouth dropped open, then he gave a snort of laughter. "I've gone after him with my fists more than once. Do you really mean to try to civilize him?"

"I hope I can. But I can't keep on striking him. There must be other ways." Her head came up. "I know nothing about you, or how you relate to him."

Edan began repotting an overgrown passionflower. "He found me in an alleyway in New York where I was staying alive by eating from garbage cans. My parents and sister had died a few weeks before from smoke inhalation in a tenement fire. I was seventeen, couldn't hold a job because I kept fighting," he smiled in memory, "starving, and had decided to turn to a life of crime. Unfortunately, or perhaps fortunately, the first person I chose to rob was Kane."

Houston nodded. "Perhaps his size was a challenge to you."

"Or maybe I was hoping I'd fail. Kane flattened me onto the street, but instead of sending me to jail, he took me home with him and fed me. I was seventeen, he was twenty-two, and already on his way to becoming a millionaire."

"And you've been with him ever since."

"And earning my keep," Edan added. "He made me work for him all day and sent me to accounting school at night. The man doesn't believe in sleep. We were up till four this morning, so that's why we were still in bed when you arrived.

"Ah!" Edan said suddenly, grinning broadly as he looked through the glass walls. "I think the barber's been here."

With much curiosity, Houston looked through the glass. Coming down the path was a big man wearing Kane's clothes, but instead of the long dark hair and beard, he was clean-shaven.

Houston looked at Edan in wonder, and he laughed as Kane walked through the door.

"Houston!" he bellowed. "You in here?"

She stepped from behind an elephant's-foot tree to look at him.

"Ain't bad, is it?" he said happily, rubbing his clean jaw. "I ain't seen myself in so long I'd forgotten how good-lookin' I was."

Houston had to laugh, for he was indeed handsome, with a big square jaw, fine lips, and with his eyes with their dark brows, he was extraordinary.

"If you're through lookin' at Edan's plants, come on back to the house. There's a lady in the kitchen cookin' up a storm and I'm starvin'."

"Yes," she said, walking out of the glasshouse ahead of him.

Once outside, he caught her arm. "I got somethin' to say to you," he said softly, looking at his boot toe, then at some place to the left of her head. "I didn't mean to jump on you this mornin'. It was just that I was asleep, and I woke up to see a pretty gal there. I wouldn't a hurt you. I just guess I ain't used to ladies." He rubbed his head and grinned at her. "But I imagine I'll learn real quick."

"Sit down here," she said, pointing to a bench under a tree. "Let me look at your head."

He sat quite still while she searched his hair for the lump and examined it. "Does it hurt very much?"

"Not at the moment," he said, then caught both her hands. "You still gonna marry me?"

He's much better looking than Leander, she suddenly thought, and when he looked at her like this, odd things happened to her knees. "Yes, I'm still going to marry you."

"Good!" he said abruptly and stood. "Now, let's go eat. Me and Edan got work to do and I got a man waitin' for me. And you got to watch them idiots with the furniture." He started back toward the house.

Houston had to half run to keep up with him. *He certainly does change moods quickly,* she thought, as she held her hat on and scurried.

By afternoon, she had rugs down in three rooms and had

two of the attic rooms cleared. The furniture that was downstairs was in no order and she had yet to decide where each piece went. Kane and Edan closeted themselves in Kane's office with their visitor. Now and again she heard Kane's voice over the movers' noise. Once he looked into the library at the gilded chairs and said, "Them little chairs gonna hold up?"

"They have for over two hundred years," she'd answered.

Kane snorted and went back to his study.

At five o'clock, she knocked on the study door and, when Edan answered it, she looked through the blue haze of cigar smoke to tell Kane she was leaving but would return tomorrow. He barely looked up from his paperwork.

Edan walked out with her. "Thank you so much for all you've done today. I'm sure the house will be what it should be when you finish."

She stopped at the doorway. "Please tell him I'll be here at noon tomorrow with his new suit, and we'll attend the garden party at two."

"I hope he'll go."

"He will," she said with more assurance than she felt.

Chapter 8

Breakfast at the Chandler house was a solemn affair, only Duncan and Houston doing justice to the steak, ham, eggs, peach pie, and buckwheat cakes. Opal looked as if she'd lost five pounds overnight, Blair's jaw was set in a hard line of anger, while Duncan seemed to range from anger to bewilderment and back again.

Houston thought about what Susan had told her this morning concerning Blair and Leander. Yesterday, Blair had been canoeing on the lake in Fenton Park with a handsome blond stranger when Leander had rowed up beside them, and the next thing anyone knew, the stranger was thrashing about in the water while Lee hauled Blair into his canoe and rowed them to shore. While everyone was laughing, Blair used a paddle to shove Lee into the mud, rescued her stranger from drowning, and rowed him back to the boat rental area.

Houston knew she should be jealous of their love play, angry at how publicly Leander was telling everyone that he preferred Blair, and jealous of all the flowers Lee was sending, but her mind kept racing to things like where she was going to place that little Jacobean desk and whom she could get to help her hang the curtains she'd found in carefully labelled packages. And then there was Mr. Taggert. She hoped he wouldn't give her too much trouble today.

"I'd like to speak to you, Houston," Duncan said after breakfast, startling Houston so much that she jumped. He led the way into the front parlor, the one used for guests—and serious discussions.

Quietly, she took a seat. This man had been her stepfather since she was a girl, and because she'd always done what he wanted and conducted herself perfectly in his image of what a lady should do, they'd never had a disagreement.

"I hear that you've agreed to marry him," he began, standing, his back to the window that faced the street.

"Yes," she answered, steeling herself for the coming storm. How was she going to plead her case? Could she say she'd asked Kane and he said he'd never murdered anyone? Or maybe she could try to explain about how much he needed her.

As if he weighed hundreds of pounds, Duncan sat down.

"Houston," he said, in a voice barely above a whisper, "I know this house hasn't been like it was when your father was alive, but I never thought you'd take drastic measures to get out of it."

She'd not expected this. "You think I'm marrying Mr. Taggert in order to leave your house?"

He stood. "That and a few other reasons." He moved to look out the window. "I know that what Leander did to you must be a humiliating experience, and at your age it must seem to be the end of the world."

He turned back to face her. "But believe me, Houston, it's *not* the end of the world. You're the prettiest young lady in town, maybe in the whole state, and you'll find someone else. If you'd like to, I'll take you to Denver and introduce you to some young men."

Rising, Houston went to him and kissed his cheek. Until this moment, she'd not known that he really cared for her. In spite of the fact that they lived in the same house, there was always a formality between them, and this was the first time she'd ever kissed him.

"I thank you so much for your kindness," she said when Duncan turned away in embarrassment. She stepped back. "I don't believe I am marrying Mr. Taggert merely because he's the one most available."

Duncan looked back at her. "Are you *sure?* Maybe you want to hold him up before the town to say, 'See, I can get another man any time I want.' You *can* get another man. Maybe one not so rich or not one with a house like Taggert's, but a man whose family you know. For all you know, there could be insanity in Taggert's family. I hear that uncle of his is nothing but a troublemaker."

Houston's head came up. "Uncle?"

"Rafe Taggert in the coal mines. The man is a thorn in Jacob Fenton's side, but Jacob keeps him on no matter what he does."

Houston turned away to hide her face. The name Taggert was fairly common, and she'd never connected her friend Jean to Kane. Maybe Jean knew Kane. And if they were related, she could vouch for Kane's family being sane.

She turned back to Duncan. "I don't believe there's insanity."

A look of frustration crossed Duncan's face. "How can you change so completely in so short a time? You were so sensible with Leander, getting to know each other before you made the commitment of marriage, but you've known this man for only days, yet you've agreed to spend the rest of your life with him."

There was no answer to give him. He was completely right. Logically, Houston knew she couldn't marry this stranger.

Except that she damn well wanted to! She covered the little smile that appeared on her lips with her hand. She couldn't adopt Mr. Taggert's language!

"Marriage is a serious matter," Duncan continued. "Think about what you're doing."

"I've already agreed to marry him," she said, as if it were an answer.

"Blair proved that until that ring is on a woman's finger, anything might happen," he said bitterly. "Don't let her . . . waywardness ruin your life. Find out about Kane Taggert. Talk to some people who know him. Talk to Marc Fenton; he might remember Taggert when he worked in the stables. I've tried to see Jacob but he can't bear to hear Taggert's name. It's your whole life, Houston; find out everything you can about the man before you commit yourself to him."

Houston knew his request was reasonable, but she hesitated before agreeing. Maybe she didn't want to find out about Kane, maybe she liked thinking of him as a mystery man who'd swept her off her feet.

Maybe she just wasn't ready for the adventure to end. But Duncan's words were sensible, and Houston was used to obeying. Briefly, she wondered what he'd do if he knew about Kane's attack on her yesterday morning and the subsequent pottery breakage. Lock her in her room no doubt. She sighed. "I will ask several people," she whispered. "I will find out all I can, and if there is nothing horribly wrong, I will marry him on the twentieth."

Duncan gave a heavy sigh. "That's all I can ask. Houston, tell me, have you always wanted money so badly? Have you considered your life in this house one of poverty?"

"Is his money one of the other reasons you think I'm marrying him?"

"Of course." He looked surprised. "Why else would you marry the great ugly thing? If it weren't for his money, no one would speak to him. He'd be just another coal miner like the rest of his family and no one would give him the time of day."

"Would he be just another miner?" she asked. "He started as a stable boy but he's earned millions. No one gave it to him.

Perhaps what I like is the man inside, the one who can pull himself up from the stable filth to achieve something in life. All I've ever done is learn how to dress properly." And he needs that knowledge, she thought, feeling a little thrill run through her body.

"What else should a lady know?" Duncan asked.

"Women today are writing books, are—." She stopped, waving her hand to dismiss the subject. "I wonder why no one is asking why a man of Mr. Taggert's wealth is marrying a woman from the Colorado mountains? He could have a princess."

"You *are* a princess," Duncan snapped.

Houston smiled at him as she moved toward the door. "I must go. I have to visit Mr. Bagly and choose a wardrobe for my future husband, then I must order a second wedding dress identical to the first one. I'm sure Blair hasn't thought to do it."

"I doubt she has either," Duncan said, reaching into his pocket. "The bank president came by yesterday with this." He handed her a piece of paper.

It was a deposit slip stating that two hundred and fifty thousand dollars had been deposited in her name.

Houston's hand on the doorknob trembled a bit. "Thank you," she murmured. "Thank you for everything and I shall do as you ask." With a smile, she left the room.

She was on the stairs before she could breathe again. She stopped and looked again at the deposit slip. He said he was going to deposit "some" money for her. Whatever faults he had, lack of generosity was not one of them. Repressing the urge to laugh with delight, she hurried up the stairs to dress for the day's outing.

An hour later, she sat inside Mr. Bagly's little shop, fabric samples all about her. One of the things she'd learned in finishing school was how to dress a man—if for no other reason than so she could argue with her husband's valet.

"He'll need a dozen business suits," she was saying to Mr. Bagly as a clerk wrote furiously. "This light-colored wool, the Oxford gray check, the Angola, and that heavy blue Scottish wool . . . for now."

"And for evening?" Mr. Bagly asked.

"The black worsted with a white marseilles vest. Now, for riding."

She chose clothes for sports, pausing at, then rejecting, the golfing knickers and clothes for afternoon receptions. For his own wedding, she chose a black cutaway, then shirts, scarves, gloves. She then chose a large supply of underwear of lisle, linen handkerchiefs, and balbriggan socks.

"Shall we leave the hats until later?"

"Yes," Houston answered. "And the canes." She looked at the little gold watch pinned to her breast. "I must go now. May I have the completed suit?"

When Mr. Bagly had brought the new suit and a complete set of accessories, including shoes, from a storage room, Houston made arrangements for him to measure Edan for clothes for the wedding. "Good luck," he called after her, as Houston sped away in her elegant new carriage. "You'll need it," he muttered under his breath.

Two hours later, Houston was dressed for the garden party, wearing a formfitting gown of dotted white mousseline de soie over yellow satin, a wide yellow ribbon across the bodice, tying in a bow on her hip. Somehow, this morning, Susan had managed to pull Houston's corset a full three-quarters of an inch tighter. Breathing was done only in the upper half of her lungs, but what did a little discomfort matter? She wanted to look her best for her first official outing with her fiancé.

Sighing as she parked before the Taggert house, she realized she must hire servants soon. Now, she needed someone to help her from the carriage. Looking around to make sure no one was about, she pulled her dress up almost to the knees and stepped down.

A low whistle came from her left. "Prettiest thing I've seen all day," said Kane, walking around the side of the house. "In fact you got better legs 'n a dancer I seen in New Orleans."

Houston tried to control her blush. "I brought your suit, and you just have time to get ready."

"Ready for what?"

She still wasn't used to seeing him without his beard. His face was bristly this morning with dark, unshaven whiskers, but they didn't hide his extraordinary good looks. How fortunate, she thought, to agree to marry a grizzly bear and have him turn into a handsome prince.

"For the garden party at two," she answered.

"Oh, that," he said over his shoulder as he started toward the door, leaving her standing.

"Yes, that." She picked up her skirts and followed him inside and toward his office. "I thought perhaps we'd have time for a few lessons before we went, just enough so you'd feel comfortable, and of course you'll want time to dress."

He stopped behind his desk, picked up a piece of paper. "I'm real sorry, but I ain't got time to go. I got too much work to do. You go on, though. You're already dressed up and all. Maybe you can take some flowers from me."

Houston took a deep breath. "Perhaps I should just give them money."

He looked at her over the paper, his expression one of surprise. "They'd like that?"

"No," she said evenly, "*they* wouldn't but I'm sure you would. That way you wouldn't have to face them."

"Are you sayin' I'm afraid of a bunch of overdressed, tea-drinkin' snobs? Why, I could buy and sell—."

Her look cut him off.

"I ain't goin'," he said stubbornly and sat down.

She walked to stand near him, wanting very much to put her hand on his shoulder, but she didn't. "It won't be so bad. You've only met the worst people of the town. I'd like to introduce you to my friends, and I promise you not one person will faint at your feet."

He looked up at her. "Not one lady'll faint when she sees me with my beard gone?"

With a smile, she moved away from him. "Are you trying to get me to say you'll be the most handsome man there?"

He made a grab for her hand, but she moved back too quickly. "Let's you and me stay here," he said. "We'll find somethin' to do together. I like that dress."

"Oh, no, Mr. Taggert," she laughed, wondering if she could tighten her corset another quarter inch. "I will not be seduced into . . . into whatever you have in mind. You must get dressed for the garden party." She'd backed up until she was pressed against the wall.

Kane moved very close to her, put both hands on the wall on either side of her head and leaned forward. "We haven't really gotten to know each other, have we? I mean, a couple should spend some time alone before they get married, shouldn't they?"

Houston deftly slid from under his arm. "Mr. Taggert," she said firmly, "I'll not be sweet-talked out of this party. I think you are afraid to go, and perhaps if you're the sort of man who lets a little gathering of people frighten him, I'm not sure you're the man I want to marry."

With an angry look, he went back to his desk. "You gotta mean streak in you a mile wide. I ain't afraid of no damn party."

"Then prove it by getting dressed and going with me." As she watched, he seemed to be fighting something inside himself, and she almost said she'd stay at home with him. Be firm, Houston, she told herself. This is what he wants you for.

He tossed the papers to his desk. "I'll go," he said in disgust. "And I hope you ain't gonna be sorry." He stormed past her and out the door.

"I hope so, too," she breathed, as she ran after him to get the suit that was still in the carriage.

While Kane dressed, Houston looked at the furniture scattered about the house and planned where it should go. After an hour and a half, when she'd begun to think Kane had left by a second-story window, she turned to see him standing in the doorway wearing the dark frock coat, white linen shirt, and slate gray trousers, a white cravat held in his hand.

"I don't know how to tie this."

Houston couldn't move for a moment. The well-tailored suit showed to advantage the extraordinary difference in width between his shoulders and his trim waist, and the dark cloth emphasized his brows and hair. With pride, she thought of appearing at the party on his arm. Maybe there was a part of her that wanted to show the town that she could get another man. She could certainly do worse than this man. Oh my, yes she could.

"Do you know how to tie this?" he persisted.

"Yes, of course," she said, coming to herself. "You'll have to sit down so I can reach your neck."

He sat on one of the little gilt chairs as if he were a condemned man.

As Houston worked on the Windsor tie, she began to talk to him. "The party is at the house of a friend of mine, Tia Mankin. There'll be long tables set with food and drink, and all you'll have to do is walk around and talk to people. I'll stay with you as much as I can."

Kane said nothing.

When the tie was done, she looked into his eyes. Was this the man on whose head she'd broken a pitcher? "It'll be over soon, then we'll come back here and have supper."

Suddenly, his arms tightened about her and he kissed her hard—as if he wanted courage from her. The next moment he was standing beside her. "Let's get this over with," he said, heading for the door.

Again, Houston was too stunned to move. Their few kisses seemed to mean nothing to him but each one left her breathless.

"Ain't you comin'?" he asked impatiently from the doorway.

"Yes, certainly," she said, smiling, and feeling very alive.

As Kane drove them the short distance to Tia's house, she gave him a few instructions. "If people are to believe our engagement, perhaps you should be attentive to me," she said cautiously. "Stay beside me, hold my arm, that sort of thing. And *please* help me out of the carriage."

He nodded without looking at her.

"And smile," she said. "Surely marriage isn't that bad."

"If I live through the engagement," he said grimly.

The people already gathered in the Mankin garden were more than curious about Kane and Houston. Trying their best to act politely, they practically ran toward the carriage, then stood back and gaped. The hairy coal miner had been replaced with a gentleman.

Kane didn't seem aware of the people's reactions but Houston was very aware of them, and, with pride, she put her hands on his big shoulders as he helped her from the carriage.

Slipping her arm through his, she guided him toward the waiting people.

"May I introduce you to my fiancé, Mr. Kane Taggert?" she began.

Twenty minutes later, when he'd been introduced to everyone, she felt him begin to relax.

"It wasn't as bad as you thought, was it?"

"Naw," he said a bit smugly. "You want somethin' to eat?"

"I would love some punch. Would you excuse me for a moment? I need to speak to someone."

She watched him for a moment as he started toward the tables of food and noticed how many women stopped to look at him. Meredith Lechner walked over to talk to him, smiling first at Houston as if for permission.

Mine, Houston thought, my very own frog-turned-prince. And it took only one lump on his head. She coughed politely to cover what might have been a giggle.

While Kane was busy, she walked toward Reverend Thomas, who stood alone on the outskirts of the crowd.

"You've certainly changed him," Reverend Thomas said, nodding toward Kane, who now had three women near him.

"The outside perhaps," she said, and her voice lowered. "I want to talk to you. Last week, in the coal town, Jean Taggert said she knew about me. How much does she know?"

"Everything," the reverend answered.

"But how—?" Houston began.

"I told her. I had to. I wanted you to have a friend, a real friend, on the inside."

"But what if I'm caught? Jean could be in even more trouble if she knows who I am. It's bad enough as it is."

"Houston," the reverend said, his eyes on hers. "You can't take all the responsibility by yourself. Jean came to me months ago and wanted to know the truth. I was glad to tell her."

Houston was silent for a moment as she watched Kane laugh at something one of the women said, and she saw the women take a step closer. It's not just me he charms, she thought.

"Did you know that Kane and Jean are related?" she asked.

"First cousins." He smiled at her startled look. "As soon as I learned about your engagement, I went to Jean. Oh, the guards were reluctant to let me in, but I do have a higher boss than theirs. Neither Jean nor any of her family's met Kane. There's some secrecy about his birth, something about his mother. Jean's guess was that she was a . . . ah, lady of the evening and Kane's father had some doubt that the child was his. That would explain why Kane was put to work at Fenton's rather than being reared by the Taggerts."

"Do you know what happened to his parents?"

"Jean felt sure they were both dead. Houston," Reverend Thomas put his hand on her arm, "are you sure you want to marry this man? I know that what Leander did must have hurt you but—."

Houston didn't feel she could listen to another lecture, no matter how well-intended. "I'm sure," she said firmly. "Now, if you'll excuse me, I must see to my fiancé before he's stolen from me."

"All right, but, Houston, if you want to talk, I'll be here."

As Houston made her way toward Kane, one person after another stopped her.

"He looks quite nice, Houston. You've done wonders with him."

"Did you really fall in love with him while you were engaged to Leander?"

"Was Lee terribly heartbroken when you told him?"

"Did you sneak out of your house to meet Mr. Taggert?"

"Houston, you must tell us *everything!*"

Finally, she made her way to Kane's side and slipped her arm through his.

"You damn well took long enough," he said under his breath. "Do you know what those women wanted to know?" he asked in a shocked tone.

"I can guess," she laughed. "Did you get something to eat?"

"Just a couple of those little sandwiches. A body could eat all of 'em and still be hungry. We have to stay here much longer? Who was that man you were talkin' to?"

"Reverend Thomas."

"Oh, yeah. You teach a class for him on Wednesdays." Smiling, he touched her nose with his fingertip. "Don't look so surprised. I know lots about you. Why don't you go sit down and I'll bring you a plate of food? That's what I seen the other men doin' for the women.''

If she were with Lee now he'd know exactly what was proper to do, she thought. And they'd have to leave the party at 3:15 because on Thursdays he—.

"You wishin' you had a man that knew what to do?" Kane asked from above her, his big shadow blocking the sunlight, a plate of food in his hand.

"Why no, I wasn't," she answered, but said no more because a mass of very wet food came tumbling into her lap.

Kane didn't move but shown in his face was the knowledge that everything he'd feared had just happened.

It was when Houston heard a woman's smothered laugh— for the entire party had come to a halt—that she reacted.

Quickly, she stood, the food falling to the ground. "Pick me up," she whispered, but he only stared at her with bleak eyes. "Sweep me into your arms, carry me to the carriage and drive away," she commanded quietly.

Kane wasn't used to obeying orders blindly, but he did this one. With ease, he picked her up.

As he carried her toward the carriage, Houston snuggled against him. On Thursdays, Leander took fencing lessons, but Mr. Taggert's Thursdays were spent in sweeping his intended off her feet.

Kane was silent until they were in the carriage and driving toward the Chandler house. "Why?" he asked. "What good did my carryin' you do?"

"Because few of the men in there have backs strong enough to carry their wives, and I think any woman would trade a little spilled food for a man who could lift her."

"You don't weigh nothin'," he said.

With a smile, she leaned toward him and kissed his cheek. "I weigh nothing to you," she said softly.

He stopped the buggy and stared at her. "You're a real lady, ain't you, Miss Chandler? A real lady."

"I hope so," she murmured and thought that it could be possible that whatever Kane Taggert wanted her to be, she just might become.

Chapter 9

Houston burst into her mother's bedroom, where Opal sat quietly embroidering a pair of cuffs.

"Mother! You have to help me," Houston said.

"Look at your dress," Opal said, rising. "Do you think it'll come clean?"

"I don't know. Mother, he's downstairs waiting for me and you must entertain him while I change. If you don't talk to him, I'm afraid he'll leave."

Opal took a step backward. "You can't mean your Mr. Taggert? You have him downstairs?"

Houston took both her mother's hands in her own. "He is very upset. By accident, he spilled some food in my lap and, oh Mother, everyone started to laugh at him. If you'd seen his face! He was completely humiliated. Please go down and talk to him for a few minutes. Don't let him leave."

Opal felt herself softening. "No one should have laughed at him if it was an accident."

"Thank you," Houston said, quickly kissing her mother's cheek before rushing from the room. She ignored Opal's cry of "What will I talk to him about?"

Susan was waiting for Houston and helped her with the back fastenings of the dress.

"It's just the front panel that's stained," Houston said, holding the dress up and examining it. "Susan, tell Mrs. Thomas to rub it with magnesia powder for the grease and—oh Heavens, every stain in the world is on it. Hold the panel over a sulfur flame, and if it still doesn't come clean, I'll use naphtha on it. But I'll do it myself. The last thing I want is the kitchen exploding. Hurry now, before it sets any worse."

When Susan returned from her errand, Houston was sitting at her desk, writing. "When I finish this note, I want you to give it to Willie to take to Mrs. Murchison. I also want you to explain to him what I need, so there's no misunderstanding."

She wrote as she talked. "Tell Willie to take the stairs in the Taggert house, the ones by the kitchen, all the way to the attics, turn left and he'll see a long corridor. The second door on the left leads to a small room filled with furniture, and along the back wall is a small Soumak carpet—no, I'll write a red figured carpet—and a large muslin bag of decorative pillows. The bag is as tall as he is, so he can't miss it. Tell him to take the carpet and the pillows downstairs to the small drawing room. Mrs. Murchison will show him where it is. Have him unroll the carpet, put the pillows along the edges of the carpet, and then bring in the large, three-arm silver candelabra from the dining room next door and set it in the middle of the carpet."

She looked up. "Can you remember all that to tell Willie?"

"Oh, yes, Miss. A picnic indoors. Did Mr. Taggert really spill the whole table of food on people?"

"Where did you hear that?"

"Ellie, who works for the Mankins' neighbors, came by."

"Well, it's not true at all. Now, go downstairs, tell Willie, and have him give this to Mrs. Murchison. And quickly, please. I'll need help dressing. Oh yes, and have him tell Mrs. Murchison I'll delay as long as possible to give her time to cook."

Houston saw to her dismay, as soon as Susan had gone, that the spilled food had soaked all her undergarments. After a quick inspection, she thought boiling would cleanse them, and she hurriedly began to undress.

From her closet she chose a dress of soft, pale green lawn with short puffed sleeves, the bodice and high neckline made of cotton guipure lace. Unfortunately, the back was laced with thirty-six tiny green buttons. She was struggling with these when Susan returned.

"What do you hear from downstairs?"

"Nothing, Miss," Susan said, beginning to fasten the buttons with a little brass hook. "Should I look? I think the parlor door's open."

"No," Houston said, but she was beginning to worry. Opal Gates was a woman who needed protection, a woman who was easily shocked. Houston had a vision of Kane using some of his vile language, of Opal fainting from shock and Kane feeling no obligation to "pick her up."

"There's no one else in the house, is there, Susan?"

"No, Miss."

"Good, because I'm going downstairs and look through the hinges. You can button me down there."

Houston tiptoed down the stairs, Susan behind her, and peeked through the parlor door.

Kane and Opal sat close to one another on the horsehair sofa, both peering together into a stereopticon.

"I've never seen the place myself," Opal was saying, "but I hear it's quite impressive."

"I lived in New York for years but I never heard of this place," Kane said. "What was that name again?"

"Niagara Falls."

Kane put the viewer down and looked at her. "You'd like to go see it, wouldn't you?"

"Why, yes, I would. In fact, Mr. Taggert, I've always had a secret dream to travel. I would like to hire my own private railroad car and travel all over the United States."

Kane took Opal's hand in his. "I'm gonna give you that dream, Mrs. Chandler. What color train would you like to have? I mean the inside. You like red?"

"I couldn't possibly—," Opal began.

Kane leaned closer to her. "I have a real weakness for ladies," he said softly. "And you, Mrs. Chandler, are as much a lady as your daughter."

There was silence for a moment between them and Susan, as she looked over Houston's shoulder, stopped her buttoning.

"Pink," Opal said. "I should like a train completely done in pink."

"You'll have it. Anything else you want?"

"I should like you to call me Opal. I'm afraid my husband, Mr. Gates, won't appreciate his wife being called by her former husband's name."

Houston held her breath to see how Kane would take the correction.

Kane took Opal's hand he was holding and kissed it heartily, not a gentleman's kiss. "No wonder you got a lady for a daughter."

"I think your mamma'll marry him if you won't," Susan said.

"Hush and finish the buttons."

"Done," Susan said, and Houston walked around the door to the front of the parlor.

"I hope I didn't take too long," she said sweetly. "You were comfortable, Mr. Taggert?"

"Yeah," Kane said, grinning. "Real comfortable. But I gotta be goin' now. I have work to do."

"Mr. Taggert," Houston said, "could you please drive me into town to the dressmaker's? I need to leave her some patterns."

A frown crossed Kane's face, but he agreed when Houston said her errand would take fifteen minutes at the most.

"Don't expect me back until evening," she whispered to her mother as she kissed her cheek good-bye and grabbed her parasol.

"You're in capable hands, dear," Opal said, smiling fondly at Kane.

When they were in Houston's carriage, she turned to Kane. "Did you and my mother have a pleasant chat?"

"You got a good mother," he said. "Where's this dress shop you want to go to? You sure you'll only take ten minutes?"

"Fifteen," she answered. "My . . . previous wedding dress was made in Denver, but I'm going to have an identical one made here."

"Identical? Oh, yeah, for the double weddin'. When is it, anyway?"

"Monday, the twentieth. I do hope you don't have to work that day and can come."

He gave her a sideways look, then smiled. "I'll be there on the weddin' day if you'll be there on the weddin' night." He laughed as her face pinkened and she turned away.

She directed him down Coal Avenue to the Westfield Block,

a long, two-story, sandstone building that ran from Second to Third Streets and contained retail stores below and offices above.

Kane tied the horse, and helped Houston out of the carriage. "I think I'll have a drink while I'm waitin'," he said, nodding toward one of the town's many saloons. "I hope bein' a husband is easier 'n bein' an intended."

Turning, he left her standing in the dusty street. There were times, Houston thought, when she missed Leander's manners.

Her business inside the dressmaker's took only seven minutes, and the woman threw up her hands in despair at the idea of being asked to make such an elaborate dress in so short a time. She sat down in shock when Houston asked her to also make a dress for Jean Taggert. In a flurry of movement, she pushed Houston from the shop, saying she needed every moment for work. Houston could tell she was thrilled at the prospect.

Now, Houston stood outside the shop, her green parasol open, and looked across the street toward the saloon where Kane was waiting for her. She hoped he didn't stay in there too long.

"Lookee here," came a man's voice. "You waitin' for us?"

Three young cowboys surrounded her and, by the smell of them, they had just come in from weeks on the trail.

"Come on, Cal," one of the cowboys said. "She's a lady."

Houston pretended the men weren't there, but silently prayed Kane would suddenly appear.

"I like ladies," Cal said.

Houston turned and put her hand on the doorknob of the Sayles Art Rooms.

Cal put his hand over hers.

"I beg your pardon," Houston said, drawing back, giving the man a look of contempt.

"Talks like a lady," Cal said. "Honey, how about you and me goin' over to the saloon and havin' a few beers?"

"Cal," one of the other cowboys said, with warning in his voice.

But Cal leaned closer to Houston. "I'll show you a real good time, honey."

"I'll show you a good time," came Kane's voice as he grabbed the back of the cowboy's shirt, and the waistband of his trousers, and sent the boy sailing to land face down in the dirty street.

When the cowboy, who was half Kane's size, lifted himself, shaking his head to clear it, Kane towered over him. "This here's a clean town," he growled. "You wanta free woman, you go to Denver, but here we take care of our women." He leaned closer to the boy. "And I damn well take care of *my* woman. You understand that?"

"Yes, sir," he mumbled. "I didn't mean no—," he began but stopped. "Yes, sir, I'm goin' to Denver right now."

"I like that idea," Kane said as he stepped back, grabbed Houston's arm and propelled her into the carriage seat.

He drove in silence to his house, then stopped. "Damn! I guess you wanted to go home." He picked up the reins again. "That kid didn't hurt ya, did he?"

"No," she said softly. "Thank you for coming to my rescue."

"Nothin' to it," he said, but he was frowning as if he were worried about something.

Houston put her hand on his arm. "Perhaps it was forward of me but I sent a message ahead to Mrs. Murchison to prepare us something to eat. That is, if you don't mind my dining with you."

He gave her a quick up-and-down look. "I don't mind, but I hope you got enough dresses to last you, since I seem to ruin 'em often enough."

"I have more than enough dresses."

"All right then," he said reluctantly, "but I got to work sometime today. You go on in and I'll put your horse away."

Once inside the house, Houston ran to the kitchen. "Is everything prepared?" she asked.

"Everything," Mrs. Murchison smiled. "And there's cold champagne waiting."

"Champagne?" Houston gasped, thinking of when Blair had drunk too much champagne and had ended up making love to Leander.

"And I've made all of Mr. Kane's favorites," Mrs. Murchison continued, her eyes softening.

"Buffalo steaks, no doubt," Houston muttered, "and another woman in love with him."

"What was that, Miss Houston?"

"Nothing. I'm sure everything will be perfect, as whatever you cook always is." Houston left the kitchen to go to the small drawing room. It was exactly as she'd envisioned it, with the candles already burning, champagne cooling, pâté and crackers set on a silver platter. The late sun coming through the windows made the room glow.

"You set this up?" Kane asked from behind her.

"I thought perhaps you'd be hungry," she began a bit nervously. The picnic had seemed a good idea, but now it looked like a setting for a seduction. "You said you'd like to talk, too," she whispered, eyes on her hands.

Kane gave a grunt and strode past her. "If I didn't know better, I'd say you wanted more than to talk. Come on and sit down here and let's eat. I—."

"Have to work," she interrupted, feeling a little hurt at his attitude. After all, she'd done this because he'd seemed so miserable when he'd dropped the food on her.

Kane walked closer to her, put his hand under her chin. "You ain't gonna cry, are you?"

"Certainly not," she said firmly. "Let's eat so I can go home. I have a great deal to do also and—."

Kane grabbed her wrist and pulled her into his arms.

Houston felt her body softening and her anger disappearing. Perhaps this was what she'd been after. She did so much like to be touched by him.

"You smell good," he said, nuzzling her neck, as his big body surrounded hers, protecting her, making her feel safe and unsafe at the same time.

"You were real nice today." He was placing little nibbling kisses along her neck. "You ain't gonna mind bein' married to a stableboy like me too much, are you?"

Houston didn't answer as she felt her knees giving way, but Kane easily held her upright as he began to make love to her left ear.

"You were the prettiest lady there today," he whispered, his soft breath sending chills down her legs. "And I liked carryin' you. In fact, I'd like to carry you upstairs to my bed right now."

Houston was tempted to say nothing and, in truth, wondered if it was possible for her voice to work.

"Eh-hem," came a loud sound from the doorway.

"Go away," Kane said, his teeth nipping along Houston's jawline.

But Houston was too steeped in years of training to continue. She pushed at Kane but didn't budge him. "Please," she pleaded, looking into his dark eyes.

With a look of disgust, he released her so suddenly she nearly fell.

Mrs. Murchison stood in the doorway, holding an enormous porcelain soup tureen. As she passed Houston on the way out, she gave her shaming looks which made Houston blush.

Trying to calm herself, Houston realized how close she'd come to blithely jumping into bed with her fiancé. But she'd promised her stepfather she'd ask questions about Kane before she married him. What if she found out he was a criminal? Would she marry him anyway? She would certainly have to if she'd been to bed with him.

Looking at him now, as he sat on the floor opening the champagne, his jacket off, the sleeves of his white shirt rolled to the elbows and showing strong, tanned forearms, she thought perhaps she should let him make love to her, then she'd have to marry him no matter what she found out about him.

But that would be cheating.

Carefully arranging her skirts, she sat on the pillows across from him. "I have a favor to ask of you," she began.

"Sure," he said, mouth full of pâté.

"I'd like to remain a virgin until my wedding."

Kane choked so badly Houston was worried about him, but he downed half a bottle of the champagne and managed to recover. "It's nice to hear you are one," he said at last, tears in his eyes. "I mean what with Westfield and all."

Houston stiffened.

"Now, don't go gettin' your back up. Here, have some of this." He held out a tulip glass of champagne. "It's good for you. So, you want to remain a virgin, do you?" he said, as he ladled creamy oyster stew into porcelain bowls. "I guess that means you want me to keep my hands off you."

He was watching her in an odd way, speculatively.

"Perhaps that would be better," she said, thinking that if he kept touching her as he had a minute ago, she'd never stay a virgin—nor want to remain one.

"All right," he said and there was coldness in his voice.

Houston's eyes widened. No doubt he thought it was because he was once a stableboy and she thought she was better than he was. "No, please," she began. "It's not what you think. I—." She couldn't tell him what she'd promised her stepfather, or that his hands made her feel far and away from being a lady. She put her hand on his bare forearm.

Kane moved away from her touch. "You made your point. Look, we have an agreement, a contract more or less, and I've been breakin' it. You said you'd pretend we were . . . in love, I guess, in public and you've done that. In private you don't have to put up with me. I'll keep my hands off you. In fact, I think it'd be better if I left now. You stay here 'n' eat and I'll go to work."

Before Houston could move, Kane had stood and was halfway across the room.

"Please don't go," she cried, leaping up to follow him, then tripping and falling on her long skirts.

He caught her before she hit the hard floor but swiftly released her once she was steadied.

"I didn't mean to insult you," she began. "It's not that I don't *like* your touch," she began, then stopped, blushed, and looked at her hands. "I mean I . . . It's just that I never . . . And I would like to remain . . . If possible," she concluded, looking up at him.

Kane was staring at her quite hard. "You don't make no sense. You want me to keep my hands off or what? All I asked for in this marriage was a lady in public. In private, this house is big enough you don't even have to look at my ugly face. It's your choice, lady."

A lady must be positive, Houston remembered from school. She put her chin in the air and her shoulders back. "I want to be your wife in private as well as in public, but I also want to remain a virgin until the wedding."

"Well, who's stoppin' you?" Kane glared at her. "Am I haulin' you upstairs by your hair? Am I forcin' you into my bed?"

"No, but you are a persuasive asker, Mr. Taggert," she shot back at him, then put her hand to her mouth.

Understanding lit Kane's eyes. "Well, I'll be damned," he said, with wonder in his voice. "Who would a thought? Oh well, maybe ladies like stableboys. Come on and sit down and eat," he said jovially. "A good asker, am I?" He grinned as she sat down across from him.

With all her heart, Houston wished she'd never brought the subject up.

The intimate little dinner Houston'd planned turned into controlled chaos. Edan came in before the soup was finished and handed Kane papers he had to read and sign. Kane invited him to eat with them, and they proceeded to talk business throughout the meal.

Houston silently watched the sun set through the long windows. Mrs. Murchison went in and out bearing great quantities of delicious food, which were consumed down to the last crumb.

Kane kept giving the woman compliments, which ranged from a mumbled "damned good" to, when she brought in an enormous baked Alaska, asking her to run away with him and live in sin. Mrs. Murchison giggled and blushed like a schoolgirl.

Houston, remembering the cook's remark that she was cooking all Mr. Kane's favorite foods, said, "What are your favorite foods, Mr. Taggert?"

He looked at her over the top of some papers. "Anything that tastes good and that includes pretty ladies."

With pinkened cheeks, Houston looked away.

At nine o'clock she rose. "I must leave now. Thank you so much for the dinner, Mr. Taggert." She really didn't think he'd notice whether she was there or not.

Kane caught the hem of her dress. "You can't leave yet. I want to talk to you."

Without yanking her skirt away, she couldn't leave, so she stood still, looking at a wall panel over the heads of the two men seated at her feet.

"I think I'm the one who should go," Edan said, beginning to gather papers.

"We ain't done yet," Kane said.

"Don't you think you should spend a little time alone with your bride?" Edan asked pointedly. "I'll tell Mrs. Murchison to go home." He stood. "Houston, thank you for dinner. I enjoyed it very much." Edan left the room, closing the door behind him.

Houston didn't move, but stood just where she was, not looking down at him.

He tugged on her skirt a few times, but when she didn't respond, he stood and looked at her. "I think you're mad at me."

Houston looked away. "That's utterly ridiculous. It's quite late, Mr. Taggert, and I must go home. My parents will be worried."

Kane put his hand on her cheek, cupping her face. "It was real nice of you to fix up this dinner with the candles an' all."

"I'm glad you were pleased. Now I must—."

He pulled her into his arms. "All night I've been thinkin' about what you said, about how I could talk you into things," he said, his lips against her neck.

"Please don't," she said, ineffectually pushing at him.

He moved his hand up to her carefully arranged hair, buried his fingers in it and slowly began to work his way through. Her thick, soft hair fell about her shoulders and Kane ran the fingers of both his hands through it.

"Pretty," he murmured, looking at her, their faces very close. The next moment he tilted her head to the side and began to kiss her in a way that made her feel as if she were dissolving. He played with her lips, pulling the lower one out with his teeth, touching the tip of his tongue to her lip.

Houston stood still as waves of feeling coursed through her body. Then, with abandon, she put her arms about his neck and pressed her body against his. Kane reacted instantly, pulling her close, bending her to fit the planes of his big body.

When he began to bend his knees and descend to the carpet and pillows, Houston didn't even consider protesting, but clung to him as if he were a life-giving force. His lips never left hers as they lay side by side on the carpet.

Kane ran his hand down her hip and thigh as his mouth travelled down her neck.

"Kane," she whispered, her head back, her leg pressed between his.

"Yes, sweetheart, I'm here," he whispered, his voice sending chills down her body.

His hand pulled her dress up to explore her legs, quickly finding the bare expanse of thigh above her gartered stockings and under her long, loose drawers.

Houston had no mind, no thoughts at all, but only felt the heavenly sensations of his hand on her skin, his lips on her face. Instinctively, she moved closer to him, wedged her leg between his even tighter.

With a groan, Kane pushed her away, lay beside her, looking at her for just a second, then stood.

"Get up," he said coldly and walked away, his back to her as he looked out the dark window.

Houston felt dirty, humiliated, cheated, as she lay on the rug, her skirts hiked about her waist. Swift tears came to her eyes as she slowly stood and tried to regain her composure.

"Go fix your hair," Kane said, not turning around. "Fix your hair and I'll take you home to your mother."

As quickly as she could, Houston fled the room, her hand to her mouth to prevent a sob coming out.

The two bathrooms downstairs were off the kitchen and in Kane's office. She didn't want to risk seeing either Edan or Mrs. Murchison so she ran upstairs to a bath near Kane's bedroom.

Once inside the marble-covered room, she gave herself over to tears. He'd wanted to marry a lady, and he was disgusted that she'd acted like a harlot. Yet this was what Blair had meant when she'd said she saw sparks when Leander kissed her. Never had Lee's kisses made her feel anything, but Kane's . . .

She looked at herself in the mirror, her eyes alive and sparkling, her mouth slightly swollen, her cheeks pink, her hair wild about her shoulders. This was not the lady he'd wanted. No wonder he pushed her away from him.

Again, the tears began to flow.

As soon as Houston left the drawing room, Kane made his way to his office, where Edan sat behind the desk, his nose in a pile of papers.

"Houston leave?" Edan asked absently. When Kane didn't answer, the blond man looked up to see Kane, with shaking hands, pour himself a water glass half full of whiskey.

"What have you done to her?" Edan asked, barely concealed anger in his voice. "I told you she wasn't like other women."

"What the hell do you know about her? And you should damn well ask what she's done to me. I want you to hitch up her buggy and take her home."

"What happened?"

"Women!" Kane said in disgust. "They never act the way they're supposed to. There's only one reason why I ever wanted to marry a lady and—."

"Fenton again," Edan said tiredly.

"You're damned right, Fenton!" Kane half shouted. "Everything I've ever done, all I've ever worked for, I've done in order to repay Fenton for what he did to me. All those years of work, the years I spent scrapin', I had one dream and that was that someday he'd come to dinner at my house. *My* house would be four times the size of his and sittin' at the foot of the table would be my wife, the woman he once denied me, his precious daughter Pamela."

"But you've had to make do with another woman," Edan said. "Isn't Houston to your liking?"

Kane took a deep drink of his whiskey. "She puts on a damn good act," he said. "She must want my money *real* bad."

"And what if she's not after your money? What if she wants a husband, children?"

Kane shrugged. "She can get 'em later. All I want is to show up Fenton. I want to sit in my own dinin' room with one of those Chandlers there as my wife."

"And what do you plan to do with Houston after this dinner? She's not a pair of shoes that you can throw away."

"I'm buyin' her some jewelry. She can keep it and, if I can't find a buyer, I'll give her this house."

"Just like that?" Edan asked. "You're going to tell her to go away, that you're through with her?"

"She'll be glad to get rid of me." He finished the whiskey. "And I don't have time for a woman in my life. Take her home, will you?" With that, he left the room.

Chapter 10

Houston cried herself to sleep that night. Her confusion was what made her so miserable. Most of her life she'd lived under the rule of her stepfather, and Duncan Gates had rigid ideas of what a lady should and should not do. Houston had always tried to live up to his ideas. Any time she'd broken rules she'd done so in secret.

With Leander, she'd conducted herself with absolute restraint. He needed a lady for a wife and Houston had become that lady. In public and in private, she'd been a lady. Her conduct was always perfect.

Yet Leander had actually wanted someone who was far and away from being a lady. The words he'd said about how wonderful Blair was were burned on her heart.

And then Kane came along, so different from Lee, with none of Lee's polish, none of Lee's sense of selfworth. But Kane'd wanted a lady, and when she wasn't one . . .

She'd never forget the look of disgust on his face after she'd rolled about on the floor with him.

How could she please a man? She'd thought Lee wanted a lady, but he hadn't. She had thought she'd learned from that experience that what men really wanted was a woman of passion. But Kane didn't. He wanted a lady.

The more she thought, the more she cried.

Later in the day, when Blair came to Houston's room, she saw her sister's red, swollen eyes and slipped into bed with her. For a while they didn't speak, but Houston began crying again.

"Is your life so awful?" Blair asked.

Sniffling, Houston nodded against Blair's shoulder.

"Taggert?" Blair asked.

Again Houston nodded. "I don't know what he wants from me."

"Anything he can get, most likely," Blair said. "You don't have to marry him. No one's forcing you to. If you'd make it clear that you want Leander, I think you could get him back."

"Leander wants you," Houston said, sitting up.

"He only wants me because I gave him what you wouldn't," Blair said. "Houston, you love Leander. Heaven only knows why, but you do, you have for years. Think what marriage to him would mean. You could live in the house he built for you, have your children and—."

"No," Houston said, taking a handkerchief from a bedside drawer. "Leander belongs to you in a way he never belonged to me. He'd much rather have you."

"No, he wouldn't! You don't know what you're saying. He doesn't like me at all. This morning at the hospital he said I was a puppet-doctor, that I did more harm than good and—." She buried her face in her hands.

"Maybe he doesn't like your doctoring but he *loves* your kisses," Houston said angrily. "Oh, Blair, I am sorry. I'm just tired and upset. Perhaps it's nerves before the wedding."

"What did Taggert do to you?"

"Nothing," Houston said, hiding her face in the handkerchief. "He's always been more than honest with me. I think perhaps I lie to myself."

"And what is that supposed to mean?"

"I don't know. I have work to do," she said as she got out of the bed. "There's so much to do to get ready for the wedding."

"You're still going to marry him?" Blair asked softly.

"If he'll have me," Houston whispered, her back to her sister. After last night, Houston thought, he may have changed his mind, and the prospect of life without Kane's moods—as well as his kisses—made a barren-looking future. She pictured herself sitting quietly in a rocker with her crochet hook.

"Do you want to help me with the wedding arrangements?" Houston asked, turning back to her sister. "Or would you rather leave everything to me?"

"I don't want to even think of marriage, not mine to Leander, and especially not yours to Taggert. Lee's just angry about what happened and I'm sure that if you—."

"Leander and I are dead to each other!" Houston snapped. "Can't I make you see that? Lee wants you, not me. It's Kane . . ." She turned away. "I'm going to marry Mr. Taggert in ten days."

Blair jumped out of the bed. "You may think that you failed with Leander, but you didn't. And you don't have to punish yourself with that overbearing oaf. He can't even handle a plate of food, much less—."

Blair stopped because Houston slapped her across the face.

"He's the man I'm going to marry," Houston said, anger in her words. "I'll not let you or anyone else denigrate him."

With her hand to her cheek, Blair's eyes filled with tears. "What I've done is coming between us," she whispered. "No man anywhere means more than sisters," she said before leaving the room.

For a moment, Houston sat on the bed. She wanted to comfort Blair but didn't know how. What was Kane doing to her that would make her slap her own sister?

And the next question was, did Kane still want to marry her?

With shaking hands, she sat down at her desk and wrote a note to her fiancé.

> *Dear Mr. Taggert,*
>   *My behavior last night was unforgivable. I'd understand if you'd like the return of your ring.*
>   *Sincerely,*
>   *Miss Houston Chandler*

She sealed the letter and had Susan give it to Willie to deliver.

When Kane received the letter, he snorted.

"Bad news?" Edan asked.

Kane started to hand the letter to Edan but, instead, slipped it into his pocket. "It's from Houston. You know, I don't think I ever met anybody quite like her. Weren't you goin' into town later?"

Edan nodded.

"Stop by one of the jewelry stores and buy a dozen rings, all different colors, and send them over to Houston's house."

"Any message?"

Kane smiled. "No, the rings oughta be enough. Now, where were we?"

At four o'clock, Mr. Weatherly, of Weatherly's Jewels and Coronation Gifts, came rushing up the steps of the Chandler house.

"I have a package for Miss Houston," he said excitedly to Susan, who answered the door.

Susan led him into the parlor where Opal and a subdued Houston sat, surrounded by lists of wedding preparations.

"Good afternoon, Mr. Weatherly," Opal said. "Could I get you some tea?"

"No, thank you," he said, looking at Houston, lights dancing in his eyes. "This is for you." He thrust a large, thin black velvet box at her.

Puzzled, but with a glimmer of hope blossoming within her, Houston took the box. All day had been miserable as she tried to plan a wedding that might not happen. And to make things worse, at noon, Mr. Gates had come home for dinner and privately informed her that he'd made an appointment for her to meet with Marc Fenton tomorrow morning. He was holding her to her promise to ask questions about Kane.

When Houston opened the box and saw the rings, she had to blink back tears of relief. "How pretty," she said with outward calm as she looked at each one: two emeralds, a pearl, a sapphire, a ruby, three diamond rings, an amethyst, one ring with three opals, a ring of carved coral and one of jade.

"Could have knocked me over with a feather," Mr. Weatherly was saying. "That blond fella that follows Mr. Taggert around came in an hour ago and asked for a dozen rings, and they were all for Miss Houston."

"Mr. Taggert didn't choose them himself?" Houston asked.

"It was his idea; the blond man said so."

Very calmly, Houston stood, the closed box of rings in her hand. "Thank you so much, Mr. Weatherly, for coming personally with the rings. Perhaps you'd like to see them, Mother," she said, handing the box to Opal. "I'm sure they need to be sized. Good day, Mr. Weatherly."

As Houston went upstairs to her room, her heart lightened. The rings themselves didn't matter, but he'd read her note and he meant to marry her. That was what was important. Of course, he hadn't asked to see her but soon they'd be married and he'd see her every day.

Upstairs, she began to dress for dinner.

Houston smiled at Marc Fenton, who sat across from her in Miss Emily's quiet, pink and white Tea Shop. Opal had taken a seat not far away, but she tried to leave them their privacy. Mr. Gates had insisted that Opal accompany Houston because he said he had no more faith in the morals of young Americans.

Marc was a good-looking man, short, stocky, blond, with wide-set blue eyes and an infectious grin.

"I hear you've made the catch of the season, Houston," Marc was saying, as he took another raisin tart onto his plate. "Everyone's whispering about how he's half barbarian and half knight-on-a-white-horse. Which one is the real Kane Taggert?" he asked, eyes twinkling.

"I thought perhaps you could tell me. Mr. Taggert used to work for you."

"He left when I was seven years old! I barely remember the man."

"But what do you remember?"

"He used to scare me to death," Marc laughed. "He ran that stable like his own private domain and nobody, including my father, trespassed."

"Even your sister, Pamela?" Houston asked, as she idly toyed with her teacup.

"So that's what you want to know about." He laughed again. "I knew nothing of what was going on. One day, both Taggert and my sister were gone. You know, to this day, I still get a little nervous when I take a horse and don't ask permission."

"Why did your sister leave?" Houston persisted.

"Father married her off immediately. I don't think he wanted to take any more chances on his daughter falling in love with another stableboy."

"Where is Pam now?"

"I rarely see her. She moved to Cleveland with her husband, had a kid, and stayed there. He died a few months ago and her kid was very sick for a long time. She's had it rough in the last year."

"Is she—?"

Marc leaned forward in conspiracy. "If you want to know more about the man you're planning to marry, you ought to talk to Lavinia LaRue."

"I don't believe I know her."

Marc leaned back with a smile. "Of course you don't. She's Taggert's light skirt."

"His . . . ?"

"His mistress, Houston. I have to go now," he said, rising, leaving money on the table.

Houston also rose, put her hand on his arm. "Where do I find Miss Larule?"

"LaRue, Lavinia LaRue, and ask down on Crescent Street."

"Crescent Street?" Houston's eyes widened. "I've never been there."

"Send Willie. He knows his way around there. Meet her somewhere private. You don't want to be seen with the Lavinia LaRues of this world. Good luck on your wedding, Houston," he said over his shoulder as he left.

"Did you find out what you wanted?" Opal asked her daughter.

"I think I found out much more than I wanted to know."

Houston spent the rest of Friday and all day Saturday making arrangements for the double wedding, ordering flowers, planning for food to be cooked and served.

"You haven't seen Kane in how many days, dear?" Opal asked.

"A matter of hours," Houston answered, not letting her mother see her face. She was not going to throw herself at Kane again. She'd made a fool of herself already and she didn't need to do it again.

On Saturday, there were other matters to consider. Mr. Gates started yelling at five in the morning, waking everyone to announce that Blair had been out all night. Opal reassured him that Blair had been out with Lee, but that made Mr. Gates worse. He shouted that Blair would have no reputation left, and that Lee would have to marry her today.

Between Houston and Opal, they managed to get him to settle down enough to eat breakfast and it was while they were eating that Blair and Leander walked into the room.

And what a sight they were! Blair was wearing an odd garment of navy blue, the skirt barely to her ankles. Her hair was down about her shoulders and all of her was covered with mud, cockleburs, and what looked to be dried blood. Lee was as bad, wearing only a shirt and trousers, holes in his pants and his sleeve.

"Lee," Opal said breathlessly. "Are those bullet holes?"

"Probably," he said, grinning good-naturedly. "You can see that I brought her back safe and sound. I need to go home and get some sleep. I'm on duty this afternoon." He turned to Blair, caressed her cheek for a moment. "Good night, doctor."

"Good night, doctor," she said, and he was gone.

For a moment no one could move, as they all stared at the bedraggled figure of Blair. For all her appearance of looking as if she'd been through three catastrophes, there was a light in her eyes that was close to fire.

Houston rose from the table and, as she got closer to her sister, she could smell her.

"Whatever is in your hair?"

Blair grinned idiotically. "Horse manure I would imagine. But at least it's in my hair and not on his chin."

Houston could hear Mr. Gates starting to move behind her. She grabbed Blair's arm firmly. "Upstairs!" she ordered.

Houston led Blair to the bathroom, turned on the tub taps

and began undressing her sister. "Wherever did you get this extraordinary suit?"

Once Blair started talking, she didn't seem able to stop. Houston unbuttoned her, unlaced a shoe while Blair got the other one, shampooed her sister's hair while Blair scoured the dirt off her skin—and all the while, Blair talked about what a wonderful day she'd had with Leander, telling the most horrifying stories about maggots, range wars, cut arteries and a wrestle with a woman. And in every story, Leander was there, saving one life after another, and at one point, even saving Blair's life.

Houston could barely believe that the Leander Blair was raving about was the remote man she'd known for years. According to Blair, Leander was close to magic when it came to being a doctor.

"Fourteen holes in that man's intestines! And Lee sewed them all," she said, as Houston rinsed her hair, then shampooed it again. "Fourteen."

And the more Blair talked, the worse Houston felt. Leander had never once looked at her as he'd looked at Blair this morning, nor had he taken her with him on his calls—not that she wanted to see the inner workings of a man's digestive system, but the sharing was what she wanted.

Blair had Leander, and after only a few days, he was hers in a way Houston had never had him. And now she didn't seem to have Kane either. Should she go to him? Eventually they'd have to see one another to talk about the wedding. Houston imagined showing up at his house. No doubt he'd say, "I knew you'd give in. You couldn't stay away too long."

All day Saturday, while Blair slept, she hoped Kane would visit her, but he didn't.

On Sunday morning, she dressed in a skirt of gray serge, a dark green blouse of plissé surah and a gray Figaro jacket, and went downstairs to join her family for church services.

When everyone was seated in the church and hymnals were open, a quiet settled on the people.

"Move over," Kane said to Houston.

Startled, she moved down so he could sit beside her. Throughout the service, he sat still, looking up at the Reverend

Thomas with a bored expression. The instant the service was over, he caught Houston's arm. "I wanta talk to you."

He half pulled her from the church, oblivious to people's attempts to socialize with them, and lifted her to the seat of his old wagon. Once seated himself, he flicked the reins to the four horses and set off so quickly Houston had to hold her hat on.

"All right," he said when he'd stopped abruptly on the south edge of town under some cottonwood trees near the waterworks plant, "what were you doin' with Marc Fenton?"

No matter how Houston remembered Kane, he was, in life, more than she imagined.

"I have known Marc all my life," she said coolly, "and I may see any friend I care to. Besides, my mother was with me."

"You think I don't know that? At least your mother's a sensible woman."

"I have no idea what you mean." She began to toy with her parasol.

"What were you doin' with Marc Fenton?" He leaned toward her in a threatening way.

Houston decided to tell him the truth. "My stepfather has made me promise to ask as many people as possible about you. Mr. Gates arranged for me to meet Marc so I could ask him about you. I would have talked to Mr. Fenton, but he refused the request." She glared at him. "And I will probably speak to a Miss Lavinia LaRue."

"Viney?" he asked, then grinned. "Gates gave you this advice? Not bad. I wonder how come he never made any money? Wait a minute, what if you ask somebody and he—or she—says I'm no good?"

"Then I'll have to reconsider our marriage," she said primly.

She wasn't prepared for his explosion of anger.

"We're supposed to be married one week from tomorrow, yet you just might call it off at any minute!? Because somebody says he don't like the cut of my shirt? I'll tell you somethin', *Miss* Chandler, you can ask ever' man I ever dealt with and ever' woman I ever slept with about me and, if they're honest, you're gonna find I ain't cheated a man in my life."

He got out of the wagon and walked under a tree, looking at the distant horizon.

"Damnation, but Edan told me a lady'd cause me nothin' but trouble. He said, 'Kane, marry some farm girl, move to the country and raise horses.' He told me not to get mixed up with no lady."

Houston managed to climb down from the tall wagon by herself. "I didn't mean to upset you so badly," she said quietly.

"Upset me!" he bellowed into her face. "I ain't had any peace since I met you. I'm rich, I ain't bad to look at, I offer you marriage and you turn me down flat. I don't hear nothin' from you, then I find out your sister's gonna marry the man *you're* so crazy in love with. But, still, you won't marry me. Then maybe you will. Then maybe you won't.

"For days you're at my house bossin' ever'body around, includin' me, and then you act like we got a bad case of measles and you don't come near the place. One mornin' I wake up and you're lookin' at me like you're starvin' and when I touch you, you break a water pitcher over my head and yell at me that I gotta respect you. But the next time I touch you, you pull me down on the floor and nearly tear my clothes off. But I respect you and I leave you a damn virgin, just like you wanted. But what do I get? Next thing I know, you're wonderin' if I want my ring back, an' it's back to maybe you ain't gonna marry me.

"This mornin' your mother come to me, told me the right suit to wear to church," he gave her a look of reproach, "and invited me to Sunday dinner."

He stopped and glared at her. "So here I am, all dressed up, with you tellin' me maybe you'll marry me, maybe you won't, and it all depends on what people say about me. Houston, I've had all this I'm gonna take. Right now you're gonna give me a yes or no and you're gonna stick to it. If you say yes now and no the day of the weddin', so help me, Houston, I'll drag you down the aisle by your hair. Now, what you got to say?"

"Yes," she said softly, and the amount of joy inside her was amazing.

"And what if somebody tells you I'm worthless? Or that I've killed people?" he asked with some hostility.

"I will still marry you."

He turned away. "You dreadin' it so much? I mean, I know

you wanted to marry Westfield, and I ain't exactly been a gentleman all the time in our courtin', but so far you've done your part of the bargain. In public, you've always acted like you didn't mind marryin' me."

Houston's relief that he hadn't been repulsed by her was so great she began trembling. She wasn't going to spend her life crocheting but was going to live with this man who was unlike anyone else.

She moved to stand in front of him. "After Sunday dinner, most young couples go to Fenton Park to walk and talk and just spend time together. Perhaps you'd like to go with me."

"I need to . . . ," he began. "If you still want to be seen with me after dinner with your family, I'm willin'."

She slipped her arm through his. "Just watch me, don't talk with your mouth full, don't shout at anyone, and above all, don't curse."

"You don't ask much, do you?" he said grimly.

"Pretend that the purchase of Mr. Vanderbilt's apartment building depends on this dinner. Maybe that will help you remember your manners."

Kane looked startled. "That reminds me. I need to—." He glanced down at her. "You know, I think I'd rather spend the afternoon sittin' in the park. It's been a long time since I took a whole day off."

Kane seemed to enjoy himself immensely at Sunday dinner. Opal fawned over him, and Duncan asked his advice. Houston watched them. They'd expected a monster and found a pleasant man.

Blair had been silent through the meal, and Houston was glad she was meeting Kane at last and could see what a generous man he was. Kane even offered to allow Mr. Gates to buy some land with him, at what Houston suspected was a bargain price.

As they were leaving, Kane said, "Your sister ain't like you at all."

Houston asked him what he meant but he wouldn't explain.

At the park, she introduced Kane to other engaged couples. For once, Kane relaxed rather than worrying about the amount of work he was missing. When a woman referred to Kane's previous mishap of dumping the food in Houston's lap, Kane stiffened, but then, when she sighed at his romantic gesture of carrying Houston, Kane ostentatiously denied that he'd done anything extraordinary.

An ice-cream parlor across from the park was open for a few hours on Sunday and Kane treated everyone to sodas and Hire's root beer.

At the end of the day, Houston returned home with stars in her eyes. She'd had no idea he could be so charming.

"I never had time to do this kind of thing before. I always thought it was a waste of time, but it's nice. You think I did all right with your friends? I didn't act too much like a stableboy?"

"Not in the least."

"Can you ride a horse?"

"Yes," she said, hope in her voice.

"I'll pick you up in the mornin' and we'll ride. Like that?"

"Very much."

Without another word, Kane put his hands in his pockets and went down the walk of the Chandler house whistling.

Chapter 11

Kane showed up on Monday morning at five o'clock, before anyone was out of bed. As soon as Houston heard the movement downstairs, she knew it could be only one person. No one ever dressed faster in a riding habit in her life.

"You took long enough," Kane said, as he led the way to two horses loaded with heavy saddlebags.

"Food," was all Kane said before mounting.

It was a good thing she'd been telling the truth when she said she could ride, she thought, hours later, as she followed Kane's horse up the side of a mountain.

They rode west, past the Taggert estate, toward the tail of the Rocky Mountains that ran along one side of Chandler. They travelled across flat land covered with fierce little chamisa plants and on until they reached the hills.

Kane led the way up the piñon-dotted hills, up higher until they reached pines and rock formations. He weaved his horse through the spruce and fir to halt before a breathtaking view of Chandler far below them.

"How did you find this place?" she whispered.

"When you play, you ride bicycles and drink tea with other people. I come up here." As he dismounted, he nodded his head toward a steep rise above them. "I gotta cabin up there, but it's pretty rough goin', not for ladies."

He began unloading food from his saddlebags as Houston dismounted by herself.

As they ate, they sat on the ground and talked.

"How did you make your money?" she asked.

"When Fenton kicked me out, I went to California. Pam had given me $500 and I used it to buy a played-out gold mine. I was able to hack out a couple thousand dollars' worth of the gold, and I used the money to buy land in San Francisco. Two days after I bought the land I sold it for half again what I paid for it. I bought more land, sold it, bought a nail factory, sold it, bought a little railroad line . . . You get the idea."

"Did you know that Pamela Fenton is a widow now?" Houston asked as if she weren't interested in his answer.

"Since when?"

"I believe her husband died a few months ago."

Kane stared at Houston for several long minutes, as if seeing her for the first time. "It's funny how things work out, ain't it?"

"How do you mean?"

"If I hadn't asked you to my house, your sister wouldn't have gone out with Westfield and you'd be marryin' him now."

She drew in her breath. "And if you'd known Pamela was free, you'd not have asked me to your house. Mr. Taggert, you're free to break our engagement at any time. If you'd rather have—."

"You ain't gonna start that again, are you?" he said, rising. "Why don't you try sayin' somethin' different sometime?"

Relief flooded Houston as she stood. "I just thought perhaps—."

Kane turned and grabbed her against him. "Damned woman, please shut up," he said as he kissed her.

Houston obeyed.

Early on Tuesday, Willie informed Houston that Miss Lavinia LaRue would meet her by the bandstand in Fenton Park at nine that morning.

Houston was met by a garishly dressed woman, short, dark, with an enormous bosom. Wonder how much is paddin', Houston thought.

"Good morning, Miss LaRue. It was good of you to meet me so early."

"It's late for me. I ain't been to bed yet. So you're the one Kane's marryin'. I told 'im he could buy hisself a lady if he wanted one."

Houston gave her an icy look.

"Oh, all right," Lavinia said. "You didn't expect me to hug you, did you? After all, you are takin' away a source of income to me."

"Is that all Mr. Taggert is to you?"

"He's a good lover, if that's what you mean but, truth to tell, he scares me. I never know what he wants from me. Acts like he can't bear me one minute, the next he can't get enough."

Houston knew she'd felt the same way but said nothing.

"What'd you wanta see me about?"

"I thought perhaps you could tell me something about him. I've really known him a very short time."

"You mean what he likes in bed?"

"No! Certainly not." She didn't like to think of Kane and another woman. "As a man. What can you tell me about the man?"

Lavinia stepped away, her back to Houston. "You know, one time I did think of somethin', but I know it was silly."

"And what was that?"

"Most of the time he acts like he don't care, but one time he saw that friend of his, Edan, out the window walkin' with a woman, and Kane asked if I liked him. If I liked him, Kane, I mean. He didn't wait for me to answer 'fore he left, but I thought then, he's a man no one's ever loved. 'Course that couldn't be true, a man with all his money must have lots of women in love with him."

"Do you love him? Not his money, but him. If he had no money—."

"If he had no money, I'd not get near 'im. I told you, he scares me."

Out of her pocketbook, Houston pulled a check. "The bank president has instructions to cash this only if he sees that you've purchased a train ticket to another state."

Lavinia took the check. "I'm takin' this because I wanta leave this two-bit town. But no money could buy me if I didn't wanta leave."

"Of course not. Again, Miss LaRue, thank you."

On Tuesday afternoon, just when Houston was getting tired of yet more wedding plans, Leora Vaughn and her fiancé, Jim Michaelson, stopped by the Chandler house on a tandem bicycle. They asked if Houston could possibly persuade Kane to rent another double bike and ride in the park with them.

After Houston had changed, borrowing Blair's Turkish pants, she rode on the handlebars up the hill to Kane's house.

"Goddamn Gould!" They could hear Kane's shouts through the open window.

"I'll ask him," Houston said.

"Do you think he'd mind if we waited inside?" Leora asked, her eyes greedily roaming over the front of Kane's house.

"I think he'd be pleased."

Houston never knew how Kane was going to greet her, but this time he seemed glad of the diversion. He was a little hesitant about the bicycle, since he'd never ridden one before, but he mastered it in minutes—then began challenging the other men in the park to races.

By late afternoon, when they returned the rented bicycles, Kane was saying he was going to buy a bicycle manufacturing plant. "Maybe I'll not make any money off it," he said, "but sometimes I like to gamble. Like recently I bought stock in a company that makes a drink called Coca-Cola. I'll probably lose ever'thing." He shrugged. "You can't always win."

In the evening they went to a taffy pull at Sarah Oakley's house.

Kane was the oldest person in the group, but all the games and diversions were new to him, and he seemed to have the most fun. He always seemed a little shocked that these young society people accepted him.

And it wasn't because he was easy to accept. He was outspoken, intolerant of any ideas he didn't agree with, and always aggressive. He told Jim Michaelson he was a fool to be content to run his father's store, that he should expand, get some business down from Denver if he insisted on staying in Chandler. He told Sarah Oakley she ought to get Houston to help her buy dresses because the ones she wore weren't as pretty as they should be. He got taffy on Mrs. Oakley's draperies and the next day had delivered to her fifty yards of silk velvet from Denver. He bent a wheel of a rented bicycle, then yelled for twenty minutes at the owner for having inferior merchandise. He told Cordelia Farrell she could get a better man than John Silverman, and that all John wanted was somebody to take care of his three motherless children.

Houston prayed for the floor to open up and swallow her when Kane invited everyone to his house for dinner on Wednesday night. "I ain't got any furniture downstairs," he said, "so we'll do it like Houston done for me one night—a rug, pillows to lay down on, candles, everything."

When three women dissolved into giggles at the look of pain and disbelief on Houston's red face, Kane said, "Did I miss somethin'?"

And Houston soon learned that everything connected with Kane involved an argument. He called it "discussin'" but it was more a verbal wrestle. On Tuesday evening, she asked him to sign some blank cards, beside her signature, which would be included in the little boxes of cake to be given away at the wedding.

"Like hell I will!" he said. "I ain't puttin' my name on somethin' blank. Somebody could write whatever they like above it."

"It's tradition," Houston said. "Everyone puts autographed cards in the boxes of cake that people take home."

"They can eat cake at the weddin'. They don't need little boxes of it. It'll melt anyway."

"It's to dream on, to make wishes on, to—."

"You want me to sign blank cards for a dumb idea like that?"

Houston lost that bout, but she won about hiring men to help the ladies from their carriages and women to turn Kane's small drawing room into a cloakroom.

"How many people you plannin' on havin', anyway?"

She looked at her list. "At last count, 520. Most of Leander's relatives are travelling in from the East. Is there someone special you wanted to invite besides your uncles and cousins, the Taggerts?"

"My *what?*"

They were off again, and again Houston won. Kane said he'd never met his relatives and had no desire to meet them. Houston, who couldn't tell him she knew Jean, or he'd no doubt ask how, said she was inviting them whether he knew them or not. For some reason, Kane didn't want them there and, after several minutes of arguing, he said they'd show up in coal miner's clothes.

Houston called him a snob. She thought she might die rather than tell him she'd already arranged for clothes to be made for his relatives—at his expense.

Before Kane could reply, Opal walked into the room, bade them good evening and sat down with her embroidery.

Kane appealed to Opal, who said, "Well then, you shall have to buy them new clothes, won't you?"

By the time Kane left, Houston felt as if she'd survived a storm at sea, but Kane seemed unperturbed. He kissed her in the hallway and said he'd see her tomorrow.

"Will everything always be an argument?" she whispered, sitting down heavily beside her mother.

"I should think it will be," Opal said cheerfully. "Why don't you take a long, hot bath?"

"I need a three-day-long one," Houston muttered, rising.

Kane stood before the tall windows in his office, a cigar clamped between his teeth.

"Are you planning to work or daydream?" Edan asked from behind him.

Kane didn't turn around. "They're all just kids," he said.

"Who are?"

"Houston and all her friends. They've never had to grow up, to worry about where their next meal's comin' from. Houston thinks food comes out of the kitchen, clothes from her dressmaker's and money from the bank."

"I'm not sure you're right. Houston seems pretty sensible to me, and I think her being jilted by Westfield made her grow up some. Those things mean a lot to a woman."

Kane turned back to face his friend. "She's consoled herself well enough," he said, his gesture encompassing the house.

"I'm not so sure she's after just your money," Edan said thoughtfully.

Kane snorted. "No doubt it's the delicate way I handle a teacup. I want you to watch her."

"You mean spy on her?"

"She's engaged to a man with money. I'd hate to have her kidnapped."

Edan raised an eyebrow. "Is that it, or are you worried she might be seeing Fenton again?"

"She spends most of every Wednesday inside that church of hers, and I want to know what she's doin'."

"So it's the handsome Reverend Thomas you're worried about."

"I'm damn well not worried about anybody!" Kane shouted. "Just do what I say and watch her."

With a look of disgust, Edan stood. "I wonder if Houston has any idea what she's getting herself into."

Kane turned back to the window. "A woman'll do a lot to get her hands on millions."

Edan didn't respond before he left the room.

Houston, dressed in the hot, padded suit of Sadie, handled her team of horses with ease as she made her way to the Little Pamela mine. She'd discussed it with Reverend Thomas and decided it was all right to talk to Jean about the forthcoming wedding. Houston still liked to think Jean was safe in her ignorance of Sadie's identity, but Reverend Thomas had, in a patronizing way, again told Houston the secrecy was long gone.

Now, as Houston travelled to the mine, she began to feel an almost overwhelming urge to talk to Jean. Jean always seemed so quiet and sensible, and even though she'd never met Kane, she was his cousin.

Houston got through the guarded gate with no trouble or challenge and went straight to the Taggert house.

Jean was waiting for her. "No problems?" she asked, then stopped and stared at Houston. "I'm glad you finally know," she said softly.

"Let's get the food distributed and we can talk," Houston said.

Hours later they were back at Jean's little house. Houston pulled a packet of tea from her pocket. "For you."

They were silent as Jean prepared the tea, then when they were both seated, Jean spoke. "So, we're to be related by marriage."

Houston held the chipped mug in her hands. "In five days. You will be there, won't you?"

"Of course. I'll pull my Cinderella gown from the closet and come in my glass coach."

"You needn't worry about any of that. I made all the necessary arrangements. Jacob Fenton has given permission for any Taggert to be allowed to come and go. My dressmaker is waiting and Mr. Bagly, the tailor, has been given instructions. All you have to do is bring your father, Rafe and Ian."

"That's all, is it?" Jean asked, smiling. "My father will be no problem, but Rafe is another matter. And unfortunately, Ian is just like his uncle."

With a sigh, Houston looked down at her mug. "Let me guess. First of all, you have no way of knowing whether Rafe will like the idea of attending the wedding or not because he is completely unpredictable. He could laugh and be happy to go, or he could possibly shout and refuse to attend."

For a moment, Jean gaped. "Don't tell me Kane is a *real* Taggert."

Houston stood and walked to gaze sightlessly out the single window, not speaking for several long minutes.

"Why are you marrying him?" Jean asked.

"I really don't know," she answered, pausing again. "Leander and I were the perfect couple," she said softly, almost as if in a dream. "In all the years we were engaged, in essence, since we were both children, I don't think we ever once disagreed. We had some . . . problems as we grew up," she thought of Lee's anger when she'd refused to let him make love to her, "but nearly always we agreed. If I wanted green curtains, Leander wanted green curtains. There was almost always perfect harmony between us."

She looked at Jean. "And then I met Mr. Taggert. I don't think he and I've yet had a harmonious conversation. I find myself yelling at him as if I were a fishwife. The day after I agreed to marry him I broke a water pitcher over his head. One minute I'll be furious with him, and the next I want to put my arms around him and protect him, then the next minute I find I want to lose myself in his strength."

She sat down, her face in her hands. "I am so confused. I don't know what anything means anymore. I loved Leander for so long, was so sure of my love for him, but right now I know that if I were offered a choice, I'd keep Kane."

She looked up. "But why? Why would I want to live with a man who makes me furious, who makes me feel like a street woman, who runs after me like a satyr, then pushes me away and says 'there'll be more of that later, honey' as if I'd been the forward one? Some of the time he ignores me, some of the time he leers at me. Sometimes he charms me. He has no respect for me; he treats me as if I were a backward child one minute, and the next he hands me unspeakable amounts of money and tells me to accomplish the work of ten people."

Houston stood quickly. "I think I must be insane. No woman in her right mind would go into a marriage like this. Not with her eyes open. I could see being so in love with a man that you'd not see his faults. But I see Kane Taggert as he really is: a man of towering vanity, a man of no vanity. Whatever you can say about him, there is a contradiction."

She sat down again, heavily. "I *am* insane. Completely, thoroughly insane."

"Are you sure?" Jean asked quietly.

"Oh, yes, I'm sure," Houston answered. "No other woman would—."

"No, I mean about being so in love with him you'd not be able to see his faults. I've always thought—or hoped—that if someone loved me they'd know all my bad points and still love me. I wouldn't want a man who thought I was a goddess, because when he found out that I have an awful temper, I'd be afraid he wouldn't love me anymore."

With a puzzled look, Houston gaped at Jean. "But loving someone means . . ."

"Yes? What *is* being in love with someone?"

Houston stood, looked out the window absently. "Wanting to be with a person. Wanting to stay with him through sickness and health, wanting to have his children, loving him even when he does something you don't like. Thinking he's the grandest, most noble prince in the world, laughing when he's said something that hurts you for the fifth time in one hour. Worrying whether he'll like what you're wearing, if he'll be proud of you, and feeling your insides melt when he does approve of you."

She stopped and was silent for several long moments.

"When I'm with him, I'm alive," she whispered. "I don't think I was ever alive until I met Kane. I was just existing, moving, eating, obeying. Kane makes me feel powerful, as if I could do anything. Kane . . ."

"Yes?" Jean asked softly. "What is Kane?"

"Kane Taggert is the man I love."

Jean burst out laughing. "Is it really such a catastrophe, being in love with one of us Taggerts?"

"The loving will be easy, but the living with might be somewhat difficult."

"You'll never be able to imagine half of it," Jean said, still laughing. "More tea?"

"Is all of your family like Kane?"

"My father takes after his mother's side of the family, I'm happy to say, but Uncle Rafe and Ian are true Taggerts. I thought this Kane, because he had money . . ."

"It probably makes him worse. Who is Ian's father? I don't remember meeting the boy."

"You haven't. He's worked in the mines for years now even though he's only sixteen. He looks like Rafe: big, handsome, angry. His father was Lyle, Rafe's brother. Lyle was killed in a mine explosion when he was twenty-three."

"And Kane's father . . . ?"

"Frank was the oldest brother. He was killed in an accident long before I was born and, I believe, even before Kane was born."

"I'm sorry," Houston said. "It must be hard for you to have to take care of so many men."

"I have help from charitable young ladies," she said, rising. "It'll be dark soon. You'd better go."

"Will you please come to my wedding? I'd very much like for you to be there and, besides, you'll see me in something a little cleaner." Houston grinned, showing off her blackened teeth.

"To tell you the truth, I somehow think I'll feel more comfortable around Sadie than the Society Princess, Miss Chandler."

"Don't say that!" Houston said seriously. "Please don't."

"All right. I'll do my best."

"And you'll go to my dressmaker's tomorrow? She needs all the time she can get to make the dress. Here's the address."

Jean took the card. "I'll look forward to it. And I'll do my best with Uncle Rafe and Ian. But I make no promises."

"I understand that from the bottom of my heart." On impulse, she clasped Jean to her. "I'll look forward to seeing you again."

On her way back to town, Houston mused on her talk with Jean. It made perfect sense that she was in love with Kane and, with the knowledge, she laughed aloud. All those years with Lee, and she'd never really been in love with him. She knew that now.

Of course, she couldn't tell anyone. It would make her seem like a woman whose love was given lightly. But it wasn't; she was sure of that. Kane Taggert was the man she loved and would always love.

She used the reins to urge the horses to move faster. She still had to wash and change her clothes. Then make arrangements for . . . A secret little smile shaped her lips as she thought of her plans for Friday night. She'd ask Leander to invite Kane and Edan to Lee's men's club and she'd ask Kane for the use of his house for a farewell dinner with her girlfriends. Just a quiet little get-together—like the one Ellie had before she got married.

Now, if Houston could only persuade that strongman she'd seen on the billboard on Coal Avenue to do what she wanted . . .

Houston was so busy musing on her plans that she didn't keep her usual vigil. Behind her, hidden by the trees, was a lone man on horseback.

Edan wore a frown as he followed her back into town.

Chapter 12

With only days left until the wedding, Houston found herself quickly running out of time. Kane's dinner on Wednesday was a great success.

"I broke my engagement to John today, Mr. Taggert," Cordelia Farrell said shyly.

"That's good news," Kane laughed as he grabbed her shoulders and kissed her heartily on the mouth. Cordelia was embarrassed but pleased. "You can do lots better 'n that ol' man."

"Thank you, Mr. Taggert."

For a moment, Kane looked puzzled. "How come ever'body calls me *Mr.* Taggert?"

"Because, Mr. Taggert," Houston said smoothly, "you've never asked *anyone* to call you Kane."

"All of you can call me Kane," he said quietly, but, looking at Houston, his eyes turned hot. "Except you, Houston. You've only called me Kane once and I liked it when you did."

Houston knew his meaning was clear to everyone and her throat went dry at the embarrassment of what he'd said.

Sarah Oakley picked up a pillow and threw it at Kane's head.

He caught it and everyone waited with breath held. Who could guess how Kane was going to react?

"Sometimes you're not a gentleman . . . Kane," Sarah said daringly.

But Kane grinned at her. "Gentleman or not, I see you took my advice and bought yourself a new dress. All right, Houston, you can call me Kane."

"At this moment, I much prefer Mr. Taggert," she said haughtily, and everyone laughed together.

All day Thursday was given over to preparing Kane's house for the wedding on Monday. Kane and Edan locked themselves in Kane's study and ignored the furniture movers, the deliveries, and the arrivals and departures of most of Chandler's tradesmen.

Friday and Saturday were more of the same, with Houston explaining and reexplaining their roles to all the people involved in the wedding. There were men and women to prepare and serve food, men to build tables for outside. There were the men who set up the enormous open-sided tents Houston'd had made in Denver. On Sunday, there were thirty-eight people doing nothing but arranging flowers.

Jean Taggert sent a message that Rafe was going to come but

young Ian was balking, and could she bring a covered dish perhaps?

When Houston read the message, she was in the kitchen, and before her on the table were two butchered cow carcasses and 250 pounds of potatoes that had just been delivered. And under the cows were three enormous wheels of cheese and 300 oranges—and she was praying the oranges weren't on the bottom.

Through all the turmoil, Houston was pleased that Kane stayed out of her way and left her to her work. He complained that he was so far behind in his own work, from lollygagging about with her, that he'd never catch up.

Only once did he give her any trouble, and that was when Leander asked Edan and him to spend the evening at Lee's men's club.

"I ain't got time to do that!" Kane bellowed. "Don't those men ever work? Lord knows but I'll have little enough time after the weddin', what with a woman always underfoot and—." He stopped and looked at Houston. "Maybe I didn't quite mean it that way . . ." he began.

Houston just looked at him.

"All right," he finally said, with disgust in his voice. "But I don't see why you women can't have your little tea party at your house." He turned on his heel and went back to his office.

"Damned women!" he muttered.

"What horrible imposition has Houston placed on you now?" Edan asked, with a hint of a smile.

"We're to spend the evenin' at Westfield's fancy club. We're to leave here by seven and not to return before midnight. What happened to the good ol' days when women obeyed and respected their husbands?"

"The first woman disobeyed the first man; the good ol' days are a myth. What does Houston want to do tonight?"

"A fancy tea party for her lady friends. I want you to stay here and watch her."

"What?"

"I don't like all those women bein' here alone. Houston's hired servants to fill the house after the weddin', but tonight only a bunch of unprotected women will be here. She's set up the dinin' room for her little party and there's a door in there that's covered with cloth, you know, the one with the flowers painted on it, and—."

"You expect me to hide inside a closet and spy on a ladies' tea party?"

"It's for their own good, and I damn well pay you enough to do a little work for me."

"A little work—," Edan sputtered.

Hours later, Houston saw Edan and noticed a bruise on his right cheek.

"How did you hurt yourself?" she asked.

"I ran into a stone wall," he said tightly and walked away.

At six, the house began to clear of workers and at six forty-five Houston's friends began to arrive, each bearing a beautifully wrapped gift.

Kane, still complaining about the injustice of having to leave his own house, climbed into the wagon beside a solemn Edan, and rode away.

Altogether, ten women plus Blair arrived at the Taggert house, and their gifts were placed on the eighteenth-century table in the dining room.

"Is everyone gone?" Tia asked.

"At last," Houston said, closing the double doors behind her. "Now, shall we get down to business?"

Edan sat inside the closet on an uncomfortable chair, a full bottle of whiskey in his hand. Damn Kane! he thought again and wondered if he could get away with murder. Any judge would surely let him off for killing a man who'd forced him to spend an entire evening watching a bunch of women drink tea.

Absently, he drank the whiskey and watched the women through the silk in the door panel. Miss Emily, a pretty, fragile, elderly lady, was banging her fist on the table.

"The third annual meeting of The Sisterhood will now come to order."

Edan held the bottle to his lips but didn't drink.

Miss Emily continued. "First, we'll hear a report from Houston on the coal camps."

Edan didn't move a muscle as Houston stood and delivered a detailed report on the injustices inside the coal camps. He'd followed her a few days before and knew of her innocent little forays to deliver fresh vegetables into the camps, but now Houston was talking of strikes and of unions. Edan'd seen men killed for less than what she was saying.

Nina Westfield began to talk of starting a magazine that the women would secretly deliver to the coal miners' wives.

Edan set the whiskey bottle on the floor and leaned forward.

There was mention of Jacob Fenton—fear of him and what he'd do if he found out about the women delivering information to the coal miners.

"I can talk to Jean Taggert," Houston said. "For some reason, Fenton seems afraid of all the Taggerts. They were given permission to attend the wedding."

"And Jean visits stores in Chandler," Miss Emily said. "I know your Kane," she said to Houston, "used to work for the Fentons, but something else is going on. I thought perhaps you might know."

"Nothing," Houston said. "Kane explodes at the mention of Fenton's name, and I don't think Marc knows anything."

"He wouldn't," said Leora Vaughn. "Marc only spends money; he's uninterested in where it comes from."

"I'll talk to Jean," Houston repeated. "Someone is stirring up a great deal of trouble. I don't want to see anyone hurt."

"Maybe I can get into the coal camps, too," Blair added. "I'll find out what I can."

"What other business is there?" Miss Emily asked.

Edan leaned back in his chair. "The Sisterhood," he breathed. These women, under the guise of lace dresses and gentle manners, were talking about wars.

The rest of the meeting was involved with various charities, of helping orphans and sick people—all the things ladies *should* do.

When the meeting was over, Edan picked up the whiskey and felt that at last he could breathe again.

"Refreshments?" Meredith Lechner asked, laughter in her voice, as she opened a large, yellow-wrapped box and pulled out a bottle of homemade wine. "Mother sent these in memory of a few meetings when she was a girl. Daddy will be told our wine cellar was robbed."

Edan didn't think he could have been further shocked, but his mouth fell open when each woman was handed a full bottle of wine and a long-stemmed glass from a wall cabinet.

"To the wedding night!" said Miss Emily, glass aloft. "To wedding nights everywhere, whether they're preceded by marriages or not."

With laughter, the women downed full glasses of wine.

"Mine first!" said Nina Westfield. "Mother and I had an awful time finding these in Denver. And then Lee almost looked in the box this afternoon."

Houston opened a blue box and withdrew a transparent black garment dripping with four-inch-wide black lace.

Edan saw that it was ladies' underwear, but not the kind for ladies.

In disbelief, he watched the women drink their bottles of wine and open presents amid shouts of laughter and boisterous comments. There were two pairs of high-heeled red shoes, more transparent underwear, and some pictures the women passed from one to another and nearly collapsed with laughter over. Chairs were discarded and the women began to dance about the room.

Miss Emily sat down at the piano that Edan hadn't noticed and started banging away.

Edan's chin hit his chest as he watched the women dance with skirts raised, legs kicking.

"It's the cancan," Nina said, out of breath. "Mother and I sneaked away from Daddy and Lee when we were in Paris and saw it."

"Can anyone try it?" Houston asked, and soon eight women were tossing their skirts over their heads to the tune of Miss Emily's playing.

"Rest!" Sarah Oakley called. "And I brought a bit of poetry to read to you."

When Edan was a boy, he and his friends had shared a copy of what the prim Miss Oakley was now reading from: *Fanny Hill.*

The women giggled and laughed as they slapped Blair and Houston on the back repeatedly.

When Sarah finished, Houston stood. "Now, my dear, dear friends, I have the pièce de résistance upstairs. Shall we go?"

Several minutes passed before Edan could move. So much for a ladies' tea party. With a jolt, he sat upright. What in the world could be upstairs? What could be more than what they'd already done? He knew that he'd as soon die as not find out what was going on.

As quickly as possible, he left the house, circled it, and saw light in the northeast corner sitting room. Ignoring thorns, he began to climb the rose trellis.

All that had happened before hadn't prepared him for what he now saw. The room was totally dark except for a large candelabra blazing with light, set behind a translucent silk screen. And between the screen and the light was a well-muscled man, scantily clad, moving his body into poses to show off his muscles.

"I've had enough of this," Miss Emily said and, with Nina on the other side, moved the screen away.

For a moment, the strongman looked bewildered, but the now-drunk women began clapping their hands and cheering, so he grinned and put more enthusiasm into his posing.

"Not nearly as big as my Kane," Houston shouted.

"I'll take him on," the strongman shouted back. "I can lick anybody."

"Not Kane," Houston said stubbornly, which made the man work harder at showing his biceps.

Edan slipped down the rose trellis to the ground. Kane'd wanted Edan to protect the ladies. Who was to protect the men from the ladies?

On Saturday morning, Kane slammed his office door for the fifth time in one hour. "Of all the days for Houston to be sick," he growled as he sat down. "You don't think she's gettin' afraid of tomorrow's weddin', do you?" he asked Edan.

"More likely something she ate—or drank," Edan answered. "I heard there were several young women of Chandler spending the day being 'indisposed'."

Kane didn't look up from his papers. "Probably just restin' for tomorrow."

"What about you?" Edan asked. "Any nerves?"

"Not a one. Real simple matter. People do it every day."

Edan leaned forward, took the paper Kane was looking at and turned it right side up.

"Thanks," Kane mumbled.

Chapter 13

The day of the wedding was so beautiful that it seemed to have been specially created for that momentous occasion. Opal woke the Chandler household at five o'clock and began the careful packing of the two wedding dresses and veils.

Houston heard her mother downstairs but she lay in bed for several minutes before she rose. She'd slept little during the night, mostly tossing and turning. Her mind was too alive with thoughts of the approaching day to sleep. She thought of Kane and prayed that in the years to come he'd learn to love her.

When Opal came to wake her, she was more than willing for the day to begin.

The three women were ready to leave for the Taggert house by ten o'clock. They travelled in Houston's carriage, with Willie behind them driving a borrowed wagon, the bed covered with muslin, the dresses concealed.

Waiting for them at the house were a dozen young women, all members of The Sisterhood.

"The tables are ready," Tia said.

"And the tents," Sarah added.

"And Mrs. Murchison has been cooking since four," Anne Seabury put in, as she took one end of the wrapped wedding dresses.

"And the flowers?" Houston asked. "Were they all put in place according to my plan?"

"I think so," one of the women said.

Miss Emily stepped forward. "Houston, you'd better look at them yourself. Someone will make sure that husband of yours stays in his office, and you can take a turn through the house."

"Husband," Houston murmured to herself as Nina ran ahead to hold Kane prisoner in his office. Everyone was going to try to insure that the bride wasn't seen before the wedding.

When she'd been assured that it was safe, Houston left her mother and Blair in the hall as she walked through each downstairs room and, for the first time, got to see the reality of the decorations that she'd planned.

The small drawing room was furnished with three long tables bearing gifts for the two brides from all over the United States. Kane had as much as said that he had no true friends in the moneyed world he dealt with in New York, but, if their gifts were any indication, it was obvious that those men considered him one of their own.

There was a little Italian inlaid table from the Vanderbilts, silver from the Goulds, gold from the Rockefellers. When the gifts had started arriving, Kane'd said that they damn well should send presents since he'd sure as hell sent enough to their kids every time they got married.

Other gifts came from Leander's relatives, and the people of Chandler had done their best to come up with the most ingenious "twin" gifts possible. There were twin brooms, twin barrels of popcorn, twin books, twin bolts of fabric. The gifts ranged from duplicate papers of dressmaker's pins to identical oak chairs from the Masons.

The room was decorated with tall potted palms set before mirrors, and the mantel dripped with red roses and purple pansies.

Houston moved to the large drawing room. This was where the close friends and relatives would mingle before and after the ceremony.

Along the baseboards, doorways, and the ceiling had been tacked the delicate twining smilax vine. Yard upon yard of the vines graced the room, weaving around the fireplace, around windows.

Set before each window were pots of ferns that filtered the morning sun and made lacy shadows on the floor. The hearth was draped with pink carnations, and entwined in the vines here and there were more carnations.

As quickly as possible, Houston finished her inspection tour of the rest of the downstairs and hurried upstairs where the others waited.

There were five hours before the ceremony, but Houston knew that there'd be a million and one last-minute details to take care of.

During the last few days, she'd spent a great deal of time downstairs, but the upstairs was still new to her. The eastern branch of the U-shaped house was guest quarters, and today Blair would be dressing in one of the suites. The center section contained Edan's rooms on one side of an aviary and hallway, and a nursery, bath, and nurse's room on the other side.

Next to the nursery was the long wing that belonged to Houston and Kane. He had a bedroom at the back, relatively small, but overlooking the gardens. Houston's room, separated from his by a marble bathroom, was by far the largest, with pale panelled walls that were set with carvings of swags and garlands to outline the paintings that had yet to be hung.

Next to her room was a large pink and white marble bath and a dressing area with walls covered in pink moiré, and beyond that a sitting room and private dining room for when she and Kane were dining alone.

"I shall never get used to this house," Tia said as she returned from an inspection of the rooms beyond the bedroom. "And look at this rooftop garden."

"Garden?" Houston asked, walking toward the double doors where Tia stood. She opened one and stepped outside into a lovely tangle of potted trees and flowers. Stone benches hid themselves amid the greenery. This had not been here the last time she saw the railed roof of the loggia that was outside her bedroom.

"Look at this," Sarah said, holding out a large white card

that was attached to an enormous fig tree. Most of the plants were protected from the Colorado sun by an overhead lattice work that made a very pretty shade.

Houston took the card.

I hope you like it, I wish you all the best in your marriage.
Edan

"It's a gift from Edan," Houston said and felt that the garden was a symbol of her happiness today.

Before Houston could say another word, the door burst open and Mrs. Murchison entered as if a storm were behind her.

"There's too many people in my kitchen!" she yelled toward Houston. "I don't know how I'm supposed to cook with all of them in there. And Mr. Kane's got too much to do already, what with losin' a day's work as it is."

"Losing . . ." Meredith said, aghast. "Do you think Houston has nothing else to—?"

Houston cut her friend off. Mrs. Murchison was under Kane's spell and no doubt she'd defend the man to the death. "I'll go down the back stairs," Houston said, ignoring the fact that Sarah was unwrapping her wedding dress. It still needed pressing and there were last-minute stitches to be taken.

Once she was downstairs, there were more catastrophes to be seen to. Several times, she heard Kane shouting from within his office, and someone pushed Houston inside the scullery when Kane stormed past on his way outside to the gardens. She envied him his freedom, and at the same time wished she could be with him. Tomorrow, she thought. Tomorrow, they'd be able to walk together in the garden.

It was only two hours before the service when she finally made it back upstairs.

"Houston," Opal said, "I think you should begin dressing now."

Houston removed her clothing slowly, thinking that when she disrobed the next time . . .

"Who in the world is that woman?" Anne asked as Houston stepped into a chemise of cotton so fine that it was a mere whisper against her skin. The top had tiny, worked buttonholes that were inserted with pink silk ribbon, and the bottom was hand-embroidered with tiny rosebuds.

"I have no idea," Tia said, joining Anne to look over the railing of the garden, "but she must be the tallest woman I've ever seen."

Sarah began tightening the laces on Houston's pink satin, hand-featherstitched corset. "I think I'm going to have to take a look," Sarah said. "Maybe she's one of Lee's relatives."

"I've seen her before but I have no idea where," Anne said. "How odd of her to wear black to a wedding."

"We have work to do," Opal said in a way that made Houston's head come up. "No one need interest herself in the private matters of any one of the guests."

Houston was quite sure that something was wrong. Ignoring her mother's stern look, she went to the edge of the rooftop garden where Tia stood. Instantly, she knew who the woman was. Even from upstairs, she looked tall and elegant.

"It's Pamela Fenton," Houston whispered, and turned back toward the bedroom.

For a moment, no one spoke.

"Probably wearing black in mourning," Sarah said, "because she lost him. Houston, which one of these petticoats do you want on first?"

Mechanically, Houston continued dressing, but her thoughts were on the fact that Kane was in the garden and the woman he once loved was walking toward him.

A knock on the door was answered by Anne. "It's the man who works with Kane," she told Houston. "He wants to see you, and he says it's urgent and he has to see you immediately."

"She couldn't possibly go . . ." Opal began, but her daughter had already snatched a dressing gown from a chair back and was on her way to the door.

Kane was standing at the far edge of his garden, looking out over the city of Chandler, smoking one of his cigars, one foot on a stone bench.

"Hello, Kane," Pamela said softly.

He waited a moment before turning to face her, and when

he did look at her, his eyes were calm, not showing what he felt. He looked her up and down. "The years have treated you kindly."

"On the outside." She took a deep breath. "I don't have much time so I'll say what I came to say. I still love you; I've never stopped loving you. If you'll walk away with me now, I'll follow you to the ends of the earth."

Quickly, he took a step toward her but stopped and walked back. "No, I can't do that," he said quietly.

"You *can!* You know you can. What do you care about any of these people? What do you care about the people of Chandler? What do you care about . . . her?"

"No," he repeated.

She moved so they were standing close. He was a couple of inches taller than she, but with her heels they were equal. "Kane, please, don't make this mistake. Don't marry someone else. You know you love me. You know I—."

"You love me so much that you left me alone," he said angrily. "You married your rich lover and . . ." He stopped, turned away from her. "I *won't* leave with you today. I'll not hurt her like that. She doesn't deserve it."

Pam sat down on the bench. "You're going to cast me aside merely because you don't want to hurt Houston Chandler? She's young. She'll find someone else. Or is she in love with you?"

"I'm sure you know the gossip. She's still in love with Westfield, but she agreed to console herself with my money. Unfortunately, I go along with the money."

"Then why? Why do you feel obligated?"

He looked at her with blazing eyes. "Have you forgotten me so completely? *I* keep my bargains."

His meaning was clear. "I thought you would have found out by now," she said softly.

"You mean found out why you left me alone with $500 to pay me for services rendered? I made an effort not to find out."

"When I told my father that he had to allow us to marry because I was carrying your child, he had me forcibly put on a train to Ohio. Nelson Younger owed my father a great deal of money, and the debt was paid when he married me."

"I was told—," Kane began.

"I'm sure you were told that I'd run away rather than marry you. No doubt my father said a few words about his daughter dallying with the stable lad, but she'd certainly not marry him. You were always so easy to get to. That pride of yours was so easily wounded."

Kane was silent for a while. "And the child?"

"Zachary is thirteen now, a wonderful boy, handsome, strong, as full of pride as his father."

Kane stood quite still, looking out over the acres of garden.

"Leave with me now, Kane," Pam whispered. "If not for my sake, then for your son's."

"My son's," Kane said under his breath. "Tell me, was this man you married good to 'im?"

"Nelson was quite a bit older than me, and he was pleased to have a child whether Zach was his or not. He loved Zach." She smiled. "They used to play baseball together every Saturday afternoon."

Kane looked back at her. "And Zachary thinks of this man as his father?"

Pam stood. "Zach would learn to love you as I do. If you and I told him the truth . . ."

"The *truth* is that Nelson Younger was Zachary's father. All I did was plant the seed."

"Are you rejecting your own son?" Pam asked with anger.

"No, I'm not. You send the boy to me and I'll take 'im. Sight unseen. It's you, Pam, I'm rejectin'."

"Kane, I don't want to beg. If you don't love me now, you could learn to again."

He took both her hands in his. "Listen to me. What happened to us was a long time ago. I don't guess I knew until now how much I'd changed. If you'd been here a few months ago, I'd have run with you to the altar, but it's different now. Houston—."

She pulled away from him. "You say she doesn't love you. Do you love her?"

"I hardly know her."

"Then why? Why turn away a woman who loves you? Why turn your back on your own son?"

"I don't know, damn you! Why do you have to show up on my weddin' day and make me miserable? How can you ask me to humiliate a woman who's been so . . . kind to me? I can't go off and leave her standin' at the altar."

Tears began to run down Pam's face as she sat down on the bench. "Nelson was kind to me also and loved Zachary so much. I tried to find you to tell you what'd happened, but you seemed to have vanished. Years later, when I began to see your name in the papers, I couldn't find the courage to write—or maybe I couldn't bear to hurt Nelson. When he died, I wanted to find you. I felt so guilty, like I was running from Nelson's deathbed to my lover's arms, but I'd waited so very long. Then Zachary became ill and, by the time he could travel to Chandler, you were engaged. I told myself it was over between us, but at the last minute, I had to see you, had to tell you."

He sat beside her, put his arm about her shoulders and pulled her head down. "Listen, love, you always were a romantic. Maybe you don't remember our fights, but I do. The only place we were good together was in a haystack. Two thirds of the time we were mad at each other. Over the years, you've forgotten all the bad parts."

Pam blew her nose on a lace-edged handkerchief. "Is Miss Chandler any better?"

"When I do somethin' she doesn't like, she hits me over the head with whatever's handy. You always ran off and hid and worried whether I still loved you."

"I've grown up since then."

"How could you? You've lived with an old man that spoiled you, just like your father did. No one's ever spoiled Houston."

Pam pulled away from him. "And is she good in bed? Is she also better at that than I am?"

"I have no idea. There's a little fire in her but she's clumsy with it. I'm not marryin' her for sex. That's always available."

Pam put her arms around his neck. "If I begged you—," she began.

"It wouldn't help. I'm gonna marry Houston."

"Kiss me," she whispered. "Remind me. Let me remember."

Speculatively, Kane looked at her. Perhaps he wanted to

know, too. He put his big hand to the back of her head and his lips on hers. It was a long kiss and he put all he had into it.

And when he moved away, they were smiling at each other.

"It *is* over, isn't it?" Pam whispered.

"Yes."

She stayed close to him. "All those years with Nelson, I believed I was in love with you but I was in love with a dream. Perhaps my father was right."

He removed her arms from his neck. "Any more talk of your father and we may come to blows."

"You aren't still angry at him, are you?"

"This is my weddin' day and I want happiness, so let's not talk about Fenton. Tell me about my son."

"Gladly," Pam said and began talking.

It was an hour later when Pam left Kane alone in the garden to finish his cigar. When he was done, he flung the butt to the ground, looked at his pocket watch and knew it was time to return to dress for the wedding.

He hadn't taken but a few steps when he came face to face with a man who, if Kane had been able to see them together, he would have known was the image of himself in about ten years' time.

Kane and Rafe Taggert stared at each other silently, rather like dogs meeting for the first time. Immediately, they each knew who the other was.

"You don't look much like your father," Rafe said with a hint of accusation in his voice.

"I wouldn't know. I never met the man—or any of his kin," Kane answered, pointing out the fact that no Taggert had ever contacted him in all the years he was growing up in Fenton's stable.

Rafe stiffened. "I hear there's blood on your money."

"I hear you don't have any—bloody or not."

They glared across the space separating them. "You ain't much like Frank, either. I'll be leavin' now." He turned away.

"You can insult me but not the lady I'm marryin'. You'll stay for the ceremony."

Rafe didn't look back, but he gave a curt nod before walking away.

"I want to talk to you," Edan said from the doorway, his eyes grim.

The many women around Houston began to protest, but she put up her hand and silently followed Edan. He led her into his bedroom.

"I know this isn't proper, but it's the only place in the house that's not crawling with people."

Houston tried to not let her emotions show because she had the distinct impression Edan was angry with her.

"I know today's your wedding, but I've got something to say. Kane knows all too well that the personal safety of the people connected to a man as wealthy as he is is often in jeopardy." He looked at her. "What I'm saying is that Kane's had me follow you a couple of times in the last week."

Houston could feel color leaving her face.

"I don't like what I've seen," he continued. "I didn't like that a young woman, unprotected, was going into a coal camp, but this Sisterhood of yours—."

"Sisterhood!" Houston gasped. "How . . . ?"

Edan grabbed a chair and put it behind her.

Feebly, Houston sat down.

"I didn't want to do it, but Kane insisted that I . . . ah, hide in a closet and be there during your tea party in case you needed protection."

Houston was looking at her hands and didn't see Edan's slight smile at the words "tea party." "How much does he know?" she whispered.

Edan took a seat across from her. "I was afraid of that," he said heavily. "How could I tell him that you're marrying him because of his connection to Fenton? You're using him and his money to further your crusade against the evil of coal. Damn! but I should have known better. With a sister like yours who'd steal her own sister's—."

Houston stood. "Mr. Nylund!" she said through clenched teeth. "I will *not* listen to you impugn my sister, and I have no idea what you're talking about when you say Kane is connected to the Fentons. If you believe my purposes are evil, we'll go now and tell Kane everything."

"Wait a minute," he said, standing, grabbing her arm. "Why don't you explain—?"

"Don't you mean that I should try to convince you that I'm innocent, that I'm not leading Kane Taggert down the aisle only to be slaughtered? No, sir, I do not answer such accusations. Tell me, did you plan to use your knowledge of me as blackmail?"

"Touché," he said, visibly relaxing. "Now that we've both shown our anger, could we talk? You'll have to admit that your actions aren't exactly beyond suspicion."

Houston also tried to relax, but it was difficult. She didn't like to think of how he'd come to know of The Sisterhood.

"How long have you been doing your Wednesday masquerades?" Edan asked.

Houston walked to the window. On the lawn below were workers looking as if they were preparing for the siege of an army. She looked back at Edan. "What we women do, we've done for generations. The Sisterhood was founded by my father's mother before there even was a Chandler, Colorado. We are merely friends who try to help each other and anyone else we can. Right now, our major concern is the treatment of the people in the coal camps. We do nothing illegal." Her eyes fastened on his. "Nor do we use anyone."

"Why the secrecy then?"

She looked at him in disbelief. "Look at your own reaction to your knowledge, and you aren't even a relative. Can you imagine how the husbands and fathers would react if they found out their delicate women spent their free afternoons learning to drive a four-horse wagon? And some of us have . . ." She stopped talking.

"I see your point. But I see theirs, too. What you're doing is dangerous. You could be—." He stopped. "You say you've been doing this for three generations?"

"We take on different problems at different times."

"And the . . . ah, tea parties?"

In spite of herself, Houston blushed. "It was my grandmother's idea. She said she went to her own wedding night knowing nothing and terrified. She didn't want her friends or her daughters to have the same experience. I think perhaps the pre-wedding celebration has evolved slowly into what you"— she swallowed—"saw."

"How many women in Chandler belong to The Sisterhood?"

"There're only a dozen active members. Some, like my mother, retire after they're married."

"Do you plan to retire?"

"No," she answered, looking up at him, because, of course, her participation could depend on him.

He turned away from her. "Kane won't like your driving the wagon into the coal fields. He won't like your being in jeopardy."

Houston moved to face him. "I know he wouldn't like it, which is truly the *only* reason I haven't told him. Edan,"—she put her hand on his arm—"this means so much to so many people. It took me months of work to learn how to act like an old woman, to be able to really become Sadie. If I stopped now, it would take more months to train someone else and, in the meantime, so many miners' families would go without the little extras I give them."

He took her hand. "All right, you can get off your pulpit. I guess it's safe enough, even though it goes against everything I believe."

"You won't tell Kane? I'm quite sure he won't be understanding in the least."

"I'm sure that's an understatement. No, I won't tell him if you swear to only deliver potatoes and *not* get involved with the unions. And about this seditious magazine you women want to start—."

She stood on tiptoe and kissed his cheek to cut him off. "Thank you so much, Edan. You are a true friend. Now I must go dress for my wedding." Before he could speak, she was at the door, but paused, her hand on the knob. "What did you mean about Kane's connection to the Fentons?"

"I thought you knew. Jacob Fenton's younger sister, Charity, was Kane's mother."

"No," she said softly. "I didn't know." She left the room.

Houston was in her bedroom only minutes when Sarah Oakley said, as she held out Houston's wedding dress, "I just saw the oddest thing."

"What was that?"

"I thought it was Kane in the garden wearing his old clothes, but instead it was a boy who looks like him."

"Ian," Houston said with a smile. "He *did* come."

"If there's anything left of him," Nina said, looking over the rail. "Two of the Randolph boys and Meredith's two brothers started laughing at him and your Ian attacked them."

Houston's head came up. "Four against one?"

"At least that many. Now they've gone behind a tree and I can't see them."

Houston took her hands off the wedding dress Sarah was still holding and went to the window. "Where are they now?"

"There," Nina pointed. "See the commotion in the shrubs? That's one heck of a fight going on."

Leaning far out the window, Houston surveyed the garden area. Most of the scene was hidden from the house by trees.

"I'll send someone to stop the fight," Sarah was saying.

"And humiliate a Taggert?" Houston said, going to the closet. "Not on your life." She again pulled on her dark blue satin dressing gown.

"What in the world are you planning, Houston?" Sarah gasped.

"I am going to stop a fight and save a Taggert from a fate worse than death: humiliation. There's no one in the back."

"Just a few dozen waiters and guests and . . ." Nina said.

"Houston, dear, aren't there some fireworks downstairs? If someone were to light them it would create a diversion," Opal said softly. She knew from experience that it was useless to tell her daughter that she needed to get dressed. Not when one of her girls wore that expression.

"I'm on my way," Nina called, running out the door as Houston put her foot out the window and onto the rose trellis.

The east lawn was alive with the explosive noise of fireworks, with early guests all looking that way, as Houston made her way diagonally across the stretch of west lawn and into the trees.

Deep in the shade of a grove of black walnut trees, Ian Taggert uselessly fought the four stout boys on top of him.

"Stop that!" Houston said in her sternest voice.

Not one boy paid her the least attention.

She moved into the flailing arms and legs, grabbed an ear and pulled. Jeff Randolph came up swinging but stopped when he saw Houston. She motioned him to stand back while she went after George and Alex Lechner, pulling up both boys by their ears.

Only Steve Randolph remained on top of Ian and when Houston touched Steve's ear, he came up flying, an uncomprehending mass of rage. The three boys standing in the background gasped when Steve sent a fist sailing toward Houston's jaw. She ducked and, seeing no other way, decked young Steven with a right. Months of handling a four-horse wagon had given her quite a bit of strength in her arms.

For a moment, no one could move as Steve slowly fell across Ian's legs.

Houston recovered first. "Steve!" she said, kneeling, slapping the boy's face. "Are you all right?"

"Damn!" Ian breathed. "I ain't never seen no lady punch like that."

Steve groaned, sat up, rubbed his jaw and looked at Houston in wonder. In fact, all five of the boys were gaping at her.

She stood. "I don't appreciate such behavior on my wedding day," she said regally.

"No, ma'am," four of the boys mumbled.

"We didn't mean nothin', Miss Blair-Houston. He—."

"I want no excuses. Now, you four go back to your parents and, Steven, put some ice on your jaw."

"Yes, ma'am," he called over his shoulder, all of them getting away as quickly as possible.

She held her hand out to Ian to help him up. "You may come with me."

He ignored her hand. "I ain't goin' into *his* house if that's what you mean," he said angrily.

"Perhaps you're right. For this fracas, I'm using a rose trellis as a staircase. Any boy who'd lose a fight probably couldn't climb a trellis."

"Lose a fight!" He was as tall as she was and, at sixteen, already big, showing promise of reaching Kane's size. He almost put his nose to hers. "In case you cain't count, there was four of 'em on me and I woulda won if you hadn't come along and interrupted."

"But you're afraid to enter your own cousin's house," she said, as if it were an observation. "How odd. Good day to you." She started briskly toward the house.

Ian began walking beside her. "I ain't afraid. I just don't wanta go inside."

"Of course."

"What's that mean?"

She stopped. "I agree with you. You aren't afraid of your cousin, you just don't want to see him or to eat his food. I understand perfectly."

She watched emotions play across his face.

"Where's this damned rose trellis of yours?"

She stood rooted to where she was and looked at him.

He stopped glaring. "All right then, where's the rose trellis you're usin' as a staircase?"

"This way."

Kane was just returning to the house when he was halted by the extraordinary sight of his wife-to-be, wearing only a garment he knew no lady wore outside her own house, climbing down the rose trellis.

More than a little curious, he stepped behind a tree to watch her and saw her fling herself into the midst of a pile of wrestling boys who were as big as she was. He was halfway there to help her when he saw her flatten a boy with a championship right.

The next minute, she was arguing in her own cool way with a big, sullen-looking boy. "Might as well give up," Kane said aloud, laughter in his voice. He'd already learned that when Houston looked like that, a man might as well give in because that delicate little lady was going to get her own way.

He laughed again when he saw the boy start up the rose trellis ahead of Houston. But as Kane watched, he saw Houston's gown snag and saw her struggle to free herself. Around the corner three men and a woman were walking and, in another minute, they'd see her.

Quickly, he ran across the lawn and put his hand on her ankle.

When Houston looked down and saw Kane, she nearly fainted. What in the world would he think of the woman he was going to marry? She knew quite well what Leander or Mr. Gates would say if they saw her now, in public, wearing her bedroom clothes, and climbing a rose trellis.

As Houston looked down at Kane, she said the only thing she could think of. "My hat isn't on straight."

She hoped that the sound he made was a chuckle.

"Honey, even I know that ladies don't wear hats with their bathrobes."

Houston was paralyzed. He didn't mind!

"Unless you want ever'body to see you like that, you'd better get inside."

"Yes," she said, recovering herself and climbing to the top while he watched. Once on the balcony, she leaned over the side. "Kane," she called to him, "your wedding gift is in your office."

He grinned up at her. "See you real soon, baby."

With that he stuck his hands in his pockets and went away whistling, nodding at the people he passed.

"Houston," Opal said from behind her. "If you don't get ready now, you're going to miss your own wedding."

"I'd rather die," she said with great feeling and returned to her bedroom.

Ten minutes later, Kane was unwrapping the package Houston'd put on his desk. Inside were two boxes of cigars and a note.

These are the finest Cuban cigars made. Each month two more boxes of the best cigars available in the world will be delivered to Mr. Kane Taggert.

It was signed with the name of a cigar store in Key West, Florida.

Kane was just lighting one when Edan entered. He held out the box to him. "From Houston. How in the world do you think she got these here in time?"

Edan took a moment to enjoy the cigar. "If I'm learning anything in life, it's to not underestimate that lady."

"Any woman who'd buy cigars like these is indeed a lady. Well," he said heavily, "I guess I better go get dressed. You wanta come help me tie things?"

"Sure."

Chapter 14

The wedding dress was of Houston's own design, simple but elaborate in its simplicity. It was of ivory silk satin cut in a long, gentle princess style with no horizontal seams from the high neck to the tip of the twelve-foot train. About the waist, extending over her breasts and flowing down her hips, was an intricate Persian design done in thousands of hand-applied seed pearls. The sleeves from shoulder to elbow were huge, their size further emphasizing the tiny waist of the dress. The tight cuffs that extended from elbow to wrist carried a repeat pattern done in pearls.

Houston stood very still as her friends attached the veil to her head. It was a five-yard-long froth of handmade Irish lace called Youghal, a bold design of wild flowers set off by spiked leaves. The complicated pattern of the lace complemented the satin smoothness of the dress.

Tia held out Houston's teardrop-shaped bouquet of orange blossoms and white rosebuds, made to reach from her hands to just graze the floor as she walked.

Opal looked up at her daughter with tears glistening in her eyes. "Houston . . ." she began but could say nothing else.

Houston kissed her mother's cheek. "I'm getting the best of men."

"Yes, I know." She handed Houston a little corsage of pink rosebuds. "These are from your sister. She thought that she'd wear red roses and you could wear pink. I guess she's right that you don't have to dress alike."

"Our veils are different," Houston said as Sarah pinned the flowers over the veil just above Houston's left ear.

"Ready?" Tia asked. "I believe that's your music."

Blair was standing at the head of the double stairs waiting for her sister. Solemnly, they embraced.

"I love you more than you know," Blair whispered. There were slight tears in her eyes as she pulled away. "I guess we should get this spectacle over."

The polished brass rails of the staircase were covered with fern leaves and at regular intervals hung clusters of three calla lilies. Beneath the arch of the stairs was a twelve-piece string orchestra now playing the wedding march.

With heads held high, both twins walked slowly down the stairs, one curving east, one curving westward. Below them, in silence, the guests looked up at the beautiful women. Their tightly-fitted dresses were identical except for the lace veils, which varied in pattern and type of lace. The color of rosebuds at the sides of their heads also distinguished one twin from the other.

When the women reached the main hallway, the crowd pulled back and the twins walked straight ahead, down the short corridor outside the library door.

Once outside the door, they paused and waited for the six organs placed around the enormous room to begin playing. Inside, seated, but now rising, were the close friends and relatives of the couples.

As Houston looked down the aisle, she saw Jean Taggert standing between her uncle and her father. And ahead of the guests, on a raised platform that was canopied in greenery and roses, stood the men—in the wrong places.

Houston should have known it was too good to be true that

all her plans would come about without anything going wrong. As it was now, she was walking up the aisle toward Leander. Quickly, she glanced at Blair to share the joke, but Blair was looking straight ahead—toward Kane.

Houston's stomach began to turn over. This wasn't just a simple mistake. With a pang, she thought of the flowers that Blair had sent her. Could Blair have arranged this so she'd not have to marry Leander? Did she want Kane?

The thought was ridiculous. Houston smiled. No doubt Blair was making a noble sacrifice and taking on Kane so Houston could have Lee. How sweet, but how wrong she was.

Still smiling, Houston looked toward Kane. He was staring at her intently and Houston was glad that he recognized her.

At least for a moment she was happy, but when his face darkened and he turned away, the smile left Houston's face.

He couldn't believe she'd arranged this switch so she could marry Leander, she thought. But of course he could.

As they drew closer to the platform, Houston tried to think of how to get out of this gracefully. Miss Jones thought she'd covered every possible situation that a lady could get herself into, but she'd never thought that a lady would find herself marrying the wrong man.

As the twins stepped onto the platform, Kane kept his head turned away, and Houston couldn't help feeling a pang of resentment that he was going to do nothing to change positions. Didn't he care if he got one twin or the other?

"Dearly beloved, we—."

"Excuse me," Houston said, trying to keep her voice low so that only the five of them could hear. "I'm Houston."

Leander understood instantly. He looked at Kane, who was still facing straight ahead. "Shall we exchange places?"

Kane didn't look at either woman. "Don't much matter to me."

Houston felt her heart sink. Leander wanted Blair and Kane would take her, too. Quite suddenly, she felt as useful as a fifth wheel on a wagon.

"It matters to me," Leander said, and the two men traded places.

Behind them, during the discussion, the audience had begun to twitter, but when Kane and Lee switched places, there was full-fledged laughter. Even though the people tried to cover their amusement, they weren't successful.

Houston stole a glance at Kane and saw the anger in his eyes.

The service was over quickly and, when Reverend Thomas said to kiss the brides, Lee enveloped Blair with gusto. But Kane's kiss was cool and reserved. He wouldn't look her in the eyes.

"Could I speak to you in your office, please?" she asked. "Alone?"

He gave her a curt nod and released her as if he couldn't bear to touch her.

The four of them walked out of the room very fast and, once outside the library, people descended. Kane and Houston were quickly separated, as one guest after another wedged his way close to the bride. There was much giggling about the mix-up at the altar. Not one person could resist the temptation to remind everyone how Lee never could seem to make up his mind about which of the twins he wanted.

Jean Taggert pulled Houston aside. "What happened?"

"I think my sister thought she was doing me a favor by giving me Leander. She was going to sacrifice herself by taking the man I love."

"Have you told Blair that you love Kane? That you wanted to marry him?"

"I haven't even told Kane. Somehow, I felt that he might not believe me. I'd rather show him how I feel over the next fifty years." In spite of herself, tears sparkled in her eyes. "At the altar, he said he didn't care whether he married me or my sister."

Jean grabbed Houston's arm and pulled her away from an approaching relative. "When you marry a Taggert, you have to be strong. His pride's been wounded and he's liable to say or do anything when he's hurt. Find him now and tell him what your sister did, or tell him it was just an error in planning—anything—but don't let him brood in silence. He'll build everything into a mountain of anger, and then there'll be no hope of reaching him."

"I asked him to meet me in his office."

"Then why are you standing here?"

With the beginning of a smile, Houston deftly flung the long train twice over her left arm and marched down the hall to Kane's office.

He was standing in front of a tall window watching the people outside, an unlit cigar in his mouth. He didn't look around when she entered.

"I'm very sorry about the mistake at the altar," she began. "I'm sure it was just a flaw in my planning."

"You didn't want to marry Westfield?"

"No! It was a misunderstanding, that's all."

He took a step toward his desk. "I gave up somethin' today because I couldn't bear the idea of humiliatin' you." He gave her a cold look. "I never could abide a liar." He tossed a piece of paper at her.

Houston bent to pick it up. It was a note, laboriously hand-lettered, that said, I'll be wearing red roses in my hair today. The name of Houston Chandler was at the bottom.

"Damn you, *Lady* Chandler! I played fair by you, but you—." He turned away from her. "Keep the money. Keep the house. You worked for it hard enough. And you won't have me to put up with. Maybe you can get Westfield to take that virginity that you're so protective of." He started toward the door.

"Kane," she called after him, but he was gone.

Heavily, she sat down on one of the oak chairs in the room.

A few minutes later, Blair came into the room. "I guess we should get out there and cut the cake," she said hesitantly. "You and Taggert—."

All Houston's rage came to the surface and she came out of the chair toward her sister with anger in her eyes. "You can't even call him by his name, can you?" she said furiously. "You think he has no feelings; you've dismissed him and therefore you think you have a right to do whatever you want to him."

Blair took a step backward. "Houston, what I did, I did for you. I want to see you happy."

Houston clenched her fists at her sides and moved closer to Blair, prepared to do battle. "Happy? How can I be happy when I don't even know where my husband is? Thanks to you, I may never know the meaning of happiness."

"Me? What have I done except try everything in my power to help you? I tried to help you come to your senses and see that you didn't have to marry that man for his money. Kane Taggert—."

"You really don't know, do you?" Houston interrupted. "You have humiliated a proud, sensitive man in front of hundreds of people, and you aren't even aware of what you've done."

"I assume you're talking about what happened at the altar? I did it for you, Houston. I know you love Leander and I was willing to take Taggert just to make you happy. I'm so sorry about what I've done to you. I never meant to make you so unhappy. I know I've ruined your life, but I did try to repair what I'd done."

"Me, me, me. That's all you can say. You've ruined my life and all you can talk about is yourself. *You* know I love Leander. *You* know what an awful man Kane is. For the last week or so, you've spent every waking moment with Leander, and the way you talk about him is as if he were a god. Every other word you say is, 'Leander.' I think you did mean well this morning: you wanted to give me the best man."

Houston leaned forward. "Leander may set your body on fire, but he never did anything for me. If you hadn't been so involved with yourself lately, and could think that I do have some brains of my own, you'd have seen that I've fallen in love with a good, kind, thoughtful man—admittedly he's a little rough around the edges, but then, haven't you always complained that my edges are a little too smooth?"

Blair sat down, and the look of astonishment on her face was almost comical. "You love him? Taggert? You love Kane Taggert? But I don't understand. You've *always* loved Leander. For as long as I can remember, you've loved him."

Houston began to calm down as she realized that what Blair had done, she'd done out of love for her sister, out of wanting

Houston to have the best. "True, I decided I wanted him when I was six years old. I think it became a goal to me, like climbing a mountain. I should have set my sights on Mt. Rainier. At least, once I'd climbed it, it would have been done. I never knew what I was going to do with Leander after we were married."

"But you do know what you'll do with Taggert?"

Houston couldn't help smiling. "Oh, yes. I very much know what I'm going to do with him. I am going to make a home for him, a place where he'll be safe, a place where I'll be safe, where I can do whatever I want."

To Houston's amazement, Blair rose from her chair with a look of fury on her face. "I guess you couldn't have bothered to take two minutes to tell me this, could you? I have been through Hades in the last weeks. I have worried about you, spent whole days crying about what I've done to my sister, and here you tell me that you're in *love* with this King Midas."

"Don't you say anything against him!" Houston shouted, then managed to calm herself. "He's the kindest, gentlest man and very generous. And I happen to love him very much."

"And I have been through agony because I was worried about you. You should have told me!"

Houston took a moment to answer. Maybe she had been aware of Blair's agony of the last few weeks, but part of her was too angry to care. Maybe she'd wanted her sister to suffer. "I guess I was so jealous of your love match that I didn't want to think about you," she said softly.

"Love match?!" Blair yelled. "I think I'm Leander's Mt. Rainier. I can't deny that he does things to me physically, but that's all he wants from me. We've spent days together in the operating room, but I feel there's a part of Leander I don't know. He doesn't really let me get close to him. I know so little about him. He decided he wanted me, so he went after me, using every method he could to get me."

"But I see the way you look at him. I never felt inclined to look at him like that."

"That's because you never saw him in an operating room. If you'd seen him in there, you would have—."

"Fainted, most likely," Houston said. "Blair, I am sorry that I didn't talk to you. I probably knew that you were in agony, but what happened *hurt*. I had been engaged to Leander for, it seemed to me, most of my life, yet you walked in and took him in just one night. And Lee was always calling me his ice princess, and I was so worried about being a cold woman."

"And you're no longer worried about that?" Blair asked.

Houston could feel the color in her cheeks rising. "Not with Kane," she whispered, thinking of his hands on her body. No, she didn't feel cool when he was near.

"You really do love him?" Blair asked, sounding as if loving Kane were the most impossible task on earth. "You don't mind the food flying everywhere? You don't mind his loudness or the other women?"

Houston caught her breath. *"What* other women?" Right away, she saw that Blair was hesitating about answering, and Houston had to use all her control to calm herself. If Blair thought she was going to once again decide what her sister should or should not do . . . "And Blair, you'd better tell me."

Houston saw her sister trying to decide and she advanced on her. "If you even consider managing my life again as you did today at the altar, I'll never speak to you again. I am an adult, and you know something about *my* husband, and I want to know what it is."

"I saw him in the garden kissing Pamela Fenton just before the wedding," Blair said all in one breath.

Houston felt a little weak, but then she saw the truth of the matter. Was this what Kane was referring to when he said he'd given up something today? "But he came to me anyway," she whispered. "He saw her, kissed her, but he married me." Nothing else could have made her happier than this. "Blair, you have made me the happiest woman alive today. Now, all I have to do is find my husband and tell him that I love him and hope that he will forgive me."

A horrible thought came to her. "Oh, Blair, you don't know him at all. He's such a good man, generous in a very natural way, strong in a way that makes people lean on him, but he's . . ." She buried her face in her hands. "But he can't stand embarrassment of any kind, and we've humiliated him in front of the entire town. He'll never forgive me. Never!"

Blair moved toward the door. "I'll go to him and explain that it was all my fault, that you had nothing to do with it. Houston, I had no idea you really wanted to marry him. I just couldn't imagine anyone wanting to live with someone like him."

"I don't think you have to worry about that anymore, because I think he just walked out on me."

"But what about the guests? He can't just leave."

"Should he stay and listen to people laughing about how Leander can't decide which twin he wants? Not one person will think that Kane could have his choice of women. Kane thinks I'm still in love with Lee, you think I love Lee, and Mr. Gates thinks I'm marrying Kane for his money. I think Mother is the only person who sees that I'm in love—for the very first time in my life."

"What can I do to make it up to you?" Blair whispered.

"There's nothing you can do. He's gone. He left me money and the house and he walked away. But what do I want with this big, empty house if he's not in it?" She sat down. "Blair, I don't even know where he is. He could be on a train back to New York for all I know."

"More than likely, he's gone to his cabin."

Both women looked up to see Edan standing in the doorway. "I didn't mean to eavesdrop, but when I saw what happened at the wedding, I knew he'd be in a rage."

Houston wrapped the train of her wedding dress about her arm. "I'm going to him and explain what happened. I'm going to tell him that my sister is so in love with Leander that she thinks that I am, too." She turned to smile at Blair. "I can't help but resent the fact that you thought that I was low enough to marry a man for his money, but I thank you for the love that made you willing to sacrifice what has come to mean so much to you." Quickly, she kissed her sister's cheek.

Blair clung to her for a moment. "Houston, I had no idea you felt this way. As soon as the reception is over, I'll help you pack and—."

Houston pulled away with a little laugh. "No, my dear

managing sister, I am leaving this house right now. My husband is more important to me than a few hundred guests. You're going to have to stay here and answer all the questions about where Kane and I've gone."

"But Houston, I don't know anything about receptions of this size."

Houston stopped at the door beside Edan. "I learned how in my 'worthless' education," she said, then smiled. "Blair, it's not all that tragic. Cheer up, maybe there'll be an attack of food poisoning, and you'll know how to handle that. Good luck," she said and was out the door, leaving Blair alone with the horror of having to manage the reception of hundreds of people.

Outside the office, Edan caught her arm and led her into the storage closet beside the north porch. He was smiling at her.

"You certainly do make a habit of spying on me," she snapped, pulling away from him.

"I've learned more in two weeks of spying on you than I have in the rest of my life, total. Did you mean what you said about loving Kane?"

"Do you think I'm a liar, too? I'm going to get dressed now. It's a hard climb to the cabin."

"You know where it is?"

"I know the general whereabouts."

"Houston, you really can't go rushing off up the side of a mountain after him. I'll go get him, explain what happened and bring him back."

"No, he's mine now—at least legally—and I'm going after him alone."

Edan put his hands on her shoulders. "I wonder if he realizes how lucky he is. What can I do to help you?"

She moved toward the door. "Could you find Sarah Oakley and ask her to come upstairs and help me change?" She paused and looked at Edan speculatively. "On second thought, maybe you could find Jean Taggert for me. She's the especially pretty lady in the violet silk dress and hat."

"Especially pretty, is she?" he asked, laughing. "Good luck, Houston."

Chapter 15

Jean helped Houston dress in record time. She fully agreed with Houston in her need to go after Kane.

When Houston was dressed, they went through the west wing to the housekeeper's rooms and down that remote staircase. Hidden among some trees, Edan was waiting with a horse laden with four bags of food.

"That should keep you for a few days," he said. "Are you sure you want to do this? If you got lost——."

"I've lived in Chandler all my life and I know this area." She gave him a hard look. "I'm not the bit of fluff people think I am, remember?"

"Did you put the wedding cake in there?" Jean asked Edan.

"In its own sweet little tin box," he said in a way that made Houston glance from one to the other and begin to smile.

"You must go, and don't worry about anything here. Just think about your husband and how much you love him," Jean said as Houston mounted.

Houston sneaked away from the wedding as secretly as she could, considering that she was surrounded by over six hundred guests. The few people who saw her were so astonished that they could say nothing. She'd pulled her hat veil down over her face and she hoped that would confuse some people, but it didn't.

As she reached the western end of the garden, she nearly ran over Rafe Taggert and Pamela Fenton walking together. She wasn't sure if it was shock or surprise, but her horse's front feet came off the ground.

Rafe looked at her with amusement. "No doubt you're the twin that married a Taggert, and now you're runnin' away."

Before she could speak, Pam answered. "If I know Kane, his pride was hurt at the altar and he ran away somewhere to lick his wounds. You aren't by chance going after him, are you?"

Houston wasn't sure how to act toward this woman who had been loved by her husband. With all the coolness she could muster, her chin quite high, she said, "Yes, I am."

"Good for you!" Pam said. "He needs a wife with your courage. I always insisted that he come to me. I hope you're prepared for his anger. It's quite frightening at times. I wish you all the luck in the world."

Houston was so astonished at Pam's words that she couldn't reply. She was torn between feeling anger at the idea of someone else knowing *her* husband, and gratitude that Pam was giving her some good advice. And, too, Pam seemed to have given up her hold over Kane. Was Kane the one in love; would Pam not have him?

"Thank you," Houston murmured as she reined her horse away from them.

She encountered no one else and breathed a sigh of relief when she was past the city limits of Chandler and heading for the country.

The first part of the journey was very easy and she had time to muse on what must be happening at Kane's house. Poor Blair! She really had meant well. She had thought Houston wanted Leander, so she was willing to make a supreme sacrifice and spend her life with a "villain" like Kane Taggert. Perhaps that's what Kane had sensed, that he was the medicine to be taken by Blair because Houston'd been wronged by her sister.

Of course, what Kane didn't understand was that none of the guests would think anything about what had happened, except as something to tease about. They would tease Leander because they had known him since he was a child. If Kane had stayed and laughed, all would have been forgotten—but Kane had yet to master the art of being able to laugh at himself.

She rode to the foot of the mountain as quickly as possible and started up the trail that she and Kane had used before. When she reached the place where they'd picnicked, she dismounted and drank some water. Above her was what looked like an impregnable piece of mountain. But Kane'd said that his cabin was up there and, if he was there, she was going to find him.

As she removed her jacket and tied it to the horse, she tried to see a path through the scrub and piñon trees. It was only after several minutes of walking about, looking at the mountainside from several angles, that she saw what could have been a trail of sorts. It went straight up the mountain, over terraced rock, and disappeared into the trees.

For a moment, Houston wondered what in the world she was doing in such a place as this on her wedding day. Right now, she should be wearing a satin dress and dancing with her husband. A thought which brought her back to the present. Her husband was at the top of this mountain—maybe. Edan could be wrong, and Kane could be on a train to Africa for all anyone knew.

After giving the horse some water, she tightened her hat on her head to give her some protection against the sun and remounted.

The way up was worse than it had looked. At times the trail was so narrow that the tree branches clawed at her legs, and she had difficulty forcing the horse to travel the narrow path. The plants that grew out of rock weren't like the soft, cared-for plants in town. These trees had to fight for life every day and they refused to bend or give way for a mere human.

A Crown of Thorns cactus caught the side of her divided skirt and tore it, leaving several long thorns in the cloth. Houston paused while she pulled thorns and fat cockleburs off her clothing and a few from her hair. So much for looking her best when she arrived, she thought, as she pushed strands of hair under her hat.

At one point, the trail took a sharp right, and the sky became hidden by the overhanging trees and rock formations. All about her were mushrooms of bizarre structure and unreal colors. Some were tiny and yellow, some as big as her foot and brilliant red. Large patches of five-inch-tall grasslike mushrooms stood upright on the forest floor.

Always, she was climbing upward, and the air was thinning as the area around her became more and more like a rain forest, rather than the semiarid region that surrounded Chandler. Twice, she had to stop and look for the trail, and once she followed a path for a mile, only to have it end abruptly in a sandy-bottomed cavelike rock formation that had a natural window at the top. The place had an odd feeling about it: half frightening, half like a place where one should attend church services.

She walked her horse out of the rocks and back onto the path, where she again tried riding.

An hour later, she had her first good luck: she found a piece of Kane's wedding suit caught on a sharp edge of rock. Her relief at finding out for sure that he was indeed at the top of the trail was great. With renewed spirit, she urged her reluctant horse upward.

She might have made it perfectly well except that it began to rain. Cold, cold sheets of water came from the sky, then, as the water collected on the overhead rocks, it flooded down on top of her, making visibility impossible. She tried to keep her head down and her eyes on the nearly invisible trail in front of her at the same time.

Flashes of lightning began to make the horse shy and dance about on the skinny little path. After quite a while of fighting both the rain and the horse, she dismounted and led the animal as she gave most of her attention to searching through the deluge for the way.

At one point, the trail ran along a little ledge, sheer rock above and below her. Houston took one step and soothed the frightened horse, took another step and calmed the horse. "If you weren't carrying the food, I'd let you go," she said in disgust.

At the edge of the cliff ledge, the lightning flashed and she saw the cabin. For a moment, she stood perfectly still and looked through the rain dripping off her nose. She had begun to doubt the cabin's existence. And now what did she do? March up to the door, knock and, when Kane answered it, tell him she thought she'd drop by and leave her calling card?

She had half a mind to turn around and leave, when all hell broke loose. The idiot horse she'd had to practically drag up the mountain called out, was answered by another horse, and so proceeded to run toward the cabin. Never mind that Houston was standing in the animal's way. She screamed as she fell into the mud and began rolling down the side of the mountain, but the blast of a shotgun aimed in her direction covered her voice. "Get the hell out of here if you wanta keep your skin," Kane bellowed over the rain.

Houston was hanging over the edge of the drop-off, clutching the roots of a little piñon tree and trying to find a place to stick her dangling feet. Surely he wasn't so angry that he'd shoot her?

Now was not the time to ask questions. She was either going to slide to her death or take a chance on Kane's temper.

"Kane!" she screamed and felt her arms giving way.

Almost immediately, his face appeared over the side. "My God," he said in disbelief as he stretched out his hand to grab her wrist.

Quite easily, he hauled her to the top, stood her on the ground and stepped back from her. He didn't seem to believe she was there.

"I came to see you," Houston said with a wet, crooked smile, as she began to weave about on her feet.

"Nice to have you," he said, grinning. "I don't get much company up here."

"Maybe it's your welcome," she answered, nodding toward the shotgun in his hand.

"You wanta come in? I gotta fire inside." His voice was highly amused—and, Houston hoped, pleased.

"I'd like that very much," she said, then squealed and jumped toward him as above her a tree limb gave a loud crack.

She was standing quite near him and, as he looked down at her, his eyes were questioning. It was now or never, Houston thought, and there was no sense in being shy or coy. "You said you'd be there for the wedding if I'd show up for the wedding night. You fulfilled your part of the bargain, so I'm here for mine."

With breath held, she watched him.

Kane's face went through several emotions before he threw back his head and laughed loud enough to be heard over the rain and the thunder. The next moment, he swept her into his arms and carried her toward the cabin. At the doorway, he stopped and kissed her. Houston clung to him and knew the arduous climb had been worth it.

Inside the little one-room cabin was a stone fireplace that filled one whole wall, and a warm, cheerful fire blazed within it.

Kane held up a blanket. "I ain't got any dry clothes up here so this'll have to do. You get out of them things while I find your horse and pen it up."

"There's food in the bags," she called as he left.

Alone, Houston began to undress, peeling the soaking garments from her cold, clammy skin. She couldn't help glancing at the door every few minutes. "Coward!" she said to herself. "You've propositioned the man and now you have to live up to your boasts."

By the time Kane returned, Houston was wrapped in the scratchy wool blanket with only her face sticking out. After a quick, smiling look of understanding, Kane put the food on the floor.

The only furniture in the room was a big bed made of pine, covered with an odd assortment of blankets that didn't look overly clean. Against one wall was a mountain of stacked canned goods, mostly peaches like she'd found in the kitchen of his house.

"I'm glad you brought food," he said. "I guess I left in too much of a hurry to get any. I don't guess Edan'd believe it, but even I get tired of peaches after a few cans."

"Edan packed the food, and your cousin, Jean, had him put in some wedding cake."

Kane straightened. "Ah, yes, the wedding. I guess I ruined the day for you, and women like weddings so much." He began to unbutton his shirt.

"Many women have weddings like the one I planned, but few have a day such as this one turned out to be."

As he pulled his wet shirt out of his pants, he smiled at her. "Your sister did all that at the weddin', didn't she? You didn't have nothin' to do with it, did you? I realized that after I got all the way up here."

"No, I didn't," she answered. "But Blair didn't mean any harm. She loves me and she thought I wanted Leander, so she tried to give him to me." As Kane began to remove his pants, Houston looked back at the fire. This was her wedding night, she thought, and her body warmed considerably.

"Thought?" Kane asked, and when she didn't answer, he persisted. "You said she *thought* you wanted Westfield. She doesn't think so anymore?"

"Not after what I said to her," Houston murmured, looking into the fire. Behind her, she could hear him rubbing himself with a towel, and she was greatly tempted to look around. Was he really as well built as the strongman she'd hired for The Sisterhood meeting?

With a swift movement, Kane knelt before her.

He was wearing only the towel about his hips, looking for all the world like a Greek god of old. The smooth, big muscles under deeply bronzed skin were indeed better than those of the man she'd hired.

Whatever Kane'd been about to say was forgotten as he looked at her. His breath caught in his throat. "You looked at me like this once before," he whispered. "That time you hit me with a water pitcher when I touched you. You plannin' somethin' like that this time?"

Houston just looked at him and let the blanket slide from her head, then down her neck, off her shoulder to hang just above her breasts. "No," was all she could think to say.

The heat of the fire was warm on her skin but nothing compared to the feel of Kane's hand on the side of her face. His fingers tangled themselves in the wet hair that flowed down her back. His thumb ran across her lower lip as he watched her.

"I've seen you dressed up a lot, but you've never been prettier than you are right now. I'm glad you came up here. A place like this is where people should make love."

Houston kept her eyes on his as his hand travelled down her neck and onto her shoulder. When he started to move the blanket away from her breasts, she held her breath, and realized that she was praying that she'd please him.

Very gently, as if she were a child, he put one arm around her shoulders and lowered her to the cabin floor. She tensed as she thought, this is it.

Kane parted the blanket so that her nude body was entirely exposed to him.

Houston waited for the verdict.

"Damn," he said under his breath. "No wonder Westfield made a fool of himself over a body like that. I've found that them curvy dresses you ladies wear are usually stuffed with cotton."

Houston had to laugh. "I please you?"

"Please me?" he said, as he held out his hand. "Just look at that. It's shakin' so bad I can't hold it still." He put his hand on the soft skin of her stomach. "It ain't gonna be easy for me to wait, but any lady'd climb all the way up here to spend the night with me deserves the best—not no quick tumble on the floor. You just sit there and I'll make us somethin' to drink. You like peaches? No!" he said as Houston began to pull the blanket about her. "You can just leave that on the floor. You get too cold you can crawl in my lap and I'll warm you."

Growing up in Duncan Gates's house had not given Houston much opportunity to learn to like the taste of liquor. But Kane took a can of peaches, poured out the juice, mashed the peaches to a pulp and mixed it with a generous amount of rum.

He handed her the concoction in the can. "It ain't a fancy glass, but it works."

Houston took a sip. She felt quite awkward wearing absolutely nothing while sitting in front of a man. But by the time she'd finished the drink, which didn't taste at all like the few sips of liquor she'd drunk before, she was feeling as if it were the most normal thing in the world to have no clothes on.

Kane took a seat across from her and watched her. "Better?" he asked as he handed her another drink.

"Much."

She was only halfway through the second can of drink when Kane took it from her. "I don't want you drunk, just relaxed."

He put his arms around her and pulled her close to him. The

drink inside Houston made her feel less inhibited than she ever had been in her life. Her arms twined about his neck and she put her lips on his.

"What did you tell your sister about you and Westfield?"

"That Lee might set her body on fire, but he did absolutely nothing for me."

"Not a good asker?"

"The worst," she said as his lips came down on hers.

His hands played along her body as he kissed her, touching her skin and sending fire through her. Some small part of her brain was aware that Kane was holding back part of himself, that he was more reserved than she was, but she didn't listen.

As his hands roamed about her body, Houston moved so she was closer to him, stretching out her body to give him freer access.

He kissed her face, her neck, his mouth running down to her breasts. When he took the pink crest in his mouth, she arched against him, and he used his hands to caress her waist and hips.

"Slow down, love," he murmured. "We have all night."

All the sensations were so new to Houston. Always, when Lee'd touched her, she'd felt like withdrawing, pulling away from him rather than wanting to explore and discover everything at once. As Kane touched her, she felt more and more wonderful, and all the fears that Lee'd instilled in her, that she was frigid, were fast disappearing.

Her hands began to explore his skin, to feel the warmth of it. The firelight made his flesh glow, and Houston so much wanted to touch all of him.

Kane pulled her closer to him, lying down with her in his arms. He removed the towel from his hips and Houston moved her hips closer to his, a little afraid of the feel of his swollen manhood.

Kane's control began to break. His breath in her ear was ragged and quick, and his gentle kisses turned hot and demanding. Houston met his force with her own.

"Houston, sweet, sweet Houston," he said as he laid her down on the blanket-covered floor and lay on top of her.

Eagerly, she clutched his body to hers. When he entered her, she gasped and quick tears of pain came to her eyes. Kane lifted himself and looked at her, and held himself back until he saw by her face that the pain was receding. He kissed her neck with little nibbling kisses, running his tongue along her ear until she moved her face and sought his mouth.

Slowly, Kane began to move inside her, and after the first few painful movements, Houston began to arch toward him in clumsy little circles. Kane put his hands on her hips and began to guide her, slowly, carefully, gracefully.

Houston put her head back and gave all her thoughts and feelings over to the new and delicious sensations Kane was sending through her body.

She began to move in a rhythm as old as time itself, and inside her she felt all the emotions she'd kept pent up, at last finding a release.

Her breath came faster and harder as she began to feel herself building into an explosion.

Kane began to move faster and she moved with him. Higher and higher her passion climbed, until she thought she might burst.

And when she did explode, she was sure she might die from the experience. "Kane," she whispered. "Oh my dear, dear Kane."

He pulled away from her just enough to look at her, and his face wore an unusual expression, one she couldn't understand.

"I didn't please you?" she asked, as her body began to tense again. "Do you think I'm frigid, too?"

He put his hand to the side of her head and kissed her softly. "No, sweetheart, the last thing I think you are is frigid. I'm not sure I know anythin' about you at all, except that you're the prettiest woman I've ever seen and you do the damnest things, like come all the way up the side of a mountain just to spend the night with me, and then my prim little lady-wife turns out to be a hot little . . . Maybe we shouldn't go into that."

He kissed her forehead. "I'm goin' outside into the rain and wash this blood off, and when I get back, let's eat. I need my strength if I'm gonna make love to you all night."

As he stood, Houston stretched, her fair skin tawny in the firelight.

As Kane watched her, an unusual thought entered his head: he didn't want to be alone, not even for the length of time it took him to go outside.

He reached out his hand to her. "Go with me," he said, and there was a plea in his voice.

"Anywhere," Houston answered.

Chapter 16

Houston walked out into the rain with her husband and wasn't even aware of the cold. Her mind was occupied with the fact that she wasn't frigid. Maybe the problem had been Leander, maybe she had been too close to him, or felt too much like his sister, to want to climb into bed with him. But whatever the reason, she was now released from her fear that there was something missing inside her.

Kane pulled her into his arms. "You look dreamy," he said. Rain was dripping down his face and onto hers. "Tell me what you're thinkin'. What does a lady think after havin' the local stableboy make love to her?"

Houston pulled away from him and stretched her arms up toward the sky. On impulse she began dancing slowly, as if she wore her satin wedding dress, holding the skirt out and moving gracefully with it. "This lady feels wonderful. This lady doesn't feel at all like a lady."

He caught her wrist. "You aren't regrettin' that your weddin' night wasn't in a silk-sheeted bed? You don't wish some other man—."

She put her fingers to his lips. "This is the happiest night of my life, and I don't want to be anywhere else or with anyone else. A cabin in the woods with the man I love. No woman in the world could ask for more than that."

He was watching her with an odd intensity, a slight frown on his face. "We better go in before we freeze to death."

Calmly, he started back to the cabin, Houston beside him, but suddenly he turned and grabbed her to him, their cold, wet skin sticking together as he kissed her.

Houston melted against him, letting him feel her joy and happiness.

With a smile, he lifted her into his arms and carried her into the cabin. Once inside, he grabbed a blanket, wrapped her in it, and began rubbing her cold body.

"Houston," he said, "you're not like any lady I ever met. I thought I had a pretty clear idea of what marriage to one of the Chandler princesses would be like, but you 'bout busted all my ideas."

She turned around in his arms, her nude body wrapped in the blanket, his bare skin glowing in the firelight. "Am I different in a good way or a bad one? I know you wanted a lady; am I not being one?"

He took a while to answer, looking at her speculatively, as if judging what he should tell her. "Let's just say that I'm learnin' a lot." He grinned. "I'll bet Gould's wife never followed him up the side of a mountain." He began kissing her neck, but stopped abruptly. "Would it be too much to hope that you know how to cook?"

"I know the rudiments, enough to direct a cook, but I don't know how to prepare a meal from scratch. You don't like Mrs. Murchison?"

"I'm happy to say that she ain't here at the moment. What I want to know is whether you can make somethin' to eat out of those bags of food."

She wiggled her arms out of the blanket and put them around his neck. "I believe I could arrange that. I never want this night to end. I was so afraid that you'd be angry with me for coming up here when I hadn't been invited. But I'm glad that we're here now and not in Chandler. This is so much more romantic."

"Romantic or not, if we don't eat soon, I'm gonna shrivel away to nothin'."

"We can't let that catastrophe happen," Houston said quickly and rolled out from under him.

Kane thought for a moment that his bride had just made a bawdy joke, but he dismissed that as an impossibility.

With the blanket loosely wrapped around her, falling off one shoulder, Houston took the bags Kane handed her and began unpacking them. He'd once again wrapped the towel about his hips as he piled more wood on the fire. She saw right away that whoever had packed the food had done an excellent job. She withdrew lidded tins, tied porcelain boxes, and muslin-wrapped packages. A note fell out of the second bag.

My dear daughter,
  I wish you all the happiness in the world in your marriage, and I think you're perfectly right in following your husband. When you return, don't be surprised to hear that Kane carried you away with him.

Very much love,
Opal Chandler Gates

Kane looked up from the fire to see Houston with tears in her eyes as she clutched a piece of paper. "Is somethin' wrong?"

She handed him the note.

"What's this mean, that I carried you away?"

Houston began unwrapping food. "It means that when we return to Chandler, your reputation as the most romantic man in town will be further enhanced."

"My *what?*"

"Yes," she said as she unwrapped a package of Vienna rolls. "It started when you carried me out of the Mankins' garden party and was added to later when people began repeating the story of how you ran the cowboys who accosted me out of town. And then there was the romantic dinner party you gave at your house with the pillows and candles."

"But it's because I ain't got any chairs, and I spilled food all over you, and was I supposed to stand around and let those cowboys bother you?"

Houston opened a can that contained creamed lobster soup. "Whatever the true reason, the result is the same. By the time we return, I expect adolescent girls to stare at you on the street, and to tell each other that they hope they marry a man who drags them away from their own weddings to a lonely mountain cabin."

For a moment, Kane said nothing, but then he grinned and came to sit by her. "Romantic, am I?" he said, kissing her neck. "I don't guess anyone'll see that it's the lady I married that's keepin' me from lookin' like a fool in front of ever'body. What's that gray stuff?"

"Pâté de foie gras," she said, spreading some on a cracker with a little pearl-handled knife Opal'd included. She put it in his mouth for him.

"Not bad. What else you got?"

There was a piece of Stilton cheese, an artichoke which Kane thought was a waste of time to eat, tomatoes, soft-shell crabs, chicken croquettes, Smithfield ham, sirloin steak in onion gravy, and fried chicken.

When Houston saw the chicken, she laughed. It hadn't been on the menu that she'd planned for the wedding. No doubt Mrs. Murchison had prepared it especially for her dear Mr. Taggert. Houston wondered how many other people had been involved in packing the food for her "secret" runaway.

"What in the world is this?" Kane asked.

"I thought the wedding might be a good place to introduce a few foreign foods to Chandler. That is a German pretzel, and some Italian pastries were served, but I don't think any were packed for us."

As Houston talked, she unwrapped more food: a cloth bag filled with fruit, a tin of Waldorf salad, a big round box filled with slices of several different pies, gingerbread, a bag of peanut candy, one of fudge. There were three loaves of bread, a box of sliced meats, cheese, and onions, a jar of olives, another of mustard.

"I don't think we'll starve. Ah! Here it is." She showed Kane the inside of a metal box that contained a large section of wedding cake.

He took the little knife from the bed, cut a piece of cake and fed it to her from his fingertips. Houston held his hand and licked away every last crumb. He put his hand to the side of her face and kissed her lingeringly.

"A body could starve to death with you around," he murmured. "Why don't you feed me before you seduce me again?"

"Me!" she gasped. "You're the one who . . ."

"Yes?" he said as he picked up a piece of fried chicken. "I did what?"

"Perhaps I won't pursue that line of thought. Would you pass me that can of soup?"

"Did you find my weddin' present to you? In that little leather trunk?"

"The one in the sitting room?" When he nodded, she said she hadn't had time to look at it. "What's in it?"

"Wouldn't that spoil the surprise?"

Houston continued eating for a moment. "I think that wedding gifts should be given on the day of the wedding. And since we are here, and the trunk is there, I'd like another gift."

"You ain't even seen what's in that trunk and, besides, how can I buy you somethin' up here?"

"Sometimes, the most precious gifts aren't purchased in a store. What I want is something personal, something very special."

Kane's face showed that he had no idea what she was talking about.

"I want you to share a secret about yourself with me."

"I already told you all about myself. You wanta know where I have money hidden in case some of my investments fall through?"

Delicately, she cut herself a piece of Camembert. "I was thinking more in the line of something about your father or mother, or perhaps about your hatred for the Fentons, or maybe about what you and Pam talked about in the garden this morning."

Kane was too stunned to speak for a moment. "You don't ask for much, do you? Anythin' else you want, like maybe my head on a platter? How come you wanta know things like that?"

"Because we're married."

"Don't you go puttin' your lady face back on. A lot of married people are like your mother and that sober ol' man she married. She calls him *Mr.* Gates out of respect, like you used to do to me. I'll bet your mother never asked Gates questions like you're askin' me."

"Well then, maybe I'm just terribly curious. After all, it was my curiosity that made me want to see your house, and that led to now, and . . ." She let her voice trail off and the blanket slide down another two inches.

Kane looked at the sliding blanket with amusement. "You sure do catch on fast. All right, I guess there is somethin' I better tell you 'cause Pam says it's gonna be all over town in just a few days."

He paused a moment, looking down at the food. "You ain't gonna like this too much, but there ain't much I can do to change it now. You 'member that I told you that Fenton kicked me off his land when I was a kid 'cause I'd been messin' around with his daughter?"

"Yes," she said softly.

"I always thought that somebody'd snitched on us and told Fenton, but today Pam said she was the one that told him." He took a deep breath, looked at her with an air of defiance, and continued. "Pam told her old man that she was expectin' my kid and she wanted to marry me. Fenton, bein' the bastard he is, sent her away to marry some ol' man that owed him money, and told me Pam never wanted to see me again."

"Is that the reason you hate Mr. Fenton?"

He looked her in the eye. "No, it ain't. I just learned all this today. The point of all this storytellin' is that Pam's come back to Chandler to live, and with her is her thirteen-year-old son who also happens to be my son. And accordin' to Pam, he looks enough like me to set a few tongues waggin'."

Houston took her time in replying. "If everyone will know this shortly, it's not really a secret, is it?"

"It was damn well a secret to me until a matter of hours ago," he said with some anger in his voice. "I didn't know I had a kid somewhere."

When needed, Houston's stubbornness could match his. "I asked for a real secret, not something that next week everyone will know and be discussing over tea. I want to know something that only you know about yourself, something that even Edan doesn't know about you."

"How come you wanta know about me? How come you can't just put the furniture away and sleep with me?"

"Because I've come to love you and I want to know about you."

"Women are always sayin' they love you. Two weeks ago you were in love with Westfield. Damn it! All right, I'll tell you somethin' that's none of your business, but you'll probably like hearin' it. This mornin' Pam came to me and told me she'd been in love with me all these years, and she wanted me to leave with her, but I turned her down."

"For me?" Houston whispered.

"Ain't you the one I married? With no thanks to that idiot sister of yours, I might add."

"Has something happened between you and Blair that makes you two snarl at each other?"

"One secret to a weddin' day," he said. "You want another secret, you gotta work for it. And the best way you can work is to get that food off this bed and take that blanket off and come rub up against me."

"I'm not sure I can stand such torture," she said, as she frantically removed food and tore the blanket away at the same time.

"I like obedient women," he said, holding out his arms to her.

"I have been trained to be the most obedient of women," she whispered, putting her lips up to be kissed.

"As far as I can tell, you ain't obeyed me once yet . . . except maybe here in this cabin. Damn it, Houston, but I never thought you'd be like this. Maybe you're more like your sister than I thought."

She pulled away from him. "You thought I was an ice princess, too?"

With a smile, he pulled her back to him. "Honey, what happens when you apply heat to ice?"

"Water?"

"Steam." He moved his hand down to her firm backside and pulled her between his legs, covering her body with his.

Houston loved the sensation of being close to him, of feeling his skin against hers. She'd been warned that the wedding night was very painful, but this night had been all the joy she'd hoped it would be. Perhaps it was Kane, and the fact that she felt approval coming from him, rather than the criticism that she'd always received from the other men in her life, but now she felt free to react in any way she truly felt.

Kane began to stroke her body, her legs, the back of her, and his touch made her feel beautiful in a way that no compliment or pretty dress ever had. She closed her eyes and gave herself to the lovely sensations of the darkened room, the sound and warmth of the fire, and this man's big, wide, hard hands going up and down her body, curving over surfaces that she'd not even been aware that she owned until this night. He stroked her hair, spreading it out on the pillow, running the back of his fingers along her cheekbones.

When she opened her eyes to look at him, she saw a softness in his face that she'd never seen before. His eyes were dark and hot-looking.

"Kane," she whispered.

"I'm right here, baby, and I'm not about to go away," he said as he began touching her again.

As she closed her eyes again, his hands became more insistent as he clutched her hips, burying his thumbs in her soft flesh. Her breath came faster as he moved to put one of his big, hard thighs across her smooth soft ones. His hands were on her breasts as his mouth sought hers and she opened to him like a flower to a bee.

Crushing her to him, his mouth clinging to hers, he put his hands on her buttocks and raised her to meet him.

Houston gasped at the first thrust, but there was no pain as she began to move with him. He pulled her closer and closer until their skin was as one person's, fusing them in this act of love.

Instinctively, Houston wrapped her legs around his waist and clutched his neck as he lifted her from the bed, supporting her weight with his arms and on his knees.

He shoved her against the rough cabin wall and increased the passion of his thrusts as Houston threw her head back and loudly exclaimed her pleasure. And when the last hard, fiery thrust came, Houston screamed.

For a moment, Kane held her suspended and she clung to him as if for her life.

After several long minutes, he eased both of them down to the bed, and snuggled her so close she could barely breathe. "A screamer," he murmured. "Who would a guessed that a lady would be a screamer?"

Houston was too exhausted to reply before she fell asleep in his arms.

Chapter 17

When Kane woke the next morning, it was full daylight. After a few long moments of grinning at Houston's nude body cuddled next to his, he caressed her bare rump.

"Time to get up and fix me some breakfast."

"Ring the bell on the table and the maid will come," she murmured as she buried her face deeper into his warm chest.

With one eyebrow raised, he looked at her. "Oh, good mornin', Mr. Gates and Leander. So nice to see you."

Houston reacted at once, sitting up poker-straight in the bed, grabbing the sheet, and wrapping it about her so that only her face could be seen.

It took her only seconds to realize that Kane was teasing. "What a terrible trick to play!" she accused, but Kane had started to laugh at the sight of her covered so primly, and all of it done so quickly. She tried her best to not laugh with him, but found it impossible.

"I guess I don't have to worry 'bout Westfield anymore," he said as he left the bed and began to rummage in the food that had been packed for them.

Houston lay back in the bed and watched him with a great deal of interest. His body was indeed better than that of the strongman she'd invited to The Sisterhood meeting, strong muscles, wide shoulders tapering to a small rear end atop heavy thighs—thighs that could rub on hers and make her body sing.

Casually, Kane turned to glance at her, but when he saw her expression, he dropped the food he was holding, stood and held out his hand to her.

She took it and he pulled her out of the bed and drew her close.

"I hadn't planned to spend much time up here, but maybe you wouldn't mind it if we spent a few days alone together, like a honeymoon, except not in Paris or some place like that."

"I've been to Paris," she whispered, moving her hips closer to his and gently rubbing against him. "And I can honestly say that here is better than there. Now, what were you saying about breakfast?"

With disbelief on his face, Kane pushed her away. "If there was one thing that I learned as a kid, it was that toys are precious and you don't wear them out on the first day."

"I'm a toy to you?"

"A grown-up toy. Now, get some clothes on and let's eat. I thought I might show you some old minin' ruins around here. I just hope I'm man enough to spend all day with you."

"I think you are," she said through her lashes as she coyly glanced down at the part of him that showed no qualms about "wearing her out."

Quite firmly, he took her shoulders in his hands and turned her around. "I got a extra shirt and pants over there and you go get dressed—and I want every button done up and nothin' left hangin' out to drive me crazy. You understand that?"

"Completely," Houston said, her back to him; she was grinning so hard that her skin was stretching.

When they were dressed and had eaten, Kane led her up the side of the mountain. Chandler was at 6200 feet elevation and now they were at about 7500 feet, making the air cold and crisp. Kane didn't seem aware of the fact that Houston wasn't used to the climbing or that her riding boots weren't made to grip the slippery rock, but led her straight up, past overhanging rock that looked as if it were about to fall on them.

"Is it much farther?" she asked once.

Turning, Kane held out his hand to help her over a particularly difficult rock. "How about a rest?" he asked as he began to remove the pack of food from his back.

"I would appreciate it very much," she said as she took the canteen he offered and drank deeply of it. "Are you sure there's a mine up here? How could they get the coal out?"

"Same way they get all coal out, I guess. What do I know about coal mining?" He was looking at her intently and, when he seemed satisfied that she was going to live, he turned away.

"Do you come up here often?"

"Whenever I can get away. Look through there at those rocks. Ever see anythin' like 'em?" Down through the mist of the valley she could see a razorback formation of rock that rose straight out of the ground, looking unnatural and dangerous. "What do you think caused somethin' like that? It's like some giant tried to pull the rock out of the ground, got it halfway up and stopped."

Houston was eating one of the pretzels that Kane had put in the pack. He'd already declared them to be one of nature's best foods, and she was to have them always on hand. "I think that perhaps a geologist would have a better explanation. Wouldn't you love to have had the opportunity to go to school and learn things such as why those rocks are shaped like that?"

Very slowly, Kane turned to look at her. "You got somethin' to say, say it. My schoolin's got me by enough to earn me a few million dollars. It ain't good enough for you?"

Houston studied her pretzel. "I was thinking more in the line of people less fortunate than you."

"I give as much to charity as anybody else does. I do my part." His jaw was set in a hard line.

"I just thought that perhaps now was a good time to tell you that I've invited your cousin Ian to live with us."

"My cousin Ian? That ain't that sullen, angry-lookin' kid that you saved from the fight, is it?"

"I guess you could describe him like that, although I rather thought he had a look of your . . . determination."

Kane ignored her last remark. "Why in the world would you volunteer to take on a problem like him?"

"He's very intelligent, but he had to quit school to help support his family. He's only a boy, yet he's been working in the coal mines for years. I hope you don't mind my asking him without consulting you first, but the house is certainly big enough, and he *is* your own first cousin."

Standing, Kane began to strap the pack on his back. As he started to walk again, this time on flatter ground, he said, "It's fine with me, but keep him away from me. I don't like kids much."

Houston started to follow him. "Not even your own son?"

"I ain't even met the kid; how am I supposed to like 'im?"

She struggled to throw her leg over a fallen tree blocking the way. Kane's pants that she wore were so large on her that they snagged on branches and caught debris inside them. "I thought perhaps you'd be curious."

His voice came from behind a clump of white-barked aspens. "All I'm curious 'bout right now is whether ol' Hettie Green's gonna sell me some railroad stock she owns."

Panting, Houston tried to catch up with him, but caught her shirt on a tree branch. Fighting to free herself, she called to him, "By the way, did you get your apartment building from Mr. Vanderbilt?"

Kane turned back to help her, gently freeing her shirt and then her hair from the rough branches. "Oh, that. Sure. Though it wasn't easy, what with bein' out here 'n' all. For what I'm spendin' in telegrams, I could own that company."

"You *don't* own Western Union?" she asked, wide-eyed.

Kane seemed to have no idea that she was teasing him. "Not much of it. Someday they're gonna hook up the telephones all over the country. Damn thing is useless as it is. Cain't call nobody outside Chandler. And who wants to talk to anybody in Chandler?"

She looked up into his eyes and said softly, "You could call your son and say hello."

With a deeply felt groan, Kane turned around and started walking again. "Edan was right. I shoulda married a farm girl, one that'd mind her own business."

As Houston practically ran to keep up with him, stumbling over fallen branches, slipping once on an enormous mushroom, she wondered if she'd gone too far, but for all Kane's words, his tone was not angry.

They walked for what must have been another mile before they came to the abandoned mine opening. It was situated on the very steep side of a hill, overlooking a broad panorama of the valley below it.

The mine went back into the earth for only about twenty feet before it collapsed. Houston picked up a piece of coal from the ground and studied it in the sunlight. When looked at closely, coal was beautiful: glossed with an almost silver quality, and Houston could readily believe that coal, with pressure and time, could become diamonds.

She looked out over the valley at the steep mountainside below. "Just what I thought," she said, "the coal is worthless up here."

Kane was more interested in the view, but gave a cursory glance to the pieces of coal on the ground. "Looks like all the rest of the stuff to me. What's wrong with it?"

"Nothing is wrong with the coal; in fact, this is high grade ore, but the railroad can't get up here. Without the railroad, coal is worthless—as my father found out."

"I thought your father made his money from sellin' things."

Houston rubbed the coal in her hand. She liked the slick feel of it and the angles made by the way the coal fractured. Many of the miners thought coal was pure and kept a piece in their mouths to suck on while they worked. "He did, but he came to Colorado because he'd heard of the wealth of coal here. He thought the place would be full of rich people dying to buy the two hundred coal stoves he nearly lost his life bringing across the 'Great Desert,' as they used to call the land between St. Joseph and Denver."

"Makes sense to me. So he sold the stoves and got started in the mercantile business."

"No, he nearly went bankrupt. You see, the coal was in Colorado all right, you could mine it with a shovel, but the railroad hadn't arrived yet, so there was no economical way to market it. Ox carts couldn't carry enough to make a profit."

"So what did your father do?"

Houston smiled at the memory of the story her mother'd told her so often. "My father had grand dreams. There was a little settlement of farmers at the foot of this mountain we're on now, and my father thought it was an ideal place for a town—his town. He gave each of the farmers one of the coal stoves if the farmer'd promise to buy all his coal from Chandler Coal Works in Chandler, Colorado."

"You mean he named the town after himself?"

"He most certainly did. I'd like to have seen the faces of the people when he informed them that they were now living in the town of Mr. William Houston Chandler, Esquire."

"And all these years I thought the town'd been named for him because he'd done somethin' like save a hundred babies from a burnin' buildin'."

"Mrs. Jenks at the library says my father was honored by the town for his many contributions."

"So how come his money wasn't made in coal?"

"My father's back gave out after one year. He shoveled coal, loaded it and hauled it to the growing population, but after a year he sold the mine to a couple of farmers' brawny sons for a pittance. A month later, he returned to the East, bought fifty-one wagonloads of goods, married my mother and brought her and twenty-five couples back to settle in the glorious town of Chandler, Colorado. Mother said that chickens were roosting on the mantel of the building that someone dared to call the Chandler Hotel."

"And the comin' of the railroad made the farmers' sons rich," Kane said.

"True, but by then my father was dead, and my mother's family had already remarried her to the highly respectable Mr.

Gates." Houston moved to look inside the mine, while Kane stayed outside.

"I guess a person gets funny ideas sometimes. This whole town thinks of your family as some sort of royalty, but the truth is, the town is named after your father only because he was enough of a braggart to want to own a town. Not much of a king, was he?"

"He was a king to my sister and me—and to my mother. When Blair and I were children, the town decided to declare my father's birthday as a holiday. Mother made an effort to tell everyone the truth, but after great frustration, she realized that the townspeople *wanted* a hero."

"And how does Gates figure in this?"

Houston gave a deep sigh. "Mr. Gates's reputation could never be of the most sterling quality because he runs a brewery, so when Queen Opal Chandler and her two young princesses were on the marriage block, he offered everything he owned. Mother's family accepted with enthusiasm."

"He wanted a real lady, too," Kane said softly.

"And he was willing to enforce his rigid beliefs of what a lady should be on the three women under his roof," Houston said through a tightened jaw.

Kane was silent for a moment. "I guess the grass always looks greener on the other side of the fence."

Houston moved to stand close to him and take his hand in hers. "Did you ever think that if you'd been raised as a son, instead of in the stables, you'd be spoiled like Marc is, instead of a man who knows the value of work?"

"You make it sound like Fenton done me a favor," he said, aghast.

"Did."

"What?!"

"Fenton *did* you a favor. I was correcting your grammar. It was part of our agreement."

"You're changin' the subject. You know, I oughta send you to New York to do business for me. You'd destroy some of those men."

She put her arms around his neck. "Could I perhaps destroy you instead?"

Chapter 18

As Houston put her arms around his neck, she saw by his expression that he seemed to be fighting something within himself, almost as if he didn't want to kiss her but couldn't keep from it.

He put his hand to the back of her head and came down on her lips as if he were a dying man. Houston clung to him, loving the feel of his big body next to hers, the power of him taking over her body.

"Kane," she whispered from somewhere deep within her throat.

He pulled away to stare down at her, his dark eyes black with desire. "What have you done to me? It's been years since what's between my legs ruled what's between my ears. But right now, I think I could kill any man that tried to take you away from me."

"Or any woman?" she asked, her lips against his.

"Yes," was all he could manage to say before he began to tear the big shirt off her.

Before, Houston had felt that Kane was withholding something in his lovemaking, that part of him was remaining aloof, not with her but somewhere else. But now he was different, no more reserve of coolness, no more holding back and watching.

With all the passion of a charging bull, Kane swept her into his arms and carried her into the opening of the abandoned mine shaft. As Houston glanced at his impassioned face, she thought, this is the man who has made millions in a few short years. This is the Kane Taggert I knew was inside. This is the man that I love—the man whom I want to love me.

Kane seemed to have no thoughts as he lowered her to the ground, his lips reclaiming hers while his hands clawed the rest of her clothes from her body, exposing her soft skin to his touch. He was ravenous as his mouth tore its way down her body.

No more was he the kind, patient, considerate lover, but in his place was a man starving with want of her. Houston thought she'd responded to him previously, but now her mind left her and she became one mass of raw, pulsating feeling.

Kane's mouth on her flesh was like a fire travelling up and down, seeping into her very bones until she was sure she'd be consumed by him.

His strong fingers clutched at her waist and pulled her close to his skin, so hot it felt as if the fire in her were searing him also. He rolled to his back, holding her and moving her body as if she were of no more weight than a child.

In one swift, fluid motion, he lifted her and set her down on his manhood. Houston gave such a half-scream, half-moan of pleasure that it echoed off the back walls of the mine and swirled about them.

Her head was thrown back, there was sweat on her neck that dampened the tendrils of her hair about her shoulders and, as she put her hands on his shoulders, she let the emotion of their lovemaking take over. She had no thoughts; at that moment she only felt—as she'd never felt anything in her life before.

Kane's hands dug into her skin as he lifted her, as she lifted herself to the frenzy of movement that their passion inspired.

Once, she opened her eyes and saw him, saw the expression on his face, his mouth partly open, his eyes closed and the deep, consuming pleasure she saw there refired her own feelings.

The pace increased.

"Kane." She thought she had whispered, but again the sound reverberated about them, swirling in the cool air, wrapping around them.

Kane didn't answer but lifted her up and down with lightning speed, and when he brought her down for that last, blinding thrust, Houston felt her body tighten as her back arched and her thighs gripped Kane's hips.

An earthshaking shudder passed through her and when it was done, she fell forward against his sweaty chest. Kane's arms held her so tightly that her ribs threatened to break, but she curled her arms against his chest, kept her legs inside his and tried her best to be even closer to him.

They lay together, the only movement being Kane's hand gently stroking her hair.

"Did you know it's started to rain?" he said softly after a while.

Houston was oblivious to anything but his body next to hers and the extraordinary experience she'd just been through. She managed to shake her head but didn't look up.

"Did you know that it's about forty degrees out there, and that I'm layin' on hundreds of those sharp little pieces of coal that you find so fascinatin', and that my left leg died 'bout an hour ago?"

Smiling, her face buried in his warm skin, Houston shook her head.

"I don't guess you have any plans of movin' within the next week or so, do you?"

Laughter was building inside Houston as she kept her face hidden and shook her head.

"And it doesn't matter to you that my toes are so cold that if I knocked 'em against somethin' they'd probably fall right off?"

Her negative response only made him hold her closer. "Could I bribe you?"

"Yes," she whispered.

"How 'bout if we get our clothes on, and then we stay in here and watch it rain, and I let you ask me questions? That seems to please you the most, as far as I can tell."

She raised her head to look at him. "Will you answer them?"

"Probably not," he said as he gently pushed her off him, but stopped midway to kiss her lingeringly, softly, and caress her cheek. "Witch," he murmured before turning away and reaching for his pants.

When he moved, Houston saw that pieces of coal were sticking to his broad back, and she began to brush them away. By some odd chance, her breasts grazed his skin repeatedly.

Kane turned around and grabbed her wrists in his. "Don't start that again. There's somethin' about you, lady, that I don't think I can resist. And you can stop lookin' so pleased with yourself." Even as he spoke, his eyes travelled down her bare body. "Houston," he half groaned as he released her and turned away, "you ain't like what I expected at all. Now, get dressed 'fore I make a fool of myself . . . again."

Houston didn't ask him what he meant about making a fool of himself *again*, but her heart raced with pleasure as she pulled on the loose clothing she'd borrowed from him. There were several buttons ripped from the shirt and the torn places made her smile.

She was barely dressed before he pulled her into his arms, and sat her on his lap as he leaned back against the wall of the mine tunnel.

The soft rain outside came down slowly, as if it never meant to stop, and Houston snuggled back into Kane's arms.

"You make me happy," Houston said as she moved his arms closer about her.

"Me? You didn't even get the present I got for you." He paused. "Oh, you mean just now. Well, you don't exactly make me sad, either."

"No, it's you who makes me happy, not the presents and not even the lovemaking—although that does help."

"All right, tell me how I make you happy." There was caution in his voice.

She was silent for a moment before she spoke. "When Leander and I had just become officially engaged, we were going to a dance at the Masonic Temple. I was looking forward to the evening very much and, I guess as a reflection of my mood, I had a red dress made. Not a deep, subdued red, but a brilliant, scarlet red. The night of the dance, I put on the dress and felt as if I were the most beautiful woman in the world."

She paused to take a breath and to remind herself that she was here in Kane's arms and safe now. "When I walked down the stairs, Mr. Gates and Leander stared at me, and I stupidly thought they were in awe of the way I looked in that red dress. But when I reached the bottom, Mr. Gates started shouting at me that I looked like a harlot and to go back upstairs and change. Leander stepped in and said he'd take care of me. I don't think I ever loved him more than at that moment."

Again, she paused. "When we arrived at the dance, Leander suggested that I keep my cloak on and tell people that I'd caught a chill. I spent the entire evening sitting in the corner and feeling miserable."

"Why didn't you tell both of 'em to go to hell and dance in your red dress?"

"I guess I've always done what people expected of me. That's why you make me happy. You seem to think that if Houston's climbing down the trellis in her underwear, then that's what ladies do. Nor do you seem to mind that I make very unladylike advances toward you." She turned her head to look at him.

After a quick kiss, he turned her back around. "I don't mind the advances, but I could do without your public appearances in your underwear. I don't guess you remember the puppies, do you?"

"I'm not sure I know what you're talking about."

"At Marc Fenton's birthday party—I guess he was about eight—I took you into the stables and showed you some black-and-white spotted puppies."

"I do remember! But that couldn't have been you, that was a grown man."

"I guess I was about eighteen, so that would make you . . ."

"Six. Tell me about it."

"You and your sister came to the party together, wearin' white dresses with pink sashes and big pink bows in your hair. Your sister went runnin' into the back and started playin' tag with the other kids, but you went and sat down on a iron bench. You didn't move a muscle, just sat there with your hands folded in your lap."

"And you stopped in front of me with a wheelbarrow that had obviously once been full of horse manure."

Kane grunted. "Probably. I felt sorry for you there all alone, so I asked you if you wanted to see the pups."

"And I went with you."

"Not until you'd looked me up and down real hard. I guess I passed 'cause you did go with me."

"And I wore your shirt, and then something awful happened. I remember crying."

"You wouldn't get near the pups, but stood way back and looked down at 'em. Said you couldn't get your dress dirty, so I gave you a shirt of mine to put on over your dress—which you wouldn't touch until I swore three times that it was clean. And what you remember as the great tragedy was that one of the dogs ran behind you and bit your hair ribbon and pulled it undone. I never saw a kid get so upset. You started cryin' and said that Mr. Gates would hate you and when I said I'd retie it you said that only your mamma could tie a bow properly. That's what you said, 'properly'."

"And you did tie it properly. Not even Mother knew that it'd come untied."

"I was always braidin' the horses' manes and tails."

"For Pam?"

"You're damned curious 'bout her. Jealous?"

"Not since you told me you turned her down."

"*That's* why you shouldn't tell women secrets."

"Would you like me to be jealous?"

Kane considered this. "I wouldn't mind it. At least you know I turned Pam down. I ain't heard nothin' like that about Westfield."

She kissed the hand that was idly fondling her breast, knowing quite well she'd told him about Leander several times. "I turned him down at the altar," she said softly.

Kane tightened his arms a bit. "I guess you did at that. Course, he ain't got near as much money as me."

"You and your money! Don't you know anything else? Like kissing, perhaps?"

"I have unleashed a monster," he laughed but showed no reluctance in obeying her wish.

"Behave yourself," he said when he at last turned her back around. "I ain't got as much stamina as you have. Don't forget that compared to you I'm an old man."

With a giggle, Houston wiggled her bottom in his lap.

"And I'm gettin' older by the minute. Now sit still! Gates was right to lock you two women up."

"Will you lock me away?" Houston whispered, leaning her head into his neck and chin.

He took so long to answer that she turned to look at him. "I might," he finally answered, then, in an obvious attempt to change the subject, he said, "You know, I ain't talked so much about stuff other'n business in years."

"What did you talk to your other women about?"

"What other women?"

"The others. Like Miss LaRue."

"I don't 'member ever talkin' to Viney about anything."

"But the nice part is afterward, lying like this together, and talking."

He ran his hand down her body. "I guess it is pretty nice at that. But cain't say as I've ever done it before. I guess after we . . . I guess I just went home. You know, I don't even 'member wantin' to lay around like this. Fat waste of time," he said, but he made no attempt to move away from her. Houston snuggled closer to him.

"Cold?"

"No, I'm the warmest I've ever been."

Chapter 19

Houston looked up at Kane from the cabin bed, watching him dress, and knew that her short honeymoon was over. "I guess we have to go," she said sadly.

"I have a couple of men comin' this mornin' and I can't afford to miss 'em." He turned to look back at her. "I wish I could spend more time up here but I can't."

There was sadness in his voice, too, and Houston decided to help rather than fight him. Quickly, she got out of bed and began to dress in her riding clothes. Kane had to help her with the ties to her corset.

"How in the world can you breathe in that blasted thing?"

"I don't think breathing has anything to do with it. I thought you liked the curves of women. With no corseting, we'd soon all have twenty-seven- and twenty-eight-inch waists. Besides, the corset supports a woman's back. They're really quite healthful."

Kane merely grunted and finished shoving food into the cloth bags. She could tell that his mind was already back on his work.

Silently, the two of them prepared for the journey down the mountain. Houston wasn't sure what was on Kane's mind, but she knew she'd never been happier in her life. Her fear that she was frigid was gone, and ahead of her was a lifetime with the man she loved.

As they were leaving the cabin, Kane paused to look back at the little room. "I sure never had a better time in that place," he said before shutting the door and walking toward the saddled horses.

Houston started to mount by herself, but Kane grabbed her by the waist and hoisted her into the saddle. She tried to hide her surprise as she looked at him. Was this the man who had left her to climb boulders all alone?

Kane ducked his head. "You look like a lady again in that suit," he mumbled.

They were silent as they started down the treacherously steep slope, and several times Kane slowed for her.

It wasn't until they were near Chandler, and they began to slow their horses to a crawl, that Houston spoke.

"Kane, you know what I've been thinking the last few days?"

He gave her a bawdy wink. "I sure do, honey, and I've enjoyed ever' minute of your thoughts."

"No, not that," she said impatiently. "I thought I'd invite your cousin Jean to live with us."

When she looked at Kane, she saw that his mouth was open.

"I doubt whether she'll accept a direct invitation because all you Taggerts are much too prideful, but I've purposely held off hiring a housekeeper and thought she might like to have the job. That would get her out of the coal camps and, besides, don't you think she and Edan would make a lovely couple?"

Kane was still gaping at her.

"Well, what do you think?"

He managed to shut his mouth and stop staring at her. "When I told Edan I was thinkin' about gettin' married, he asked me if I was ready to let a woman in my life. He 'bout laughed his fool head off when I said I didn't plan to let marriage change my life. I'm beginnin' to see why he was laughin'. Who else you gonna invite to live at my house? The town drunk? But I tell you, I draw the line at preachers. I like preachers even less 'n kids. Course, it don't matter who *I* like——." He broke off as Houston, her back rigid, urged her horse ahead.

For a moment, he didn't move but watched her, then, in a spurt of speed, he caught up with her. "You ain't gonna get mad, are you, honey? You can invite whoever you want to live in that big house. It don't matter none to me." It was the first time in his life that he'd ever tried to coax a woman out of a bad mood and he was awkward at it.

He grabbed her horse's bridle. "I ain't even seen this woman. What's she look like? Maybe she's so ugly that I won't be able to stand lookin' at her." He was sure that he saw the faintest glimmer of a smile on her lips. So . . . humor was the way.

"Jean was wearing violet chiffon over purple satin, with tiny brillants at the shoulder and——."

"Wait a minute!" he interrupted. "You mean that little black-haired, green-eyed wench with the curvy backside and the great ankles? In fact, I saw her get out of the carriage and her calves ain't bad either."

Houston glared at him. "You were looking at other women on our wedding day?"

"When I wasn't watchin' you climbin' up and down the rose trellis. Come to think of it, you sure looked mighty good in your underwear." He moved his hand to caress her arm.

In the distance was the civilization of town and the people who would make demands on their time. Now was their last chance for privacy.

As if reading her thoughts, Kane dragged her off the horse and into his arms and they came together as if it were to be their last night alive.

And when they entered the Taggert house two hours later,

there was dirt on their clothes, cockleburs in their hair, and their faces were flushed. Kane was holding Houston's hand until Edan appeared.

Edan took one look at them and, when he'd recovered his speech, he said to Houston, "I see you found him. Kane, there are four men waiting for you and half a dozen telegrams. And Houston, I think those servants you hired are in a state of war."

Houston felt Kane give her hand one last squeeze, and then he disappeared down the hall. She started up the stairs to her bedroom to change clothes. Reality had come back to them.

Ten minutes later, Kane came to say he had to leave on urgent business and would be back as soon as it was finished. He was gone for three days.

Chapter 20

Within four hours after Kane had left, Houston knew that being a wife was what she was meant to do. Blair could have her ambition, her need to reform the world, but Houston just wanted to manage a household for the man she loved.

Of course, running Kane's house was rather like directing an army during wartime, but she'd been trained for her position as General of the Army.

The first thing she did was write a note to Jean Taggert begging her to spend a few days helping with the housekeeping arrangements. Then Houston wrote a letter to Jean's father telling him that she planned to ask Jean to stay and be her housekeeper. Houston prayed that Sherwin Taggert would want his daughter to get out of the coal camp.

When she gave the notes to a new footman to deliver, Houston had her first taste of what was upsetting the servants so badly. The footman seemed to think it was beneath him to go to a coal camp, and, being American, he didn't hesitate to express his opinion.

Houston very calmly asked him if he wanted his job or not, and, if he did, he was to do what she asked and to not belittle the relatives of the man who was feeding him. When that was settled, and the footman on his way, Houston went downstairs and began sorting out the duties of the other people she'd hired. Most of the people she'd chosen were now sitting on the bare floors, refusing to do anything until they knew exactly the limits of their responsibilities. Houston saw immediately why Miss Jones had strongly recommended that experienced servants be hired.

By the morning of the second day, Houston had seven maids cleaning the house, four footmen bringing furniture down from the attics, and three assistants helping Mrs. Murchison in the kitchen. Outside, she had a coachman, two stableboys, and four young, strong-backed boys to help in the gardens.

It was while she was in the garden introducing herself to Mr. and Mrs. Nakazona and trying to explain to them as best she could, since neither spoke the other's language, that the boys were to be under the Japanese family's rule, that she saw Ian's face in an upstairs window.

This morning, while helping her dress, Susan had informed Houston of the awful brawl Rafe Taggert had caused after the wedding guests left. Susan had just happened to hear some of it. Young Ian had boasted that he hated his cousin Kane and would never live in his house. Rafe had said that it was an empty boast since no one had asked Ian to live there. Ian'd said that Houston had but he'd die before he accepted.

It was at that point that Rafe and Ian had had the fight, which the larger Rafe easily won. Rafe'd said Ian was going to stay with his cousin and receive all the benefits that money can buy, even if Rafe had to beat Ian every day for the rest of his life, and he'd said he'd find Ian if he tried to run away.

So, for the last few days, Ian had been holding himself prisoner in the room where Houston had left him. Mrs. Murchison had been the only one to see him when she took trays of food and books to him.

"Books?" Houston'd asked.

"The boy seems to love them," Susan said. "Mrs. Murchison says he reads all day long and that it isn't good for him. She thinks he should join the boys' baseball team and get outside some."

Now, when Houston had most of the other people under control, she turned her thoughts to Ian. If the boy was going to live with them, he was going to be part of their family.

Upstairs, she knocked on his door and, after several minutes, he told her to come in. From his flushed face, Houston had an idea he was hiding something, and she thought she saw the edge of a book sticking out from under the bed.

"You're back," he said as if it were an accusation.

"We returned yesterday," she said, and was sure he knew that. "Do you like your room?"

The big, light, airy room was twice as big as the Taggert house at the mine camp, but there was no furniture in it except for a bed covered with a dirty blanket—evidence of Ian having lain on it for days.

"It's all right," Ian mumbled, looking at the toe of his heavy work boot.

The Taggert pride, Houston thought. "Ian, could you help me this afternoon? I have four men hired to help me arrange furniture, but I think I'm going to need a supervisor, someone to make sure that they don't hit the edges on the doors as they bring it down, that sort of thing. Could you help me?"

Ian hesitated, but he agreed.

Houston was curious as to how Ian'd handle his new responsibility, and she was sure he'd be a little tyrant. But he surprised her. He was careful, observant, and very serious. Only at first, when he used his size and adolescent strength to establish his authority, did he show any anger. By late afternoon, he was so completely in control that Houston merely had to point to where she wanted a piece of furniture placed.

She was watching Ian with amazement, as he skillfully guided a large desk down the main staircase, when Edan spoke from behind her.

"Kane was like that. People like those two have never been

children. Your footmen sense that, and that's why they're willing to obey a kid."

She turned to face him. "Do you know how to play baseball?"

Edan's eyes sparkled. "Sure do. You thinking of starting a team?"

"I almost have enough men. I think I'll call Vaughn's Sporting Goods and order some equipment. You think I could learn to hit a ball with that stick?"

"Houston," he said, as he turned back toward Kane's office, "I think you could do anything you set your mind to."

"Dinner at seven," she called after him. "And we dress for dinner."

She could hear Edan's laughter as he went back to the office.

The meal was pleasant and Edan's quiet patience with Ian seemed to melt some of the boy's tense anger.

But the next day was different. When it was time for dinner, Houston was dressed in pale green silk faille with a green net overlay embroidered with cut-steel bugle beads, a large pink cameo at her waist. She hadn't seen Kane since he'd returned that afternoon, and he hadn't changed out of the heavy work clothes he'd worn on his business trip. But she wasn't about to start an argument with him. Let him come to the table and be the only one in his dirty canvas.

Edan, looking strikingly handsome in his dark dinner clothes, was waiting for her at the head of the stairs, and Ian, wearing one of Edan's new suits that was only a little too big, was standing in a shadow of the hallway.

Houston, without saying a word, took Edan's offered arm, then held out her other arm for Ian. For several long moments, he didn't move, but when Houston just stood there, as stubborn as he was, Ian came forward and took her other arm.

There was more than enough room for the three of them to walk down the stairs together.

"Ian," Houston said, "I can't thank you enough for helping me the last couple of days."

"I need to earn my keep," he mumbled, looking away from her in embarrassment, but he was pleased with her thanks.

"Where the hell is everybody?" Kane shouted from the

bottom of the stairs, then looked up and saw them. "You all goin' somewhere? Edan, I need you." As he said this, his eyes were on Houston alone. The other two didn't exist as far as he was concerned.

"We're going in to dinner," Houston said, as she forcibly held Ian's arm to her. He'd tried to jerk it away when Kane appeared. "Would you join us?"

"Somebody has to earn a livin' around here," he snorted as he turned on his heel and returned to his office.

During dinner, as course after course was brought into the room, Houston led the conversation to what Ian had been reading over the last few days. This was a topic that hadn't been mentioned last night.

Ian nearly choked on a piece of tenderloin. His uncles Rafe and Sherwin had encouraged his reading, but he'd learned to read in secret for fear of being thought of as a sissy. "Mark Twain," he said with an air of defiance when he'd cleared his throat.

"Good," Houston said. "Tomorrow, I'm arranging for a tutor to come and give you lessons. I think that will work out better than going to school, since you'd be quite a bit larger than the other children. And besides, I rather like having you here."

Ian gaped at her for a moment. "I ain't goin' to no school to be laughed at and called names. I'll go back to the coal mines and—."

"I perfectly well agree with you," Houston interrupted. "And tomorrow, we'll have you fitted for your own clothing. Ah, the sorbet. I think you'll like this, Ian."

Edan was laughing at the expression on Ian's face. "You might as well give in, boy. Nobody wins an argument with this lady."

"Except *him*," Ian said.

"Especially not him," Edan answered.

They were just starting dessert when Kane came in. Houston had persuaded Ian to tell them the story of *Huckleberry Finn*, but when Kane entered he stopped talking and looked down at his plate.

"Sure is takin' a long time to eat," Kane said, putting his foot on a chair and helping himself to a handful of grapes from the arrangement in the center of the table.

The look Houston gave him made him sit down in the chair. She nodded to a footman, who set a place in front of Kane and served him. After a moment of surprise, Kane began to eat the chocolate charlotte with gusto, so much gusto that the others started watching him. Kane put his spoon down and looked a bit like he wanted to run from the room.

Ian was surreptitiously watching his cousin and Edan was concentrating on his food.

Houston had left the head of the table for Kane and was sitting next to Ian, across from Edan, but Kane didn't take the head seat, sitting next to Edan instead. Houston caught Kane's eye and held up her fork, and he began to follow her directions on how to eat with some semblance of manners. To start the conversation again, she told of getting the gardeners to work and how well the Japanese family had taken to having help.

Kane told of how he'd met the Nakazonas, and Edan added to the conversation with a story of bringing in the plants from all over the world, and Ian asked what the tree was outside his window. It was stilted, but it did resemble conversation and, best of all, it was pleasant. When the meal was finished, the four of them went away smiling.

Kane and Edan went back to work after dinner while Ian and Houston went to the small drawing room. Houston embroidered pillow cases while Ian read and, after using some persuasion, she got him to read aloud to her. He had a good voice and a flair for reading dialogue. Edan joined them for a while.

At bedtime, Houston went up alone, Kane being firmly ensconced inside his office, cigar smoke seeping out from under the door. Sometime during the night, he crawled into bed with her, pulled her close to his big, warm body and went to sleep immediately.

Houston woke to the heavenly sensation of Kane's hand roaming over her legs and hips. She turned her face toward him before even opening her eyes, and he fastened his lips onto hers as he began to make love to her gently, slowly, languidly.

It wasn't until their passion was spent that Houston at last opened her eyes.

"Wanted to make sure it was your husband?" Kane asked, smiling down at her. "Or would any man do, this early in the mornin'?"

She decided to answer his teasing with some of her own. "How would I know about other men? Should I try to find out?"

A frown crossed his face as he rose.

She put her arms around him, her bare breasts against his back. "I was only teasing; I have no desire for any other man."

He pulled away from her. "I got to get to work and earn enough money to feed that army you hired."

Houston lay in bed and watched him until he disappeared into his bathroom. There was a part of him that she knew nothing about.

A knock on the door gave her no more time to think.

"Miss Houston," Susan said. "Miss Jean Taggert is downstairs with her father and all their belongings in a wagon, and they want to speak to you."

"I'll be right down," she called, reluctantly getting out of bed, wishing that Kane had stayed with her. He was already at work by the time Houston was dressed.

Downstairs, she led Jean into the small drawing room. "I'm so glad you've decided to accept my offer," Houston began. "I really do need a housekeeper."

Jean waved her hand. "You don't need to continue the lie. I know why you're offering me the job, and I know more than you do that you'll have to teach me everything, and that I'll be more of a hindrance than of any use. But more important than my pride is getting my family out of the coal mines. Rafe blackmailed Ian into leaving, and my father has blackmailed me. I've come to ask for more charity than you've already offered. I'll work myself into a stupor for you, if you'll let my father live here with me."

"Of course," Houston said quickly. "And, Jean, you're family, you don't really have to be my housekeeper. You can live here as a guest, with no duties or obligations except to enjoy yourself."

Jean smiled. "I'd go crazy in two weeks. If my father is welcome, then I'll stay."

"Only if you sit at the table with us for meals. It's a big table and almost empty. Now, may I meet your father?"

When Houston saw Sherwin Taggert, she knew why Jean wanted to get him out of the mines. Sherwin was dying. Houston was sure that Jean knew it, and that her father did also, but it was also apparent that no one was going to mention the fact.

Houston found Sherwin to be a gentle, polite man and, within minutes, he had the rest of the staff running to make him comfortable. There was some argument as to where the elder Taggert would stay, but Jean won when she put her father in the downstairs housekeeper's rooms with a door leading outside to the gardens and placed near the stairs that led to the upstairs room Jean chose.

At luncheon, Kane stayed in his office, but Edan joined the growing group who sat down to meals. Ian relaxed visibly when he saw his uncle and Jean, and the meal became very pleasant. Sherwin told a funny story of a happening in the mine and, while everyone was laughing, Kane came into the room. Houston introduced him to his relatives, and he looked about for a seat. Since Jean was seated next to Edan, Kane stood still for a moment until Houston motioned for a footman to pull out the chair at the head of the table.

Through the rest of the meal, Kane sat quietly, saying very little but watching everyone, and especially watching the way Houston ate. She ate slowly, prolonging the meal and giving Kane plenty of time to see which fork she was using.

Toward the end of the meal, Houston turned to Ian. "I have some good news for you. Yesterday, I sent a telegram to a friend of my father who lives in Denver and asked him if he'd like to move to Chandler and be your teacher. Mr. Chesterton is a retired British explorer. He's been all over the world, up the Nile, to the pyramids, to Tibet; I doubt if there's anywhere he hasn't been. And this morning, he agreed to come here. I think he'll make you a marvelous teacher, don't you?"

Ian could only stare at her. "Africa?" he said at last.

"That among others." She pushed back her chair. "Now,

who'd like to play baseball? I have equipment, a playing field chalked out on the north lawn, and a book of instructions. Unfortunately, I have no idea what a word of it means."

"I think Ian could show you some of the basics," Sherwin said, eyes twinkling. "And I imagine that Edan knows a few rules, too."

"You'll join us, Edan?" Houston asked.

"I'd love to."

"And you, Jean?"

"Since I have no idea how to even begin running a house like this, I may as well make myself useless on a baseball diamond."

"And Kane?" Houston asked her husband as he began to pull back from the group. He wore a puzzled expression.

"I have some work to do, and, Edan, I need you to help me."

"I guess that leaves me out of baseball," Edan said, rising. "I'll see you at dinner."

Once in Kane's office, Edan watched his friend pace the floor and look out his window at the others on the baseball field. Edan wondered if Houston had purposely put the diamond outside Kane's office. Twice, Edan had to repeat questions before Kane answered them.

"She's really pretty, isn't she?" Kane asked.

"Who?" Edan asked, pretending ignorance as he looked through the morning's batch of telegrams, studying the offers for land, factories, stocks, whatever Kane was buying or selling at the moment.

"Houston, of course. Damn! Look at that Ian. Playing! At his age, I was working fourteen hours a day."

"And so was he," Edan said. "And so was I. Which is why he's playing now," he said as he dropped the telegrams on the desk. "Everything here can wait for a few hours. I think I'll go out and enjoy the sunshine, and listen to something else besides money."

He paused at the door. "You coming?"

"No," Kane said, his eyes on the papers. "Somebody better stay here and . . ." He looked up. "Hell, yes, I'm comin'. How far can a body hit that ball with that bat? I'll put a hundred on it that I can beat you and anybody else out there."

"You're on," Edan said, leading the way out the door.

Kane took to baseball like a child to candy. It took three swings before he first hit the ball—and no one had the nerve to tell him of the three-strikes-and-you're-out rule—but when he hit it, the ball flew through the air and smashed a second-story window. He was disgustingly pleased with himself and from then on proceeded to give everyone advice.

Once, Kane and Ian almost went after each other with bats, but Houston managed to separate them before it became bloody. To her consternation, both men turned on her and told her to mind her own business. She retreated to Sherwin's side.

"Ian will feel at home now," Sherwin said. "He and Rafe argued all the time. He misses the discussions."

Houston groaned. "Discussions are what Kane calls them, too. You don't think they'll hurt each other, do you?"

"I think your Kane has too much sense to let it go that far. It's your turn to bat, Houston."

Houston didn't care for trying to hit the ball that came flying at her, but she very much enjoyed it when Kane put his arms around her and snuggled up against her to show her how to hold the bat. Ian shouted that Kane was giving the opposing team an unfair advantage and, while Kane was shouting at his young cousin, Houston slammed the ball past second base.

"Run!" Jean shouted. "Run, Houston, run."

Houston took off as fast as she could, holding her skirt up almost to her knees. Edan, on first, just stood there grinning at her with delight, but Kane tore across the field, grabbed the ball and went running for Houston. She looked up, saw him coming and thought that, if he hit her, she'd never survive the impact. She started running faster, hearing in the background everyone shouting at Kane to stop before he hurt Houston.

He caught her at home base, grabbing her by the ankles and slamming her face down into the dirt. But she stretched out her arm and touched the plate.

"Safe!" Sherwin yelled.

Kane jumped up and started yelling at his smaller uncle and Ian, on the same team as Kane, joined in the shouting. Sherwin just stood there quite calmly.

Jean helped Houston up and examined her for cuts and bruises. Houston looked fondly at her shouting husband and said, "He does like to win, doesn't he?"

"Not any more than you do," Jean said, looking at a huge tear in Houston's skirt, and the dirt on her face.

Houston touched her husband's arm. "Dear, since we've beaten you so badly today, perhaps we could stop now for refreshments, and you can try again tomorrow."

For a moment, Kane's face darkened, then he laughed, grabbed her in his arms and twirled her around. "I've beat ever' man on Wall Street at one time or another, but you, lady, I ain't never beat at nothin'."

"Stop bragging and let's get something to eat," Edan said. He turned to Jean and held out his arm. "May I?"

The two couples walked toward the house together, Sherwin and Ian behind.

Chapter 21

It was as if the baseball game broke the ice with the entire family. Kane stopped staying in his office during meals, and Ian stopped being quiet. Kane told Ian he was a dreamer and didn't know anything about the real world. Ian, who considered Kane's words a dare, suggested—in language that made Houston threaten to make him leave the table—that Kane show him some of the "real" world.

Kane began to introduce Ian to the world of business, showing him stock-market reports and teaching him how to read a contract. In only days, Ian was talking in terms of thousands of dollars being paid for land in cities he'd only read about.

One day, Houston saw Sherwin doodling on a scrap of

paper. Later, she saw that it was a very accurate rendition of one of the Colorado mockingbirds. She ordered, from Sayles, a large, portable watercolor kit and presented it to Sherwin with an elaborate lie, saying that she'd found it in the attics, and did he know anyone who'd want it? She was afraid of the Taggert pride and thought he might refuse the paints.

Sherwin had laughed so knowingly that Houston'd blushed. He'd accepted the paints and kissed her on the cheek. After that, he spent most of his time in the garden painting whatever took his fancy.

Twice, Houston visited Blair at the new Westfield Infirmary for Women, staying for hours and getting to know her sister again after all the years of separation. And one day, Leander called her to ask about hiring servants for Blair and him. Lee was cautious and hesitant about talking to her, and she remembered the time he'd tried to speak to her in the church when the engagement had been announced, and how rude she'd been.

"Lee," she began, "I'm glad the way things worked out. I'm really happy with Kane."

He was slow to answer. "I never meant to hurt you, Houston."

She smiled into the telephone. "I was the one who insisted that Blair trade places with me. Maybe I knew that the two of you were better as a couple than we were. Shall we forget it and be friends?"

"That would be my fondest wish. And, Houston, that man you married is a good one."

"Yes, he is, but what makes you say so?"

"I have to go, and thanks for the advice on the housekeeper. Blair's even worse than I am at these things. I'll probably see you in church on Sunday. 'Bye."

She frowned at the telephone in puzzlement, then shrugged and went back to the library.

It was three weeks after they were married that Houston told Kane that she was now ready to decorate his office. She had thought perhaps he might object, but she wasn't prepared for the violence of his objections. In expressing his opinion of her tampering with his private space he used words she'd never heard before—but it didn't take much intelligence to understand them.

Edan and Ian stood in the background and watched with interest to see who was going to win this battle.

Houston had no idea how to handle this, but she was determined. "I am going to clean and put proper furniture in this room. Either you let me do it now, when you can supervise and voice your approval, or I'll do it when you're asleep."

Kane leaned over her in a threatening manner and Houston bent backward, but she didn't relent.

Kane slammed from the room so hard the door nearly came loose from its hinges. "Damned women!" he shouted. "Can't let any man alone, always changing everything, can't stand for a man to be happy."

As Houston turned to look at Edan and Ian, they both gave her weak smiles and left the room.

Houston'd had an idea that the room was dirty and messy, but when she got into it, she found it to be a pigsty. It took six people an hour and a half to clean all of it, including the marble lions' heads on the fireplace. When it was clean, Houston had the footmen remove Kane's cheap oak desk and replace it with a partners' desk, William Kent style, built in 1740. There were three chair openings in the big, dark desk, two for the partners, one for a visitor. She placed two comfortable leather chairs at the desk and, for Kane, an enormous chair upholstered in red leather. When she'd first seen this chair in the attic, she had known where it was meant to go, and who was to sit in it.

When the desk was in place, Houston sent all the servants away except Susan, and they started sorting out the contents of the cabinets. She knew it would be useless to try to file the documents that were jammed in every available place, so she had Susan bring hot irons and they ironed the wadded papers and placed them neatly in the desk drawers.

Flanking the fireplace were two glass-doored wall cabinets, both filled with papers and, in one of them, four whiskey bottles and six glasses that hadn't been washed within the last four years.

"Boil these," Houston said, holding them out as far as she

could. "And see that Mr. Taggert has fresh glasses in here every morning."

In the glass cabinets she placed a collection of small brass statues of Venus.

"Mr. Kane will like those," Susan giggled, looking at the exquisite, plump, nude women.

"I think they were bought with him in mind."

On the north wall were two cabinets concealed in the panelling, and Houston gasped when she opened the first one. Mixed in with the papers were stacks of money, some tied together, some wadded into balls, some loose that floated to the floor when the door was opened.

With a sigh, Houston began to sort it out. "Tell Albert to call the hardware store and have them send me a cashbox immediately, and get another couple of hot irons and we'll see if we can get this to lie flat."

With her eyes wide in astonishment, Susan went to do as she was bid.

When Kane saw his office, he looked at it for a long time, noting the draperies of deep blue brocade, the collection of statues of pretty women, and the red chair. He sat in the chair. "At least you didn't paint the room pink," he said. "*Now*, will you let me get back to work?"

Houston smiled as she passed him and kissed him on the forehead. "I knew you'd be pleased. Whether you admit it or not, you like pretty things."

He caught her hand. "I guess I do," he said as he looked up at her.

Houston left the room feeling as if she were floating, and grinned all through her fitting at her dressmaker's.

Two days later, they gave their first dinner party and it was a major success. Houston invited only some of her friends whom Kane had already met so he'd feel comfortable, and Kane turned out to be a charming host. He poured champagne for the ladies and escorted everyone on a grand tour of his house.

It was only later, during the entertainment, that Houston wanted to disappear. She'd hired a travelling clairvoyant to come after dinner and perform. Kane fidgeted in his chair for the first ten minutes, then started talking to Edan, who sat next to him, about a piece of land he wanted to buy. Houston nudged him once and he turned to her and said, much too loudly, that he thought the man was a fraud and he refused to sit there another minute.

In front of everyone, he got up and left the room. Houston, her back rigid, signalled to the psychic to continue.

Later, after their guests had departed, Houston found her husband at the bottom of the garden. She followed winding dirt paths downward to the flat, grassy bottom. The steep hill, the house on top of it, was at her back, while before her stretched a secret, magic place of shadowy trees and plants, with only the sound of birds around them.

"I didn't like that man, Houston," Kane said, not turning from where he stood leaning against a tree, smoking a cigar. "There's no such thing as magic, and I couldn't sit there and pretend there is."

She put her fingers to his lips to stop his words, then slipped her arms around his neck. He bent to kiss her, bending her entire body to fit with his.

"How'd a lady like you get hitched up with a stableboy like me?"

"Just lucky, I guess," she answered before kissing him again.

One of the things that Houston liked best about Kane was his lack of knowledge about what was right and what was improper. There were people not far from them, servants who could easily decide to take an evening stroll, gardeners who could come searching for a forgotten tool—but none of this bothered Kane.

"You wear too damn many clothes," he said as he began unbuttoning her dress, slipping the satin off her shoulders as he progressed.

When she was standing in her underwear, her dress a heap at her feet, he slipped his arm under her knees and carried her across the lawn, through a tangle of flowers to a marble pavilion containing a statue of Diana, goddess of the hunt.

He placed her on the grass at the foot of the goddess and carefully removed her clothing, piece by piece, kissing each part of her body as it was exposed.

Houston was sure she'd never felt so good in her life, and her passion was very slow to build since she wanted to prolong this time together forever.

He stroked and caressed her body until she was dizzy. The world seemed to be spinning and twirling about, and her fingers began to tingle.

When at last he moved on top of her, he was smiling, as if he knew what her thoughts were. She clung to him, pulling him closer and closer until they were one person.

He continued to move slowly, prolonging her ecstasy, slowly bringing her to new heights of passion.

"Kane," she whispered repeatedly, "Kane."

When at last he exploded within her, she shivered, her whole body shuddering with the force of her own release.

He lay on top of her, bronze skin in the moonlight, sweat glistening on his skin, and held her close to him. "What have you done to me, woman?" she thought she heard him whisper.

Slowly, he moved off her. "Warm enough? You want to go inside?"

"Never," she said, snuggling against him, the mountain air cool on her damp skin. She looked up at the statue above them. "You know, don't you, that Diana is the Virgin Goddess? Do you think she'll resent our intrusion?"

"Probably jealous," Kane snorted, running his hand up and down the smooth skin of her waist and hip.

"Why do you think Jacob Fenton paid Sherwin for working in the mines when it's obvious that he's too weak to actually earn his salary?"

The groan Kane gave as he rolled away from her was heartfelt. "I can see that the honeymoon is over. Or, with you, maybe it's still on, since you only started these questions after we got married. I reckon you can get dressed by yourself. I got some business to finish before I can go to bed." With that, he left her alone.

Houston was torn between wanting to cry and being glad that she had asked Kane what she had. There was something deep between the Fentons and the Taggerts, and she was sure that Kane could never be truly happy until he was rid of what bothered him.

The next night, Houston woke shivering and somehow knew that her sister's life was in danger. She'd heard her mother's often-repeated story of how one afternoon when Houston was six years old she'd dropped her mother's best teapot and started crying that Blair was hurt. They'd finally found Blair by the side of an arroyo, unconscious, her arm broken from having fallen from a tree. Blair was supposed to have been attending a dancing lesson.

But the odd bond between the twins had not appeared since then—until now. Kane called Leander, then held Houston for over two hours until she stopped shaking. Somehow, Houston sensed the danger was over, stopped shaking, and fell into a deep sleep.

The next day, Blair came to Houston's house and spent the afternoon telling her what'd happened that had indeed endangered her life.

It was four days later that Zachary Younger burst into their lives. The Taggerts were just sitting down to dinner when the boy, a footman running after him, stormed into the dining room and yelled that he'd heard that Kane was his father, and that he already had one father and didn't want another one. He left in the next breath.

Everyone seemed to be stunned except Kane. He sat down while the others remained standing and asked the maid what kind of soup they were having tonight.

"Kane, I think you should go after him," Houston said.

"What for?"

"Just to talk to him. I think his heart was broken when he found out that the man he thought was his father wasn't."

"Pam's husband *was* the boy's father as far as I can tell. And I sure as hell didn't tell him any different."

"Perhaps you should explain that to the child."

"I don't know how to talk to no kid."

Houston looked at him.

"Damned woman! In another year, I'll be broke 'cause I'll have spent all my time doin' whatever fool things you dream up for me to do."

As he started out the door, Houston touched his arm. "Kane,

don't offer to buy him a single thing. Just tell him the truth and invite him to meet his cousin Ian.''

''Why don't I invite him to live here and help you think up things for me to do?'' He went out the door muttering about ''starvin' to death.''

Kane walked out the door slowly, but Zach was moving even slower. He caught up with him. ''You like to play baseball?''

Zach turned, his handsome young face full of fury. ''Not with you I don't.''

Kane was taken aback by the boy's anger. ''You ain't got no reason to be mad at me. From what I hear, your father was a good man and I never said otherwise.''

''The people in this nothing town say *you're* my father.''

''Only in a manner of speakin'. I didn't even know you existed until a few weeks ago. You like whiskey?''

''Whiskey? I . . . I don't know. I never drank any.''

''Come on inside then. We'll have some whiskey and I'll explain to you about mothers and fathers and pretty girls.''

Houston was nervous all afternoon as Kane and his son spent hours locked together in his office. And when at last Zachary left, he looked at Houston from under his lashes, his face red, his mouth smirking.

''Zachary was certainly looking at me oddly,'' she said to Kane.

Kane studied the fingernails of his left hand. ''I explained to 'im about makin' babies, and I guess I got carried away.''

Houston's jaw dropped a fraction.

Kane grabbed an apple. ''I got to work tonight 'cause Zach is comin' over tomorrow to play baseball with me and Ian.''

He gave her a sharp look. ''You sure you're all right? You look a little green. Maybe you oughta rest a while. Takin' care of this house might be too much for you.'' He kissed her cheek before he returned to his office.

It was four days later that Kane decided to visit Vaughn's Sporting Goods and see what other game equipment was available. His and Edan's team had been soundly beaten by the team of Ian and Zachary. Ian, having spent most of his young life inside a coal mine, was awed by Kane and not yet sure enough of himself to accuse Kane of not playing by the rules. After all, it *was* Kane's bat.

Zach had no such qualms. He made Kane follow every rule to the letter and would not let his father be what Kane called "creative." So far, Kane'd had to forfeit every game because he refused to follow any rule that someone else had made. He wanted to rewrite the baseball rule book.

Now, he and Edan were in the sporting goods store choosing tennis equipment, bicycles, and an entire gymnasium set of Indian clubs and pulleys.

On the other side of the counter was Jacob Fenton. He rarely left his house now, preferring to stay at home and read his stock reports and curse the fact that his only son wasn't interested in business in the least. But lately, his future had brightened, because his daughter, whom he'd dismissed as worthless long ago, had returned to his house with her young son.

Young Zachary was all that a man could hope for in a son: eager to learn, interested, extremely intelligent, and the boy even had a sense of humor. In fact, Zach's only flaw was his growing attachment to his father. On afternoons when he should have been at home studying how to manage the coal mines he'd someday inherit, he was at his father's playing games. Jacob had decided to fight fire with fire and buy the boy all the sporting equipment he could find.

Kane, his arms full of tennis racquets and two pairs of fifteen-pound dumbbells, turned a corner and came face to face with Jacob Fenton. Kane stood there staring, his face rapidly starting to show his rage.

Jacob had no idea who this big, dark man was except that he looked vaguely familiar. The suit the young man wore obviously cost him some money.

"Excuse me, sir," Jacob said, trying to pass.

"Don't recognize me out of the stable, do you, Fenton?"

Jacob realized that this man reminded him of Zachary. And he knew quite well why Taggert's face showed hatred. He turned away.

"Wait a minute, Fenton!" Kane called. "You're comin' to my house for dinner two weeks from today."

Jacob paused for a moment, his back to Kane, and gave a curt nod before briskly leaving the store.

Kane was silent as he put his purchases on the counter and Edan handed the storekeeper a long list of equipment. "Send all this to my house," he said, not bothering to identify himself before he walked outside and climbed into his old wagon.

When Edan was beside him, he clucked to the horses. "I think I'll get me somethin' better to drive around in than this ol' wagon."

"Why? So you can impress Fenton?"

Kane looked at his friend. "What's in your craw?"

"Why are you inviting old man Fenton to dinner?"

Kane's jaw stiffened. "You damn well know why."

"Yeah, I know why: to show him that you've done better than he has, to show off your pretty house and your pretty silverware and your pretty wife. Have you ever thought what Houston's going to say when she finds out that you want her just as much as you want a new carriage?"

"That ain't true and you know it. Houston's a lot of trouble sometimes, but she does have her compensations," Kane said, smiling.

Edan calmed his voice. "You said before that after Houston had served her purpose and sat at the foot of your table with Jacob Fenton as your guest, you were going to get rid of her and go back to New York. I believe you said that you were going to buy her off with jewelry."

"I gave her a whole trunkful of jewels and she ain't even opened it yet. She seems to like other things instead of jewels."

"She damn well likes you and you know it."

Kane grinned. "She seems to. Who knows, though? If I didn't have any money—."

"Money! You bastard! You can't see what's in front of you. Don't invite Fenton. Don't let Houston know why you married her. You don't know what it's like to lose the ones you love."

"I don't know what the hell you're talkin' about. I ain't plannin' to lose nothin'. All I'm gonna do is have Fenton over for dinner. It's what I've worked for most of my life, and I'm not gonna deny myself the pleasure."

"You don't even know what pleasure is. Both of us have

worked because we had nothing else. Don't risk everything, Kane, I'm begging you."

"I ain't givin' up nothin'. You don't have to come if you don't want to."

"I wouldn't miss your funeral, and I won't miss this."

Chapter 22

As Houston adjusted the *une fantaisie* in her hair, she found that her hands were shaking badly. The last two weeks had been nerve-racking. When Kane had come home and told her that he planned to invite the Fentons to dinner, she'd been very happy because she saw this as a way to close the rift between the two men.

But her happiness had soon turned to despair. She'd never known Kane to be so concerned about anything before. He repeatedly asked her if whatever she was planning for the dinner was of the best quality. He inspected the engraved invitations, had Mrs. Murchison cook the entire elaborate dinner beforehand so Kane could inspect each dish. He stood over the footman's shoulder as the man polished the hundred-year-old Irish silver. He went through Houston's closet and said that she had nothing really good enough to wear to this dinner, and insisted that she wear a dress of white and gold and even chose the fabric himself from the selection that the dressmaker brought to the house. He had new clothes made for everyone and hired two tailors to come to the house the night of the dinner to help the men dress. He even had new uniforms made for all the servants, and Houston had to talk him out of forcing the footmen to wear their hair powdered, as he'd seen in one of Houston's fashion magazines that the Prince of Wales' servants did.

By the end of the two weeks, everyone was praying for this

evening to be over. So far, Sherwin and Jean had turned coward and said they weren't feeling well enough to attend. Ian, his courage boosted from his past days of association with Zach, said he wouldn't miss the fireworks for the world. And besides, Fenton, as the mine owner, was his image of the Devil. He was looking forward to sitting, as an equal, at the same table with his enemy.

If the President had been coming to visit, no more care could have been taken—and no group of people could have been more nervous than this household. Houston feared that one of the maids would pour a bowl of soup in Fenton's lap and Kane would try to murder the girl on the spot.

But what was making Houston's hands shake was that Kane had promised to tell her what was between him and Fenton. It seemed that she'd wanted to know forever, but now she had an urge to tell Kane she didn't want to know.

Adding to her fear was a telephone call yesterday from Pamela Fenton. Pam had begged Houston to call the dinner off, saying that she had a bad feeling about what was going to be said. She said that her father's heart wasn't strong and that she was afraid of Kane's temper.

Houston had tried to talk to Kane, but all he had said was that Houston didn't understand. She had told him she was willing to try to understand if he'd explain things to her.

And that was when he'd said that he'd tell her everything before the dinner party.

Now, sitting before the mirror, inspecting herself, she found herself shaking.

She gasped when she saw Kane behind her.

"Turn around," he said, "I have something for you."

She turned back toward the mirror and, as she did so, Kane slipped a cascade of diamonds about her neck. They fitted high on her neck like a tall collar, with looping strands falling over her collarbone. There were long, double-strand earrings to match.

He stepped back to look at her. "Good," he said, and took her hand in his and led her to his bedroom.

Without saying a word, very aware of the cool diamonds

around her throat, she sat down in the blue brocade chair in front of an inlaid round table.

Kane went to a panel in the wall, slid aside part of the molding and released a little handle. The panel moved back to expose a safe built into the wall.

"Very few people in the world know the whole of the story I'm about to tell you. Some people know parts of it and have guessed at the rest of it, but they've been wrong. I've only been able to piece it together after years of work."

From the safe he removed a leather portfolio, opened it, and handed Houston a small photograph. "This is my mother."

"Charity Fenton," she whispered, looking at the pretty woman in the picture, very young, both her eyes and hair dark. She looked up to see surprise on Kane's face. "Edan told me who she was."

"He told you everything he knows." He gave her a photograph of four young men, all looking nervous and out of place in the photographer's studio. Two of the men looked like Kane. "These are the four Taggert brothers. The youngest is Lyle, Ian's father, next is Rafe, then Sherwin, then my father, Frank."

"You look like your father," she said.

Kane didn't reply but put the rest of the contents of the portfolio on the table. "These are originals or copies of all the documents that I could find pertaining to my parents or to my own birth."

She only glanced at the papers, blinking once at a copy of a family tree that showed a Nathaniel Taggert who'd married a twelve-year-old French duchess, but soon looked up as she waited for him to continue and tell her the story behind the papers, to explain his many years of hatred for his mother's family.

He walked to the window, staring down at the garden. "I don't guess you know anything about Horace Fenton, since he died long before you were born. He was Jacob's father. Or at least Jacob thought Horace was his father. The truth was that Horace gave up tryin' to have his own kids, so he adopted the newborn baby of some people travellin' to California after they were killed by a stampede of horses. But Jacob was only a few

years old when Horace's wife finally had a little girl, and they
named her Charity because they felt so lucky.

"From what I could find out, there's never been a kid more
spoiled than Miss Charity Fenton. Her mother took her
travellin' all over the world, her father bought her ever'thing
she even thought she wanted."

"And how was Jacob treated?" Houston asked.

"Not bad. Ol' Horace spoiled his daughter, but he taught his
adopted son how to survive—maybe so Jacob could support
Charity after her father died. Jacob was trained to run the
empire that Horace'd built.

"I'm not sure how they met. I think Frank Taggert was
elected to present some grievances to Fenton about the
sawmill—that was before the coal mines were opened—and
he met Charity. Anyway, they took to each other pretty fast,
and she decided that she wanted to marry Frank. I don't guess
it crossed her little spoiled mind that her father would ever
deny her anything.

"But Horace not only refused to let his daughter marry a
Taggert, he locked her in her room. Somehow, she managed to
escape and spend two days with Frank. When her father's men
found her, she was in bed with him, and told her father she
was gonna have Frank Taggert even if her life depended on it."

"How terrible for her," Houston whispered.

Kane took a cigar from a drawer by the bed and lit it. "She
got him, though, because two months later she told her
parents she was pregnant."

"With you," Houston said softly.

"With me. Horace kicked his daughter out of the house and
told her she was no daughter to him. His wife went to her bed
and stayed there until she died four months later."

"And that's why you hate the Fentons, because you are
rightfully an equal heir with Jacob, but you were sent to the
stables."

"Equal, hell!" Kane exploded. "You ain't heard half the
story. Charity moved down to the slums where the Taggerts
lived, the only place they could afford on what Fenton paid
'em, and hated it. Of course, nobody would talk to her since

she was one of the Fentons, but, from what I heard, her uppity ways didn't help none.

"Two months after she married Frank Taggert—and I have the marriage certificate there—he was killed by some fallin' timbers."

"And Charity had to go home to her father."

"He was an unforgivin' bastard. Charity'd tried to make it without him, but she nearly starved. I talked to a maid that used to work for Fenton, and she said that when Charity returned she was filthy, thin and heavily pregnant. Horace took one look at her and said that she'd killed her mother and that the only way she could stay was as a servant. He put her to work in the scullery."

Houston rose to stand beside her husband and put her hand on his arm. She could feel him trembling with emotion. Kane's voice quietened. "After my mother put in fourteen hours of scrubbin' Fenton's pots, she went upstairs, gave birth to me, and then very calmly hung herself."

Houston could only gape at him. "No one helped her?"

"No one. Fenton had put her in an attic room far away from the other people in the house, and if she did call out, no one could have heard her."

"And what did Horace Fenton do?"

"He was the one that found her. Who knows? Maybe his conscience bothered him and he went to make up to her, but he was too late. She was already dead.

"Not many people could tell me much of what happened after that, so I had to piece it together. Horace arranged for a wet nurse for me, then spent a day closeted with a battery of lawyers and twenty-four hours after Charity had hung herself, he put a pistol to his head and fired."

Houston sat down. There was nothing for her to say. She thought of Kane having to live with this tragedy all his life. "And so you were raised by the Fentons."

"I damn well wasn't 'raised' by anybody," he shouted. "When Horace Kane Fenton's will was read two days after his suicide, it was found out that everything he owned had been left to Charity's son."

"You?"

"Me. Jacob didn't own a cent of it. He was left as guardian to Kane Franklin Taggert, aged three days."

"But I don't understand," Houston said. "I thought . . ."

"You thought that I was born penniless. Jacob didn't leave the room for hours after the will was read, and when he and the lawyers did leave, he'd managed to bribe every one of them—and to forge a new will that said he inherited everything."

"And you?"

"People were told that Charity's baby had died at birth, and I was sent to spend the first six years of my life on one farm after another. Jacob was afraid that if I stayed with one family, I might find out some of the truth of my birth."

"Or that the Taggerts might find out about your being alive. I can't imagine Rafe letting his nephew be cheated out of his inheritance."

"Money gives power, and none of the Taggerts ever had any."

Houston walked across the room. "And Jacob didn't want to give up everything he'd worked for all those years. He must have thought of Horace as his father, yet at the last minute he was disowned as if he meant nothing. And everything was given to an infant."

"Are you takin' his side?!"

"Certainly not. I'm just trying to ascertain why he would do such a dreadful thing. What if he held the money in trust for you, and when you came of age, you decided to throw him out?"

"I wouldn't have done that."

"Of course, he had no way of knowing that. So what now? Will you prosecute him?"

"Hell, no. I've known about this for years."

"You aren't planning to take the money back, are you? Right now, your own son is living with the Fentons, and you wouldn't send him out of his home, would you?"

"Wait just one damned minute before you start takin' Fenton's side in all this. All I ever wanted to do was have

Fenton someday sit down at *my* table, which was bigger than his, and to have a first-class lady at its head."

Houston looked at him for a long moment. "Perhaps you should tell me the rest of the story. Why are you having Mr. Fenton to dinner, and where do I fit into this?" she asked quietly. For some reason, she could feel fear creeping over her body.

Kane turned his back to her. "All those years that I worked in the stables, all the times I cleaned Fenton's boots, I thought I was gettin' above myself when I imagined myself in that big house of his. Pam and I started foolin' around, and the next thing I know, she's packed up and gone and left me $500 and a fare-thee-well-it-was-a-pleasure. Ol' Jacob pulled me into his office and screamed that I'd never get what he'd worked so hard for. At the time, I thought he meant Pam.

"I took the money and went to California, and after a few years, when I'd made some money, I began to wonder about what Fenton meant when he threw me out. I hired some men to search out the answers for me. It took a while, but I finally learned the truth."

"And you planned revenge on Mr. Fenton," Houston whispered. "And I was part of your plan."

"In a manner of speakin'. At first, all I wanted was enough money so I wouldn't have to worry about bein' a stableboy again, but after I learned the truth about what'd been stolen from me, I began to imagine havin' Fenton to a dinner party at my house, and my house would be five times as big as his. And sittin' at the foot of the table would be Pam, the daughter he said I wasn't good enough for."

"But you couldn't get Pam."

"I found out that she was married and had a kid—I didn't know that the kid was mine—so I had to give up the idea of her. Of course, I had to build my house in Chandler because, if it was any place else, nobody would know that the stableboy had made good. And I wanted Fenton to be able to see it every day. So I started thinkin' who would do as well as Pam at my table, and I knew that the only real ladies in this town were the Chandler twins.

"I hired somebody to find out about you two, and I saw right away that Blair wouldn't do. Fenton might laugh that all I could get was a woman nobody else would have."

"You had to have a real, true, deep-down lady," Houston whispered.

"That I did. And I got one. I was a little upset when I first asked you and you turned me down, but I knew you'd come around. I got more money 'n Westfield'll ever have, and I knew you'd marry me."

He removed his watch from his pocket. "It's time to go downstairs. I been waitin' for this for a long time."

He took Houston's elbow and escorted her to the stairs.

Houston was too numb to speak. She'd been asked to marry him because he wanted an instrument for revenge. She'd thought he wanted her because he needed her, that he'd come to like her, if not love her, over the past months, but the truth was, he was only using her.

Chapter 23

Houston sat through the dinner feeling as if her skin had turned as icy as the diamonds around her neck. She moved and spoke as if in a dream. Only her years of training helped her as she led the conversation and directed the servants in serving the meal.

On the surface, nothing seemed to go wrong. Pam seemed aware of the tension and helped as best she could. Ian and Zach talked of sports, Jacob looked at the food on his plate, and Kane watched it all with a look of pride on his face.

What had he planned to do with me after I'd served my usefulness, she kept wondering. Did he plan to go somewhere else, now that he'd done what he wanted to in Chandler? She remembered every complaint he'd made about trying to do business in this boring little town. Why hadn't she ever wondered *why* he'd built this house? Everyone in town had asked that question while it was being built, but after Houston had been swept away by him, she'd stopped asking questions.

He'd marched into town and gone straight up to Jacob Fenton and announced his arrival, asking the older man how he liked his house. Why hadn't Houston realized that everything in Kane's life was ruled by his feelings for the Fentons?

And Houston had only been a part of the revenge.

That's all she was to the man she'd given her heart to, a tool to be used in the game he wanted—had—to win.

And the man she'd chosen to love was the sort of man who could dedicate his life to an unholy emotion such as revenge.

The food she ate stuck in her throat, and she had to force herself to swallow. How could she have been so wrong about a man?

When at last the long meal was finally over, Houston rose, preparing to lead Pam into the small drawing room, leaving the men to their cigars.

The two women talked about ordinary matters—clothing, where to buy the best trims, the best dressmakers in town—and did not say anything about the meal they'd just been subjected to. But twice, Houston caught Pam looking at her in a speculative way.

Kane led Jacob Fenton into his office, where he offered the man one of the cigars that Houston had given him and hundred-year-old brandy in a glass of Irish crystal.

"Not bad for a stableboy, huh?" Kane began, looking at Fenton through a haze of cigar smoke.

"All right, you've shown me your big house. Now what do you want?"

"Nothin'. Just the satisfaction of seeing you here."

"I hope you don't expect me to believe that. A man who would go to so much trouble to show me what he's done in life isn't going to stop with a dinner party. But I warn you that if you try to take away what's mine, I'll—."

"You'll what? Bribe more lawyers? All three of those bastards are still alive, and if I wanted to, I could pay them more than you own just to tell the truth."

"That's just like a Taggert. You always take what you don't own. Your father took Charity, a sweet, pretty little thing, and subjected her to horrors that caused her to hang herself."

Kane's face turned red with his rage. "Horace Fenton caused my mother's death, and you stole everything I owned from me."

"You owned nothing. It was all mine. I'd been running the business for years, and if you think I was going to stand back and see it all turned over to a squalling baby, I'd have seen it dead first. And then you, a Taggert, wanted to take my daughter away from me. You think I was going to peacefully let you do to my daughter what your father did to my sister?"

Kane advanced on the smaller, older man. "Take a good look at this place. *This* is what I would have done to your precious daughter. *This* is how I would have treated her."

Jacob stubbed out his cigar. "Like hell you would have. Did you ever think that maybe I did you a favor? It's your hatred of me that's made you rich. If you'd won Pamela, and received the money from *my* father, you probably would never have worked a day in your life."

He started for the door. "And, Taggert, you try to take back from me what you think you own and I'll prosecute that pretty wife of yours for illegal entry into the coal camps."

"What?" Kane gasped.

"I wondered if you knew," Jacob smiled. "Welcome to the world of the rich. You never can be sure whether people want you or your money. That sweet little lady you married is up to her ears in sedition. And she's using every connection you have, including yours to me, to start what may develop into a bloody war. You'd better warn her that if she doesn't slow down, I'll stop honoring her relationship to the Taggerts. Now, good night, Taggert." He left the room.

Kane sat alone for a long time in the room. No one bothered him as he drank most of a bottle of whiskey.

* * *

"Miss Houston!" Susan said as she burst into the drawing room where Houston was pacing the floor. "Mr. Kane wants you to come to his office right away. And he looks awful mad."

Houston took a deep breath, smoothed the front of her gown and started down the hall. Jacob had bid her a pleasant good evening and left two hours ago with his daughter. Houston had done nothing but think since the Fentons had left. Never before had she thought about where her life was leading her. Always before, it had seemed that she'd taken what life had handed her. Now, it was time to make some of her own decisions.

He sat at his desk, his jacket off, his shirt open halfway down his chest, a nearly empty bottle of whiskey in his hand.

"I thought you were working," she said.

"You ruined it all, you and your lying ruined it all."

"I . . . I have no idea what you're talking about," she said, sitting down in one of the leather chairs across the desk from him.

"You not only wanted my money, you wanted my connections to the Taggerts. You knew that Fenton would let you do your illegal work because of your relationship to me. Tell me, did you and your sister think up this whole scheme? How were you plannin' to use Westfield in all this?"

Houston stood, her back rigid. "You're making no sense to me. I only learned of your mother's name the day of our marriage. I couldn't have used something I knew nothing about."

"I told Edan once that you were a good actress, but I had no idea how good a one. You almost had me believin' what you were sayin' about marryin' me for love, but all the time you were usin' my name to get into the coal camps."

Involuntarily, Houston gasped.

Kane stood and leaned across the desk toward her. "I worked all my life for this night and you destroyed it. Fenton threatened to prosecute my lovin' wife and tell the world about how you've been usin' me. I can see the headlines now."

Houston did not back down from his stare. "Yes," she said softly, "I do go into the coal camps, but it has nothing to do with you, since I was doing it long before I met you. You are so obsessed with your money that you think everyone wants it.'' She moved away from the desk.

''In the last few months,'' she continued, ''because of you, I've learned a great deal about myself. My sister said that I'm the unhappiest person she's ever known, and she's been afraid that I might take my own life. I never realized that she was telling me the truth, because until I met you I'd never experienced happiness. Until I began to spend days with you, I never questioned why I didn't, as you said, 'Tell 'em all to go to hell' and dance in my red dress. But with you, I've learned how good it feels to do things for myself, to not always be trying to please other people.

''And now, I feel I can make some of my own decisions. I don't want to live with a man who'd build a house like this and marry a woman he didn't want to marry, all in an attempt to repay some old man who was trying to protect what was rightfully his. I can understand, and almost forgive, Mr. Fenton's actions, but I can't understand yours. You may think I married you for your money, but I married you because I fell in love with you. I guess I loved a man who lived only in my imagination. You aren't that man. You're a stranger to me, and I don't want to live with a stranger.''

Kane glared at her for a moment, then stepped back. ''If you think I'm gonna beg you to stay, you're wrong. You been a lot of fun, baby, more than I expected you to be, but I don't need you.''

''Yes, you do,'' Houston said quietly, trying to control the tears gathering in her eyes. ''You need me more than you could possibly know, but I can only give my love to a man who is worthy of my respect. You're not the man I thought you were.''

Kane walked to the closed door and opened it, making a sweeping gesture with his arm to let her pass.

Houston, somehow, managed to walk past him and out into the night. She never once thought of packing clothes or taking anything with her.

A carriage stood outside in the drive.

''You're walking out, aren't you?'' Pamela Fenton asked from inside the carriage.

Houston looked up at the woman with such a ravaged face that Pam gasped.

"I knew something awful had happened. My father has the doctor with him now. He was shaking as if his bones would break. Houston, get in. I have a house here now, and you can stay with Zach and me until you have things settled."

Houston only stared at the woman, until Pam climbed down from the carriage and half pushed her, half pulled her into the vehicle. Houston had no idea where she was. All she thought of was that now everything was over, that all she'd had was gone.

Kane burst into the large upstairs sitting room that Ian and Edan shared. Edan was alone, reading.

"I want you to find out anything you can about Houston goin' into the coal camps."

"What do you want to know?" Edan said, slowly putting his book down.

"When? How? Why? Anything you can find out."

"She dresses up as an old woman every Wednesday afternoon, calls herself Sadie, and drives a wagonload of vegetables into the camp. Inside the food she hides medicines, shoes, soap, tea, anything she can get in there and gives it to the miners' wives. Later, Jean Taggert returns the scrip the women pay Houston."

"You've known all this and haven't bothered to tell me?" Kane bellowed.

"You sent me out to watch her, but you never bothered to ask me what I found out."

"I've been betrayed on all sides! First, that lying little bitch, and now you. And Fenton knew everything that was goin' on."

"Where's Houston, and what have you said to her?"

Kane's face hardened. "She just walked out my front door. She couldn't face the truth. As soon as she knew I was onto her little scheme of usin' me and my money to get what she wanted, she ran out. Good riddance. I don't need the money-grubbin'—."

Edan grabbed Kane by the shoulder. "You stupid son of a bitch. That woman's the best thing that ever happened to you, and you're too goddamn stupid to see it. You have to find her!"

Kane shrugged away. "Like hell I will. She was just like all them others; she was just a higher-priced whore."

Kane never even saw the right that plowed into his face and sent him sprawling. Edan stood over the big dark man as Kane rubbed his jaw.

"You know something?" Edan said. "I've about had it, too. I'm tired of hiding away from the world. I spent my twenties closeted inside ugly rooms with you, doing nothing but working to make money. And for what? The only thing you ever bought was this house, and you did that because you wanted revenge. Houston told me once that I was as bad as you, hiding away, staying at your beck and call, and I've come to think she's right."

Edan stepped away and rubbed the knuckles of his hand. "I think it's time I found my own life. Thanks to you, I've been paid for the years I've dedicated to your goals, and I have a few million stashed away. I'm going to take them and do something with my life."

He put out his hand to shake, but Kane ignored him.

Later, Kane saw Ian, Jean and Sherwin get into the wagon with Edan, which meant that only the servants were left, and he didn't wait until morning before he fired them.

Chapter 24

Houston wasn't even aware of her surroundings as she stood in the middle of Pam's bedroom.

"First, we'll put you in a tub of hot water, then you can tell me what's going on."

Houston stood completely still as Pam left to fill the tub. She wasn't sure she was fully aware yet of what had happened tonight. She'd fallen in love with a man who was using her.

"It's ready now," Pam said, pushing Houston into the pink tiled bathroom. "You get undressed while I call and see how my father is. And Houston! don't just stand there looking as if the world were about to end."

Through years of training, Houston obeyed as well as any trained animal, and when Pam returned, she was lying in the big tub, up to her neck in suds.

"Dr. Westfield finally calmed my father down," Pam said. "He's too old to go through nights like this one. Whatever did Kane say to him? The only thing that I know of that could upset him so badly would be something about Zachary. If Kane thinks that he's going to take my son away from me, he'd better be prepared to fight—."

"No," Houston said tiredly. "He's not after his son. Nothing so noble."

"I think you should tell me."

Houston looked up at this woman whom she really didn't know, a woman who was once the love of her husband's life. "Why are you helping me? I know you still love him."

Pam narrowed her eyes for a moment. "So he told you, did he?"

"I know he . . . refused your invitation."

Pam laughed. "That's tactful of you. I guess he didn't bother to also tell you that I, too, realized we'd never make it together? We came to a mutual understanding that if we married we'd probably kill each other within three months. Now, tell me what happened between you and Kane. It's all family, if that's what you're thinking, and it's going to come out sooner or later."

If Kane decided to take the Fenton money that was legally his, it would indeed all come out, Houston thought. "Do you know who Kane's mother was?" she asked softly.

"I have no idea. I don't think I ever considered that he had a mother, probably because he seemed too self-sufficient to need something as simple as a mother. I guess I assumed he'd arrived on earth all by himself."

Houston sat in the hot water and told the story of Charity

Taggert slowly, trying not to color the tale with her own viewpoint.

Pam had pulled up a pink upholstered brass wire chair. "I had no idea," Pam said at the end of the story. "You're saying that everything my father owns is legally Kane's. No wonder he's so angry at my father, and no wonder my father is shaking with fear. But, Houston, you didn't walk out on Kane tonight because he wasn't born a pauper. What else happened?"

It was more difficult for Houston to tell about herself, to admit that she was second choice to Pam and that, now that she'd fulfilled what Kane needed her for, she was useless to him.

"Damn him!" Pam said, standing and pacing the floor. "He would feel completely justified in telling you that he'd married you for what he thinks he needs. He is the most spoiled man I ever met in my life."

Houston, showing the first signs of life, rolled her head upward to look at Pam.

"He likes to imagine that his life was one of great misery, but I can tell you that *he* was the real ruler of our household when he lived there. People look down on me for having fallen in love with the stable lad, but that's only because they never had someone in their stables like Kane Taggert."

She sat down in the seat again, leaning forward, her face angry. "You know him. You've seen his temper and the way he orders everyone about. Do you think he was ever any different, merely because he was supposed to be someone's servant?"

"I don't guess I really thought about it," Houston said. "Marc did say that Kane was a tyrant."

"Tyrant!" Pam gasped, getting up again. "Kane ran everything. More than once, my father had to miss business appointments because Kane said he couldn't have a carriage or a horse, that the animals weren't ready to travel. At dinner, we ate what Kane liked because the cook thought his tastes were more important than Father's."

Houston remembered the way Mrs. Murchison had succumbed to Kane's teasing and how the woman adored him.

"He was always a handsome boy and knew how to get

whatever he wanted out of women. The maids cleaned his rooms, they did his laundry, they took meals to him. He didn't run Fenton Coal and Iron, but he ran our household. I can't imagine what he would have been like if he'd known that all the money was legally his. Perhaps my father did him a favor. Maybe living in the stables taught him some humility, because he certainly wasn't born with it."

Pam fell to her knees by the tub. "You have my permission to stay here as long as you want. If you want my two cents, I think you were right to leave him. He can't marry a person in order to enact some plan of revenge. Now, get out of that tub while I fix you a toddy that will help you sleep."

Again, Houston did as she was told, drying herself with one of Pam's pink towels and slipping into Pam's chaste nightgown.

Pam returned with a steaming mug in her hand. "If this doesn't make you sleep, it'll make you not care that you're awake. Now, get into bed. Tomorrow has to be better than today."

Houston drank most of the concoction and was asleep very soon. In the morning, when she woke, the sun was already high in the sky and she had a headache. Draped over the end of the bed was her underwear and a dressing gown. A note from Pam said that she had to go out and for Houston to help herself to breakfast downstairs and to tell the maid if she needed anything.

"Edan," Jean Taggert was saying, "I can't thank you enough for all you've done tonight. There was no need for you to stay up with me."

They were standing in the corridor of the Chandler Hotel. Both of them looked tired. After they'd left Kane's house, they'd come to the hotel. Ian had gone to bed immediately, but Sherwin had been extremely upset by the night's happenings and, in his weakened state, he'd begun coughing and couldn't catch his breath. He gasped that he was afraid that Jean and Ian would have to return to the coal fields.

Edan called Dr. Westfield, and Lee was there in minutes,

already dressed from having just seen to Jacob Fenton. Edan also roused the hotel staff and had hot water bottles and extra blankets brought. He sent a bellboy to get the druggist out of bed to fill a prescription for Sherwin.

Jean was able to stay by her father throughout the night and try to reassure him that she and Ian would not return to the mines, while Edan tended to all the necessary details.

Now, with the sun just coming up, Sherwin asleep at last, they stood outside his door.

"I can't thank you enough," Jean said for the thousandth time.

"Then stop trying. Would you like some breakfast?"

"Do you think the dining room is open at this hour?"

Edan grinned at her as he pushed a loose strand of hair out of her eyes. "After last night, this hotel is so afraid of me that they'll do anything for me."

He was right. A weary-looking clerk escorted them into the dining room, removed two chairs from a table by the window and went to drag the cook out of bed. Unfortunately, the cook lived four miles out of town and it took him a while to get there. Neither Jean nor Edan noticed that breakfast took over two hours to arrive.

They talked about when they'd grown up, Jean telling about taking care of all the men in her life, of her mother dying when Jean was eleven. Edan told of his family, of their deaths in the fire and of how Kane had taken him in.

"Kane was good for me. I didn't want to love anyone again. I was afraid that they'd die, too, and I didn't think I could bear being left alone again."

He put down his napkin. "Are you ready to go? I think the business offices should be open by now."

"Yes, of course," she said, rising. "I didn't mean to keep you from your work."

He caught her by her elbow. "I didn't mean me, I meant us. You and I are going to a realtor to buy a house today. It'll have to be something large to have room for all of us."

She moved out of his grasp and turned to look at him. "All of us? I don't know what you mean, but Ian, Father and I couldn't possibly live with you. I'll get a job in town, perhaps

Houston can help me, and Ian can go to school and work afterwards, and Father—."

"Your father would hate himself for being a burden to you both, and Ian is too big to go to school with the others and he'd be better off with his tutor. And you couldn't earn enough to support them. Now, come with me and help me find a big house, and you can be my housekeeper."

"I couldn't possibly do that," she said, aghast. "I can't be a housekeeper to an unmarried man."

"Your father and cousin will be there as chaperones in case I try to molest you and, then again, from what I've seen of married life in the last few months, I rather like the idea. Come on, Jean, close your mouth and let's go shopping. We'll probably have to buy furniture and food and all sorts of things before we can get out of this hotel. Do you think the staff will volunteer to help us if they know their help will get rid of us faster?"

Jean was too stunned to say another word as Edan led her upstairs to her father's room to tell him where they were going. In the end, Ian, Jean and Edan went to the realtor's.

Houston sat at Pam's dining table, listlessly poking at a bowl of oatmeal.

Pam burst into the room, pulling off long, white chamois gloves. "Houston, the entire town is on fire with gossip about last night," she said without a greeting. "First of all, after you left, it seems that Kane and Edan had a brawl in an upstairs bedroom. One of the maids said that the fight went on for hours and, when it was over, Edan left the house in a storm."

"Edan left, too?" Houston asked, wide-eyed.

"Not only Edan, but also the other Taggerts: Jean, Ian and Sherwin. And when they were gone, Kane marched downstairs and fired all the servants."

Houston leaned back in her chair and gave a great sigh. "He said he was tired of all of us taking so much of his time. I guess he can work all he wants now . . . or go back to New York and work there."

Pam unpinned her Strada hat, fluffing the ostrich plumes atop the white Italian straw. "I haven't told you the half of it.

Edan and Jean took up residence at the Chandler Hotel and kept the staff up all night, waiting on Sherwin who was, as far as I could find out, near death's door, and this morning they bought a house together."

"Edan and Jean? Is Sherwin all right?"

"Gossip says he's fine and, yes, Edan and Jean bought that enormous Stroud place at the end of Archer Avenue, across from Blair's hospital. And after they signed the papers—Edan paid cash for the house—Jean went back to the hotel and Edan went to The Famous and bought, I hope I get this right, three ladies' blouses, two skirts, a hat, two pairs of gloves, and assorted underwear. That nasty little Nathan girl waited on him, and she kept after the poor man until he admitted that the secret woman he was buying the clothes for was approximately the exact same size as Miss Jean Taggert. If Edan doesn't marry her after this, her name won't be worth much in this town."

She paused for a moment. "And, Houston, you might as well know that the Chandler Chronicle is hinting that there's another woman involved in everything that happened last night."

Houston picked up her coffee cup. The local paper didn't faze her. Mr. Gates had complained for years that the paper was nothing but a gossip rag consisting of reports on the most bizarre deaths from around the world and inane articles about where each English duke's family was wintering. He stopped delivery of the paper after it carried a half-page story in which an Italian man declared Anglo-Saxon women to be the best kissers in the world.

"Wherever did you hear all this?" Houston asked.

"Where else but Miss Emily's Tea Shop?"

Houston almost choked on her coffee. The Sisterhood! she thought. She had to call an emergency meeting to let them know that Jacob Fenton knew about the women disguising themselves and illegally entering the coal camps. All the man had to do was get angry enough at Kane and he could have the women arrested.

"May I use your telephone?" Houston asked. "I have some calls to make."

Chapter 25

Houston called her mother first and interrupted Opal in a fit of crying. After Houston'd managed to calm her mother without giving her too much information, she persuaded Opal to help her call some of the members of The Sisterhood. The only suitable meeting place, where they were sure of not being overheard, seemed to be the upstairs of the teashop.

"At two o'clock, then," Houston said as she hung up and began calling the others who were on the telephone system.

When the women finally met in Miss Emily's parlor, they all looked askance toward Houston. She was sure they were dying to hear the truth of what had happened last night when everyone left Kane's house. She walked to the front of the women who stood waiting.

"Last night, I found out some very important information," she began. "Jacob Fenton knows about our going into the coal camps. I'm not sure exactly how much he knows, but I called this meeting to discuss it."

"But the guards don't know, do they?" Tia asked. "Is it only Fenton himself who knows? Has he told others? How did he find out?"

"I don't know any of those answers. All I know is that he's aware that we disguise ourselves and go into the camps . . . and he's threatened to prosecute me."

"You?" Blair gasped. "Why you, particularly? Why not all of the drivers?"

Houston looked at the floor. "It has to do with my husband and Mr. Fenton, but I don't believe that I will be arrested."

"I don't think we can chance it," Blair said. "You'll have to stop driving."

"Wait a minute!" Miss Emily said. "Fenton must have known about this for a long time. He didn't just learn about it yesterday and come storming to your house to threaten you. Is that right, Houston?"

She nodded.

"It's none of our business, of course, but am I safe in saying that a great deal happened at the Taggert house last night, and that it's likely that Fenton's declaration of his knowledge of you was only part of what happened?"

Again, Houston nodded.

"My guess is that Fenton has decided that what we do isn't all that harmful, and so he allows us to go safely into the camps. If I'm correct, and I do know Jacob, he's probably had a few laughs about the silly women dressing up and enjoying themselves. I say that we continue the visits. For myself, I feel better knowing that, in a way, we're protected."

"I don't like it!" Meredith said.

"And how do you propose secrecy?" Sarah asked. "It doesn't matter about Fenton, anyway. He overlooks half of what goes on at the camps. Remember last year when that union official was found beaten to death? The official verdict was 'death by person or persons unknown'. Surely, Fenton knew who did it, but he keeps his hands clean. Do you think he's going to prosecute the daughters of the leading citizens of Chandler? My father, after removing some of my hide, would go after Fenton with a shotgun."

"If we're an object of humor, and we're protected by the mine owner himself, then what's the use of all the secrecy?" Nina asked. "Why don't we wear lace dresses and travel in pretty carriages and just distribute the goods?"

"And which miner will let his wife accept charity from the rich town women?" Miss Emily asked. "I think we should keep on with things just as they are. Houston, I want you to consider this very seriously: do you think Fenton'll press charges against you or the other women?"

And risk exposing that he'd stolen everything from a three-day-old baby, Houston thought. "No," she said. "I don't think I'll be arrested. I say that we proceed as always. The few men who know what we do have a vested interest in keeping our secrets. If that's everything, I say we adjourn and go home."

"Just a minute," Blair said, standing. "Nina and I have something to say."

Together, Blair and Nina told of an idea they'd been working on for weeks, of a ladies' magazine that, in code, informed the miners of what was going on throughout America concerning the organization of unions. They showed sample articles and talked of distributing the magazine as a gift to the women in the coal mines.

The women of The Sisterhood were hesitant at first to agree. They'd already experienced fear when they'd learned of Fenton's knowledge.

"Are we committed or not?" Miss Emily asked, and the women began discussing the new magazine.

Hours later, it was a quiet group who left Miss Emily's parlor, each woman thinking about the possibility of arrest of either herself or one of her friends.

"Houston," Blair said as the others left. "Could we talk?"

Houston nodded, but couldn't bring herself to tell her sister what'd happened. Blair just might start blaming herself again, and Houston didn't need more misery right now.

"You want to tell me what happened last night?" Blair asked when they were alone. "The gossip says that you left him. Is that true?"

"True enough," she said, refusing to cry. "I'm staying with Pamela Younger, Jacob's daughter."

Blair looked at her sister for a long time but offered no advice nor any comment. "If you need me, I'm here to listen, but in the meantime you'll need something to keep you busy. The first issue of Lady Chandler's Magazine will have to be submitted to the Coal Board for approval and I want it to be as safe and innocuous as possible. I need articles on how to clean clothes, how to take care of your hair, how to dress like a duchess on a coal miner's salary, that sort of thing. I think you'll do a great job of writing them. Can you go with me now and we'll buy you a typewriter? I'll show you how to use it this afternoon."

Houston hadn't thought about how she'd spend her time when she didn't have Kane to care for, but now she realized that, if she didn't do some work, she'd sit at Pam's and curse herself for being such a fool as to love a man like Kane Taggert. "Yes," she said, "I'd like to be busy. I've had some ideas about how the miners' wives could brighten up the cabins and how they could add a little beauty to their lives."

Blair put Houston to work with so much to do that Houston didn't have time to think about anything. As soon as Houston got one article completed, Blair had an idea for another one. Pam was so interested in Blair's magazine that she converted her kitchen into a stain-removal center and tried to find a really effective way to clean velvet. The entire house reeked of ammonia by the end of the day, but Houston was able to report that "two tablespoons of ammonia and two of warm water rubbed well into the velvet with a stiff brush" did the job. Blair said she might make it the headline story. Pam smiled at this, but Houston knew her sister was being sarcastic.

The writing gave Houston a perfect excuse to stay inside and not face the townspeople. Pam left the house often, telling no one where she was going, and was able to keep Houston up to date on the gossip, reporting that Kane stayed alone in his big house with no servants and no friends.

"And no relatives. That should make him happy," Houston said. "Now, he can work uninterrupted, with no interference."

"Don't be bitter, Houston," Pam said. "Regretting what could have been makes a person miserable. I know. What do you think of including this dye recipe in the first issue? A pennyworth of logwood and a pennyworth of soapbark. I've renewed my black felt hat with it twice, and it worked quite well."

"Yes, of course," Houston said absently, as she scrubbed away the ink that filled the typewriter keys. Blair had told her that when Remington first issued the typewriter, the keys were constantly jamming together. When the owners looked into the matter, they found that the typists were too fast for the mechanics of the machine, so they decided to make the keyboard as difficult as possible to use. They placed the most frequently used keys all over the board so the typist would have to reach constantly, and thus she'd be slowed down. By chance, the top letters spelled QWERTY.

Two weeks after Houston left Kane, the railroad car that he'd had made for Opal arrived, causing a great stir in the town. With tears running down her face, Opal went to Houston and talked about what a wonderful man she'd left, and how could she do such a thing, and a woman wasn't a woman without a baby and, with Houston not even having a husband, it was all too horrible to contemplate.

Houston managed to tell her mother that it was Kane who didn't want her, not the other way around. It wasn't quite the truth but, somehow, lies to one's mother, to placate her, were acceptable.

Houston returned to her typewriter and tried not to think of what was past.

Opal Chandler Gates slowly made her way up Hachette Street toward the Taggert Mansion. She was supposed to be shopping downtown this morning, and Mr. Gates had never questioned why she was wearing her new fox-trimmed suit with the little matching fox hat, but then men rarely understood the importance of clothing. Today, she had to look her best, for today, she was going to beg Kane to take Houston back—if he'd indeed thrown her out as Houston'd intimated.

Houston could be so rigid, Opal thought. She was so much like her father in that. Bill would be friends with someone but, if that person broke his trust, Bill would never, *never* forgive him. Houston had a tendency to do that. Opal knew that after what Leander had done to Houston, he could disappear for all Houston cared.

And now, something had to be done about Kane. Opal was sure that Kane had done something dreadful, something clumsy and awkward and stupid. But then, that was one of Kane's most appealing characteristics: he was as rough as Houston was polished. They were perfectly suited, and Opal meant to see them together again.

At the big front door of the house, she knocked but there

was no answer, so she opened it and went inside. The hall echoed with emptiness and the lonely feeling of an unoccupied house.

Opal ran her finger along a table in the hall. It was amazing how much dust could collect in two short weeks.

She called Kane's name, but there was no answer. She'd only been in the house once before and didn't know her way around very well. It took quite a while to walk through both the downstairs and the upstairs. While she was upstairs, in Kane's bedroom, she looked out at the gardens and saw him walking across the lawn.

She practically ran down the stairs and across the grass that badly needed mowing. Following a twisting path downward, she found him at the bottom, standing near a tree, smoking one of his lovely, fragrant cigars, and staring into space.

He turned to look at her as she approached. "And what brings you here this mornin'?" he asked cautiously.

Opal took a deep breath. "I hear you got angry and tossed my daughter out of your house."

"Like hell I did! She walked out on me! Said somethin' about she didn't respect me."

Opal sat down on a stone bench under the tree. "I was afraid of that. Houston's just like her father was. Would you tell me what happened? Houston won't tell me a word. That's also just like her father."

Kane was silent as he looked back into the garden.

"I know it's private, and if it has anything to do with . . . well, the bedroom, I know Houston is probably a little frightened, but I'm sure that if you're patient—."

"Frightened! Houston? You're talkin' about the woman that married me? She ain't afraid of nothin' in bed."

Opal fidgeted with her gloves, her face red. "Well, then, perhaps it was something else." She waited. "If you're worried about secrecy, I assure you—."

"Ain't nothin' much secret in this town. Look, maybe you can understand what made her so mad, I can't. You know I used to work in Fenton's stables? Well, all the time I worked there I was never allowed upstairs in his house, and I always used to wonder what it'd be like to be master of a big house like that. And later, when I wanted to marry Fenton's daughter, he said I wasn't good enough for her. So I left and started makin' money, yet in the back of my mind was this dream that someday I'd have him to dinner at my house, which was bigger than his, and I'd have a lady-wife sittin' at the end of the table.''

It took Opal a few moments to realize that this was the end of his story and she was going to have to piece together the rest of it. ''My goodness,'' she said after a moment. ''Do you mean that you built this enormous house and married my daughter to fulfill your dream?''

There was no answer from Kane.

Opal smiled. ''Well, no wonder Houston left when she found out. She must have felt quite used.''

''Used! She was damn well usin' me, too. She married me for my money.''

Opal looked at him seriously, all smiles gone. ''Did she? Do you have any idea how hard Mr. Gates worked to keep her from marrying you? In fact, many people advised her not to marry you. But she did. And as for money, neither she nor Blair have to worry about money. They aren't rich, but they have enough to buy all the dresses they need.''

''Considerin' Houston's dress buyin', that's a fortune,'' he mumbled.

''Do you think Houston wants more, the kind of riches only you can give her?'' Opal continued. ''Does she strike you as greedy?''

Kane sat down on the bench.

Opal put her arm about his big shoulders. ''You miss her, don't you?''

''I've only known her a few months, but I guess I . . . got used to her. Sometimes I wanted to strangle her because she was always makin' me do things I didn't wanta do, but now . . . Now, I miss steppin' on her hairpins. I miss havin' her interrupt me and Edan. I miss Edan. I miss baseball with Ian and my son. I miss—.'' He stood, his face angry. ''Damn her! I wish I'd never met her. I was a happy man before I met her and I will be again. You go tell her I wouldn't have her back if she came crawlin'.''

Kane started up the path toward the house, Opal hot on his heels.

"Kane, please, I'm an old lady," she called after him, trying to keep up.

"Ain't nothin' old about a lady," he shouted over his shoulder. "I shoulda stayed with prostitutes," he mumbled. "They only want money."

Opal only caught up with him when he was inside his office, papers in his hand. "You have to get her back."

"Like hell I do. I don't *want* her back."

Opal sat down, fanning herself, out of breath. Surreptitiously, she adjusted her new health corset that was boned with thin blades of steel. "If you had no hope of getting her back, you'd be on a train to somewhere else."

Kane sat in his red leather chair, silent for a moment. "I don't know how to get her back. If she didn't marry me for my money, I don't know how I won her in the first place. Women! I'm better off without her." He looked at Opal through his lashes. "You think she'd like a present?"

"Not Houston. She has her father's morals. Apologies and declarations of love won't do it either. She is so rigid. If there were some way to make her move back in and give you a little time, perhaps you could convince her that you didn't just marry her in order to repay Mr. Fenton—who really can't be blamed for not allowing his daughter to marry the stableboy."

Kane opened his mouth but closed it again. His eyes lit. "I do have a way, but . . . No, it wouldn't work. She'd never believe I'd do such an underhanded, dirty trick."

"It sounds perfect. Tell me."

Kane hesitantly told her and, to his disbelief, Opal thought the idea splendid. "Ladies!" Kane muttered.

Opal stood. "Now, I must go. Oh yes, dear me, I almost forgot. The reason I came was to tell you that the train car arrived and I couldn't possibly accept it. It's really too expensive a gift. You'll have to take it back."

"What in the world would I do with a pink train? You can travel in it."

Opal smiled fondly at him. "Dear Kane, we all have our

dreams; unfortunately, if they come true, sometimes they aren't as nice as the dream. I'd be scared to death to travel."

"Well then, park it somewhere and have it for your tea parties. Are you sure this thing with Houston'll work? I don't know if I *want* her to believe that I'd do somethin' like that."

"She'll believe you, and I think that's a very good use for the train, but you could have it redone in another color."

"If you don't accept that thing, I'll move it to your front yard."

"Since you're blackmailing me . . . ," she said, eyes twinkling.

Kane groaned as she kissed his cheek. "I feel that everything will go well now. Thank you so much for the train, and we'll have you and Houston to dinner next week. Good-bye."

Kane sat for a long time, muttering about women in general and ladies in particular.

Chapter 26

Houston had to stifle a yawn as she hurried down Lead Avenue, trying to get her errands done before it started to rain. She was tired after the turmoil at Pam's house last night that had kept all of them up late.

Zachary had gone to see his cousin Ian at the new house Edan had bought and asked him to go to Kane's to play baseball. Before Ian was half through expressing his opinion of Kane, Zach put his head down and rammed the older, larger boy in the stomach. They fought a bloody battle for thirty minutes before Edan found them and separated them.

When Zach returned to Pam, his collar clutched by Edan, Jacob was there visiting. He saw his precious grandson covered in dried blood, his face scratched, bruises forming. And touching him was someone connected with Kane Taggert.

Another war began.

Pam, worried about her son's health, wasn't concerned with who and why, but Jacob was. Immediately, he began attacking Edan.

"Your fight's not with me," Edan said, then left the house.

Jacob started demanding answers from Zach, and when the older man realized that Zach'd been defending his father, Jacob's anger knew no bounds. His wrath turned to Pam and included comments on her fitness as a mother and allusions to how she came to have Zach in the first place.

For the first time, Houston saw Pam's temper, and Houston understood why Kane had turned her down the day of the wedding. Both Pam and her father said things they couldn't possibly mean; neither seemed to have any control. If Kane and Pam had tried to live together . . . Houston didn't like to think of what could have happened.

Zachary entered the fight, torn between protecting his mother and wanting to be on the man's side. Both Pam and Jacob started yelling at him.

"That's not the way to handle a Taggert," Houston whispered to herself.

She stepped into the middle of the red-faced, screaming people. "Zachary," she said, in a voice that was at once cool and commanding. Startled, they all stopped to look at her.

"Zachary, you will come with me and we will wash you. Mr. Fenton, you will call your carriage and return to your home. You may send flowers of apology later. And you, Pamela, may go upstairs to your room and bathe your wrists with cologne and lie down."

She stood there quite still, her hand outstretched to Zachary, until Pam and Jacob moved to obey her. Meekly, the boy took her hand and followed her into the kitchen. He was much too old to allow a woman to wash his face and hands, but he sat there quietly and let her tend to him as if he were four. After a few minutes, he began telling her about the fight.

"I think you were perfectly right to defend your father," Houston said.

Zach's mouth dropped open. "But I thought you didn't like him anymore."

"Adults fight differently than children do. Now, put on a clean shirt and you and I will visit Ian."

"That bas—," Zach began but cut himself off. "I never want to see him again."

"You *will* see him again," she said, leaning forward until they were nose to nose.

"Yes, ma'am," was Zach's answer.

Houston and Zachary spent hours with Edan and the rest of the Taggerts. Houston felt as if she'd stepped into the middle of someone's honeymoon, as Jean and Edan kept giving each other looks when they thought no one else was looking.

Sherwin took over the boys and had them both in the back garden pulling weeds and moving rocks. By the time Houston and Zach returned home, he was too tired to be angry at anyone, and he and Ian had a date tomorrow to play baseball with some of the town boys, all of whom Houston had called and invited.

When at last she'd climbed into bed, after having heard Pam's three apologies and four thanks, she was exhausted. On the table by the bed was a vase of two dozen red roses from Jacob Fenton to "Lady" Houston.

Now, she was still tired as she ran to catch the streetcar before the rain began again.

She was nearly at the corner, approaching the Chandler Opera House, when thunder cracked, the skies opened and the rain began—and a hand pulled her into the alleyway. Houston's scream was covered by the thunder.

"You'll have ever'body in here if you don't be quiet," Kane said, his hand over her mouth. "It's just me, an' all I wanta do is talk to you for a minute."

Houston glared at him through the rain that was running down her face.

"This is the same place that I pulled you in that first time, you remember? I asked you why you'd defended me to that bad-tempered little woman. This is sorta like an anniversary, ain't it?"

His face softened as he spoke and, as he let his hand on her mouth relax, Houston let out a scream to wake the dead.

Unfortunately, the rain covered her scream, and the people within hearing distance had moved indoors.

"Damn you, Houston!" Kane said, replacing his hand. "What's wrong with you? All I wanta do is talk. I'm gonna take my hand away and if you scream I'll stop you. You understand me?"

Houston nodded, but the moment he released her, she pivoted on her left foot and started out of the alleyway. Kane, with a curse of disbelief, made a grab for her and the stitching at the waistband of her dress tore away.

Houston turned back to him, her face furious as she looked down at her dress, now attached only for a few inches at the front. "Can't you ever listen to what a person says? I don't want to talk to you. If I did, I'd be living with you," she shouted above the rain. "I want to go home. I don't care if I never see you again."

As she again turned to leave, Kane reached out for her. "Houston, wait. I have somethin' I wanta say."

"Use the telephone," she said over her shoulder.

"You little bitch," Kane said through clenched teeth. "You're gonna listen to me, no matter what I have to do."

He made a grab for her, succeeded in pulling the rest of her skirt away and they both fell into the mud that was about three inches of soft ooze from several days of rain. Houston fell on the bottom, burying her face in the wetness, while Kane, on top, remained relatively clean.

Houston managed to lift the upper half of her body out of the sucking mud. "Get off of me," she said, her lips closed to prevent the mud from entering her mouth.

Kane rolled to one side. "Houston, honey, I didn't mean to hurt you. All I wanted was to talk to you."

Houston turned so she was sitting up in the mud, but didn't try to rise as she used her skirt, now completely torn loose and hanging about her hips, to wipe some of the filth from her face. "You never mean to hurt anyone," she said. "You just do whatever you want, no matter who gets in your way."

He was grinning at her. "You know, you look pretty, even like that."

She gave him a hard look. "What is it you have to say to me?"

"I . . . ah, I want you to come back to live with me."

She continued wiping her face. "Of course you do. I knew you would. You lost Edan, too, didn't you?"

"Damn it, Houston, what do you want me to do, beg?"

"I want absolutely nothing from you. Right now, my only wish is to go home and take a bath." She started to rise, struggling over the suction of the mud and her torn skirt.

"You can't forgive nobody for nothin', can you?"

"Like you can't forgive Mr. Fenton? At least, I don't use others to get what I want."

Even through the rain, Houston could see Kane's anger staining his face. "I've had enough," he said, advancing on her and pinning her against a wall. "You're my wife and by law you're my property. I don't care if you respect me or love me or whatever else you think you gotta have, you're returnin' to live with me. And, what's more, you're gonna do it right now."

She looked at him with as much dignity as she could manage, considering the state of her face. "I'll scream all the way through town, and I'll leave your house at the first opportunity."

He leaned toward her, bending her backward.

"You know that brewery your stepfather owns? A year ago, he had some money problems that he didn't tell nobody about. Two months ago, in secret, he sold the place to an anonymous buyer, somebody that lets him remain manager."

"You?" Houston whispered, her back against the wet brick wall.

"Me. And last month, I bought the Chandler National Bank. I wonder who'd be hurt if I decided to close the place?"

"You wouldn't do that," she gasped.

"You just said that I do whatever I want, no matter who gets in my way. And right now, I want you to move back into my house."

"But why? I never meant anything to you. All I ever meant to you was something to further your revenge on Jacob Fenton. Surely, someone else would be better—."

He ignored her words. "What do you say? Will you martyr yourself to save the whole town? My house and my bed bein' the stake you'll burn at, of course."

Suddenly he grabbed her chin in his hand, his fingertips roughly caressing her damp, gritty skin. "Can I still make you burn? Can I still make you cry out in pleasure?"

He bent his head as if he meant to kiss her but stopped a breath away from her lips. "You ain't got any choice at all as far as I can see. You either come home with me right now or I foreclose on a whole lot of people. Are your uppity morals more important than the food in people's mouths?"

She blinked at the water in her eyes, whether from tears or the rain she wasn't sure. "I'll live with you again," she said, "but you have no idea how cool the Lady of Ice can be."

He didn't answer her but lifted her into his arms and carried her to his waiting wagon. Neither spoke on the way up the hill to the Taggert mansion.

Houston didn't have a great deal of difficulty remaining cool to her husband, and only once was she tempted to falter. She remembered too well why he'd married her and what a fool she'd been to think she was in love with such a selfish man. At least Leander had been honest when he'd told her what he wanted of her.

Houston did the bare minimum of what was required of her to run the house and no more. She rehired the servants but planned no entertainments, and she spoke to Kane only when necessary and refused to react when he touched her—which had been the most difficult part.

The first night she was in his house had been the worst. He'd come to her bedroom and slowly pulled her into his arms. Houston had refused to let her body betray her. She'd stood as rigid as a steel pole and thought about Sunshine Row at the mining camp. It was probably the most difficult thing she'd ever done in her life, but she wasn't going to fall into bed with him after the way he'd used her. Nor had she let her reserve break when he'd moved away from her and looked at her with the eyes of a sad puppy. She thought he'd used his good looks to advantage to get what he wanted.

The next morning he came to her room and lifted a small chest from the floor. Houston knew that it was his wedding gift to her, and she'd always known what was in it, but she'd waited for him to present it to her. And now, when he dumped about a million dollars' worth of jewels in her lap, all she could think about was that they were so cold—about as cold as her insides felt.

Kane stood back and watched for her reaction.

"If you mean to try to buy me—," she began.

He cut her off. "Damn it, Houston! Was I supposed to tell you about Fenton *before* we were married? I had a hard enough time as it was, what with you tryin' to get Westfield even when we were standin' at the altar." He waited a moment. "You ain't gonna deny that you wanted Westfield?"

"It doesn't seem to matter what *I* want. You are an expert at getting your own way. You wanted a house to impress Mr. Fenton, you wanted a wife to impress him. It doesn't matter that the house cost millions and the wife is a human being with feelings of her own. It's all the same to you. You have to have your own way, and look out, anyone who tries to thwart you."

Kane left the room without another word.

The jewels glowed in Houston's lap and, without another glance, she turned the blanket down to cover them as she stepped out of bed.

She spent the days in her sitting room reading. The servants came to her to ask questions, but otherwise she stayed alone. Her only hope was that Kane would see that she didn't want to live with him and would release her.

A week after she'd returned, he came storming into her room, papers from the bank in his hand.

"What the hell are these supposed to mean?" he shouted. "The account of Mrs. Houston Chandler Taggert has been charged for bath powder, two yards of ribbon, and for paying the telephone bill of the Taggert household."

"I believe I'm the only one who uses the telephone, therefore I should pay the expenses."

He sat down in a chair across from her. "Houston, have I ever been stingy with you? Have I ever complained about how much you spend? Have I ever done or said anything that makes you think that I'd ever withhold money from you?"

"You have accused me of marrying you for your money," she said coolly. "Since your money is so precious to you and not to me, you may keep it."

He started to speak, but closed his mouth. After a long moment of looking at the bills, he said softly, "I'll be goin' to Denver tonight, and I'll be gone for about three days. I'd like you to stay in the house. I don't want you doin' anything to get in trouble, like tryin' to start a riot at the coal mines."

"And what will you do to innocent people if I do? Will you throw three families into the snow?"

"If you haven't noticed, it's still summer." He walked to the door. "You don't know me very well at all, do you? I'll tell the bank to send your bills to me. Buy whatever you want." With that, he left her alone.

As soon as he was gone, she went to the window to look at Chandler below. "You don't know me very well, either, Kane Taggert," she whispered. "You'll not be able to keep me chained inside this house."

Three hours later, after she saw Kane drive away from the house, she called Reverend Thomas and told him to prepare a wagon because, tomorrow, Sadie would visit the Little Pamela mine.

Chapter 27

Houston, dressed as Sadie, eased the wagon up the hill toward the coal mine and, as she maneuvered the horses around a long, deep rut in the road caused by the recent heavy rains, she thought she heard a sound in the back of the wagon. Last summer, a cat had been caught under the canvas that was tied down so tightly, and she was sure that was what was making noise now.

She flipped the reins to the horses and concentrated on getting up the hill. At the gate, she prayed the cat, or, by the sound, several cats, would be still long enough for her to get past the guards. She'd hate to have the men's curiosity aroused so they'd feel compelled to search her wagon.

She breathed a sigh of relief when she was past the guards and into the camp. She'd called Jean this morning and, in between Jean's breathless announcement that Edan had asked her to marry him, Jean had said that Rafe was now working the graveyard shift and would be at home when she brought her wagon. Rafe didn't know about Houston, but he was willing to introduce Sadie to another woman who'd help her with the distribution of the vegetables and the contraband goods. Jean didn't know whether the new woman was aware of Sadie's true identity or not.

Houston pulled the wagon over in front of the Taggerts' company house and halted just as Rafe came out the door.

"Mornin' to you," Sadie called as she struggled to get her fat old body down from the wagon.

Rafe nodded in her direction, looking at her so hard that Houston kept her head down, the sloppy hat shading her face. "I hear you're gonna find me somebody else to help me get rid of this stuff. Now that Jean's gone to be a lady, I don't guess I'll get to see much of her." Sadie began to untie one corner of the canvas. "I got me some cats caught under here and I got to get 'em out."

She glanced up at Rafe as she tossed the canvas back and picked up a head of cabbage, meaning to brag a bit on her fine produce. But when she looked back at the wagon, her knees buckled under her and she grabbed the side of the wagon for support. Under the head of cabbage was Kane Taggert's face and he gave her a lusty wink.

Rafe grabbed Sadie with one hand and looked into the wagon at the same time.

Kane sat up, food falling over the side of the wagon. "Are you deaf, Houston? Couldn't you hear me callin'? I thought I was gonna pass out, since I couldn't breathe. Damn it, woman! I told you not to go into the mines today."

Rafe looked from one person to the other before he took Houston's chin and held her face up to the light. If you were looking for it, you could see the makeup. Over the years, Houston'd become an expert at keeping her face down and she'd soon learned that people rarely look at each other critically. They saw at first glance that she was an old woman and they never questioned that first impression.

"I didn't believe it," Rafe said under his breath. "You'd better get inside and start talkin'."

Kane stood beside her, gripped her elbow painfully and half pushed her inside the little house of Rafe's.

"I told you not to do this," Kane began. He looked at his uncle. "You know what the ladies of Chandler are doin'? There's three or four of 'em that dress up like this and they carry illegal things inside the food."

Houston jerked away from Kane's grasp. "It's not as bad as you make it sound."

"What's more, Fenton knows about the women and he can prosecute 'em at any time. He must hold half the leadin' citizens in the palm of his hand, and they don't even know it."

Rafe looked at Houston for a moment. "What sort of illegal goods?"

"Nothing much," she answered. "Medicines, books, tea, soap, anything we can fit inside the vegetables. It's not what he makes it seem. And as for Mr. Fenton, since he does know and hasn't done anything about it, perhaps he's protecting us, seeing that nothing interferes with our trips. After all, we hurt no one."

"No one!" Kane gasped. "Honey, someday I'm gonna explain to you about stockholders. If Fenton's stockholders found out about you, and how you're takin' profit out of their greedy little mouths, they'd string all of you up. But before Fenton swung, he'd use all you women, and all the daddies and husbands he could, to get himself off. I'm sure Fenton loves what you're doin', 'cause he knows that, any time he wants it, he has power over Chandler's leadin' citizens—just so long as his investors know nothin' about nothin'."

"Just because you'd blackmail a person, doesn't mean that other people would do the same thing. Perhaps Mr. Fenton—."

She stopped, because Rafe was shoving her out the door. "I think you better go tend to your wagon. The woman that's gonna help you lives next door. Just knock on the door and she's ready." With that, he shut the door behind her.

"How long's this been goin' on?" Rafe asked Kane. "And what's she do with the money she's paid for the food?"

Kane didn't know all the answers to his uncle's questions, but between them they were able to figure out most of the story. Rafe agreed with Kane about why Fenton allowed the women into the mine camp.

"He'd sell 'em out in seconds," Rafe said. "So what're you plannin' to do now? You gonna let her keep on drivin' the wagon and risk gettin' hurt someday? If the guards found out that she'd played 'em for the fool for a couple of years, they'd act first and ask who was protectin' her later."

"I told her she wasn't to go into the mines today and you see how she obeyed me. The minute she thought I was out of sight, she bought a load of vegetables to bring up here."

"*She* paid for 'em?"

Kane pulled out a chair and sat down. "She ain't too happy with me right now, but she'll come around. I'm workin' on her."

"If you wanna talk about it, I can listen," Rafe said as he took a seat across from his nephew.

Kane had never talked to anyone in his life about his personal problems, but lately, things were changing rapidly. He'd told Opal some of his problems and now he wanted to tell his uncle. Maybe a man could help him.

Kane told Rafe about growing up in Fenton's stables, about his dream of building a bigger house. Rafe nodded in understanding, as if what Kane said made perfect sense to him.

"Only thing was, Houston got real mad when I told her why I'd married her, and she walked out the front door. I got her to come back but she ain't exactly happy about it."

"You say that you'd planned to have her sittin' at your table, but what about afterward?"

Kane started looking at his fingernails. "I didn't want a wife and I thought she was in love with that Westfield that jilted her, so I was sure she'd be glad to see the last of me after the dinner with Fenton. I thought I'd give her a box of jewelry and then I'd go back to New York. Damnest thing was, though, I gave her the jewelry, but she didn't even look at it."

"So why don't you just leave her and go back to New York?"

Kane took a while to answer. "I don't know, I kinda like it here. I like the mountains, and it ain't hot here in the summer like it is in New York and—."

"And you like Houston," Rafe said, grinning. "She's a pretty little thing, and I'd rather have a woman like her than the entire state of New York."

"So how come you ain't married?"

"All the women I like won't have me."

"I guess that's the same with me. When I didn't really care whether Houston married me or not, and thought somebody else'd do just as well, she kept tellin' me that she loved me, and now, when I don't think I could live very well without her, she looks at me like I was a pile of horse manure."

The two men were silent for a moment, the air heavy with their feelings of injustice.

"You want some whiskey?" Rafe asked.

"I need some," Kane answered.

As Rafe turned away to get the whiskey, Kane, for the first time, looked around at the house. He calculated that the whole place would fit into his dressing and bathing area. The house was dirty in a way that no cleaning could remedy. There was no light to speak of in the room, and the air gave off a smell of the deepest poverty.

On the mantelpiece were a tin of tea, two cans of vegetables and what looked to be half a loaf of bread wrapped in cloth. Kane was sure that that was all the food in the house.

Quite suddenly, Kane remembered the rooms above the stables where he'd grown up. He'd sent his sheets and clothes to the Fenton laundress to be cleaned and, when he'd grown up, he'd coaxed the maids into cleaning his rooms. And there'd always been food in abundance.

What was it that Houston had said she was taking to the miners? Medicines, soaps, tea? Whatever she could hide in a head of cabbage. Never had Kane actually had to worry about food. And no matter where he'd lived, he'd never lived like this.

As he looked up at a corner where the roof obviously leaked, he wondered how his mother, raised with all the finest in life, had survived in a house like this as long as she did.

"Did you know my mother?" Kane quietly asked, as Rafe set a tin cup of whiskey on the table.

"I did." Rafe was watching this man who was his relative, both familiar and unknown at the same time. Sometimes Kane moved in a way that made Rafe think it was Frank sitting in front of him—and then he had a way of looking at people that made him think of pretty little Charity.

Rafe took a seat at the table. "She lived with us for just a few months, and it was hard on her, but she was a game little thing. We all thought Frank was the luckiest man on earth. You should have seen her. She worked all day cleanin' and cookin' and then, just before Frank got off his shift, she'd doll herself up like she was ready to meet the President."

Kane stared at his uncle for a moment. "I heard she was a spoiled brat and snubbed all the other women and they hated her."

Rafe's face showed his anger. "I don't know who told you that, but he's a damned liar. When Frank was killed, she just didn't care about livin' anymore. She said she was goin' home to have the baby because she knew Frank would want the best for his child, and she wanted to share her baby with her father. The bastard!" Rafe said under his breath. "The next thing we heard was that Charity and the baby had died and her father had killed hisself in grief. Sherwin and me were glad that Charity's last moments had been happy, and that her father had accepted her back right away. None of us knew about you, or knew that Charity had killed herself, until years later."

Kane wanted to ask why Rafe hadn't done anything about it when he found out, but he put his mug to his mouth and drank instead. He'd told Houston that money gave a man power.

What could any of the Taggerts have done when they could barely scratch out a living? And besides, he hadn't done so badly on his own.

"I was thinkin'," Kane said, looking down at his cup. "You and me got off to a bad start, and I was wonderin' if there was anything I could do to help . . ." Even as he said the words, he knew he shouldn't have. Houston said that he used his money and used people. He looked at his uncle and saw that Rafe was holding himself rigid, waiting for Kane to finish his sentence. "Ian likes to play baseball a lot and so does Zach, and now I don't get to see them too much, so I was wonderin' if maybe I could start a baseball team with the kids here. I'd buy all the equipment, of course."

Rafe relaxed. "The kids'd like that. Maybe you can come on Sunday mornin' when they're not down in the mine. You think Fenton'll agree?"

"I sorta think he will," Kane said, finishing his whiskey. "I guess I better go look for my wife. The way she's feelin' about me right now, she just might leave me here."

Rafe rose. "You better let me find her, and I guess you'll have to ride home in the back of the wagon. If the guards saw you leave when you didn't enter, they'd get suspicious, and then the other ladies that drive wagons could get in trouble."

Kane nodded. He didn't like the idea but he knew the sense of it.

"Kane," Rafe said as he stood by the door. "If I could give you some advice about Houston, it'd be to just be patient with her. Women have odd ideas about things that men can't begin to understand. Try courtin' her. You did somethin' that won her in the first place, so maybe you can repeat it if you try courtin' her all over again."

"She don't much like presents," Kane muttered.

"Maybe you're not givin' her the right presents. One time, a girl was real mad at me, and what made her come 'round was when I gave her a puppy. Just a little mutt, but she loved it. She was *real* grateful, if you know what I mean." With a smile and a wink, Rafe left the cabin.

* * *

Houston waited all the way back to Kane's house for his explosion, but it never came. He climbed onto the wagon seat with her after she was out of sight of the guards and, although Houston never said a word, he talked to her about the scenery and some about his business. A few times she started to reply, but she stopped herself. Her anger at him was too deep, and she couldn't soften toward him. He'd soon realize that she could never love him again, and he'd have to release her from being his prisoner.

At home, he said good night to her politely and went to his office. The next day, he came to her sitting room at lunch time and, without a word, took her hand and led her down the stairs to the kitchen, where he picked up a picnic basket from Mrs. Murchison. Still holding her hand, he led her down the paths of the garden to the very bottom—to the statue of Diana where they'd once made love.

Houston stood rigid while he spread the white linen cloth and the food, and he had to pull her to make her sit on the cloth. All through the meal, which she just nibbled at, Kane talked to her. He told her more about his business, telling her what a difficult time he was having without Edan to help him.

Houston didn't reply to anything he said, but her silence didn't seem to bother him.

After they'd finished eating, Kane turned around and put his head in her lap and continued talking. He told her about talking to Rafe about his mother. He told her about how dingy Rafe's house had been and how his own quarters, when he was growing up, hadn't been nearly as bad.

"You think there's somethin' I could do to get Uncle Rafe away from the mines? He's not a young man any longer, and I'd like to do somethin'."

Houston didn't speak for a moment. She'd never heard such a question from Kane. "You can't offer him a job because he'd think it was charity," she said.

"That's what I thought. I don't know what to do. If you have any ideas, will you let me know?"

"Yes," she said hesitantly, and into her mind's eye came the picture of Rafe walking with Pamela. They made a striking couple.

"I have to go back to work now," he said, startling her by kissing her quickly and sweetly as he rose. "Why don't you stay here and enjoy the garden?"

He left her alone and Houston wandered about looking at the plants, and in the rose garden she borrowed a pair of clippers from a gardener and snipped a few blooms. It was the first time since she'd arrived that she'd done anything that wasn't absolutely necessary. "Just because the master is horrible is no reason to hate the house," she said to herself to justify carrying the roses inside.

When Kane came to dinner, the house was full of freshly cut flowers, and he did little more than grin at Houston all the way through the meal.

The next day, Blair came to luncheon, talked about her friend from Pennsylvania, Dr. Louise Bleeker, who'd come to help in the clinic, and asked if Houston was all right. For some reason, Blair no longer seemed to hate Kane.

"Things aren't much better," Houston said, toying with her meal. "And you?"

Blair hesitated. "Lee will get over it, I'm sure."

"Over it?"

"He's a bit angry with me right now. I, ah . . . made a journey in the back of his buggy. But let's talk about you."

"Let's talk about the magazine. I have two new articles for you."

On Sunday, Kane roused Houston from bed, remaining far back from her, not getting too close to her sleepy form inside the warm bed. He tossed on the bed a dress of deep rose zephyr-gingham that was trimmed with narrow bands of black velvet ribbon. "Wear that and get dressed as fast as you can," he ordered before leaving the room.

Minutes later, he returned wearing corduroy trousers, a bright blue flannel shirt and navy suspenders. He stood for a moment looking at Houston in her underwear, the tight corset pushing her breasts up above the lace-edged chemise, her legs encased, from the knee down, in black silk stockings with little butterflies going up one side, and wearing tiny black leather high-heeled shoes.

He gaped at her for a moment, then turned and left the room as if, if he stayed any longer, he might not live through it.

Houston dropped the robe she'd grabbed but not bothered to cover herself with and let out a sigh. She told herself that it was a sigh of relief and not the sigh of regret that it sounded like.

He didn't tell her where they were going when he lifted her into the buggy that he'd given her, but started driving. Houston didn't ask him where they were headed, but her face showed her surprise when they turned up the road to the Little Pamela mine.

The guards allowed them to pass without so much as a challenge or a question and, once through the gate, people came out of the houses and began following them. Houston started to wave to a few women she knew.

"They don't know you when you're clean," Kane warned her.

She couldn't help looking around, as more and more people began following them, and there were enormous smiles on the children's faces.

"What have you done?" she asked.

"There," he answered, pointing. In front of them was the only open area in the camp, the mine mouth in the background. In the center of the dirt field were wooden crates.

Kane halted the buggy and two boys with black-rimmed eyes held the horse as he helped Houston down. When they were standing on the inside of the circle of people who had gathered around the boxes, Kane grinned and said loudly, "Go to it, boys."

As Houston watched the boys tear into the crates, Rafe walked up behind them.

"The boxes came two days ago, and I didn't think you'd mind if I told 'em what was inside. They've been dancin' around and nervous with excitement since then," Rafe said, as he put his hand on his nephew's shoulder.

Houston looked at that hand on her husband's shoulder with astonishment before turning back to see what the boys had found in the crates. They withdrew baseball equipment: uniforms, bats, gloves, balls, catchers' face masks.

Kane turned to Houston, his face showing his expectation.

Had he done all this just to impress her, she wondered. She looked about the circle of parents who looked on their sons adoringly. "And what did you get for the girls?"

"Girls?" Kane asked. "Girls can't play baseball."

"No? What about tennis, archery, bicycling, gymnastics, fencing?"

"Fencing?" Kane said, his face turning to anger. "I guess nobody can please you, can they, Miss Ice Lady? Nobody's up to your standards, are they?" he asked before turning away and walking toward the boys, who were swinging bats and tossing balls in the air.

Houston moved away from the crowd. Perhaps she had been a little too hard on him. Perhaps she should have said something nice about his trying to help the boys. It was what she'd always wanted to happen and, when it did, she was ungrateful.

At least, she could make the best of the day and not stand sulking in a corner. She stepped forward and spoke to a little girl near her and began explaining some of the rules of baseball. Within minutes, Houston had a crowd around her of women and girls, and even some men who had never seen the game before. By the time Kane and Rafe had organized the boys into teams, Houston had started a cheering section to applaud the boys' progress, no matter how inept it was.

Two hours after they arrived, a four-horse wagon came barrelling into the midst of the people. Everyone stopped dead still, thinking that it must mean that a disaster had occurred.

The driver, red-faced and sweating, was Mr. Vaughn, who owned the sporting goods store. "Taggert!" he yelled at Kane as he controlled the sweaty horses. "This is the last time that I make an order like this for you. I don't care if you buy my whole store, I ain't workin' on Sunday for nobody."

"Did you bring everything?" Kane asked, moving to the back of the wagon that was covered with canvas. "And stop bellyachin'. With the prices I've paid you in the last months, I *do* own your store."

The crowd laughed, enjoying the power money gave a man

to say what he wanted to anyone. But Houston was watching the back of the wagon.

"Well, look at this," Kane said, pulling out a tennis racquet. "I don't think we can hit a baseball with this." He turned to a little girl standing by him. "Maybe you could use this."

The child took the racquet but didn't move. "What is it?" she whispered.

Kane pointed to Houston. "See that lady there? She can show you how to use it."

Houston walked straight to her husband, put her arms about his neck and kissed him, much to the delight of the people around them. When he wouldn't let her go, Houston pushed at him.

"I guess I finally found the right present," he said to someone over her shoulder as he pressed her close.

As Houston moved away from him, she heard Rafe laugh.

The rest of the afternoon, Houston didn't have much time to think as she organized games of tennis and showed girls how to use the archery equipment. There were balls, hoops and sticks, jump ropes, jacks, dolls, paper dolls. She had her hands full just trying to portion out the goods fairly, and the mothers helped her soothe the girls who thought they weren't getting their fair share.

Before Houston knew it, it was sundown, and Kane came to her and put his arm about her shoulders. As she looked up at him, she knew that she still loved him. Perhaps he wasn't the man she had first thought he was, perhaps he was capable of living his life for the sole purpose of revenge, and maybe today was only a show of his hatred for Jacob Fenton, but at the moment, she didn't care. She'd promised to love him for better or worse and his obsession with revenge was part of the worse. As she looked up at him, she knew that she'd always love him, no matter what he did, no matter what dreadful motives he had for the things he did. She would stand by him and love him even if he took everything the Fentons owned.

"You ready, honey?" he asked.

"Yes," she said and meant the word from the bottom of her heart.

Chapter 28

Kane didn't look at Houston as they left the coal camp and drove past the sullen guards. He held the reins tightly and kept his eyes on the road ahead.

Houston looked at nothing else but him, wondering how she could have so little pride as to admit to being in love with a man who used her. But as she looked at him, she knew that she couldn't help herself.

At the foot of the hill, just before the road turned back to the main highway, Kane stopped the wagon. The sun was going down in a riot of pinks and oranges, setting the horizon on fire. The cool mountain air was growing cooler, the air was fragrant with the scent of sage, the road was littered with the silvery pieces of coke from the ovens, and blowing in the gentle breeze were feathery seedpods.

"Why are we stopping?" she asked, as he came around to her side of the wagon and lifted his arms to her.

"Because, love," he said, pulling her down into his arms, "I don't think that I can wait any longer to make love to you."

"Kane . . ." she began to protest, "we can't stop here. Someone might come along."

She said no more because he was holding her in his arms, drawing her closer to him, his hands beginning to caress her back. Houston leaned into him with all the fervor she felt.

He drew back from her, touching her cheek with a rare gentleness. "I missed you, honey," he whispered. "I missed you a lot."

The next minute, all gentleness was gone as his mouth swooped down on hers and hungrily caught her lips under his own.

Houston was as eager for him as he was for her. Her body

melted against his, her curves fluidly conforming to the hard planes of his body.

The next minute, he pushed her away and looked at the expression of rapture and desire he saw on her face. With a look of fortitude, he moved away from her and went to the back of the wagon and removed the piece of canvas. After he'd spread it on the ground, behind the privacy of piñon trees and juniper shrubs, he held his hand out to her.

Slowly, Houston walked toward him, watching him, her mind a blank except for thoughts of the pleasure to come.

His hands were shaking as he began to undress her, slowly working the tiny buttons loose one by one. "I've been thinkin' about this for a long time," he said softly. The dim evening light made shadows of his lashes across his face, making him look younger and very vulnerable. "You asked me once about other women. I don't guess I ever even thought about a woman once I was outta bed with her—in fact, I don't think I thought about her while I was *in* bed with her. And worst of all, I sure as hell never told a woman all the things I've told you in the last few months. Are you a lady or a witch?"

As his hand slid inside her dress, touching her skin, finding her breast and sending the warmth of his touch throughout her body, Houston put her arms around his neck, pressed her lips to his. "I'm a witch who's in love with you," she whispered.

Kane grabbed her to him so close that she felt her ribs giving way, and only a squeal of protest made him loosen his grip.

There was no more talk as Kane attacked her with all the pent-up desire that he had stored. And Houston responded in the same manner.

With exuberance, they both began tearing at each other's clothes, and the still night air was filled with the sound of bits of fabric tearing when a reluctant button refused to slide through the hole.

Houston wasn't given time to remove her hose and high heels before Kane was on her, his hot mouth running over every bit of skin that he could find. She dug her nails into his flesh and pulled him closer and closer until they were one person.

As she started to open her mouth, Kane closed it with his

own. "You scream here, Ice Lady, and you'll get us some unwanted visitors."

Houston had no idea what he was talking about and had no intention of wasting her time finding out. Yet every few minutes, Kane would clamp down on her mouth with whatever was handy and Houston kissed whatever he placed there.

She had no idea of time or of how long they were there, because her thoughts were taken up with Kane's body that was sometimes on top of hers, sometimes under, beside, sitting and, even once, she thought, standing. Her hair was plastered to her face with sweat, hanging down her back in wet tendrils—and everywhere she was surrounded by Kane's skin: hot, damp, moving, delicious skin that was hers for the tasting and the touching. Her long-stored desires, her nearness to losing the man she loved, made her insatiable. They came together, then broke apart, reunited and at last came together for the last final, paralyzing thrust.

They slept for a few minutes, locked together, their skin fused.

Kane roused after a while and pulled the end of the canvas over them and snuggled his jacket about Houston's bare upper body. He looked at her for a moment in the moonlight, at her sleeping face, smoothed back her drying hair. "Who woulda thought that a lady like you . . ." he whispered, before trailing off, pulling her to rest on his shoulder and lying back on the canvas.

Houston woke an hour later to Kane's hand running up and down her body, his thumb playing with the pink tip of her breast. She smiled at him in a dreamy way.

"I got all a man can ask for," Kane said, moving to his side. "I got a naked woman in my arms and she's smilin' at me." He put his big thigh between hers. "Hey, lady, you wanta get tumbled by the stableboy?"

She rubbed her hips against his. "Only if he's very gentle and doesn't frighten me with his barbarian ways."

Kane gave a grunt as his mouth followed his hand. "When a man wants somethin', he uses a gun or a knife, but, honey, the weapons you use scare me to death."

"You look terrified," she said, as she took his ear lobe between her teeth.

This time they made love leisurely, taking their time, and not feeling frantic or rushed, and when they were finished, they lay still, in each other's arms, and slept. Sometime during the night, Kane rose and unhitched the horses from the wagon. When Houston sleepily asked him what he was doing, he said, "Once a stableboy, always a stableboy," before coming back to the canvas that was their bed.

Before the sun came up, they stirred and wakened and began to talk. Kane lay on his back, Houston draped around him, and talked about how much pleasure he'd had in seeing the children with the toys that he'd given them. "Why do some of the boys look like raccoons?"

It took Houston a while to understand what he meant. "They work in the mines and haven't yet learned how to wash the dust out of their eyes."

"But some of those boys were just babies, or at least not much older. They couldn't . . ."

"They do," Houston answered, and they were silent for a moment. "You know something I'd like to do for all the mines instead of just one?"

"What?"

"I'd like to buy about four wagons, something like a big milk wagon, but inside would be shelves of books, and the wagons would travel to all the camps and would be a free lending library. The drivers could also be librarians or teachers, and they could help the children, and the adults, too, to choose books."

"Why don't we hire men to drive the wagons?" Kane asked, with a twinkle in his eye.

"Then you like the idea?"

"It sounds fine to me, and a few wagons have to be cheaper than that train I bought your mother. How's she doin' with that thing, anyway?"

Houston smiled at him in the growing light. "She says that you gave her the idea. She had it moved to her backyard and now she uses it for her own personal retreat. I hear that Mr. Gates was so angry that he could barely speak."

As the sun lightened the sky, Kane said they should return home before the morning traffic started. All the way home, Houston sat close to him and, several times, he stopped and kissed her. Houston told herself that the Fentons didn't matter and that she would love Kane no matter what he did to take his revenge.

At home, they took a bath in Houston's big, gold-fixtured tub and ended with more water on the tile floor than inside the tub. But Kane absorbed most of it when he covered the floor with twenty-one thick white Turkish towels, then laid Houston on the floor and made love to her. Houston's maid, Susan, nearly walked into the room, but Kane slammed the door in her face and they laughed together as they heard the girl run across the hardwood floor of Houston's bedroom.

Afterward, they went downstairs to the biggest breakfast two people ever ate. Mrs. Murchison came out of the kitchen and personally attended them, grinning and smiling and obviously pleased that Kane and Houston were reconciled.

"Babies," she said, on her way out the door. "This house needs babies."

Kane nearly choked on his coffee as he looked at Houston with terror on his face. She refused to look at him but smiled into her own cup.

Just as Mrs. Murchison reentered the room bearing a platter of pan-fried beefsteaks dripping brown gravy, they heard the rumble. It felt as if it came rolling under their feet, something deep and dark and evil. The glasses on the table rattled and, from upstairs, they could hear the sound of breaking glass.

With a scream, Mrs. Murchison dropped the platter.

"What the hell was that?" Kane asked. "An earthquake?"

Houston didn't say a word. She'd heard that sound only once before in her life but, once heard, it was never, never forgotten. She didn't look at Kane or the servants, who were already running into the dining room, but went straight to the telephone and picked it up.

"Which one?" was all she said into the receiver, not bothering to tell the operator who she was.

"The Little Pamela," she heard before the cold instrument slipped from her hand.

"Houston!" Kane yelled into her face as he grabbed her shoulders. "Don't you dare faint on me now. Was that a mine?"

Houston didn't think she'd be able to speak. There was a knot of fear closing her throat. Why did it have to be *my* mine, she kept hearing inside her head as her mind's eye saw all the children. Which boys who'd played ball yesterday were now dead?

She looked up at Kane with bleak eyes. "The shift," she whispered. "Rafe was on the last shift."

Kane's hands tightened on her shoulders. "It was the Little Pamela then?" he whispered. "How bad?"

Houston's mouth opened but no words came out.

One of the footmen stepped out of the group of now-silent servants gathered in the hall. "Sir, when the explosion is bad enough to smash windows in town, then it's very bad."

Kane stood still a minute, then went into action. "Houston, I want you to get every blanket and sheet in this house and load it into the big wagon and bring it to the mine. You understand me? I'm gonna get dressed and go on up there ahead of you. But I want you to come as soon as possible, you understand that?"

"They'll be needin' rescuers," the footman said.

Kane gave him a quick look up and down. "Then get out of them fancy duds and get on a horse." He turned back to Houston. "Alive or dead, I'll get Rafe out." After a quick kiss, he bounded up the stairs.

Houston stood still for a moment before she began to move. She couldn't change what had happened but she could help. She turned to the women left standing near her. "You heard the master. I want every sheet and blanket put into the wagon within the next ten minutes."

One of the maids stepped forward. "My brother works at the Little Pamela. May I go with you?"

"And me," said Susan. "I've mended a few broken heads in my time."

"Yes," Houston answered as she hurried up the stairs to change out of her lacy morning gown. "I'm afraid we'll need all the help we can get."

Chapter 29

Kane had never had much experience with disasters; his battles had usually been on a one-to-one basis, so he was unprepared for what met him at the site of the Little Pamela mine. He heard the screams of the women from far away and he thought that, as long as he lived, he'd never get the sound out of his head.

The gate to the camp was open and unguarded, only a woman sitting there rocking her baby and crooning to it. Kane and the four men with him slowed as they entered the camp, and as more women, some of them running, some of them just standing and crying, came into view, the men dismounted.

As Kane walked past one woman, she grabbed his arm in an iron grip.

"Kill me!" she screeched in his face. "He's gone and we have nothing! Nothing!"

Kane was unable to stop her from pulling him inside the shack. Rafe's cabin was a mansion compared to this place. Five filthy children, wearing little more than rags, stood in a corner clutching at one another. Their gaunt faces and big, sad eyes told of their constant hunger. He hadn't seen these children when he'd come yesterday, but then, he didn't remember being in this part of the camp where the houses were hovels of tarpaper and flattened tin cans.

"Kill us all," the woman screamed. "We'll be better off. We'll starve now."

On the board that seemed to serve as a table was a half loaf of old bread, and Kane could see no more food in the house.

"Sir," the footman who'd entered behind Kane said. "They'll need help with the bodies."

"Yes," Kane said softly and left the hut, the woman crying

loudly behind him. "Who are these people?" he asked, once they were outside.

"They can't afford to pay the rent for the company houses at two dollars a room, so the company rents them land at a dollar a month and they build their own houses out of whatever they can find." He nodded toward the slum area of shacks of corrugated tin, powder cans, and Kane thought he saw pieces of the crates that yesterday had contained the baseball equipment.

"What will happen to the woman if her husband is dead?"

The man's mouth turned grim. "If she's lucky, the company will pay her six months' wages, but then she and the kids are on their own. Whatever happens, the company will say that the explosion was caused by the miners."

Kane straightened. "At least we can help now. Let's go get this woman some food."

"Where?" the man asked. "Four years ago, there was a riot and the miners attacked the company store, so now there's always only a bare minimum of goods, including food, in any one camp." His mouth twisted. "And the town won't help, either. We tried to get City Hall to help us when the last mine went up, but they said we had to go through 'channels'."

Kane started walking toward the center of the camp where the mine was. Before the mouth of the mine lay three sheet-draped bodies; two men carried another body to the open doors of the machine shop, where he could see Blair and two men at work. Kane walked to the stand beside Leander. "How bad is it?"

"The worst," Leander said. "There's so much gas in the mine that the rescuers are passing out before they reach the men. We can't tell exactly what happened yet, or how many are dead, because the explosion went inward instead of outward. There could be tunnels of men still trapped in there alive. Somebody get her, will you?" Lee called as he jumped on the elevator that would take him down into the mine.

Kane caught the woman in question as she ran toward a burned body that was being hauled from the mine. She was a frail little thing, and he picked her up in his arms. "Let me take you home," he said, but she only shook her head.

Another woman came up to them. "I'll take care of her."

"Do you have any brandy?" Kane asked.

"Brandy?" the woman spat at him. "We ain't even got any fresh water." She helped the woman Kane was holding to stand.

Two minutes later, Kane was on his horse and tearing down the side of the mountain toward Chandler. He passed Houston on the way up and she called to him, but he didn't slow his pace.

Once in town, he kept going at full speed, nearly running over a half-dozen pedestrians who all shouted questions at him. Most of the citizens of Chandler were standing outside looking up toward the mountain that held the Little Pamela mine and speculating on what had happened.

Kane thundered through town and up Archer Avenue until he came to Edan's house. Across the street, the new Westfield Infirmary was alive with activity. He hadn't seen Edan since the night they'd parted so bitterly.

Edan was walking across the front porch, a saddled horse waiting for him, when Kane skidded to a stop, reining his horse so hard the animal's front feet came off the ground.

Kane dismounted and ran up the steps all in one motion. "I know you ain't got much use for me anymore, but I don't know who else has got the brains to help me organize what I want to do, so I'm askin' you to forget your feelin's at the moment and help me out."

"Doing what?" Edan asked cautiously. "I'm planning to go help at the mine. Jean's uncle is up there and—."

"He happens to be *my* goddamn uncle, too!" Kane exploded in Edan's face. "I've just spent the last hour up there and they got more rescuers than they know what to do with, but they don't have much food and no water, and the explosion flattened a bunch of the houses—if you can call those shacks that. I want your help in gettin' together some food and shelter for the people, for the rescuers, and for the women that're standin' around screamin'."

Edan looked at his former employer for a long hard minute. "From what Jean could find out on the telephone, it's going to take a long time to get all the bodies out. We'll have to rent wagons to haul everything up to the mine, and we ought to try to get a train for . . . for the bodies. Today, we'll need food that doesn't have to be cooked."

Kane gave Edan a brilliant smile. "Come on, we got to get to work."

Jean had just come onto the porch, her face ghostly white.

Edan turned to her. "I want you to call Miss Emily at the teashop and tell her to have all her sisters meet me at Randolph's Grocery as soon as they can get there. Be sure you talk to Miss Emily herself, and be sure you say 'sisters'. Jean! This is very important, do you understand me?"

Jean nodded once before Edan gave her a quick kiss and mounted his horse.

Once in town, Kane and Edan separated and went to anyone who they knew owned a freight wagon. Most of the owners volunteered their services and, throughout Chandler, there was a feeling of togetherness as their concern for what had happened in the camp drew them together.

Six young ladies met them in front of Randolph's and Kane took only seconds telling them what was needed before the women took over, sweet Miss Emily bellowing orders in the voice of a gunnery sergeant.

As the wagons pulled up in front of the store's big back doors, the women loaded cases of canned beef, beans, condensed milk, crackers and hundreds of loaves of bread. When a crowd of curious people began to gather, Miss Emily put them to work helping to load the cases of food.

Edan saw to the filling of a water wagon.

Pamela Fenton came running down the hill, holding her hat on, Zachary in front of her. "What can we do?" she asked loudly over Miss Emily's orders.

Kane looked down at his son and a feeling of thankfulness spread through his body. This child of his would never be exposed to the constant danger of the mines. He put his hand on the boy's head and turned to Pam. "I want you to get as many friends as you can to help you and find every tent in this town. Go up to my house and find out what Houston did with those big tents she had for the weddin'. Then, I want every one of those tents taken up to the mine."

"I don't think Zach is old enough yet to see what's happened up there," Pam said. "Sometimes those explosions can be—."

Kane's temper had played no part in the day's happenings, but now he let it loose. "It's *you!*" he yelled into her face. "It's you Fentons that caused all this. If the mines weren't so dangerous, and your father would part with his precious money, none of this would have happened. This boy is *my* son and, if the boys up there can die in the mines, he's not too delicate to see the deaths that your father caused. Now, woman, you get busy and do what I say or I'll remember who you are and remember that right now my dearest wish is to see your father dead."

When Kane stopped, he was aware that all the many townspeople around him had stopped to stare at him, pausing, frozen in motion, as they gaped.

Edan stepped down from a wagon, the first one to move. "Are we going to stand here all day? You!" he yelled at a young boy. "Load that case of beans and you, move that wagon before that horse runs into the back of the other one."

Slowly, the people began to return to their duties, but Kane's mind was on the deaths that had been caused by Jacob Fenton. In spite of what he'd said to Pam, he wouldn't allow Zach to travel on any wagon to the site of the mine disaster until he was ready to drive one himself.

It was nearly sundown when Kane climbed into a seat and started the trip up to the Little Pamela mine. Zach was beside him, and the boy didn't speak until they were well on their way.

"Did my grandfather really kill the people? Was it really his fault?"

Kane started to tell his son just what he thought of Fenton, of how the man wanted money so badly that he had cheated Kane out of what was his, but something inside him made him stop. Whatever else the old man was, he was Zachary's grandfather, and the boy had every right to love him.

"I think sometimes that people get confused about money. They think that money can give them everything that they want in life, and so they go after it any way that they can. It doesn't matter whether they have to cheat or steal to get it, or even that they may take the money away from someone else, they think that gettin' the money is worth all they have to do."

"My mother said that you're richer than my grandfather. Does that mean that you stole it, too? Did you cheat people?"

"No," Kane answered softly. "I guess I was lucky. All I had to do was give up my life to get the money."

They were quiet as they travelled the rest of the way to the mine, and Kane experienced again the horror of first entering the scene of the explosion.

By the mouth of the mine lay eight bodies, undraped, before they were taken away to the machine shop where Blair, another female doctor, and two male doctors were working.

Houston, her hair straggling about her cheeks, her dress soiled, came to the back of the wagon as Kane let down the board.

"This is wonderful of you," she began, as she lifted a case of condensed milk and started to hand it to a waiting woman. "You really have no part in this. You—."

Kane took the heavy case from her. "I live here too, and in a way these mines belong to me. Maybe if I'd collected on Fenton, I could have prevented this from happening. Houston, you look tired. Why don't you take the wagon back and go home and rest?"

"They need everyone. The rescuers are succumbing to the gas and they're having difficulty reaching the men."

"Here! Give me a drink of that," said a familiar voice behind them, and Kane turned to see his uncle Rafe downing a mug of water.

Houston was sure that she'd never seen Kane's smile so big or showing so much gladness before. He thumped his uncle on the back so hard that the mug went flying across the ground. Rafe said a few well chosen words about Kane's exuberance, but Kane just stood and grinned until Rafe stopped cursing and winked at Houston before he went back to the mine mouth.

Kane went to the mine where he saw Leander, blackened from the smoke of the explosion, just coming up from the inside. He handed Lee a dipper of water. "Many more?"

Lee drank the water greedily. "Too many." He held up his hands and looked at them in the fading light. "The bodies are burned and, when you touch them, the skin comes off on your hands."

There was nothing Kane could say, but his thoughts went to the man who was responsible for all this.

"Thanks for the food," Lee was saying. "It's been more help than you know. Tomorrow, more people will be here, the press, relatives, the mine inspectors, government people, and the curious. Food is something that sometimes gets overlooked. I better get back now," he said, turning away.

Kane made his way through the growing number of people, found Houston and his son and put them on one of the empty freight wagons. "We're going to organize the rest of the food," was all he said as he started down the hill. When Houston's head nodded against his shoulder, he put his arm around her and held her so she could sleep the rest of the way into Chandler.

Houston and Zach slept for a few hours in the back of the wagon while Edan and Kane wakened townspeople and purchased goods to be taken to the mine. In the morning, they went to the high school and asked that the children be dismissed for the day so they could help gather the needed goods.

The students purchased vegetables, jam, fruit; they talked their mothers into cooking the food and boiling hundreds of eggs. They collected clothes, dishes, firewood, and carried everything to receiving stations.

And all day, the news came down from the mountain: twenty-two bodies found so far, so burned, bloated, and mutilated as to make identification almost impossible. Twenty-five more bodies were expected to be found by the rescuers who were working in two shifts. So far, one rescuer had died.

At midday, Kane drove a heavily laden wagon to the mine and, as he unloaded bundles of blankets and hundreds of diapers, he saw the rescuers coming to the surface and more than one of them vomited on the ground.

"It's the smell," said a man beside Kane. "The bodies down there smell so bad the men can't stand it."

For a moment, Kane stood there staring, then he grabbed someone's saddled horse and tore down the mountainside—heading for Jacob Fenton's house with all the speed he could muster.

He hadn't been up the drive to that house since he'd left years before, but the familiarity was so strong that he felt that he'd never been away. He didn't wait to knock on the door but rammed his foot through the leaded-glass panel and walked through the door that barely stayed on its hinges.

"Fenton!" he bellowed as servants came running from every part of the house, two footmen grabbing his shoulders to restrain him, but he shrugged them off as if they weighed nothing. He knew the arrangement of the downstairs of the house well enough and soon found the dining room, where Jacob sat eating alone, at the head of the table.

They looked at each other for a moment, Kane's face red with his rage, his body heaving.

Jacob waved his hand to dismiss the servants. "I don't imagine you came here for dinner," he said, calmly buttering a roll.

"How can you sit there when the people you've killed are on that mountain?" Kane managed to get out.

"There I beg to differ with you. *I* have not killed them. The truth is, I have done everything in my power to keep them alive, but they seem to have a suicidal bent. Could I offer you some wine? This is a very good year."

Kane's mind was full of the sights and sounds of the last few days. His ears seemed to ring with the sound of women's crying, and he wasn't aware of it, but he hadn't eaten in nearly two days. Now, the smell of the food, the cleanliness of the room, the quiet, all went together to make him sway on his feet.

Jacob stood, poured a glass of wine and, as he pulled out a chair for Kane, he set the glass before him. Kane didn't notice that Jacob's hand was trembling as he held the wine.

"Is it very bad?" Jacob asked, as he walked to a sideboard and removed a plate, which he began filling.

Kane didn't answer as he sat in the chair, looking at the wine. "Why?" he whispered after a moment. "How could you kill them? What is worth the death of those people? Why couldn't you have been satisfied with taking all the money that was left to me? Why do you have to have more? There are other ways of making it."

Jacob put a full plate of food in front of Kane, but the younger man didn't touch it. "I was twenty-four when you were born, and all my life I had thought that I was the owner of what I'd grown up with. I loved the man I thought was my father . . . and I thought that he cared for me."

Jacob straightened his shoulders. "At that age, one tends to be idealistic. The night Horace killed himself, I found out that I was nothing to him. His will stated that I could remain your guardian until you were twenty-one years old, and then I was to turn everything over to you. I was to walk out with the clothes on my back and nothing more. I don't think you can imagine the depth of the hatred I felt that night for the squalling infant that had ruined my entire life. I don't think I had a rational thought as I sent you away to a farm woman to wet-nurse and then bribed the lawyers. That hatred kept me going for years. It was all I could think of. If I signed a paper, I knew that somewhere there was a four-year-old child who actually owned what I was buying or selling. I sent for you once when you were young, so I could see for myself that you weren't worthy of what my father had left you."

Jacob sat down, across the table from Kane. "The doctor says that at most I have only a month or two to live. I haven't told anyone, but somehow I wanted to tell you the truth before I died."

He picked up his full glass of wine and sipped it. "Hatred hurts the one who hates more than it does the hated. All those years that you lived here, I'd see you and I was sure that you were trying to take everything that I owned. I lived in fear that you'd find out the truth and take what was mine and my children's. And when you wanted Pam for your wife, it seemed that all my fears had come true. Later, I thought that I should have seen your marriage to my daughter as a solution, but at the time . . . I don't think that I had any rational thoughts then."

He drank deeply of the wine. "There you are, Taggert, a

dying man's last confession. It's all yours; you can take it if you want. This morning, I told my son the truth about who owns my property because I don't have the strength or the inclination to fight you any longer."

Kane sat back in the chair and, as he looked at Fenton and saw the gray tinge under his skin, he realized that he no longer hated the man. Houston had said that his hatred of Jacob Fenton had spurred him on to achieve what he had, and perhaps she was right. In fact, she had pointed out the injustice of Horace cutting Jacob out of his will.

Kane took a drink of the wine that was in front of him and looked at the food. "Why did you have to starve the miners to make your money?"

"Starve the miners?" Jacob gasped, his eyes bulging. "Doesn't anyone in the world understand that I barely break even with the miners? The only money I make is in Denver at the steel mills, but everyone looks at the poor mistreated miner and accuses me of being Satan."

He stood and began to pace around the room. "I have to keep the coal mines under lock and key or the unionists will come in and incite the miners to demand more money, fewer hours. You know what they want? They want to elect a check weighman. Look, I know as well as anyone that the scales are fixed, and that the miners dig more coal than they're credited for, but if I were honest and paid them what they earned, I'd have to charge more per ton for the coal, and then I'd not be competitive, and I'd never get more contracts and then they wouldn't have any more jobs. So who gets hurt the most if I let them hire honest weighmen? I can hire coal miners by the hundreds, but I don't think they can get jobs so easily."

Kane looked at the older man for a moment. He understood about business, and he knew that sometimes compensations had to be made. "What about the mine safety? I hear you use rotten timbers and—."

"Like hell I do. The miners have their own pride system. You can ask your uncle if I'm not right. They brag about how they can tell just how far they can go before the roof caves in. I have mine inspectors in there all the time, and they find that the men won't take the time to shore up as they go."

Kane picked up the fork by the plate of food in front of him and slowly began to eat, but then found that he was ravenous and began to shovel it in. "You don't pay them for the time they spend shoring, do you? They're paid by the tonnage they get out, aren't they?"

Jacob took a chair across from Kane and put another thick slice of beef on his plate. "I hire them as subcontractors and it's up to each man to fulfill his part of the contract. Did you know that I pay men to inspect the miners' hats? The idiots open the cap to light cigarettes and send the whole place up. The inspector has to check that the caps are welded shut to prevent them from killing each other."

Kane, his mouth full, was gesturing with his fork. "One minute, you treat 'em like children and lock 'em up and the next minute, they have to be subcontractors and take the responsibility for their own . . . what's it called when you have to work and don't get paid for the work?"

"Dead work," Jacob supplied. "I do the best I can and still keep the miners working. I'd like to buy my coal from someone else and just make steel, but I can't see putting so many people out of work. Every time something like this happens," he motioned in the general direction of the Little Pamela, "I say that I'm going to close the mines. There's a vast amount of competition to supply coal to the mills in Denver, and I could close all seventeen mines around Chandler and they wouldn't even be missed. But you know what would happen to this town if I closed the mines? It'd be a ghost town in two years."

"So, according to you, you're just doin' the whole town a favor."

"I am, in a way," Jacob said righteously.

"I imagine you're payin' your stockholders, ain't you?"

"Not as much as I'd like, but I do the best I can."

Kane was cleaning the bottom of the second plate of food with a piece of bread. "Then you'd damn well better start doin' better. I happen to have a little money of my own and I just might decide to use it to bring a few lawsuits against the principals of Fenton Coal and Iron, and I think that all production—steel and coal—might be shut down while this thing was in court."

"But that would ruin Chandler! You couldn't—."

"I somehow think that the owners of FC&I might have enough self-interest to keep that from happening."

Jacob looked at Kane for a long time. "All right, what do you want?"

"If the men need inspectors to protect them from themselves, I want inspectors, and I want the kids out of the mines."

"But the children's small bodies can do things that the adults can't!" Jacob protested.

Kane merely gave him a look and went on to the next point, trying to remember everything that Houston had told him about the problems in the mines. Jacob protested every aspect of Kane's complaints; from libraries, "reading just makes them discontented"; to church services, "and pay preachers for every religion? We'd have religious wars if we tried to make them all go to the same service"; to better housing, to which Jacob said that the miners living in the shacks were really healthier because of all the fresh air coming through the cracks in the walls.

They talked and argued through the afternoon, with Jacob constantly refilling Kane's wineglass. By about four o'clock, Kane's words began to slur and his head rested against his chest. When he finally nodded off to sleep in the midst of telling Jacob that perhaps unions weren't as bad as Jacob seemed to think, the older man stood and looked down at Kane's big body sprawled in the chair.

"If I'd had a son like you, I could have conquered the world," he murmured before leaving the room and sending a servant for a blanket to cover Kane.

It was full night when Kane woke, stiff and sore from sleeping in the chair, and for a moment he didn't know where he was. The room was dim, but on the table he could make out the outline of a cloth-wrapped package and knew without a doubt that the package contained sandwiches.

With a smile, he stuffed the food into his pocket and left the house. Somehow, he felt lighter than he had in years, and as he rode back to the mine, he felt new hope that from now on his life was going to be different.

At the mine, Reed Westfield, Leander's attorney father, was

just entering the elevator to go back into the tunnel to continue the rescue operation. Kane caught the man with Reed by the collar. "Go get somethin' to eat. I'll go on this trip."

As the machinery started, Kane told Reed a quick story of how all that Jacob Fenton owned was legally Kane's.

"I don't want that hangin' over the man's head any longer, and I don't need the money. I want you to draw me up a paper sayin' that I turn everything over to him and whoever he wants to leave it to, and I want it done soon because the old man is dyin'."

Reed looked at Kane through weary eyes and nodded. "I have an office full of clerks with nothing much to do. Is tomorrow morning soon enough?"

Kane did no more than nod because, as they reached deeper into the mine, his face contorted at the smell.

Chapter 30

On the third day after the explosion, a total of forty-eight bodies had been taken from inside the mine, and seven were still unaccounted for. In the afternoon of the second day, four bodies had been found on their knees, their hands cupped over their mouths. They'd survived the major explosion, but the afterdamp, the gases, had killed them.

In town, the businesses were draped with black and flags were flown at half-mast. As the hearses drove through the streets in an unending stream, the people walked about with bare, bowed heads.

The fiancé of Sarah Oakley had been killed as he walked home from helping with the rescue of the miners. Too tired to watch where he was going, or to be aware of his surroundings, he didn't see or hear the train before it overtook him, killing him instantly.

Leander and Kane, with help from Edan, had demanded, and received, the promise of a rescue station to be built on land that had been donated by Jacob Fenton. No one dared say so but everyone was of the opinion that Kane had gone to Fenton's house and demanded the gift of the land.

Houston spent the day attending funerals and trying to comfort widows and seeing that children had enough to eat.

"I think this is what you want," Reed Westfield said, handing Kane a piece of paper as they stood before the mine entrance. "After this is settled, we can draw up a longer form, but I believe that should hold up in court."

Kane scanned the document and quickly saw that it said that he gave all rights to the holdings of the Fentons to the trust of Jacob Fenton, to dispose of however he wished.

"If you'll sign it, I'll witness it and file it. I have a copy here that you can give Fenton."

Kane smiled at Reed. "Thanks," he said, as he took the fountain pen from Reed and signed the paper. He held the copy up. "I think I'll take this to him right now. Maybe it'll make up to him for parting with that land, and I might mention that he ought to start a program to train men in mine rescue."

Reed returned Kane's grin. "I think the man might have remained richer before you gave him the rights to his property."

As Kane rode down the hill toward Chandler, he looked about the camp and thought of the horror of the last few days. There was still much to do, and he had some ideas about how to prevent future explosions and how to act if there were more disasters. He planned to talk to Edan about his ideas, and Leander would be a good one, too, and even Fenton. When Kane thought of Jacob's approaching death, he felt some sadness. After all, he had grown up seeing the man most of his life until he was eighteen. And now, the owner of the mines would be Zachary, after Marc, that is. Somehow, Kane thought, everyone seemed to forget Marc.

As he rode up the drive to the old Fenton house, he saw that the front door was standing open. The jamb had been repaired from where he'd kicked it in the day before and the glass replaced, but now it was wide open.

He dismounted, and called into the house as he entered, but there was no answer. Jacob's office was at the back of the house, and Kane clearly remembered that the last time he'd been in this room was when Jacob had thrown him out for wanting to marry Pam. As he put the paper on the desk, he wondered how different his life would have been if he'd married Pam and not had the opportunity to make his own fortune. For one thing, he wouldn't be married to Houston.

With that thought, he again wondered if Houston would have married him if he hadn't had a few million in the bank.

He called out again, but there was still no answer so he started to leave the house through the kitchen, a way that was very familiar to him. The kitchen was also empty and the back door was standing open. As he reached the door, he saw the narrow stairs leading to the upper floor.

When he'd been growing up, he'd always wanted to see the upstairs of the house, had even imagined owning the house one day.

He laughed as he thought of the house he'd built because he was angry at not being able to see the upstairs of the Fenton house.

With his hand on the bannister, curiosity overrode his common sense and he bounded up the stairs two at a time. Hurriedly, like a thief afraid of getting caught, he went down the hall and looked into the bedrooms. They were very ordinary, with heavy, ornate, dark furniture and heavy, depressing curtains and wallpaper. "Houston has much better taste," he mumbled and then laughed at his snobbery.

He was still smiling when he came to the head of the front staircase, but his smile vanished instantly.

At the foot of the stairs, in a crumpled heap, lay Jacob Fenton—obviously dead.

Kane's first thought was that he'd come too late and now Jacob would never know that at last he was the legal owner of all he'd worked so hard to have. And, too, Kane felt sadness. All those years that Kane had worked in New York, all he could remember were the times he'd polished Fenton's boots, but right now what he remembered were the times he'd given Jacob a hard time, embarrassed him in front of guests, argued with him about when he could and could not have his own horses, and all the times Kane'd tickled the cook and talked her into putting onions into the gravy, both of them knowing that onions gave Jacob such indigestion that he didn't sleep all night.

Slowly, Kane started down the stairs, but he'd only taken one step when Marc Fenton and five of his young friends burst into the hall. By the state of their clothes and their loud voices, they looked as if they were just returning from all night on the town.

"If Taggert thinks that he's gonna take *my* inheritance away," came Marc Fenton's slurred voice, "he's gonna have to fight me. Nobody in this town will believe Taggert over me."

The two women, wearing yellow satin, one with a red feather boa, the other with four peacock feathers in her hair, and the three men, all shouted agreement with Marc.

"Where's the whiskey, love?" one of the women asked.

As a group, the people stopped to stare at the body of Jacob Fenton lying at the foot of the stairs. It was Marc who looked up and saw Kane standing at the head of the stairs.

"I came to see your father—," Kane began but Marc never gave him a chance to finish.

"Murderer!" Marc screeched and started up the stairs in one leap.

"Wait a minute!" Kane shouted, but no one paid him the least attention as the three other men jumped him also. All five men went rolling down the stairs and Kane thought that since he was the only one who was sober, he would probably be the only one who was hurt. In spite of the fact that it was four against one, Kane was winning the fight.

But then one of the women slammed Kane over the head with a heavy brass statue of David preparing to slay the giant.

The four men unsteadily got to their feet and looked down at the unconscious form of Kane.

"What do we do now?" one of the women whispered.

"Hang 'im!" Marc shouted, starting to pick up Kane, but when he made no progress, and none of the others offered to help, he looked up, pleading, "He killed my father."

"There ain't enough whiskey in the world to get me drunk enough to hang a man as rich as he is," one of the men said. "While he's out, let's take him to the jail. Let the sheriff deal with him."

There was some argument from Marc, but he was too drunk to put up a great deal of fight, and so the four of them struggled to heave Kane's big body into the back of a buckboard that had been left standing outside the house. Not one of them seemed to give the body of Jacob another thought as they left him on the floor, the doors of the house wide open.

"Here, drink this," Edan was saying as he held Kane's head.

With a groan, Kane tried to sit up, but the pain in his head made him lean back against the cold stone wall. "What happened?" He looked up to see Edan, Leander and the sheriff hovering over him.

"It was all a mistake," Lee said. "I told the sheriff about the paper and why you went to Fenton's."

"He was dead?" Kane asked. "He looked like it from where I stood." Kane's head came up sharply, causing him more pain. "The last thing I remember is Marc Fenton and some drunks pullin' me down the stairs."

Edan sat down on the cot where Kane was stretched out. To his right were the bars of the jail. "As far as we can tell, the servants found Jacob Fenton dead about three minutes before you walked into the house. For some reason, they all decided to go get help and so left the body alone and the house open. Then Marc and his friends came in from an all-night spree and saw you standing at the top of the stairs and thought you'd pushed him down. You're lucky, because Marc wanted to hang you from the front porch."

Kane rubbed the knot on the back of his head. "Hangin' couldn't hurt more than this does."

"You're free to go, Mr. Taggert," the sheriff said. "And I suggest that you get out of here before your wife finds out. Women take on so when their husbands are put in jail."

"Not Houston," Kane said. "She's a lady to the core. She'd be calm if they hanged me." Even as he said the words, a new thought came to him. How *would* Houston react if she thought he were a murderer? Hadn't he heard one time that all the property of murderers was confiscated by the state? Or was it that a person couldn't inherit from a person he'd killed?

"How many people know about this?" Kane asked. "The Fenton servants can testify that I'm innocent, but has that fact spread around town yet?"

"I called Lee the minute I saw young Fenton push you out of the wagon," the sheriff said, puzzled.

"Everyone is too concerned with the mine explosion to care much who gets thrown in jail," Leander said. "All the reporters are at the Little Pamela trying to figure out new ways to describe the bodies," he added with a grimace.

"What are you planning?" Edan asked, his eyes narrowed.

Kane was silent a moment. "Sheriff, you mind if I stay in here overnight? I'd like to play a little practical joke on my wife."

"Joke?" the sheriff asked. "Women don't usually appreciate a joke, no matter how good it is."

Kane looked up at Lee and Edan. "Can I count on you two keepin' quiet for twenty-four hours?"

Edan stood and, at the look on Lee's face, he said, "My guess is that he wants to see if Houston will stand by him if he tells her that he'll probably be convicted as a murderer. Am I right?"

Kane started studying the dust in a far corner of the room. "Somethin' like that."

Both Lee and the sheriff snorted.

"I ain't interferin' in love," the sheriff said. "Mr. Taggert, if you wanta set up residence in this jail, be my guest, but the city of Chandler is gonna bill you as if this were the finest hotel in San Francisco."

"Fair enough," Kane answered. "Lee? Edan?"

Leander merely shrugged. "It's up to you. I've known Houston for most of my life, and I never knew anything at all about her."

Edan looked at Kane for a long moment. "When Houston

passes this test—and she will—will you give up your obsession of doubting her so we can get back to work? Vanderbilt
has probably bought the eastern seaboard by now."

Kane drew his breath in sharply. "Well, he can sell it back to
us starting tomorrow, as soon as I get out of this place," he said
with a grin.

When the men were gone, Kane lay down on the cot and
went to sleep.

Houston had a three-month-old baby in her lap, trying to
get the child to sleep, and a two-year-old and a four-year-old
in a bed beside her. They were some of the many children
who'd lost their fathers in the last few days. Their mother was
beside herself trying to figure out how she was going to
support herself and her small children in the years to come.
Houston and Blair and other members of The Sisterhood had
been campaigning to get the local merchants to try to find jobs
for the women, and Houston was one of the volunteers to help
in an impromptu child-care center—something new that Blair
had seen in Pennsylvania.

When the sheriff's deputy came to the little house and asked
for her, she had no idea what he wanted.

"Your husband has been arrested for the murder of Jacob
Fenton," the young man said.

It took Houston a moment to react, and her first thought was
that Kane's temper had at last gotten the better of him.
"When?" she managed to whisper.

"Sometime this mornin'. I wasn't there so I don't know
much about it, but ever'body in town knows that he threatened ol' man Fenton's life, not that anybody blames him,
'cause we all know that Fenton's guilty as sin, but it ain't
gonna help Taggert none. They hang you for killin' a bad man
as well as a good one."

Houston gave him her iciest look. "I will thank you to not
judge and condemn my husband before you hear the facts."
She put the baby into the boy's arms. "Here, you may take care
of the babies while I go see my husband."

"I can't do that, Blair-Houston, I'm on city time. I'm a
deputy sheriff."

"I had the impression that you believed you were a judge. Check her diaper and see if she needs changing, and if the others wake up, feed them and entertain them until their mother returns in about two hours."

"Two hours!" she heard the boy wail as she left the cabin.

Houston's carriage was waiting outside for her and she made the trip to the jail in record time. The little stone building was built into a hill at the far edge of town. Most of the prisoners were drunks sleeping off Saturday night, and the real cases were usually taken to Denver to be tried.

"Good morning, Miss Blair-Houston," the sheriff said, getting to his feet and hastily putting his paper down.

"Mrs. Taggert," she corrected. "I'd like to see my husband immediately."

"Why, of course, Mrs. Westfield-Taggert," he said, removing the keys from a nail in the wall.

Kane was asleep on the cot and Houston saw the dried blood on the back of his head. She went to him, touched his face as she heard the cell door being locked behind her.

"Kane, darling, what have they done to you?" She began to kiss his face and he started to wake.

"Oh, Houston," Kane said as he rubbed his head. "What happened?"

"You don't remember? They say that you killed Jacob Fenton. You didn't, did you?"

"Hell, no!" he blurted, then paused as Houston went to her knees and put her head in his lap. "At least I don't think so. I . . . ah, I really don't remember too well."

With her cheek against his thighs, his hand in her hair, she was determined not to show her fear. "Tell me what you do remember."

He began his story slowly. "I went to see Fenton, and nobody was home so I went upstairs lookin' for him. When I got to the front of the house, there he was lyin' at the bottom of the stairs. Dead. The next minute, Marc Fenton and some others came in and started yellin' that I'd killed him. There was a fight, and I got hit over the head with somethin' hard, and I woke up here. I think there's talk of a lynchin'."

Houston looked up at him with fear in her eyes and after a

moment she stood and began to walk about the cell. "That's a very weak story."

"Weak!" Kane gasped, then calmed. "Houston, honey, it's the truth, I swear to you."

"You were the only one in the house? There were no witnesses that he was already dead when you entered?"

"Not exactly that way. I mean, nobody saw me come into the house, I don't think, but maybe somebody saw Fenton dead earlier."

"That won't matter. If someone saw him die, that would make a difference, but you could have been hiding in a closet for hours for all they know. Did someone actually see him die?"

"I . . . I don't know, but Houston—."

She came back to sit on the bed by him. "Kane, everyone in town heard you say that you wished Jacob was dead. Unless you have an eyewitness to his death, we'll never prove that you're innocent. What are we going to do?"

"I don't know, but I think I'm beginnin' to worry. Houston, there's somethin' I wanta tell you. It's about the money."

"Kane," she said softly, looking up at him. "Why *were* you at Mr. Fenton's house? You weren't really planning to murder him?"

"Hell, no," he said quickly. "I had Mr. Westfield draw up a paper sayin' that I was releasin' all my claims to the Fenton property, and I was takin' the paper to Fenton. What I wanta talk to you about is my money. If they convict me, they're gonna confiscate everything I own. You'll not only be a widow, you'll be a pauper. Your only chance to save any of the money is to leave me right now before I go to trial. If you do that, Westfield can arrange for you to have a few million."

Houston was barely listening to the last part of what he was saying. Her face showed how stunned she was. "Why did you go to Fenton's?" she whispered.

"I told you," Kane said impatiently. "I wanted to give him a paper sayin' I had no hold on his property. Poor ol' man, he was dead when I got there and never saw the paper. But, Houston, what matters is that you have to save yourself and you've gotta do it now. If I'm taken out of here and lynched, it'll be too late."

Houston felt that she was in a dream. Ever since she'd found out that Kane had married her to enact a plan of revenge, she had never felt the same. She'd admitted that she loved him in spite of what he felt about her, but in her heart she'd always known that some part of her would withhold her complete love.

"You've given up your revenge, haven't you?" she asked softly.

"Are you on that again? I told you that all I wanted was to have him at my table at a house that was bigger than his. If I could afford it, what was wrong with it?"

"But you also wanted a lady-wife at the table, too. You married me because—."

"You married me for my money!" he shot at her. "And now you're gonna lose ever' penny of it when they hang me for a murder I didn't commit."

Houston stood. He hadn't said, in so many words, that he loved her, but he did. She knew it. She knew it with every fiber in her body. He had married her as part of a stupid plan of revenge, but in the end, he'd fallen in love with her and, because of that love, he could forgive an old man who'd wronged him.

"I have to go," she said. "I have a great deal of work to do."

If she'd looked at Kane, she would have seen the look of pain on his face. "I guess you gotta talk to Mr. Westfield about the money."

"Someone," she murmured, pulling at her gloves. "Perhaps Mr. Westfield isn't the right person." Absently, she kissed his cheek. "Don't worry about a thing. I know exactly what to do." With that, she called to the sheriff and he let her out.

Kane stood in the middle of the cell for a moment, unable to move. She had certainly jumped at the chance to get rid of him, he thought. He climbed on the cot to look out the window and, as he saw Houston speeding away in her shiny carriage, he had to blink his eyes to clear the water. Sunlight, he thought, stepping down.

Easy come, easy go, he told himself. He'd done all right without a wife before, and he'd do all right again.

"Sheriff," he called. "You can let me out now. I found out what I wanted to know."

"Not on your life, Taggert," the man answered, laughter in his voice. "The city of Chandler needs the revenue that I'm gonna charge you for a night's accommodations."

Without a word of protest, Kane went back to the cot. He didn't really care where he spent tonight.

Chapter 31

"You're sure you know what you're doing?" Houston once again asked Ian.

Solemnly, Ian nodded as he glanced back at the small wooden crate in the back of the wagon. Beside him sat Zachary, his eyes straight ahead and alive with excitement. He wasn't yet old enough to be fully aware of the dangers of what they'd planned.

"It isn't in any danger of going off by itself, is it?" Houston asked.

"No," Ian answered, but he couldn't help glancing back at the little wooden box that held the dynamite.

Houston's hands on the reins were white with the strain of holding them as tightly as she was.

It had taken nearly twenty-four hours to arrange what was going to happen tonight. She had known what she wanted to do, and right away she had also known that no adult would help her. When she'd asked Ian, she'd explained to him that he was taking a risk and could get into serious trouble if he was openly involved, but Ian had said that he owed Houston for all that he had now, and he was willing to risk anything. Much to

Houston's chagrin, Ian'd asked young Zachary to come along, saying that they needed someone to hold the horses.

Tonight, at midnight, Houston had met Ian at the Little Pamela mine and, counting on the confusion caused by the mine explosion, they'd broken the chains on the dynamite shack and stolen enough to blow away about two city blocks. Against Ian's protest of the time it would take, Houston had rechained and relocked the shack.

Slipping about, neither of them very good at hiding the fact that they were doing something illegal, they managed to get the box into the waiting wagon. A few people said hello to Houston, but they'd seen her often in the last few days and thought nothing of her presence.

She and Ian were halfway down the mountainside when they met Zachary walking toward them. He'd climbed out his window, using a knotted rope, hours ago and had planned to walk all the way to the mine.

"You're to do nothing but stay with the horses, nothing more," Houston warned. "And, as soon as your father and I get on the horses, I want both of you out of there. Ian, can you get back into Edan's house all right?"

"Of course."

"And you, Zach?"

Zachary swallowed hard, because the rope had given way when he was still four feet off the ground. There was no way he could slip back into his house unnoticed. "Sure," he answered. "No problem at all."

Houston didn't relax as they neared the sleeping town. It was three o'clock when they reached the jail. Earlier, she'd hidden two saddle horses outside the jail, their bags laden with food, clothes and enough cash to carry them through a couple of months in hiding.

She stopped the wagon quite a distance from the jail and watched nervously as Ian removed the box of dynamite. She knew that he had trained in the mines as a shot-firer, but she wasn't convinced that he knew how to blow up the side of the stone jail.

Just as she opened her mouth to speak, Ian started talking.

"I'll put a few sticks in the base of that wall that's in the hill, then, when it blows, the entire wall will come sliding down. It'll be like opening a very large window. Kane will have to jump down from the floorboards onto a horse, and then you'll be off. It couldn't be simpler."

"A very simple plan, for which we could all go to prison for the rest of our lives," she murmured.

Yesterday, when Kane had told her that he might be hanged for a murder that he didn't commit—and, when Houston was honest with herself, she admitted that she didn't really care whether he was a murderer or not—she knew that something had to be done to get him released. The town's sympathy would be on Kane's side after the way he'd helped with the disaster, but the trial would probably go to Denver, and Fenton Coal and Iron was a powerful force in Denver. She did not think he'd have a fair trial and, with no witnesses except to say that Kane had been found at the top of the stairs with a dead Jacob at the bottom, she had no doubt that Kane would be found guilty.

After only a moment's soul-searching, she knew what had to be done. She had to get him out of the jail, and even if it meant that they had to spend the rest of their lives in hiding, she meant to do it. They'd go to Mexico, and she thought that she could get Blair to send them enough money to live on. As long as Kane kept a quiet profile and didn't call too much attention to himself, she thought they could get away from the American law. It was too bad that Kane was so well known in so many parts of the country, so they couldn't possibly hide in the United States.

Houston's only regret was that she wouldn't be able to say good-bye to her family and her friends. She probably wouldn't even be able to write to them, as her letters might lead to Kane's capture.

But she knew what had to be done, and she felt that as long as she had Kane she could be happy, no matter where they lived or in what hardship.

Now, in the darkness, she directed Zach to get the horses from their hiding places, to tighten the girths and to bring the horses closer to the jail.

Her hands were trembling as she helped Ian insert the sticks of dynamite into the chinks of the stone wall. When everything was set, she motioned Ian to let her stand on his shoulders so she could see inside the window.

"Tell him to put the mattress around his head," Ian said as he lifted her.

"We don't have enough dynamite to hurt him, do we?" she asked.

"The heels on those boots of yours hurt, so don't waste my time askin' damn fool questions."

Houston looked into the dark cell and saw Kane sprawled across the little mattress, parts of him hanging over the side. She tossed a pebble into the cell.

He didn't even move and it took six stones, one of them glancing sharply off his chest, before he woke.

"Kane!" she said as loudly as she dared.

"What?" he asked, sitting up. "Is that you, Houston? What're you doin' here in the middle of the night?"

She motioned for him to come to the window. "I don't have time to explain now but Ian and I are getting you out of jail. We're going to dynamite this wall away, so I want you to get into the farthest corner and put that mattress around as much of you as you can cover."

"You're what?" Kane gasped. "Dynamite! Listen, Houston, there's somethin' I have to tell you."

"Houston!" Ian said from below her. "Them little heels are killin' me. Are you gonna stay up there all night?"

"I have to go," she said. "Just get in the corner, and when the wall is gone, I have horses ready. I love you." With that, she bent and got off Ian's shoulders.

Kane stood by the window of the cell for several long moments. She hadn't run off to get the money, but instead, she'd set up a plan to blow the side of the jail out and rescue him. He put his hands in his pockets and started to whistle a little tune, smiling at the thought of Houston being so concerned about him.

It was while he was whistling that he heard an odd sound, like something on fire.

"Dynamite!" he gasped, grabbed the mattress and leaped

into the corner of the room. Nothing could have prepared him for the noise of the explosion. It was as if the top of his head had been taken off—and the noise went on and on.

Houston, Ian and Zach hid behind a boulder as the wall to the jail came tumbling down. The dynamite removed the foundation to the two-story wall and the stones above it fell rather gracefully, leaving a clear view of the interior of the jail. Kane was huddled in a corner and, when the dust began to settle, he made no attempt to move.

"We've killed him," Houston cried and started running, Ian behind her.

"Probably just deafened him. Kane," Ian shouted above the sound of the rock that was still falling, and when Kane made no response, Ian scrambled up the rock and into the three-walled cell.

Ian pulled the mattress off but Kane couldn't understand a word he said, so Ian had to use gestures. For some reason, Kane seemed to have been made stupid by the explosion, since he kept shaking his head at Houston, and Ian had to nearly push him onto the rock pile so he could get to the ground.

Houston waited on a horse and, as Kane got close to her, she saw that he kept putting his hands to his head as if he were in great pain. He seemed to want to say something, but Houston wouldn't give him time as Ian and Zach started pushing him onto the other horse.

"Go home, both of you," she ordered as she saw that people were rushing down the street toward them after hearing the explosion.

"Let's go," she shouted to Kane and he followed her down the south road of town and out into the dessert.

Houston rode as fast and as hard as she could spur her horse, looking back occasionally to Kane who followed her with a blank, odd look on his face.

The sun came up, and still they rode, slowing just enough to allow the horses to breathe. At noon, they stopped at a stage station, a desolate place in the middle of the barrenness between Colorado and New Mexico, and Houston paid an outrageous price for two fresh horses.

"He all right?" the station manager asked, nodding toward Kane as he leaned against the building and hit his head with his hand.

Houston handed the old man a twenty dollar bill. "You haven't seen us."

He took the money. "I mind my own business."

Houston tried to talk to Kane, but he just dumbly stared at her moving mouth and followed her only after she motioned him to do so.

What they ate during the day, they ate while on their horses, never stopping even after the sun set. Only once did Kane try to speak, but when he couldn't seem to hear himself, he made gestures that Houston finally realized meant that he wanted to know where they were going.

"Mexico," Houston shouted four times before he seemed to understand.

Kane shook his head, but Houston urged her horse on faster and ignored him. No doubt, he didn't want her to get into trouble with him, but she wasn't going to let him talk her into returning. If he was to live his life in exile, she was going to live with him.

Kane caught her horse's reins and pulled until she had to slow down.

"STOP!" he bellowed. "WE'LL STAY HERE FOR THE NIGHT."

Every word was at the top of his lungs and Houston blinked several times at the volume breaking the still night air.

Kane didn't say another word as he dismounted and led his horse over a small hill and into a grove of trees. Houston followed his lead as he unsaddled his horse and made a camp for the night. She wanted to go on longer, to put more distance between them and the posse from Chandler, but perhaps Kane had been hurt in the blast and needed rest. It would take a long time before the citizens could be organized, so perhaps they had time.

She had the saddle in her hands when she glanced toward Kane and saw that he was looking at her in a way that was almost frightening.

Very slowly, he took the saddle out of her arms, tossed it to the ground, and after one look that she couldn't interpret, he was upon her.

He was like a hungry animal and, after Houston got over her surprise, she reacted in kind. Buttons flew off her dusty riding suit like corn popping in a skillet. His mouth was all over her body at once, with his big, strong hands tearing away all that inhibited his contact with her skin.

"Kane," she half-cried, half-laughed. "Kane. My only love, my true love."

He didn't seem to need words as he pushed her nude body to the ground and thrust inside her with the strength of the dynamite they'd set off that morning. Houston felt as if she were like the stone wall crumbling and, as they moved together in a sweaty, fierce passion, she was sure that this was all she needed in life, and that what she'd done today had been right.

When at last they erupted together, Houston shivered with the force of her passion and the depth of her love for this man.

They lay together for a while, Kane holding her tightly in his arms, as if he never meant to let her go. And Houston clung to him just as tightly, afraid now when she thought how close she'd come to losing him, how close he'd come to being hanged.

After a long while, Kane stood and went to the horses to care for them. Houston started to help but he motioned her to lie still, tossing her a blanket to cover her from the cool night air.

Even when he built a fire, he wouldn't let her help. Houston started to protest that perhaps they'd be seen, but Kane shouted that she should trust him, and she did. She was glad to turn over the mastery of this wild escape to him, and she was glad to lie back and be waited on. He brought a plate of beans to her, with a tortilla and a cup of dreadful coffee. But Houston thought it was the most delicious meal of her life.

When they'd finished eating, Kane put out the fire, lay down beside her and pulled her into his arms. In minutes, both of them were asleep.

Chapter 32

When Houston woke, it was full light and Kane was holding her and smiling angelically.

"We have to go," she said, sitting up, shrugging off his hands and pulling on the remnants of her torn clothing. The front of her riding habit was missing so many buttons that it was decidedly indecent. "They'll be after us soon, and I don't imagine they'll stop to rest this long."

He caught her arm. "Hot after the murderer, right?"

"I really don't think this is any time for laughter."

"Houston, I want you to tell me what you have planned. Why are you runnin' toward Mexico?"

"I'll tell you as we get the horses saddled," she said and stood, waiting impatiently until Kane also rose. "I think we can hide in Mexico," she said, putting the saddle blanket on her horse.

"For how long?"

"Forever, of course," she answered. "I don't think that the law ever forgives one for murder. I think we can live there quite frugally, and I hear that people don't ask as many questions there as they do in this country."

He caught her arm. "Wait a minute. You mean that you're plannin' to live in Mexico with me? That if I'm an outlaw, you're gonna be one, too?"

"Yes, certainly, I'm planning to live with you. Now, will you please saddle your horse so that we can ride?"

Houston didn't say any more because Kane grabbed her about the waist and twirled her around. "Honey, that's the best thing that anybody's ever said to me. You don't care about the money after all."

"Kane!" she said, exasperated. "Please put me down. They'll find us and you'll—."

She stopped because he planted a hearty kiss on her mouth.

"Ain't nobody comin' after us, unless it's the sheriff 'cause he's mad at you for tearin' up his jail. Oh, Houston, honey, I wish I could see that man's face."

Houston took a step back from him. What he was saying made no sense to her, but in the pit of her stomach was a little feeling of fear. "Perhaps you should explain that remark."

Kane drew three circles in the dirt with his toe. "I just wanted to see how you . . . ah, felt about the fact that I wasn't a rich man anymore."

She gave him a look that had stopped many a forward cowboy. "I would like to know about Jacob Fenton."

"I didn't tell you a single lie, Houston, it's just that I guess I didn't tell you all of it. I did find him dead at the foot of the stairs, and I was taken to jail for his murder, but the truth was that the servants had run out of the house and knew he was already dead. Although, I didn't ask if any of them actually *saw* him die. That was real clever of you to think of that."

"So why were you in jail when I got there? Why weren't you released immediately?"

"I guess I was, sorta. Houston, honey," he held out his arms to her. "I just wanted to know for sure that you liked me for myself and it wasn't my money you wanted. You know, when you walked out of that jail after I told you that I'd lose my money, I thought for sure that you were goin' to Westfield to see what you could get before I was hanged."

"Is that what you thought of me?" she said under her breath. "You think that I'm that low a human being that I'd leave the man I love alone to face a murder trial and not lift a finger to help?" She turned toward the horse.

"Houston, baby, sweetheart, I didn't mean nothin'. I just wanted to know for sure. I didn't have any idea you'd do somethin' as damn fool as . . . Well, I mean, I had no idea that you'd blow the jail to kingdom come and near kill me."

"You seem to have recovered well enough."

"Houston, you ain't gonna be mad, are you? It was just a

little joke. Ain't you got any sense of humor? Why, ever'body in town will—."

"Yes," she said, glaring at him. "Go on. What will everybody in town do?"

Kane gave her a weak grin. "Maybe they won't notice."

She advanced on him. "Won't notice that I removed the entire side of a jail that had two-foot-thick stone walls? Perhaps they all slept through the explosion. Yes, perhaps they *will* just drive past the building and not even notice. And maybe the sheriff will forgo telling the story of the decade about how one of the Chandler twins stuck dynamite into the wall to rescue a husband who wasn't even charged with murder. Maybe every person for miles around won't be laying bets as to when I'll find out my error and whether *I'll* be charged with murder." She turned back to the horse, every muscle in her body aflame with anger.

"Houston, you have to understand my side of it. I wanted to know if it was me you loved or my money. I saw an opportunity to find out and I took it. You can't blame a man for tryin'."

"I most certainly *can* blame you. Just once, I'd like you to listen to me. I told you that I loved you—you, not your money—yet you never heard a word I said."

"Oh, well," he shrugged, "you said that you couldn't live with a man you couldn't respect, either, but you came back, and it didn't even take all that much persuadin'. I guess you just can't help yourself." He gave her a crooked grin.

"Of all the arrogant, vain men I have ever met, you are the worst. I am very, very sorry that I ever rescued you. I wish they had hanged you." With that, she mounted her horse.

"Houston, baby, you don't mean that," Kane said as he climbed onto his horse and began to ride beside her. "It was just a joke. I didn't mean no harm."

All day long they rode, and every minute, Kane was either presenting arguments to her or thinking of further excuses as to why she should be grateful to him for what he had done. He said that Houston could be more sure of her feelings for him now. He tried to make her see the humor of it all. He chastised her for using boys to help her and warned of the danger she'd placed them all in. He tried anything he could think of to get a reaction out of her.

But Houston sat on her horse as rigid as a human body could be. Her thoughts were on the people of Chandler. After the horror of the mine disaster, they'd want something to lighten their mood and they'd no doubt milk this story for every drop of humor. The sheriff would embellish it for all it was worth, and the Chandler Chronicle would probably run a series of articles on the whole affair, starting with the wedding and ending with . . . ending with a man who should have been hanged.

When Houston thought of Kane, her blood boiled, and she refused to listen to a single word he said. The fact that she had given him her love and he had doubted it so publicly, doubted her in such a spectacular, outrageous way, was particularly humiliating.

She had her first taste of what was to come when they stopped at the stage station and traded horses. The old man asked if they were the couple from Chandler that he'd heard about. He could hardly recount the story for laughing so hard, and when they left, he tried to return the twenty dollars Houston had given him.

"That story was worth a hundred dollars to me," he said, slapping a grinning Kane on the back. "I owe you eighty dollars."

Houston put her chin in the air and went to her horse. She was doing her best to pretend that neither man existed.

Once they were on the trail again, Kane started talking to her with renewed vigor, but he lost a lot when he kept pausing to laugh.

"When I saw you standin' there, and you were sayin' that you were gonna bust me out and save me from the hangin' tree, I couldn't think of what to say, I was that stunned, and then when Ian started yellin' that the heels on them little boots of yours—," he had to pause to wipe the grin off his face. "Why, Houston, you'll be the envy of every woman west of the Mississippi. They'll all wish they had the courage and the bravery to rescue their husbands from the jaws of death and—."

He stopped to clear his throat and Houston glanced at him. He was unsuccessfully trying to control his laughter.

"When I think of the look on your face atop that horse. What're those women that wear horns on their heads? Lady Vikings, that's what you looked like, a lady Viking come to rescue her man. And the look on Zachary's face! If my head hadn't been hurtin' so much—."

He broke off because Houston kicked her horse's side and raced ahead of him.

Whatever Houston had expected, when she reached Chandler, it was worse. Ignoring Kane as best she could, she rode on the outskirts of the town to the north side so she would see as few people as possible on her way to Kane's house.

It was six o'clock in the morning when they rode up the hill to the Taggert house, but already there were about twenty couples who just "happened" to be strolling in front of the house. Most of the Taggert servants were in the front drive talking to the townspeople.

Houston held the front of her destroyed habit together and mustered as much dignity as she could and rode to the kitchen entrance, while Kane dismounted at the front and all the people ran to him.

"Probably wants to brag," Houston murmured. Somehow, she managed to get through the kitchen and Mrs. Murchison's smiles and unsubtle questions.

Upstairs, Houston dismissed Susan and drew her own bath. After a short time in the tub, she climbed into her bed and went to sleep. She heard Kane enter the room at some time, but she pretended to be fast asleep and he went away.

After nine hours of sleep and a huge meal, she felt physically better, but her mood was worse. When she walked in her rooftop garden, she could see the street and the extraordinary number of people who were strolling in front of the house.

Kane came into her room once to tell her that he was on his way up to the Little Pamela to see if any help was needed, and he asked Houston to go with him. She shook her head in refusal.

"You can't hide in here forever," he said angrily. "Why aren't you proud of what you did? I sure as hell am."

After he had left, Houston knew he was right, that she had to face the townspeople and the sooner she got it over, the better. She dressed slowly in a serviceable blue cotton, went downstairs and asked that her buggy be hitched.

It didn't take Houston but ten minutes to find out that Kane's prediction of how the people of Chandler would react was dead wrong. She was not being cast as a heroine who'd rescued her husband, but as a silly, flighty woman who went hysterical first and asked questions later.

She drove her little buggy through the back side of town and up the road to the Little Pamela. Perhaps at the mine they'd need so much help that they wouldn't have time to talk about her escapade.

No such luck. The victims of the disaster wanted something to laugh about and Houston's escapade was their target.

She did the best she could at holding her head high while she helped to clear the debris and tried to make arrangements for the relocation of the widows and orphans.

Her real complaint was that Kane was enjoying everything so much. At the wedding, he'd been hurt because the people believed that any woman would prefer Leander over him, but now he had very public proof that Houston was in love with him.

Houston kept thinking of all the times he could have told her that he wasn't really being charged with murder. He could certainly talk fast enough when he wanted to, so why was he so tongue-tied the night she informed him that she'd just inserted dynamite under his feet?

As the day wore on, and the people became more bold about asking her questions ("You mean you didn't ask the sheriff what his chances were or talk to an attorney? Leander was in on all of it. He could have told you. Or you could have . . ."), Houston wanted to hide. And when Kane walked past her, gave her a hearty punch in the ribs, a wink and said, "Buck up, honey, it was only a joke," she wanted to cry that it might be a joke to him, but to her the public humiliation was horrifying.

Toward evening, she saw Pamela Fenton standing nose to nose with Kane and, on the cool evening breeze, she heard the words, "At the wedding, you said that you wouldn't humiliate her. What do you think you've done now?"

The thought that someone was fighting her case was gratifying to her.

At home, she had dinner in her room and Kane made one more attempt to talk to her, but she just looked at him. He stormed out of the room, complaining that she had no sense of humor and was too damn much of a lady too damn much of the time.

Houston cried herself to sleep.

Chapter 33

The next day, Houston was arranging flowers in a large vase in the hall outside Kane's office. She was still angry, still too hurt and humiliated to speak to him, and she couldn't bear the thought of leaving the safety of her own house.

Kane had the door to his office open and with him were Rafe, Leander, and Edan. Kane'd called a meeting to discuss the possible consequences of the mine explosions. Kane had been concerned when he found out that the miners' widows would probably not be given any compensation.

Houston listened to the men discussing the future of Chandler and she felt a great deal of pride at what her husband was doing. She wondered how she could ever have believed that he would foreclose on the people whose mortgages the Chandler National Bank held. Yesterday, Opal'd had a long talk with Houston and told her why Kane had used blackmail to get Houston to come back to live with him.

"He loves you so much," Opal'd said, "and I don't see why you have to be angry with him now."

It might have worked, except at that moment she heard three

women in the hall giggling like schoolgirls. They'd come to see Houston and "catch up on the latest news" was what they told the maid. Houston politely declined to see them, or anyone else.

Now, standing in the hallway, she listened with pride to the reforms her husband was planning, but then she heard Leander ask a question that caused her back to stiffen.

"Is this a bill from the City of Chandler?" Lee asked.

"Yeah," Kane answered. "The sheriff wants five hundred dollars cash to repair the jail. I think it may be the only bill I ever *wanted* to pay."

"Maybe you could have a grand openin' and Houston could cut the ribbon," she heard Rafe say.

There was a long silence. "If she ever speaks to him again," Edan said.

There was another pause.

Leander spoke next. "I don't think you ever know a person. I've known Houston most of my life, but the Houston I knew and the one who'd blow out the side of a jail aren't the same woman. A few years ago, I took her to a dance and she wore a very becoming red dress, but Gates had said something that had hurt her feelings and she kept clutching her cloak so every inch of that dress was covered. She was so nervous by the time we reached the dance that I said that if she wanted to keep wearing the cloak it was fine with me. Damned if she didn't spend the whole evening sitting in a corner looking like she was about to cry."

Houston's hand paused as she held a flower. It was odd how the same episode could be seen in two ways. Now that she looked back on it, maybe she had been silly to be so upset about a red dress. Now, she seemed to remember that Nina Westfield often wore just that shade of red that had caused Houston so much anguish that night.

Smiling, Houston continued with the flowers.

"If she was gonna break out of the mold, she could've done it with less danger to my hide," Kane said. "You don't know what it's like to have somebody tell you that they've just lit dynamite under your feet and there ain't nowhere you can run."

"You can stop bragging," Edan said. "You loved what she did and you know it."

Houston's smile grew broader.

Leander laughed. "Too bad you didn't get to see what happened after the explosion. Everybody thought another mine had gone up and we ran out of our houses in our underwear. When we saw the jail, with half of it blown away, we just stood there; not one of us could understand what had happened. It was Edan who first remembered that you were in the jail."

A little laugh escaped Houston, but she got it under control.

"Listen," Edan said, "as soon as I saw that jail, I knew Houston was involved. While the rest of you've been worshipping at her feet over the years and telling yourselves what an ice princess she is, I've been following her around. Under her prim little exterior is a woman . . . Well, you wouldn't believe some of the things that woman does on a regular basis."

Houston had more difficulty controlling her laughter. Edan sounded half-appalled, half-admiring. She thought of the time he'd hidden and watched the pre-wedding party. The day he'd told her that he'd seen it, she hadn't allowed herself to think about anything except that he'd heard about their plans for the mines, but now she thought of the boxer, and the cancan, and, oh Heavens, *Fanny Hill*. At the time, she'd been terrified that Kane would find out some of the things that she did, such as The Sisterhood's stag parties, and infiltrating the mine camps, but, in the end, he'd caught her in nearly all of it and her life hadn't ended. The night she wore that red dress, she was sure that if she showed it to anyone, her reputation would be ruined and she wouldn't be a fit wife for Leander.

But look at what she'd done in the last few months! There was the time she had climbed down the rose trellis in her underwear. Then there was inviting all those people to live with them and telling Kane—who had to support them— about it later.

The more she thought, the more the laughter bubbled inside her. Before they were married, she was quite sure who was marrying Kane Taggert. He requested a lady, and she was sure that she could fill the bill. But when she began to remember the things she'd put him through, and all the times he'd said, with that special look of disbelief on his face, that he'd had no idea what he was getting when he married a real, true, deep-down lady, Houston could no longer control her laughter. It exploded from her in a sound that made the vase on the table tremble.

She grabbed the side of the table and kept on laughing as her knees grew weak.

Immediately, the men came running out of the room.

"Houston, honey, you all right?" Kane asked as he took her arm and started to pull her upright. But it was like trying to get a piece of seaweed to stand.

"I covered my red dress because I didn't want anyone to think I wasn't a lady," she cried, "but then I blew out the side of the jail." She put her hands over her stomach as she fell the last few inches to sit on the floor. "Was my hat on straight?" she asked. "Was it on straight the night I challenged the boxer to a muscle showdown?"

"What's she talkin' about?" Kane asked.

Edan was beginning a smile, and it broadened as he said, "You lost it while you were dancing." He started to laugh. "Houston, I took a bottle of whiskey with me that night because I thought I'd be bored watching a ladies' tea party." By the time he finished, he was on the floor with Houston. "And Miss Emily!" he gasped. "I can't walk past her shop with a straight face."

Houston was laughing too hard to speak clearly. "And Leander! I was so careful all those years. I never let you know about Sadie or any of the other things."

Leander, smiling, watched. "You know what she's talking about?" he asked Kane.

Rafe answered. "This sweet little empty-headed lady that looks too delicate to do anything but embroider, regularly handles a four-horse wagon."

"I can drive twelve," she declared and that sent Edan and her into new peals of laughter.

"And she has a right that can flatten boys as big as she is," Kane said with pride, "and she can leave her own weddin' to follow her pigheaded husband when he's made an ass of himself in front of the whole town, and she can pay my mistress to get outta town and she can scream." He stopped when he said the last and began to look embarrassed.

Leander looked down at Houston on the floor, her arms around Edan, both of them weak with laughter, and he turned to Kane, saw the way the man was watching Houston with a mixture of pride and love. "And to think that I called her an ice princess," Lee murmured.

Kane rocked back on his heels, his thumbs in his belt loops and said, "I melted the ice."

Both Lee and Rafe shouted with laughter, as much at Kane's pride as at his words.

Rafe nodded down at Houston. "You better do somethin' with that piece of ice 'fore she melts and runs down into the cracks in the floor. I don't think you wanta lose her."

Kane stooped and lifted Houston into his arms. "I ain't *never* lettin' this lady go."

Houston, still laughing, snuggled against him as he carried her toward the stairs.

"No sir," Kane said, "Ain't nothin' separatin' us. Not other ladies or kids of mine that she don't know about or the hangman. I guess that's why I love her so much. Ain't that right, Houston?"

Houston looked up at him with stars in her eyes.

He put his head toward hers and whispered so the others couldn't hear. "When I get you upstairs, you're gonna explain to me what a 'muscle showdown' is. And don't you start laughin' again. Houston!"

Twin of Fire

Prologue

"Surprise!" eleven people shouted as Blair Chandler entered the dining room of her Uncle Henry's house. She was a pretty young woman, with dark brown hair highlighted with red glints, wide-set blue-green eyes, a straight, aristocratic nose and a small, perfectly shaped mouth.

Blair paused for a moment, blinking back tears of happiness, as she looked at the people in front of her. There were her aunt and uncle, Alan beside them, watching her with love in his eyes, and surrounding him were her fellow medical students—one woman and seven men. As they beamed at her with pleasure, standing behind the table heaped with gifts, she couldn't seem to remember the past few years of struggle to graduate and earn her medical degree.

Aunt Flo, with the grace of a young girl, hurried forward. "Don't just stand there, dear. Everyone is dying to see your gifts."

"This one first," Uncle Henry said, holding out a large package.

Blair thought she knew what was in the box, but she was afraid to hope. When she tore away the wrapping and saw the leather case with the clean, new medical instruments, she sat down heavily in the chair behind her, unable to speak. All she could do was run a finger over the brass plate on the bag. It read: Dr. B. Chandler, M.D.

Alan broke the awkward silence. "Is this the woman who put the rotten eggs in the surgeon instructor's wardrobe? Is this the woman who stood up to the entire Philadelphia Board of Hospitals?" Bending, he put his lips close to her ear. "Is this the woman who placed first in the exams at St. Joseph's and became the first woman to intern on their staff?"

It was a moment before Blair could react. "Me?" she whispered, looking up at him, her mouth open in disbelief.

"You won your internship," Aunt Flo said, her face beaming. "You're to start in July, just as soon as you return from your sister's wedding."

Blair was looking from one person to the other. She had tried her best for St. Joseph's, had even hired a tutor to help her prepare for the tests, but she'd been told that this city hospital, as opposed to a women's clinic, did not accept female physicians.

She turned to her Uncle Henry. "You've had a hand in this, haven't you?"

Henry swelled his big barrel chest with pride. "I merely made a wager that if my niece didn't score higher than anyone ever had on their test, they didn't have to give her a position. In fact, I told them you'd even consider giving up medicine and staying home to take care of Alan. I don't think they could resist the chance to see a lady doctor brought to her senses."

For a moment, Blair felt a little weak. She'd had no idea that so much had been riding on that treacherous three-day test.

"You made it," Alan laughed. "Although I'm not sure I like being the consolation prize." He put his hand on her shoulder. "Congratulations, sweetheart. I know how much you wanted this."

Aunt Flo handed her a letter that gave confirmation that she had indeed been accepted at St. Joseph's Hospital for internship. Blair clutched the paper to her breast and looked at the people around her. Right now, she thought, my entire life is stretching before me—and it is perfect. I have family, friends; I am going to be allowed to train at one of the finest hospitals in the U.S.; and I have Alan, the man I love.

She rubbed her cheek against Alan's hand as she looked at the shiny medical instruments. She was going to realize her lifelong dream of becoming a doctor and marry this kind, loving man.

All that remained was for her to return to Chandler, Colorado, and attend the marriage of her twin sister. Blair was looking forward to seeing her again after all these years, and to the two of them sharing their happiness about the men they'd chosen, about the lives they'd chosen for themselves.

And while she was in Chandler, Alan was going to visit and meet her mother and sister. They would formally announce their engagement then, the wedding to be held after both she and Alan finished their internships.

Blair smiled up at her friends, wanting to share her happiness with everyone. Just another month, and all that she'd worked for would begin.

Chapter 1

Chandler, Colorado
May 1892

Blair Chandler was standing quietly in the ornate front parlor of the Chandler house, amid heavy, dark, carved furniture dressed with little lace doilies. It didn't matter that her mother had remarried many years ago and her new husband, Duncan Gates, had ended up paying for the house, the townspeople still thought of it as having belonged to William Houston Chandler—the man who'd designed it, had it built, and died before he could make the first payment.

Blair kept her eyes downcast, covering their blue-green light that was flashing now in anger. She'd been in her stepfather's house for a week, and all the coarse-looking little man did was yell at her.

To all the world, she looked to be a respectful young woman, standing there in her proper white blouse and dark cord skirt, most of the voluptuousness of her hourglass figure concealed in folds of cloth. And her face held such a quiet, gentle prettiness that no one would have guessed the spirit beneath. But anyone who was around Blair for long knew that she could hold her own in an argument.

Which was why Duncan Gates didn't lose a minute in telling her how to become a "proper" lady. And his idea of what a lady was did not include a young woman who had been trained to be a doctor and was especially good at gunshot wounds. He couldn't appreciate the fact that Blair's sewing ability worked just as well on a perforated intestine as it did on a sampler.

He ranted and raved, as he'd done for a week, and Blair took it until she could stand no more, then she began to give him back some of his own. Unfortunately, that was usually when Blair's mother or sister stepped in and prevented further words from being spoken. It hadn't taken Blair long to learn that Mr. Gates ruled his household, and the women in it, with an iron fist. He was allowed to say what he pleased, but no woman was allowed to thwart him in any way.

"I'm hoping that you will come to your senses and give up this medicine nonsense," Gates was shouting at her now. "A lady belongs in the home and, as Dr. Clark has proven, when a woman uses her brain, her female functions suffer."

Blair gave a great sigh, barely glancing at the worn pamphlet that Mr. Gates held aloft. Dr. Clark's booklet had sold hundreds of thousands of copies and had done an enormous amount of damage to the furthering of education for women. "Dr. Clark did not prove anything," she said tiredly. "He said he'd examined a flat-chested fourteen-year-old female student and, from that one examination, he concluded that if women used their brains, their reproductive systems would suffer. I don't consider that conclusive evidence at all."

Mr. Gates's face began to turn red. "I'll not have language like that in my house. You may think that because you call yourself a doctor you have a right to indecent behavior, but not in my house."

The man was beginning to pass what Blair could tolerate. "Since when is this *your* house? My father—."

At that moment, Blair's sister, Houston, stepped into the room and put herself between them, giving Blair a look of anguish. "Isn't it time for dinner? Perhaps we should go in," Houston said in that cool, reserved voice of hers—a voice that Blair was beginning to hate.

Blair took her place at the big mahogany table and all

through dinner answered Mr. Gates's nasty-tempered questions, but her mind was on her sister.

Blair had looked forward to returning to Chandler, to seeing her sister and mother, to again seeing her childhood playmates. It had been five years since she'd been back and, the last time, she'd been seventeen, preparing to enter medical school and bursting with enthusiasm about her new studies. Perhaps she'd been too wrapped up in her own thoughts to really see the atmosphere in which her mother and sister were living.

But, this time, she'd felt the oppression as soon as she got off the train. Houston had met her, and Blair was sure that she'd never in her life seen a more perfect specimen of a rigid, frigid, unbending woman. She looked like a perfectly formed woman who just happened to be made out of ice.

There were no exuberant huggings at the train station, nor were there exchanges of gossip as they were driven back to the Chandler house. Blair tried to talk to her sister, but she only received that cool, remote stare. Even the name of Leander, Houston's fiancé, brought no warmth to Houston's demeanor.

Half of the short trip was made in silence, Blair clutching her new surgical bag, afraid to let it out of her hands, while they drove through Chandler.

The town had changed a great deal in the five years since Blair had seen it. There was a feeling of newness about the place, that things were building and growing. The western town was so different from cities and towns in the East, where traditions were already established.

The buildings, with their false fronts, a style someone had called Western Victorian, were either new or under construction. Chandler had been merely a pretty piece of land with a magnificent amount of surface coal when William Chandler had arrived. There'd been no railroad, no town center, no name for the few stores that were serving the scattered ranchers in the area. Bill Chandler soon remedied that.

When they pulled into the drive of the Chandler house—or mansion, as the townspeople liked to call it—Blair smiled up at the ornate three-story building with pleasure. Her mother's garden was green and lush and she could smell the roses.

There were steps from the street up to the house now because the hill in the street had been levelled for the new horse-drawn trolley cars, but it hadn't changed much otherwise. She walked across the deep porch that wrapped around the house and went through one of the two front doors.

It didn't take Blair ten minutes inside the Chandler house to see what had taken all the spirit out of Houston.

Standing inside the doorway was a man with a solidness that any self-respecting boulder would envy—and the look on his face matched the shape of him.

Blair had been twelve years old when she'd left Chandler to go to Pennsylvania to live with her aunt and uncle so she could study medicine. And in the intervening years, she'd forgotten just what her stepfather was like. Even as Blair smiled at him and offered him her hand, he started telling her what a bad woman she was and that she wouldn't be allowed to practice her witchcraft doctoring under his roof.

Bewildered, Blair had looked at her mother in disbelief. Opal Gates was thinner, her movements slower than Blair remembered, and before Blair could reply to Mr. Gates's remarks, Opal stepped forward, hugged her daughter briefly, and led her upstairs.

For three days, Blair said very little. She became a bystander who watched. And what she saw frightened her.

The sister she remembered, the one who laughed and played, the one who used to delight in the twin game of trading places with her sister, and causing trouble, was gone— or buried so deep that no one could find her now.

The Houston who used to organize games, the Houston who was always so creative, Houston the actress, was now supplanted by a steel-backed woman who owned more dresses than the rest of the town put together. It seemed that all of Houston's creativity had been rechannelled into the choosing of one stunning dress after another.

On her second day in Chandler, Blair found out from a friend something that gave her hope that her sister's life wasn't completely without purpose. Every Wednesday, Houston dressed as a fat old woman and drove a four-horse wagon loaded with food into the coal camps that surrounded Chandler. This was quite dangerous since the camps were locked and guarded to prevent the infiltration of unionists. If Houston had been caught delivering illegal goods to the miners' wives—goods not bought at the company store—she could be prosecuted; that is, if the guards didn't shoot her first.

But on the third day, Blair gave up the little hope she'd found, because on the third day she re-met Leander Westfield.

When the Westfields had moved to Chandler, the twins had been six-year-olds, and Blair had been confined to her room with a broken arm and so had missed meeting the twelve-year-old Leander and his five-year-old sister. But Blair'd heard all about him from Houston. Disobeying her mother, Houston had slipped into Blair's room to tell her that she'd met the man she was going to marry.

Blair had sat there and listened with wide-eyed attention. Houston had always known what she wanted, always seemed like an adult.

"He's just the sort of man I like. He's quiet, intelligent, very handsome, and he plans to be a doctor. I shall find out what a doctor's wife needs to know."

If possible, Blair's eyes had opened wider. "Has he asked you to marry him?" she'd whispered.

"No," Houston had answered, pulling off her still-clean white gloves—if Blair'd had on those gloves for even thirty minutes, they'd have been soiled black. "Men as young as Leander don't think of marriage, but we women have to. I have made up my mind. I shall marry Leander Westfield as soon as he finishes medical school. This is subject to your approval, of course. I couldn't marry someone you didn't like."

Blair had been honored that Houston had given her this power, and she'd taken her responsibility seriously. She'd been a little disappointed when she'd met Leander and found that he wasn't a man at all but just a tall, slim, good-looking boy who rarely said anything. Blair had always liked the boys who ran and threw rocks and taught her how to whistle with two fingers in her mouth. After a few initial unpleasant encounters with him, she had begun to see what people liked about Lee after Jimmy Summers had fallen out of a tree and broken his leg. None of the other children had known what to do and just stood back and watched Jimmy cry in pain, but Lee had taken over and sent someone for the doctor and someone else for Mrs. Summers. Blair had been quite impressed with him and, as she'd turned toward Houston, Houston had nodded her head once, as if to say that this episode had reaffirmed her decision to become Mrs. Leander Westfield.

Blair was willing to admit that Leander did have a few good qualities about him, but she'd never really liked him. He was too sure of himself, too smug . . . too perfect. Of course, she had never told Houston she didn't like him and, too, she had thought maybe he'd change, become more human as he grew older. He didn't.

A few days earlier, Lee had come to pick up Houston to take her to an afternoon tea and, since Opal was out and Mr. Gates at work, Blair had a chance to talk to Lee while Houston finished dressing—it usually took her an eternity to get fastened into one of those lace and silk concoctions she always wore.

Blair thought that they'd have a common ground for conversation since they were both doctors, and that he'd no longer antagonize her as he had at one time.

"I'll be interning at St. Joseph's Hospital in Philadelphia next month," she began, when they were seated in the front parlor. "It's supposed to be an excellent hospital."

Leander just looked at her with that piercing look of his that he'd had since he was a child. It was impossible to tell what he was thinking.

"I wonder," she continued, "do you think it would be possible for me to make rounds with you at the Chandler Infirmary? Maybe you could give me some pointers that I could use when I start training next month."

Lee took an infuriatingly long time to answer. "I don't think that would be advisable," was all he said at last.

"I thought that between doctors . . ."

"I'm not sure the Board of Directors would consider a

woman a fully qualified doctor. I might be able to get you into the women's hospital."

In school, they'd been warned that they would be treated like this at times. "It may surprise you to know that I plan to specialize in abdominal surgery. Not all female doctors want to become glorified midwives."

Leander arched one brow and looked her up and down in an annoying way that made Blair wonder if all the men in Chandler believed that women were idiots who shouldn't be let out of the house.

Still, she was determined not to judge him. After all, they were adults now and childhood animosities should be put aside. If he was the man Houston wanted, then she should have him—Blair didn't have to live with him.

But days later, after she'd spent time with her sister, she began to question the idea of a marriage between Leander and Houston, because, if anything, Houston was even more rigid when Lee was present. The two of them rarely spoke to each other, nor was there any of the putting of heads together and giggling as there was between most engaged couples. They were certainly not like she and Alan, Blair thought.

And tonight, at dinner, things seemed to come to a head. Blair was tired from the constant harassment of Gates, and she was sick at seeing her sister in this horrible atmosphere of oppression. When Gates kept after Blair, she exploded and told him that he had ruined Houston's life, but he wasn't going to ruin hers, too.

Blair regretted having said that as soon as it was out and she meant to apologize, but just then his royal highness, Leander Westfield, entered and everyone looked up at him as if a demigod had come into the room. Blair had a vision of Houston as a virgin sacrifice to be given to this cold, unfeeling man. And when Leander dared to call Houston his bride, as if he already owned her, Blair could stand no more and ran from the table in tears.

She had no idea how long she had been crying before her mother came to her, held her in her arms and cradled her like a child.

"Tell me what's wrong," Opal whispered, stroking her daughter's hair. "Are you so very homesick? I know Mr. Gates hasn't made your visit pleasant, but he means well. He wants you to have a home and children and he's afraid that, if you're a doctor, no man will have you. You won't have to stay with us much longer, then you can go back to Henry and Flo and start work at the hospital."

Her mother's words made Blair cry harder. "It's not me," she sobbed. "I can leave. I can get out of here. It's Houston. She's so miserable and it's all my fault. I went off and left her to that awful man and now she's so very unhappy."

"Blair," Opal said firmly, "Mr. Gates is my husband and, whatever else he is, I respect him and I cannot allow you to speak that way about him."

Blair raised tear-stained eyes to her mother. "I don't mean him. He's here now, but Houston can get away from him. I mean that Leander."

"Lee?" Opal asked, incredulous. "But Leander is a darling boy. Why, every young lady in Chandler was dying to be asked for even a dance with him, and now Houston is going to marry him. You can't mean you're worried about Houston marrying Lee?"

Blair moved away from her mother. "I have *always* been the only one to see what he's like! Have you ever really looked at Houston when he's around? She freezes! She sits there as if she's afraid of the world and of him in particular. Houston used to laugh and have a good time, but now she doesn't even smile. Oh, mother, right now I wish that I'd never left. If I'd stayed here, I could have prevented Houston from agreeing to marry that man." She ran back to her mother and buried her face in her lap.

Opal smiled down at her daughter, pleased by her caring concern. "No, you shouldn't have stayed here," she said softly. "You would have become like Houston and believed that the only thing a woman can do is to make a home for her husband, and then the world would have lost a fine doctor. Look at me." She lifted Blair's face.

"We can't really know what Houston and Lee are like when

they're alone. No one can know what's in another's personal life. I imagine you have a few secrets of your own."

Immediately, Blair thought of Alan and her cheeks pinked. But now was not the time to talk of him. He'd be here in a few days, and then maybe she'd have someone who agreed with her.

"But I can see the way they are," Blair persisted. "They never talk, never touch, I never see either one of them look at the other with love." Blair stood. "And, the truth is, I never have been able to stand that pompous, upright, shining citizen, Leander Westfield. He's one of those spoiled rich kids who's been handed everything on a silver platter. He has never known disappointment or hardship or struggle or ever heard the word no. When I was in school, the neighboring male medical school allowed the top five women from my female college to attend some classes. The men were quite polite until we women began to score better on the tests than they did— and then we were asked to leave before the end of the term. Leander reminds me of all those smug young men who couldn't stand the competition."

"But, dear, do you really think that's fair? Just because Lee reminds you of others doesn't mean that he's actually like them."

"I've tried several times to talk to him about medicine and all he does is stare at me. What if Houston decides she wants to do something with her life besides match his socks? He'll come down harder on her than Gates ever has on me, and it won't be temporary, either. Houston won't be able to get away."

Opal was beginning to frown. "Have you talked to Houston? I'm sure that she can explain to you why she loves Leander. Perhaps in private they're different. I do think she loves him. And no matter what you say, Leander is a good man."

"So is Duncan Gates," Blair said under her breath. But she was learning that "good" men could kill a woman's soul.

Chapter 2

Blair tried her best to talk to Houston, tried to reason with her, but Houston just got a tight look on her face and said that she loved Leander. Blair wanted to cry in frustration, but as she followed her sister downstairs, she began to concoct a plan. They were going into town today, Blair to pick up a medical journal Alan was sending in care of the Chandler Chronicle office and Houston to do some shopping, and they were going with Lee.

So far, she'd been polite to Leander, but what if she forced him to show his true colors? What if she made him show what an unmoveable, hardheaded tyrant he really was? If she could prove that Lee was as oppressive and narrow-minded as Duncan Gates, then maybe Houston would reconsider spending her life with him.

Of course, Blair could be wrong about Lee. And if she was, if Lee was a considerate, open-minded man—like Alan—then Blair would sing the loudest at Houston's wedding.

As soon as they reached the first floor, there was Leander waiting.

She was mute as she followed the two of them out the door. They never looked at each other and certainly never touched. Houston just walked slowly, probably because her corset was so tight she couldn't breathe, Blair thought, and allowed Lee to help her into his old, black carriage.

"Do you think a woman can be anything besides a wife and mother?" Blair asked Lee, when he started to help her into the carriage. She kept Houston in her corner vision, to make sure her sister heard Lee's answer.

"You don't like children?" he asked, surprised.

"I like children very much," she answered quickly.

"Then I guess it's men you don't like."

"Of course I like men—at least some men. You aren't answering my question. Do you think a woman can be anything besides a wife and mother?"

"I guess that depends on the woman. My sister can make a damson plum conserve that will make your mouth cry with joy," he said, eyes sparkling and, before Blair could reply, gave her a wink, grabbed her by the waist and half tossed her into the carriage.

Blair had to calm her temper before she could speak again. It was quite obvious that he wasn't going to take her seriously. At least he has a sense of humor, she admitted reluctantly.

They drove down the streets of Chandler and Blair tried to keep her mind on the sights. The old stone opera house's doors had been repainted, and there looked to be at least three new hotels in town.

The streets were full of people and wagons: cowboys just in from remote ranches, well-dressed Easterners wanting to capitalize on Chandler's prosperity, a few men from the coal fields, and residents of the town who waved and nodded to the twins and Leander. Shouts of, "Welcome back, Blair-Houston," followed them down the streets.

Blair glanced at her sister and saw that she was looking toward the west, at the most monstrously big house she'd ever seen. It was a white house, perched on a high hill, the top of which had been flattened by one Mr. Kane Taggert in order to build the oversized hulk that loomed over the entire town.

Blair knew that she couldn't be fair about the house, because for years all her mother and Houston had written her about was that house. They had ignored births, deaths, marriages, accidents—nothing that went on in Chandler was considered important if it didn't relate to that house.

And when it had been completed, and the owner of the house had invited no one to see the inside of it, the despair in the letters Blair'd received was almost humorous.

"The whole town still trying to get inside the place?" Blair asked, as she tried to reorganize her thoughts. If Leander never took her questions seriously, never gave her a straight answer, how was she going to prove anything to Houston?

Houston was talking about that monstrous house in an odd, dreamy voice, rather as if she thought of it as a fairy castle, a place where dreams came true.

"I'm not so sure all the things people say about him are rumors," Leander was saying, referring to Houston's mention of Taggert. "Jacob Fenton said—."

"Fenton!" Blair exploded. "Fenton is a conniving, thieving man who uses entire lives of people just so he can get what he wants." Fenton owned most of the coal mines around Chandler and kept the people locked inside the camps as if they were prisoners.

"I don't think you can blame Fenton alone," Lee said. "He has stockholders; he has contracts to fulfill. There are others involved."

Blair couldn't believe what she was hearing and, as they paused to let a horse-drawn trolley pass, she glanced at Houston and was glad she was hearing this. Leander was defending the coal barons, and Blair knew how deeply Houston cared about the miners.

"You've never had to work in a coal mine," Blair said. "You have no idea what it means to struggle daily just to live."

"And I take it you do."

"More than you do," she spat. "You got to study medicine at Harvard. Harvard doesn't allow women."

"So, we're back to that," he said tiredly. "Tell me, does every male doctor get blamed for a few, or have you singled me out particularly?"

"You're the only one marrying my sister."

He turned to look at her, eyebrows raised in surprise. "I had no idea you were jealous. Cheer up, Blair, you'll eventually be able to find your own man."

Blair clenched her fists at her sides, looked straight ahead, and tried to remember her original purpose in even speaking to this man who had such an overinflated sense of his own worth. She hoped Houston appreciated what she was doing for her!

Blair took a deep breath. "What do you think of women as doctors?"

"I like women."

"Ah ha! You like women as long as they're in their place and not in your hospital."

"I believe you said that, not me."

"You said that I wasn't a 'real' doctor and couldn't make rounds with you."

"I said that I thought the Hospital Board wouldn't accept you. You get their permission and I'll show you all the bloody dressings you want to see."

"Isn't your father on the board?"

"I don't control him any more now than I did when I was five—maybe less so."

"I'm sure he's just like you and doesn't believe that women should be doctors."

"As far as I remember, I haven't made a statement as to my personal beliefs concerning women in medicine."

Blair felt as if she were about to scream. "You're talking in circles. What *do* you think about women in medicine?"

"I think that would depend on my patient. If I had a patient who said he'd rather die than be treated by a woman, I wouldn't let a female doctor near the man. But if I had a patient who begged me to find a lady physician, I guess I'd scour the earth if I had to."

Blair could think of nothing else to say. So far, Leander had managed to turn around every word she'd said.

"That's Houston's dream house," Leander said when the trolley car had passed, making an obvious attempt to change the subject. "If Houston didn't have me, I think she'd have joined the line of women fighting for Taggert and that house of his."

"I *would* like to see the inside," Houston said in a faraway voice, then asked Lee to let her off at Wilson's Mercantile.

When Houston had gone, Blair felt no need to even speak to Leander, and he didn't seem to feel that it was necessary to make conversation, either. It was on the tip of her tongue to ask him more questions about the hospital, but she didn't want more of his clever little retorts.

He let her out at the Chandler Chronicle office and she stopped to talk to some of the people she'd known all her life, all of whom called her Blair-Houston because they couldn't tell the twins apart. She hadn't heard the name in years and wondered how Houston felt about always being a part of a whole, never quite her own person.

She picked up her new medical journal at the newspaper office and started down Third Street on the wide wooden boardwalk toward Farrell's Hardware, where she was to meet Houston and Leander.

Lee was there alone, leaning against the railing, the carriage drawn by that big black and white spotted horse of his nearby. There was no sign of Houston, and Blair thought of waiting in the shoe shop across the street until her sister showed up. But Lee saw her and shouted loud enough for the entire town to hear, "Planning to turn tail and run?"

Blair straightened her spine, crossed the dusty street and went to meet him.

He was grinning at her in a smirking way that made her wish she were a man and could challenge him to a duel.

"I don't think that what you're thinking is very ladylike. What would Mr. Gates say?"

"Nothing that he hasn't already said to me, I'm sure."

Lee's expression changed instantly. "Houston told me he was being pretty rough on you. If there's anything that I can do to help, let me know."

For a moment, Blair was bewildered, both at his change in attitude and at his offer of help. She thought he despised her. Before she could speak, Houston appeared, her face flushed and distracted looking.

"I'm glad you showed up now because you just saved your sister from a fate worse than death. She was about to have to say something pleasant to me."

"I beg your pardon," Houston said.

Lee took her elbow and escorted her to the carriage. "I said that you'd better get home now so you can start getting ready for the governor's reception tonight."

He helped Houston into the carriage, then reached for Blair.

With a glance at her sister, Blair knew that she had to try again to show her what Leander was really like.

"No doubt you're a believer in Dr. Clark's theory concerning the overuse of a woman's brain, too," she said loudly.

Leander, his hands on her waist, gave her a blank look for a moment, then began to smile. After a lusty look up and down, he said, "Blair, I don't think you have anything to worry about. It looks to me like all your brains are going to the right places."

Blair sat in the carriage, listening to Leander's chuckling, and thought that surely no other sister had endured what she was going through for hers.

As they were leaving town, two big, beefy men, driving a wagon that was so dilapidated that no respectable farmer would have had it, yelled at Leander to halt. The dark man, a fearsome, bearded, dirty-looking brute, addressed Houston in an aggressive way that Blair had never seen her allow in a man before. If there was one thing that Houston knew how to do, it was to stop men who were too forward.

Houston nodded politely to him and he bellowed at the horses and left in a cloud of dust.

"What in the world was that about?" Leander asked. "I didn't know you knew Taggert."

Before Houston could answer, Blair said, "*That* was the man who built that house? No wonder he doesn't ask anyone to it. He knows they'd turn him down. By the way, how could he tell us apart?"

"Our clothes," Houston answered quickly. "I saw him in the mercantile store."

"As for no one accepting his invitation," Lee said, "I think that Houston might risk plague or anything else for that matter to see that house."

Blair leaned forward, across her sister. "Did you receive letters about that house?"

"If I could sell the words by the pound, I'd be a millionaire."

"Like him," Blair answered, looking up at the house that dominated the west end of town. "He can keep his millions, and he can keep his dinosaur of a house."

"I think we've agreed again," Lee said, acting surprised. "Do you think this'll become a habit?"

"I doubt it," Blair snapped, but her heart wasn't in the remark. Maybe she'd been wrong about him.

But twenty minutes later, she was just as worried about her sister's future as ever. She'd left Lee and Houston in her mother's garden alone, then remembered that her journal was still in Lee's buggy. Hurrying downstairs to catch Lee before he left, she was a witness to a little drama between the couple.

Leander, reaching behind Houston's head to shoo a bee away, made her stiffen. Even from where Blair stood, she could see the way her sister drew away from being touched by Lee.

"You don't have to worry," he said in a deadly voice. "I won't touch you."

"It's just until after we're married," she whispered, but Lee didn't reply before he stormed past Blair and drove away very fast in the carriage.

Leander stormed into his father's house and slammed the door behind him, rattling the stained glass. He took the stairs two at a time and at the landing turned left and headed for his room, the room that he was to give up as soon as he married Houston and moved into the house he'd bought for her.

He nearly ran over his father, but didn't apologize or slow down.

Reed Westfield, glancing up at his son as he passed, saw the look of anger on his face and followed him to his room. Leander was already throwing clothes into a valise when Reed arrived.

Reed stood in the doorway for a moment and watched his son. Even though they looked nothing alike, Reed being short, stocky, and having a face with all the delicacy of a bulldog, they had much the same temperament. It took a great deal to rouse the Westfield ire.

"Is it an emergency patient that needs your attention?" Reed asked, as he watched his son throw clothes at the case on the bed, and, in his rage, miss half the time.

"No, it's women," Lee managed to say through clenched teeth.

Reed tried to hide a smile, coughed to cover it. In his legal practice, he'd learned to hide his own reaction to whatever his clients said. "Have a spat with Houston?"

Leander turned to his father with a face full of fury. "I've *never* had a spat or a fight or an argument or any disagreement whatsoever with Houston. Houston is utterly, totally perfect, without flaw."

"Ah, then it's that sister of hers. Someone mentioned that she was badgering you today. You won't have to live with your sister-in-law, you know."

Lee paused in his packing. "Blair? What's she got to do with anything? She's the most enjoyment I've had with a woman since I got engaged. It's Houston who's driving me to drink. Or, more correctly, she's the one forcing me to leave Chandler."

"Hold on just a minute," Reed said, taking his son's wrist. "Before you jump on a train and leave all your patients to die, why don't you sit down and talk to me and tell me what's made you so mad?"

Lee sat in a chair as if he weighed a ton, and it was several minutes before he could speak. "Do you remember why I asked Houston to marry me in the first place? Right now, I can't seem to remember a single reason that made me do it."

Reed took a seat across from his son. "Let me see—if I remember correctly, it was pure, clean, old-fashioned lust. When you returned from Vienna and the last of your medical studies, you joined the legion of men, young and old, following the luscious Miss Houston Chandler around town, begging her to attend whatever you could think of, anything, just so you could be near her. I believe I remember your rhapsodizing about her beauty and telling me how every man in Chandler had asked her to marry him. And I also remember the night you asked her yourself and she accepted you. I think you walked around in a daze for a week."

He paused for a moment. "Does that answer your question? Have you decided now that you *aren't* lusting after the lovely Miss Houston?"

Leander gave his father a serious look. "I've decided now that that shape of hers, that walk of hers that has grown men fainting in her wake, is all show. The woman is a block of ice. She is completely frigid, without any emotion at all. I cannot marry someone like her and spend the rest of my life trying to live with a woman who has no feelings at all."

"Is that all that's wrong?" Reed asked, obviously relieved. "Good women are supposed to be like that. You wait, after you're married, she'll warm up. Your mother was very cool to me before we were married. She broke her parasol over my head one evening when I got too fresh. But later, after we were married . . . well, things got better—much better. You take the word of someone who's more experienced in these matters. Houston is a good girl and she's had to live with that bigot Gates all these years. Of course she's nervous and frightened."

Leander listened to his father's words carefully. He'd never planned to spend his life in Chandler. Instead, he'd planned to intern in a big city, work on the staff of a big hospital and eventually have his own practice and make a lot of money. He had lasted but six months before he decided to come home where he was needed, where he would have more important cases than a rich woman's hysteria.

All the time he'd been away from Chandler, Houston had written him letters, gossipy letters about what went on in the town and later about her finishing school. He'd always looked forward to the letters and looked forward to once again seeing the little girl who'd written them.

The night he'd returned home, his father threw a party of welcome and the "little girl" walked into the room. Houston had grown into a woman with a figure that made Lee's palms sweat, and as he was gaping, an old friend had punched him on the arm.

"It's no use trying. There isn't a single man in town who hasn't asked for her hand in marriage—or for anything else she'll part with—but she'll have none of us. I think she's waiting for a prince or a president."

Lee had grinned smugly. "Maybe you boys don't know how to ask. I learned a few tricks while I was in Paris."

And so he had become a contestant in the local race to see who could get Miss Chandler to marry him. He still didn't understand what had happened. He had taken her out to a few parties, and at about the third one, he'd asked her to marry him, saying something to the effect of, "I don't imagine you'd want to marry me, would you?" He had expected her to refuse; then he could laugh with the men at his club, saying that he'd tried, too, but alas, he also had failed.

He had been shocked when Houston had accepted his proposal immediately and asked if the twentieth of May would be a date that suited him, all in the same breath. The next morning, he had seen his picture in the paper as being engaged to Houston, and the article further stated that the happy couple was choosing her ring that morning. After that, he'd never had a moment to think about what he'd done when he'd proposed. If he wasn't at the hospital, he was at a tailor's shop or agreeing with Houston about what color the draperies should be in the house he'd suddenly found himself buying.

And now, just weeks before the wedding, he was having second thoughts. Every time he touched Houston, she moved away from him as if he were repulsive. Of course he knew Duncan Gates, knew how the man never missed an opportunity to put a woman in her "place." His father had written a few years ago that Gates had tried to bar women from the new ice-cream parlor that had opened in town. His reasoning was that it would encourage women to be lazy, to gossip, and to flirt. All of which, Reed had written, had proven true—and the men were delighted.

Leander took a long, thin cigar from his pocket and lit it. "I've not had much experience with 'good' girls. Before you married Mother, did you worry that she might not change?"

"Worried about it night and day. I even told my father that I refused to marry her, that I wouldn't spend my life with a woman made of stone."

"But you changed your mind. Why?"

Reed made an apologetic little smile. "Well, I . . . I mean I . . ." He turned his head away, in what looked to be embarrassment. "If she were here today, I think she'd want me to tell you. The truth is, son, I seduced her. I gave her too much champagne and sweet-talked her for hours and seduced her."

He turned back abruptly. "But I'm not advising you to do that. I'm advising you to learn from what I did. You can get into an awful lot of trouble that way. To this day, I think you came about two weeks earlier than was proper."

Leander was studying the tip of his cigar. "I like your advice and I think I'll take it."

"I'm not sure I should have told you this. Houston is a lovely girl and . . ." He stopped and studied his son for a moment. "I trust your judgment. You do what you think is best. Will you be here for dinner?"

"No," Lee said softly, as if in deep thought. "I'm taking Houston to the governor's reception tonight."

Reed started to say something but closed his mouth and left the room. He might have reconsidered saying what he thought if he'd known that later his son called a saloon to order four bottles of French champagne to be sent to his new house, then asked the housekeeper to prepare a dinner that began with oysters and ended with chocolate.

Chapter 3

Blair sat in her room on the top floor of the Chandler house and tried to concentrate on an article about peritonitis, but, instead, her eyes kept moving to the window where she could see her sister cutting roses in the garden below. Blair could see that Houston was humming, smelling the roses and, in general, enjoying herself.

For the life of her, Blair couldn't understand Houston. She'd just had an argument with her fiancé, he'd stormed away in anger, yet Houston wasn't in the least upset.

And then there was that episode in town with that man Taggert. Blair had never seen Houston so responsive to a man to whom she hadn't been formally introduced. Houston was a stickler for rules and etiquette, yet she'd greeted that ill-clad, hairy man as if they were old friends.

Blair put her journal down and went to the garden.

"All right," Blair said as soon as she reached her sister. "I want to know what's going on."

"I have no idea what you're talking about." Houston looked as innocent as a baby.

"Kane Taggert," Blair answered, trying to read her sister's face.

"I saw him in Wilson's Mercantile and later he said good morning to us."

Blair studied Houston and saw that there was an unnatural flush in her cheeks, as if she were very excited about something. "You're not telling me everything."

"I probably shouldn't have involved myself, but Mr. Taggert looked as if he were getting angry and I wanted to prevent a quarrel. Unfortunately, it was at Mary Alice's expense." Houston then told a story about Mary Alice Pendergast's baiting of Taggert, of referring to him as a coal miner, of turning her nose up at him. And Houston had taken Taggert's side.

Blair was stunned that Houston would involve herself in something that wasn't any of her business, but worse, Blair didn't like the look of Taggert. He looked capable of doing anything to anybody. And, too, she'd heard many references to the man and his cronies, men like Vanderbilt, Jay Gould, Rockefeller. "I don't like your getting mixed up with him."

"You sound like Leander."

"For once, he's right!" Blair snapped.

"Perhaps we should mark this day in the family Bible. Blair, after tonight, I swear I'll never even mention Mr. Taggert's name."

"Tonight?" Blair had a feeling that what she should do right now was run, not walk, to the nearest place of safety. When they were children, Houston had been able to involve her in several projects with unhappy endings—all of which Blair had been blamed for. No one could believe that sweet, demure Houston was capable of disobedience.

"Look at this. A messenger brought it. He's invited me to dinner at his house." Houston pulled a note from inside her sleeve and handed it to Blair.

"So? You're supposed to go somewhere with Leander tonight, aren't you?"

"Blair, you don't seem to realize what a stir that house has caused in this town. *Everyone* has tried to get an invitation to see the inside of it. People have come from all over the state to see it, but no one has ever been invited in. Once, it was even put to Mr. Taggert that an English duke who was passing through should be allowed to stay in the house, but Mr. Taggert wouldn't even listen to the committee. And now *I've* been invited."

"But you have to go somewhere else," Blair persisted. "The governor will be there. Surely he's more important than the inside of any old house."

Houston got an odd look on her face, the same one she'd had that morning when she'd gazed up at that hulking house. "You couldn't understand what it was like. Year after year we watched the train unload its goods. Mr. Gates said the owner didn't build a spur line to the house site because he wanted everyone to see everything going all the way through town. There were crates of goods from all over the world. Oh, Blair, I know they must have been filled with furniture. And tapestries! Tapestries from Brussels."

"Houston, you cannot be in two places at once. You promised to go to the reception and you must go," she said flatly, hoping to end the matter. Of the two men, Leander was definitely the lesser evil.

"When we were children, we could be in two places at once," Houston said, as if it were the simplest statement in the world.

Blair was sure her breath stopped. "You want us to trade places? You want *me* to spend an evening with Leander, pretending I like him, while you go see some lecherous man's house?"

"What do you know about Kane to call him lecherous?"

"Kane, is it? I thought you didn't know him?"

"Don't change the subject. Blair, please trade places with me. Just for one night. I'd go another night but I'm afraid Mr. Gates would forbid it, and I'm not sure Leander would want me to go either, and I'll never get another opportunity like this. Just one last fling before I get married."

"You make marriage sound like death. Besides, Leander would know I wasn't you in a minute."

"Not if you behaved yourself. You know that we're both good actresses. Look at how I pretend to be an old woman every Wednesday. All you have to do is be quiet and not start an argument with Lee, and refrain from talking about medicine and walk like a lady instead of looking like you're running to a fire."

Blair's mind was reeling. Ever since she'd returned to Chandler she had been frantically worried about her sister, afraid that all her spirit had been suppressed. This was the first sign of life Houston'd shown in a week. It was like when they were children, getting into scrapes, pretending to be each other, and laughing hilariously together later.

But what about Leander? All he had to do was start teasing Blair about being a lady doctor and . . .

Her head came up. Leander never teased Houston, and for one night she'd *be* Houston. And, too, this would be her chance to reassure herself that Leander really was the wonderful man both Opal and Houston said he was. She would be able to satisfy herself that, when they were alone, Lee and Houston were right for each other, that they were in love.

"Please, please, Blair. I hardly ever ask you for anything."

"Except to spend weeks in the house of our stepfather whom you know I detest. To spend weeks in the company of that self-congratulating man I think you intend to marry. To—," Blair said, but she was smiling. She could return to Pennsylvania in peace if she were sure her sister was going to be happy.

"Oh, Blair, please. I really do want to see this house."

"It's just his house you're interested in, not Taggert?"

"For Heaven's sake! I've been to hundreds of dinner parties and I haven't yet been swept off my feet by the host. Besides, there'll be other people there."

"After the wedding, would you mind if I told Leander he spent an evening with me? Just to see the look on his face would be worth everything."

"Of course you may. Lee has a very good sense of humor, and I'm sure he'll enjoy the joke."

"I somehow doubt that, but at least I'll enjoy it."

"Let's go get ready. I want to wear something befitting that house, and you'll get to wear the blue satin Worth gown."

"I should wear my knickerbockers, but that would give it away, wouldn't it?"

Blair followed Houston into the house, pleased by the entire arrangement. It wouldn't be easy to impersonate Houston and that slow, lazy walk of hers, but Blair considered it a challenge and looked forward to it.

Blair started having second thoughts about the whole affair when she felt Houston tightening the corset strings. Houston didn't have any qualms about enduring a little pain for the sake of beauty, but Blair kept thinking about how her internal organs were being reorganized by the whalebone instrument of torture. But when she put the dress on and saw herself with the exaggerated hourglass figure like Houston's, she wasn't displeased at all.

Houston watched her sister in the mirror. "Now you look like a woman." She glanced down at the skirt and blouse she wore, feeling the lightly tied corset underneath. "And I feel as light as a feather."

They paused for a moment and studied each other in the mirror. "No one will know one of us from the other," Houston said.

"Not until we speak," Blair answered, turning away.

"You don't have any problems. At least as me, you can get away with not speaking."

"And does that mean that I talk too much?" Blair shot back at her.

"It means that if Blair were quiet, we'd never get out of the house because Mother'd call a doctor."

"Leander?" Blair asked, and they both laughed.

Later, as they were both dressed and ready to go out for the evening, Blair supposedly to spend the evening with her friend, Tia Mankin, she got to see something that few people ever saw: she saw herself as others saw her.

At first, she was so busy concentrating on trying to be Houston, imitating her walk, the way she entered a room, the way she looked at people as if from far away, that she didn't see the way Houston was mimicking her.

Mr. Gates walked into the room and said very politely that both young women looked lovely. Houston, as Blair, leaned her head back and used her superior height to look down at the man. "I am a doctor and being a doctor is more important than being pretty. I want more out of life than just being a wife and mother."

Blair opened her mouth to protest that she never sounded like that and that she'd never attack a man who hadn't attacked first, but as she looked at the faces around her, she saw that no one thought what Houston had said was out of character.

She almost felt sorry for Mr. Gates when the little man's face blew up like a fish's and his skin turned red. Before she knew what she was doing, she stepped between her sister and the angry man. "It's such a nice night," she said loudly. "Blair, why don't you and I sit in the garden until Leander comes?"

When Houston turned around, she had a look of anger and hostility on her face such as Blair had never seen before. Do I really look like that? she wondered. Do I really start most of the arguments with Mr. Gates?

She wanted to ask Houston those questions, but before they could get outside, Leander arrived to pick them up.

Blair stood back and watched Houston pretending to be her and, almost immediately, she wanted to protect him. He was courteous, smiling, polite and oh, so very good-looking. She'd never noticed before that Leander was enough to stop a heart or two. He was a serious-looking man with green eyes, a long thin nose and full lips. Black hair, overly long, scraped the collar of his coat. But what Blair was interested in wasn't his surface good looks, but the expression in his eyes. It was as if those eyes hid secrets that he told no one.

"Houston?" he asked, bringing her back to reality. "Are you all right?"

"Of course," she said briskly, trying to imitate her sister's coolness.

As Leander put his hands on her waist and lifted her into the carriage, she smiled at him and he smiled back, quickly, briefly, but it warmed her and she was glad to have this time with him.

They were no more than in the carriage when Houston started on Leander.

"How do you keep peritonitis from spreading?" she asked in a hostile voice that made Blair look at her in wonder. What was she so angry about? And where had she learned about peritonitis?

"Sew both layers of the intestine together and pray," Lee said quite sensibly, and correctly.

"Have you heard of asepsis here in Chandler yet?"

With her breath drawn in, Blair looked up at Lee to see how he'd take this question. Blair thought it was downright insulting, and she wouldn't blame Lee if he gave Houston a piece of his mind. But Lee only glanced at Blair, winked quickly, and told Houston that the doctors in Chandler did indeed wash their hands before surgery.

Blair couldn't help smiling up at him, and she felt that the two of them were in this together. Houston kept on baiting Lee as Blair leaned back in the seat and watched the stars, not bothering to listen to her sister's ranting.

When at last they came to Tia's house, she was very glad. And when Houston was gone and Blair and Lee were alone, she breathed a deep sigh.

"It's rather like the aftermath of a bad rainstorm," she said, looking up at Lee and half dreading his comments about her other self.

"She doesn't mean anything. All doctors are like that when they leave medical school. You're very aware of the responsibility of your profession."

"And it changes later?"

"It does, but I'm not sure how to explain it. I guess you come to learn your limitations and aren't so sure that you can save the world single-handedly."

Blair relaxed against the back of the carriage and thought

how kind of him it was that he didn't say anything bad about Houston's attacking him. And he'd called her a doctor.

It felt quite natural when she slipped her arm through his and didn't move to the other side of the buggy now that her sister was gone. She didn't notice the odd way that Leander looked at her, but Blair was quite pleased with the evening.

Chapter 4

Chandler, Colorado, was at the base of the Rocky Mountains with an altitude of seven thousand feet and, as a result, the air was always thin, clear and cool. The summers were pleasant during the day, and when the sun went down, the mountain air made shawls necessary.

Blair sat next to Lee and took deep breaths, inhaling the crisp fragrance of the mountains. She hadn't realized she'd missed it as much as she had.

They had not driven half a mile when a man rode up in a flurry of dust, his horse panting, and yelled at Leander. "Westfield! Somebody needs help. There's a woman down on River Street that just tried to kill herself."

Blair had never seen the man before, and she didn't think she wanted to again. He looked like a cartoon of a gambler, with his coal black hair and his little mustache and, worse, the way he smirked as he stared at her.

He took off his straight-brimmed hat and tipped it to her. "I could understand that maybe you're too busy to come, Doc."

Blair glanced at Lee and saw that he was hesitating, and she knew that it as on her account. "I'll go with you, Lee. Maybe I can be of some help."

The man, a gambler or not, said, "River Street ain't no place for a lady. Maybe I should watch out for her while you go to the suicide."

That settled Lee as nothing else had. He cracked the whip over the horse's head and yelled, "Hang on," to Blair all in one breath.

Blair slammed against the back of the carriage seat and grabbed the roof support as Lee went flying. She closed her eyes in terror twice, as Lee narrowly missed three other carriages. The people saw him coming and started getting out of his way long before he reached them. She heard several shouts of encouragement and guessed that the sight of Lee tearing through the streets was a familiar one.

He halted the horse in the northeast corner of town, across the Tijeras River and between two railroad tracks—a place Blair had never seen or been curious about. In one motion, he tied the horse, grabbed his bag, leaped to the ground, and ordered Blair to remain in the buggy.

After a quick glance at the leering face of the gambler, she followed Lee into the house with the red lights on the outside. Lee went up the stairs as if he knew where he was going, but Blair couldn't help looking around.

Everything seemed to be red. The walls were red, the carpets were red, the furniture was upholstered in red with red fringe. And what wasn't red was made of very dark wood.

At the head of the stairs, she saw a tight group of women in various stages of undress and, just as she reached them, they began backing away from the door.

"I need help, I told you," Blair heard Lee shouting as she pushed her way through the crowd.

Lee glanced up at her. "I told you to stay in the car." On the bed in front of him was a pale, thin young woman, actually little more than a girl, writhing in pain that Blair guessed was from swallowing an alcohol-based disinfectant.

"Carbolic?" Blair asked, and as she saw Lee removing a stomach pump from his bag, she knew what had to be done.

Blair didn't lose a moment going to work. With a voice of authority, she ordered three women, one wearing only her corset and a thin black wrapper, to hold the girl's arms and legs, and another one to fetch towels. When a tall, well-dressed woman who looked as though she knew how to give orders came into the room, Blair sent her after two raincoats, and when the coats were there, Blair watched Lee until he had a free hand, then she slipped it into the sleeve of one oiled, waterproof garment. She then put the other raincoat on over her sister's dress.

Lee talked to the girl, soothing her even as he pushed the pump down her throat, and when the carbolic came up, it came with all the contents of her stomach, splattering everyone in the room.

Gagging, sick, weak, covered in filth, the girl clung to Lee, and he held her, while Blair quietly organized the cleaning.

"Nothing is that bad," Lee said, holding the girl as she began to cry. "Here, I want you to drink this," he said, giving her water and two tablets.

He didn't release her until she began to relax and at last fall asleep. Gently, he laid her on the bed and looked up at the tall woman Blair had sent after the raincoats. "Clean her up and send her to the Infirmary tomorrow. I want to talk to her."

The woman nodded silently, looking up at Lee with big, worshipful eyes. She turned to Blair. "I hope you appreciate this man, honey, ain't many like him. He—." The woman stopped at a look from Lee.

"We have to go." With surprise, he glanced down at the raincoat he wore and then looked across the patient's bed at Blair.

"I learned it from my doctor-sister," she said in answer to his silent question and suddenly worried about how Lee would react to her help with the girl.

But as Lee packed his instruments, took her arm and led her outside, he made no mention of her expertise. The people around them mumbled thanks and looked at both Lee and Blair with dull eyes, and Blair thought the young women were thinking that any one of them could have been the girl on that bed.

"Do you come here often?" she asked Lee on the way down the stairs.

"About once a week a doctor is here for one reason or another. I guess I've been here as often as any of them."

At the carriage, Lee paused in front of Blair and she was sure he'd say that he knew who she was. "I really appreciated your going with me on the case and that I didn't have to leave you somewhere first. It meant more to me than you'll know."

She gave a smile of relief. "You were very good with the woman, fast, as careful as possible."

With a slight smile, he touched the hair at her temple. "You're sounding like Blair again, but whatever the reason, I thank you for the compliment."

When Blair was in medical school, she had had a teacher who warned them that the curse of young female doctors was that they tended to fall in love with whichever man was the best surgeon. The instructor had said that all a new female intern had to do was see a doctor remove an ovarian cyst that was difficult, and she'd soon be swooning over him.

At this moment, Blair thought that Lee was one of the best-looking men she'd ever seen. He'd handled the technical side of the case quite well, but, more, his compassion was such as she'd never seen matched. When he moved toward her to kiss her, she realized that she wanted him to kiss her as herself, as Blair, rather than as Houston.

She turned her face away.

Leander dropped his hand from her face instantly, and the anger in his eyes was frightening. He turned away, every movement showing his anger.

Blair felt a moment of panic. Right now, she was Houston and not Blair, and of course she would kiss the man she loved.

Blair caught his arm. He stopped and looked at her, his eyes blazing with fury, and it took a great deal of courage not to step back. Boldly, she put her arms around his neck and touched her lips to his.

He stood there as if he were made of stone, not moving, not responding to her advances.

For a moment, it occurred to Blair that Dr. Leander Westfield was certainly a spoiled man if he reacted so severely to his fiancée's refusing him a single kiss. As he continued to show no reaction, she thought of this as a challenge, like getting through the first year of medical school.

She stood on tiptoe and began to show a little passion to this unyielding man.

She wasn't prepared for his reaction—nothing that had ever

happened to her in her lifetime had prepared her for his reaction.

He caught her head in his hand, twisted her head around and applied his mouth to hers with a passion that made her breath disappear. And Blair reacted in kind. She pressed her body against his and only clung harder when he pushed his knee between her legs and thrust his tongue into her mouth.

"Excuse me," came a voice with laughter in it, and it was several moments before Lee pulled away.

Blair stood there with her eyes closed and was glad of the support of the carriage behind her or she probably would have fallen. She was vaguely aware that it was the dreadful gambler-man who was there, and that he was smirking at them even while he spoke to Lee, but she didn't really care. Perhaps Houston's reputation was ruined forever, but the last thing Blair was thinking about was her sister.

"Ready?" she heard Lee saying softly in her ear when the man was gone. She could feel the warmth of his body so near hers.

"For what?" she murmured, then opened her eyes.

"Houston, we don't have to go to the reception," Lee said.

Blair stood up straighter and remembered who she was and where she was and that she was with her sister's fiancé. "Yes, of course we do," she said shyly, not meeting his eyes and ignoring the fact that his hands lingered much too long on her waist as he helped her into the carriage.

Once seated, she kept her eyes on the road ahead. So *this* is why Houston loves him, she thought. And to think that she'd worried that they were too cool to each other in private.

She glanced at him once as he turned to her, and his eyes were alive, sparkling—and hungry.

She gave him a weak smile and told herself to think of Alan. Alan. Alan!

Blair managed to get herself under control somewhat, but, still, her senses were reeling, so that she wasn't aware that Lee had driven them across the river and into the deep recesses of Fenton Park. Midnight Lane spread before them as Lee halted the horse next to the park bandstand and moved to help her out of the carriage.

"Why are we stopping?"

"I have the smell of carbolic in my nose and I thought the fresh air would help get rid of it."

He smiled at her as he lifted her from the carriage, and she had to turn away from him or she knew she'd be in his arms again. "You really were very good with the girl tonight."

"You said that," he answered, releasing her as he took a cigar from his pocket and lit it. "Why did you go with me tonight? You never have before."

Blair caught her breath. She had to think fast. "I guess I was worried about this afternoon. You seemed awfully angry," she said, hoping it sounded plausible.

He cocked his head to one side and looked at her through a cloud of smoke and moonlight. "You've never seemed to worry about *that*, either."

What in the world had she stepped into? Blair wondered. And why hadn't Houston warned her about whatever Lee was talking about?

"Of course I worry, Lee," she said, turning away, her hand on the bandstand. "I always worry when you're upset with me. I won't let it happen again."

He was silent for so long that she turned to look at him. He was watching her with the same hungry eyes she'd seen before.

"Lee, you're making me blush. Shouldn't we go to the reception?" Blast Houston! she thought. Once again she'd allowed her sister to talk her into doing something that was going to get her, Blair, into trouble. She hoped seeing that oversized house was worth this.

Slowly, Lee's hand reached out to touch her arm. She backed away and came up against the wooden bandstand.

He threw his cigar down and advanced a step toward her.

Blair gave him a little smile, grabbed her skirts and ran up the stairs to the center of the bandstand. "We used to have the loveliest concerts here," she said, backing up, as she watched him moving toward her. "I remember wearing pink and white and . . ."

Her voice trailed off as he stood before her and she could

back no further. As she looked up at him, feeling the warmth of his body near hers, he held out his arms to her and she went to him.

There was no music except the sounds of the night, but Blair was sure she heard violins as Lee waltzed her about the bandstand. Closing her eyes, her skirts over her arm, she followed him as if in a trance, giving no thought to any moment but this one. And when he pulled her close and kept waltzing, his legs pressed against her own, she gave herself over to feelings such as she'd never experienced before.

She wasn't aware of time passing as he held her, nor did she remember that she was supposed to be her sister or that this man who held her so intimately was a stranger. She was only aware of the present, there was no past, no future.

When he began to kiss her neck, her cheek, her temple, she leaned into him, slipped her arms around his neck and kept dancing slowly, seductively.

"You said you could be different," he whispered, but Blair didn't hear any words. "Come, kiss me once more before we have to leave."

Only some of the words reached her brain. She didn't want to leave, wanted this moment never to end, and when he kissed her again, it weakened her more than before, and Lee had to hold her against him or her knees would have given way.

He pulled back and for a moment she couldn't move, her eyes closed, her head back.

When she did look at him, he was grinning—an expression of delight on his face such as she'd never seen before. She smiled, too.

"Come on, sweetheart," he laughed, sweeping her into his arms. "I want to show you to the world."

Once Lee'd put her in the carriage, Blair's mind began to work again. This evening was not going as she'd planned. She'd wanted to find out if her sister was marrying the right man and, instead of making a scientific study, every time Leander touched her, her knees turned to jelly.

"This is utterly ridiculous."

"What is?" Lee asked from beside her in the carriage.

"That . . . that I should have acquired this raging headache all of a sudden. I think I ought to go home."

"Here, let me look."

"No," Blair said, leaning away from him.

His long, strong fingers took hold of her chin as he moved his face closer to hers. "I don't see any signs of pain," he whispered, "except maybe this little vein right here," he said, kissing her forehead at her hairline. "Does that help any?"

"Please," she whispered, trying to turn away. "Please don't."

After a slow, lingering caress, he took the reins to the horse and drove them out of the park.

Blair put her hand to her breast and her pounding heart. At least they would be in a public place, she thought, and then he'd take her home, and she'd once again be able to be herself—and keep this dangerous man in his place, which was in her sister's arms, not hers.

Later, someone told Blair that there had indeed been a reception for the governor, and that she had attended and met him, and had managed to speak in a coherent manner, but she couldn't remember any of it. She had seemed to always be in Leander's arms for those few hours, dancing across a floor of glass and seeing nothing but his eyes, drowning in the green depths of them.

She remembered several people telling her that they'd never seen her looking lovelier or seen Lee so happy. There were a thousand questions about the wedding and Blair knew none of the answers, but it didn't matter because Lee was always there to take her away to the dance floor again.

If they had talked, she remembered nothing of what they had said. She thought only of his arms and his eyes and how he made her feel.

It was when a boy brought a message to say that Lee was needed elsewhere that she came to her senses and realized that this magic night was over. She felt like Cinderella, and now she had to pay the price for her wonderful night.

"You may stay and I'll get someone to take you home," Lee said. "Or you can go with me."

"You," was all she said and he took her to his waiting carriage. They didn't speak on the drive through the quiet streets of Chandler, but Blair knew that she was long past any coherent thoughts.

He reached over, took her hand in his, and when she looked at him, he smiled. For a moment, Blair remembered her sister and knew that she shouldn't be here now, that what she'd seen tonight was too intimate a thing to share, that these smiles and kisses were for Houston, and Blair had no right to intrude on their love. Until this night, she'd had no idea that the twin bond was as strong as it was, that she could spend one evening with the man her sister loved and, through that bond, could react so strongly to this man, could almost feel that it was she who was in love with him.

"Warm enough?" Lee asked and she nodded.

Warm enough, cold enough, drunk enough, sober enough, she thought.

Leander stopped the carriage in front of a house that Blair'd never seen before. "Is your patient here? I thought we were going to the Infirmary."

Lee lifted his arms for her. "I'd like to think that my presence has made you forget the house we chose."

Before Blair could cover her error, he continued.

"I thought maybe we could talk about some of the plans for the wedding. We haven't been able to talk much lately."

"But what about your patient? Shouldn't we—"

He swung her down. "There is no emergency, nor is there a patient. I wanted an excuse to get out of there and I'm afraid I used my profession. You don't mind, do you?"

"I really must get home. It's already late and Mother will probably be waiting up for me."

"I thought your mother was a heavy sleeper and you had trouble waking her?"

"Well, yes, she is, but what with Blair home, she's changing." Blair smiled at his puzzled frown and quickly said that she'd love to talk about the wedding. She swept past him and stopped at the locked door, hoping that he wouldn't ask her too many more questions.

The interior was lovely, feminine without excluding the masculine. Blair was sure that Houston had decorated it. In the parlor, a small fire was burning against the Colorado mountain chill, and in front of it was a low table set with candles, roast duckling, caviar, oysters, chocolate truffles and four silver buckets filled with ice and French champagne. Fat pillows surrounded the table.

Blair took one look at Lee standing there in the firelight and at the food and the champagne and thought, I'm in trouble.

Chapter 5

The way Leander stood there looking at her made Blair feel as if the blood were draining from her body. She'd spent the last week near this man and she'd never noticed that he had any special powers over women, especially not over her. It had to be the twin bond that was making her react this way. Houston was certainly a sly one who managed to conceal all this passion under her cool persona. No one, not even her own sister, had ever guessed what fires lay beneath that haughty-seeming exterior. And how Houston must have laughed to herself at Blair's fears that she and Lee weren't compatible!

Of course, Blair thought, if I were engaged to a man who made me tremble every time he so much as brushed against me, I don't think I'd allow another woman to be alone with him—not even my own sister, or perhaps especially not my own sister.

But even as Blair thought those words, she told herself that she *did* have a man who made her tremble with his every touch. Well, perhaps not with every touch, but with enough touches to make her love him.

As she looked at Lee again, at the way his upper lip curled and at the burning intensity of his eyes, she knew that if she were honest, she would have to admit that *no* man anywhere had ever made her feel like this before, nor had she had any idea that this kind of passion was possible.

"I think I should go home. I think I forgot to do something," Blair mumbled.

"Such as?" He was advancing on her in slow, steady steps.

"Stay there," she answered, swallowing hard.

Lee took her arm. "You aren't afraid of me, are you? Come over here and sit down. I've never seen you like this. Not that I don't like it, but . . ."

Blair tried to relax, tried to remember that she was supposed to be her sister. If she told Lee now of the trick the twins had been playing on him all evening, he'd be furious—perhaps furious enough to break the engagement. She thought that if she could keep him talking, if they could eat a little, drink very little, then maybe she could get him to take her home. Anything, so long as she didn't allow this man to touch her.

She took a seat on one of the pillows and helped herself to a raw oyster. "I haven't seen you very often as Dr. Westfield," she said, not looking up at him, but she heard the sounds of a bottle of champagne being opened.

"Never, as I remember. Have a strawberry," he said, as he dipped the berry in champagne, ignored her extended hand and put it into her mouth.

He was bringing his mouth to hers when Blair choked on the fruit. Lee handed her a glass which she drank from gratefully. Unfortunately, it was champagne and, almost instantly, she could feel it going to her head.

"Never?" she asked, trying to suppress the lightheaded, dizzy, happy feeling that was beginning to overwhelm her. "That seems like an awfully long time."

"Too long for most things." He took her fingertips and began to nibble them.

She pulled away from his touch. "What's that?" she asked, pointing to a bowl.

"Caviar. It's said to be a wonderful aphrodisiac. Would you like some?"

"No, thank you." She was drawn to the wineglass that Lee'd refilled. As she sipped it, she said, "How *do* you prevent peritonitis?"

He moved closer to her, spearing her with his hypnotic eyes. "First, you have to examine the patient." He put his hand on her stomach and began to move it around in a slow, easy way. "I feel the skin, the warm, alive skin and then I move lower."

Blair, in one frantic motion, managed to move away, and knocked her glass of champagne over so it ran down the table and onto Lee's hand.

He pulled back with a laugh. "I'll put more wood on the fire."

She thought he seemed awfully pleased with something. "I really think I should go home. It must be awfully late."

"You haven't touched your food." He took a seat on the pillow next to her.

"I'll eat if you'll talk. Tell me how you became a doctor. What made you want to do it?"

He paused in putting choice bits of food on her plate and looked at her speculatively.

"Did I say something wrong?"

"No, but you've never asked me that before."

Blair wanted to shout that that was because she'd never really talked to him before. She took a deep drink of wine to cover her embarrassment, while Lee put chicken in wine sauce on her plate. "Maybe it was seeing you with the girl tonight."

He stretched his long, lean form out beside her, inches away, pants tight around his thighs, wine in hand, looking at the fire. "I wanted to save people. Did you know that Mother died not because she was having a baby at forty-five but because the midwife had just come from another delivery and hadn't washed her hands?"

Blair paused with her fork on the way to her mouth. "No," she said quietly, "I didn't know. It must have hurt when Blair asked about aseptic conditions."

He turned to look at her, smiling. "Blair doesn't bother me at all. Here, have another oyster."

Blair didn't know whether to be glad or offended by his

comment that she didn't bother him at all. "You certainly upset her. Did you know that she thinks you're just like Mr. Gates?"

Lee's mouth dropped open a fraction. "What an absurd idea. Why don't you relax here beside me?"

Blair moved toward him before she even considered what she was doing, but she stopped. Maybe it was the champagne that was making her so forward. Of course, that didn't explain how she'd behaved on River Street, or in the park, or at the reception. "No, thank you," she said in a prim little Houston-voice. "I'm quite fine where I am. Do you plan always to work at the Infirmary?"

With a sigh, he looked back at the fire.

"You didn't have to become a doctor to help people, did you?" she persisted. "You could have built a hospital, couldn't you have?"

"Thanks to my rich grandfather who left me a trust, yes, I could have. But I wanted to do something on my own. If I could ever find another doctor who's interested, I'd like to open a women's infirmary, something a great deal more complete than that two-bit clinic that's set up for them now. I'd like a decent place where women like my mother could be treated. But all the doctors say gynecology is treating women whose illnesses are in their heads."

"What about Blair?" she asked, suddenly alert.

"Blair? But she's a wo—." He broke off at the look in her eyes. "Perhaps. When she's finished her training. Let's not start talking about her again. Come over here."

"I really think I should go . . . ."

"Houston!" he snapped. "Is this the way it's always going to be? Will you always refuse me?" His voice was showing his growing anger. "If we get married, will you still refuse me then?"

"*If?*" Blair whispered. "*If* we get married?" What had she done to cause this? Could he be thinking of calling off the wedding after only one evening with Blair? Was Houston so much warmer to Lee than this that he considered her reactions tonight unforgivably cold?

"Sweetheart, let's not argue." He opened his arms to her.

Blair hesitated only a moment before she remembered Houston's caution about not arguing with Lee. Perhaps if she kissed him just a few more times, then he'd be satisfied and take her home to safety.

She went to him, let him hold her, her body full against his and, as he began to kiss her, she forgot about everyone except the two of them.

Leander held her close to him in a way that was almost desperate, almost as if he feared that she'd disappear, and Blair was acutely aware that this could be the only time in her life that she would be near this man who made her feel like this. His mouth held hers in a deathless grip, never letting her go as she clung to him.

When his hands went to her back and his skillful surgeon's fingers began to unfasten the hooks and eyes at the back of her dress, she had no thoughts about stopping him. The dress began to fall away and, as her shoulders became visible, Lee kissed them, ran his hands over her skin until it tingled.

Within moments, the dress was in a heap beside them and the rustle of the pink silk taffeta petticoat between them was a further spur to their growing passion. Leander's long legs moved over the stiff fabric, twisting it and pulling it from her body at the same time.

Blair couldn't move away from his lips and her hands buried themselves in his long, clean hair and she could smell the deep male scent of it.

"Leander," she whispered, as his lips moved down her arm and his hands rid her of two more petticoats. Satin, taffeta, and the softest of cottons surrounded them, cocooning them together in the warm glow of the firelight.

His hands on her body seemed to be everywhere, stroking her, caressing her, removing clothing with infinite care and slowness, sliding each piece of fabric down her skin, exposing more of her to his touch.

With his hand on her leg, running up and down over her silk stocking, his lips on her earlobe, she realized that he was still wearing his clothes and she began tugging at them.

In removing his own clothing, he did not use the care he did with hers, but instead, pulled it off with a force just short of violence.

In medical school, Blair had seen many men nude, and once she had seen Alan with his shirt off, but she had never seen a warm, alive man with dark, sunbrowned skin coming at her with the fire in his eyes that Lee had now. For a moment, she pulled back from him as he moved to draw her back into his arms.

There was caution in his eyes when she withdrew from him, but Blair didn't see it. All she saw was Lee—his skin, his lovely skin, curving around firmly muscled shoulders, tapering down to his flat stomach. With interest, she looked downward, curious as to the difference between a man who was alive and one who was dead—the only way she'd seen a man who was fully nude before today.

"Do I pass inspection?" he asked, and his voice was husky.

Blair didn't answer as she drew him to her and put her arms around that skin that glowed so.

Leander wasted no more time in removing the rest of her clothing, slipping the garters off the hose and even unbuttoning her shoes, all without ceasing his caressing of her, so that by the time Blair was completely bare, she was beginning to feel that her passion was rising to a level that might eventually cause her to burst.

Nothing she had ever felt before prepared her for the feeling of her skin against Lee's. With a gasp of pleasure, she clung to him, slipped her leg between his and tried to get closer to him.

Lee pulled her over on top of him, kissing her, his hands running down her back, over her thighs, and back up her buttocks, lingering by her sides at her breasts.

His mouth never left hers as he rolled her to her back and slowly spread her legs with his own.

In theory, Blair knew how the human species reproduced itself. They'd had special classes for unmarried women at her medical college, but none of the teachers had mentioned the passion involved in the act. She had not guessed that a woman felt this way, that it wasn't an act purely for the purpose of procreation, but it was an act of love and lust.

She was ready for Lee when he entered her, but it still hurt, and she gasped with the pain. He lay still for a moment, his breath hot on her neck, his lips quiet as he waited for some sign from her.

Blair recovered from the first moment of pain and began to move her hips slowly, her hands on his back and moving downward over his hips. Only Lee's jagged breathing in her ear showed her the supreme effort he was exerting to control himself with her, to hold back so he didn't hurt her.

It was only when she began to move that he followed her lead and very slowly began to make love to her.

There was no pain as Lee made slow, gentle strokes and Blair, awkward at first, moved with him. After a few moments, the slowness left them both and their passion showed itself in a frenzy. They could not get enough as they arched against each other, clinging, clutching, trying the impossible of getting closer until at last they exploded together.

Blair held on to Lee as if she were afraid to let go. Their sweaty bodies stuck together, even their skin melded into one.

"I love you," Leander whispered into her ear. "I'm not sure I did before. I'm not sure I knew you before tonight. I'm not sure either of us is the same person as yesterday, but I do know that I love you and, Houston, I've never loved another woman."

For a moment, Blair couldn't understand why the man in her arms had called her by her sister's name.

Remembrance came to her all too swiftly. With a feeling of sheer horror, she started to pull away from Lee. "I have to go home," she said, and her voice showed all that she felt.

"Houston," Lee said, "it's not the end of the world. We'll be married in two weeks, and then we'll spend all our nights together."

"Let me up! I have to get home."

He looked at her for a long moment, as if he were deciding whether or not to be angry, but at last he smiled. "You can be as shy as you want, sweetheart. Here, let me help you with that."

Blair couldn't even look at him. It had been the most wonderful experience of her life, but it hadn't really belonged to her. She had cheated her sister, cheated the man she was to marry, and lied to this man who . . . who . . .

Under her eyelashes, she looked at Lee as he helped her with her corset strings. If she wasn't careful, she'd be back in his arms and, if he asked her, she'd probably board the next train with him and forget all about her obligations to other people.

"You certainly seem to know your way around a woman's underclothing," she snapped at him.

Lee chuckled as he held the taffeta petticoat for her to step into. "Well enough, I guess. Shall I do your garters for you?"

Snatching her hose out of his hand, she sat on a chair and began to roll them onto her legs, trying her best to ignore him. What in the world had she done? Houston was going to hate her. And what would Lee say when he found that his bride was a virgin—again? And what would Alan say if he knew? How could she explain to him? Would anyone believe her if she said that he'd touched her and after that she'd had no more control over her own body? Maybe all the things that Duncan Gates said about her were true.

"Houston," Lee said, kneeling in front of her. "You look as if you're about to cry." He took her hands in his. "Look at me, sweetheart. I know how you've been raised, and I know you meant to stay a virgin until we were married, but what happened tonight was between us and it was all right. I'll be your husband in very little time, and then we can enjoy each other as often as we want. And if you're worried about the morality of what we did, I'm a doctor and I can tell you that many, many women who enter marriage have spent some time alone with the men they love."

He was making everything worse. The man she loved was not the man she'd just made love to, and the man she was to marry had not taken her virginity.

She stood. "Please take me home," she said, and Leander obeyed her.

Chapter 6

"Good morning," Leander said with uncharacteristic jubilation to his father and sister, Nina, who sat at the breakfast table.

Nina, twenty-one and very pretty, paused with her coffee cup on the way to her mouth. "Then it's true what I heard," she said.

Lee helped himself to an enormous plateful of food from the sideboard.

"Sarah Oakley called first thing this morning and told me that last night at the reception you and Houston couldn't take your eyes—or hands—off each other. She said that she'd never seen two people so in love."

"Did she now?" Lee asked. "And just what was so unusual about that? I *have* asked the beautiful lady to marry me."

"But there have been times when you looked as though you wanted to run away rather than stay with your lovely bride."

Lee smiled at his sister. "When you grow up, baby sister, maybe you'll know a little more about the birds and the bees." As he put his plate down across from her, he reached over and kissed her on the forehead.

Nina nearly choked on her food. "That does it," she said, looking up at her father. "He's either mad or he's finally fallen in love."

Reed was leaning back in his chair and watching his son with great interest. When Lee looked up at him and winked, his worst fears were confirmed.

"You sure know a lot about women, Dad," Lee grinned and Reed burst out laughing.

"I don't think I want to know what that little exchange was

about," Nina said primly as she rose to leave. "I think I'll call Houston and give her my condolences."

"Tell her I'll pick her up at eleven," Lee said with his mouth full. "And I'll bring a picnic basket."

Reed stayed in his chair and lit his pipe, something he rarely did in the morning, and watched his son eat. Usually, Leander ate slowly and carefully, but today he was wolfing food as if there were no tomorrow. He seemed to be lost in a world of his own, a world of happiness and plans for the future.

"I've been thinking about that women's hospital lately," Lee said, as he bit into a two-inch-thick biscuit. "Actually, Houston made me think of it. Maybe it's time that I start looking into building the thing, or maybe I'll buy that old stone warehouse at the end of Archer Avenue. With some work and some money, that place could be just what I need."

"Houston had this idea?" Reed asked.

"Not really, but she helped. I have to get to the hospital, and later I'm to meet Houston. I'll see you." He grabbed an apple and, at the doorway, he paused to look back at his father. "Thanks, Dad," he said, just the way he did when he was a boy, and today he reminded Reed of the boy he'd once been, before he took on the responsibility of planning marriage.

All morning, Lee whistled at the hospital and his cheer was infectious. Before long, the entire hospital was smiling and grumbling less about the work to be done. The young prostitute who'd tried suicide the day before benefited the most from Lee's good humor. He talked to her about the joy of being alive and then got her a position on the nursing staff at the women's clinic, promising to watch over her and to help her in the future.

At ten minutes to eleven, he jumped in his carriage and drove downtown to pick up a basket that he'd had Miss Emily prepare at her tea shop.

"So it's true," Miss Emily said, smiling and making her pink-and-white face crinkle into tiny tissue paper wrinkles. "Nina has been talking about her lovesick brother all morning."

"My sister talks entirely too much," Lee said, but he was smiling. "I don't know what's so unusual about my being happy, because I'm marrying the most beautiful woman in the world. I've got to go," he said, as he rushed out of the shop.

He left his horse and buggy to the care of the Gates's stableboy, Willie, took the steps two at a time and raised his hand to knock.

"You can go in," came a voice from the shadowed side of the deep porch. "They're expecting you."

Leander looked into the shadows and saw Blair there, her face turned away, but he could see that her hair was straggling and her face streaked. He went to her. "Has something happened? Is Houston all right?"

"She's fine!" Blair snapped, starting to rise.

Lee caught her arm. "I want you to come over here and sit down so I can look at you. You don't look well at all."

"Leave me alone!" she half cried, half shouted. "And don't touch me!" She jerked away from him, ran down the stairs and out of sight around the house.

As Lee was standing there in open-mouthed astonishment, Houston came onto the porch, pulling on gloves of white lace.

"Was that Blair shouting? You weren't having another one of your arguments, were you?" she asked.

Lee turned to her with a look of pure joy, his eyes going up and down her, as if he wanted to drink in all of her. "It was Blair," he said in answer to her question.

"Good," Houston said, "I was hoping you'd see her. She's been like that all day. For some reason, I think she's been crying. I thought you might know what was wrong with her. She won't answer any of my questions."

"I'd have to examine her," Lee said, as he helped her into the carriage, but as soon as he touched her, he couldn't seem to let go, and held on to her waist.

"Lee! People are watching."

"Yes, of course," he grinned, "but we'll soon remedy that."

He didn't trust himself to speak much on the way out of town, only occasionally glancing at Houston, noting the way she sat so far to the side of the carriage, away from him as she always had until last night. He couldn't help smiling to himself to think that this cool young woman was the same one who hadn't been able to resist him last night.

He hadn't slept much, but had lain awake reliving every moment he'd spent with Houston. It wasn't so much the sex, he'd had that with women before and hadn't fallen for them, but it was something about her attitude that had made him feel wonderful, powerful, as if he could do anything.

He drove them to a secret place he'd found once when he'd been called to set the broken leg of a prospector and been caught in a summer storm. It was a secluded place amid enormous rocks, with tall trees swaying overhead, a spring trickling out of the rocks. He'd never brought anyone here before.

He stopped the carriage, jumped out, tied the horse and went to get Houston. As he lifted her in his arms, he let her slide down and pulled her close to him, hugging her so that she couldn't breathe. "I thought about nothing else but you last night," he said. "I could smell your hair on my clothes, I could taste your lips on mine, I could—."

Houston pulled away from him. "You what?" she gasped.

He touched the hair at her temples with the backs of his fingers. "You aren't going to be shy with me today, are you? You aren't going to be the way you were before last night, are you? Houston, you've proven to me that you can be different, so there's no need to go back to being the ice princess. I know what you're really like now, and I can tell you that if I never see that cool woman again, I'll be even happier. Now, come here and kiss me like you did last night."

Houston pushed free of him. "Are you saying that last night I wasn't like I usually am? That I was . . . better?"

Smiling, he advanced on her. "You know you were. You were like I've never seen you. I didn't know you could be like that. You'll laugh at this but I was beginning to believe that you were incapable of any real passion, that beneath your cool exterior was a heart of ice. But, if you can have a sister like Blair who starts fires at the least provocation, surely some of it had to rub off."

He took her wrist in his hand and pulled her to him, ignoring the way she resisted. He also ignored the way she tried to turn her head away when he put his mouth on hers.

The lips under his were unresponsive, held together rigidly, hard. At first, he was amused that she was trying to keep herself under control and doing such a damn fine job of it, but as the kiss continued, and she still made no response, he pulled away from her in anger.

"You're carrying this game too far," he said. "You can't be wildly passionate one minute and frigid the next. What are you, two people?"

Something in Houston's eyes gave him the first seed of doubt. But of course he was wrong. He took a step backward.

"That's an impossibility, isn't it, Houston?" he said. "Tell me that what I'm thinking is wrong. No one can be two people, can she?"

Houston just stood there and looked at him with stricken eyes.

Lee walked away from her and at last sat down heavily on a rock. "Did you and your sister trade places last night?" he asked softly. "Did I spend the evening with Blair and not with you?"

He barely heard her whispered, "Yes."

"I should have known from the first: how well she handled that suicide and she didn't even know it was the house I'd bought for her—you. I don't think I wanted to see. From the moment she said she wanted to go on the case with me to see if she could be of any help, I was so stupidly pleased that I never questioned anything after that. I should have known when I kissed her . . .

"Damn both of you! I hope to hell you enjoyed making a fool of me."

"Lee," Houston said, her hand on his arm.

He turned on her angrily. "If you know what's good for you, you won't say a word. I don't know what possessed either of you to play such a dirty little trick, but I can tell you that I don't like being the butt of such a joke. Now that you and your sister have had a good laugh at my expense, I have to decide what to do about last night."

He half shoved her into the carriage and cracked the whip over the horse as they tore back into town. At the Chandler house, he didn't get out but let Houston get herself, and all her yards of skirts, out of the carriage unaided. On the porch, waiting, was Blair, her face red and swollen from crying for hours on end. Leander glared at her with a mixture of anger and some hatred before he yelled at the horse and took off again.

He paused for only moments at his father's house before mounting a big roan stallion and taking off for the mountains at breakneck speed. He didn't know where he was going, but he knew that he had to get away and think.

He climbed with the horse until the animal could go no farther, then dismounted and led the horse, straight up, over rocks, across arroyos, through cacti and mean little under-brush. When at last he came to the top of a ridge, when he could go no higher, he pulled the rifle from the horse's saddle, jammed it against his leg and fired it up into the air, emptying it. Once the air had cleared of screaming birds and gunsmoke, he yelled at the top of his lungs, giving vent to his frustration and anger.

"Damn you, Blair!" he shouted. "Damn you to hell."

The sun was setting as Reed Westfield walked into the library. As he reached for the light switch, he saw the glow of one of his son's cigars.

"Lee?" he asked, as he pushed the button for the lights. "The hospital was calling for you."

Leander didn't look up. "Did they find someone?"

Reed studied his son for a moment. "They found someone. What happened to the man who left here this morning? Don't tell me that Houston regretted what happened last night? Women do that. Your mother—."

Lee looked at his father with bleak eyes. "Spare me more of the advice about women. I don't believe I can stand any more."

Reed sat down. "Tell me what's happened."

Lee flicked the ash off his cigar. "I believe that, as they say, all hell is about to break loose in a few minutes. Last night," he paused to take a breath and calm himself. "Last night, the Chandler twins decided to play a game. They thought it'd be great fun to switch places and see if they could fool poor stupid Leander. They did quite well."

He jammed his cigar into an ashtray and stood, walking to

the window. "I was fooled all right, and not because Blair did such a good job of pretending to be her sister. In fact, she did little more than dress like Houston. Blair assisted me in a medical case without my giving her any instruction; she was interested in my life, something Houston's never cared much about; Blair asked me about my dreams and hopes for the future. In other words, she was the perfect woman whom every man dreams about."

He turned back to look at his father. "And she was the perfect lover. I guess every man's vanity wants a woman who can't resist him. He likes to think that he can talk her into anything. So far, all the women I've known have been interested in the money I had in the bank. I've had women who weren't interested in me when they thought I was a lowly, unpaid doctor, but when they learned that my mother was a Candish, their eyes began to sparkle. Blair wasn't like that. She was—."

His voice trailed off as he turned back to face the window.

"Houston isn't interested in your money," Reed said. "She never has been."

"Who knows what Houston wants out of life. I've spent months with her and I don't know anything about her. To me, she's a cold woman who does nothing more than look pretty. But Blair is alive!"

He said the last with such passion that Reed narrowed his eyes. "I don't think I like the sound of that. Houston is the woman you're going to marry. I know Blair is a forward girl, and it's a shame about what happened last night, but I tried to warn you that that kind of thing could get you in trouble. I'm sure Houston will be angry, but if you court her enough and send enough flowers, she'll eventually forgive you."

Lee looked at his father. "And what about Blair? Will she forgive me?"

Reed walked to the big walnut desk that dominated the room and took a pipe from a box. "If she's the kind of girl who'd sleep with her sister's intended, then I imagine she already knows how to get over this sort of thing."

"And just what is that supposed to mean?"

"Exactly what it sounds like. She's been back East all these years, going to school with men, studying things she has no right to know anything about, and trying to be a man. Girls like her know from experience how to recover from affairs of one night's duration."

Leander took minutes to get his emotions under control. "I'm going to forget you said that, but I want you to know that if you ever say anything like that again, I'll walk out the door and never come back. It's none of your business, but Blair was a virgin until last night. And in two weeks' time I mean to make her my wife."

Reed was so flabbergasted that he just stood there opening and closing his mouth like a fish out of water.

Lee took a seat and lit another cigar. "I think I'd better tell you all I know of what's happened. As I said last night, for some reason, the twins decided to trade places so it was Blair I took to the reception. I had already planned to do my best to seduce her and, if I found her unwilling, I was going to break off the engagement. I think I was expecting to have to do that, since I was sure that no one, or at least not me, could break through that coating of ice that surrounds Houston."

He held the cigar out, and a faint smile curved his lips as he remembered last night. "Within five minutes of being alone with her, I was so pleased with Blair that I never thought of questioning who she was or why she was behaving so differently. There was an emergency on River Street and she went with me, unlike Houston who always insisted that I drop her at one of her friends' houses. We went to the reception and later to our house. Altogether, it was the most pleasurable evening of my life."

"So now, you think you have to marry her," Reed said with heavy-sounding finality. "Couldn't you give it some time? You hardly know her. Marriage is forever. You'll have to spend your life with this woman, and one night's acquaintance isn't enough to base that on. Just because she's feisty in bed doesn't mean—." He stopped at Lee's look.

"All right," Reed continued. "So now, you ask for the young lady's hand in marriage. What happens to Houston? Do you just walk away from her? Women take these things quite hard, you know."

"Since all this was started by the twins, I don't feel too bad. They should have thought of the consequences."

"They could hardly have known that you would choose that night to decide the fate of your future. Before you ask Blair to marry you, why don't you wait a month or so? That'll give both of you some time to think about what you're doing."

"It's too late for that. Besides, I don't think Blair would marry me."

"Don't . . . ?" Reed began. "If she'll sleep with you, why the hell won't she marry you?"

In spite of the anger in his father's voice, Lee began to smile. "I'm not sure she likes me. She thinks I'm a bigot like Gates, and I honestly believe that if I asked her to marry me, she'd laugh in my face."

Reed threw up his hands in despair. "I don't understand any of this."

At that moment, the front door was thrown open, and immediately there was the sound of shouting throughout the house.

Lee rose from his chair. "That will no doubt be the outraged Mr. Duncan Gates. I went to his brewery an hour ago and told him that I had deflowered his stepdaughter and, to make amends, I would marry the wayward girl. He is bringing Blair and the four of us are going to discuss the matter. Don't look so glum, Dad. I mean to have her and I'll use any method I can to get her."

Chapter 7

"I have absolutely no intention of marrying him. None," Blair said for the twentieth time.

"You are soiled, unfit," Duncan raged. "No one else will have you."

Blair tried her best to keep calm and not show the turmoil that was boiling inside her. Gates had been shouting at her and trying to intimidate her for three solid hours. She thought about her Uncle Henry's calmness, how he'd look at what had happened with some humor, and they would sit down and talk about the situation as if they were sane adults. But not Gates. He had the medieval idea that now that she was no longer a virgin, she should be cast down to the dogs—or to Leander, which was about the same thing as far as Blair was concerned.

"May I ask why you don't want to marry my son?" Reed Westfield asked.

Blair could feel animosity coming from the man, like heat waves on the desert. "I have told you that I have been accepted to intern at a major hospital in Pennsylvania and I plan to take the offer. Besides, I don't love your son. He is engaged to my sister and, as soon as possible after their wedding, I will return to Pennsylvania, and no one in this town need ever see me again. I don't know how to make myself more clear than that."

"You've ruined your sister's life!" Gates shouted. "You don't think she can marry him after this?"

"Are you insinuating that Leander was . . . ah, unsoiled, as you put it, before last night?"

Duncan's face turned red.

"Calm down, Duncan," Reed said. "Blair, there must be some way that we can work this out to everyone's satisfaction. Surely, you must have *some* feelings for my son."

Blair looked at Lee, who was standing at the back of the room and appearing to enjoy everything. Not any feelings that she could tell publicly, she thought, and as if Lee could read her mind, he smiled at her in such a way that she blushed and had to look away. "I told you before," she said. "I was pretending to be my sister, and I was acting the way I thought she would act with the man she loved. I don't think I should be punished for being an excellent actress."

Reed lifted one eyebrow. "I don't think any actress carries her role that far."

"And I'll not have Houston's name dragged through the

mud by you or anyone else," Duncan shouted. "She wouldn't have done what you've done. She's a good girl."

"And I'm not, is that it?" Blair asked, torn between tears and outrage.

"A decent woman wouldn't—."

"I've heard all I want to hear," Lee said, stepping forward. "Would you leave us now? I want to talk to Blair alone."

Blair wanted to protest that she didn't want to see him alone, but perhaps he wasn't as bad as all of them shouting at her.

"Would you like some sherry?" he asked, when they were alone.

"Please," she answered, taking the glass with shaking hands.

He frowned when he saw her hands. "I had no idea that he was as bad as that. Houston'd told me, but I hadn't imagined half of it."

Blair drank the wine gratefully and hoped it would calm her nerves. "If you didn't think he was so bad, why did you enlist his help in your preposterous scheme?"

"I wanted all the help I could get. I thought—correctly— that if I went to you on my own, you'd laugh in my face."

"I'm not laughing now."

"All right, then let's get this settled. The invitations are at the printer's, and all that has to be changed is your name for Houston's."

Blair jumped up from her chair. "Of all the stupid ideas I have ever heard, that's the worst. Can't you hear me? I don't *want* to marry you. I don't want to spend another minute in this dreadful town. I want to go home and I want my sister to get her fiancé back. What can I say to you people to make you understand? I want to go home!"

In spite of her good intentions, she collapsed in the chair, put her face in her hands and burst into tears. "He's right," she cried, "I've ruined Houston's life."

Lee knelt before her and very gently pulled her hands down. "Don't you understand that I want to marry *you*, not Houston?"

She looked at him for a moment, felt his warm hands on her wrists and considered the matter, but before she could let herself be persuaded, she got up and went to stand before the window.

"You belong to my sister. Since she was a child, she has planned to marry you. She has a trunkful of linens embroidered with an *L* and an *H* intertwined. She's never wanted to be anything but Mrs. Leander Westfield. She loves you, don't you know that? And what I love is medicine. Medicine has been my life since I was twelve and now I've earned this internship and I want to take it and marry Alan and live happily ever after."

Leander lost the concerned look he was wearing and stood bolt upright. "Alan? And just who the hell is he?"

"Since I've returned to this town, no one has asked me about my life in Pennsylvania. Gates shouts at me that I'm immoral, Mother just sits and sews, Houston spends most of her time ordering new dresses, and you . . . you just stand there giving me orders."

Several emotions went across Lee's face. "Who is Alan?"

"The man to whom I'm engaged. The man I love. The man who is coming to Chandler in two days to meet my family and tell them that he would be honored to marry me."

"*I'm* asking for that honor."

"I'm sure that you fell in love with me after one night." To her surprise, Leander said nothing to this.

He toyed with a letter opener on the desk. "What if I make you want to marry me? What if by the end of two weeks you *want* to walk down that aisle to me?"

"There's not a chance in the world of that happening. Alan will be here soon and, besides, I told you, you belong to Houston."

"I do, do I?" he said and, in one stride, he was across the room to her and had her in his arms.

His kiss was as draining to her senses as it had been last night when she'd pretended to be her sister. She was weak when he released her.

"Now, tell me I don't have a chance." He moved away from her. "Did it ever occur to you that this Alan might not want you after you explain why your name is on the wedding invitation?"

"He's not like that. He's a very understanding man."

"We'll see how understanding he is. You're going to marry me two weeks from now, and you'd better get used to the idea."

Blair somehow managed to remain calm until Mr. Gates took her back to the Chandler house—and then she saw Houston's face. Her sister looked as if nothing in life mattered anymore. Blair had been worried about Houston's future, had been so concerned that she'd wanted to go out with Leander just to assure herself that her sister would be all right. And what she'd managed to do was destroy Houston's entire future.

Blair begged her sister to answer, but Houston refused to speak to her, and even when Blair burst into tears, Houston wouldn't relent.

Mr. Gates fairly pushed Blair up to her room on the third floor and locked the door behind her. Even when Opal came to the door and asked to see her daughter, Gates refused to open it.

Blair sat for a long time inside the dark room, her eyes too dry to cry since she'd been crying all day and quite a bit of the night. Now, she had to make a plan to get herself out of this mess. She wasn't going to be forced to stay in this town and marry a man she didn't want to marry, nor was she going to give up her internship at St. Joseph's Hospital.

She sat quietly until she heard no more sounds from inside the house, and then she went to the window. As a child, she'd managed to climb to the ground by using the long, serpentine branches of the old elm tree on the east side of the house. If she jumped, she thought she could make the largest branch of the tree—and if she missed . . . She didn't like to think of that.

Hurriedly, she packed a soft bag with a few clothes and tossed it to the ground, waiting a moment for the sounds of alarm. So far, so good. No one seemed to have heard her. She slipped into a divided skirt and climbed onto the window ledge, holding on with one hand and reaching as far as she could with the other. She could just barely reach the tree branches. She pulled back, knowing that there was no way that she could get to the tree except by jumping. She crouched in the window, and with one big leap, sent herself hurtling through the air, grabbing the tree branch as she went by.

She hung there, suspended in the air, and she could hear the slight cracking of the wood. It took several tries but she managed to get her legs around the branch just before her arms gave out. Using all her strength, while hanging upside down by her hands and ankles, and feeling the bark and sharp places scratch her skin through her clothing and hose, she managed to propel herself to the trunk of the tree. Once there, she took a moment to catch her breath before beginning the descent.

When she was finally on the ground, she looked back at the house with a feeling of triumph. They weren't going to make her stay where she didn't want to.

A sound to her left made her whirl about.

A match was lit and the flame showed Leander's face as he held the match to a cigar. "Need some help with your bag?" he asked, when he looked at her.

"What are you doing here?" she gasped.

"Protecting what I've come to think of as mine," he said, smiling.

"You were standing here while I was fighting for my life at the top of that tree?"

"Not quite the top, and I didn't see that you were in any real danger. Who taught you to climb like that?"

"Certainly not you. You were too busy saving lives to learn how to climb trees when you were a boy."

"What odd ideas you have about me. I can't imagine where you got them. Now, if you've had your nightly exercise, I suggest that we get you back into the house. After you, my lady," he said, making a sweeping bow toward the tree.

"I have no intention of returning to that house. There's a train to Denver in a little while and I will be on it."

"Not if I tell Gates. I'm sure that he'll be after you with a shotgun."

"You wouldn't!"

"Do you forget that I was the one who started this in the first place? I don't plan to let you leave Chandler now or ever."

"I think I'm beginning to hate you."

"You didn't hate me last night," he said softly. "Now, do you want a repeat demonstration of just how much you don't hate me or do I help you back into your boudoir?"

Blair gritted her teeth. He had to sleep sometime and when he did, she'd be ready to escape.

"Stop looking at me as if you'd like to have me on a platter for breakfast and come on." He grabbed the lowest branch of the tree and swung himself up, holding out his hand to her.

Reluctantly, she took his hand and let him pull her up. She did get some satisfaction from the fact that she did very little to help, and he had to pull her dead weight.

When they were at the roof, he helped her into the window, leaned forward and whispered, "How about a good-night kiss?"

Blair, with a little smile, leaned toward him as if she meant to kiss him and, at the last minute, slammed the window down so that Lee had to jump to keep his fingers from getting caught. From behind the glass, she puckered her lips into a kiss before she pulled the shade down to block him from view.

As she was smiling, she heard a crack of wood from outside, a muffled cry, then a heavy thud.

"He's fallen," she gasped, as she threw open the window and stuck her head out. "Lee!" she called as loud as she dared.

To her surprise, he put his head around the window jamb and kissed her quickly and firmly. "I knew you couldn't resist me."

With that, he jumped to the longest branch and was on the ground in record time. "You should have let *me* teach you how to climb trees," he laughed up at her and then sat down under the tree as if he planned to spend all night there.

Blair slammed down the window and went to bed.

Chapter 8

On Sunday morning, Gates told Blair to get dressed for church, and she was to look as much like a lady as she could manage.

Breakfast was a sullen meal, with Houston more rigid than usual, and both she and Opal looked as if they'd been crying most of the night. Duncan's face seemed to be permanently set in the mask of a martyr who was suffering for everyone.

Immediately after the awful meal, Opal said that she didn't feel well enough to attend church and retired to her room. Gates got Blair into a corner and told her that she was killing her mother with her wicked ways.

Church was the worst. The minister seemed to think that what had happened between the twins was a great joke and made the congregation laugh when he said that Lee had changed his mind about which twin he wanted to marry.

After the service, people gathered around them, wanting to know what was going on, but Houston just stood there looking as if she were made of steel. And when Leander tried to talk to her, she answered him with barely concealed anger, so of course he decided to take his fury and frustration out on Blair. He grabbed her arm and half dragged her to his waiting carriage.

Blair was thrown against the seat of the buggy as Lee took off and headed for the south of town. It wasn't until they were out of town that he slowed down.

Blair straightened her hat. "Did you think that she'd smile at you and say something pleasant?"

He halted the buggy. "I thought she'd be reasonable. It was the two of you who started the whole game. I never meant to publicly humiliate her."

"All you have to do is help me get back to Pennsylvania, and you can go back to Houston on bended knee and I'm sure she'll have you."

He looked at her for quite a while. "No, I won't do that. You and I are going to be married. I brought a picnic basket and I thought we could have lunch." He wrapped the reins around the brake handle, climbed down and went to help Blair down. But as he came around the horse, he paused. "I seem to have a rock in my shoe," he said, and leaned against a tree to remove it.

Blair sat there for a moment and watched him, thinking about her sister's face during the announcement in church; thinking that she didn't want to remain in Chandler or become this man's wife; then she grabbed the reins, flicked them, and yelled to the horse to go while Leander stood there wearing only one shoe. He chased her for a while, but he soon stopped when he stepped on something with his stockinged foot and started limping.

When she was safely out of reach of him, she slowed the horse and returned to Chandler. She had to find a way to escape the town. After this morning's announcement, she couldn't very well board a train without some curiosity being aroused. Being a Chandler in a town named Chandler had drawbacks. Tomorrow, Alan would arrive and perhaps he'd help her. In spite of what she'd told Lee, she had some worries about whether Alan would still want her after what had happened.

The minute Blair saw the Chandler house, she knew something was wrong. Opal was sitting on the porch, and when she saw Blair, she jumped up.

"Do you know where your sister is?"

Blair hurried up the stairs. "Has she run away? Let me change and we'll start looking for her."

"It's worse than that," Opal said, sitting down in the porch swing. "That awful man, Mr. Taggert, came to the church and told everyone that he and Houston were going to be married, that it was to be a double wedding with you and Leander. What is happening to my family? Mr. Gates says that that man Taggert has killed people to get what he has, and I can't help but feel that Houston is taking this man because she lost Leander and she wants to show the town that she can get another husband. And he must be very rich. I'd hate to think that she's marrying the man for his money."

Blair sat down in the swing beside her mother. "This is all my fault."

Opal patted her daughter's knee. "You always were easy to talk into anything. Don't look so surprised, dear, I know my daughters quite well. For all that Houston looks as though butter wouldn't melt in her mouth, I know she was the one who used to talk you into the most daring things. You've always had the very biggest of hearts and always wanted to help people, which is why I'm sure that you'll make a very good doctor."

"If I ever get out of here and can continue my education," Blair said bleakly.

Opal toyed with a clematis vine running up the side of the porch. "I've been thinking about you and Lee. You might not think so at the moment, but he really is a very fine man. I don't think anyone knows him very well. He was always so quiet around Houston, but in the last few days, he's been more animated than I've ever seen him."

"Animated! Is that what you call it? He orders me about, tells me I am going to marry him, says that a woman can't be his partner in the clinic he wants to build and, in general, is a narrow-minded pig of a man."

"And did you think that on Friday night?"

Blair turned her face away to hide a blush. "Perhaps I didn't then, but I'd had a great deal of champagne, and there was moonlight and dancing and things just happened."

"Mmmmm," Opal said noncommittally. "However you saw that night, I don't think Lee saw it the same way."

"I'm not sure I care how he saw it. The problem now is Houston. I have returned to this town and effectively ruined her life, and now she says that she's planning to marry that ugly Midas, Kane Taggert. How are we going to prevent that from happening?"

"Mr. Gates and I are going to talk to her as soon as she returns home and see if we can persuade her to believe that there is another solution to this problem, other than the drastic one she seems set on."

Blair looked out through the greenery surrounding the porch and toward the white corner of the Taggert mansion. "I deeply and sincerely hate that house," she said with feeling. "If Houston hadn't wanted to see it so badly, we wouldn't have changed places, and I wouldn't have spent the night with Leander and, now, if she didn't want that house so much, she wouldn't be considering marrying that barbarian."

"Blair, you should rest this afternoon. Read some of the books you brought, and let us worry about Houston. By the way, where is Lee? Why didn't he bring you home?"

Blair stood. "I think I will rest. I didn't get much sleep last night. And Lee will probably be by in a while to pick up the carriage. Under no circumstances do I want to see him."

Opal hesitated a moment before she agreed. "I'll send Susan up with a tray. You rest, dear, because, if I know this town, tomorrow will be hectic. Just as soon as everyone hears about your marriage to Lee and Houston's to that man, I'm sure . . . Oh my, I don't even like to think about it."

Blair didn't want to either and, gratefully, she went to the sanctity of her room, where she stayed for the rest of the day.

Monday was worse than Blair ever imagined it could be. Breakfast was dreadful. Gates kept yelling, his mouth stuffed with food, that Blair had ruined her sister's life. Since Blair tended to agree with him, it was difficult to defend herself. Opal kept crying, while Houston managed to look faraway, as if she weren't hearing any of it.

After breakfast, people began to arrive in droves— wagonloads of them bearing food and flimsy excuses as to why they were there. It'd been so long since she'd lived in a small town that she was appalled at how nosy the people were. There didn't seem to be anything that they considered none of their business. Paramount was the answer to why Lee was now marrying Blair. And they were very curious about Taggert, asking Houston thousands of questions about him and what his house was like.

At eleven, Blair went into the house, to put away one of the numerous pies that someone had brought, and managed to slip out the back door without anyone seeing her. She practically ran the two miles to the train station and she felt, with every step, that she was getting closer to freedom. When Alan came, he would be able to straighten out the entire mess, and then Houston would be able to marry Leander and Blair could return home.

Impatiently, she waited for the train to pull into the station and when it did, at last, she thought the steam would never clear. But through the mist, she saw him and began to run with the train, following him until he could jump off and take her in his arms.

She didn't care that the people of Chandler watched them, or that they thought that she was engaged to another man—all that mattered was that she was with Alan again.

"What a wonderful welcome," he said, holding her close.

She pulled back to look at him. He was still as handsome as she remembered, still with his blond-haired, blue-eyed wholesome good looks, a few inches taller than she was.

She had started to say something when she saw that his attention was directed to something over her shoulder. She turned quickly—but not quickly enough.

Leander deftly slipped his arm about her waist and managed to pull her to him and away from Alan in one motion. "So, you must be Alan," he said smoothly, with a warm smile. "I've heard so much about you. Of course, there aren't many secrets between lovers, are there, sweetheart?"

"Release me!" she said under her breath while trying to smile at the look of puzzlement on Alan's face. While shoving an elbow in Lee's ribs, she told Alan, "May I introduce my sister's fiancé? This is Leander Westfield. And this is Alan Hunter, my—."

Lee cut her words off by squeezing her ribs with his hand, and even three sharp elbowings in his side didn't make him release her. He extended his hand to Alan. "Excuse Blair, won't you? She's a little excited today at getting to see an old and dear friend. I am *her* intended. She and I are to be married in two weeks, actually less than that now, isn't it, dear? Just a few short days and you will become Mrs. Leander Westfield. I know the anticipation is making you a bit nervous and forgetful, but let's not give your friend the wrong impression." He smiled angelically at Alan.

"This isn't the way it seems," Blair began. "This man is crazy, and he has some very strange ideas." With one big push, she managed to move away from Lee. "Alan, let's go somewhere and talk. I have a great deal to tell you."

Alan looked up at Lee, who was several inches taller than he. "I think we do need to talk." He held his arm out to her. "Shall we go?" He looked over his shoulder at Lee. "You may carry my bags, young man."

Lee successfully pushed himself between the couple. "I would generally take great delight in carrying the bags of a friend of my wife-to-be, but today I have a little problem. Yesterday, I had to walk four miles in new shoes, and my feet are too blistered to endure any extra weight. My doctor has insisted that I put no stress on them. Come along, Blair, we'll meet your little friend at the carriage."

"You beast!" Blair spat up at him as he pulled her toward the carriage. "And just what doctor would prescribe an asinine remedy like that?"

"Dr. Westfield at your service," he said, as he helped her into the carriage.

"That's an unusual horse," Alan said as he threw his bags in the back, referring to the Appaloosa that pulled Lee's carriage.

"The only one in this area," Lee said proudly. "Wherever I go, people can see that horse and recognize it, so if they need help, they can find me."

"What kind of help?" Alan asked, as he climbed into the carriage.

"I'm a doctor," Lee answered, as he cracked the whip over the horse and sent the buggy flying before Alan was fully seated next to Blair.

It was a hair-raising ride that Lee took them on, and the citizens of Chandler, thinking he was on an emergency case, moved out of his way. He halted in front of the house he'd bought for Houston.

"I thought this would be a good place to talk."

Blair's eyes widened. She hadn't seen the house since the

night she and Lee'd . . . "I need to talk to Alan, not you, and definitely not *here*."

"The scene of the crime, so to speak? Well, I guess we could go to Miss Emily's Tea Shop. She has a private room."

"Much better, but I'd like to be alone with Alan. Houston and I—." She stopped, since Lee had taken off like lightning again and thrown her and Alan against the back of the buggy.

"And here are our little lovebirds, now. Lee, you should have told us about you and Blair," Miss Emily said. "When Nina told us you were the lovesick young swain, we all thought it was Houston."

"I guess it's true that love is blind," Lee said, winking at the older woman. "Could we have the private dining room? An old friend of my fiancée's has come to visit, and we'd like to talk."

Miss Emily took one look at Alan and smiled. "You have to meet Nina, Leander's sister, such a pretty young lady."

By the time they got into the private dining room, and tea and cakes had been set before them, Blair was grimacing, Alan was still looking puzzled, but Lee was smiling proudly.

"If you don't mind, I'll tell Alan the truth," Blair said, as soon as the door was closed. "My sister, Houston, wanted to go somewhere and—."

"Where?" Lee interrupted.

She glared at him. "If you must know, she had received an invitation to see that monstrous house of Taggert's that night and she wanted to go, and the only way she could was if I posed as her and went to the reception with you. Anyway," she turned back to Alan and her voice lost its anger, "my sister wanted to trade places for the evening, like we used to do when we were children, so we did. Except I didn't know what I was getting myself into because *he*," she glanced at Lee, "kept getting angry at me, I mean Houston, and I kept trying to get away from him but he wouldn't let me. And then, the next day, he found out we'd traded places, and now he stupidly thinks I want to *marry* him."

Alan was quiet for several moments. "The story seems to be missing a few pieces."

"I'd say about half of it's missing," Lee said. "The truth is, the twins did exchange places, and I don't for the life of me know why I didn't see it right away. I was engaged to Houston, who's a cool little thing, so I should have guessed it wasn't her because when I touched Blair she practically ignited."

"How dare you say such a thing!"

Lee looked completely innocent. "I'm just telling the truth, sweetheart. I took her to my house for a late supper and, well, let's just say that we had the wedding night a couple of weeks early."

"Alan, it wasn't like that. I was Houston and *she* loves him, Heaven only knows why, because *I* don't even like the man. He's bigoted, egotistical and thinks a woman couldn't be a partner in the clinic he wants to open. I just want to go home and work in St. Joseph's and marry you, Alan. You have to believe that."

Alan was frowning as he ran his fork across the table-cloth. "You must have some feeling for him or you wouldn't have—."

"I told you," Blair interrupted, her face showing her anxiety. "I was Houston. Alan, please believe me. I'll leave with you right now."

"Over my dead body," Lee said.

"Ah! at last a pleasurable thought," she said, smiling at him with her eyes narrowed.

Alan interrupted them as he turned to Lee. "Tell me, do you plan to drag her down the aisle by her hair?"

"I have nearly two weeks. By the day of the wedding, she'll be begging to marry me."

"Are you sure of that?" Alan asked.

"Positive," Lee answered.

"Shall we put it to a test? On the twentieth she either leaves with me or marries you."

"Agreed."

"Agreed!?" Blair rose from the table. "I don't think I want either one of you. I'll not be bargained over like a head of cattle."

"Sit down." Lee put his hand on her shoulder and pulled her back into her chair. "You say you're in love with him, yet you can't resist me, so who else do you want to choose from?"

"I don't want to choose at all. I want to marry Alan."

"That's what you say today, but you've only just met me," Lee said smugly. "Of course, it was an impressive first meeting, but—. Here! sit down." He looked back at Alan. "We need some rules set up. First, she has to agree to stay in Chandler until the twentieth. No leaving town. And second, she has to accept my invitations. She can't sequester herself in Gates's house or only go out with you. Anything else is open territory."

"That sounds fair enough to me. What about you, Blair?"

Her first thought was to walk out of the tearoom and leave them both there, but first, she wanted to know the consequences. "What if I don't agree?"

"If you don't agree, and I take that to mean you plan to slip out of town," Lee said, "I'll send Gates after you in Pennsylvania, and after he finishes telling his story, you won't have a medical career. On the other hand, if on the twentieth, you should mistakenly choose Alan, I'll buy your train ticket and I'll somehow pacify Gates."

She considered this for a moment, then looked at Lee. "All right, but I'll give you warning now. I don't want to marry you, and I'm going to make you feel nothing but relief on the twentieth when I leave this bigoted little town with Alan, because I'm going to make your life as miserable as possible between now and then."

Lee turned to Alan. "I love a woman with fire in her veins. May the best man win." He extended his hand and Alan shook it. It was settled.

Chapter 9

The day after Alan arrived, Blair was stretched on her back on a quilt spread across the grass under a tree in Fenton Park. Alan was reading an article to her about the latest advancements in the treatment of diphtheria while she watched the clouds moving overhead, listened to the buzzing of the bees and heard the laughter of the other people in the park on this beautiful day.

"Blair, did you hear me? I was reading Dr. Anderson's report. What do you think?"

"About what?" she asked dreamily, turning onto her stomach. "Oh!" she said, startled. "I guess I wasn't listening. I was thinking about my sister and what happened yesterday."

Alan closed the book. "Care to share your thoughts?"

"That man Taggert sent her a carriage and horse and, along with it, the world's largest diamond. Houston wasn't even ruffled. She just very calmly clutched that ring to her heart, walked out to that carriage and drove away, and she didn't get home until after nine o'clock. By then, Mother was prostrate with grief because her daughter was selling herself, so I had to spend hours trying to quiet her before she could sleep. And this morning, Houston left before daylight—which started Mother crying again."

"And she isn't worried about you?" Alan asked, as he put the medical text down and leaned against the tree.

"I think that both she and Mr. Gates believe that I'm getting a better man than I deserve—or at least Gates thinks that. I'm not sure what Mother thinks. She's too worried about how Houston's life has been ruined."

Alan ran his fingers along the edges of the book. "And you still think that I shouldn't be introduced to your mother and stepfather?"

"Not yet," she said, sitting up. "You can't imagine what Gates is like. If he heard that I'd—." She stopped because the last thing she wanted to do was to remind Alan of why she'd become engaged to Lee in the first place. But she knew that if Gates heard that she'd slept with one man while being engaged to another, her life would be more miserable than it was already. That man never missed a chance to point out to her that she was ruining her sister's life so that Houston thought she had to marry a man for his money, anything so she could save herself from humiliation in front of the entire town—humiliation that was entirely caused by Blair and her immorality. Night and day, that's what she heard from her stepfather.

She gave Alan a weak smile. "Let's not talk about anything unpleasant on this lovely day. Why don't we go for a walk or, better yet, why don't we rent a canoe and go out on the lake? I haven't had any practice on the water since I left the rowing team in the fall."

"I would like that," he said, rising and offering his hand to help her up.

They folded the blanket, took the book, and started toward the small rental shop beside Midnight Lake, where they rented a canoe. There were several couples on the lake and they called out in greeting.

"Good morning, Blair-Houston," they said, looking with interest at Alan, and some of them hinted that they'd like to be introduced, but she didn't oblige. Houston might feel an obligation to satisfy the curiosity of the townspeople, but Blair didn't think she had to.

She leaned back in the canoe while Alan paddled, her face protected from the fierce high-altitude sun of Chandler by a large hat, letting her hand trail in the water; she nearly fell asleep.

"Good morning!" came a voice that made her sit upright. She looked into Leander's face as he rowed alongside them.

"What are you doing here?" she asked, jaw clenched. "Go away."

"According to your mother, I'm out with you. Well, Hunter, you don't look altogether comfortable with that paddle. Maybe it's too much city living."

"Will you get out of here and take your snide remarks with you? We were perfectly peaceful until you came along."

"Careful with your temper, people are beginning to look, and you wouldn't want them to think there was anything wrong in paradise, would you?"

"Paradise? With you? You're nothing but a—."

Leander interrupted her. "Hunter, can you give me a hand? I seem to have caught my foot under this seat and it's beginning to swell."

"Alan, don't do it," Blair warned. "I don't trust him."

But it was too late. Alan, newly out of medical school and very aware of his responsibilities as a healer, could not resist a plea for help. He instantly put the paddle down and leaned over the side to help Lee—and as soon as he was stretched across the water, Lee gave the canoe a shove, and Alan, after a moment of struggle, fell into the lake. Blair instantly leaned over to help Alan, but Lee grabbed her about the waist and hauled her into his boat.

There was laughter surrounding them, and the sound of Alan thrashing in the water as he tried to get back into the canoe, and there was the sound of Blair flailing at Lee to make him let her go. Somehow, he managed to row them the few feet to shore using just one oar, while holding Blair with his other arm and suffering as little physical injury as possible from her flying fists.

Once on shore, he stood before her and grinned like a little boy who'd just done a magnificent feat.

"My hat," Blair said through clenched teeth and Lee, still grinning, went to the little wooden boat to get it.

And when he had his back turned and he was off guard, Blair grabbed a discarded paddle and pushed him in the back with all her might. To her great joy, Leander went face down in the mud at the edge of the lake.

But Blair didn't have time to enjoy her success, because she saw that Alan was still floundering in the water. She thanked heaven for her years on the women's rowing team as she made her way out to Alan in Lee's boat.

"I never learned to swim," he said, as she leaned over to help him over the side. "Just to tread water."

They managed to get him inside the boat, Alan coughing, dripping water and weak, after what, to him, had been a harrowing experience. Blair glanced toward shore and saw Lee standing there covered with mud, and that gave her some satisfaction.

Expertly, she turned the boat and rowed them to the other side of the lake to the rental place.

She took care of the rental while Alan stood to one side and sneezed, then got them a hired carriage to take them back to the Imperial Hotel where he was staying.

Blair was so angry that she didn't even look at Alan all the way through town to the hotel. How dare Leander treat her like that in public—or in private for that matter, she thought. She had made herself perfectly clear that she wanted nothing to do with him, yet he insisted on forcing himself on her.

She followed Alan up the stairs to his room. "If I ever get my hands on that man, I'll kill him. He is the most insufferable creature! Thinking that I could ever possibly want to marry someone like that is just a perfect example of his self-centeredness. Give me your key."

"What? Oh. Here. Blair, do you think you should go into my room with me? I mean, how do you think it will look?"

Blair took the key from him and opened the door. "Could you imagine living with that man? He is like a very large spoiled boy who has to have his own way. Now, he's decided that he wants me, probably because I'm the first woman to ever say no to him, and so he sets out to make my life miserable." She stopped and looked at Alan as he stood dripping on the hotel room floor. "Why are you standing there in those wet clothes? You should get undressed."

"Blair, I don't think you should be here, and I certainly don't plan to undress in front of you."

Blair began to come back to her senses and realized where she was. "You're right, of course. I guess I was too angry to think. Will I see you tomorrow?"

"If I don't die of pneumonia before then," he said with a smile.

She smiled back at him, started to leave, then, on impulse, she turned back and flung her arms around him as she pressed her mouth to his.

He held her tentatively at first, as if he didn't want to get her wet, but as Blair applied more pressure and more passion, he held her closer, turning his head as he became more involved in the kiss.

Blair pulled away. "I have to go," she said softly, as she moved toward the door. "I'll see you tomorrow."

Alan stood still for a while after Blair'd gone, not bothering to change out of his wet clothes. "You *didn't* say no to him, Blair," he whispered, "and when I kiss you you have to go, but he can make you stay all night."

On Thursday morning, Blair burst into the Chandler house, tears running down her face, and ran upstairs to her room. She had to plow through several bouquets of flowers before she could get to the bed. Sweeping aside a half dozen boxes of chocolates, she flung herself on the bed where she spent an hour weeping. Leander Westfield was making her life impossible. Yesterday he'd once again ruined a pleasant afternoon with Alan. She and Alan had gone on a picnic in the country and Lee had shown up, firing a six-gun in the air to frighten the horses, and trying to pull Blair atop his horse. But, again, she'd managed to thwart him by making the horse rear, and she got away.

Alan had stood there watching them, not able to participate since he knew very little about the temperament of horses that weren't attached to a carriage. In fact, Blair'd had a difficult time talking him into taking a ride, rather than renting a buggy as he preferred to do.

When Blair had gotten away from Lee and his rearing horse, she mounted one of the horses that she and Alan had rented— the other one had run away at the sound of Lee's pistol—and spent some moments persuading Alan to mount behind her.

Blair'd spent a great deal of her childhood on a horse, and she needed all her skill now, as she raced to get away from Lee. As she turned back to look at him once, with Alan holding on to her for dear life, Alan screamed in fear. They were fast approaching a tree, and the horse was going to hit it if he wasn't given room to pass it.

Leander saw the danger at the same time and, in a lightning-fast movement, swerved his horse so hard that the animal unexpectedly reared, throwing Lee into the dust. Because of his action, Blair and Alan were able to get away safely.

Unfortunately, or fortunately from Blair's point of view, Lee's horse kept on going, heading for the safety of his stable.

Alan was clutching both Blair and the saddle as she kept up a brisk pace back to town. "Aren't you going to give him a ride? It's miles back to town."

"It's only about six miles," she answered over her shoulder. "And, besides, he should be used to walking by now."

That had been Wednesday, and compared to today, that had been a day of thanksgiving. Early this morning, Gates had started on Blair because he'd finally heard what had happened at the lake, and how Blair had been seen with another man, and how she'd humiliated Lee before everyone.

Blair didn't want to argue with him, so she said that she was to meet Lee at the hospital this morning. She lied and said that Lee wanted to talk to her about medicine, but the truth was, she was hoping Lee wouldn't be at the hospital, because she certainly didn't want to see him.

Gates insisted that she go with him as he left for work, and when he dropped her off, he waited to see her go through the doors. Like a prisoner, she thought.

The inside of the hospital was familiar to her, and the smell of carbolic, wet wood and soap was like coming home. No one seemed to be around, so she started wandering about the wards, peering inside the rooms, glancing at the patients and wishing that she could get back to Pennsylvania and go to work.

It was on the third floor that she heard something that she identified at once: the sound of someone trying to breathe.

She became Dr. Chandler instantly, running into the room, seeing the older woman choking and beginning to turn blue. Blair didn't waste a second before she began pushing on the woman's chest and then using her own lungs to force air into the woman.

She hadn't applied two breaths before she found herself forcibly pulled away.

Leander pushed so hard that she nearly fell as he began clearing the woman's throat. Within minutes, the patient was breathing evenly again and he turned her over to a nurse.

"You come to my office," he said to Blair, barely looking at her.

What followed for Blair was twenty minutes of a tongue-lashing such as she'd never had before in her life. Lee seemed to think that she was trying to interfere in his work and that she could have killed his patient.

Nothing Blair said made any difference to his rage. He said she should have called for help rather than worked on a patient that she knew nothing about, that the treatment she'd tried might have been the wrong one and she could have done more harm than good.

Blair knew he was right and, even as he spoke, she began to cry.

Leander relented, stopped his tirade, and put his arm around her.

Blair drew away, screaming that she hated him and she never wanted to see him again. She ran down the stairs and hid inside a doorway while he ran past looking for her. When the way was clear, she left the hospital and caught a trolley car home—where she was now, crying and never wanting to see that horrible, hideous man again.

At eleven, she managed to pull herself together enough to leave the house to meet Alan. She told her mother she was meeting Lee to play tennis and Opal merely nodded, mistakenly trusting her daughter.

Opal was sitting on the back porch, trying to enjoy the spring afternoon and not worry about her daughters, her embroidery in her hands, when she looked up to see Leander standing in the doorway. "Why, Lee, what a pleasant surprise. I thought you and Blair went to play tennis. Did you forget something?"

"Mind if I sit down and join you for a while?"

"Of course not." She looked at him. Rarely was Lee's handsome face marred by a frown, but today he looked as if he were deeply worried about something. "Lee, is there something you'd like to talk about?"

Leander took his time in answering as he withdrew a cigar from his inner coat pocket and motioned to Opal for permission to smoke. "She's out with a man named Alan Hunter, the man she says she's going to marry."

Opal's hands stopped sewing. "Oh, dear, yet another complication. You'd better tell me all of it."

"It seems that she accepted this man's marriage proposal in Pennsylvania and he was to come Monday and meet you and Mr. Gates."

"But by Monday, Blair'd already . . . And the announcement of your marriage had been made, so . . ." She trailed off.

"It was my doing that our engagement was announced. Both Houston and Blair wanted to keep quiet and forget any of it'd ever happened. I'm almost ashamed to admit that I blackmailed Blair into remaining in Chandler and participating in the competition."

"Competition?"

"I met Hunter at the train station on Monday, and I talked him into competing with me for Blair's hand. I have until the twentieth to win her, because on the twentieth she's going to decide whether she wants to marry me or leave town with Hunter."

He turned to Opal. "But I think I'm losing, and I don't know how to win her. I've never had to court a woman before, so I'm not really sure what has to be done. I've tried flowers, candy, and making a fool of myself in front of the entire town—all the things I thought women liked, but nothing seems to be working. On the twentieth, she's going to leave with Hunter," he repeated, as if it were the most tragic of thoughts and, with a sigh, he told Opal what had been going on in the last few days, told her about the lake incident and then the time with the horses and ended with this morning at the hospital when he had, admittedly, been a little rough on Blair.

Opal was thoughtful for a moment. "You love her a great deal, don't you?" she said with surprise in her voice.

Lee sat up straighter in his chair. "I don't know whether it's love exactly . . ." He glanced at Opal, then seemed as if he realized he was fighting a losing battle. "Well, all right, maybe I am in love with her, so in love that I don't even mind looking like the town idiot—if only I get her."

He quickly began to defend himself. "But I'm not about to go to her looking moony-eyed and tell her that I did an unmanly thing like fall in love with her on the first night I spent with her. It's one thing to have your roses thrown back in your face, but I'm not sure I'd like to have the same thing done to my declarations of undying love."

"I think you may be right. Do you know how this other man is courting her?"

"It's something I clean forgot to ask."

"He must be the 'friend' who keeps sending her medical books. Blair reads one, and an hour later she leaves the house, saying she's meeting you."

"I have a room full of medical books, but I can't imagine sending one to a woman. I guess I have to agree with Mr. Gates when it comes to medicine. I wish she'd give up this absurd idea and settle down and—."

"And what? Be more like Houston? You had a perfect homemaker, yet you fell in love with someone else. Did you ever think that if Blair gave up her medicine she'd not be Blair?"

There was silence between them for a few moments.

"At this point, I'm willing to try anything. So you think I should send her some medical textbooks?"

"Lee," Opal said softly. "Why did you become a doctor? When did you first know that you wanted to dedicate your life to medicine?"

He smiled. "When I was nine and Mother was ill. Old Doc Brenner stayed with her for two days and she lived. I knew then that that's what I wanted to do."

Opal looked out across her garden for a moment. "When my daughters were eleven, I took them to Pennsylvania to visit my doctor brother, Henry, and his wife, Flo. We had no more than arrived when Flo, Houston, and I came down with a fever. It wasn't serious, but it kept us in bed and left the care of Blair to the staff. My brother thought she looked lonely, so he invited her to go on his rounds with him."

Opal paused to smile. "I didn't learn what went on until days later, when Henry was so excited that he could no longer contain himself. It seems that Blair disobeyed Henry when he told her to stay away from the patients he was treating. The first day, Blair helped her uncle in a difficult, messy birth, keeping her head clear, never panicking, even when the woman began to hemorrhage. By the third day, she was assisting him in an emergency appendectomy performed on a kitchen table. Henry said he'd never seen anyone so suited to medicine as Blair was. It took me a while to get over the shock of the thought of my *daughter* being a doctor, but when I talked to Blair about it, there was a light in her eyes that I'd never seen before, and I knew that if at all possible I was going to help her become a doctor."

She paused to sigh. "I hadn't reckoned on Mr. Gates. When we returned to Chandler, all Blair could talk about was becoming a doctor. Mr. Gates said that no girl under his protection was going to do anything so unladylike. I stood back for a year and watched Blair's spirit gradually become smothered. I think the final straw was when Mr. Gates forbade the library to loan Blair any more books on the subject of medicine."

Opal gave a little laugh. "I think that was the only time that I ever stood up to Mr. Gates. Henry and Flo had no children, and they begged me to let Blair come live with them, promising that Henry would take the responsibility of seeing that Blair received the best education money could buy a woman. I didn't want to see my daughter go, but I knew it was the only way. If she'd stayed here, her spirit would have been broken."

She turned to Lee. "So you see how much medicine means to Blair. It's been her entire life since she was just a girl and now—." She broke off as she pulled an envelope from her pocket. "This came the day before yesterday, from Henry. He sent it to me so I could break the news to Blair as gently as possible. The letter says that even though she qualified to intern at St. Joseph's, even though she placed first in the three-day-long testing, the Philadelphia City Commissioner has vetoed her placement, because he says it's an impropriety to have a lady working so closely with men."

"But that's—," Lee burst out.

"Unfair? No more unfair than your asking her to give up medicine and stay home to see that the maid irons your shirts the way you want them."

Lee looked out at the garden, smoking his cigar, thinking.

"Maybe she'd like to visit a few cases with me in the country. Nothing too difficult, just some routine checks."

"Yes, I do think she'd like that." She put her hand on his arm. "And Lee, I think you'll see a different Blair from the one you've seen up 'til now. Because Blair tends to be a bit outspoken, people sometimes don't see the size of her heart. If you continue to make Mr. Hunter look like a fool in front of her, she'll never forgive you, much less begin to love you. Let her see the Leander this town knows, the one who repeatedly gets out of bed at three o'clock to listen to Mrs. Lechner's complaints of mysterious pains. And the man who saved Mrs. Saunderson's twins last summer. And the man who—."

"All right," Lee laughed. "I'll show her that I'm actually a saint in disguise. Do you think she really *does* know anything about medicine?"

It was Opal's turn to laugh. "Have you ever heard of Dr. Henry Thomas Blair?"

"The pathologist? Of course. Some of his advances in disease detection have been—." He stopped. *"He's* Uncle Henry?"

Opal's eyes twinkled in delight. "The same, and Henry says Blair is good, very good. Give her a chance. You won't be sorry."

Chapter 10

Blair's day was not improved by her tennis game with Alan. During her schooling, her uncle had emphasized the importance of exercise. He said that vigorous physical exercise would help improve her ability to think and to study. Therefore, Blair had joined the rowing team, had learned to play tennis with some of the other students, and, when she could, she'd participated in gymnastics, bicycling, and done a little hiking.

She beat Alan at tennis.

Alan was looking distracted as he walked toward the side of the court. Throughout the game, he'd watched over his shoulder, with an expression on his face that showed that he thought someone was going to appear at any moment.

Blair was very annoyed when the game was finished, because she suspected that Alan's worry about Leander was keeping him from playing well.

"Alan, I almost think you're afraid of him. So far, we've beaten him every time."

"You have beaten him. I'm useless in this country. Now, if we could meet in a city, perhaps I'd have a chance."

"Leander has studied all over the world. I'm quite sure he's as at home in a ballroom as on a horse," she said as she cleaned off her racquet.

"A Renaissance man?" Alan said archly, an edge to his voice.

Blair looked up at him. "Alan, you look as if you're angry. You know how I feel about the man."

"Do I? What I know are the facts, that you went out with him once and ended up spending the night with him, yet when I touch you, you seem to have infinite control."

"I don't have to listen to any of this." She turned away.

He caught her arm. "Would you rather that Westfield said it? Would you rather that he were here now with his blazing six-guns and his ability to trick a gullible young medical student?"

She gave him a cool look worthy of her sister. "Release my arm."

He did so immediately, his anger leaving him. "Blair, I'm sorry, I didn't mean what I said. It's just that I'm so tired of looking the fool. I'm tired of staying in my hotel room and of not being allowed to meet your parents. I feel like the one who's unwanted, rather than Westfield."

She felt herself giving in to him. His anger was perfectly understandable. She put her hand to his cheek. "I wanted to leave with you that first day, but you wanted a competition. You agreed to it, and now my future life as a doctor is in jeopardy. I can't leave Chandler with you until the twentieth. But have some faith that I *will* leave with you."

He escorted her to within a block of her house, and when they parted, Blair felt the tension in Alan. He was worried and nothing Blair said seemed to make any difference.

At the house, she went to her room, glad for once that her mother didn't give her an itemized list of the flowers and candy that Leander had had delivered while she was out. Instead, Opal merely greeted her pleasantly and went back to her sewing, while Blair had to practically drag herself up the stairs.

She was determined not to spend the afternoon crying, as she'd spent the morning, so she stretched out on the bed and tried to read a chapter about burn victims in a book that Alan had lent her.

At three, Susan, the upstairs maid, came in with a tray of food. "Mrs. Gates said I was to bring this up to you and to ask if you needed anything else."

"No," Blair said listlessly, pushing the food out of reach.

Susan paused at the door, running her apron along the door frame. "Of course, you heard about yesterday."

"Yesterday?" Blair asked, without much interest. How could Alan think that she was interested in Leander? Hadn't she made it clear to everyone involved that she wanted nothing whatever to do with him?

"I thought maybe since you were asleep when Miss Houston came in last night, and then you left so early this morning, that you might not have heard about Mr. Taggert and the awful mess he made at the garden party yesterday, and how he carried Miss Houston out, and then he came here and I do believe that your mother almost fell in love with him, and he's going to buy her a pink train and—."

Susan had Blair's attention now. "Slow down a minute and tell me everything." She curled her legs on the bed and began to eat the food in front of her.

"Well," Susan said slowly, obviously enjoying being the center of attention. "Yesterday, your sister showed up at Miss Tia Mankin's garden party—the one you were invited to but didn't go to—and standing next to her was this divine man, and at first no one recognized him. Of course, I was only told this because I wasn't really there, but I got to see him later and everything they said was more than true. I never thought that that big dirty man could look so good. Anyway, he came to the party and all the women gathered around him, and then he took food to Miss Houston and spilled it in her lap. Nobody could say a word for a minute, but somebody started to laugh, and the next thing you know, Mr. Taggert picked Miss Houston up and carried her out of the garden and put her in that pretty new buggy he bought her."

Blair had a mouthful of sandwich and tried to wash it down with milk. "Didn't Houston say anything? I can't imagine her allowing a man to do that in public." Truthfully, she couldn't imagine her sister allowing that in private, either.

"I *never* saw anything like that with Dr. Leander, but not only did Miss Houston allow it, she brought him here and asked your mother to entertain him in the parlor."

"My mother? But she cries every time she hears the name of Taggert."

"Not after yesterday. I don't know what it is about him she likes, other than his looks, because the man scares me to death, but she almost fell in love with him. I helped Miss Houston change clothes, and when we got downstairs, your mother was asking him to call her Opal, and he was asking her what color train car he could buy her."

Susan took the empty tray off the bed. "But something awful must have happened after Miss Houston left with the man, because she came home last night in tears. She tried to hide it from me when I helped her undress, but I could see that she was crying. And today, she hasn't eaten and she's stayed in her room all day." She gave Blair a sly look as she paused at the doorway. "Just like you. This house ain't a happy place today," she said just before she left the room.

Immediately, Blair left her room and went to her sister. Houston was lying on the bed, her eyes red and swollen and looking a picture of misery. The first thought that Blair had was that her sister's unhappiness was her fault. If she hadn't come back to Chandler, Houston would still be engaged to Leander, and she wouldn't be considering marrying a man who spilled food all over her and mauled her in public.

Blair tried to talk to Houston, telling her that if she made it clear that she still wanted Lee, she could probably still have him, and she wouldn't have to sacrifice herself to that man Taggert. But the more Blair talked, the more Houston closed up. She would say nothing except that Leander no longer loved her, and that he wanted Blair in a way that he'd never wanted her.

Blair wanted to tell her sister that if she'd just wait until the twentieth, she could have Lee. She wanted to tell about the blackmail scheme, and about Alan and how much she loved him, but she was afraid that would make Houston feel worse, as if she were the consolation prize. All Houston could seem to talk about was the fact that Lee had rejected her, that he wanted Blair, and that Taggert was making her miserable, although she wouldn't tell Blair exactly what the man had done to her.

And the more Houston talked, the worse Blair felt. She'd gone out with Leander in the first place because she'd been worried that he wasn't good for her sister. She'd been worried because Houston hadn't been upset after Lee had been angry with her. But now, Houston had a totally different kind of man and she spent the entire day in misery. If only she hadn't interfered!

Houston was standing by her bed, trying to stop the flood of tears cascading down her face.

"You may think that you failed with Leander, but you didn't. And you don't have to punish yourself with an overbearing oaf. He can't even handle a plate of food, much less—."

Blair stopped because Houston slapped her across the face.

"He's the man I'm going to marry," Houston said, anger in her voice. "I'll not let you or anyone else denigrate him."

With her hand to her cheek, Blair's eyes began to fill with tears. "What I've done is coming between us," she whispered. "No man anywhere means more than sisters," she said before leaving the room.

The rest of the day was even worse for Blair. If she'd had any doubts as to why Houston was marrying Taggert, they were put to rest just before dinner when a dozen rings were delivered from the man. Houston took one look at them and her face lit up like a gaslight on high. She fairly floated from the room, and Blair wondered if the presents of the carriage and thirteen rings were going to be enough to make up for having to live with a man like Taggert. From the look on Houston's face, it seemed as if she thought so.

Dinner came, and Houston's cheerfulness made Blair feel terrible, but she knew the uselessness of trying to talk to her sister about anything.

When the telephone rang during dinner, Gates told the maid to tell whoever it was that no one was going to talk on the newfangled thing. "Think they have the right to make you talk to them just because they can make that thing ring," he grumbled.

Susan came back into the room and her eyes were on Blair. "It's very important, the caller said. I'm to say it's a Miss Hunter."

"Hunter," Blair said, her soup halfway to her mouth. "I'd better answer it." Without asking Mr. Gates's permission, she half ran to the telephone.

"I don't know any Hunters," Gates was saying behind her.

"Of course you do," Opal said smoothly. "They moved here from Seattle last year. You met him at the Lechners' last summer."

"Maybe I did. I seem to remember. Here, Houston, have some of this beef. You need fattening up."

"Hello," Blair said tentatively.

Instead of Alan's voice as she expected, she heard Leander. "Blair, please don't hang up. I have an invitation to extend to you."

"And what do you plan to do to Alan this time? You've used guns, horses, you've nearly drowned him. Did you know that we played tennis today? You could have thrown balls at him or hit him with the racquet."

"I know that my conduct hasn't been the best, but I'd like to make it up to you. I'm going to be on call all day tomorrow to handle any emergencies that come up, and I have several patients in the country that I need to see. I thought you might like to go with me."

Blair couldn't speak for a moment. To spend the entire day doing what she was trained for? To not have to loll about, going from one pastime to another, but to learn something?

"Blair, are you there?"

"Yes, of course."

"If you'd rather not, I'll understand. It'll be a long day, and I'm sure you'll be exhausted by the end of it, so—."

"You pick me up whenever you need to. I'll be ready at the crack of dawn, and tomorrow we'll see who gives out first." She hung up the telephone and went back to the table. Tomorrow she'd be a doctor! For the first time in days, she didn't feel the burden of the weight of responsibility for hurting her sister.

Nina Westfield heard the pounding on the door for some minutes before someone answered it.

A white-faced maid came into the parlor, her hands trembling. "Miss, there's a man out here, he says he's Mr. Alan Hunter, and he says he's come to kill Dr. Leander."

"My goodness. Does he look dangerous?"

"He's just standin' there and bein' calm, but his eyes are wild and . . . he's very handsome. I thought maybe you might be able to talk to him. He doesn't look like the killin' kind to me."

Nina put her book aside. "Show him in, then get Mr. Thompson from next door to come over, and send someone to get my father. Then send someone to keep Lee at the hospital. Invent an illness if you have to, just keep him away from home."

Obediently, the maid left, and in a moment she escorted Mr. Hunter into the parlor.

Nina didn't think he looked like a killer at all, and she extended her hand to him in friendship, ignoring the maid's gasps when she closed the door to the room. When Mr. Thompson showed up a few minutes later, Nina sent him home, saying that it had all been a mistake, and when her father came, she introduced Alan and the three of them sat and talked until late.

Unfortunately, no one thought about Leander, who was trying to help the man who'd been their family butler for sixteen years. The butler was writhing with pains that no one could pinpoint, although Lee kept trying. And every time Lee left the room, the butler called the Westfield house and was told that the dangerous man was still there, so the butler went back and developed a new symptom.

Which was why Leander got only four hours sleep before the first emergency call came in, and since it was four thirty he hesitated to awaken the entire Chandler family, and instead he climbed the tree to get into Blair's bedroom.

Chapter 11

There was only the faintest hint of bluish-gray dawn when Leander climbed the tree and crossed the porch roof to Blair's bedroom. He felt like a schoolboy about to get caught in a prank. Here he was, twenty-seven years old, a doctor; he'd spent years in Europe; had visited some of the grand salons, but now he was climbing a tree and slipping into a girl's bedroom as if he were a naughty boy.

But when he entered the room and saw Blair outlined by the thin sheet, he forgot all inhibitions. The last few days had been miserable. He'd found her and knew that, as he wanted his own soul, he wanted this woman, but he could see her slipping away from him. Something about her made him clumsy, awkward, and everything he did was wrong. He'd tried to impress her, tried to make himself look good compared to that incompetent, weak, frightened little blond mouse she thought she loved. Lee knew Hunter wasn't man enough for her.

For a moment, he stood over her, liking that she was soft and sweet, as she had been the one night when she hadn't been angry with him.

That night had changed his life, and he was determined to have her like that again.

With a smile, and a feeling that he couldn't help himself, he pulled the sheet back and slipped into bed with her, shoes and all. There wasn't time for prolonged lovemaking and now, before she woke, while he could still think, he knew that the third floor of Duncan Gates's house was not the place.

He kissed her temple as he pulled her into his arms and, sleepily, she snuggled closer to him as he kissed her eyes and cheeks. When he touched her lips with his, she slowly came awake, moving her body nearer his, her thigh sliding between his as his hand moved down to draw her gown up and caress her bare flesh.

His kiss deepened, his tongue touching hers, and she responded eagerly, pushing at him as she tried to get closer.

It was Lee's watch fob piercing her stomach through her thin nightgown that made her waken—but not fully.

"I thought you were a dream," she murmured, as her hand caressed his cheek.

"I am," Leander said hoarsely. Never in his life had he been required to use such control. He wanted to take her gown off, to caress all her warm, lovely flesh, to feel her skin against his. He wanted to run his unshaven cheeks against the soft flesh of her stomach and hear her squeal in feigned protest.

Blair suddenly sat straight up. "What are you doing here?" she gasped.

He put his hand over her mouth and pulled her down beside him, where she began kicking her heels and pushing at him. "If you want to go with me, you have to go now, and since it's not daylight yet, I didn't want to bang on your front door and wake the whole house. Will you stop making so much noise? Gates will be in here, and if he sees you like this, he'll probably parade you downtown in sackcloth and ashes." He moved his hand away as she calmed.

"That's preferable to what you have planned," she said in a loud whisper. "Get off me."

Leander didn't move an inch. "If I'd had time, I would have climbed in here without my . . . ah, shoes," he said, rubbing his leg up and down between hers, still holding her quite close.

"You are a vain, lecherous—."

She broke off because he pinned her arms above her head and kissed her, gently at first, deepening until she couldn't breathe, then gentle again. When he pulled away, there were tears in her eyes as she turned her head aside. "Please don't," she whispered. "Please."

"I don't know why I should have any mercy," he said, releasing her hands but keeping her trapped under most of his body. "You've shown me no mercy in the last few days." At the look in her eyes, he moved off her. "If I leave the way I came, down the tree, will you get dressed and meet me out front?"

Her eyes lost the look of a trapped animal. "And we'll go on call?"

"I never saw a woman look forward to blood and gore before."

"It's not that, it's the helping of people that I like. If I can save one life, then my life—."

He kissed her quickly before climbing out of the bed. "You can give me the new doctor speech on the way. Ten minutes, all right?"

Blair could only nod and was out of the bed almost before Lee was out the window. She didn't give a thought to how unusual their behavior was, because nothing in her life had been ordinary since she'd returned to Chandler.

Out of the small closet in her room, beside some of Houston's stored winter clothes, Blair took a garment that she was very proud of. She'd had it made in Philadelphia by the old, established tailoring firm of J. Cantrell and Sons. She'd worked with them for weeks on designing and fitting a suit that would fill all the needs she could imagine in future emergencies as a doctor and yet remain modest. In the tailor's shop, she'd tried wearing it astride a wooden horse, making sure that it was short enough to be safe and long enough to be respectable.

The jacket was cut with perfect military simplicity; the skirt looked full and feminine, but it was actually divided into two so it had the safety and comfort of bloomers. The suit was made of the finest, most closely woven, navy blue serge that money could buy, with several deep pockets that disappeared into the folds of the fabric, a buttoned flap over each pocket so that no precious instruments could be lost. There was a simple red cross on the sleeve to designate the suit's purpose.

Blair tied on a pair of high laced black calfskin shoes—boys' style rather than the fashionably narrow shoes that tortured women's feet into submission—grabbed her new physician's bag, and hurried downstairs to meet Leander.

He was leaning against the carriage smoking one of his thin little cigars, and for a moment, Blair dreaded going anywhere with him. No doubt she'd spend all day fighting his hands moving all over her, and she'd never get to do anything to help with a patient.

He took one quick look at her outfit and seemed to nod in approval before jumping into the carriage and leaving Blair to help herself get in.

As soon as she climbed into Lee's carriage, he started off in the way that Blair was beginning to prepare herself for. She held on for dear life.

"Where is this first case?" she shouted over the sounds of the carriage tearing along the road south out of Chandler.

"I don't usually do these calls anymore, since I work in the hospital most of the time," he shouted back at her. "So some of the cases I haven't seen, but this one I happen to know. It's Joe Gleason, and his wife's sick. I'm sure it's another baby. Somehow, Effie manages to produce one every eight months." He gave her a sideways look. "Ever caught a newborn?"

Blair nodded and smiled. Since she'd lived with her uncle, she'd an advantage that the other students in her college did not have: she'd been able to work with patients rather than just learn theory from books.

After a ride that left Blair's side bruised from slamming against the side of the carriage, Leander halted in front of a little log cabin that was at the foot of the mountains, the bare yard in front of it full of chickens, dogs and an endless number of thin, dirty children—all of whom seemed to be fighting each other for space.

Joe, little, scrawny, mostly toothless, shooed children and animals out of his way with equal disdain. "She's in here, Doc. It ain't like Effie to lay down durin' the day, and now she's been in bed for four days, and this mornin' I couldn't wake her up. I been doctorin' her the best I could, but don't nothin' seem to help."

Blair followed the two men into the house, looking at the wide-eyed children as she listened to the beginning of Joe's tale of what had happened.

"I was choppin' wood and the axe head flew off and hit Effie in the leg. It didn't cut her real bad but she bled a lot and felt dizzy, so she went to bed—in the middle of the day! Like I said, I doctored her the best I could, but now I'm worried about her."

The little room where the woman lay in a motionless heap was dark and foul smelling.

"Open that window and get me a lantern."

"The wagon man said the air weren't good for her."

Leander gave the man a threatening look, and Joe ran to open the window.

As Joe got the lantern, Lee took a seat by the woman's bed and pulled back the covers. On her leg was a filthy, rancid, thick bandage. "Blair, if what's under here is what I think it is, maybe you—."

Blair didn't give him a chance to finish. She was examining the woman's head, lifting her eyelids, taking her pulse, and at last bending to smell her breath. "I think this woman is drunk," she said with wonder, as she looked about the room. On the crude little table next to the bed was an empty bottle labelled *Dr. Monroe's Elixir of Life. Guaranteed to cure whatever ails you.*

She held it aloft. "Have you been giving this to your wife?"

"I paid good money for that," Joe said indignantly. "Dr. Monroe said it'd do her a world of good."

"Is this thing from Dr. Monroe also?" Lee asked, motioning toward the thick bandage.

"It's a cancer plaster. I figured if it could cure cancer, it'd sure cure Effie of a little cut. Is she gonna be all right, Doc?"

Lee didn't bother to answer the man as he began shoving pieces of wood into the old stove that sat in the corner of the room and put a kettle of water on to boil. As they waited for the water to boil and, later, while Lee and Blair were scrubbing their hands, she asked questions.

"Have you given her anything else?" she asked, dreading the man's answer.

"Just a little gunpowder this mornin'. She was havin' a hard time wakin' up, and I thought gunpowder would help perk her up."

"You damn well may have killed her," Lee said, then his face whitened a bit as he started prying away the edges of the filthy bandage from the unconscious woman's leg just above the knee. As he looked at the flesh under the bandage, he grimaced. "Just what I thought. Joe, go boil me some more water. I'll have to clean this up." The little man took one look under the bandage and hurried from the room. Lee, his eyes on Blair's, pulled the filthy fabric back so she could see.

Tiny, squirming maggots covered the swollen, raw cut.

Blair didn't allow herself to react as she took instruments from Lee's bag and handed them to him. She held an enamelled basin while Lee began to carefully pick out the maggots.

"These things are really a blessing in disguise," Lee was saying. "Maggots eat the putrefied part of the wound and keep it clean. If these"—he held one aloft on the point of his tweezers—"weren't here, we'd probably be amputating now. I've even heard that doctors used to put maggots on a wound just so the worms could clean it."

"So maybe it's good that this place is so filthy," Blair said with distaste, looking about the nasty little room.

Lee looked at her speculatively. "I would have thought that this sort of thing would have been too much for you."

"I have a stronger stomach than you think. You ready for the carbolic?"

As Lee cleaned the wound further, Blair was always ready

with whatever he needed, always half a step ahead of him. He handed her the needles and thread, and Blair sewed the raw edges of the cut while Lee stood back and watched her every movement. He grunted when she finished sewing and let her apply clean bandages to the wound.

Joe arrived to tell them the water was boiling.

"Then you can use it to boil these rags you call sheets," Lee said. "I don't want any more flies getting under that bandage. Blair, help me get these sheets out from under her. And I want some clean clothes for her, too. Blair, you can change her while Joe and I have a talk."

Blair didn't attempt to bathe the woman, but she was sure that the wound on her leg was the cleanest spot on her body. She managed to insert the woman's big body into one of Joe's night rails while the woman lolled about and grinned sometimes in her drunken stupor. Through the open window, she could see Lee and Joe at the side of the cabin, Lee towering over the little man, yelling at him, punching his chest with his finger and generally scaring the man to death. Blair almost felt sorry for Joe, who'd only been doing the best he knew how for his wife.

"Where's the doc?"

She turned to see a man wearing the chaps and denim shirt of a cowboy standing in the doorway, his face anxious.

"I'm a doctor," Blair said. "Do you need help?"

His deep-set eyes in his thin face looked her up and down. "Ain't that Doc Westfield's rig outside?"

"Frank?" Lee asked from behind them. "Is something wrong?"

The cowboy turned around. "A wagon fell down an arroyo. There were three men on it, and one of 'em's hurt pretty bad."

Lee said, "Get my bag," over his shoulder to Blair as he hurried to the carriage, and it was already moving by the time she got there. Silently, as she tossed the two bags to the floor of the carriage, grabbed the roof support and put her foot on the runner, she thanked Mr. Cantrell for the design of her suit that gave her such mobility.

Lee did grab her upper arm with one hand, as he held the

reins with the other, and helped haul her inside as the horse broke into a full gallop. When she was seated, the bags held firmly between her feet, she looked at Lee and he winked at her—a wink with some pride in it.

"This is the Bar S Ranch," Lee shouted, "and Frank is the foreman."

They followed the cowboy, Lee making the buggy go nearly as fast as the lone rider, for about four miles before they saw any buildings. There were four little shacks and a corral precariously pasted onto the side of Ayers Peak.

Lee grabbed his bag, tossed the reins to one of the three cowboys standing nearby and went into the first shack, Blair, bag in hand, on his heels.

There was a man lying on a bunk, his left sleeve soaked with blood. Lee deftly cut the fabric away and a spurt of blood hit his shirt. The encrustation of dried blood on the cowboy's shirt had temporarily sealed the cut artery and kept the man from bleeding to death. Lee pinched the artery with his fingers and held it; there was no time to think about washing.

The cowboys stood over them, barely giving them room, as Blair poured carbolic over her hands and, with a gesture that was as practiced as if they'd been working together for years, Lee released the artery while Blair's smaller fingers took hold. Then Lee disinfected his hands, threaded a needle and, while Blair held the wound open, he sewed. In another few minutes, they had the wound closed.

The cowboys stepped back and their eyes were on Blair.

"I think he'll be all right," Lee said, standing, wiping the blood off his hands with a clean cloth from his bag. "He's lost a lot of blood, but if he pulls through from the shock, I think he'll make it. Who else?"

"Me," said a man on another bunk. "I busted my leg."

Leander slit the man's pant leg, felt the shin bone. "Somebody hold his shoulders. I'll have to pull it into place."

Blair looked about the room as three men moved in front of her to hold the cowboy's shoulders. Leaning against a wall was an enormous man, with arms the size of hams. His big, wide face, that looked as if it'd seen many fights, was white with what Blair recognized to be pain, and he was cradling one arm with the other.

She went to him. "Were you in the wagon accident?"

He glanced down at her, then away. "I'll wait for the doc."

She started to turn away. "I'm a doctor, too, but you're right, I'd probably hurt you more than you could stand."

"You?" the man said; then, as Blair faced him, she saw his face turn even paler.

"Sit down," she ordered and he obeyed, sitting on a bench near the wall. As carefully as she could, she removed his shirt and saw what she'd guessed was wrong with him: that big shoulder of his had become dislocated in the fall. "It's going to hurt some."

He arched his eyebrow at her from under a brow beaded with sweat. "It's doin' that now."

All the cowboys were gathered around Lee as he set the broken leg, and one in the back of the watching crowd had a whiskey bottle to his lips. Blair snatched it away from him and handed it to her patient. "This'll help."

Blair wasn't sure she was physically strong enough to do what she knew had to be done, but she also knew she couldn't stand by and wait for Leander to finish while this man suffered. She'd set a dislocation only once before, and that had been for a child.

With a deep breath and a prayer, she began to flex his forearm, then pressed it against the wall of his massive chest. Grabbing a box of canned goods, she stood on it and, with great effort, managed to raise his big arm high in the air and rotate it. She repeated the procedure, trying not to cause him more pain. She was sweating and panting with the exertion of trying to move that big arm inside a joint that was as big as her hips.

Suddenly, the humerus snapped back into place with a loud click and the deed was done.

Blair stepped back off her box, and she and her patient grinned at each other.

"You're a fine doctor," he said, beaming.

Blair turned around and, to her surprise, everyone in the room, including the two other injured men, were watching her.

And they stayed there, staring silently while Blair bandaged the man's shoulder with her best basket-weave pattern, making it pretty as well as comfortable and useful.

Leander broke the silence when she'd finished. "If you two are ready to stop congratulating each other, I have more patients to see to." His words were at odds with the sparkle of pride in his eyes.

"Ain't you one of them Chandler twins?" a cowboy asked, walking with them to the buggy.

"Blair," she answered.

"She's a doctor, too," Frank said, and they were all looking at her strangely.

"Thanks, Dr. Westfield *and* Dr. Chandler," the man with the dislocated shoulder said as they climbed into the carriage.

"Might as well get used to calling her Westfield, too," Leander said as he snapped the reins. "She's marrying me next week."

Blair couldn't say a word, since she nearly fell out of the carriage as Leander's horse leaped ahead.

Chapter 12

Leander slowed the horse when they were away from the line shacks.

"My father's housekeeper packed us a lunch. I'll stand while you get it out, and we'll eat on the way to the ranch."

Lee stood in the carriage, like a gladiator in a chariot, and Blair lifted the seat. "What an awful lot of room," she said, surprised, looking at the blankets, a shotgun, boxes of ammunition, extra harness, and tools that were stored under the hinged seat. "I don't believe I've seen a compartment with that much room before."

Leander frowned at her over his shoulder, but she didn't see him. "That's the way it came," he mumbled.

Blair stuck her head farther into the compartment, looking at the sides of it. "I don't believe it is. I think it's been altered, something removed to make the space larger. I wonder why."

"I bought the thing used. Maybe some farmer wanted to carry his pigs back there. Are you going to get the food or are we going to starve to death?"

Blair took a big picnic basket out of the hole and sat back down. "It's big enough to hold a man," she said, as she withdrew a box of fried chicken, a jar of potato salad, and a jar of iced lemonade from the basket.

"Are you going to talk about that all day? What if I tell you some stories about when I was interning in Chicago?" Anything, Leander thought, to get her mind off that space back there. If the coal mine guards were half as observant as Blair, he wouldn't be alive today.

He ate chicken with one hand, held the reins with the other and told her a long story of a young man who'd been brought in by the police one night and, because he was already blue from not breathing, he was pronounced to be as good as dead—but Leander had thought there was hope. He'd tried rhythmical manipulations, but when there was no response, he'd examined the patient and found that his eyes were pinpoints, so Leander had guessed that the man was a victim of "knockout drops": opium.

"Are you going to eat all of that potato salad yourself?" Lee asked and, when Blair started to hand him the jar with the fork in it, he said he couldn't possibly eat it and the chicken and drive the buggy. So, Blair had to move so that she was sitting beside him and could feed the salad to him.

"Go on with your story."

"I realized that the only way to keep the man from going into a coma was to continue artificial respiration until he revived. None of the other doctors would waste his time on a man they considered as good as dead, so they went to bed and the nurses and I took turns trying to save the man."

"I'm sure the nurses *would* help you," she said.

He grinned at her. "I didn't have much trouble with them, if that's what you mean."

She shoved a large forkful of salad into his mouth. "Are you going to brag or are you going to tell the story?"

Leander continued telling of the long night of trying to save the man, of how he'd taken an icy cloth and repeatedly flicked the man on his bare stomach, then there was heart stimulation, and gallons of black coffee. He and the nurses had worked in relays all night, walking him until morning, when they'd thought he was out of danger and they could put him in bed and let him sleep.

Lee had had fewer than two hours sleep that night before he was due back on duty, and when he made morning rounds, he went into this patient's room, ready to be modest in the blaze of this man's praise for working so hard to save his life.

"But what the man said was, 'See, doctor, see, they did not get my watch. It was safe inside my pants, hidden from the thieves that poisoned me.'"

"He didn't even acknowledge that you'd done all that for him?" Blair asked in disbelief.

Leander smiled at her, and in a moment she began to see the humor of the situation. There were times when being a doctor wasn't the glory that one expected, but it was just plain hard work.

They finished the lunch and, as they travelled, Blair got Lee to tell her more stories about his experiences as a doctor, both in America and abroad. In turn, she told him about her Uncle Henry and her schooling, where the teachers had been so rough, saying that the women would be competing with male doctors who expected the women to be ill-trained, so, of course, the women had to be the best. She told him about the gruelling three-day test that she'd had to take to get into St. Joseph's Hospital. "And I won!" she said and went on to tell Leander about the hospital. She wasn't aware of the way that Lee was looking at her as she talked about her future at the hospital.

In the early afternoon, they reached the outskirts of the Winter ranch, and Lee drove them to the big old ranch house to visit the rancher's eight-year-old daughter who was recovering from typhoid.

The little girl was perfectly fine, and Lee and Blair stayed for a cup of milk warm from the cow and an enormous chunk of corn bread.

"That's all the pay we'll probably get," Lee said, as they got back into the carriage. "Doctors don't get rich in the country. It's good you'll have me to support you."

Blair started to say that she had no plans to stay in Chandler or to marry him, but something made her stop. Maybe it was the way he'd hinted that she really was a doctor, and that when—if—they were married, she would still practice medicine. And considering the prejudice and bigotry in this town, that was saying a lot.

They were barely off the rancher's land when a cowboy rode up to them, his horse stopping on its back legs and raising a cloud of dust over them. "We need some help, Doc," the cowboy said.

To Blair's disbelief, Lee did not take off immediately with his usual lightning speed.

"Aren't you from the Lazy J?"

The cowboy nodded.

"I want to take the lady back to Winter's ranch before I go with you."

"But, Doc, the man's been gut shot and he's bleedin'. He needs somebody right away."

Yesterday, Blair would have been furious that Lee wanted to exclude her from a case, but she knew now that he wasn't against her helping him with the patients, so it had to be something else. She put her hand on his arm. "Whatever happens, I'm in this, too. You can't protect me." There was a hint of threat in her voice that said that she'd follow him if he left her behind.

"They ain't shootin' now, Doc," the cowboy said. "The lady'll be safe while you patch Ben up."

Leander glanced at Blair, then skyward. "I hope I don't live to regret this," he said, as he snapped the whip over the horse, and they were off.

Blair grabbed the side of the carriage and said, "Shooting?" But no one heard her.

They left the horse and carriage some distance away and the cowboy led them to the ruins of an adobe house, stuck on a steep hillside, a section of the roof fallen in.

"Where are the others?" Lee asked and looked to where the cowboy pointed through the trees toward another ruin.

Blair wanted to ask questions about what was going on, but Lee put his hand in the small of her back and pushed her forward into the ruin. When her eyes adjusted, she saw a man and a fat, dirty woman sitting on the floor below what was left of a window, rifles across their shoulders, pistols by their sides, spent shells all around them. In the corner were three horses. With her eyes wide as she looked around, she was sure that she was in the midst of something she didn't like.

"Let's sew him up and get out of here," Lee said, bringing her back to the task at hand.

In the darkest part of the shack, on the floor, was a man holding his stomach with his hands, his face white.

"Do you know how to give chloroform?" Lee asked, as he sterilized his hands.

Blair nodded and began to remove bottles and candles from her bag. "Can he hold his liquor?" she asked the people in the room.

"Well, sure," the cowboy said hesitantly, "but we don't have no liquor. You have some?"

Blair was very patient. "I'm trying to figure out how much chloroform to give him, and a man who takes a lot of whiskey to get drunk requires more chloroform to put him under."

The cowboy grinned. "Ben can outdrink anybody. Takes two bottles of whiskey just to make him feel good. I ain't never seen him drunk."

Blair nodded, tried to estimate the weight of the man and began to pour chloroform onto a cone. When he began to go under, he fought the gas, and Blair stretched her body across the top of him while Leander held the man's lower half. Thankfully, he didn't have too much strength left and couldn't do much damage to his wound.

When Lee pulled away the man's pants and they saw the hole the gunshot had made in his stomach, Blair suspected there wasn't much chance for him, but Lee didn't seem to think that way as he cut into the man's abdomen.

A friend of Uncle Henry's, a doctor who specialized in abdominal surgery, had once visited them from New York and he had been there when a little girl was brought in who'd fallen on the broken half of a bottle. Blair had been in the surgery when the man'd removed the glass from the child's stomach and repaired three holes in her intestines. That single operation had so impressed Blair that she'd decided to specialize in abdominal surgery.

But, now, as she watched Leander, threading one needle after another for him, she was awed. The bullet had entered the man at his hipbone and travelled crosswise to leave at the bottom of his buttocks, puncturing his intestines over and over as it made its way through.

Leander's long fingers followed the bullet's pathway, sewing layers of intestines as he went. Blair counted fourteen holes that he sewed together before he reached the man's skin and the exit hole of the bullet.

"He's to eat absolutely nothing for four days," Leander was saying as he sewed the man back together. "On the fifth day he can have liquids. If he disobeys me and sneaks food, he'll be dead within two hours because the food will poison him." He looked up at the cowboy. "Is that clear?"

No one answered Lee because just then about six bullets came whizzing into the ruined shack.

"Damn!" Lee said, cutting off the last stitches with the scissors Blair had handed him. "I thought they'd give us enough time."

"What's going on?" Blair asked.

"These idiots," he said, not bothering to lower his voice, "are having a range war. There's usually one or two going on around Chandler. This one's been on about six months now. We might be here for a while until they decide to take another break."

"Break?"

Lee wiped his hands. "They're quite civilized about it all. When a person's wounded, they cease fire until a doctor can be found and brought in to wherever they're holed up. Unfortunately, they feel no such obligation to stop until the doctor's out again. We may be here until morning. Once I was stuck someplace for two days. And now you see why I wanted you to stay at Winter's ranch."

Blair began cleaning and putting the instruments back into the two medical bags. "So now we just wait?"

"Now we wait."

Lee led her behind a low adobe wall that had once been a room partition. He sat down in the farthest corner and motioned for Blair to sit next to him, but she wouldn't. She felt that she should stay as far away from him as possible and so leaned against the opposite wall. When a bullet hit the wall two feet from her head, she practically leaped into Leander's open arms and buried her face against his chest.

"I'd never have guessed that I could like a range war," he murmured and began to kiss her neck.

"Don't start that again," Blair said, even as she turned her head so he could reach her lips.

It didn't take Lee long to realize that he couldn't continue this pursuit, not here and now with so many people present and bullets flying around them. "All right. I'll stop," he said and smiled at the look on Blair's face.

She didn't move away from him but stayed in his arms, since his nearness made her feel very safe and the sounds of the bullets seem farther away. "Tell me where you learned to sew up intestines like that."

"So, you want more sweet talk. Well, let's see, the first time . . ."

Blair seemed insatiable. For hours they sat snuggled together, Blair asking endless questions about how Leander had learned things, what cases he'd had in the past, what was his most difficult case, his funniest, why he'd become a doctor in the first place, on and on, until, to give himself a break, he began to ask her questions.

The sun went down, there was a lull in the shooting now

and then, but for the most part it kept on all night. Lee tried to get Blair to sleep, but she refused.

"I see you're watching him," she said, nodding toward the man who'd been shot. "You have no intention of sleeping nor do I. What do you think his chances of living are?"

"It all depends on infection, and that's controlled by God. All I can do is sew him up."

The sky began to grow light and Leander said he needed to check his patient, who was beginning to stir.

Blair stood to stretch, and the next minute a sound reached her that made her forget everything except her profession. It was the sound of a bullet connecting with flesh.

Blair moved away from Lee and ran around the corner of the low wall just in time to see what had happened. The man who had not spoken had been shot in the chin and the woman had grabbed a handful of fresh horse manure and was about to apply it to the open wound.

Blair didn't think about the bullets flying over her head as she launched herself from a standing position and leaped on top of the big woman.

Startled, angry, the woman began to fight Blair and Blair had to protect herself from the woman's fists—but, under no circumstances was she going to allow that woman to put horse manure on an open wound.

Blair was so set on her purpose that she wasn't even aware when she and the woman went rolling out the wide opening where the door used to be.

One minute, Blair was trying to remove the woman's hand from her hair, and the next minute, there was the thunder of rifle fire directly above them.

Both women stopped their fighting and looked up to see Leander standing between them and the shack across the way, a rifle at his hip, blazing as fast as he could cock it and fire.

"Get the hell inside," he yelled at the women, and the next minute, he let out a stream of profanity directed at the men in the other shack, telling them that he was Dr. Westfield, and that he knew who they were, and if they ever came to him for help, he'd let them bleed to death.

The firing ceased.

When Leander walked back into the shack, Blair was cleaning the chin of the injured man.

"If you ever do anything like that again, so help me—." He broke off as he couldn't seem to find a threat bad enough.

He stood over Blair very quietly as she sewed the man's chin and bandaged it, and when she had put on the last bit of adhesive plaster, he grabbed her arm and pulled her upright.

"We're getting out of here this minute. They can all shoot each other for all I care. I'll not risk you for any of them."

Blair barely had time to grab her bag before Lee pulled her out of the cabin.

"Your union man came last night," Reed greeted his son as soon as Lee walked into the house.

As Leander rubbed a sore place on his back where a wooden plank had gouged it all night, he looked up at his father in alarm. "You didn't let anyone see him, did you?"

Reed gave his son a withering look. "All he's done is eat and sleep, which looks to be something that you haven't done in days. I hope you didn't keep Blair out all night. Gates is after your hide as it is."

Lee wanted nothing more than to eat and take a nap before he had to be at the hospital, but it didn't look as if he were going to have time. "Is he ready to go?"

Reed was quiet for a moment, watching his son, feeling that this might be the last time he ever saw him alive. He always felt this way before Lee left to take one of the unionists into the mine camps. "He's ready," was all Reed said at last.

Wearily, Lee went to the stables and sent the stableboy on an errand while he hitched a horse to his carriage. His Appaloosa was too tired after being out all night, so Lee took one of his father's horses. Watching to see that no one could see them, he went to the door to get the man waiting beside his father. Lee only glanced at the young man, but he had the same light in his eyes that all the unionists had: a light of fire, an intensity that burned with such heat that you knew there was no need to talk to the men about the danger that they faced, because these men wouldn't care. What they were doing, the cause they were fighting for, was more important than their lives.

Leander had removed most of the implements of his profession from the compartment in the back of his carriage—the big space that Blair had been so curious about—and now the man slipped inside. There was no talking, because all three men were too aware of the possibilities of what could happen today. The coal-camp guards would shoot to kill first, then ask questions of the dead men.

Reed handed Lee a papier-mâché cast that slipped into grooves in the sides of the compartment above the level of the man, a cast that at quick glance looked like a pile of blankets, a shotgun, rope, and a saw—things that any man might have in his carriage. On top, Lee put his medical bag.

For a moment, Reed touched his son's shoulder, then Lee was in the carriage and off.

Leander drove as quickly as he could without causing the hidden man too much pain. Two weeks ago, he and his father had had another discussion about what Lee was doing, Reed saying that Lee shouldn't risk his life to get these unionists into the camps, that even if he were caught and somehow managed to live, no court in the country would uphold what he was doing.

As Lee drove closer to the road that turned off to the coal camps, he went slower, watching about him as best he could to see that no one was near who shouldn't be. With a smile, Lee remembered when he'd defended the man who owned the coal mines around Chandler, Jacob Fenton, to Blair. He'd made excuses for Fenton and said that the man had to answer to stockholders, that he wasn't fully responsible for the miners' plight. Lee often said things like that to throw people off the track. It wouldn't do for them to find out how deeply he felt about the mistreatment of the miners.

Coal miners were given two choices: they either obeyed the company rules or they were out of work. It was as simple as that. But the rules were not for men, they were for prisoners!

Everything to do with the mines was owned by the company. The men were paid in currency that could be exchanged only at the company stores, and a man could be fired if he were found to have bought something at a store in town. Not that the men were allowed out of the camps to go into town. The mine owners argued that the coal camps were towns, and that the miners and their families didn't need anything from the surrounding town. And the owners said that the guards at the gates, who allowed no one in or out, were keeping out unscrupulous thieves and fast-talking men; the guards were "protecting" the miners.

But the truth was, the guards were there to keep out agitators. They were there to keep away all possibility of union organizers coming into the camps and talking to the miners.

The owners couldn't abide the possibility of a strike, and they had the legal right to post armed guards at the entrances and to search the vehicles that went in or out.

There were very few carriages that were allowed inside: some old women in town brought in fresh vegetables, a couple of repairmen were allowed in now and then, the mine inspectors, and there was a company doctor who made rounds, a man who was so poor a doctor that he couldn't support himself in private practice. The company paid him mostly in whiskey and, in gratitude, he ignored most of what he saw, declaring the company not at fault in every accident case, so that no benefits were due the widow and orphaned children.

A year ago Lee had gone to Fenton and asked permission to go into the camps—at no expense to the mine owner—to examine the health of the miners. Fenton had hesitated, but then he'd given permission.

What Lee had seen had horrified him. The poverty was such that he could barely stand it. The men struggled all day under the earth to make a living, and at the end of the week they could barely feed their families. They were paid by the amount of coal they brought out, but a third of their time was spent on what the miners called "dead work," work for which they received no pay. They themselves had to pay for the timbers that they used for shoring the mines, because the owner said that safety was the miners' responsibility, not his.

After the first days in the coal camps, Lee'd gone home and

not been able to say much for days. He looked at the rich little town of Chandler, saw his sister come home from The Famous with fifteen yards of expensive cashmere, and he thought of the children he'd seen standing in the snow with no shoes on. He remembered the men standing in line for their pay and hearing the paymaster tell them what they were being charged for that week.

And the more he thought, the more he was sure that he had to do something. He had no idea what he could do until he began to see articles in the newspaper about the organization of unions in the East. Aloud, he wondered to his father whether unionists could be persuaded to come to Colorado.

Reed, as soon as he realized what his son was thinking about, tried to dissuade him, but Lee kept going to the camps, and the more he saw, the more he knew what he had to do. He took the train to Kentucky and there met his first union organizers and talked to them about what was happening in Colorado. He learned about the early unsuccessful attempts at unionization in Colorado, and he was warned that his involvement could get him killed.

Leander remembered holding an emaciated little three-year-old girl in his arms as she died from pneumonia, and he agreed to help however he could.

So far, he'd managed to bring three unionists into the camps, and the owners were aware that they'd been there and that someone was helping the miners, so they were more and more on guard.

Last year, a big coal miner by the name of Rafe Taggert had begun to hint that he was the one to blame, that he was the one who was bringing the organizers into the camps. For some reason, the man believed that neither the guards nor the owner would harm him, that no "accidents" would be arranged to get him out of the way. There were rumors that Taggert's brother was once married to Fenton's sister, but no one was sure. Since coal miners had to move around a great deal as one mine after another closed, not many people had been in this area long enough to remember something that may or may not have happened over thirty years ago.

But whatever the reason, the suspicion was on Rafe Taggert, and no one had so far suspected the handsome young doctor who so kindly offered his time to help the miners.

As Lee pulled into the gate area of the Empress Mine, he did his best to act nonchalant and exchange banter with the guards. No one checked him and he drove to the far end of the camp to let the man hide in the trees until Lee could go from house to house to start getting a meeting together. Only three men would meet with the organizer at a time. The young man would stay there all day and into the night, risking his life every minute. And Lee would go from house to house looking at the children and telling the men where to meet the organizer and, with each telling, he was putting his life in peril, because he already knew that one of these men was an informer.

Chapter 13

Blair woke on Sunday morning feeling wonderful. She stretched long and hard, listened to the birds outside her window and thought that it must be the best of days. Her mind was full of all the things that she and Lee had done the day before. She remembered the way he'd repaired the man's intestines, his long fingers expert, knowing what he was supposed to do.

She wished Alan could have seen him operating.

Suddenly, she sat upright. Alan! She'd completely forgotten that she was to meet him at four o'clock yesterday. She'd been so worried about Houston, about how her sister had made a fool of herself over those rings, and then the call from Lee had come, and she'd sensed he was just asking her to go with him out of a sense of duty. She had never dreamed that she'd be away all night.

Susan came to tell her that the family would be leaving for

church soon after breakfast and that Mr. Gates had requested that she go with them. Blair hopped out of bed and hurriedly dressed. Perhaps Alan would be at church and she could explain that she'd been away working.

Alan was there, three pews ahead of them, and no matter what Blair did, he wouldn't look around after his initial glance. To make her feel worse, he was sitting next to Mr. Westfield and Nina. After church, Blair managed to get near him for a few minutes in the little yard outside the building.

"So, you were out with Westfield," Alan began the moment they were alone. His eyes were angry.

Blair stiffened in spite of her good intentions to be humble. "I believe you were the one to agree to a competition, not me, and part of the arrangement was that I not refuse Leander's invitations."

"All night?" He managed to look down his nose at her even though they were nearly the same height.

Blair at once felt defensive. "We were working, and we got caught in the midst of a range war and Leander says that—."

"Spare me his words of wisdom. I have to go now. I have other plans."

"Other plans? But I thought maybe this afternoon—."

"I'll call you tomorrow. That is, if you think you'll be home." With that, he turned on his heel and left her standing there.

Nina Westfield came by to tell her that Lee had to work at the hospital the rest of the day. Blair climbed into the carriage with her mother and stepfather and was only vaguely aware that Houston wasn't with them.

At home, Opal was fussing about the dining room, arranging flowers on the table, setting it with the best tall silver candelabra.

"Are you expecting company?" Blair asked idly.

"Yes, dear, *he's* coming."

"Who is?"

"Houston's Kane. Oh, Blair, he is such a lovely man. I just know you're going to love him."

Minutes later, the door opened and Houston came in leading her big millionaire by the arm, as if he were a prize piece of game that she'd just bagged. Blair had first seen him earlier in church, and she admitted that he was good-looking —not as handsome as Leander, or even Alan—but more than presentable, if you liked that overly muscular type.

"If you'll sit here, Mr. Taggert, next to Houston and across from Blair," Opal was saying.

For a moment, everyone just sat there looking at their plates or about the room, no one saying anything.

"I hope that you like roast beef," Mr. Gates said as he began to carve the big piece of meat.

"I'm sure to like it better'n what I usually get; that is, until Houston here hired me a cook."

"And who did you hire, Houston?" Opal said, with a bit of ice in her voice, reminding her daughter that lately she'd been leaving the house, and been gone for hours, with no one knowing where she was.

"Mrs. Murchison, while the Conrads are in Europe. Sir, Mr. Taggert might have some suggestions for investments," she said to Mr. Gates.

From then on, Blair thought, there was no stopping the man. He was like an elephant in the midst of a flock of chickens. When Mr. Gates asked him about railroad stock, Taggert raised his fist and bellowed that railroads were dying, that the whole country was covered with railroads and there was no more decent money to be made in them—"only a few hundred thousand or so." His fist came down on the table and everything—including the people—jumped.

Compared to Taggert's temper and loudness, Gates was a kitten. Taggert brooked no disagreement whatever; he was right about everything, and he talked in terms of millions of dollars as if they were grains of sand.

And if his bellowing and arrogance weren't enough, his manners were appalling. He cut his slice of roast with the side of his fork, and when it went sliding across the table toward Blair, he didn't even pause in telling Gates how to run the brewery as he pulled the meat back onto his plate and kept on eating. Ignoring the three vegetables that were served, he piled about two pounds of mashed potatoes onto his plate and

emptied the gravy boat on top of the white mountain. Before
he was finished, he'd eaten one half of the ten-pound roast. He
knocked over Houston's teacup, but she just smiled at him and
motioned for the maid to bring a cloth. He drank six glasses of
iced tea before Blair saw Susan secretly pouring his glass from
a separate pitcher. Blair then realized that Houston had
arranged for Taggert to drink dark beer with ice in it. He talked
with his mouth full and twice had food on his chin. Houston,
as if he were a child, touched his hand, then his napkin, which
was still folded beside his plate.

After a while, Blair stopped trying to eat. She didn't like
food flying toward her or the silverware jumping or the way
that loud, overbearing man monopolized the conversation.
Conversation ha! He might as well have been giving a speech.

The worst part was the way Houston, her mother and Gates
hung on his every word. You would have thought his words
were gold. And perhaps they were, Blair thought with disgust.
She'd never thought much about money, but perhaps money
was all-important to other people. It certainly seemed to be so
important to Houston that she was willing to subject herself to
this awful, hideous man for the rest of her life.

Blair grabbed the candelabra before it fell over, as Taggert
reached for more gravy. Cook must have made it in a wheelbarrow, she thought.

Just then, Taggert paused long enough in his proposal of
allowing Gates to buy in on a land sale to glance at Blair.
Suddenly, he stopped talking altogether and pushed back his
chair.

"Honey, we better be goin' if you wanta get to the park
while it's still light."

Heaven help, Blair thought, that he should have manners
enough to ask if anyone else was finished eating. He was ready
to leave, and he autocratically demanded that Houston leave
with him. Dutifully, Houston followed him.

"Why, Lee," Opal said with a smile, twisting her neck
around to look up at him, making the little oak rocker creak. "I
didn't hear you come in." She took a closer look at him. "You

look happier than you did a few days ago. Has something happened?" There was a hint of an I-told-you-so look on Opal's face.

Lee gave her a quick peck on the cheek before sitting down in the chair next to her on the back porch. He was tossing a big red apple back and forth in his hands. "Maybe it's not that I want your daughter, it's that I want you for a mother-in-law."

Opal kept on sewing. "So, today, you think there's a chance that you'll get my daughter. If I remember correctly, the last time we talked, you were sure you could never win her. Has anything changed?"

"Changed? Only the entire world." He bit into his apple with gusto. "I'm going to win. I'm not only going to win, but it's going to be by a landslide. That poor kid Hunter doesn't have a chance."

"I take it you've found the key to Blair's heart, and it isn't flowers and candy."

Leander smiled, as much to himself as to her. "I'm going to court her with what she really likes: gunshot wounds, blood poisonings, respiratory infections, amputations, and whatever else I can find for her. She'll probably love spring roundup around here."

Opal looked horrified. "It sounds dreadful. Must it be so drastic?"

"As far as I can tell, the worse the going is, the better she likes it. As long as somebody's there to make sure she doesn't get in over her head, she'll be fine."

"And you'll be the one to take care of her?"

Leander rose. "For the rest of her life. I believe that's the sound of my loved one now. You'll see, in less than a week, she'll be running down the aisle to me."

"Lee?"

He paused.

"And what about St. Joseph's?"

He winked at her. "I will do my best to never let her find out. I want her to turn them down. Who are they to say that she can't work for *them*?"

"She's a good doctor, isn't she?" Opal beamed with pride.

"Not bad," Lee said, chuckling, walking back into the house. "Not bad for a woman."

Blair met Leander in the parlor. Yesterday had turned out to be awful. Alan had not called, she'd heard nothing from Lee, and all day, she'd worried about Houston and that awful man she was selling herself to. So it was with some trepidation that she met Lee now. Was he going to be the doctor Lee or the one who insulted her at every turn?

"You wanted to see me?" she asked cautiously.

Leander wore an expression that she'd never seen before, one of almost shyness. "I came to talk to you, that is, if you don't mind listening to me."

"Of course not," she said. "Why should I mind talking with you?" She sat down on a red brocade chair.

Leander had his hat in hand, threatening to twist it into shreds, and when Blair motioned for him to sit, he merely shook his head no.

"It's not easy to say what I've come to say. It's not easy to admit defeat, especially in something that has come to mean so much to me as the winning of you for my wife."

Blair started to say something, but he put his hand up. "No, let me say what I must without interruptions. It's hard for me, but it has to be said because it's all that I can think about."

He walked to the window, still twisting his hat in his hands. She'd never seen him nervous before.

"Saturday, the day we spent together as doctors, was a monumental day in my life. Until that day, I would have wagered anything that I owned that a woman couldn't be a good doctor, but you proved me wrong. On that day, you showed me that a woman can not only be a good doctor, but might even become better than most men."

"Thank you," Blair said, and a small thrill of pleasure ran through her at his words.

He turned back to face her. "And that's why I'm giving up the race."

"The race?"

"The competition, then, whatever you call it. I realized

yesterday, while I was working alone in the hospital, that I had changed after the day we spent together. You see, I've always worked alone, but on that day when we worked together . . . Well, it was like everything that I'd imagined and more. We fit together so well, so rhythmically, almost like lovers." He stopped and looked at her. "I meant that allegorically, of course."

"Of course," she mumbled. "I'm not sure that I understand any of this."

"Don't you see? I may have lost a wife, but what I've gained is a *colleague!* I might treat a woman with little or no respect, might trick her to show that her friend is such a Willie boy that he can't row, swim or even ride a horse, but I could never, never do that to a fellow doctor whom I've learned to respect and even admire."

Blair was silent for a moment. There was something wrong in what he was saying about Alan, but his words of praise were too sweet to cause her to quibble over details. "Are you saying that you no longer want to marry me?"

"I'm saying that I respect you, and you've said that you want to marry Alan Hunter, and I now know that I cannot stand in your way. You and I are equals in the medical profession, and I cannot further humiliate a fellow doctor in the manner that I have in the past few days. Therefore, you are no longer held captive here. You may leave with the man you love at any time, and I can assure you that I'll do everything in my power to keep Gates from letting anyone know about your loss of . . . of chastity."

Blair stood. "I'm not sure that I understand. I'm free to go? You aren't blackmailing me any longer, and you won't cause Alan further embarrassment? And you're doing all this because you believe that I'm a good doctor?"

"That's exactly right. It took me a while to come to my senses, but I have. What kind of marriage could we have if it was based purely on lust? Of course, we do have a mutual attraction to one another, and perhaps that one night was extraordinary, but that isn't a basis for marriage. What you and Alan have is real, that you can spend time together and talk, that you have mutual interests, and I'm sure that you have the same . . . ah, reactions to his touch that you have to mine. Maybe you two have made love several times in the last few days, for all I know.''

''I beg your pardon!''

Leander hung his head again. ''I'm sorry. I didn't mean to insult you again. I always seem to put my foot in my mouth around you. Now, you'll never listen to what else I have to say.''

''I'll listen,'' she said. ''Tell me the rest of it.'' She was feeling strangely let down. Of course, the fact that he respected her as a doctor was wonderful, but at the same time she wanted something else, and she didn't know what it was.

When he looked back at her, his eyes were glowing intensely. ''I know you want to get back to Pennsylvania, and I don't blame you, but working with you was such a joy and a pleasure and, since I know that I'll never have the chance again because I'm sure that you'll never want to come back to Chandler after what's happened in the last few days, I'd really like to ask if I could have the honor of working with you for the next few days. My father has agreed to persuade the board to allow you into the hospital under my care, and you and I can work together until after Houston's wedding. Oh, Blair, I could show you my plans for the women's clinic. I've never shown them to anyone before, and I'd really like to share them. Maybe you'd even help me plan it—if you had time, that is.''

Blair walked to the far side of the room. She didn't think that she'd ever enjoyed anything as much as she'd enjoyed that day with Leander, and if they were no longer engaged, perhaps Houston would not feel that she had to marry that man Taggert and—.

''And Alan can work with us. Gosh, if he's half as good as you are . . . Is he?''

Blair came back to the present and realized with a bit of guilt that she hadn't even thought of Alan. ''You mean, is he as good as I am? I guess so. Of course he is! Although I don't think he's had the opportunity to work with doctors as I have. I mean, I was very lucky. My Uncle Henry is quite well respected, and ever since I was little more than a child, I've assisted in surgery and helped with emergency cases and had the opportunity to assist many eminent men, but—." She stopped. "Of course, Alan is an excellent doctor," she said firmly.

"I'm sure he is, and I'm sure it'll be a joy working with both of you. By the way, did Alan take that exam for St. Joseph's Hospital?"

"Yes, but he didn't—."

"Didn't what?"

Her mouth was set in a firm line. "They only accepted the six highest scorers."

"I see. Well, perhaps it was a bad day for him. May I come for you tomorrow morning at six? Until then, my library is always open to a fellow colleague." He quickly kissed her hand and then was gone.

Chapter 14

Blair was dressed and ready to leave at five thirty the next morning. She sat on the edge of her bed and puzzled over what to do. Should she wait downstairs or would he come through the window again as he'd done last time?

When the downstairs clock chimed six, she opened her door and thought she heard the front door. She flew down the stairs and got there just as a sleepy Susan was opening the door to Leander.

"Good morning," he said, smiling. "Ready to go?"

She nodded in answer.

"You can't go, Miss Blair-Houston. You haven't had anything to eat and Cook doesn't have breakfast ready yet. You'll have to wait until she gets dressed."

"Have you eaten?" she asked Lee.

"It seems as though I haven't eaten in days," he answered, smiling back at her, and again she was impressed by how good-looking he was, with those green eyes. And for some reason, she was reminded of the night they'd spent together. It was odd that she should think of that now, because she hadn't remembered it in days. Perhaps it was that now he wasn't trying to enrage her.

"Come into the kitchen and I'll fix you some breakfast. Even I know how to fry eggs and bacon. Mr. Gates's meal will probably be late and the entire household'll catch it, but we'll not be here to hear what he has to say."

A half hour later, Lee leaned back from the big oak kitchen table and wiped his mouth. "Blair, I had no idea that you could cook. It seems too much to hope for in a woman, one who can cook, a woman who can be a man's friend, a colleague," his eyes and voice lowered, "a lover." With a sigh, he looked back at her. "I swore to myself that I wasn't going to be a sore loser, that I was going to give up gracefully." He gave her a sweet little-boy smile. "You'll have to forgive me if I forget some-times."

"Yes, of course," she said nervously and realized that she was once again thinking of that night together. That night, when she'd been free to kiss him, when his hands . . .

"They aren't clean?"

"I beg your pardon?" she said, coming back to the present.

"You were staring at my hands and I wondered if maybe something was wrong with them."

"I . . . Are you ready to go?"

"Whenever you are," he said, rising and pulling back her chair.

Blair smiled at him and thought of that ill-mannered man Houston said she planned to marry and thought that there was no comparison between him and Lee.

On the way to the hospital, he asked her about Alan and she told him that he was to meet them at the infirmary. He did, looking sleepy and a bit sullen at seeing Leander and Blair arriving together.

The day was a hard, long one. It seemed that every patient was Lee's sole responsibility, and the three of them had to do the work of a dozen people. At one o'clock, four men who'd been hurt when the end of a tunnel of the Inexpressible Mine had collapsed were brought in. Two of them were dead, one had a broken leg, but the fourth man was hovering between life and death.

"He's a goner," Alan said, "might as well leave him."

But Blair was looking at the man's eyes, closed now, but she saw that he was struggling to live. She couldn't tell what was hurt inside him, but she thought that maybe he had a chance. By all rights, he should be dead now, yet he wanted to live enough that he was hanging on.

Blair looked at Lee, and for a moment he was reminded of the union organizers' eyes.

"I think there's a chance. Can we open him and see? I think he wants to live," she persisted.

"Blair," Alan said in an exasperated voice, "anyone can see that he can't live more than minutes. His whole insides must be crushed. Let him die with his family."

Blair didn't even look at Alan, but kept her eyes on Lee. "Please," she whispered. "Please."

"Let's get him to the operating room," Leander bellowed. "No! don't move him. Keep him on that table and we'll carry it."

Blair was right, but so was Alan. His insides were crushed, but not as badly as they'd thought when they'd first opened him. His spleen was ruptured and it was bleeding a lot, but they managed to remove it and clean some of the other wounds.

Because of the internal bleeding, they had to work fast and, without anyone being conscious of what was happening, Alan was pushed out of the way. Leander and Blair, who worked so well together and who had the experience, sewed as fast as Mrs. Krebbs could thread needles. She was Leander's favorite nurse and had been with him since he'd returned to Chandler. Alan, realizing that he couldn't work as fast as Leander and Blair, stepped back and let the three of them repair the man's mashed insides.

When they had sewed him shut, they left the operating room.

"What do you think?" Blair asked Lee.

"Now is when God comes into the matter, but I think that you and I did the best we could." He grinned at her. "You were damned good in there. Wasn't she, Mrs. Krebbs?"

The stout, gray-haired woman grunted. "We'll see if the patient lives," she said as she left the room.

"Not given to compliments, I take it," Blair said, as she scrubbed the blood from her hands.

"Only when you deserve them. I'm still waiting for mine. Of course, I've only been here two years."

As the two of them laughed together, Blair wasn't aware of Alan standing against the wall watching them.

Once out of surgery, they went back to the wards and, late in the day, attended a child who had been scalded. And as the day wore on, Blair and Leander seemed tireless, but Alan followed them feeling more and more as if he were completely unneeded. Twice, he tried to talk to Blair about going home, but she'd hear none of it. She stayed next to Leander's side every minute. By ten that night, Alan was drooping.

"Come into my office," Lee said at eleven. "I have some beer and sandwiches there, and I want to show you something."

Alan sat in a chair and hungrily ate his sandwich while Lee unrolled plans and spread them across his desk. "These are my plans for the women's infirmary, a place where a woman can go for any ailment and get competent treatment. I'd like a training center, too, for women to be taught how to look after their children's health." He stopped and smiled at Blair. "No horse manure or cancer plasters."

She smiled back at him and realized that his face was inches from hers and that he was moving toward her with an expression on his face that she'd seen only once before—*that* night. Before she knew what she was doing, she was leaning toward him in a way that seemed very natural to her, and it seemed perfectly normal that he should kiss her.

But, only a breath away from her lips, he pulled back abruptly and began to roll the plans. "It's late and I'd better get you home. It looks like we've worn Alan out. Besides, it's useless for me to show you these plans. You won't even be here. You'll be in a big city in an established hospital, and you won't have the nuisance of having to build a place from scratch, of having to plan where you'll put the equipment, of whom you'll hire, of planning just what you'll teach and whom you'll treat." He stopped and sighed. "No, in your city hospital, you'll have everything already planned. It won't be hectic like this new clinic will be."

"But that doesn't sound bad. I mean, it might be fun to decide how you want things. I'd like to have a burn clinic or maybe a special isolation ward or—."

He cut her off. "That's kind of you to say but at a big city hospital, the people pay their bills."

"If a big hospital is so good, then why didn't you stay in one? Why did you leave?" she asked indignantly.

With a show of great reverence, he put the plans back into the safe. "I guess I like feeling needed more than I like security," he said, turning back to her. "There are more than enough doctors in the East, but out here it's a challenge to keep up with all the work. The people here *need* a doctor more than they do there. I feel as if I'm doing some good here, and I didn't there."

"Is that why you think I want to return East? For security? You don't think that I'm up to all the work here?"

"Blair, please, I didn't mean to offend you. You asked me why I didn't want to work at a big, safe, orderly, comfortable hospital in the East, and I told you, that's all. It has nothing to do with you. We're colleagues, remember? I'd never dream of telling you what you should or shouldn't do. In fact, if I remember correctly, I'm the one who's taking obstacles out of your path. I gave up my intention of marrying you so you could return East, marry Alan, and work in your hospital just like you say you want to. What else can I do to support you?"

Blair had no answer for him, but she felt unsettled inside. At this moment, the thought of working in St. Joseph's Hospital seemed selfish, as if she were seeking glory instead of trying to help people as she should be doing.

"Speaking of Alan," Lee was saying, "I think we'd better get him home."

Blair had completely forgotten Alan and now turned to see

him slumped forward in his chair, dozing. "Yes, I guess we'd better," she said absently. She was thinking too hard about what Leander had said. Maybe a big hospital was "safe," but the people there got just as sick as they did in the West. Of course, there were more people to treat them there, and here they didn't even have a decent hospital for women. In Philadelphia, they had at least four infirmaries for women and children, and of course there were women doctors in practice there, and everyone knew that women would sometimes suffer a disease for years before they'd let a man examine them.

"Ready?" Lee asked, after he'd wakened Alan.

Blair thought about what Lee'd said all the way home, and she lay awake in bed for a while and thought about it, too. Chandler certainly needed a female doctor, and she could train with Leander and help run that new clinic of his, all at the same time.

"No, no, no!" she said aloud, as she hit the pillow with her fist. "I am *not* going to stay in Chandler! I am going to marry Alan, train at St. Joseph's Hospital, and I am going to set up practice in Philadelphia!"

She settled down to go to sleep but as she drifted off, she thought of the many women in Chandler who had no female doctor to tend to them. She had a restless night.

On Wednesday morning, Lee came to the house to visit her, and Blair found that she was very glad to see him.

"I don't have to be at the hospital until late this afternoon, and I thought you might want to go riding with me. I stopped by the hotel and asked Alan to go with us, but he said he was tired after yesterday and he didn't like to ride anyway. I don't imagine you'd like to go with me alone, would you?"

Before Blair could say a word, Leander continued. "Of course you wouldn't," he said quickly, looking down at his hat in his hands. "You can't go out with me alone, since you're engaged to another man. It's just that the whole town thinks that I'm to marry you in five days, and no other young lady will go out with me." He turned to leave. "I didn't mean to burden you with my problems. My loneliness isn't your concern."

"Lee," she said, grabbing his arm to keep him from leaving

the room. "I . . . I did want to discuss that blood poisoning case with you, maybe—."

Leander didn't give her a chance to finish. "That's great of you, Blair, you're a real friend," he said, as his face split into a grin that made Blair's knees weak. The next moment, he had his hand on the small of her back and he half pushed her out the door to the side yard where two saddled horses waited.

"But I can't wear this," she protested, looking down at her long skirt. "I need a divided skirt and—."

"You look fine to me, and so what if you show a little ankle? I'm the only one who'll be there, and I've seen all of you, remember?"

Blair didn't get a chance to say another word before he lifted her and put her on top of the horse, and she was busy trying to arrange her skirts so she had some modesty left. She prayed that Houston wouldn't see her like this. Houston might one day forgive her sister for stealing the man she was to marry, but she'd never, never forgive her for being seen in public wearing the wrong clothes.

Leander grinned back at her and she forgot all about her sister and that she was with a man she shouldn't be with.

He led her far out into the country. They rode side by side for a while, and Blair got him to talk more about the women's infirmary and tell her some of his plans. And she told him some of her ideas. Only once did he say, wistfully, that he wished he had someone to work with him. Cautiously, Blair asked him if he'd consider a woman doctor. Lee said he'd more than consider her, and for the next half hour he did nothing but tell her how they'd work together on this new infirmary if she stayed in Chandler. Before long, Blair was caught up in the fantasy, and she was talking about how they could work together and all the miracles they could accomplish. Together, they'd wipe out all illness in the state of Colorado.

"And then the three of us could move to California and cure that state," Leander laughed.

"Three?" Blair asked blankly.

Lee gave her a look of reproach. "Alan. The man you love, remember? The man you're going to marry. He'll be in on this, too. He'll have to have a part in the new infirmary, too. And he'll help us like he did yesterday."

It was strange, but Blair could barely recall Alan being at the hospital yesterday. She remembered the way he hadn't wanted to help the man who'd been crushed, but had he been in the operating room with them?

"Here we are," Lee was saying, as she followed him into an enclosed place between gigantic rocks. He dismounted and unsaddled his horse. "I never thought I'd be able to bear this place again after what happened here."

Blair stepped back as he unsaddled her horse. "What did happen here?"

He paused with the saddle in his hands. "The worst day of my life. I brought Houston here after the night we'd made love, and I found out that the woman I'd spent the most wonderful night of my life with wasn't the woman I was engaged to."

"Oh," Blair said meekly, wishing she hadn't asked. She stepped back as Leander pulled a blanket from his saddlebags and spread it on the ground, then watered the horses from a little spring nearby and began to spread food on the blanket.

"Have a seat," he said.

Blair was beginning to think that she shouldn't have come out here alone with him. He was easy to resist when he was being obnoxious and tossing Alan into the lake, but the last time they'd been alone and Lee had been this nice, they'd ended up with their clothes off and making love. Blair looked up at Lee standing over her, the sun making a crescent around his head and thought that, under no circumstances whatsoever, must she let him touch her. And she mustn't let the conversation stray to what had happened between them. She must *only* talk about medicine.

They ate what Lee had brought and Blair talked to him about all the worst cases she'd ever seen in her life. She needed to remember the gory details, because Lee had taken off his jacket and stretched out inches away from her. His eyes were closed, and all he had to do was murmur a response now and then to Blair's stories and she suspected he was falling asleep. She couldn't help looking at him as she talked, those long,

long legs, and she thought about how they felt next to her own skin. She looked at his chest, broad, strong, his pectorals straining against the thin cotton of his shirt. She remembered how his chest hairs felt against her breasts.

And the more she remembered, the faster she talked, until the words seemed to clog in her mouth and refused to come out. With a sigh of frustration, she stopped talking and looked down at her hands in her lap.

Leander didn't say anything for a long while, and she thought perhaps he was asleep.

"I never met anyone like you," he said softly, and Blair couldn't help but lean slightly forward to hear him. "I never met a woman who could understand how I felt about medicine. All the women I've known raged at me if I was late picking them up for a party because I was sewing some man back together. Nor have I met any woman who was interested in what I did. You are the most generous, and the most loving, person I've ever met."

Blair was too stunned to speak. Sometimes, she thought she had fallen in love with Alan because he was the first young man who hadn't reviled her for the way she was. There were many times when Blair had tried to be like her sister, to be quiet and genteel, to not tell a man, when he said something stupid, that what he'd just said was stupid, but she couldn't seem to help herself. And as a result of her laughter, of her honesty, she had never had very many suitors. In Pennsylvania, men had seen how pretty she was and been interested, but when they'd found out that she was going to be a doctor, they were interested no longer. And if they had stayed around, they'd soon learned that Blair was very smart, and that was death to a woman. All she had to do was beat a man at chess, or do an arithmetic problem in her head faster than he could, and there would no longer be any interest in her. Alan was the first man she'd ever met who wasn't repulsed by her abilities—and Blair had decided that she was in love with him within three weeks of their first meeting.

Now, Leander was saying that he *liked* her. And when she thought of all the things she'd done to him in the last few days, the times she'd left him in the desert to walk back to town, she was astounded that he could stand the sight of her. He was either a remarkable man or he liked punishment.

"I know that you'll be leaving town in a few days, and maybe I'll never see you again, so I want to tell you what that one night we had together meant to me," he said in a voice that was little more than a whisper.

"It was as if you couldn't help yourself that night, as if my simple touch made you come to me. It was so flattering to my vanity. You've called me a vain man, but I'm vain only when I'm with you because you make me feel so good. And to have found the woman of my life . . . a friend, a colleague, a lover without equal, and now to have lost her."

Blair was inching toward him as he spoke.

Lee turned his head away from her. "I want to be fair about what has happened. I want to give you what you want, what will make you happy, but I hope you don't expect me to be at the train station when you leave with Alan. I imagine that on the day you leave with him, I shall get rip-roaring drunk and tell my problems to some red-haired barmaid."

Blair sat upright. "Is that what you like?" she said stiffly.

He looked back at her in surprise. "Is what what I like?"

"Red-haired barmaids?"

"Why, you stupid little—." Instantly, his face was flushed red with anger, as he stood and began to shove the blanket, pulling it out from under her, and food into the saddlebags. "No, I don't like red-haired barmaids. I wish I did. I was fool enough to fall in love with the most pigheaded, blind, idiotic, stubborn woman in the world. I never had any trouble with a woman in my life until I met you, and now all I have is trouble."

He slammed the saddle on the horse. "There are times when I wish I'd never met you."

He turned back to her. "You can saddle your own horse, and you can find your own way back to town. That is, if you're not too blind to see the trail, because you sure are blind about people."

He put one foot in the stirrup and then, on impulse, turned back to her and took her in his arms and kissed her.

Blair had completely forgotten what it was like to kiss Lee, forgotten that overwhelming sensation. She couldn't have told you who she was when he was touching her, because all sensation left her except for the touch of this one man.

"There," he said angrily, drawing back from her, then having to give her a little shake to make her open her eyes. "I've had blind patients who saw more than you do."

He walked away from her and started to mount his horse, then mumbled, "Oh, hell," and saddled her horse for her and put her in the saddle. He led her a chase back into Chandler, and when he stopped before her house, he said, "I expect you at the hospital at eight tomorrow morning."

She barely had time to nod before he left her alone.

Chapter 15

Bleak was the only way to describe Blair's mood when she got home. She wasn't sure what was wrong with Leander, nor did she understand why she was so upset.

Her mother was in the family parlor surrounded by hundreds of boxes. "What's this?" Blair asked absently.

"They're wedding gifts for you and Houston. Would you like to open some of yours now?"

Blair just glanced at the presents and shook her head. The last thing she wanted was to be reminded of the wedding that might or might not take place—not that Leander still wanted to marry her.

She called Alan's hotel and left a message that they were to be at the hospital tomorrow morning at eight, then went upstairs to fill the bathtub.

When she came back downstairs an hour later, Houston was home, a rare thing for her since she always seemed to be out with Taggert, and she was in a flurry of activity as she opened presents and talked to Opal a mile a minute about the plans for the wedding. Houston exclaimed over the gifts from the East, things from Vanderbilts, the Astors, names that Blair had only heard of, and now Houston was marrying one of their exclusive society.

Listlessly, she sat on one of the sofas.

"Have you seen the dress, Blair?" Houston asked as she turned around, holding a big cut-glass bowl that must have cost someone the earth.

"What dress?"

"Our wedding dress, of course," Houston said patiently. "I'm having yours made just like mine."

Blair felt that she couldn't stand to be in the room with so much enthusiasm. Maybe Houston could be put in a thrill of delight by a few presents, but she couldn't. "Mother, I don't feel too well. I think I'll go to bed and read for a while."

"All right, dear," Opal said, as she dug into yet another box. "I'll send Susan up with a tray. By the way, a young man called and said he wouldn't be at the hospital tomorrow. A Mr. Hunter, I believe," she said.

If anything, Blair began to feel worse. She'd neglected Alan shamefully in the last few days.

The morning came all too soon, and Blair's mood wasn't much improved. At least, the patients at the hospital kept her mind off her own problems—that is, until Leander came. His black mood made hers seem like a beam of sunshine. Within two hours, he managed to yell at her four times, telling her that if she wanted to be a doctor, she had to learn a few things. Blair wanted to yell back at him but, after one look at his face, she wisely said nothing except, "Yes, sir," and tried to do what she could to obey his orders.

At eleven, she was bending over a little girl whose broken arm she'd just set, when Alan came up behind her.

"I thought I'd find you here—with him."

Blair gave the little girl a smile. "Alan, I'm working."

"We're going to have a talk now, in front of the entire hospital or alone."

"All right, then, come with me." She led him down the

corridor to Leander's office. She didn't know the hospital very well, and it was the only place she knew where they could be private. She just hoped that Lee wouldn't come back and discover them in there.

"I should have guessed this is where you'd go. His office! You must feel comfortable in here. No doubt you're in here often enough." To his consternation, Blair collapsed in a chair, put her hands to her face and began to cry.

Alan was on his knees before her in an instant. "I didn't mean to be cross with you."

Blair tried to control her tears, but couldn't. "Everyone is cross with me. I never seem to please anyone. Mr. Gates never leaves me alone. Houston hates me. Leander can barely speak to me, and now you . . . ."

"What's Westfield got to be angry about? He's winning hands down."

"Winning?" Blair pulled a handkerchief from her pocket and blew her nose. "He's not even in the competition. He said he could see that I loved you, and so he was no longer going to compete."

Alan stood and leaned against the desk. "Then why are you spending day after day with him? You haven't been two feet from his side for a week."

"He said that he'd like to work with me for the few days left of my stay. He said he'd never worked so well with anyone before. And he extended the invitation to both of us."

"Of all the underhanded—," Alan began, pacing the room. "He is lower than I thought. I never heard of such a sneaky, dirty trick." He looked back at Blair. "He knows you're infatuated with anything to do with medicine, so he uses that to get near you, and of course he'd invite me! The man's had years of experience and training over mine, so he looks great while I look like an idiot."

"That's not true! Leander said he wanted to work with me, and we *do* work well together. It's as if we read each other's minds."

"From what I hear, it's been that way since the first night you went out."

"Now who's being underhanded?"

"No more than he is," Alan shot back. "Blair, I'm tired of looking like a fool. I'm a student doctor competing in an operating room with a man with years of experience. I grew up in a city, but I'm competing in a canoe and on horseback. There's no possible way that I can look good against him."

"But you don't understand. Leander *isn't* competing. He no longer *wants* to marry me. I'm staying in Chandler until my sister gets married, and then you and I will leave together. I still have hopes that Houston will marry Leander."

He watched her for a moment. "I believe that some part of you actually believes what you're saying. Let me tell you something: Westfield has *not* left the race. The poor man is competing so hard it's a wonder he has any breath left. And if you believe you're not getting married on Monday, why haven't you put a stop to all the wedding plans your sister is making? Do you plan to sit in the front row and watch your sister get married while you're surrounded by two of everything? What are you going to do with all those presents?"

He put his hands on the arms of the chair and leaned his face into hers. "As for Houston marrying your beloved doctor, I don't think you *could* sit there and watch that."

"That'll be enough, Hunter," came Leander's voice from the doorway.

"It's not nearly enough," Alan said, advancing on Leander.

"If it's a fight you want—."

Lee stopped when Blair placed herself between the two men.

"Blair," Alan said, "it's time you made a decision. I will be on the four o'clock train out of this town today. If you're not there, I'll leave alone." With that, he left the room.

Blair stood there alone with Lee for a moment and neither said anything, then Lee put his hand on her arm.

"Blair," he began, but she moved away.

"I think Alan's right. It's time I made my decision and stopped playing childish games." With that she swept past him and walked the two miles to her house.

When she got home, she very calmly took a pen and paper and began to make a list of the pros and cons of leaving with

Alan. There were five good, strong reasons that she could come up with of why she should leave with him. They ranged from being able to get out of this bigoted town to allowing Houston to no longer feel pressured to marry her millionaire.

The only reason she could think of for *not* leaving with Alan was that she'd never get to see Leander again. She'd not be able to work with him on that new infirmary of his—of course, if what Alan had said was true, maybe Leander had shown her his plans just as a ruse to win the competition.

She stood. If she didn't get to work on the clinic here, in Pennsylvania, St. Joseph's Hospital was waiting for her.

She glanced down at her uniform and knew that that one garment was the only thing that she'd take with her. She couldn't walk out the door carrying a bag other than her medical bag, or there'd be questions. All she could take was what she was wearing. She crumbled the list in her hand and kept it there. She might need it to remind her why she was doing this.

Downstairs, her mother was arranging gifts, and Houston was out. Blair tried to say a few words to her mother, to say good-bye without saying the exact words, but Opal was too busy counting pieces of silver.

With her chin in the air, Blair went out the door and walked the long way to the train station. As she walked, she looked at the bustling little town with different eyes. Maybe it wasn't as bad as she'd originally thought. It wasn't Philadelphia, but it had its compensations. Three carriages rattled by carrying people who called out to her, "Hello, Blair-Houston," and the double name for once didn't seem so bad.

As she neared the train station, she wondered what would happen after she'd gone; if Houston would marry Lee, if her mother would understand Blair's disappearance, if Gates would hate her more than he did already.

She arrived at the train station at three forty-five and quickly saw that Alan wasn't there yet. She stood on the platform, her medical bag beside her, fiddled with the list in her hand, and thought about how this could be her last few minutes in the town named for her father. After the scandal she'd caused—

stealing her sister's fiancé, then running off with another man four days before the wedding—she doubted whether she could come back before she was about ninety years old.

"Ahem," came a voice that she recognized, and she turned abruptly to see Leander sitting on a bench behind her.

"I thought I'd come to say good-bye," he said, and Blair went to stand in front of him. The list fell from her hand and, before she could pick it up, Leander took it and read it.

"I see I lost out to Uncle Henry and to your guilt over Houston."

She snatched the list from his hands. "I have done something unforgivable to my sister, and if I can remedy what I've done, I will."

"She didn't look too unhappy to me the last time I saw her. She was looking at Taggert like he hung the moon."

"Houston likes his money."

Lee snorted. "I may not know much about that woman, but I know she isn't in love with money. I think what she likes is a little more, ah . . . personal."

"You're crude."

"Then I guess it's good that you're marrying somebody perfect like Hunter, and not somebody crude like me. Just because I do things to your body that make you cry with pleasure, because we enjoy each other's company, because we work together so well—those aren't reasons to marry me. I hear you even beat Hunter at tennis."

"I'm glad I'm not marrying you. I never wanted to, ever." A sound made her glance down the track and she saw the train.

Leander stood. "I'm damned well not going to wait here to see you make an ass of yourself." He shoved his hands into his pockets. "You're going to be miserable, and you deserve it." He turned on his heel and left.

For a moment, Blair almost ran after him, but she caught herself. She'd made her decision and she was sticking to it. This would be better for everyone concerned.

The train pulled into the station, but Alan still wasn't there. She stood and walked down the platform while two men got off the train and a man and a woman got on.

The conductor started to motion the train forward.

"You have to wait. There's someone supposed to be here."

"If he ain't here, then he's missed the train. All aboard."

With disbelief, Blair watched the train pull out of the station. She sat down on the bench and waited. Perhaps Alan was just late and meant to catch the next train. She sat there for a total of two hours and forty-five minutes, but Alan didn't appear. She asked the ticket manager if a man fitting Alan's description had bought a ticket. He'd purchased two tickets early that morning—for the four o'clock.

Blair paced the platform for another thirty minutes, then began to walk home.

So this was how it felt to be jilted, she thought. Funny, but she didn't feel bad at all. In fact, the closer she got to home, the lighter she felt. Maybe tomorrow she could work at the hospital with Leander.

When Blair walked into the house it was as quiet as a tomb, and the only light on was in the family parlor. She walked in, and to her surprise, her mother and Leander were sitting there, talking as quietly as if they were at a funeral.

When Opal saw her daughter, she very calmly, very slowly, dropped her embroidery and fainted. Leander stared at Blair so hard his mouth fell open, his cigar dropped out and set the fringe on a little footstool on fire.

Blair was so pleased with their reactions that she stood there grinning at them. The next moment, Susan came into the room and began screaming.

The screaming revived them all. Lee put out the fire, Blair slapped her mother's hands until she recovered, and Susan went off to make tea.

As soon as Opal was sitting upright, Leander grabbed Blair's shoulders, jerked her to her feet and began shaking her. "I hope that damned dress of yours fits because you're marrying me on Monday. You understand that?"

"Leander, you're hurting her," Opal cried.

Lee didn't pause in shaking Blair. "She's *killing* me! You understand, Blair?"

"Yes, Leander," she managed to say.

He pushed her down on the sofa and stormed from the room.

With shaking hands, Opal picked up her sewing from the floor. "I believe I've had enough excitement in the last two weeks to last me a lifetime."

Blair leaned back on the couch and smiled.

Chapter 16

For three days, Leander kept Blair so busy at the hospital that she had no time to think. He came for her early in the morning and returned her late in the evening. He took her to the warehouse on Archer Avenue and told her of his plans to renovate the place into a women's clinic. Right away, Blair had some ideas of her own, and Lee listened quietly and discussed them with her.

"I think we can have it ready in two weeks, since the equipment is already on its way from Denver," Lee said. "I'd planned it as a surprise, a wedding present, but I've had more than my share of surprises lately and can't stand any more."

Before Blair could say a word, he ushered her out of the warehouse and into his buggy and drove her back to the hospital. She was relieved that what Alan had said wasn't true, that Lee hadn't been lying about the clinic just to win the competition.

As the hours accumulated and the wedding grew closer, Blair wondered why Lee had wanted to marry her. He made no attempt to touch her, and they never talked except to discuss a patient. A few times, she caught him watching her, especially when she was working with other doctors, but he always turned away when she looked up.

And every day, Blair came to respect Lee more and more as a

doctor. She soon realized that he could have made a great deal of money if he'd stayed in a big city hospital but, instead, he chose to remain in Chandler where he was seldom paid for anything. The hours were long and hard, the sheer amount of work overwhelming, and the rewards, for the most part, intangible.

On Sunday afternoon, the day before the wedding—when Blair was feeling a little queasy from Houston's pre-wedding party the night before—he called her into his office. It was an awkward meeting for both of them. Leander kept staring at her in a way that made her arms break into gooseflesh, and all she could think of was that tomorrow she was going to walk down the aisle to him.

"I've written a letter to St. Joseph's Hospital, telling them that you'll not be accepting their position."

Blair took a deep breath and sat down heavily in a chair. She hadn't thought about having to give up the internship.

Lee leaned forward on the desk. "I was thinking that maybe I've been a bit highhanded." He began to study his nails. "If you want to call tomorrow off, I'd understand."

For a moment, Blair was so bewildered she couldn't say anything. Was he saying that he didn't want to marry her? She stood quickly. "If you're trying to get out of this after all you've done to force me to marry you, I'll—."

She couldn't say any more because Leander had leaped from behind the desk, grabbed her shoulders and kissed her in a hard, intense way that left her speechless.

"I don't want out," he said when he had released her and Blair had managed to get her weak knees under control. "Now, get back to work, doctor. On second thought, go home and rest. If I know your sister, she has three dresses for you to try on, and your mother will have a hundred things for you to do. I'll see you tomorrow afternoon." He grinned broader. "And tomorrow night. Now, get out of here."

Blair couldn't help smiling back at him, and she kept smiling all the way home.

But her smile disappeared as soon as she entered the Chandler house. Mr. Gates was furious because she had been working at the hospital on a Sunday and not at home helping her sister with the wedding arrangements, especially when poor Houston wasn't feeling well today. Blair was tired, too, and she was nervous about the wedding, and she was close to tears before the odious man got through yelling at her. Opal seemed to understand what her daughter was feeling and quickly got Mr. Gates to go to his study, as she took Blair into the garden to start writing thank-you notes.

Blair was still smarting from Mr. Gates's attack when she sat down with her mother.

"How could you marry a man like him, Mother? How could you subject Houston to him? At least I got away, but Houston's had to stay here all these years."

Opal was silent for a few minutes. "I guess I didn't consider you girls when I fell in love with Mr. Gates."

"Fell in love with him! But I thought that your family forced you to marry him."

"Where in the world did you get such an idea?" Opal asked, aghast.

"I think Houston and I must have decided it on our own. We couldn't see any other reason for your marrying him. Perhaps we liked to think that after our father died, you were too distraught to care whom you married."

Opal gave a little laugh. "You both were so young when William died, and I'm sure that as children you'd remember him as the most wonderful of fathers, always doing things, creating things, making excitement wherever he went."

"He wasn't like that?" Blair asked cautiously, dreading to hear awful things about her adored father.

Opal put her hand on her daughter's arm. "He was all and more than you remember. I'm sure you don't remember half of his spirit, his flamboyance, or his courage or ambition. Both of you girls have inherited much from him." She sighed. "But the truth is that I found William Chandler the most exhausting man on earth. I loved him dearly, but there were days when I had tears of relief in my eyes when he finally left the house. You see, I'd been raised in the belief that a woman's role in life was to sit in the front parlor and direct servants while she embroidered. The most strenuous thing I had planned to undertake was counted cross-stitch. All those little squares to count!"

She leaned back in her chair and smiled. "Then I met your father. For some reason, he decided he wanted me, and I don't really think I had much say in it. He came into my life with his extraordinary handsomeness, and I don't think I ever even considered saying no to him.

"But then we were married, and there was one crisis after another to handle, all of them caused by Bill's lust for life. Even when William produced children, he made twins; one child wasn't enough for him."

She looked down at her hands, and there were tears in her eyes. "I thought I'd die, too, after Bill passed away. I didn't seem to have a reason for living, but then I began to remember things that I had once enjoyed, such as needlework, and of course I had you girls. Then Mr. Gates came along. He was as different as night and day from Bill, and he liked what Bill used to call my 'busywork.' Mr. Gates had rigid ideas of what a woman should and should not do. He didn't expect me to spend Sunday afternoons climbing mountains with him as Bill used to. No, Mr. Gates wanted to provide a lovely home for me, and I was to stay in that home and tend to my children and give tea parties in the afternoons. As I got to know the man more, I found that he was easy to please, and that the things that came naturally to me quite often were the ones that he expected from me. With your father, I was never quite sure what I was supposed to do."

She looked up at Blair. "So I found I was in love with him. What I wanted to do and his ideas of what I should do matched perfectly. I'm afraid that I didn't really think of you girls, or realize how much like Bill both of you were. I knew you were like your father, and so I arranged for you to live with Henry, but I thought Houston was like me, and she is to some extent. But Houston is also like her father, and it comes out in odd ways, such as her dressing as an old woman and going into the mine camps. Bill would have done something like that."

Blair was silent for a long time as she thought about what

her mother had said, and she wondered if she could ever love Leander. She'd known for sure that she was in love with Alan, but she hadn't been exactly devastated when he'd jilted her. There was too much bound up in what had happened. She couldn't look at Lee without remembering that her sister had loved him so much and for so long, and now Houston was going to have to watch him marry someone else.

Blair didn't sleep much the night before the wedding, and it seemed that all the demons of the night were still there in the morning. The bright sunlight of the day couldn't rid her of her sense of doom.

For the last few days, she'd managed to forget for whole minutes that she was marrying her sister's intended, but then she'd always believed that it would never actually happen. She had thought that somehow she'd get out of marrying Leander, and Houston could have him back.

At ten o'clock, they left for Taggert's house, where the wedding was being held, Opal and the twins riding in Houston's pretty little carriage, one of the many gifts from Taggert, the stableboy behind, driving a big wagon that Houston had borrowed, the wedding dresses hidden inside muslin in the back. They were silent all the way to the house. When Blair asked Houston what she was thinking, Houston said she hoped that the lilies had arrived undamaged.

Blair knew that this was further proof that her sister's major interest in the man she was marrying was his monetary worth.

And once Blair saw Taggert's house, she was sure that Houston had sold herself to the god of money.

The house looked as if it were carved out of a mountain of marble: cool and white and vast. The downstairs was dominated by a big, sweeping, double staircase that curved up two sides of a hallway that was bigger than that in any house Blair'd ever seen.

"We'll come down there," Houston said, pointing toward the stairs. "One of us on each side." Surrounded by a bevy of prettily dressed girlfriends, she sauntered away and started an inspection of the house, while Blair stood where she was.

"It takes a while to get used to," Opal whispered to her daughter. There was a feeling about the place that it wasn't real, that it was out of a fairy tale and that it would disappear as quickly as it had appeared.

"Houston plans to *live* in this?" Blair whispered back.

"It does seem smaller when Kane is here," Opal assured her. "I think we should go upstairs now. There's no telling what Houston has planned for us."

Blair followed her mother up the wide stairs, looking over her shoulder all the time to the floor below. Everywhere she looked, she saw exotic arrangements of flowers and greenery, and on the landing she paused to look out the window to the grounds below. They were beautiful, with a lush lawn and shrubberies.

Opal paused beside her. "That's the service yard. You should see the *garden*."

Blair didn't say any more as she followed her mother up to the second floor and the private family rooms.

"Houston's put you in here," Opal said, opening the door to a tall-ceilinged room with a white marble fireplace that was carved with swags and flowers. The couches, chairs, and tables in the room should have been in museums.

"This is the sitting room and through here is the bedroom and that's the bath. Each guest room has a sitting room and a bath all its own."

Blair ran her hand along the marble basin in the bathroom and, although she'd never seen any before and couldn't be sure, she thought the fixtures might be gold. "Brass?" she asked her mother.

"He wouldn't have it in his house," Opal said with some pride. "Now, I must go and see if Houston needs any help. You have hours before you need to be ready, so why don't you take a nap?"

Blair started to protest that she couldn't possibly sleep, but then she looked at the enormous marble tub and thought that she'd like to make use of it.

As soon as she was alone, she filled the tub with steamy hot water and climbed into it, the water relaxing her instantly. She stayed in there a long time, until her skin began to wrinkle, and then stepped out and dried with a towel so thick it could have been a pillow. She wrapped herself in a pink cashmere robe and went into the bedroom, where she promptly fell asleep on the big, soft bed.

When she woke, she felt rested and clear-headed, and she remembered her mother's words of there being a garden in the back of the house. Quickly, she dressed in her usual simple skirt and blouse and left the room. Not wanting to use the main staircase, since she could hear muffled voices below, she went down a corridor past closed doors and eventually found a back staircase that led into a maze of kitchen and storage rooms on the first floor. Every inch of these rooms was filled with people scurrying back and forth and creating wonderful smells of food. Blair had a difficult time getting through the crowd. Several people saw her, but no one had time to comment on a bride being in the kitchen two hours before the wedding began. Blair was only concerned that Houston didn't see her. No doubt Houston had a timetable and she would keep to it no matter what happened. Houston would never find time to slip away into the garden.

Behind the house was a lawn that was now covered with enormous tents, and tables with pink linen tablecloths, and hundreds of vases of flowers. Men and women in uniforms were hurrying in and out of the house to put food and condiments on the tables.

Blair hurried past these people, too, and went to what looked to be the garden below. When she first stepped into the edge of the garden, she was unprepared for what she saw. Before her rolled acres of winding paths, appearing and disappearing amid plants such as she'd never seen before. Tentatively, she began to follow a path.

The commotion of the wedding preparations disappeared behind her and, for the first time in days, she felt free to think.

This was her wedding day, but right now she couldn't remember how she had got here. Three weeks ago, she was in Pennsylvania and she had her entire future mapped out. But how different everything had turned out! Alan had run away rather than marry her. Her sister had lost the man she loved and was now marrying one of the richest men in the country— without any love involved.

And everything was Blair's fault. She had come home to see her sister married and had instead managed to make her into a mercenary. Houston might as well have put herself on the auction block and taken the highest bidder.

As Blair strolled about the garden, frowning over her thoughts, she saw Taggert coming down the path. Before she thought about what she was doing, she turned abruptly and went the other way before he saw her. She'd gone no more than a few feet when she saw an extraordinarily tall woman, who looked vaguely familiar, hurrying along the same path as Taggert. Blair couldn't remember where she'd seen her before.

She shrugged her shoulders, dismissing the woman, and kept walking.

Her thoughts were fully occupied with what was going to happen today, and she was trying to puzzle out exactly how it had come about, when she suddenly remembered who the tall woman was.

"That's Pamela Fenton," she said aloud. Houston and Blair had been at the Fenton house often when they were children, to ride Marc's ponies or to attend one of his numerous parties, and his older sister Pam had been nearly grown then and they had been in awe of her. Then she'd left home suddenly, and there had been whispers about what had happened for years afterward.

So she's come back after all these years, and she'll be at the wedding, Blair thought with some pleasure. Idly, she wondered what Pamela had done so long ago to cause the town to gossip about her. There was something about a stableboy, wasn't there?

Blair stopped where she was. The scandal had indeed been about a stableboy in her father's stables. She'd fallen in love with him, and her father had sent her away as a result of that love affair.

And Kane Taggert was that stableboy!

Grabbing her skirts, Blair ran along the path toward where

both Taggert and Pam had gone. She was several feet away when she halted.

She watched in disbelief as Kane Taggert took Pamela Fenton's face in his hands and kissed her with a great deal of passion.

With quick, hot tears in her eyes, Blair fled down the paths toward the house. What had she done to her sister? Houston was going to marry this monstrous man who kissed a woman two hours before he was to marry another.

And it was because of Blair that this was happening.

Chapter 17

Anne Seabury helped Blair into the elaborate wedding dress that Houston had designed. It was an elegantly simple dress of ivory satin, high necked, big sleeved, and as tight as the steel-ribbed corset could make it. Hundreds, maybe even thousands, of tiny seed pearls were sewn about the waist and at the cuffs. And the veil was of handmade lace such as Blair had never seen before.

As she glanced in the mirror, she wished that she was donning this dress under happier circumstances, that she was going to go down that aisle with a smile on her face.

But she knew that was impossible, since she'd already done what she knew she had to do. As soon as she'd seen that monster Taggert kissing another woman, she had returned to the house and sent the man a note. She had told him that she'd be wearing red roses in her hair, and she instructed the maid to tell him that he was to be sure and stand on the left, not the right as was originally planned.

Blair wasn't sure of the legality of what she was doing, since the licenses gave the proper names of which twin was to marry which man, but perhaps she could buy her sister a little time if the minister pronounced Leander and Houston man and wife instead of marrying her to that lecherous man Taggert. She didn't like to think of the consequences if the marriage was legal and she found herself married to Taggert.

She sent pink roses to her sister and asked her to please wear them.

At the head of the stairs, Blair grabbed her sister to her. "I love you more than you know," she whispered before starting the descent, then, with a sigh, said, "Let's get this spectacle over." With every step, Blair felt that she was moving closer to her execution. What if the marriage was legal and she found herself married to that dreadful man and had to live in this mausoleum of a house?

Inside the enormous room that was supposed to be a library, but could have been an indoor baseball field, she saw Taggert next to Leander on a platform that was draped, hung, and piled with roses and greenery.

Blair kept her head high and her eyes straight. She knew that, by now, Houston must have seen what was going on, that she was, after all, going to get to marry the man she loved.

Blair looked ahead at Kane Taggert, and as she walked down the aisle toward him, she saw his brows draw together in a straight line. He knows! she thought. He knows that I'm not Houston.

For a moment, Blair was amazed at this. Right now, she doubted if even her own mother could tell which twin was which, but somehow, this man knew. She glanced at Leander and saw that he was giving Houston a slight smile, a smile of welcome. Of course, Leander was trusting, she thought; he had no reason to suspect anyone of any bad deed since he was incapable of doing anything bad himself. But Taggert, on the other hand, was reputed to have done many bad things to get his money, so he'd be looking for treachery and could therefore tell the twins apart, Blair reasoned.

Blair didn't look at her sister as they took their places on the platform. Leander took Houston's hand in his, while Taggert turned away from both twins and the minister.

"Dearly beloved, we—," the minister began, but Houston cut him off.

"Excuse me, I'm Houston."

Blair looked at her sister in astonishment. Why was Houston ruining what had been so carefully arranged?

Leander gave Blair a hard look. "Shall we exchange places?" he said to Taggert.

Taggert merely shrugged his big shoulders. "Don't matter much to me."

"It matters to me," Leander said and moved to trade places with Taggert.

Lee took Blair's hand in his and nearly squeezed it off—but she felt little pain. Taggert had publicly admitted that Houston didn't matter to him, that he didn't care whether he married her or someone else. Blair had never asked herself why Taggert wanted to marry Houston, and now she wondered if it was because she was the only one who'd have him.

Leander pinched her and she looked up in time to say, "I do."

Before she was aware of what was happening, the ceremony was over, Leander was grabbing her in his arms and preparing to kiss her. To the audience, it must have looked like a kiss of great enthusiasm, but in truth, Lee whispered in her ear with a great deal of vehemence. "I want to see you outside. Now!"

Tripping over the twelve-foot train of her heavy satin dress, Blair tried to keep up with him as he half dragged her down the aisle. People descended on them as soon as they were in the hall, but Leander didn't let go of her hand as he pulled her into a large, panelled room at the end of the corridor.

"Just what was that all about?" Leander began, but didn't let her answer. "Do you hate the idea of living with me so badly that you'd go to such lengths to get out of it? Would you rather have a man you don't even know than me? Anyone but me, is that it?"

"No," she began, "I didn't even think about you. I just thought about Houston. I didn't want her to feel that she had to marry that awful man."

Leander looked at her for a long moment, and when he

spoke, his voice was quiet. "Do you mean that you were willing to marry a man you dislike just so your sister could have the man you think she wants?"

"Of course." Blair was a bit bewildered by his question. "What other reason would I have for making the switch?"

"Only that you thought that marriage to anyone would be preferable to marriage to me." He grabbed her arm. "Blair, you're going to settle this right now. You and Houston are going to talk to one another, and I want you to ask her why she wanted to marry Taggert—and I want you to listen to her answer. You understand me? I want you to really listen to her answer."

Ignoring the hundreds of people around them, all of whom were whispering and laughing about the mix-up at the altar, Leander pulled Blair through the crowd as he asked where Houston was. She wasn't difficult to find, as she sat alone in a small room that was littered with papers.

"I think you two have a few things that need to be said to one another," Leander said through his teeth to Blair as he half pushed her into the room and closed the door behind her.

Alone, the twins didn't speak to each other. Houston just sat in a chair, her head down, while Blair hovered near the door.

"I guess we should get out there and cut the cake," Blair said tentatively. "You and Taggert—."

Houston came out of her chair looking as if she had suddenly been turned into a harpy. "You can't even call him by his name, can you?" she said, anger in every word. "You think he has no feelings; you've dismissed him and therefore you think you have a right to do whatever you want to him."

Surprised, Blair stepped back from her sister's anger. "Houston, what I did, I did for you. I want to see you happy."

Houston's fists were clenched at her sides and she advanced on Blair as if she meant to challenge her to a fight. "Happy? How can I be happy when I don't even know where my husband is? Thanks to you, I may never know the meaning of happiness."

"Me? What have I done except try everything in my power to help you? I've tried to help you come to your senses and see that you didn't have to marry that man for his money. Kane Taggert—."

"You really don't know, do you?" Houston interrupted her. "You have humiliated a proud, sensitive man in front of hundreds of people, and you aren't even aware of what you've done."

"I assume you're talking about what happened at the altar? I did it for you, Houston. I know you love Leander and I was willing to take Taggert just to make you happy. I'm so sorry about what I've done to you. I never meant to make you so unhappy. I know I've ruined your life, but I did try to repair what I'd done."

"Me, me, me. That's all you can say. You've ruined my life and all you can talk about is yourself. *You* know I love Leander. *You* know what an awful man Kane is. For the last week or so, you've spent every waking moment with Leander, and the way you talk about him is as if he were a god. Every other word you say is, 'Leander.' I think you did mean well this morning: you wanted to give me the best man."

Houston leaned toward her sister. "Leander may set your body on fire, but he never did anything for me. If you hadn't been so involved with yourself lately, and could think that I do have some brains of my own, you'd have seen that I've fallen in love with a good, kind, thoughtful man—admittedly he's a little rough around the edges, but then, haven't you always complained that my edges are a little too smooth?"

Blair sat down. "You love him? Taggert? You love Kane Taggert? But I don't understand. You've *always* loved Leander. For as long as I can remember, you've loved him."

Some of Houston's anger seemed to leave her and she turned away to look out the window. "True, I decided I wanted him when I was six years old. I think it became a goal to me, like climbing a mountain. I should have set my sights on Mt. Rainier. At least, once I'd climbed it, it would have been done. I never knew what I was going to do with Leander after we were married."

"But you do know what you'll do with Taggert?"

Houston looked back at her sister and smiled. "Oh, yes. I

very much know what I'm going to do with him. I am going to make a home for him, a place where he'll be safe, a place where I'll be safe, where I can do whatever I want."

Blair stood and it was her turn to clench her fists. "I guess you couldn't have bothered to take two minutes to tell me this, could you? I have been through Hades in the last weeks. I have worried about you, spent whole days crying about what I've done to my sister, and here you tell me that you're in *love* with this King Midas."

"Don't you say anything against him!" Houston shouted, then calmed. "He's the kindest, gentlest man and very generous. And I happen to love him very much."

"And I have been through agony because I was worried about you. You should have told me!"

Houston idly ran her hand along the edge of the desk that sat in the middle of the room. "I guess I was so jealous of your love match that I didn't want to think about you."

"Love match?!" Blair exploded. "I think I'm Leander's Mt. Rainier. I can't deny that he does things to me physically, but that's all he wants from me. We've spent days together in the operating room, but I feel there's a part of Leander I don't know. He doesn't really let me get close to him. I know so little about him. He decided he wanted me, so he went after me, using every method he could to get me."

"But I see the way you look at him. I never felt inclined to look at him like that."

"That's because you never saw him in an operating room. If you'd seen him in there, you would have—."

"Fainted, most likely," Houston said. "Blair, I am sorry that I didn't talk to you. I probably knew that you were in agony, but what happened *hurt*. I had been engaged to Leander for, it seemed to me, most of my life, yet you walked in and took him in just one night. And Lee was always calling me his ice princess, and I was so worried about being a cold woman."

"And you're no longer worried about that?" Blair asked.

The color in Houston's cheeks heightened. "Not with Kane," she whispered.

"You really do love him?" Blair asked, still not able to

comprehend this fact. "You don't mind the food flying every-where? You don't mind his loudness or the other women?"

Blair could have bitten out her tongue.

"What other women?" Houston asked, eyes narrowed. "And Blair, you'd better tell me."

Blair took a deep breath. It would have been all right to tell Houston what she had seen before she'd married the man, but now it was too late.

Houston advanced on her sister. "If you even consider managing my life again as you did today at the altar, I'll never speak to you again. I am an adult, and you know something about *my* husband, and I want to know what it is."

"I saw him in the garden kissing Pamela Fenton just before the wedding," Blair said all in one breath.

Houston whitened a bit, but she seemed to be under control. "But he came to me anyway," she whispered. "He saw her, kissed her, but he married me." A brilliant smile lit her face. "Blair, you have made me the happiest woman alive today. Now, all I have to do is find my husband and tell him that I love him and hope that he will forgive me."

She stopped suddenly. "Oh, Blair, you don't know him at all. He's such a good man, generous in a very natural way, strong in a way that makes people lean on him, but he's . . ." She buried her face in her hands. "But he can't stand embar-rassment of any kind, and we've humiliated him in front of the entire town. He'll never forgive me. Never!"

Blair started toward the door. "I'll go to him and explain that it was all my fault, that you had nothing to do with it. Houston, I had no idea you really wanted to marry him. I just couldn't imagine anyone wanting to live with someone like him."

"I don't think you have to worry about that anymore, because I think he just walked out on me."

"But what about the guests? He can't just leave."

"Should he stay and listen to people laughing about how Leander can't decide which twin he wants? Not one person will think that Kane could have his choice of women. Kane thinks I'm still in love with Lee, you think I love Lee, and Mr. Gates thinks I'm marrying Kane for his money. I think Mother is the only person who sees that I'm in love—for the very first time in my life."

"What can I do to make it up to you?" Blair whispered.

"There's nothing you can do. He's gone. He left me money and the house and he walked away. But what do I want with this big, empty house if he's not in it?" She sat down. "Blair, I don't even know where he is. He could be on a train back to New York for all I know."

"More than likely, he's gone to his cabin."

Both women looked up to see Kane's friend, Edan, standing in the doorway. "I didn't mean to eavesdrop, but when I saw what happened at the wedding, I knew he'd be in a rage."

Houston expertly wrapped the train of her wedding dress about her arm. "I'm going to him and explain what happened. I'm going to tell him that my sister is so in love with Leander that she thinks that I am, too." She turned to smile at Blair. "I can't help but resent the fact that you thought that I was low enough to marry a man for his money, but I thank you for the love that made you willing to sacrifice what has come to mean so much to you." Quickly, she kissed her sister's cheek.

Blair clung to her sister for a moment. "Houston, I had no idea you felt this way. As soon as the reception is over, I'll help you pack and—."

Houston pulled away with a little laugh. "No, my dear managing sister, I am leaving this house right now. My husband is more important to me than a few hundred guests. You're going to have to stay here and answer all the questions about where Kane and I've gone."

"But Houston, I don't know anything about receptions of this size."

Houston stopped at the door beside Edan. "I learned how in my 'worthless' education," she said, then smiled. "Blair, it's not all that tragic. Cheer up, maybe there'll be an attack of food poisoning, and you'll know how to handle that. Good luck," she said and was out the door, leaving Blair alone to the horror of having to deal with the enormous, elaborate reception.

"Why did I ever open my big mouth about that school Houston chose?" she mumbled, as she straightened her dress, tried to breathe inside the tight corset, and left the room.

Chapter 18

The reception was worse than Blair had imagined it could be. People were always running out of this or that and, the minute Houston was out of sight, no one seemed to know what to do. And then, there were what seemed to be hundreds of Lee's relatives to meet, all of them asking questions about the unusual exchanging of twins. Opal began spreading the rumor that Houston's husband had taken her away on a white horse (probably one with wings, Blair thought), and all the young ladies were whispering that Kane was the most romantic of men. All Blair could think of was that she was certainly glad that her switch had failed and she wasn't going to have to spend her wedding night with Taggert.

Some man was asking Blair how he should serve what looked to be a hundred-pound wheel of cheese when she looked across the guests to see Leander watching her, and a small blush began to spread over her body. Whatever else she minded about Lee, spending the night with him was not one of them.

He pushed his way through the crowd of people, gave a few curt directions to the man with the cheese, and pulled Blair away with him into the garden, out of sight of the people. "Thank heavens a man only has to go through this once in his life. Did you know that Mr. Gates is crying?"

She felt good being here with him in the shade, away from the noise and the crowd, and she wished he'd kiss her. "He's probably happy to see the last of me in his house."

"He told me that now he could relax, because now he knew you'd be happy. Now, you were going to do what the Lord made women for. You'd have a good man—that's me—to take care of you, and at last you'd be fulfilled."

He was looking at her in a way that made her feel very warm.

"You think you *will* be fulfilled with me?" he asked in a husky whisper and began to move toward her.

"Dr. Westfield! Telegram!" came the voice of a boy, and the next minute he was standing there, shattering their aloneness.

Leander gave the boy a nickel and told him to help himself to the food as he began to open the telegram, his eyes on Blair. But the next minute, all his attention was on the paper in front of him.

"I'll wring her neck," he said under his breath, his face beginning to turn red with anger.

Blair took the telegram from his hand.

I HAVE JUST MARRIED ALAN HUNTER STOP WOULD YOU TELL FATHER AND BLAIR STOP I WILL RETURN IN THREE WEEKS STOP DO NOT BE TOO ANGRY STOP LOVE NINA

"Of all the underhanded . . . ," Lee began. "Father and I will go after her and—."

Blair cut him off. "And do what? She's already married and, besides, what's wrong with Alan? I thought he'd make a very good husband."

Quickly, the anger left Leander. "I guess he will at that. But why couldn't she have stayed here and been married in public? Why did she have to run away as if she were ashamed of him?"

"Nina and I have been friends all our lives, and I imagine that she was afraid of me. After all, I didn't get to marry the man I had originally planned to marry, so perhaps she thought I'd be angry about how Alan left me at the train station. No doubt he left me for Nina."

Leander leaned against a tree and took a cigar from his pocket. "You seem awfully cool about this. I gave you the chance to back out. You could have gone back to Pennsylvania. You had the chance."

Later in her life, Blair thought that that was the moment she fell in love with Leander. He'd made such a fool of himself to win her, yet here he stood like a sulky little boy, saying that she didn't have to marry him, that he would have let her go.

"And what would you have done if I'd boarded a train? I seem to remember your shaking me and telling me that I *was* going to marry you and that I had no say in the matter," she said softly, as she moved to stand in front of him, her hand touching his collar. Around her was spread yards of the heavenly silk satin, the beading gently flashing colors in the soft light of the garden.

He watched her for a moment, then tossed the cigar to the ground and grabbed her to him in a kiss of great passion, holding her close to him, trying to merge their bodies into one. He pulled her head to his shoulder, almost smothering her as he hugged her in a way that a mother holds a child that has almost been lost. "You *did* choose him, you went to the train to go with him."

Blair tried to untangle herself and the cascading veil from his grasp. She wanted to look at him. "That's behind us now," she said, as she looked into his eyes and thought about the man behind that handsome face. She remembered the many times she'd seen him working to save a life, especially the day they'd brought in an old cowboy who'd been gored by a bull, and when Lee had been unable to save him, and the man had died on the operating table, Blair was sure there'd been tears in Lee's eyes. He'd said he'd known the old man for years, and it would hurt to know that he was gone.

Now, she stood within his grasp, and she knew that she'd married the right man. Alan hadn't really loved her, nor she him. Not if he could one minute demand that she choose, and a few hours later leave her standing at the train station. And she remembered how relieved she'd been when he hadn't shown up.

"A great deal has happened between us," she said, as she ran her hand down his cheek. It was so nice to be able to touch him, as she'd wanted to since their first night together. He was hers from now on, totally and completely hers. "But today marks a new beginning, and I'd like to start with a clean slate. You and I work well together, and we have . . . other things in common," she said, as she moved her hips just slightly against his. "I want this marriage to work. I want us to have children, and I want us to keep in practice together, and I want us to . . .

love each other." She said the last hesitantly, because all he'd ever said was that he desired her, and love had never entered the picture.

"Children," he murmured, pulling her even closer. "Especially, let's make children." He began to kiss her as if he were starving.

"Here they are," someone shouted. "Now, stop that. You have a whole lifetime for that. Now, you have to come and join the party. The cake has to be cut."

Reluctantly, Blair pulled away from her husband. Another few minutes of his kisses and she'd be rolling about the grass with him. She'd already proven that she had no control when it came to him.

With a sigh, Lee took her hand in his and led her back to the mass of people gathered on one of Taggert's too smooth, too big lawns.

Immediately after the cake cutting, the guests separated them and several women started asking Blair hundreds of questions about where Houston had gone.

"That man swept my daughter off her feet," Opal said in a demure way that didn't allow for any disbelief. "Both my daughters have married strong men who knew exactly what they wanted and went after it."

Two of the women in Opal's audience looked as if they were about to swoon at the romance of the stories.

"Mother," Blair said, holding out a dish. "Have a slice of ham." She leaned forward so only Opal could hear her. "Now I know where Houston and I get our acting ability."

Opal smiled at the women, took the dish from Blair and gave her a quick wink.

With a laugh, Blair went away, leaving her mother to brag about her new sons-in-law.

At sundown, there was dancing in the library, and of course Leander and Blair had to lead the dancing. Several people asked if it had been she that night at the governor's reception and not Houston. Both Blair and Lee laughed secretly, and he swept her away in his arms again, whirling her about the polished dance floor.

"It's time we left these people and went home. I don't think

I can wait much longer to make you mine," Leander whispered in her ear as he held her.

Blair didn't even nod, but tightened the train about her arm and quickly left the room to go upstairs to change into her going-away clothes. Her mother came to help her and Opal was silent until Blair stood ready.

"Leander's a good man and I know you've had some problems, but I think he'll make you a good husband," Opal said.

"I do, too," Blair said, looking radiant in an electric blue suit that Houston had chosen for her sister. "I think he'll make the best of husbands." And I *know* he'll make the best of lovers, she thought, then kissed her mother quickly and ran down the stairs to meet Leander.

Amid showers of rice so heavy that their health was threatened, they left the Taggert mansion for the pretty little house that would be their home.

But once they were away from the crowd, Blair began to feel timid and shy. From now on, her life would be tied to this man whom she knew only in a professional way. What did she know about him personally? What had he done in his life besides study medicine?

At the house, Lee swept her into his arms and carried her over the threshold, took one look at her white face and said, "This isn't the woman who risked her life to keep a man's chin clean, is it? You're not afraid of me, are you?"

When Blair didn't answer, he said, "What you need is some champagne. And we both know where that will lead, don't we?"

He set her on the floor in the entry hall and turned right into the dining room. Blair hadn't really seen the house, and now she went left into the parlor. Behind the parlor was a tiny bedroom for guests. The furniture was heavy and dark, but the room was still pleasant, with blue-and-white striped wallpaper and a border of pale pink roses along the top. She took a seat on a satin-covered sofa.

Leander returned with two glasses of champagne and a bottle chilling in a silver holder on a tray. "I hope you like the place. Houston did it. I don't think I cared much what she did." He sat at the other end of the couch, away from her, seeming to sense her shyness.

"I like it. I don't know much about decorating houses, and Houston's much better at that than I am. I would probably have asked her to do the house anyway. But now she has Taggert's."

"Did you two get that straightened out?"

The champagne was making Blair relax and Lee refilled her glass. "Houston said that she'd fallen in love with Taggert." Blair's face showed her disbelief. "I can't imagine my sister with that loud, overbearing boor. Why she would prefer him over you is . . ." She stopped, looking embarrassed.

Leander was grinning at her. "I thank you for the compliment." He leaned across the couch and began to toy with the curls that were escaping the neat chignon that Houston had fixed that morning, and, slowly, he began to remove the pins from her hair. "Opposites always seem to attract. Look at you and me. Here I am a fine surgeon, and you're going to be a fine wife and mother and put all my socks in their proper place, and you'll see to the house so it's a comfortable place for a man to come home to and—."

Blair nearly choked on the champagne. "Are you saying that you expect me to give up medicine to wait on you?" she sputtered. "Of all the misinformed, *stupid* ideas I have ever heard, that one is the worst." With a great deal of anger, she slammed her glass down on a side table and stood. "I always tried to tell Houston that you were like Gates, but she wouldn't listen. She said you weren't at all like him. I'll tell you one thing, Leander Westfield, if you married me thinking that I'd give up medicine, we might as well call this whole thing off now."

Leander sat on the couch as she stood over him raging, then, halfway through her speech, he slowly rose to stand in front of her. And when she began to wind down, he smiled at her. "I think you have a great deal to learn about me yet. I'm not sure why you're so ready to believe the worst about me, but I hope to prove to you that I'm not what you think. And I plan to spend the rest of my life teaching you. But lessons don't start until tomorrow," he said, as he put his arms around her and pulled her to him.

Blair clung to him, and when his lips touched hers, she felt as if she never wanted to let go. She knew that she knew nothing about him. She didn't know why he'd wanted to marry her, whether he had merely tolerated her working with him so that he could win the competition as Alan had said, or if he had enjoyed that time together as much as she had.

But right now, she didn't care. All she thought about was his arms around her, his body near hers, the heat he was producing that was making her feel wonderful.

"I've waited a long time for this to happen again," he said, wrapping her hair about his wrist, his other hand caressing her neck and cheek. "Go upstairs and get ready. I'm going to be a gentleman tonight, but I'll never be one again, so you might as well take advantage of this once. Stop looking at me like that and go. I'm sure your sister bought you some outrageous—but proper—nightgown for tonight, so go get it on. You have about ten minutes. Maybe."

Blair didn't want to leave him, but she did and she went upstairs, around the narrow, curving stairs and into the bedroom. There were three bedrooms upstairs: the master bedroom, one for guests and one a tiny nursery. Her clothes were hung in the closet, all her shoes beside Leander's, and for a moment she thought she'd never seen anything as intimate as those shoes next to each other.

On the bed was indeed a beautiful robe of white chiffon with swan's-down about the hem and sleeves, a gown of white satin to go under it. Blair shook her head at the extravagance of the things, but the next moment she was dying to get into them. Sometimes, she was frustrated by Houston's seemingly useless life, but this wedding made her admire her sister as nothing else had. The wedding itself had required the planning of a military general and no detail had seemed too small to attract Houston's attention. She'd even remembered to have her sister's clothes moved to her new house during the wedding, so they'd be here when she returned with Leander.

Blair was only half into the robe when Lee came up the stairs and, by the look in his eyes, he didn't seem to care that it was hanging off her shoulder in a very unkempt way. He bounded across the room and had her in his arms in seconds. In fact, his enthusiasm was so great that Blair took a step backward, tripped on the hem of the robe, and fell back onto the bed. Lee went with her and they fell into the feather bed, bits of swan's-down from the robe floating around them.

They started to laugh, and Lee rolled over, his arms still about her, pulling her with him, kissing her, tickling her, making Blair squeal with delight. The lovely robe came off and she was in the thin satin gown, and he was nibbling at her shoulders and growling like a bear, making her laugh harder. His hands went up and down her thighs while she made halfhearted protests about nothing in particular.

The telephone downstairs began to ring before their play turned serious.

"What's that?" Blair asked, lifting her head.

"I don't hear anything," Leander murmured, his face buried in her neck and travelling lower.

"It's the telephone. Lee, you have to answer it. Someone may be ill and need you."

"Anyone who'd disturb a man on his wedding night deserves what he gets."

Blair pushed away from him. "Lee, you don't mean that. When you became a doctor, you did so because you wanted to help people."

"But not tonight, not now." He tried to pull her back into his arms, but she resisted and the damn telephone kept ringing. "Why did I have to marry a doctor?" he mumbled, as he stood and adjusted his clothes while giving Blair looks that made her giggle and look away. "Don't you go away. I'll be right back," he said before he went down the stairs. "Right after I kill whoever it is on the telephone."

As soon as he picked up the receiver, the operator began to talk. "I hate to disturb you tonight of all nights," she began, "but it's your father, and he says it's urgent."

"It'd better be," Lee said. Then she put Reed on the line.

"Lee, I hate to bother you, but it's an emergency. Elijah Smith is about to die of a heart attack if you don't come right away."

Leander drew in his breath. Elijah Smith was their code name for trouble at the mine. Reed often reported to Lee over the telephone while Lee was at the hospital, and they'd worked out a series of messages. Poor Mr. Smith got everything from poison ivy to smallpox, but a heart attack was what they'd agreed to use to signal the worst that could happen: a riot.

Lee rolled his eyes toward the ceiling, toward the room where his bride waited. "How much time do I have?"

"They needed you an hour ago. Lee, don't go; someone else can take the case."

"Yeah, like who?" Lee spat, taking his anger out on his father. There was no one outside the mines who knew what was going on inside them. And Lee felt responsible for any rioting, since he was the man who brought the unionists in. "I'll be there as fast as I can," Lee said before he hung up the telephone.

As he went up the stairs, feeling as if the worst thing in his life had just happened, he suddenly realized that he had to give Blair a reason for leaving. He was no longer a bachelor who answered to no one. He now had a wife who deserved an explanation as to where he was going. At the moment, he was feeling so miserable that he couldn't think of a lie—and heaven forbid that he should tell her the truth! With Blair's total lack of a self-preservation instinct, she'd no doubt insist on going with him. And if he didn't have enough to worry about, he couldn't have her in danger, too.

The best way was to do it quickly and get out of the house.

He had never moved faster in his life, and considering that there were what seemed to be tears fogging his eyes as he looked at Blair lying there in that thin little piece of cloth, every nook and cranny of her delicious body showing, he should have been given an award. He didn't say much at all, except that he had to go and he'd be back as soon as possible. He ran down the stairs and was out the door before Blair could even move.

At his father's house, he was still feeling miserable and thinking that the miners could riot all night as far as he was concerned.

Reed told Lee that an informer had let the guards know about the unionist, and that the stupid man had gone back into the camp without Lee. He'd sneaked down the back side of the mountain and was being very bold when the guards heard about him. Now, the armed guards were searching each house and making threats against innocent people.

Leander would be able to get into the camp, and if he could find the unionist before the guards did, he might be able to save the man's life—and the lives of the miners who were being falsely accused of bringing the man in.

Lee knew that he was the only one who could do this, and he set to readying his carriage.

"If Blair comes to you, don't even hint at where I've gone. If you tell her I'm on a case, she'll want to know where it is, and she'll want to help. Make up something, but, whatever you do, don't tell her the truth. Anything would be better than the truth because she'd tear into the middle of the riot and I'd have to save both her *and* the unionist."

Before Reed could ask what sort of story his son had in mind, Lee was off with a cloud of dust and rocks spewing behind him.

Chapter 19

Blair's mouth didn't close for several minutes after Leander left their house. She couldn't believe that one minute he was there, and the next he was gone.

Her first reaction was anger, but then she smiled. It must have been a serious case that would take Lee away on his wedding night, something that was life and death—and something that was dangerous, she thought, sitting upright. If it weren't serious, no doubt with guns blazing or outlaws terrorizing people, Lee would have taken her with him.

Blair tossed the covers aside and hurriedly dressed in her medical uniform. Leander was going into something dangerous, and he'd need her help.

Downstairs, she picked up the telephone. Mary Catherine was on the switchboard at this time of night. "Mary, where did Lee go?"

"I don't know, Blair-Houston," the young woman answered. "His father called him, and the next thing Leander said was that he was on his way. Not that I listened in, of course. I'd never do that."

"But if you did happen to hear a few words, what would they have been? And don't forget the time I didn't tell Jimmy Talbot's mother who broke her best cut-glass pitcher."

There was a pause before Mary Catherine answered. "Mr. Westfield said that some man I've never met was having a heart attack. That poor man. It seems that every time Mr. Westfield and Leander talk on the telephone, it's about this Mr. Smith who has one ailment after another. Last month he had at least three diseases and Caroline—she's on the day shift— said that Mr. Smith was ill twice. I don't think he's going to live very long, but then he seems to heal quickly between illnesses. He must be awfully important for Leander to leave you on your wedding night. You must," Mary Catherine paused to let a rude little giggle escape, "miss him very much."

Blair wanted to tell the woman what she thought of her constant eavesdropping, but she merely whispered, "Thank you," and put the receiver down, vowing to never again say anything private on the telephone.

In the stable behind the house, Lee's carriage was gone, and the only horse there was a big, mean-looking stallion that Blair had no intention of trying to ride. The only way to get to her father-in-law's house was to walk. The cool mountain air gave her energy, and she half ran up and down Chandler's steep streets to the Westfield house.

She had to pound on the door to wake up the household and a sleepy, sullen housekeeper came to the door, Reed just behind her.

"Come into the library," Reed said, his face a strange ashen color. He was fully dressed but looking old and tired. Blair was sure that he was up because he was worried about Leander. What in the world had her husband gotten himself into now?

"Where is he?" Blair asked as soon as they were alone in the well-lit library that was filled with the smoke from too many pipes.

Reed just stood there, his face taking on more of a resemblance to a bulldog.

"He's in danger, isn't he?" Blair asked. "I knew he was. If it were an ordinary case, he'd take me with him, but something's wrong with this one." Still, Reed didn't say anything. "The telephone operator said that he often goes to look after a Mr. Smith. I would imagine that I could find out where the man lives, and I can go from house to house and ask if anyone's seen Leander tonight. If I know him, he left in his usual flurry, and I'm sure several people saw him." Blair's face began to have the same look as Reed's—of complete determination. "My husband is going into something dangerous, as he did that day when he knowingly went into a range war, and he's walking into it alone. I believe that I can help. There may be others wounded, and if Lee were hurt," she stumbled over her words, "he would need attention. If you won't help me, I'll find someone who will." She turned away from him to leave.

Reed was bewildered for a moment. She might not be able to find Lee, but she'd certainly manage to stir up a great deal of trouble, and she'd make people aware that *something* was important enough to take him away on his wedding night. And, of course, people would hear about the riot in the mine, and all that had to happen was for one person to put two and two together and connect Leander and the mine riot. He *had* to tell Blair something that would stop her here and now, something so awful that she'd go home and not wake the town searching for Leander. Damn, but why hadn't Lee married Houston? *She'd* never have questioned her husband's whereabouts.

"There's another woman," Reed blurted before he thought about what he was doing. His own wife wouldn't have let anything stop her except the thought of his love going to someone else. Why didn't women ever feel secure that they were loved? Blair should certainly know, since Lee had done so much to prove to her just how much he loved her.

"Woman?" Blair asked, turning back to him. "Why would he go to another woman? Was she ill? Who is Mr. Smith and why is he always ill? Where is my husband?"

"The ah . . . woman tried to kill herself because of Lee's marriage," Reed said and knew that now his relationship with his son was over, because Lee would never forgive him as long as either of them lived.

Blair sat, or rather fell, into a chair. *"That* kind of woman," she whispered.

At least, he had gotten her off Mr. Smith, Reed thought, and at the same time cursed all telephone operators everywhere.

"But what about Houston? He was engaged to her. How could he be in love with someone else?"

"Lee . . . ah, thought this woman was dead." On the table before Reed was a newspaper, and on the front page was an article about a gang of robbers that had been in the Denver area, but were now beginning to move south. The leader of the band was a Frenchwoman. "He met her in Paris, and she was the great love of his life, but he thought she'd been killed. I guess she wasn't, because she came to Chandler to find him."

"When?"

"When what?"

"When did this woman come to Chandler?"

"Oh, months ago," Reed said offhandedly. "I think maybe you'd better let Lee finish this story. I think I've said enough already."

"But if she came months ago, why did Leander continue his engagement to my sister?"

Reed rolled his eyes skyward, and again the newspaper caught his eye. "She, this woman he loved, was . . . involved in something Lee didn't approve of. He had to do something to distract himself."

"And my sister was that distraction, and then later I was." She took a deep breath. "So, he was in love with this woman and thought she'd been killed, so he returned to Chandler and asked Houston to marry him. And then I came along, and one twin was as good as another, and of course his honor made him feel he was obligated to me. That explains why he'd consider marrying a woman he didn't really love. Is that it?''

Reed ran his finger around the inside of his collar, which suddenly felt as if it were choking him. "I guess that'll do as well as any explanation," he said aloud and then muttered, "Now, I have to explain myself to my son."

Blair felt very heavy as she left the house and began to walk home. Reed had sent for his stableboy to drive her home, but Blair had dismissed him. This was her wedding night and supposedly one of the happiest times of her life, and if she couldn't spend it with her husband, she certainly didn't want to spend it with another man. But her happiness had turned into a nightmare.

How Leander must have laughed at her when she told him that she hoped to make their marriage work. He hadn't cared whom he married. Houston was pretty and would make a good doctor's wife, so he asked her to marry him, but then Houston was cool to him, so when Blair jumped into bed with him on their first night out, he decided to marry her instead. Whatever did it matter, when his heart was already given to another woman?

"There she is!" came a man's voice from behind Blair.

It was just growing light, and she saw a small man on horseback and he was pointing toward her. For a moment, Blair felt a little pride that she was already being recognized in the streets as a doctor. She stopped and looked up at the man and the three men behind him.

"Is someone hurt?" she asked. "I don't have my medical kit with me, but if you'll give me a ride to my house, I'll get it and I can go with you."

The cowboy looked shocked for a moment.

"If you'd rather have my husband, I don't know where he is," she said with some bitterness. "I think you'll have to make do with me."

"What's she talkin' about, Cal?" one of the men in the back asked.

Cal put up his hand. "No, I don't want your husband. You'll do just fine. You wanta ride with me?"

Blair took the hand he offered and let him pull her up to mount in front of him. "My house is—," she said, pointing, but he didn't let her finish.

"I know where your house is Miss High and Mighty Chandler. Or I guess it's Miz Taggert now."

"What is this?" Blair said, startled. "I'm not—." But the cowboy put his hand over her mouth and she could say no more.

Leander put a hand to the small of his back and tried to ease it against the jolting of the hard wagon seat. He had to admit that he had an awful case of feeling sorry for himself. Last night should have been spent in the arms of his new wife, in a soft bed, making love to her, laughing together, getting to know each other. But instead, he'd been climbing down the side of a mountain and then back up it again with a semiconscious man slung over his shoulder.

When he had got to the mine last night, the gates were locked and there was no sign of a guard, but he could hear the sounds of shouting in the camp and some women screaming words of anger. He hid his horse and carriage in the trees and went up the mountain and down the steep side and got into the camp the back way. He ran under cover of the houses and the dark to the house of one of the miners who he knew would likely take the risk of hiding the unionist.

The miner's wife was there, wringing her hands because the guards were searching every house and the unionist was hidden in the weeds at the back of the outhouse—and he was bleeding and moaning. No one dared go to him because if he were found, it would be death to anyone found with him. If the guards kept up their search and found nothing, and no trace of an infiltrator, they'd not harm the miners, but if he were found . . . The woman put her face in her hands. If the unionist were found there, she and her family'd be thrown out of the camp with no jobs nor any money.

Lee gave her a few words of sympathy but didn't spend much time talking. He went to the weeds at the back and hauled the short, stocky man across his shoulders and began the long, arduous task of trying to sneak him out. The only way out was straight up the side of the mountain, and that's the way Lee went.

He had to pause several times, both to rest and to listen. The sounds below seemed to be quietening. There were always many saloons in a mining camp, and the men too often spent most of their wages on drink. Now, Lee could hear the drunks singing as they staggered home, probably unaware that their houses had been searched—as was the right of the mine owner's representatives.

Lee stopped at the crest of the mountain and tried to see, in the moonlight, the man's wounds. He'd started bleeding again when Lee'd moved him. Lee wrapped the man's wounds as best he could to stop the bleeding, then started across the crest, and then down to where his buggy was hidden.

He couldn't possibly put the man into the cramped little compartment in the back, so he propped him up beside him and drove as carefully as he could.

He took the road north toward Colorado Springs. He couldn't return with the man to Chandler, or there'd be too many innocent questions about who he was and where he'd been hurt. Lee didn't want to risk being found out. He'd never be able to help anyone again if there were any suspicions attached to him.

On the outskirts of town lived a friend of his, a doctor who wasn't inclined to ask too many questions. Lee put the wounded man on the doctor's surgery table and mumbled something about finding the man on the trail. The old doctor looked at Lee and said, "I thought you got married yesterday. You were out lookin' for half-dead men on your weddin' night?"

Before Lee could answer, the old man said, "Don't tell me nothin' I don't want to know. Now, let's have a look at him."

Now, returning to Chandler, it was two o'clock in the afternoon. Lee was past being tired. All he wanted to do was eat, sleep, and see Blair. He'd spent most of the past several hours planning a story to tell her about where he'd been. He thought he'd tell her that he'd been called to a shootout between members of a gang of bank robbers and that he hadn't wanted to risk her coming along and getting hurt. It had a ring of truth, and he thought he could get away with it. He just prayed that she wouldn't ask him why he had to go when there were other doctors in Chandler who could have gone. Also, there would be no account of the shooting incident in the paper.

If worse came to worst, he planned to act hurt that she didn't trust him and that she seemed to want to start their marriage off on the wrong foot.

At home, he was almost relieved when Blair wasn't there. He was too tired to do his best in the telling of a major lie. He stuck some ham between two thick slices of bread and went up to the bedroom. The room was a mess, with Blair's clothes tossed on the bed, the bed unmade. He glanced at the closet, saw right away that her medical uniform was gone and knew that she'd gone to the hospital. He'd have to do some talking, for the men of the board to continue to allow her to work there. Last time, he'd had to promise to take on nearly every shift before they'd let him bring her into the operating room. He'd nearly worked himself into a stupor, but it had been worth it. He'd won Blair in the end.

He ate half the sandwich, crawled onto the bed, hugged Blair's discarded satin nightgown to him and went to sleep.

When he woke, it was eight o'clock, and he knew right away that the house was empty—and instantly, he began to worry. Where was Blair? She should have been home from the hospital by now. As Leander rose, starting to eat the other half of the now-stale sandwich that was lying beside him on the bed, he saw that her medical bag was on the floor of the closet.

For just a moment, his heart stopped beating. She'd never, never leave the house without taking that bag. It was a wonder that she hadn't carried it down the aisle with her when she'd married him.

But now, it was there on the floor.

He threw the sandwich down and went tearing through the house shouting her name. Maybe she'd come back while he was asleep, and the house just *seemed* empty. It took only minutes to find that she was nowhere, inside or out.

He went to the telephone and told the operator to give him the hospital. No one there had seen Blair since the wedding. After enduring some rude jests, saying that Blair'd already realized her mistake and run away from him, Lee put the phone down.

It rang almost instantly.

"Leander," it was the day operator, Caroline, "Mary Catherine said that Blair called your father right after you left last night to go treat your poor Mr. Smith. Maybe he knows where she is."

Lee bit his tongue to keep from telling Caroline to stop eavesdropping, but maybe this time he had reason to be grateful to her. "Thanks," he murmured and went out to saddle his stallion and get to his father's house in record time.

"You told her *what?!*" Leander yelled at his father.

Reed seemed to shrink under his son's anger. "I had to come up with a story fast. And the only thing I could think of, that was guaranteed to keep her from following you, was a story of another woman. From what I've heard of your recent escapades together, I thought fire, war, or union riots just might make her tear into the thick of things."

"You could have come up with another story—*any* other story but that my one true love was here and that I married Blair because I'd lost my real love."

"All right, if you're so smart, you tell me where you were supposed to be that would keep her from following you."

Lee opened his mouth, but closed it again. If Reed had told her of a disaster, no doubt Blair would have come to help. He knew bullets flying toward her didn't stop her. "Now what do I do? Tell her my father is a liar, that there is no other woman?"

"Then where were you on your wedding night? Other than climbing up and down the side of a mountain and hauling a wounded unionist to safety? What will your little wife do next time you're called away?"

Lee groaned. "Probably something really stupid like hiding in the back of my buggy and joining in the fracas. What *am* I going to do?"

"Maybe we should find her first," Reed said. "We'll start

looking as discreetly as possible. We don't want the town to realize that she's walked out, or there'll be questions."

"She hasn't walked out," Lee spat. "She's . . ." But he didn't know where she was.

Chapter 20

Leander and his father looked for Blair all night. Lee had an idea that she might walk when she was upset, and so they combed the streets. But she was nowhere to be found.

By morning, they'd decided to pass the story around that she'd gone to a medical emergency without telling anyone where she was going and that Lee was worried about her. At least, this story allowed them to ask questions about her in the open.

There was some teasing about Lee losing his wife on the first day of their marriage, but he managed to weather it well. His one and only concern was for Blair and where she was. She was so headstrong, and they had so little to base their marriage on, that he was afraid that she'd returned to her uncle in Pennsylvania and that he'd never get her to return. He'd gone through hell trying to get her to marry him, and he certainly didn't want to have to go through anything like that again in order to persuade her to live with him.

By afternoon, he was exhausted and he collapsed on their still unmade bed and slept. He'd have to telegraph Dr. Henry Blair tomorrow morning and tell the man to keep Blair there until he could come and get her.

He was wakened by a heavy hand on his shoulder.

"Westfield! Wake up."

Sluggishly, Lee turned over to see Kane Taggert standing over him, the man's face showing anger. In his hand was a piece of paper. "Where's your wife?"

Lee sat up, ran his hand through his hair. "I think she may have left me," he said. It was of no use trying to conceal the truth. Soon, the entire town would know.

"That's what I thought. Look at this."

He thrust a dirty, torn piece of paper into Lee's hands. On it, in primitive block letters, was the message:

WE HAVE YOUR WIFE. LEAVE $50,000 AT TIPPING ROCK TOMORROW. YOU DON'T SHE DIES.

"Houston?" Leander asked. "I'll get my gun and go with you. Do you know who has her? Have you told the sheriff yet?"

"Wait a minute," Kane said, lowering his big form to sit on the bed. "Houston's fine. Me and her've been gone since the weddin'. We just got back this mornin', and this was on my desk with a lot of other mail."

Lee stood as if lightning had struck him. "Then they have Blair. I'll get the sheriff or . . . That man'll never find her. I'll go by myself and—."

"Hold on a minute. We got to think about this. When I got back this mornin', there was a man to see me, a man that'd come down from Denver, and on the way here he was robbed by a new gang that seems to wanta make their headquarters outside Chandler. This little man was real upset, sayin' that all Westerners were outlaws and that they even captured women. It seems he'd heard one of the men that came ridin' up durin' the robbery say that they'd got 'her.' That could mean your wife."

Leander was changing clothes, into denim pants, chaps, a heavy cotton shirt, and a gun on the belt at his hips. Some of his original fury was leaving him and he was beginning to think. "Where was the man held up? I'll start there."

Kane rose and Lee gave only a glance at the man's heavy work clothes. "I figure this is my fight, too. They want my money, and it's my wife they think they got." He looked at Lee out of the corner of his eye. "When I saw this note and realized that it was Blair that they had, I figured this town would have been turned upside down lookin' for her but, as far as I can tell, don't nobody know she's missin'. I think there's some reason you wanta keep quiet about this."

Lee started to tell him that he didn't want her many friends upset, but he didn't. "Yeah," he said, nodding, "there's a reason." He waited, but Taggert said nothing more. "You know how to use a gun? How to ride?"

Kane gave a grunt that sounded somewhat like a bear. "Houston ain't civilized me that much. And don't forget that I grew up here. I know this area, and I have an idea where their hideout is. Twenty miles north of here is a box canyon that's almost hidden from the outside. You could walk past it and not even see it. I got caught in there in a flash flood once."

For a moment, Lee hesitated. He didn't know this man, didn't know if he could be trusted or not. For years, he'd heard stories about the illegal means Kane had used to obtain his money, that nothing else mattered to the man but money. But here he was telling Lee that he was willing to help—and willing to respect Lee's right to keep secret whatever he wanted kept secret.

Lee tied the holster of the gun to his leg. "You got a gun with you?"

"I got enough for a small army outside on my horse, and I also got the fifty grand they want. I'd rather give the money away than risk shootin' around a lady," he said, grinning. "After all, she did wanta marry me a couple of days ago."

At first, Lee didn't remember what he meant, but then exchanged grins with him. "I'm glad it worked out the way it did."

Kane ran his hand over his chin and seemed to be laughing at some private joke. "Me, too. More glad than you know."

Fifteen minutes later, they were saddled, their bags packed with food, and on the trail out of town. Lee had left a message with the operator to tell his father that he'd gone to see about Mrs. Smith. Lee didn't even listen to the operator's murmurs of sympathy about the poor Smith family.

Once outside the town limits, they rode hard, Lee's big horse eating up the miles. Kane's animal was a magnificent beast that carried the two hundred and fifty pounds or so of the man with relative ease. Lee's only thoughts were of Blair, and he hoped she was safe and unharmed.

Blair struggled again against the ropes that held her to the heavy oak chair. Once, she'd managed to escape, so they'd tied her to a chair, and yesterday she'd managed to turn the chair over, but before she could get untangled from it, *that* woman had come into the room and ordered the chair to be nailed to the floor. Blair sat there for hour after hour and watched the woman as she gave orders to her men.

She was called Françoise and she was the leader of the outlaws. She was tall and pretty, slim, with long black hair that she obviously took an inordinate pride in, wore a gun belted about her hips, and was smarter than all the men who rode with her put together.

And Blair knew immediately that this was the woman Leander loved.

Everything fit what Reed had said. She was French, speaking with an accent so heavy that at times her men had difficulty understanding her, and she was involved in something that Lee could not approve of. Blair couldn't help feeling her opinion of Lee fall somewhat because he loved a woman who was capable of such dishonesty.

She sat in that hard chair and watched the woman with unconcealed hostility. Because of her, she'd never have her husband to herself, she'd never be able to erase the past from his mind. Maybe men liked the glamour of being in love with a criminal. Maybe Leander wanted to nurse his broken heart all his life.

The woman stood in front of her for a moment and watched Blair's eyes blazing above the gag. Then she pulled a chair from under an old table and sat across from her.

"Jimmy, remove the cloth," she said to the big bodyguard who was always with her. She said it as, "Jeemy, remove zee cloth."

Once it was gone, she motioned the big man away so that they were alone in the room. "Now, I want to know why you look at me with such hatred. You do not look at the men that way. Is it because I am a woman, and you do not approve of a woman who is so skilled as I am?"

"Skill? Is that what you call it?" Blair asked, flexing her sore jaw. "Just because men are such fools that they can't see through a woman like you, doesn't mean that I am. I know what you are."

"I am so glad that you do, but then I don't believe I have ever lied to anyone."

"You can stop lying to me for one. I know all about you." She lifted her head somewhat and tried to muster what pride she could. "I am Leander's wife."

Blair had to admit that the woman was certainly a good actress. One after another, emotions passed across her face. They ranged from puzzlement to disbelief, and ended with humor.

The woman stood, her back to Blair. "Ah, Leander," she said at last. "Dear Leander."

"There's no need to act so smug," Blair shot at her. "You may think you have him and that he'll always be yours, but I'll make him forget everything that ever happened between the two of you."

When the woman turned back to face Blair, her face was serious. "How could he forget what we had? No one alive could forget something like that. It happens only once in a lifetime. So, he has married you. How long ago?"

"Two days. You should know, since he spent our wedding night with *you*. Tell me, how did you try to kill yourself? You look as if you've recovered well enough. Perhaps it was merely a play for sympathy and not a true attempt at suicide. I can't imagine that you'd be a good loser when it came to someone like Leander."

"No," she said softly. "I didn't want to lose Leander, but I didn't want anyone else to have him, either. Did he tell you why we are no longer together?"

"He didn't tell me a word about you. After finding out what you've become, I'm sure he can barely stand to think of you. Reed told me. But perhaps you don't know Lee's father, since you're not the sort of woman a man can bring home to his family. Lee thought you were dead, and he left Paris thinking you were dead. He returned to Chandler." Blair thought of all the stories he'd told her about his years in Europe, and he'd never even hinted about another woman. But maybe it was too painful a subject for him to talk about.

"I'm going to win him," Blair said. "He's my husband, and neither you nor anyone else is going to take him from me. He'll come for me and you may see him again, but you won't have a chance with him."

"Paris, was it?" the woman said, smiling. "Perhaps this Leander Taggert and I—."

"Taggert? Leander's no Taggert. Houston married Tag—." She stopped. Something was wrong here, but she didn't know what.

Françoise put her face close to Blair's. "What is your name?"

"Dr. Blair Chandler Westfield," she said, frowning.

Immediately, the woman turned on her heel and left the cabin.

Blair slumped back into the chair. She'd been here for nearly two days now, and she'd had very little sleep and even less food, and she was beginning to have trouble fully comprehending what was going on.

After they'd taken her, they'd blindfolded and gagged her and then ridden for what seemed like hours. Most of the time, she'd concentrated on keeping the hands of the cowboy who rode behind her in the saddle from running all over her body. He kept whispering that she "owed" him. For the life of her, Blair couldn't remember having met the man before or having done anything to him.

She moved all over the horse, as far as she could, to get away from him, and when the horse began to grow restless and prance, one of the other men ordered the man in the saddle with her to leave her alone, saying that she belonged to Frankie.

That idea sent a shiver up Blair's spine. Just who was Frankie and what did he want with her? She still had hopes that they needed her medical services but, because they hadn't let her get her bag, she doubted it.

When they'd removed the blindfold, she was standing in front of a rundown little shack, a porch with a fallen post on one end. Around her were six men, all small and stupid-looking like the one who'd taken her. There was a small corral to her right, and a few other outbuildings here and there. And everything was surrounded by high, sheer cliff walls. White rock kept them protected—and hidden—like a fort. At the moment, Blair couldn't even see the entryway into the canyon, but realized it must be small enough that the cabin could block it from view.

But she soon lost interest in her surroundings, because on the porch appeared Frankie, the Frenchwoman who was the love of her husband's life. Hate, anger, and jealousy combined to make Blair speechless as she gaped up at this woman who was the leader of this two-bit band of semimorons.

Someone pushed Blair into the shack: a dirty, dark little place with two rooms, one with a table and a few broken chairs, the other with a bed. Supplies were on the floor in the main room.

For the first twenty-four hours, they'd been fairly lax in their guarding of Blair, but after four attempts to escape—she'd almost succeeded in one of them—they'd tied her to the chair, and then ended by nailing it to the floor.

Now, her wrists were raw from the rough rope and from pulling on it for long hours, and Frankie had decided that perhaps a little less food would help her stay in place and keep her from again trying to scale the rock wall that protected them.

Blair wasn't sure her mind was functioning properly. It seemed so long since she'd eaten or rested, and there was this horrid woman who was her husband's lover. Part of her said that Leander had to be part of this, part of her said that Frankie had done it on her own, that she wanted to see Leander again. And if Lee saw her again, would he want Blair, or would he this time go with the woman whom Reed had called his one true love? Of course, Leander *had* left her on their wedding night to go to this woman. She had that kind of power over him. So who was to say that Leander wasn't hiding behind the cabin somewhere, that he hadn't arranged everything so that he and Frankie could be together?

There were tears running down Blair's face when Frankie

came into the room, with the cowboy who'd abducted Blair in tow by his ear, as if she were his schoolteacher. There were bright red handprints on the boy's face where he'd been slapped.

"She is the one?" Frankie asked the boy. "You are the one who says he knows. Do you know or do you lie to me to settle an old debt?"

"It's her. I swear it is. Her husband tossed me in the dirt, and he's worth millions."

Frankie, in disgust, pushed the boy away. "How stupid I was to send a boy to do a man's job. You see this?" She held up a torn newspaper. "They are identical twins. One is married to a rich man, and one is . . ." She turned to glare at Blair, who was listening with wide-eyed interest. "And one is my dear, beloved Leander's wife."

Blair was much too upset, hungry, tired, and too ready to believe what she thought to be true, to hear the sarcasm in the woman's voice.

"Get out of here," the Frenchwoman shouted at the boy. "Let me think what's to be done."

She might have thought faster if she'd known that at that moment a man was lying on his stomach on the rock above, his rifle aimed and ready, three more rifles at his side. And another man waited at the entrance to the hidden canyon to receive a signal from the man above.

Chapter 21

Blair was sure that her spirits had never been lower in her life. Maybe it was a combination of hunger, thirst, fear, everything combined, but it suddenly seemed that very few people in her life had ever really loved her. Her stepfather had always hated her, and in school, the only man who'd ever been interested in her had ended by jilting her, and now her husband was actually in love with another woman—and always had been. She didn't actually believe that she could get him back. Back? She'd never had him to begin with.

"I need to go to the outhouse," she mumbled to Françoise at dawn, when the woman returned to the shack. Blair had waited as long as possible, because the last time she'd gone, Françoise had sent one of her outlaws to guard Blair, and then she'd caught the man peeping through a knothole.

"I shall go with you this time," the Frenchwoman said as she untied the knots on Blair's wrists.

When Blair stood, she was dizzy and began to sway on her feet. The lack of circulation in her body was making her extremities cold.

"Come on," the woman said, jerking Blair. "You didn't look too tired when you were scaling that wall."

"That might have been what did it," Blair said, as the woman caught her arm and half dragged her from the shack.

The outhouse stood near the entryway into the box canyon, as if someone had planned to keep guard from inside that malodorous place. Blair went inside while Françoise stood outside, a rifle across her shoulder, keeping watch.

Blair had no more than closed the door when she heard a muffled scream. With some curiosity, but also with a feeling of dread that something awful had happened, she leaned forward to look out the convenient knothole. The next moment, the door was rattled and, when it was found to be locked, she was knocked backward by the force of an enormous fist, knuckles wrapped, coming through the weathered boards of the door. Before she could straighten up and look for a weapon to protect herself, the sound of shooting came from outside.

The hand that was coming through the door fumbled for and opened the latch. Blair poised herself to leap at the man who was trying to take her.

When the door was opened, she jumped and landed against the big, hard form of Kane Taggert.

"Stop that!" he ordered when she started beating him with her fists. "Come on, let's get you two out of here. Another minute, and they'll see that you're missin'."

Blair quietened and glanced down at Françoise, tucked under Taggert's left arm as if she were a sack of flour. "Is she hurt?"

"Just a nick on the chin. She'll wake up in a little while. Run for it."

Blair ran through the narrow opening, ducking the bullets that seemed to be coming from everywhere. Behind her was the big body of Kane and she wondered who it was shooting from the cliff above them. She prayed that it wasn't Houston.

Kane tossed Françoise's unconscious body across the saddle of his horse. "I hadn't figured on her. Get up there," he said, as he picked Blair up and dropped her into the saddle behind the inert form of the Frenchwoman. "Tell Westfield that I'll stay here a while and keep 'em busy down there. The three of you head on up to the cabin and I'll meet you there." With that, he slapped the horse on the rump and started Blair up the hill.

Blair hadn't gone but a few feet when Lee jumped out from the trees and grabbed the horse's reins. The grin he wore threatened to split his face. "I see you're all right," he said, as he put his hand on her leg and caressed it.

"And so is she," Blair said with all the haughtiness she could muster, as she gave him Kane's message. "I'm sure you had Taggert rescue her for yourself."

Leander gave a groan and looked at the woman as if he'd just noticed her. "I hate to ask this, but is she the French-woman who is the leader of the gang that kidnapped you?"

"I'm sure you know who she is as well as anyone. Tell me, did you arrange for me to be taken?"

Lee swung up on his horse. "No, but I may arrange for something lethal to happen to my father. Let's not waste any more time. Taggert says there's a cabin hidden up in the mountains. We'll stay there while he gets the sheriff and a posse. Let's go—and stop giving me death looks!"

Blair tried her best to maneuver the big horse up the mountainside to follow Lee, but it wasn't easy. Françoise began to wake and moan, and when her movements caused the horse to shy, Lee stopped and looked back at the women. With a sigh of exasperation, he glanced at Blair's face, then away. He pulled the Frenchwoman onto his horse in front of him, and told her that if she knew what was good for her, she'd be quiet.

Blair turned her nose up in the air and moved away from them both.

Kane caught up with them by taking a shortcut up a steep bit of rock that the horses couldn't travel and met them before they'd gone very far.

Lee dismounted but stayed close to his horse—and to Françoise. "What's going on?"

"They're after us," Kane said, as he drank from a canteen. "My guess is that they'll stay around until they get her back." He nodded his head toward Françoise. "I don't think they're much without her." Kane looked at the woman who was sitting on the horse with her spine straight. "I think you'd better watch her. She's pretty smart."

"I'll take care of her," Lee said. "I think they'll look for us south, on the way back to Chandler. We'll be safe enough, but you'll have them on your tail. Why the hell did you take her, anyway? She'll be more trouble than she's worth."

Kane stoppered the canteen and shrugged his big shoulders. "I was behind her and, at first, I thought she was some other woman they'd captured. Then she turned around, and I saw that she was carryin' a rifle so I clipped her one on the chin. It occurred to me that she might be useful."

"Makes sense, but I don't relish trying to take care of her until you get back. I wouldn't mind a dozen men, but two women?"

Kane put his hand on Leander's shoulder. "I don't envy you one bit. I'll see you in a few hours, Westfield. Good luck." He helped Blair from his horse and mounted and was down the mountain, out of sight, in minutes.

"Why aren't we going with him?" Blair asked.

"We didn't know how they'd treated you, so it was decided that you and I'd stay higher up on the mountain in a cabin while Taggert went to get the sheriff." Lee's eyes lit up and he took a step toward her. "I thought maybe we'd have some time to ourselves, just the two of us."

Both of them seemed to have forgotten the presence of Françoise, although Lee still firmly held the reins to the horse on which she sat. The terrain around them was much too steep and wild to try to escape.

The Frenchwoman slid off the horse and put herself between Blair and Leander, who were moving toward each other as surely as magnets.

"Oh, Leander, my chérie, my darling," she said, putting her arms around him and plastering her body against his. "You must tell her the truth. We cannot keep what we feel for each other a lie any longer. Tell her that you want only me, and that this was all planned by you. Tell her."

Blair turned on her heel and started down the mountainside.

Leander had the dual problem of trying to untangle himself from the dark woman's grasp and of keeping his jealous wife from running into the outlaws who were looking for them. He couldn't release the Frenchwoman, so he held onto her wrist, and the horse, and started chasing Blair.

"Darling," Françoise said, as Lee pulled her along, "you're hurting me. Let her go. You know she never meant anything to you. She knows the truth."

With every word, Blair blindly hurried faster down the steep slope.

Lee stopped long enough to turn back to Françoise. "I've never hit a woman, but you are tempting me. Blair," he called, "you can't keep running. There are men with guns looking for us."

Françoise sat down on the solid rock that was the mountainside, put her face in her hands and began to cry. "How can you say such things to me? How can you forget our nights in Paris together? What about Venice? And Florence? Remember the moonlight in Florence?"

"I've never been to Florence," Lee said, as he grabbed her by the arm and pulled her up; then, when she wouldn't walk, he tossed her over his shoulder and went skidding down the mountain after Blair, catching her by the back of her skirt. Thanks to the expert tailoring of J. Cantrell and Sons, the fabric held. He kept pulling, as Blair did, and finally, he sat on the rocky surface and pulled her into his lap.

It occurred to him that he was a ridiculous sight, with one

woman draped over his shoulder, bottom end up, and another one held on his outstretched leg. When Françoise started to move, he smacked her on her rump. "You stay out of this."

"Whenever you touch me there, I obey you," Françoise said in a purring voice.

Blair started to get up, but Lee held her.

"Blair," he began, but she wouldn't look at him. "I have never seen this woman before today. I did *not* meet her in Paris. I have never been in love with anyone except you, and I married you because I fell in love with you."

"Love?" Blair said, turning to look at him. "You never said that before."

"I have, but you never listened. You were too busy telling me that I was in love with Houston. I didn't love her, and I certainly never loved this . . . this . . ." He looked at the ample rear end that was beginning to strain his shoulder. He shrugged her off, but kept her wrist in his grasp.

Blair was starting to lean toward Lee. Maybe he was telling her the truth. She did so want to believe him.

"You lie very well, Leander," Françoise said. "I never knew that about you. Of course, then, you and I only knew one another one way." She leaned toward him. "But such a way. Ooh là là."

Blair tried to get out of Lee's lap, but he held her firmly, and with one look at his wife's face, he gave a heavy sigh and took the wrists of both women and led them up the mountain.

Blair followed him but only reluctantly. It was a long, hard climb. They had to walk across an area that was covered with fallen trees, repeatedly stepping high up and over. The air was getting thinner as they travelled upward, and it was more difficult to get the oxygen needed to counteract the exertion of the climb.

All the while, Lee kept his hold on Françoise and every time he tried to help Blair, she pushed his hand away.

The cabin was between two steep-sided ridges, hidden so well that they walked past it twice before they saw it, and then they came upon it suddenly, as if it had just appeared out of nowhere.

There wasn't much land in front of the cabin, as the mountainside fell away sharply, but outside was a breathtaking view. The grass was ankle deep and was interspersed with three colors of daisies and clumps of wild roses.

The floor of the forest was soft with hundreds of years' worth of decayed vegetation and so their passage had been silent.

Lee didn't say a word as he motioned for Blair to watch Françoise while he checked the cabin to make sure it was empty. And when he was sure that it was safe, he motioned for the women to enter.

It was an ordinary little cabin: two rooms and a little loft over the door, filthy from years of being invaded by animals and negligent men, but it was obviously a private place, and that was what they wanted.

Blair watched without much interest as Lee tied Françoise to a post in the cabin, giving her freedom to move somewhat and not gagging her.

He had a bandanna in his hand, ready to cover her mouth, but he couldn't seem to bring himself to use it. "I don't think your men will find us here. I'll be outside listening, and if I hear anything, I'll put this on you."

"Chérie, you aren't going to keep up this charade, are you? She knows about us. She told me everything."

"I'll bet she did," Lee said, tightening the ropes. "She told you enough that you can continue this lie. What's in it for you?"

Françoise just looked at him.

When Blair looked up at the two of them, they were staring deeply into one another's eyes.

Lee turned back as if to say something to Blair, but he seemed to change his mind when he saw her expression. He picked up his rifle. "I'll be outside if you need me. There's food in the saddlebags."

With that, he left the women alone.

Slowly, Blair began to remove what food there was in the saddlebags that Lee'd thrown on the old table near the post where Françoise was tied. There was a fireplace in the cabin, but heaven only knew when the chimney had been cleaned last and, besides, they didn't need smoke to advertise their whereabouts.

While Blair put cheese and ham on bread and ate, Françoise talked, never letting up in her declarations of what she and Leander had meant to each other.

"He'll come back to me, you know," Françoise said. "He always does. No matter how hard he's tried to leave me, he couldn't. He'll forgive me for whatever I've done, and this time he'll join me. We'll ride together, love together. We'll—."

Blair grabbed a sandwich and a canteen and left the cabin.

Chapter 22

Lee was some distance from the cabin and so well concealed that Blair didn't see him until he called to her.

"What's happened?" Lee asked, as he took the sandwich from her and managed to caress her wrist at the same time.

"Don't touch me," she said, jerking her arm away as if he'd tried to hurt her.

Lee's expression changed to anger. "I've had about all of this I can take. Why don't you believe me when I say that I've never met her before? Why do you believe her over me, your husband?"

"Because your *father* told me about her. Why shouldn't I believe him?"

"My father lied to you because I told him to!" Lee snapped.

She took a step backward. "Lied? So you admit it? What would take you away on our wedding night? There was no medical emergency. I somehow doubt that your mysterious Mr. Smith actually exists, so where were you?"

Leander didn't answer for a moment, as he turned to look

back at the distant forest and eat his sandwich. He wasn't going to compound his problems with another lie. "I can't tell you," he said quietly.

"You won't tell me." She turned away, heading for the cabin.

He caught her arm. "No, I *can't* tell you." His face showed his rising anger. "Damn it, Blair! I've not done anything to deserve your mistrust. I was *not* out with another woman. Lord, but I can barely handle one woman, much less two. Don't you realize that it had to be something important, something dire, to take me away on my wedding night? Why the hell can't you trust me? Why do you believe my father, who was lying on my behalf, and that bitch in there who makes her living by stealing?"

He dropped her arm. "Go on, then. Go ahead and believe her. That's just what she wants. I'm sure she'd like nothing better than to see us at each other's throats. It'd be much easier for her to escape one captor than two. If she keeps on, and you continue believing her, another couple of hours and you'll *help* her escape just to get the two of us apart."

Feeling quite weak, Blair sat down on the grass. "I don't know what to believe. She seems to know so much about you, but then I have no right to expect you to be faithful. You didn't want to marry me in the first place. It was only a competition."

Leander grabbed her upper arm and hauled her to her feet. "Get back to the cabin," he said with teeth clenched, then turned his back to her.

Blair was bewildered by everything. Her head down, her feet dragging, she started back to the cabin. One time Aunt Flo had complained to her husband that Blair knew nothing about life. "If a man told her she'd broken his heart," Aunt Flo said, "Blair'd look in some medical text to find out how to sew it back together. Medicine is not all there is to life."

Blair stopped and turned back toward Lee. "Have you really never been to Florence?" she asked softly, but the sound carried in the silent forest.

He took a moment before he turned to look at her. His face was unyielding. "Never."

Cautiously, Blair took a step toward him. "She's not really

your type, is she? I mean, she's too skinny and doesn't have enough on top *or* bottom, does she?''

"Not nearly enough." Still, his face didn't change as he watched her approach.

"And she wouldn't know a hernia from a headache, would she?''

He watched her until she was standing in front of him. "I wouldn't have made a fool of myself in front of the town if I'd loved someone else.''

"No, I guess you wouldn't have.''

His rifle in one hand, he held out one arm to her and she snuggled against him, her head against his chest. His heart was beating wildly.

"You owe me a wedding night,'' she whispered.

Suddenly, he grabbed her hair, pulled her head back and kissed her deeply, his tongue touching hers.

When Blair turned her body to his and pressed her knee between his legs, he let her go, gently pushing her away.

"Go back inside,'' he growled. "I need to keep watch and I have some thinking to do—and I certainly can't think with you near.''

Reluctantly, she moved away from him.

"Blair,'' he said, when she was no longer touching him, "I'm beginning to come up with a plan. I haven't worked it out yet, but don't let her''—he nodded toward the cabin—"know that you know she's lying. Pretend that you believe what she says. I think I can use your anger.''

"I'm glad to be useful,'' she muttered before returning to the cabin.

Jealousy was a new emotion to Blair. Never before had she experienced it. She sat in that dirty little cabin and listened while Françoise recounted her grand passion with Leander. Part of her wanted so badly to believe Lee, but part of her was sure this awful woman was telling the truth. Blair had to sit on her hands or she would have leapt for the woman's throat. She did her best to think of other things.

After a while, Blair got herself under control enough to realize that what Françoise was saying was very general.

"And your sister . . .," Françoise was saying, "ah, her name is . . ."

"Charlotte Houston," Blair said absently, wondering where Lee could have gone on their wedding night if it wasn't to another woman.

"Yes, Charlotte," Françoise was saying. "I had to fight Charlotte for many months, but then when she married Taggert . . . I imagine Lee felt obligated—."

"He must have discussed her with you at length," Blair said, suddenly alert.

"When he could get away. The truth is, I am already married, and we thought my husband would never release me, but he will. You see, I found out that I was going to be free on the night he married you."

"So, he left me to go to you," Blair said. "Of course, now I'm free and you're shackled to the post, but I'm sure it'll work itself out. Excuse me, I think I'll get a breath of air."

When Blair walked out of the cabin, she felt as if she'd lost twenty pounds. She felt light and happy and free. No matter what Lee'd said, there'd been some doubt about his relationship with the Frenchwoman. But now, Blair was sure he'd been telling the truth.

As she stood on the porch and breathed deeply of the clean, cool air, an iridescent hummingbird came up to inspect the red insignia on her shoulder. Blair held very still and watched the little bird hovering about her, smiling at it before it realized that she was nothing edible and flew away. Still smiling, she walked down to where Leander hid in the grasses.

She sat down beside him without saying a word, listening to the wind in the aspens overhead.

"She didn't know Houston's name," she said at last, and when he looked at her with curiosity, she continued. "I haven't always been a part of your life, but Houston has. I don't imagine anyone you've ever known hasn't heard her name, if for no other reason than for the sheer quantity of letters that Houston wrote you."

Lee put his arm around her, chuckling and shaking his head. "You don't believe me, but you do believe her. I guess I'll have to take whatever I can get."

She leaned against him and they just sat there together, listening to the wind, not saying a word. Blair thought how close she'd come to missing this moment. If she'd had her way, she'd be in Pennsylvania with Alan right now. Alan who was so small, Alan who wasn't even a doctor yet, and would probably never be as good as Leander was, Alan who didn't know which end of a gun to hold, Alan who would have probably gone to the sheriff and would never have rescued his wife on his own.

"Thank you for rescuing me," she said, and she meant for rescuing her from more than just her kidnappers.

Lee moved to look at her, then pushed her away, as if she had turned to poison. "I want you to go sit by that tree," he said, and there seemed to be a quiver in his voice. "I want to talk to you, and I can't do it with you so near me."

Blair was so flattered that she moved to all fours and put her face in front of his. "Maybe you regret leaving on Monday night," she said, her lips almost touching his.

Lee drew back from her. "Go!" he ordered, and there was a threat in his voice. "I can't keep watch and do what I want to do to you at the same time. Now, get over there and be still."

Blair obeyed him, but his words were sending little chills up and down her spine. In a few hours, Taggert would have the sheriff in the mountains and they'd take the outlaws and Lee could hand over Françoise, and then they'd be alone. She thought of their one and only night together, and when she looked up at him through her lashes, she heard him catch his breath.

She was very pleased when he looked away.

"I've had time to come up with a plan that just might work," he said, as he looked out across the forest. "What I want you to do is help the woman to escape. Tonight, I'll say something that could mean I plan to sneak off with Françoise—maybe we could have an argument. I'm sure you could manage that," he said, as he turned to look back at her. "What the hell!" he gasped as he looked at her.

"My stocking was loose," Blair said innocently, as she lifted her slim leg and adjusted the tight black cotton garment, wishing with all her might that she were wearing silk. Maybe there was something to Houston's wardrobe. No doubt Houston had worn nothing but the sheerest of silks on her honeymoon.

"Blair," Leander said. "You are trying my patience."

"Mmmmm," she said, lowering her leg. "What were you saying about an argument?"

Leander looked away, and Blair saw that his hand was trembling. "I said that I want us to stage an argument, and afterward I want you to let Françoise see you put something in my coffee. Make her think that you're going to make me sleep through the night rather than go to her."

"You wouldn't go to her, would you?"

"I'm saving my energy for later," he said, in such a way, looking at her through his thick lashes, that Blair's heart began to pound.

Lee looked back at the forest. "I want her to escape. I can tie the knots so that she can get away, but it will take her a couple of hours to work free. And while she's working them, I plan to run a little errand."

"While you're supposed to be sleeping?"

"As far as I can tell, she's a cautious woman. She doesn't take too many chances with her life, so I want her to feel safe, that I'm in a drugged sleep and you want her to escape. She didn't even try to escape when we were travelling up here," he said, almost as an afterthought.

"It was too steep. She couldn't have."

"Did you try to escape out of that box canyon?"

Blair smiled at him. "How did you know that?"

"A wild guess, based on your recklessness and disbelief that anything can harm you. Now, are you willing? Do you think you can give a good performance?"

Blair grinned at him. "We're here together now because of my extraordinary acting ability."

He returned her smile. "Go back in now, and listen to Françoise. Make her think that you believe every word she says. Make her think that you're ready to murder me."

Blair stood and looked down at him. "I'm not going to let anything happen to you until I get my wedding night," she said, then when Lee started to rise, she ran back to the cabin, making sure that she raised her skirts high enough to let him see a great deal.

"You can have her for all I care!" Blair shouted at Lee. "You can spend the rest of your life together and I hope you're both hanged," she yelled as she ran from the cabin, leaving Leander and Françoise together.

She kept running up the hill, not pausing to look back until she was out of sight of the cabin. Once she was hidden by the trees, she collapsed on the ground and sat there to catch her breath. Below, she could barely see Lee as he began to look for her.

She smiled as she watched him. She was sure that he'd had no idea just how good an actress she could be and that now he was worried that she'd believed what she'd shouted at him. It had been a good fight, long and loud, with lots of anger. Blair had shouted about Lee's father, about his leaving her on their wedding night, about having taken her away from Alan, about his sister taking the man she'd loved. That one had thrown him. He'd stood there looking at her as if he half believed her.

Now, Blair was out of breath and she wanted to stay away from the cabin long enough to make it look as if she were truly angry. And, too, she wanted to think about where Lee was going tonight. Was this another one of his secret visits? Was their entire life together going to be full of these secret disappearances of his? Would he ever tell her what he was doing that was so private that even his wife couldn't be told the truth?

As Blair watched the cabin, and saw Leander looking for her, she decided that there had to be a way to make him trust her. She didn't want to be so ill informed of his life that some woman who didn't even know him could make her believe that she knew something that his wife didn't.

As she was sitting there, lost in thought, she was oblivious to the sounds that were coming from behind her. When she did hear them, she was almost paralyzed, realizing that it was probably Françoise's gang that had at last found them. Very slowly, she turned to look up the hill.

What she saw more than paralyzed her. Coming down the

hill were two big black bears—and they were heading toward her.

No one had ever moved faster. Blair shot up and started running before her feet were firmly on the ground. She was at the cabin before she glanced over her shoulder and saw that the bears weren't behind her. Cautiously, she stopped and looked around. There were only the sounds of the forest and no sign of the bears. Curious, she walked to a tree at the edge of the clearing and looked back up the hill. Ordinarily, she would have run to safety, but part of her remembered that she was in the midst of a game with Leander and she couldn't give it away by running into his arms now.

Very slowly, she crept back up the hill, always checking that the way behind her was clear. If the bears were lurking somewhere, she wanted to know about it so she could tell Lee.

About ten feet from where she had been sitting, and only a few yards from the cabin, was a small cave, and from the tracks around it, Blair thought that it must have been used by generations of bears.

"So that's why the cabin is abandoned," she murmured and started down the hill. It was nearly sunset and she had to pretend to give Lee the drug that was to make him sleep.

Later, she thought that she'd done it all very well, and she doubted if even Lee had seen her put the headache powder in his coffee—but she'd made sure that Françoise had. For a moment, she'd been tempted to put a little ipecac into his drink after she'd seen Lee looking at Françoise when he thought no one was watching him.

Within minutes after Lee had drunk the coffee that had been heated on the tiny fire he'd made behind the cabin, Lee was yawning and saying that he had to sleep. After several minutes of telling Blair how to guard the prisoner, he went into the other room, and they could hear him fall onto the dirty little cot.

Françoise looked at Blair in such a way that Blair wanted to cut the woman loose and challenge her to a fistfight. But, instead, she checked the woman's bindings.

"At least, he won't be spending the night with you," Blair said. "I'm going to sleep." She looked the Frenchwoman up and down as she was tied to the pole. "I hope you're comfortable."

"And what if I escape? How will you explain that to him?"

"With relish," Blair answered. "What do I care what you do as long as you're away from my husband? Besides, I learned a few things about knots in medical school. You won't get out of those so quickly."

Blair went into the other room, and she thought how Lee had been right, that Françoise was extraordinarily careful of her life. How many prisoners asked permission before trying to escape?

A quick check of the cot and she saw that Lee had already sneaked out of the cabin through the open window. Blair made a pile of blankets that she hoped would look like a body and went out the window after him.

She walked for several minutes, but she heard nothing. He seemed to have disappeared. She was heading east, the cabin at her back, and, she hoped, toward where Lee was going. Of course, he hadn't seen fit to tell her any of his plans, but she guessed this might be the direction he'd be taking, for whatever he planned to do. She hid when she heard a sound behind her.

"All right, come out of there."

She heard the voice, and it sounded like Lee's, but it wasn't the voice he used with her. It had a hard, metallic sound to it—and it was accompanied by the clicking of the hammer of a gun being pulled back. With a sheepish look, Blair stepped out of her hiding place.

Muttering a curse, Lee reholstered his gun. "Why aren't you at the cabin where I left you? Why aren't you guarding that woman?"

"I wanted to know where you were going."

"*Not* to meet another woman. Now, go back to the cabin. I have some unfinished business to attend to, and I don't have much time, and I can't do anything with you around."

"If you're not meeting someone else, then where are you going? I thought we were supposed to wait for—."

"What do I have to do? Tie you up, too?"

"Then I was right. You *are* somehow involved with those

robbers and that woman. Or else you could tell me where you're going. Oh, Leander, how could you?" She started to turn away, but he caught her arm and spun her around.

"All right, I'll tell you! The Inexpressible Mine is less than a mile from here, and I plan to sneak down the back side, break into the explosives shed, steal some dynamite and blow the end of that canyon up. I can't get all of them, but I can trap most of that gang inside the canyon—especially if I use their lady-leader as bait."

Blair blinked several times, then took a step toward him, her eyes glistening. "It'll take less time if you just take me with you." Before he could speak, she continued. "I can help. I can climb. I almost climbed out of the canyon where the robbers held me. Please, please, Leander." She grabbed him and began kissing his neck and face. "I'll obey you and never get in your way, and if anybody gets hurt, I'll thread the needles for you."

Leander knew he was a beaten man. "I didn't know when I was well off with a dull, obedient lady like Houston," he said under his breath, as he started walking at a quick pace.

Blair bit her tongue to keep from telling him that her sister secretly drove a huckster wagon into the mine camps. Instead, she just smiled back at him and began to follow him through the dark forest toward the mine.

Chapter 23

Leander set such a hard pace down the mountainside that Blair almost wished she hadn't gone with him. She could be safe now, asleep, instead of half falling down the dark, steep cliff. Twice, she skidded down on her back, but managed to catch herself before she fell too far. Lee seemed to be saying that since she'd been fool enough to want to come with him, she had to look out for herself.

They finally came out at the bottom of the steep ridge and looked out over the little mining community.

"I guess it's useless to ask you to stay here, isn't it?"

"Entirely," she replied.

"All right, then, stay close to me. Don't get more than two feet from me. I want to know where you are every minute. You understand? And if I tell you to run, that's just what I want you to do. No questions, no arguments. And be as quiet as you can."

Blair nodded in answer to his warnings and began to follow him down into the camp.

It was late and most of the lights were out. Only a few saloons were still open and busy. They ran from the cover of one building to another, and Blair could feel her heart pounding with excitement.

"We'll have to break into the company store first. I'll need a crowbar to get that lock and chain off."

They crept to the back of a large building that was nearly in the center of the town. Three times, they had to duck when people walked by.

"Blair," Lee whispered, "I've got to break this glass. I want you to laugh to cover the sound. Make it a loud laugh, like a pros—like a lady of the evening. No one will pay attention to a familiar sound like that, but they'll come running to the sound of breaking glass."

"Leander," she said stiffly, "I am not as experienced as you are. I have no idea how a lady of the evening laughs."

"Suggestively. Sound like you're trying to get me to go into the woods with you so you can do pleasurable things to my body."

"That should be easy," she said, and meant it.

Lee wrapped his hand in his handkerchief and prepared to smash through the glass in the door. "All right. Now!"

Blair tossed her head back and gave a raucous laugh that filled the air, and when Lee looked back at her, there was admiration in his eyes.

"I'll take you up on that offer as soon as possible," he said, even as he reached inside and opened the door. "Stand over here and be ready to run if someone sees us."

Blair stood to one side of the door and watched Lee as he made his way about the store looking for a crowbar. Behind her were stacks of canned goods, bags of flour, a barrel of crackers. On one shelf were six little barrels of honey. Looking at them, Blair smiled, as they reminded her of the bears.

Suddenly, without having a specific plan, she grabbed a rucksack from a pile on the floor and shoved two barrels of the honey into the bag and put it on her back. By the roll of wrapping paper on the counter was a pencil so, quickly, she tore off a corner and wrote a note.

"What are you doing?" Lee demanded.

"Leaving an IOU, of course. After tomorrow, I'm sure the entire town will know we blew up part of a mountain, and people will know we had to have stolen the dynamite. Unless you usually carry some in your medical bag. You weren't planning to just take this without saying who did it, were you? Someone else would be blamed."

Lee looked at her for a moment. "Good thinking," he said at last. "There'll be no reason for secrecy tomorrow. But I don't want to be caught tonight. Let's go. Wait a minute. What do you have on your back?"

"Honey," she answered, and she didn't give him time to ask more questions before she left the store ahead of him. He closed the door carefully and, unless you looked for it, you couldn't see the broken glass.

Lee led her through the camp, back to the outskirts, and once it occurred to her that he knew the place awfully well. But then, she'd heard that he sometimes treated injured miners.

They walked over ground that was crunchy from slag, and the slight wind blew coal dust into their eyes. Behind the railroad tracks, behind a fifty-foot-tall mountain of coal dust waste, behind the long rows of ovens where the sulfur was burned from the coal, was the explosives shed.

Rubbing her eyes, Blair stood in the shadows while Lee pried the door off the shed. As quickly as possible, he shoved sticks of dynamite under his shirt and wired the door shut. He wouldn't leave it hanging open for a passerby to help himself to what was inside. Whoever opened it next would still have a difficult time.

"Let's go," he said, and Blair began the steep ascent to the top. At times, the ground was directly in front of her face and she had to pull herself up.

Lee was waiting for her at the top, but he didn't give her time to catch her breath. They nearly ran to the cabin. "I'm going to saddle my horse and leave it in front. I thought you might get out of bed to get something to eat, and you might forget and leave a knife within her reach. I'll be waiting outside to follow her when she goes back to the canyon."

"We," was all Blair said, but the way she looked at him made him sigh.

"All right, but get inside now and wait for me."

"I have to tend to a personal matter first—in the bushes," she said, and she didn't know whether she was blushing from her words or from the fact that she was lying.

Lee didn't even look at her as he saddled his horse. Blair ran up the side of the hill toward the bears' den. Cautiously, she approached the black hole of the cave, listening for any sounds. Holding her breath in fear, she picked up a rock and smashed it against the corked hole in one of the barrels of honey she'd taken from the pack on her back, then listened again for sounds of movement. Still quiet.

Turning the barrel so the honey ran onto the ground, she began to make her way down the mountain toward the cabin, leaving a thick trail in the leaves and grass.

Lee's horse stood ready and saddled in front of the cabin, and Blair managed to remove the cork from the second barrel of honey without any noise before she tied it on the back of the saddle. For a moment, she hesitated about what she was doing, because if Françoise took too long to cut herself loose and the bears smelled the honey first, then the bears could go for the horse before it had a rider. Timing was everything.

She climbed in the cabin window and saw, even in the dark, Lee frowning at her because she'd taken so long. As quickly as she could, she removed her medical uniform. She wanted to look as if she'd just wakened.

Françoise was lying on the floor and Blair could see that there were raw places on her wrists where she'd tried to get out of the bindings. Blair's stomach lurched. She'd taken a vow to relieve suffering, and she hated to be the cause of pain in anyone.

Françoise opened her eyes as Blair walked by.

"I guess I haven't recovered since you tried to starve me," Blair said, as she sliced a piece of cheese from the chunk on the corner of the table. "It won't be long now before the sheriff will be here."

"If he were coming, he's had time. The man who came with Leander has been killed by now."

"Too bad," Blair said nonchalantly. "He's Taggert, the one with the money."

With a fierce yawn, Blair put the knife on the table and picked up the piece of cheese she'd cut. "I'm going back to bed. Sleep well," she laughed before leaving the room.

As soon as she was out of sight of the woman, she began to dress, slowly and silently, while she placed herself so that she could see Françoise. The outline in the moonlight showed that the woman lost no time in taking the knife from the table and even less time in cutting her bindings. She was out the door in seconds.

"Let's go," Lee said as soon as he heard his horse take a step.

"Let me guess, more walking," Blair said heavily, feeling very tired.

"When we get through with this, you can stay in bed for a week," Lee said. "With me."

"That sounds restful," Blair said sarcastically.

Lee led her down a sheer rock face. She had an idea that if she were to see this place in daylight, she'd refuse to try to climb it. As it was, she didn't seem to have a choice. They had to beat Françoise back to the box canyon.

Lee stopped abruptly and below them lay the canyon. It was quiet around the darkened little cabin, and she wasn't sure there was anyone in there.

"They're waiting for her. I don't think they make a move without her telling them what to do."

"Lee, it's taken Taggert a long time, hasn't it? Do you think he's all right?"

"I don't know. There were many of them against one of him." He moved to the mouth of the canyon and began to place the dynamite. "As soon as we get them sealed in here, I'll ride back to Chandler and get help."

"Ride? On what?"

"Here, hold this," he said, handing her a fuse. "I'll show you later. Now, it's all set. We just have to wait for our lady outlaw."

They sat there in silence for a few minutes. "She should be here by now. I hope she isn't lost."

"Or gone elsewhere," Blair added. "Lee, I think I should tell you something. It's about the honey. I—."

"Quiet! I think I hear something."

It was nearing daylight and in the hazy dawn they could just see the outline of a rider on horseback. The horse was giving the rider a very hard time, and the slim woman was having difficulty controlling it.

"Up there! Now!" Lee ordered Blair, and she began to run to the safety of the higher rocks.

The next minute, all hell broke loose. Françoise began screaming and, in the canyon below, men started running and shooting their guns before they even knew what was wrong. Blair stopped on her way up to look back, and she saw the Frenchwoman on the big stallion, fighting to control the animal, and behind her were two bears, loping along, stopping now and then to lick the rocky ground.

Blair heard a muffled sound from Lee, and the next thing she knew, he was tearing up the hill, his arm catching her about the waist. All the while, he was whistling in an odd way, two short, piercing tones, then repeated.

"Get down," he said and shoved Blair so that she scraped her elbows on the rock. She scooted forward until she could see into the chaos in the canyon below. The horses in the corral were going crazy now that the bears were in the canyon with them, and the people were running around trying to shoot the bears, calm the horses and escape the confusion. Françoise was pulling on the reins of Lee's horse, and screaming and pointing at the entryway, as she tried to get the men to listen to her.

Suddenly, Lee's big horse reared and dumped her onto the ground, then the animal turned and started running toward the entrance, oblivious to the bears that stood in his way.

"He'll get caught in the blast," Lee said, standing to see better into the canyon. There was a great deal of sadness in his voice when he spoke of the inevitability of losing his beloved horse.

The horse kept running and the bears got out of its way.

Less than a minute later, the dynamite exploded, closing the entrance to the canyon and trapping the outlaws inside. Lee was knocked to the ground by the blast, but the dust hadn't settled before he was running down toward the opening. When he was halfway down, his big horse came running to him with rolling, terrified eyes. Lee hugged the animal's head and talked to him to quiet him.

"What the hell were those bears for?" Lee yelled at Blair, who'd followed him down. They could hear the shouts and shots in the canyon below, and the dust hadn't settled yet from the explosion.

"I didn't mention it, because I knew you'd patronize me, but it's been too long," Blair said, almost shouting, not letting him frighten her. "Taggert's been gone more than enough time. I knew the outlaws were going to find us before long, and then we'd be stuck in that cabin with a dozen men shooting at us. They can climb out of that canyon fairly easily, but I thought that maybe, if it were timed right, the bears could delay things. I do hope no one hurts the bears. All they wanted was the honey."

Lee started to say several things to her, but nothing seemed to fit. "I've never seen a woman who didn't have a sense of danger. Don't you realize that you could have been hurt?"

"So could you," she said, with her chin in the air.

He grabbed her by the arm, not yet ready to forgive her. "Now, I'm afraid to leave you here while I go for the sheriff."

He didn't have a chance to say anything else because at that moment, the sheriff and six men came running up the mountainside. They were completely out of breath.

"You all right, Doc?" the sheriff asked, panting, his big chest heaving. For all his gray hair, he was a man in good condition, and he'd made it up to the canyon in very little time. He'd known exactly where the canyon was after Taggert had described it—and he also knew, better than anyone else in town, Leander's propensity for taking things into his own hands. "Taggert said you were in trouble." The next moment, his mouth fell open as he looked over the rim into the canyon below. The people were like toys as they ran around the rock walls and looked for ways to get out. "You do this, Doc?"

"Me and the Missus," Lee said in a drawl that made Blair giggle.

The sheriff pulled back from the edge while the men of the posse kept watching. "Don't let none of 'em escape," he said over his shoulder, as he stood there looking at Blair and Leander. "It looks like you found your match, boy," he said to Lee and there was anger in his voice. "How come you couldn't wait for me to get here? Why'd you have to take the law in your own hands? Somebody could have been hurt by this. Those people down there have killed men. And that Frenchie leader's meaner'n a snake. I've warned you about this sort of thing before. One of these days you ain't gonna come out of one of your do-gooder scrapes alive."

"What's he talking about?" Blair whispered, having never seen the sheriff angry at anyone before. She'd known him all her life, but he was a gentle, quiet man to her.

"What took you so long?" Lee asked, ignoring Blair's question and the sheriff's anger. "We were afraid something had happened to Taggert."

"He got nicked on the head by a bullet and was out for a few hours. That's why it took me so long to get here. We just learned of you capturin' that woman a few hours ago. But it looks like we're too late. She get away?"

"She's down there," Lee said.

"Not for long, she ain't," one of the men of the posse said. "That's a woman climbin' up the side of the canyon."

Blair looked toward the man and, as she did, her peripheral vision caught sight of a movement. She saw one of the sheriff's men, almost hidden by a tree, put his rifle to his shoulder and aim. He's going to shoot her, Blair thought, and she knew that no matter how bad a person was or what he'd done, she couldn't stand by and watch that person be killed. Blair took a flying leap at the man and managed to land close enough that she hit his leg and knocked his aim off. The rifle fired into the air well above Françoise's head.

But Blair hadn't thought about the consequences to herself, and the next moment she was trying to hang on to the cliff edge, her feet dangling over the side.

The sheriff and Lee reacted instantly, each man on his belly, grabbing an arm and pulling her to safety.

"She's the one for you all right," the sheriff said, his voice heavy with disgust, as he helped pull Blair on to the safety of the rocky ledge. "You just be real careful of her and don't let her get hurt."

"I'm doing everything I can to protect her from herself and from me," Lee said solemnly.

Blair sat on the ground at the feet of the two men, dusting herself off and looking down into the canyon where she'd almost fallen.

"All right, boys," the sheriff said. "Somebody volunteer to stay here and watch 'em while we go get some help. And they all better be *alive* when I get back."

"Sheriff, you mind if you don't mention our names—or Taggert's—in this? And could you send somebody over to the company store of the Inexpressible and claim our IOU for the crowbar and the dynamite?" Lee paused and smiled a moment. "And send the bill to my father. He owes me." He turned, the reins to his horse in one hand, and took Blair's hand in his other.

"Where you off to now?" the sheriff called as they went up the mountain.

"On my honeymoon," Lee called over his shoulder.

"You be careful. That Frenchie escaped, and I don't imagine she has any love for the two of you."

As Lee waved to the sheriff, he whispered to Blair, "Love is just what I have on my mind."

Chapter 24

Blair started walking, but she didn't last long. The combination of little food, less sleep, and even more excitement, at last got to her. When she started to stumble, Lee picked her up and put her on his horse and led the way. Blair nodded off to sleep and the times that she nearly fell from the horse, Lee was there to catch her and put her back on.

They seemed to travel for days and, at one point, Blair was sure that she'd never even seen a bed in her life, much less slept in one.

The sun was hanging low in the sky when they finally stopped and Lee lifted her from the horse. Listlessly, she opened her eyes to look at a large log cabin with a stone foundation.

"Where are we?" she asked, but wasn't really sure that she cared. All she wanted to do was sleep.

"It's my father's hunting cabin. We'll stay here for a few days."

Blair nodded and closed her eyes as Lee carried her inside the cabin. She was vaguely aware that he was taking her up some stairs, but she was too tired to be sure. By the time he placed her on a bed, she was sound asleep.

She awoke to an odd sound outside the window, and as she blinked the sleep out of her eyes, she grew curious as to what the sound was. She tossed the cover back, then gasped when she found herself to be nude. There was a man's shirt on the end of the pine bed and she put it on. Looking down from the window, she saw cows dotting the landscape, and below the window a cow and calf were chomping grass and making the sound that had wakened her.

The cabin was on a slight hill in a clearing in the forest, mountains on all sides, tall trees a few yards from the cabin. The grass was laced with wild rose bushes that were just beginning to bloom.

A sound on the stair behind her made her turn. Lee was just coming up with a tray in his hands, the smell of the food making her mouth water.

"I thought I heard you," he said, smiling at her and looking with interest at her bare legs below the shirt. Blair self-consciously slipped back into the bed and Lee put the tray across her lap.

He removed the cloth that covered the food. "I'm afraid there's no fresh food, but we have everything that's ever been canned or preserved." There was ham and bacon, cheese, peaches, corn muffins, and a tiny dish of wild strawberries.

"It's a feast and I'm starving," she said, and started to eat with gusto.

Lee lounged across the foot of the bed and watched her with a steady intensity that began to make her blush. She was more than aware that now all obstacles to the wedding night were at last removed.

"How long did I sleep?" she asked, mouth full of food.

Lee removed his pocket watch in a slow, easy way that made her pause in her eating. He looked at it, then put it on the little table next to the bed, as if he had no intention of putting it back into his pocket.

"Fourteen hours," he said.

Blair stuffed a corn muffin into her mouth so fast that she nearly choked. "You said that this was your father's cabin. Have you been here often?"

Leander began to unbutton his shirt, taking his time over each button, then slowly pulling it out of his pants. "Since I was a kid," he said.

His eyes on hers were intense and serious—and the way he

was looking at her through his lashes was making her nervous. She began to eat faster. "Did you come up here for elk?"

Lee, his eyes never leaving hers, began to unbutton the placket of his trousers.

It didn't take a second glance to show that he was wearing no underwear. Blair's hand began to tremble.

Lee stood and let his trousers slip to the floor.

Blair looked up at him, her eyes on his, her hand halfway to her mouth with a piece of bacon, while he bent toward her and removed the tray and bacon, and set them on the floor.

"You're not Houston now," he said.

For a moment, Blair was afraid of him. She'd fought him every minute for the past few weeks, and she'd felt so guilty about what she'd done to her sister that now she couldn't really believe that it was all right to give in to him.

Lee bent toward her and she moved backward until her head came into contact with the headboard. Part of her wanted to move away, but the other part—the biggest part—would have died before moving.

Very gently, Lee's lips touched hers. He didn't press her or touch her in any other way. There was just this lovely man with this magnificent, nude body bending over her and kissing her.

Blair started sliding down in the bed, or perhaps running down into it would better describe it, rather like butter melting. Lee stayed with her, bending as far as he could until he lost balance and fell on top of her.

From then on, there was no more slowness. Blair opened her mouth to his kiss, and Leander became like a wild man: kissing her with passion, his hands tearing at her hair, running all over her body, ripping the shirt from her. Blair was caught by his passion. For weeks, she'd wanted him, and now he was hers to touch and hold, to help her get rid of this ache that had been caused by holding back for too long.

They clutched each other and rolled on the bed together, their mouths eating at all the bare flesh they could find, hands seeming to multiply, for they were everywhere. Blair had images running through her head of all the times she'd seen

Leander and wanted to touch him. She remembered his hands tying delicate knots in surgery, and she'd wanted those hands to touch her. There were times when she'd watched him walk, and she'd thought of his body moving on top of hers. Now, she ran her hands down his back and over his buttocks, so firm and small and beginning to move in a way that made her sure that she was on fire.

He seemed to sense when she was ready, and when he entered her, she gave a little scream and Lee's mouth came down on hers, and she drew on it hungrily.

His movements became rapid and she matched his speed with her own, clinging to him with her hands, mouth, legs. And when he began to move harder and faster, she stiffened, lifting her hips to his, allowing him more access to her body.

And when they finished, Blair again screamed and her body jerked into a spasm of passion as Lee collapsed onto her. Minutes later, Blair relaxed, and for a moment, her body trembled as she clung to him, keeping her legs tight about his waist, determined to never let him go.

They lay together for several minutes before Blair began to relax and released the death hold she had on Lee.

She caressed the damp curls about his neck, running her fingers over the muscles in his shoulders, feeling his skin. He was so new to her, yet, in a way, it was as if they'd always been together. There was so much about him that she didn't know, so much that she wanted to learn.

He raised himself on one elbow and looked at her. "Downstairs I have a hip bath and water heating in the fireplace. Like a bath?"

For a moment, she looked at him, in the light from behind his head, and she realized how precious that head had become to her. Was it just her idea or was he actually the best-looking man in the world?

"Keep looking at me like that and you won't get a bath before next Tuesday."

Lee lifted one eyebrow at Blair's mischievous smile, wrapped her in a blanket and carried her downstairs to the first floor. One end of the cabin was dominated by an enormous stone fireplace flanked by two large windows. The other end contained a kitchen that was littered with dirty dishes, the survivors of Lee's cooking binge. The long walls were stone to about three feet, logs above that, with several windows here and there.

Before the fireplace was a tin tub, taller at one end than the other, now full of cold water that Lee said was from the nearby stream. As Blair stood there, feeling somewhat shy, Lee poured hot water into the tub and then led her toward it. When she still just stood there, he pulled the blanket from her and set her into the water.

The water felt heavenly and she leaned back against the tub and let herself relax. She was aware of Lee standing over her and watching. He'd put on his trousers, but he was shirt-less—and stunning: all that dark skin of his stretched over muscles hard from a life spent mostly out-of-doors.

"I married the boy next door," she murmured, smiling.

He knelt at the foot of the tub. "Why did you try to make my life miserable when we were children?"

"I didn't do any such thing," she said, as she began to wash her arms.

"What do you call mud in my face; snowballs flying at me from nowhere, and the time you told Mary Alice Pendergast I was in love with her? Her mother showed my mother love notes that were supposedly from me."

"Because you were taking Houston," she said softly. "She was my *twin,* but suddenly you were there and she seemed to like you more than me."

When Lee didn't say anything, she looked up to see his eyes piercing into hers. He didn't seem to believe her. She hadn't thought of that time when they were children for years. She *had* hated him, hated him from the first moment she saw him. But why? Everyone else seemed to like him, and Houston adored him, but she couldn't stand being near him. She used to leave a room when he entered.

"Maybe . . . ," she whispered.

"Maybe what?"

"Maybe I wanted to be your friend."

"But you couldn't, since Houston'd already put her brand on me?" He lifted her foot from the tub, took the soap and began washing her, his long fingers sliding far, far up her leg.

"You sound as if you weren't involved, but you did ask her to marry you. You must have loved her." Blair watched his hands, *felt* his hands.

He began to soap her toes. "I *guess* I asked her to marry me. Sometimes, I don't seem to remember having said those words to anyone. I think it was a passage of manhood. *Every* man in Chandler asked Houston to marry him."

"Did they?" Blair asked with interest. "Houston never said a word about anything like that. Only Alan asked me to marry him. All the other men were—."

"Fools," he said quickly, washing her foot with great care.

"But I'm so different," she said, and in spite of everything she could do, tears began to form in her eyes. "I've always tried to be like other women, someone like Houston, soft and gentle, but instead I had to become a doctor. And then, I received higher grades than all the other students, male or female, and I could see the men's eyes change when they looked at me. And—."

"You could stand a little work on your suturing," he said, as he dropped her leg and took her right foot into his hands.

"And whenever I beat a man at anything, he—." Her eyes widened. "What?"

"Your stitches, when you're in a hurry, are too big. You need to work on them."

Blair opened her mouth to speak but closed it. She wanted to tell him that her stitches were perfect, but she realized that that wasn't the issue here. He wasn't going to allow her to feel sorry for herself. With a smile, she looked at him. "Will you show me how?"

"I'll show you how to do *anything*," he said, with a look that made her feel very warm, then he resumed washing her. "Those men were fools. No man who's sure of himself would be afraid of any woman. It just took you a while to come home to me."

"Home. Home to my sister's fiancé," she sighed.

Leander was quiet for a moment, washing her hand, soaping

it, clasping her fingers with his. "I guess if I had a brother and all the women were after him, and none of them wanted me, I'd be jealous too."

"Jealous! I am not—." She had never thought of it before, but maybe she was jealous of Houston. "She's everything I ever wanted to be. I didn't *want* to be a doctor, I *had* to be one. What I wanted to be was like Houston and keep my gloves clean. She has so many friends. She had you."

He didn't even look up as he began to wash her right arm. "No, she never had me."

Blair kept on talking. "Houston does everything so well. She has an easy way of making friends. People for miles around love her. If Houston'd been leading the Southern troops, they would have won the War Between the States. No one can organize quite the way she can."

"She certainly organized you. Organized you into taking me off her hands."

"You! Oh, no, that just happened. That was entirely my doing. Houston was innocent in that."

"Blair," he said softly, "the night of the governor's reception, I was going to tell Houston the engagement was off."

"Off? I know you said something like that, but you surely didn't mean it."

He paused in washing her. "I don't know Houston at all. I don't think I ever did, but I can see things in you that I think are in Houston, too. Houston just covers whatever she's thinking with those damned white gloves of hers. For some reason, she decided when she was a kid to marry me. I wasn't a person to her, just a goal. Maybe it was like you and medicine, except that your goal was right. I think Houston wanted a reason to back out of our engagement because she had begun to see it wasn't going to work."

"But you didn't see her the night Mr. Gates told her I was to marry you."

"What if you'd studied medicine for years, and then found out the sight of blood made you faint? That carbolic gave you hives?"

"I would have . . . died," she said at last.

"I think I gave Houston hives. We got so we could barely

stand each other. We never talked, never laughed, and she curled her lip if I tried to touch her.''

''I can't imagine that!'' Blair said in genuine horror.

Grinning, he began to wash her upper chest, his hands sliding around her neck and up her cheeks. ''Maybe part of her realized that you and I were right for each other, and that's why she sent you out with me.''

''But she just wanted to see Taggert's house and—.''

''Now, there's a laugh! The lovely Miss Ice Princess Houston Chandler never backed down for any man in her life, but from the first time she set eyes on Taggert, she began to thaw. Remember the time we saw him in town, and he stopped and leered at Houston? I didn't realize it then, but I should have been jealous, that is if I had been in love with Houston as I was supposed to be. But I remember being more curious than anything else.''

''Taggert,'' Blair said. ''I can't imagine how any woman could want that awful man.''

''He was certainly ready to risk his life to help us,'' Lee said. His slick, soapy hands were sliding lower down her chest. ''Frankie's gang thought you were Houston. They demanded fifty grand for ransom. Taggert not only brought a gun, he brought money.''

Blair didn't hear what he was saying because his hands slid over her breasts. She lifted her arms to entwine with his, leaning back against the tub, enjoying the sensation of having him touch her.

He moved to stand before her, then lifted her from the water, her wet skin sticking to his. ''I've waited a long time for this,'' he said.

Leander seemed to be particularly adept at removing his clothing because by the time he'd carried her the three steps to the couch, he was bare. His first passion was spent, and this time he seemed to want to do little more than explore her body. Blair felt as if she were being tortured. He knocked her hands away when she reached for him and only allowed himself the pleasure of touching all of her body with his hands, his mouth, rubbing against her skin with his until she was nearly senseless with desire.

When he moved on top of her, she was clutching at him, but he was infuriatingly slow, refusing to hurry, taking his time with long, slow strokes. By the time he began to move faster, Blair was in a frenzy, feeling that she might explode from wanting him so badly.

When at last the peak came, it was such that she was sure for a moment that she had died. Her body ached and trembled, quivered, as she clung to Lee.

He pulled back, smiling at her. "I knew we'd make a great team."

She was serious as she said, "Is lovemaking the only reason you wanted to marry me?"

His face also turned serious. "That and your suturing."

"You!" she gasped, hitting at his ribs with her fist.

But Lee moved off her. "Come on, get up. Let's take a walk. I have some places to show you."

She wasn't used to seeing him without clothing. The only other nude men she'd ever seen were cadavers stretched out on cold marble slabs. Lee looked more alive than anyone she'd ever seen.

"Oh, no, you don't," he laughed, taking her hand and pulling her off the couch. "Get upstairs and get dressed. There're some old clothes in the chest at the head of the stairs. Get them on." He smacked her firm, bare bottom as she went up the stairs.

Blair opened the chest and began to rummage for clothes, but there was a mirror on the wall and she paused to look at herself in it. Her skin was glowing, her cheeks were rosy and her eyes brilliant. Of course, her hair, usually pulled back tightly so it wouldn't interfere with her work, was now standing out in a wild lion's mane about her head.

Could it be true that Leander loved her? He certainly didn't seem to mind her company, and he'd fought awfully hard to win her. Or did he just want a practicing surgeon-partner and an eager bedmate?

"You've got three minutes," Lee yelled from downstairs.

"What's my punishment if I'm not ready?" she called back.

"Abstinence."

With a laugh, Blair began to dress hurriedly in heavy canvas pants and a flannel shirt. The pants were too short, but she managed to get the upper and lower halves of her body covered. The waist was so big she had to hold it in her hand.

Downstairs, Lee was shoving food into a rucksack.

"Do you have a belt?" she asked.

When he glanced at her, she released the waistband and, with an impish grin, let the pants drop to the floor. She was rewarded by Lee's groan.

He turned away toward the woodpile and picked up a length of rope, then went to her, knelt, and put the rope through the belt loops. As he raised her pants, he kissed her legs all the way up, so that by the time the trousers were in place, Blair was swaying on her feet.

Lee walked to the door. "Come on, let's go." This time he was the one with the impish smile.

Weak-kneed, Blair followed him outside.

Chapter 25

Blair followed Lee as he walked along a narrow elk trail, through scrub oak, across a meadow, as he wound up the side of a mountain. The bark of the aspens had been chewed by the elk, killing many of the trees, and they had to walk across the fallen logs. Everywhere were the droppings of the big animals that had now gone north for the summer.

Lee pointed out a hawk to her and named some of the flowers. He seemed to sense when he was going too fast and slowed for her, holding back scratchy little oak trees to make the way clear.

At the top was a narrow ridge, falling off on both sides, with huge fir trees going down one side, and a vista that showed miles of hazy blue mountains on the other. Lee sat down, leaned against a fallen tree and opened his arms to her. She cuddled next to him gratefully, holding his hand in hers and toying with his fingers.

"What did the sheriff mean when he said we were two of a kind?" she asked.

Lee had his eyes closed, the sun warm on his face. "I got into trouble a couple of times when I was a kid. I guess he's not forgiven me."

Blair sat upright. *"You!? You* got into trouble? But you were always a paragon of virtue, every mother's dream."

Not opening his eyes, but smiling, he pulled her back against him. "You know as little about me as possible. I'm not what you seem to think."

"Then tell me how you got into trouble and why I didn't hear about it. I'm sure that in Chandler it would have made front-page news: Saint Leander Does Something Less Than Perfect."

Lee grinned broader. "You didn't hear of it because my father somehow managed to keep it quiet and, also, because it happened in Colorado Springs. What I did was get myself shot twice."

"Shot?" she gasped. "But I didn't see any scars."

Lee grunted. "You've yet to *look* at me. I get near you and you pounce on me."

"I do no such——." Blair stopped because what he said was true. "How did you get shot?" she asked meekly.

"I went with Dad to Colorado Springs when I was about fourteen. He had to talk to a witness for a client of his, and he was to meet the man at a hotel not far north of the bank. We'd just eaten dinner and were leaving the hotel when suddenly guns started firing and somebody yelled that the bank'd been robbed. I looked down the street and saw half a dozen men with bandannas over their faces riding toward us.

"I guess I didn't think, I just acted. There was a buckboard in the alley, hitched with four horses and loaded with feedbags. I jumped into the seat, yelled at the horses and drove the wagon into the street and blocked the outlaws' exit."

"And they shot you."

"I couldn't very well jump off the wagon. The horses would have run ahead and left the street clear."

"So you just sat there and held the horses," Blair said with some awe.

"I stayed there until the sheriff caught up with the bank robbers."

"And then what?"

He smiled. "And then my dad pulled me off the wagon and carried me to a doctor who gouged one bullet out—the other one went through my arm. He also let me get drunk, and I swear the hangover was worse than the holes in me."

"But, thanks to you, the robbers were caught."

"And spent years in jail. They're out now. You even met one of them."

"When?" she asked.

"The night we went to the reception. Remember when we went to the house on River Street? The suicide case? Remember the man outside? I don't think you liked him very much."

"The gambler," she said, thinking of the way the man'd looked at her.

"Among other things. LeGault spent ten years in prison after that robbery in Colorado Springs."

"Because of you," she said. "He must hate you, since you're the one who caught him."

"Probably," Lee said, without much interest. He opened his eyes and looked at her. "But then, I believe you used to hate me, too."

"Not exactly hate . . . ," she began, then smiled. "Where did you go on our wedding night?"

"Want to see my bullet scars?"

She started to say something about his refusal to answer her, but she compressed her mouth into a tight little line and said no more.

He put his fingertip under her chin. "Honeymoons aren't the place for anger, or for sulky looks. How about if I tell you about the time I delivered triplets?"

She didn't say a word to him.

"One of them was breech."

Still nothing.

"And they were a month early, and they were each born an hour apart, and to keep them alive we had to . . ."

"To what?" she asked after several minutes of silence.

"Oh, nothing. It wasn't very interesting. It was only written about in three journals. Or was it four?" He shrugged. "It doesn't matter."

"Why was it written about?"

"Because our method of saving them was . . . But you probably wouldn't be interested." With a yawn, he lay back against the log.

Blair leaped on him, her hands clenched into fists. "Tell me, tell me, tell me," she shouted at him while Lee, laughing, began to roll across the grass with her. He stopped when she was on the bottom.

"I'll tell you, but you have to tell me a secret about yourself."

"I don't *have* any secrets," she said, glaring at him, reminded of his refusal to tell her where he'd gone.

"Oh, yes, you do. Who put the snakes in my lunch pail and the grasshoppers in my pencil box?"

She blinked a couple of times. "I'm not sure, but I think it might have been the same person who put the taffy in your shoes, who sewed the sleeves of your jacket closed, who put hot peppers in your sandwiches, who—."

"At my mother's garden party!" he said. "I sat there and ate those sandwiches and thought everyone else's were hot, too, and that I was just a coward because they were about to kill me. How did you manage it?"

"I paid Jimmy Summers a penny to release his muddy dog when I dropped my spoon. The dog ran into the garden, and you, always the rescuer, ran to get rid of the dog. Everybody watched you, so I had plenty of time to doctor the sandwiches on your plate. I thought I'd burst to keep from laughing. You sat there sweating, but you ate every bite."

He loomed over her, shaking his head. "And the dried cow pie in my favorite fishing hat?"

She nodded.

"And the pictures of Miss Ellison on my slate?"

She nodded.

"Did anyone besides me ever catch you?"

"Your father did once. Houston said you were going fishing, so I sneaked over to your house, dumped out the worms you'd just dug and put a garter snake in the can. Unfortunately, your father caught me."

"I would imagine he had a few words to say. He hated any pranks of Nina's."

"He said that I was *never* going to be a lady."

"And he was right," Lee said solemnly, beginning to rub about on her. "You aren't a lady at all. You're a flesh and blood woman." He grinned. "Lots of flesh in all the right places."

Her eyes widened. "Are you planning to take my virtue, sir? Oh, please, sir, it's the only thing I have left."

"You don't deserve even that for what you've done, young lady," he said, leering, lowering his voice. "You've been tried and found guilty, and you are to be punished."

"Oh?" she said, arching a brow. "Taffy in my shoes?"

"I was thinking more along the lines of your becoming my love slave for the rest of our lives."

"Isn't that a little severe for a bit of taffy?"

"It's for the hot peppers and the—." His eyes widened. "Did you put the sneezing powder on my crackers? And the soot on my father's binoculars the day I took them to school?"

She nodded, beginning to feel a little guilty about the sheer volume of pranks she'd played on him.

He was looking at her with some awe. "I knew you did some of them but I'd always thought John Lechner did most of them. You know, I saw him four years ago in New York and I remembered all the things I *thought* he'd done to me, and I'm afraid I was barely civil to him."

"You didn't retaliate?"

"About a hundred times. I spent years with bruises from fights with John." He grinned. "And to think: he was innocent. As for the ones I knew you did, what could I do? You were six years younger than me and, besides, just thinking of the whipping my father gave me after that one time I did punch you was enough to make me think twice about striking a girl."

"So now I have to pay for some childhood foolishness," she said with an exaggerated sigh. "Life is hard."

"That's not all that's hard," he said with a one-sided smirk. "It's a good thing I'm a doctor and impossible to shock."

"It wasn't your doctoring that attracted me."

"Oh? And what did attract you to me?"

"Your persistence in trying to get my attention. I withstood it long enough but can stand no more."

"If you insist," she said tiredly.

"I love obedient women," he murmured as he ran his hand under her shirt and began to caress her rib cage, moving his hand up to touch her breasts.

Blair was astonished that she could want him again after only a few hours, but when her fingertips touched his warm skin, it was as if it were the first time. She hadn't thought of the pranks she'd played on him in years. At the time, she'd thought she did them because she hated him, that she was getting even with him for taking Houston away. But now, she wondered if all she'd wanted was his attention.

When he lifted his head and started to unbutton her shirt, she took his face in her hands. "I don't understand what you mean to me," she whispered.

Lee gave her a soft, gentle smile. "Not yet? Well, stay by me and it'll come to you. One thing about you, Blair, you sure can put up one hell of a fight. Do you think you'll come to fight *for* me as strongly as you've fought *against* me?"

"I don't know," she said, confused. She was so torn about this man. He'd been her enemy for most of her life. She'd fought him every way she could. And in spite of what Lee had said, she'd effectively managed to sabotage her sister's wedding. Why? Why had she fallen into bed with a man she swore she hated?

Lee took her hands in his and kissed the palms. "While you're trying to find the answers to life, we're wasting time." He finished unbuttoning her shirt.

They made love slowly, almost delicately, Lee watching her face to see her reactions. He kissed each of her fingertips, lingering over them, and the sensation of feeling the warm, moist interior of his mouth went through all of her. He kissed her breasts, ran his hands all over her skin.

And when he came to her, it was gentle, sweet, prolonged.

Later, he held her very close, tucking her legs between his, wrapping himself around her, trying to enclose her body within his.

Blair lay within the circle of his arms, listening to clicking grasshoppers, the high-pitched whistle of a hummingbird, and the wind. The smell and taste and feel of Lee seemed to fill her. How much she wanted this moment never to end.

"When we get home, you'll have to hire somebody to take care of my socks," he said softly.

"Your what?" she asked vaguely, holding on to him as if her life depended on it.

"My socks and my shirts—and I like my boots kept polished. And you'll need somebody to clean the place, make the bed and feed us."

Blair was silent for a moment before she began to understand what he was saying. Since she was a girl, all she'd cared about—or learned anything about—was medicine. She had absolutely no idea how to run a house.

She gave a big sigh. "Think anyone'd like to marry us?"

She could feel Lee chuckle. "We can ask. I met a lady criminal who—." He stopped when Blair put her teeth to his skin and threatened to bite.

"Lee," she said, as she moved back to look at him. "I really, truly don't know anything about running a house. My mother tried to teach me but—."

"You climbed trees."

"Or escaped to somewhere. Aunt Flo tried, but Uncle Henry kept saying that there was time, and then he'd take me into the surgery to help him. I guess there wasn't time. Next year, I was planning to enroll in a course in housewifery so I'd be prepared when I married Alan."

"A course, huh? One where they teach you how to get the toilet clean and how to scrub the floors?"

"Think it would have been that bad?"

"Probably worse."

She put her head back into his shoulder. "I *told* you not to marry me. Now you see why no one else wanted to. Houston's so much better at this than I am. You should have kept her."

"Probably," he said solemnly. "I'd certainly never have to worry about her borrowing my scalpel."

"I never borrow yours," she said indignantly. "I have my own."

"Yes, but Houston does know how to run a house. I imagine her husband's socks will always be clean and in order."

Blair pushed away from him. "If that's what you want, you can just go to her—or to any other woman for that matter. If you think I'm going to dedicate my life to your underwear, you're mistaken." She sat up and angrily began to pull on her trousers.

"Not even *one* sock?" he asked in a pleading way.

Blair glanced at him and saw that he was laughing at her. "You!" she laughed and fell back into his arms, where he hugged her fiercely. "You didn't tell me about the triplets."

"What triplets?"

"The ones you delivered and that were written about in four journals."

He looked at her as if she'd lost her mind. "I've never delivered triplets in my life."

"But you said . . . Oh, you!" she gasped, laughing.

He ran his hand up her trousered legs and over her bare back. "How about walking down to the river? We can eat there."

"And talk about the clinic," she said, as she stood and put on her shirt. "When do you think the equipment will arrive? And you never did tell me exactly what you ordered. Lee, if you don't want to work there all the time, I thought I might write a friend of mine, Dr. Louise Bleeker. She's quite good and Chandler is growing by leaps and bounds, so I'm sure we could use another doctor."

"Actually, I was thinking of hiring Mrs. Krebbs to help in the clinic."

Blair paused in buttoning her shirt. "Mrs. Krebbs! Do you know what she's *like*? One day, a little boy came to the hospital with a chicken bone caught in his throat and dear Mrs. Krebbs suggested I wait for a *real* doctor to arrive."

"And she's still alive today?" he asked, wide-eyed.

She squinted up at him. "Are you teasing me again?"

"I never tease women who look like you do." He looked down at her gaping shirt that was unbuttoned to just above her navel. "Come on," he said before she could answer. "If we're going to talk business, let's at least walk while we do it."

Chapter 26

Leander and Blair, holding hands, ran up the hill to the cabin. They stopped now and then to kiss, and Lee began to tug on Blair's clothes and she on his until, when they reached the rise just before the cabin, they were both unbuttoned to the waist.

But the fun stopped when they looked up the hill toward the cabin, for there on the front porch stood Reed Westfield.

Lee's face instantly turned somber, as he put himself between Blair and the cabin and began to button her shirt. "Listen to me," he said gently. "I think I'll have to go away again. I don't imagine my father'd come here unless it were an emergency."

"Emergency? I can—." Something in his eyes made her stop and her jaw harden. "Is it *that* kind of emergency? One where I'm to be excluded, where I can't be trusted? The emergency that is for men only?"

He put his hands on her shoulders. "Blair, you have to trust me. I would tell you if I could, but for your own good—."

"For my own good, I should remain ignorant. I understand completely."

"You don't understand anything!" Lee said, his fingers gripping her tightly. "You're just going to have to trust me. If I could tell you, I would."

She jerked away from him. "I understand perfectly. You *are* just like Mr. Gates. You have rigid ideas of what a woman can and cannot do, and I can't be trusted enough to be told what you're doing when you so mysteriously disappear. Tell me, what do you plan to allow me to do now that we're married? That is, besides manage your household and gleefully share your bed? May I continue practicing medicine, or am I too incompetent to do that, too?"

Lee rolled his eyes skyward, as if looking for help. "All right, have it your way. You seem to think I'm a monster, so I'll be one. My father is here for an important reason, and I have to leave you now. I can't tell you where I'm going or I would. What I'd like you to do now is to return to Chandler with my father, and I will be home as soon as possible."

Blair didn't say another word as she walked past him, up the hill and toward the cabin. It was difficult for her to even look at Reed. He'd never liked her since she was a child and he'd caught her playing a prank on his precious son. When Lee'd said he wanted to marry Blair, Reed had participated in that dreadful interrogation Gates had subjected her to. And later, Reed had point-blank, directly, lied to her, making up that story about Lee and a Frenchwoman.

So now, as she walked past him and into the cabin, she could be neither warm or even especially cordial. She greeted him coolly and went inside.

Even when she was alone, she wouldn't allow herself to unbend. What had she expected except to be treated this way? Lee said he loved her, but what man wouldn't love a woman who was as enthusiastic a bed partner as she was? And Lee's sense of honor would make him feel obligated to marry her, since she'd been a virgin that first night.

Blair went upstairs to remove the men's clothing she was wearing and put her medical uniform back on. The window was open and through it she could hear voices. When she looked outside, she could see Lee and his father at some distance from the cabin and, from the look of their gestures, they were angry with each other.

Lee was squatting in the grass, chewing on a stem, while Reed was using every inch of his heavy body to lean over his son in an intimidating way. To Blair, it looked as if Reed were threatening Lee.

In spite of herself, she leaned closer to the window. Some words floated to her, words that Reed was punctuating with a finger pointed at Lee. ". . . danger . . ." ". . . risk your life . . ." ". . . Pinkerton . . ."

She drew back. "Pinkerton?" she whispered, as she fastened

the last buttons on her uniform. What did Lee have to do with the Pinkerton Detective Agency?

For a moment, she sat on the bed. She hadn't had much time to think about where Lee'd gone on their wedding night. Reed had lied to her and she'd believed him. She was willing to believe that Lee loved someone else; she was willing to believe that he was running into a den of outlaws to save the leader from blood poisoning. But what if Lee were involved in something else, something . . . She hesitated to even think about what he could be involved in. Maybe he was *helping* the Pinkertons. But the way Reed was warning his son, Blair didn't think so.

Leander was involved in something illegal. She knew it, felt it. And that's why he couldn't tell her what he was doing. He wanted her to remain innocent.

Slowly, with heavy feet, Blair went downstairs and arrived at the door just as Lee was entering. "I have to go," he said, watching her.

Blair looked up at him. What act of criminality was Lee into? And why? Did he need money? She thought of the new medical equipment he'd ordered from Denver. It must have cost a great deal, and everyone knew that a doctor made very little money. Of course, Lee'd inherited money from his mother, but who knew how much that was? Was he doing this so he could open his clinic? So he could help people?

"I know," she said, putting her hand on his arm.

As he looked at her, he seemed to sigh with relief. "You're not angry anymore?"

"No, I don't think I am."

He kissed her in an achingly sweet way. "I'll be back as soon as I can. Dad will take you home now."

Before another word was said, he was on his big stallion and riding down the mountain, out of her sight.

Blair mounted the horse Reed had brought for her, and they started the long trek home in silence. Most of the trail, between pine trees, across tiny streams, was, of necessity, single file. Blair was puzzling over Lee's disappearances, telling herself her conclusion was wrong, and praying that he wasn't in danger.

A few miles outside of Chandler, when the land flattened and the terrain dried, Reed reined his horse to ride beside her.

"I think you and I got off on the wrong foot," Reed said.

"Yes," she answered honestly. "From when I was about eight."

He looked puzzled for a moment. "Ah, yes, the pranks. You know, I wouldn't have known about them except that my wife found out about a few of them. Lee never said a word about them. Helen said they were being executed by a girl. She said boys were smart, but they weren't clever like girls, and these pranks were quite clever. She was very interested after I told her I'd seen you exchanging the fishing worms with a snake. 'Blair Chandler,' she said. 'I might have guessed she was the one. She always has had an extraordinary interest in Lee.' I don't know what she meant by that, but I do know that she laughed a great deal whenever she heard about another prank."

"If Lee didn't tell her, how did she find out?"

"Nina sometimes, Lee's teacher at other times. Once Lee came home from school with a stomachache, and after Helen'd put him to bed, she returned to the kitchen to see Lee's lunch pail slowly moving across the table. She said she nearly died of fright before she could open it enough to see what was inside. It was a horned toad, which she gratefully put in her flower garden."

"No wonder you weren't too happy when Lee said he was going to marry me," Blair said.

Reed was quiet for a moment, moving easily with his horse. "I'll tell you my big worry about you and Lee, and it has nothing to do with the pranks. The truth is, my son works too hard. Even as a boy, he used to take on three jobs at once. For some reason, Lee thinks the world's problems are his responsibility. I was proud when he said he wanted to become a doctor, but I was worried, too. I was afraid he'd do just what he's done—take on too much. He works in the hospital, and he manages the place even though Dr. Webster has the title of administrator. Lee also takes the case of anybody in town. Four nights a week he runs off on calls. And he still visits people in the country."

"And you were afraid I'd be more of a burden to him?" Blair whispered.

"Well, you have to admit that excitement does happen around you. I wanted Lee to marry someone as different from him as possible, someone like Houston who's so like Opal, someone who'd stay home and sew and make a home. It's not that I've ever had anything against you, but just look at what's happened in the last few weeks since you returned to Chandler."

"I see what you mean," Blair said, as one picture of excitement after another passed through her mind. "I don't think Lee's had much rest, has he?"

"He nearly killed himself while trying to impress you with what a good doctor he was." He paused and smiled at her. "But somewhere along the way, I began to see how much he wanted you."

"Yes, I believe he does," she murmured, wondering if the wanting of her was leading him into doing whatever he was doing in secret.

She and Reed rode into Chandler in silence, the last few miles in starlight. He left her at the house she shared with Leander, and Blair went inside with a heavy heart. Was he in debt for this place, too?

She took a quick bath and wearily climbed into the empty bed. It seemed that she was destined to spend every night in this house alone.

At six the next morning, she was awakened by the telephone ringing. Groggily, she made her way downstairs.

The operator, Caroline, said, "Blair-Houston, four freight wagons from Denver have just arrived and the drivers are waiting for Leander at the old warehouse on Archer Avenue."

"He can't go, but I'll be there in fifteen minutes."

"But it's the doctor equipment and Leander needs to tell them where it goes."

"According to my diploma, *I* am a doctor," Blair said icily.

"I'm sure I didn't mean anything. I was just passing the message along." She hesitated. "Why can't Leander go?"

Nosy woman! Blair thought. She wasn't about to tell her Lee

was on another of his mysterious missions. "Because I exhausted him," she said, and hung up the phone with a smile. *That* should give them something to gossip about.

Blair tore up the stairs and minutes later she was running down the street while still pinning her hair up. By the time she got to the top of Archer Avenue, she saw the men lounging against the wagons and looking impatient.

"Hello, I'm Dr. Westfield."

One burly man, mouth full of tobacco juice, looked her up and down for a moment, while the other men peered around the wagon frames—as if they were trying not to show interest in a freak of nature. The first man spat a big wad of juice.

"Where do you want this unloaded?"

"Inside," she said, pointing to the warehouse.

Immediately, there were problems. She had no key, nor had she any idea where Lee kept a key to the place. The men just stood there looking at her skeptically, as if this were what they would have expected from a woman who called herself a doctor.

"It's too bad we can't get in," she said sadly, "because my stepfather owns the Chandler Brewery, and he promised a barrel of beer, as thanks, to the men who helped me with the new equipment. But I guess—."

The sound of breaking glass cut her words off.

"Sorry, ma'am," said one of the men. "I guess I leaned against the window too hard. But it looks like maybe somebody little could get through here."

A moment later, Blair was inside and unbolting the heavy front door for them. With the sunlight coming in, she could see the place: cobwebs hanging down, the floor littered, the ceiling with at least three leaks. "Over there," she said absently, pointing to a corner that at least looked dry, if not clean. While the men unloaded, she walked through the one vast room and tried to imagine how it would be arranged for the clinic.

The men brought in oak tables, cabinets with little drawers, tall cabinets with glass doors, big sinks, small boxes of instruments, cases of bandages and cotton, everything for a fully equipped infirmary.

"Seem to be enough?"

She turned to Lee, standing there, surveying the crates and furniture.

He was watching her with eyes narrowed, a lit cigar between his lips. His clothes were dirty and he looked tired.

"More than enough," she said, and wondered how much it had cost him. "You look exhausted. You should go home and sleep. I'm going to get some women in here to clean this place."

With a smile, he tossed her a key. "This is to spare the rest of the windows. Come home soon," he said with a wink and then was gone.

For a moment, Blair felt tears come to her eyes. Whatever he was doing, he was doing so he could help other people, of that she was sure. Whatever this equipment had cost him, he was willing to do *anything* to pay the price.

When the men had finished unloading, they gave her a ride back to her house and she called her mother, explaining about the beer. Opal said that Mr. Gates was so pleased that Blair was at last married to a decent man that she was sure he'd give the men a barrel of beer.

After calling her mother, Blair called Houston. Houston would know whom to get to clean the warehouse. Sure enough, by ten o'clock, the place was full of women with cloths about their heads, brooms flying, huge pails of water full of big mops and scrub rags, working.

By eleven, Blair had talked to Mr. Hitchman, who'd built the Chandler house, and arranged for his two sons to start the remodelling according to Leander's plans.

At two, Lee came back and, through the noise and dust, she told him what she'd arranged.

Protesting that she couldn't possibly leave, she allowed him to pull her out to his carriage and drive her into town to Miss Emily's Tea Shop.

Miss Emily took one look at Blair and sent her to the back with an order to wash all of her body that was possible because all of it was dirty. When Blair returned, Lee was waiting behind a table loaded with little chicken sandwiches and cakes iced with strawberry frosting.

Blair, ravenous, began stuffing herself and talking all at once. ". . . and we can use the tall cabinet, the one with the countertop, in the surgery, and I thought that big sink could go—."

"Slow down a minute. All the work doesn't have to be done in a day."

"I don't think it can be. It's just that this town needs a place for women. Years ago, Mother took me to see the Women's Infirmary here. Is it still as bad?"

"Worse than you can imagine," Lee said seriously, then took her hand and kissed it. "So, what are you dallying for? Let's get out of here and go to work. By the way, I called your sister and she's hiring a maid and a housekeeper for us."

"Two?" Blair asked. "Can we afford two?"

He gave her a very puzzled look. "If you don't eat all of Miss Emily's merchandise." He looked aghast when she immediately put down the sandwich she'd picked up.

"What's brought this on? Blair, I'm not as rich as Taggert, but I can certainly afford a couple of maids."

She stood. "Let's go, shall we? I have a plumber coming later."

Still wearing a look of puzzlement, Lee followed her out of the teashop.

Chapter 27

Françoise slammed the glass down on the table and saw, with disgust, that the glass was too heavy, too crude, to break. "It's all her fault," she muttered.

Behind her, a man spoke, causing her to jump. She turned to look up at LeGault, tall, thin, dark—slimy. He had a habit of entering and leaving rooms without a sound. He toyed with his little mustache. "Blaming her again?"

Françoise didn't bother to answer him as she stood and walked toward the window. The shades were drawn and the heavy plush curtains closed. No one must see her, for she was in hiding. She'd been inside this room for over a week now. The men in her band were either in prison or in a hospital. The bears that woman had enticed into the canyon had caused men and animals to panic to the point where one man was trampled by sharp horses' hoofs. Two men had been shot, and another's leg had been mauled by an angry bear. By the time the sheriff's men got the canyon mouth open, the outlaws were crying to be taken into custody.

And all because of one woman.

"I am still blaming her," Françoise said with anger. Mostly what she hated was being played for a fool. That idiot band of men who followed her hadn't had sense enough to find her, yet she'd been holed up practically under their noses.

In the last week, she'd had time to go over every detail of what had happened, and she now saw how that woman had used her. She saw the way Blair had pretended to be angry with her handsome husband, had pretended to drug him, then had "forgotten" the knife so Françoise could get away.

"I don't guess you've considered the doc's involvement in this," LeGault said with a smirk. "Only the woman is guilty, right?"

"She was the instigator." Françoise shrugged. "She is the one I would like to see repaid."

"And I'd like to see Westfield repaid," LeGault said.

"And what has he done to you?"

LeGault rubbed his wrists. He was careful to keep the scars covered—scars made by the iron manacles he'd worn in the prison where Westfield had put him. "Let's just say that I have reason enough to want to see him get some of what he's given me." He paused. "Tonight, the messenger arrives with news. I hope he'll know the day of the shipment."

"No more than I do," Françoise said with feeling. "After this job is done, I'm heading east, to Texas."

"And leave your dear, devoted gang behind?" LeGault said tauntingly.

"Idiots! It will do them good to rot in jail for a few years. About tonight: do you think I could go with you? I'll do anything to get out of here for a while."

"Anything?"

"Anything that will not ruin our partnership," she said with a smile, thinking she'd rather walk into a pit of rattlesnakes than sleep with LeGault. "It will be night and no one will see me. I need air and this waiting is making me miserable."

"Sure. Why not? I have to meet the man in the middle of nowhere, up behind the Little Pamela mine. But if someone recognizes you, don't expect me to stay by you. No one's after me, and I plan to keep it that way."

"Don't worry about me tonight. You have to worry about how to get the boxes we steal out of Chandler, while I hide and you stay in plain sight."

"Don't worry about that. I'll come up with something," he said at the door. "I'll come back for you at midnight."

Hours later, they rode out of town, avoiding the lights on the houses, even the lights on the carriages. Françoise kept her hat down over her face and, in her thick coat and big pants, she didn't look at all like a female.

They met their messenger, and the news was pleasing to them. Smiling, they started down the mountainside to where their horses were hidden.

"Quiet! I hear something," LeGault said, as he jumped for cover behind a boulder.

Françoise hid, too, just as they saw two men emerge from the trees, the moonlight clearly outlining them. One, a short, stocky man, seemed nervous, while the other, tall, slim, the moonlight glinting off a revolver at his side, was calm and watchful. He paused while the short man climbed into a carriage that was well concealed behind a clump of piñon. Still watching, he struck a match and lit a cigar.

"Westfield!" Frankie gasped and LeGault shushed her.

They watched as the tall man, Leander, drove away—but there was no other man in the carriage with him.

"Where did he go?" Françoise asked when the carriage was gone, as she turned around to lean against the rock.

"Hidden," LeGault said thoughtfully. "Now, why would our righteous, do-gooder doctor be hiding a man in his buggy in the middle of the night?"

"Isn't that a coal mine down there?"

"Sure, but what does that matter? Think he's plannin' to steal a couple tons of coal?"

"He and that bitch of his stole dynamite from somewhere, probably from the coal mine."

LeGault played with the tip of his mustache. "He's awfully familiar with coal mines."

"You can stay here all night with your puzzle, but it's too cold for me. We have much planning to do yet, and not much time to do it in."

LeGault didn't say a word as he followed Françoise back to the horses. "This woman Westfield married," he said, hands on the pommel, "she's a Chandler, isn't she?"

"Like the town name, yes."

"Very much like the town name. The most respectable, unsuspected name in the town."

"What are you thinking?"

"You saw Westfield and his bride together. What would you guess she'd be likely to do for him?"

"Do?" Françoise thought of the way the woman'd looked at the doctor, as if he might disappear at any moment—and if he did start to fade, she was going to grab on to his coattails. "I believe she'd do anything—everything—for that man."

LeGault gave a smile that showed perfect, even white teeth. "I don't know what we saw here tonight, but I'm going to find out. And when I do, I'll see how we can use it. We need a way to move that shipment out of Chandler."

Françoise began to smile also. "And who better to do it than a Chandler?"

Leander and Blair worked on the clinic for three days, along with several crews of workers, before they got it ready. On the evening of the third day, Lee climbed a ladder and nailed up the big sign: Westfield Infirmary for Women.

When he stepped down from the ladder, he saw Blair grinning up at the sign with the expression of a child who has tasted ice cream for the first time. "Come inside," he said. "I have a celebration planned for us." When Blair didn't move, he caught her hand and pulled her inside.

Under an oak lid, inside a galvanized sink, were two bottles of champagne in ice.

Blair backed away. "Lee, you know what happens to me when I drink champagne."

"I'm not likely to forget," he said, as he popped the cork and grabbed a crystal glass, filled it and handed it to her.

Blair took a cautious sip, looked at him over the rim, then drained the glass and held it out for a refill.

"Not upset about St. Joseph's? Don't wish you could intern there?"

She kept her eyes on the wine Lee was pouring into her extended glass. "And miss working with the man I love? Hey!" she said, as Lee kept filling and the glass overflowed. She looked up to see him watching her with hot eyes.

"For how long?" he whispered.

Blair tried to be nonchalant. The words had come out unexpectedly. "Maybe forever. Maybe I've loved you since I first met you. Maybe I tried everything I could to hate you, probably because Houston claimed you first, but nothing seems to have worked. No matter what I did to you, you always came out on top."

Lee was standing a foot away from her, but the heat in his eyes was drawing her closer. "So I passed your tests, did I? Rather like Hercules and his tasks."

"It wasn't quite that bad."

"No? People are still asking me if I'd like to go rowing. And, of course, there was that last-minute switch at the altar, and everyone wants to know if I know which twin I *did* marry."

"But there are no more snakes in your lunch pail," she said solemnly.

Leander put his wineglass, then hers, down on the edge of the sink and stepped toward her. "You have a lot to make up to me."

"I shall always keep your scalpels sharp," she said, stepping back.

Leander just stood there, not saying a word, as he watched

her. It was nearly dark outside and very dim in the surgery of the hospital. With his eyes locked on hers, Lee began to remove his clothing, inch by inch exposing warm, dark skin, long muscles playing, moving.

Blair stood transfixed where she was, her eyes hypnotized by him, watching his fingers on buttons, watching him as he exposed himself bit by delicious bit. His legs were long and thick-thighed, big muscles about his knees, calves strong and heavy. Her breath deepened and her throat dried as she saw him standing before her nude, his desire for her rampant.

Still watching her, he sat down on a long, low bench, his legs apart, his body ready for her.

"Come to me," he whispered in a voice that came from somewhere inside him.

Blair didn't bother to remove any outer clothing but released the drawstring of her pantalets and stepped out of them as she walked. Her full cord skirt covered them as she straddled him, slipping down on his manhood easily. She wrapped her leather encased feet about his calves for a moment, pulling herself down, closer and closer to him, feeling him against her skin.

Then, on tiptoe, she began to move up and down, slowly at first, watching. His face was expressionless, devoid of lines, angelic almost, as the pleasure began to dissolve over him. A moment later, she arched against him, bringing her knees up to the bench. Lee's hands slid under the skirt, began to move up and down her thighs, clutching her, helping her to move.

Lee's eyes closed for a second, opened, then he leaned his head back and slid downward. Blair moved her hands from his shoulders to his neck and began to move harder and faster, her thighs straining, tightening, as Lee caught her buttocks in his hands and helped her move.

She arched once, hard, backbreakingly hard, holding on to Lee as her body tightened and froze for a moment in a final ecstasy.

Lee held her, even though she almost fought him, not allowing her to fall, himself shuddering with the grip of his passion.

For a moment, Blair didn't know where she was, as she came out of her powerful arch and clung to Lee.

After a moment, he pulled back and smiled at her. "It's nice to have mutual interests."

"Hello. Is anyone here?"

"It's your father," Blair said in horror.

Lee lifted her off him. "Go out there and stall him while I get dressed."

"But I can't—," she began, thinking that he'd know from the look of her what she'd been doing.

"Go!" Lee commanded and gave her a small shove toward the doorway.

"There you are," Reed greeted her, then took one look at Blair's flushed face and began to smile. "I guess Lee's here, too."

"Yes," she said, and her voice cracked. "He'll . . . a, be out in a minute. Could I offer you some refreshment?" She stopped as she remembered that the only thing they had was champagne.

Reed's eyes sparkled. "Come outside. I have something I want to show you."

With a glance over her shoulder, she saw that Lee wasn't ready yet, so she followed Reed outside. Standing in front of the clinic was a pretty little carriage, black exterior, black leather seats, a black box in the back to hold supplies. Blair touched the brass rail that held up the canopy. "It's lovely." She thought it was odd that Reed would buy such a carriage for himself, as it had a decidedly feminine air about it.

"Look at the front of it," Reed said, his ugly little bulldog face still beaming at her.

She looked up to see Leander coming out of the door, and he seemed to be as puzzled by the carriage as she was.

Blair bent over to see that there was a brass nameplate just under the single seat. Dr. Blair Chandler Westfield, it read.

It took Blair a moment to understand. "For me? The carriage is for me?"

"I can't have my new daughter running about the streets of Chandler on foot, and I know this son of mine won't let that old buggy of his out of his sight, so I thought you'd better have one of your own. Do you like it?"

Blair stood back for a moment and looked at the buggy. It seemed that this was what she needed to finish establishing that she was really a doctor. "Yes," she cried. "Oh, yes!" And the next moment, she ran to hug Reed and kiss his cheek, and before he could get embarrassed, she was climbing into the carriage and looking at every nook and cranny. She opened the box in the back. "It's not nearly as big as yours, Lee. Maybe we can have it enlarged. I'm sure that I'll need to carry lots of things."

"Such as rifles, maybe? Look, if you think I'm going to allow you to run around the country all alone in your new carriage, you're deeply mistaken. Dad, I wish you'd asked me about this. Giving her freedom is like letting a self-destructive tornado loose. She'll run off on one case after another and end up getting herself killed."

"And I guess you're so much better," she said, looking down at him from the seat. "You walk into range wars. At least, I went into the thing not knowing what it was."

"That's worse," Lee said. "All someone has to say is that he needs help, and you're off. You have no sense of taking care of yourself. Look at what happened with the gang that kidnapped you. You jumped on the horse with the man and didn't even ask where he was taking you."

"Wait a minute," Reed said, and there was laughter in his voice. "I guess I didn't think of any of that. Maybe I learned with you, Lee, that I couldn't stop you from doing whatever you wanted to do. Maybe Blair's like you."

"She has no sense about what's safe for her to do," Lee said sullenly.

"And you do?" Reed's eyes bored into his son's.

Blair watched them, and she was further convinced that Lee was doing something dangerous, but she was sure that it was something that would eventually help other people.

Reed glanced at the brown horse that was hitched to the buggy. "I've sent for an Appaloosa like Lee's, but the horse hasn't come yet. I thought you'd want to be recognized like Lee is."

"They're going to recognize her because *I* will be beside her," Lee said with determination.

Blair didn't answer that, but merely gave him a little smile with lifted eyebrows that made her think he was going to jump into the seat with her—and she didn't like to think what he was going to do to her.

Reed let out a loud laugh and hit his son roughly on the shoulder. "I hope she leads you a chase as hard as the one you led your mother and me. Maybe you'll understand some of what we went through." He put his hand up to help Blair down. "Did I ever tell you about the time Lee exchanged the rat poison in the attic for bread crumbs? We had every rat in my wife's hometown in our house before we found out what was going on."

"No, you didn't," she said, looking up at Lee's back as they entered the clinic. "And I certainly would like to hear more."

Chapter 28

Blair and Leander had been married only a couple of weeks when the Westfield Clinic was officially opened. Of course, she hadn't finished her internship, but both she and Lee knew it was only a formality. Blair'd had years of practice in hospitals.

The day the clinic opened, Blair was so nervous she spilled her coffee and dropped her corn muffin on the dining room floor. Guiltily, she grabbed the muffin and glanced toward the door to the kitchen.

Lee put his hand over hers. "She doesn't bite, you know."

"Maybe she won't bite you, but I'm not so sure about me." Days ago, the housekeeper-cook Houston'd hired had come to their house and Blair found her to be a formidable woman: a tiny body with stiff steel-gray hair, hard black eyes, and a little slash of a mouth. Mrs. Shainess barely came up to Blair's shoulder, but whenever she entered the room, Blair stiffened. The little woman made Blair feel clumsy and unsure of herself. The first day she'd arrived, she'd gone through Blair's small wardrobe, saying tersely that she was looking for garments that needed repairing or cleaning. She'd sighed as she'd handled Blair's few pieces of clothing, and for hours later, the house smelled of chemicals as the woman cleaned those clothes.

That night, when Blair and Lee returned from the hospital, Mrs. Shainess drew him aside for a private discussion. Afterward, with a smile, Lee told Blair that Mrs. Shainess did not think she had a wardrobe befitting a lady and that Blair was to see Houston's dressmaker tomorrow.

Blair tried to protest, but Lee would not listen. She was worried enough as it was that Lee was in debt without her adding to his expenses. So, the next day, when she went to the dressmaker's, she planned to order very, very little, but she found that Lee had already called and ordered twice as much as Blair thought she'd ever need. Still, she couldn't help being pleased by the beautiful clothing, and she drove home quickly in her new carriage, planning to thank him in the best way she knew how.

But when she entered the drawing room, Lee was engrossed in a letter he held—and when Blair came into the room, he crumpled it, struck a match to it and burned it in the fireplace.

Blair didn't ask him about the letter because she didn't want to hear him tell her again that she wouldn't understand. All her enthusiasm about the new clothes left her, and she spent the evening trying to come up with rational explanations for Lee's actions: he was helping someone; he needed money; he was a criminal; he was a Pinkerton agent.

At night, they made love slowly and Blair clung to Lee. She was getting to the point that she didn't care *what* he was doing. He could secretly own all the gambling houses on River Street and she wasn't sure it would matter to her.

On the first day that the Westfield Clinic was officially open, Lee was called away to help at the Windlass Mine, where the end of a tunnel had collapsed. Blair wanted to go with him, but he sent her off to the clinic to help the needy patients.

When she opened the door at eight that morning, Lee's nurse, Mrs. Krebbs, and three patients were already waiting. Mrs. Krebbs, as cool as ever, nodded slightly to Blair and went to the surgery to check the supplies and instruments.

"This way," Blair said, guiding her first patient into the examining room.

"Where's the doctor?" the woman asked, clutching her handbag to her bosom, as if someone meant to steal it.

"I am a doctor. Now, if you'll have a seat and tell me what's wrong, I'll—."

"I want a *real* doctor," the woman said, backing against the door.

"I assure you that I am a certified doctor. If you'll just tell me—."

"I ain't stayin' here. I thought this was gonna be a real hospital with real doctors."

Before Blair could say another word, the woman was out of the door and hurrying toward the street. Blair kept her anger under control as she ushered in the next patient.

The second woman flatly said that Blair couldn't possibly know what was wrong with her because her illness wasn't pregnancy. Blair had difficulty understanding this until she realized the woman thought Blair was a midwife. The woman left before Blair could explain. The third woman left after she found out that the handsome Dr. Westfield, who she'd met last summer in Denver, wasn't going to examine her.

For hours after the third patient left, no one came to the clinic, and Blair had visions of the telephone catching fire from all the scorching gossip that was passing across its wires. At four o'clock, a salesman touting a pink liquid made for "female problems" came by. Blair was polite but ushered him out quickly. She went back to straightening towels that were already straight.

"They want a man," Mrs. Krebbs said. "They want a trained doctor like Dr. Leander."

"I *am* a trained doctor," Blair said through her teeth.

Mrs. Krebbs sniffed, put her nose in the air and went into another room.

Blair locked the door at six o'clock and went home.

At home, she didn't tell Lee about her lack of patients. He'd gone to so much trouble and expense to start the clinic that she didn't want to bother him. Besides, he was worried enough as it was.

She filled the tub for him, then prepared to leave as he undressed.

"Don't go. Stay and talk to me."

She felt a little shy at first as he stripped and got into the tub. Somehow, this was more intimate than making love.

Lee leaned back in the tub, a faraway look in his eyes, and began to tell her of what he'd been through that day. He told of pulling two bodies out of the mine rubble, of having to amputate a man's foot while in the pit. She didn't interrupt him and he went on to describe the feeling of being inside the mine: the weight of the surrounding walls, the lack of fresh air, the total darkness, no room to stand, no room to move.

"I don't know how they do it, how they can walk into that day after day. At any moment, a roof may fall on them. Each day, they face a thousand ways to die."

She had his foot out of the water and was washing it. "Houston says that for the men to join together in a union is the only way they'll accomplish anything."

"And how would Houston know that?" Lee snapped.

"She lives here," Blair said, surprised. "She hears things. She said that someone is bringing union activists into the camps, and there's going to be a revolution before long. And—."

Lee snatched the cloth from her. "I hope you don't listen to gossip like that. Nobody—neither the miners nor the owners—wants a war on his hands. I'm sure things can be handled peacefully."

"I hope so. I had no idea you cared so much for the miners."

"If you'd seen what I saw today, you'd care, too."

"I wanted to go with you. Maybe next time . . ."

Lee leaned forward and kissed her forehead. "I don't mean to snap. I wouldn't want you up there and, besides, you have all your many patients in the clinic to heal. I wonder what our pretty little housekeeper has for supper tonight?"

Blair smiled at him. "I hope you don't think I had courage

enough to ask. I'll go down in the deepest mine with you and face falling roofs, but deliver me from Mrs. Shainess's kitchen.''

''Falling roofs—that reminds me. How are you and Mrs. Krebbs doing?''

Blair groaned, and as Lee dressed, she launched into a soliloquy about Mrs. Krebbs. ''She may be an angel in the operating room, but elsewhere she is a witch.''

By the time Lee was ready to go downstairs to dinner, he was smiling again and gently arguing about whether Mrs. Krebbs's good qualities outweighed her bad.

That night, they snuggled against each other and fell asleep together.

The second day the clinic was open was worse: no one came. And when Blair got home, Lee received one of his cryptic phone calls and was out the door and didn't return until midnight. He crawled into bed beside her, dirty, exhausted, and she experienced male snoring for the first time. She gently touched his shoulder a couple of times and had no effect on him, so, with one big shove, she pushed him onto his stomach and he quietened.

On the third day, as Blair sat at her too-neat desk, she heard the outside doorbell jangle, and when she went into the waiting room, she saw her childhood friend, Tia Mankin. Tia was suffering from a persistent dry cough.

Blair listened to her complaints, prescribed a mild cough syrup, and was smiling broadly when the next patient arrived, another childhood friend. As the day wore on, and one friend after another came in with a vague complaint, she wasn't sure whether to laugh or cry. She was glad that these young women still considered themselves her friends, but part of her was feeling frustrated at the lack of real patients.

In the late afternoon, Houston drove up to the clinic in her pretty little carriage and told Blair she thought she was expecting, and would Blair please examine her to see if she was? Houston wasn't pregnant, and after the exam, Blair showed her around the clinic. Mrs. Krebbs had already gone home and the twins were alone.

''Blair, I've always admired you so much. You're so brave.''

"Me? Brave? I'm not brave in the least."

"But, look at all this. It's happened because you knew what you wanted and then went out and got it. You wanted to be a doctor, and you let nothing stand in your way. I used to have dreams, too, but I was too cowardly to pursue them."

"What dreams? I mean, besides Leander?"

Houston waved her hand. "I think I chose Lee because he was such a respectable dream. Mother and Mr. Gates approved so heartily of him, and in turn I got their approval." She stopped and smiled. "I think there was a part of me that enjoyed all those tricks you played on Lee."

"You knew about them?"

"Most of them. After a while, I began watching for them. I was the one who suggested to Lee that John Lechner was the culprit."

"John was always a bully, and I'm sure he deserved whatever he got from Lee. Houston, I had no idea you thought of yourself as a coward. I so badly wanted to be perfect like you."

"Perfect! No, I was just frightened, afraid of disappointing Mother, of enraging Mr. Gates, of not living up to what the town expected of a Chandler."

"While I seemed to make everyone angry without even trying. You have so many friends, so many people love you."

"Of course they do," Houston said with some anger in her voice. "They'd 'love' you, too, if you did as much for people as I do. Someone will say, 'Let's have a social,' then someone else will say, 'We'll get Blair-Houston to do all the work.' I was too cowardly to ever say no. I have organized socials that I didn't even attend. How I dreamed of telling them no. I used to imagine packing a bag and climbing down the tree outside your bedroom and just running away. But I was much too cowardly. You said I had a useless life and it has been."

"I was jealous," Blair whispered.

"Jealous? Of what? Surely not of me."

"I didn't realize I was until Lee made me see it. I've won awards, scored high on tests, had many honors, but I know I've always been lonely. It hurt when Mr. Gates said he didn't want me, but he did want you. It hurt when you wrote me of all the men you danced with one evening after another. I'd be studying a chapter on the correct way to amputate a leg, and I'd stop and reread one of your letters. Men have never liked me as they have you, and sometimes I thought I'd give up medicine if I could be a normal woman, one who smelled of perfume and not carbolic."

"And how many times I've wished I could do something important besides choose the colors of my next dress," Houston sighed. "Men only liked me because they thought I was, as Leander once said, pliable. They liked the idea of a woman they could browbeat. To most of the men, I was a human dog, someone to fetch their slippers for them. They wanted to marry me because they knew what they were getting: no surprises from Houston Chandler."

"Do you think that's why Lee asked you to marry him?"

"Sometimes, I'm not sure he *did* ask me. We saw each other a few times after he returned, and I guess I so expected to marry him that, when the word marriage came up, I said yes. The next morning, Mr. Gates asked if it was time yet for the announcement in the paper. I nodded, and the next thing I knew the house was full of people wishing me a lifetime of happiness."

"I know about the citizens of Chandler and their curiosity. But you loved Lee all those years."

"I guess so, but the truth is, we never seemed to have much to say to each other. You and Lee talked more than he and I did."

Blair was quiet for a long while. It seemed ironic that all these years she'd envied her sister, and at the same time her sister was envying her.

"Houston, you said you used to have dreams that you were afraid to pursue. What were they?"

"Nothing much. Nothing like you and medicine. But I did think I might be able to write—not a novel or anything grand, but I thought I'd like to write articles for ladies' magazines. Maybe about how to clean silk charmeuse or how to make a really good facial mud."

"But Mr. Gates would hate that, wouldn't he?"

"He said those women who wrote were probably adulteresses who'd been thrown out by their husbands and had to support themselves."

Blair's eyes widened. "He doesn't mince words, does he?"

"No, and I let him bully me for years."

Blair ran her finger along a cabinet top. "And your husband doesn't bully you? I know you said you loved him, but now it's . . . I mean, it's after the ceremony and you've lived with him." No matter how many times Houston said she loved the man, Blair would never be able to believe her. Yesterday, she'd seen Taggert in front of the Chandler National Bank. The bank president, half Taggert's size, was looking up at the big man and talking as fast as he could. Taggert had just seemed bored as he looked over the man's head at some place down the street, then he'd taken out a big gold pocket watch, looked at it, then down at the little bank officer. "No," Blair'd heard him say before he walked away. He was impervious to the man's entreaties to stay and listen.

And that's how Blair thought of him: impervious. How could Houston love a man like him?

When Blair looked up, Houston was smiling. "I love him more every day. What about you and Lee? At the wedding, you said you didn't believe he loved you."

Blair thought of this morning, of their exuberant coupling that had tumbled them out of bed, and of later when Mrs. Shainess had nearly slammed breakfast on the table. When the woman's back was turned, Lee had rolled his eyes in such a way that Blair had started giggling. "Lee's all right," she said at last and made Houston laugh.

Houston began to pull on her gloves. "I'm glad everything worked out as it did. I'd better go. Kane and the rest of my family will be needing me." She paused a moment. "What a lovely word. I may not have a medical degree, but I am *needed*."

"*I* need you," Blair said. "Was it you or Mother who organized all my 'patients'?"

Houston's eyes widened. "I have no idea what you mean. I merely came here because I was hoping I was expecting. I plan to come back at least once a month, or any other time I'm not feeling well."

"I think you should visit your husband more often, not me, if you want a baby."

"Like I hear you're exhausting Lee every night and morning?"

"I what?" Blair began, then remembered her telephone boast. Of course it was all over town.

"By the way, how is Mrs. Shainess working out?"

"Dreadful. She doesn't approve of me."

"That's nonsense. She's bragging to everyone about her lady-doctor." She kissed Blair's cheek. "I must go. I'll call you tomorrow."

Chapter 29

The next morning, early, Blair looked up from her desk to see Nina Westfield, now Hunter, standing before her.

"Hello," Nina said softly, her eyes half pleading. "Wait," she said, when Blair started to rise. "Before you say anything, let me do some explaining. I just got off the train and came directly here. I haven't seen Dad or Lee, but if you say you can't bear the sight of me, I'll leave on the next train and you'll never have to see me again."

"And miss thanking you every day for the rest of my life?" Blair asked, eyes sparkling.

"Thanking . . . ?" Nina said, then realized what Blair meant and, the next minute, she was pulling her sister-in-law out of the chair, hugging her and crying on her neck. "Oh, Blair, I've been so worried that I haven't really enjoyed what I've done. Alan kept saying that you loved Lee but just didn't know it. He said you and Lee were much more suited to one another than you and he were. But I wasn't *sure*. To me, Lee's a brother. I couldn't imagine choosing to live with him. I mean—." She pulled away, blowing her nose and sniffling.

Blair was smiling at her. "I'd offer you tea, but we don't have any. How about a cup of cod liver oil?"

That made Nina smile, as she sat down heavily in an oak chair. "I think this may be the happiest moment of my life. I was so afraid you'd be angry, that the whole town would be angry with me."

"But no one in town knew Alan and I were engaged. They thought Lee and I were to be married."

"But you wanted Alan," Nina persisted. "I know you did. I know you went to meet him at the train."

Blair's curiosity was peaked. "I want to hear the whole story."

Nina looked down at her hands. "I really hate to tell you everything." She looked up, tears beginning to form again. "Oh, Blair, I was so unutterably devious and underhanded. I did everything I could to get Alan. You never had a chance."

"If I shoot you, I promise I'll sew the wound myself."

"You can joke, but you won't after you hear about the things I did." She blew her nose again, and, while looking at her hands, she began. "I met Alan the night he decided to kill Lee."

"What? Leander? He was going to *kill* Leander?"

Nina shrugged. "He was just angry, and I understood so well how he felt. Lee has such a highhanded way about him. When I was little, he used to decide what was good for me and what was bad. It used to make me so angry that I wanted to strangle him."

"I know the feeling," Blair said. "He hasn't changed a great deal."

"When I saw Alan, I knew he wasn't going to kill anyone, he was just enjoying the idea. I invited him into the parlor, and it was quite easy to get him to talk and tell me what was going on. He told me he was in love with you, but I knew that Lee'd already made up his mind that you were going to marry him, so I didn't think Alan had much of a chance. I knew Lee'd win."

"How could you possibly know that?"

Nina looked surprised. "I've lived with Lee all my life. He

wins. He always wins. If he decides to play baseball, his team will win. If he enters a fencing tournament, he'll win. Dad says he's even forced dying patients to live. So, of course, I knew he'd win in this competition, whether the prize wanted to be won or not. But anyway"—she ignored Blair's look of astonishment—"I knew how Alan felt, and we started commiserating with one another, comparing examples of Lee's domineering ways. Then Dad came home, and I introduced Alan and we sat up late talking about medicine and life in Chandler compared to life in the Northeast. It was a very pleasant evening."

Nina paused a moment. "After that, Alan began to seek me out whenever Lee did something especially devious, like pushing Alan out of the operating room, making Alan look like an incompetent. He's going to be a very good doctor; he just has a lot of training to do yet."

"I think he will, too," Blair said softly. "So you and Alan fell in love."

"I did. I think he did, too, but he wasn't aware of it. I don't mean any disrespect, but I think that after Alan saw you here, he was a little afraid of you. He said that in Pennsylvania the two of you had had a very sedate courtship, holding hands in the park, studying together, but when he came here . . ." Nina's eyes brightened. "Really, Blair, jumping on and off horses like a circus performer, blithely pulling a man's intestines out onto a table so you could reach something underneath, beating him at tennis—no wonder he turned to someone else."

"Lee didn't turn away," Blair said defensively.

"Exactly my point! You and Lee are just alike, always tearing from one thing to another. You exhaust us mere mortals. Anyway, I don't think it occurred to Alan that you and he *shouldn't* get married. After he told you to meet him at the train, he came to me and told me what he'd done. By then, I knew I was in love with him and I didn't think you were, but you were too stubborn to admit that you weren't, or maybe all of you were too obsessed with winning your nasty little competition to look at the issues."

Nina took a deep breath. "So I decided to take matters into my own hands. I thought that if my brother could play some devious tricks to get what he wanted, I could, too. At three thirty, before he was to meet the four o'clock train, I asked Alan to come to the kitchen with me. I heated some molasses, not hot, but just so it was warm and runny; then, while he sat there playing with those blasted train tickets, I 'tripped' and spilled about a quart of it all over him. I must admit I did a good job. I managed to get it in his hair and all the way down to his shoes."

Blair couldn't speak for a moment. "But I stayed at the station for hours," she managed to whisper.

"I . . . ah . . ." Nina stood. "Blair, if my mother were alive, I'd never be able to face her again." She looked back at Blair, her pretty face flaming red, squared her shoulders defiantly and said in one breath, "He went to the bathroom, handed his clothes out to me, but I dropped his watch, it rolled inside the bathroom, I ran after it, the door slammed behind me and the outer key fell out."

Blair thought about this a moment, then began to smile. "You locked yourself inside the bathroom with a naked man?"

Nina set her jaw, put her chin in the air and gave a curt nod.

Blair didn't say a word but went to a side cabinet and withdrew a bottle of whiskey and two glasses. She poured an ounce in each glass and handed one to Nina. "To The Sisterhood," she said and downed the whiskey.

Nina, with a big grin, downed hers also. "You really aren't angry? I mean, you don't mind being married to Lee?"

"I think I might be able to stand the torture. Now, sit down and tell me what your plans are and how is Alan? Are you happy with him?"

Once Nina started, she couldn't stop. She didn't like Pennsylvania much and she said she'd almost persuaded Alan to return to Chandler when he finished interning. "I'm afraid his feelings for you and Lee aren't the friendliest, but I have hopes of working on him. I came back to see if I could persuade you to forgive me and to bear Dad and Lee's wrath."

"I don't think Lee—," Blair began, but Nina cut her off.

"Oh, yes, he will. Wait until you've known him as long as I have. He's a lamb when he's pleased, but when one of the women under his care does something he doesn't approve of, then look out! And Blair," she toyed with her parasol, "I need someone to take over the miners' pamphlets."

Blair's senses were immediately alert. "You mean the paper that may incite the miners to riot, to go on strike?"

"It's merely to inform them of their rights, to point out that if the miners united, they could accomplish a great deal. Houston and the others who drive the huckster wagons are taking them to the mines where they deliver vegetables, but that's only four mines. There are thirteen others. We need someone who has access to *all* the mines."

"You know those places are locked up. Even Leander's buggy is checked—. Nina! you can't think of trying to get Lee to deliver the papers?"

"Not on your life! If he even knew I was aware that there were coal mines, he'd lock me away. But I did think that, with you being a doctor and having the Westfield name, you could maybe see some of the women of the camps."

"Me?" Blair gasped, then stood. This bore thinking about. If she were caught with those papers in her carriage, she'd be shot immediately. But then she thought of the poverty of the mine camps, the way the people had to forfeit all American rights in order to earn a living.

"Nina, I don't know," she whispered. "This is a serious decision."

"It's a serious problem. And Blair, you're home again. You aren't just another body in a big city anymore. You're a part of Chandler, Colorado." She stood. "You think about it. I'm going home to see Dad now, and maybe Lee and you can come over later for supper. I have only two weeks before I have to return to Alan. I wouldn't have asked you, but I don't know anyone else who has access to the mines. Just let me know what you decide soon."

"All right, I will," Blair said absently, her mind completely taken with the idea of delivering seditious news into a camp guarded by men with guns.

All afternoon, as she wandered about the empty clinic, and as she tried to read a medical journal Lee had lent her, she considered the possibilities of what she was being asked to do. Nina had hit on something about Blair: she didn't really consider herself a part of Chandler. When she'd left the town, in her mind she'd left for good. She'd never planned to return, but now she had to face it: she was either a part of the community or she wasn't. She could stay in her clean clinic and occasionally patch broken bodies, or she could help prevent bodies from being broken.

And what if her own body were broken?

Her thoughts went round and round, and she never seemed able to reach a conclusion.

She and Lee ate dinner with his father and sister, and when Nina pulled her aside to question her, Blair said she hadn't decided yet. Nina smiled and said she understood—which made Blair feel even worse.

The next morning, Blair's head ached. The empty infirmary echoed with her steps, and Mrs. Krebbs said she had some shopping to do and left. At nine o'clock, the doorbell jangled and Blair hurried to what she hoped was a patient.

A woman and a little girl, about eight, stood there.

"May I help you?"

"You the lady-doctor?"

"I am a doctor. Would you like to come into my office?"

"Sure. Course." She told the girl to sit and wait while she followed Blair.

"What seems to be your problem?"

The woman sat down. "I ain't strong like I used to be, and I find I need help now and then. Not a lot of help, just a little."

"We all need help at times. What kind of help do you need?"

"I might as well come out and say it. Some of my girls, you know, on River Street, have been sold dirty opium. I thought maybe, with you bein' a doctor, you could get us some pure stuff from San Francisco. I figure you doctors got ways to check it to make sure it ain't bad, and maybe you could afford to buy it in large quantities and sell it. I can find you all the buyers you need and—."

"Please leave my office," Blair said quite calmly.

The woman stood. "Well, ain't you Miss High and Mighty? Too good for the likes of us, are you? Did you know the whole town is laughin' at you? You callin' yourself a doctor and just sittin' here in this empty place and won't nobody come to you. And ain't nobody *gonna* come, either."

Blair walked to the door, held it open for her.

With her nose in the air, the woman grabbed the child's hand and left, slamming the outer door behind her, the bell falling with a thud to the floor.

Without a trace of anger, Blair sat down at her desk and picked up a piece of paper. It was a household account of expenses Mrs. Shainess had given her that morning. Blair was supposed to add the twenty-two figures and check that Mrs. Shainess's total was correct.

She was looking at the paper when suddenly her eyes blurred, and the next thing she knew, she had her head on the desk and she was crying. She cried softly, tears that fought their way up from her stomach, before she lifted her head to search for a handkerchief.

She gasped when she saw Kane Taggert sitting in the chair across from her. "Do you enjoy spying on people?"

"Haven't done it enough to know," he said, looking at her with concern.

She floundered through desk drawers for a moment before snatching the big handkerchief Kane offered.

"It's clean. Houston won't let me out the door without an inspection."

She didn't answer his attempt at levity, but just turned away from him and blew her nose.

He reached across the desk and picked up the paper of accounts. "This what was makin' you cry?" He barely glanced at it. "It's seven cents off," he said, as he put the paper down. "Seven cents make you cry?"

"If you must know, I got my feelings hurt, that's what. Plain, old-fashioned, got my feelings hurt."

"Care to tell me about it?"

"Why? So you can laugh at me, too? I know your kind. You'd

never go to a woman doctor, either. You'd be like all the men and most of the women! You'd never trust a woman to cut you open."

His face was serious. "I ain't never been to any doctor, so I don't know who I'd want cuttin' on me. I guess, if I hurt enough, I'd let anybody work on me. Is that why you were cryin'? Cause nobody is here?"

Blair put her hands down on the desk, her anger, and energy, leaving her. "Lee once told me that all doctors were idealistic, at first. I guess I was worse than most. I thought the townspeople'd be thrilled to have a clinic for women. They are—if Leander is here running it. They see me and they start asking for a 'real' doctor. My mother has been here for three ailments in two days, and a few women I've known all my life have come. And, now, to add to my grief, the Chandler Hospital Board has suddenly decided that they really don't have enough work for another doctor."

Kane sat there and watched her for a while. He didn't know much about his sister-in-law, but he did know she usually had the energy of two people, and now she sat there with a long face and eyes with no light in them.

"Yesterday," he began, "I was in the stable without a shirt on—don't tell Houston—and I rubbed up against the back wall and got a lotta splinters in my back. I can't reach 'em to dig 'em out." He watched as she lifted her head. "It ain't much, but it's all I can offer."

Slowly, Blair began to smile. "All right, come into the surgery and I'll have a look."

The splinters weren't very big, or in too deep, but Blair treated them with great care.

As Kane lay on his stomach on the long table, he said, "How'd your doorbell fall off? Somebody mad at you?"

That's all it took for Blair to tell him about the woman wanting opium, how she'd said everyone was laughing at her. "And Lee's worked so hard for this clinic, and it's been his dream for years, and now he's always on one case after another in the mines, and I have charge of this place and I'm failing him."

"Looks to me like the sick people are failin' you. It's their loss."

She smiled at the back of his head. "It's nice to hear you say that, but you wouldn't have come unless . . . Why *did* you come?"

"Houston's rearrangin' my office."

He said it with such fatality that Blair laughed.

"It ain't funny. She puts the silliest little chairs everywhere, and she likes lace. If I get back and my office is painted pink, I'll . . ."

"What will you do?"

He moved his head to look up at her. "Cry."

She smiled at him. "She paints it pink and I'll come over tomorrow and we'll repaint it. How's that for a deal?"

"The best I've had all day."

"All done," she said a minute later and began to clean her instruments, as he put his shirt and coat back on. She turned to look at him. "Thank you," she said. "You've made me feel much better. I know I've been unkind to you in the past, and I apologize."

Kane shrugged his big shoulders. "You and Houston are twin sisters, so you've got to be somethin' alike, and if you're half as good at doctorin' as she is at runnin' things, you must be the best. And I have a feelin' things are gonna change for you. Pretty soon, ladies are gonna be beatin' down your door with all kinds of diseases. You'll see. You just stay here and clean up this place real good, and tomorrow I bet there'll be some patients here."

She couldn't help grinning at him. "Thank you. You've done a world of good for me." On impulse, she stood on tiptoe and kissed his cheek.

He smiled at her. "You know, for a minute there, you looked just like Houston."

Blair laughed. "I think that may be the highest compliment I've ever received. I guess I do have some work to do. If that shoulder bothers you, let me know."

"I'll bring every broken bone to you, Dr. Westfield, and all my pink walls," he said as he left the clinic.

Blair began to whistle as she started clearing her desk of paperwork, and immediately realized that she didn't know whether the account list was seven cents over or under and had to add it herself. The rest of the day, she felt better than she had in days.

Once, she stopped and thought how kind Kane had been in trying to cheer her, after the way she'd treated him. Perhaps there *was* reason for Houston to love him.

At home, in his dark panelled office, Kane turned to his assistant, Edan Nylund. "Last week, after I bought the Chandler National Bank, didn't they send us some papers?"

"About a twenty-pound stack," Edan said, pointing, but not looking up, as Kane took the papers and thumbed through them.

"Where'd Houston go?"

He had Edan's interest now. "To her dressmaker's, I believe."

"Good," Kane said. "Then we've got the rest of the day, maybe the rest of the week." He strode out of the room, papers in hand.

Edan's curiosity got the better of him and he found Kane in the library, using the telephone. Since the system only connected one house in Chandler to another, and Kane's business dealings were usually out of state, Edan'd never seen Kane use the instrument before.

"You heard me," Kane was saying to the person on the other end. "The mortgage on that ranch of yours is due next week, and I have every right to call it in. That's right. You get an interest-free ninety-day extension if your wife shows up at the Westfield Infirmary tomorrow and is treated by Dr. Blair. She's about to have a baby? Good! She drops it in the office in my sister-in-law's lap and I'll give you a hundred and eighty days. Damn right, you can send your daughters. Yeah, all right. Another thirty days per daughter that shows up tomorrow with somethin' wrong with her. But if Blair gets wind of this, I foreclose. You understand me?

"Damn!" he said to Edan, as he put down the receiver. "This is gonna cost me. Look in there and see who else has a loan due or's been turned down for an extension, and then I want you to see how much whoever owns the Chandler Hospital will sell it for. We'll see if their board of directors will refuse to hire the owner's sister-in-law."

By the next morning, Blair's good mood was gone, and she had to nearly drag herself to work. Another long day with little to do, she thought, walking the distance rather than driving her new carriage. But when she was half a block from the clinic, Mrs. Krebbs came running.

"Where have you been? The place is overrun with patients."

For a moment, Blair couldn't move, but then she ran to the door. The waiting room was a mess: children screaming, mothers trying to quiet them, and one woman groaning with what looked to be labor pains.

Fifteen minutes later, Blair was cutting the umbilical cord of a newborn girl.

"180," the mother murmured. "Her name is Mary 180 Stevenson."

Blair didn't have time to ask any questions before the next patient was brought in.

The next afternoon, a woman brought a little boy to the clinic, an undersized eight-year-old who looked six, a boy who'd already spent two years inside a coal mine. He died in Blair's arms, his frail little body having been crushed by coal falling from a train car.

Blair called Nina, said, "I'll do it," and hung up.

Chapter 30

Blair drove her carriage down the road, away from the Inexpressible Mine and back toward Chandler. Nina had lost no time in arranging for her to take the pamphlets to the mine, perhaps because she was afraid Blair would change her mind.

So this morning, Blair had called Dr. Weaver, a young man she'd met at the Chandler Infirmary, and asked him to look after the clinic because she'd been called to a mine emergency. The man'd been happy to oblige.

At the Westfield house, Nina'd done her best to hide the pamphlets under a makeshift piece of wood that was to serve as a false bottom in the back compartment of Blair's new carriage. Throughout Nina's instructions, Blair was so scared that she could barely speak.

At the mine entrance, the guards had teased her, saying that Dr. Westfield had certainly changed since his last visit, but they let her in. She had to ask some coal-dust-covered children how to find the house of the woman who was to help her, and she found the woman, lying on the bed faking illness, to be as nervous as she was. The woman hid the pamphlets under a floorboard and Blair left the camp as quickly as she could manage.

The guards, sensing she was nervous and, with the normal vanity of men, thinking it was their presence that was making her so, teased her more as she left.

She was a mile from the mine before she began to shake, and within twenty minutes, she was shaking so badly her hands couldn't hold the reins. She pulled off the road to hide among some rocks, stepped down from the buggy, and when her knees gave way, she sat down on the ground and began to cry tears of relief that it was over.

Her shoulders were still shaking when suddenly two strong hands caught her and pulled her upright.

She looked into Leander's eyes blazing with fury.

"Damn you," he said, before he crushed her against him.

Blair didn't ask questions about how he knew what she'd done—she was too grateful that he was there. She clung to him, and even though he was already nearly crushing her ribs, she wanted him to hold her tighter.

"I was so afraid," she said into his shoulder, standing on tiptoe to bury her face in the soft skin of his neck. "I was so frightened." Tears poured down her face, ran into her mouth.

Lee just held her close to him and stroked her hair, never saying a word while she cried.

It took a while before her tears stopped and her body quit shaking. When she had the courage to release her death grip on Lee, she pulled away and began searching her pockets for a handkerchief. Lee handed her his, and after she'd blown her nose and mopped up her face, she glanced up at him. What she saw made her step backward.

"Lee, I . . . ," she began, taking another step back, until she halted against a boulder.

His eyes were on fire. The teasing, smiling, tolerant Lee that she'd always seen was nowhere near this enraged man.

"I don't want to hear a word," he managed to choke out. "Not a word. I want you to swear you'll never do this again."

"But I—."

"Swear it!" he said, advancing on her and catching her forearm in his hand.

"Lee, please, you're hurting me." She wanted to calm him down, to make him see the need of what she'd done. "How did you know? It was secret."

"I'm in the mine camps every day," he said, glaring at her. "I hear what goes on. Damn you, Blair, when I heard you were to deliver those papers, I couldn't believe it at first." He nodded toward the wet handkerchief that was crumpled in her hand. "At least, you did realize the danger you were in. Do you know what those men would have done to you? Do you have any idea? You might have begged them to kill you after they got through. And they have the law on their side."

"I know, Lee," she said with passion. "They have every legal right to do whatever they want to do. And that's why *someone* has to inform the miners of their rights."

"But not *you!*" Lee bellowed into her face.

She blinked from the blast and curved her backbone against the rock. "I have access to the mines. I have a carriage. I am the logical one to do it."

Lee's face turned so red she thought he might explode as he lifted his hands toward her throat, but caught himself and moved away. As he turned his back to her, she saw his upper body rise and fall with his deep breaths. When he turned back, he appeared to have controlled himself somewhat.

"Now, I want you to listen to me and listen very carefully. I know that what you did was for a very good cause, and I know that the miners need to be informed. I even appreciate the fact that you're willing to risk your life to help others, but I cannot allow you to do this. Am I making myself clear?"

"If I don't, who will?"

"What the hell do I care?" he yelled, then took another couple of deep breaths. "Blair, you are the person I care about. To me, you are more important than all the miners in the world. I want you to swear that you'll not do anything like this again."

Blair looked at her hands. She had been more afraid this morning than she'd ever been before in her life. Yet, some part of her felt that today she'd done the most important thing in her life. "Yesterday, a little boy died in my arms," she whispered. "He'd been crushed in—."

Lee grabbed her shoulders. "You don't have to tell me a thing. Do you know how many children have died in *my* arms? How many arms and legs I've cut off men trapped under beams and rocks? You've never been inside a mine. If you had to go inside . . . It's worse than you think it is."

"Then, something has to be done," she said stubbornly.

He dropped his hands, started to speak, but closed his mouth, then tried again. "All right, let me try another tactic. You're not cut out for this. A few minutes ago, you were a mess. You don't have the personality that it takes to do something like this. You're very courageous when it comes to saving lives, but when you're involved in something that could lead to a war and the loss of lives, you fall apart."

"But it needs to be done," she pleaded.

"Yes, maybe it does, but it has to be done by someone other than you. What you feel shows on your face too easily."

"But how will the miners be told? Who else has access to the mines besides you and me?"

"Not *us*," Lee exploded again. "*Me! I* have access to the mines, not you. I don't know why you were allowed past the guards. I don't want you up here. I don't want you going down into the mines. Last year, I was trapped underground for six hours after a timber gave way. I can't allow the possibility of something like that happening to you."

"Allow?" she asked, and found her fear leaving her. "What else aren't you going to 'allow'?"

He arched an eyebrow at her. "You can take what I've said anyway you want, but the end result is the same: you cannot go into the mines again."

"I guess it's all right for you to sneak off to wherever you go in the middle of the night, but I'm to be the docile little wife and stay at home."

"That's absurd. I've never thwarted you in any way before. You wanted a women's clinic, I gave it to you. And now you can stay there."

"And let you go to the mines, is that it? I guess I'm too much of a coward to go into the mines. You think I'd be afraid of the dark?"

Lee didn't say anything for a moment, and when he did speak, his voice was little more than a whisper. "You're not a coward, Blair, I am. You're not afraid to do something that terrifies you, but I'm too terrified of losing you to ever let you do it again. You may not like the way I say it, but in the end it's all the same: you have to stay out of the mine camps."

Blair seemed to feel every emotion she'd ever experienced go through her at once. She was angered at Lee's highhand-edness. Just as Nina had said, his forbidding her to do something infuriated her. But she also thought about what he'd said, that she just plain wasn't any good at the job. Houston went into the camps, but even if her wagon were searched, the guards'd only find tea and children's shoes. It wasn't the same as what Blair had carried. And Lee had said he was worried about what damage the pamphlets could cause. She'd read one of the things and it was full of vicious hatred, the kind of angry words that made men act first and consider what they'd done later.

She looked up at Lee as he watched her. "I . . . I didn't mean to scare you so badly," she stuttered. "I—." She didn't say any more, as Lee held out his arms to her and she ran to him.

"Do I have your promise?" he asked, burying his face in her hair.

Blair started to say that she couldn't give it, but then she thought that maybe there was a different way to get the information into the mines, a more subtle way, one that wasn't likely to get anyone shot.

"I promise that I will never again carry unionist papers into a mine camp."

He pulled her head back to look at her. "And what if someone calls me to a mine disaster, and you answer the telephone?"

"Why, Lee, I'll have to—."

His hand tightened on the back of her head. "You know something, I really like this town, and I'd hate to have to move, but it may become imperative to leave and go to, say, some place in east Texas where there aren't any people to speak of. Some place where my wife *can't* get into trouble." He narrowed his eyes. "And I'll ask Mrs. Shainess and Mrs. Krebbs to live with us."

"Cruel and inhuman punishment. All right, I'll stay out of the mines unless you're with me. But if you ever need me—."

He kissed her to silence. "If I ever need you, I want to know where you are—*always*. Every minute of every day. Understand me?"

"There are many times I don't know where you are. I think that in all fairness—."

He kissed her again. "When I left the hospital, they were unloading two wagons of injured cowboys, a stampede, I believe. I really ought to—."

She pushed away from him. "What are we standing here for? Let's go!"

"That's my girl," Lee said, as he followed her back to her carriage and his horse.

"Open the gate!"

Pamela Fenton Younger sat atop her horse before the gate to the Little Pamela mine, glaring down at the two guards.

Both guards stared up at her. There was something quite intimidating about a six-foot-tall woman atop a seventeen-hand-high black stallion that was prancing so high its ironclad hoofs showed. Even though they were separated from the animal by a heavy wooden gate, the men stepped back when the horse jerked its head and did a half turn.

"Did you hear me? Open the gate."

"Now, wait a minute—," one of the guards began.

The other guard punched him in the ribs. "Sure thing, Miss Fenton," he said, as he pulled aside the gate for her, then jumped back as she went charging through.

"The mine owner's daughter," the guard was explaining behind her.

Pamela rode directly to the entrance of the mine shaft, the horse's hoofs kicking up a cloud of coal dust. "I want to see Rafferty Taggert," she said, holding the horse on a tight rein, its eyes rolling wildly. "Where is he?"

"On shift," someone said. "Tunnel number six."

"Then bring him up. I want to see him."

"Now, see here—," a man said, stepping forward.

Another man, older, pushed his way toward the nervous horse. "Good mornin', Miss Fenton. Taggert's below, but I'm sure that, for you, someone can bring him up."

"Do that," she said, with a hard pull on the reins to further assert her dominance over the big animal. With a curled lip, she looked about the coal camp, at the dirt, the poverty. When she was a child, her father had insisted she accompany him to this place, to show her where their wealth came from. Pam had looked at everything and said, "I think we're poor."

The place still disgusted her. "Saddle a horse for him and have it waiting. I'll meet him by the bend in Fisherman's Creek." She had to wait while the stallion made a full turn before she could look at the mine supervisor. "And if he's docked even a penny, you'll hear about it." With that, she let the horse have its head and tore back through the camp, cinders flying behind her.

She didn't have to wait long for Rafe. The name of Fenton might have evil connotations for some people but those who worked for Fenton Coal and Iron jumped when a Fenton spoke.

Rafe sat on a mangy horse much too small for his big body. His face and clothes were black with coal dust, but the whites of his eyes showed his anger. "Whatever you want takes first place, doesn't it? Princess Fenton gets whatever she demands," he said as he dismounted, looking her squarely in the eyes.

"I don't like that place."

"Nobody does, it's just that some of us have to earn a livin'."

"I didn't come to fight you. I have something important to tell you. Here." She handed him a bar of soap and a wash cloth. "Don't look so surprised. I've seen coal dust before."

With one more glare at her, he took the soap and cloth, knelt by the stream and began to lather his face and hands. "All right, tell me why you want me."

Pam sat down on a flat rock, stretching her long legs toward him. Her tall, hard, black hat made her seem even taller than she was, but the little black veil gave her face a look of mystery and femininity.

"When I was seven years old, my father lost the duplicate key to his private desk drawer. I found it and put it in my treasure box. When I was twelve, I discovered what the key opened."

"And you've been spying ever since."

"I keep myself informed."

He waited, but she said nothing else. When he turned, his face clean, she handed him a towel. "So what have you found out?"

"My father hired Pinkerton men months ago to find out who's bringing unionists into the coal camps."

Rafe took his time drying his forearms. They were muscled from years of wielding a sledgehammer. "So, what have your Pinkertons found?"

"Not *my* Pinkertons, my *father's*." She picked a flower of Queen Anne's lace from beside her and toyed with it. "First of all, they found that four young women of Chandler, all from prominent families, are disguising themselves as old women and bringing illegal goods into the camp. Illegal being anything that my father doesn't make a profit on." She looked up at him. "One of the women is your nephew's new wife."

"Houston? That fragile little . . ." He drifted off. "Does Kane know?"

"I doubt it, but then I'd have no way of knowing, would I?"

She watched him intently. When both she and Kane had been quite young, they'd had an affair that they'd thought was their secret love, but in truth had been the hottest gossip of the town. When she'd met Kane's Uncle Rafe, weeks ago at the twins' wedding, he'd seemed to her to have all the characteristics of Kane that she'd liked, but Rafe also had a gentle side that she'd never seen in the younger man. For days after the wedding, she'd hoped he'd call her or send her a note, but he'd made no effort to contact her. The damned Taggert pride! she'd cursed. And it made her wonder why a man like Rafe worked in a coal mine. There had to be a reason why. He wasn't married, wasn't under the burden of a family to support.

"Why do you stay here?" she asked. "Why do you put up with that?" She nodded toward the road that led up to the mine.

Rafe took a rock in his hand and tossed it, looking out over the little stream. "My brothers were here and Sherwin was dying. He had a wife and daughter to feed and wouldn't take help from me or anyone else."

"Taggert pride," she murmured.

"I went to your father and agreed to work if he'd give my salary to Sherwin. Your father likes to have Taggerts grovelling for his money."

She ignored his last remark. "That way, Sherwin kept his pride and you got to help your brother. What did you get out of it besides a permanent cramp in your back from four-foot-tall ceilings?"

He looked up at her. "It's only for a few years—or was. My brother and his daughter have gone to live with Kane and Houston."

"But you stay."

Rafe looked back at the stream and didn't answer.

"The Pinkerton report said there were three suspects who could be bringing the unionists in. One was a man named Jeffery Smith, the second was Dr. Leander Westfield and the last was you."

Rafe didn't look at her or speak, but his hand clutched and unclutched a rock.

"You don't have anything to say?"

"Are the Pinkertons working as miners?"

"I doubt if they wear uniforms," she said sarcastically.

He stood. "If that's all you have to say, I need to get back to work. I guess you don't know which men are the Pinks?"

"Not even my father knows," she said, standing beside him. "Rafe, you can't go on doing this. You don't have to stay here. I can get you a better job if you want—any kind of job."

He gave her a look from narrowed eyes. "Call it Taggert pride," he said, as he started for his borrowed horse.

"Rafe!" she caught his arm. "I didn't mean—." She stopped and dropped her arm. "I wanted to warn you. Maybe you don't like the way I did it, and maybe you don't like my father's name, but I wanted to give you a chance to decide what you want to do. My father can be a ruthless man when he wants something."

He didn't move or speak, and when she looked up at him, he was looking at her in a way that made her heart jump into her throat. Without conscious thought, she stepped forward into his arms.

His kiss was slow and gentle and she felt as if she'd been looking for this man all her life.

"Meet me here tonight," he whispered. "Midnight. Wear something easy to get out of." With that, he mounted his horse and was gone.

Chapter 31

After the horror of the morning, and then seven hours of mending the young men who'd been hurt in the stampede, Blair was exhausted. She was so tired that she didn't even get angry when Lee received one of his calls that made him ride out without telling anyone where he was going.

At dusk, she started the drive home, stopping off at the telegraph office to send her friend, Dr. Louise Bleeker, a message:

NEED YOU STOP HAVE MORE WORK THAN I CAN HANDLE STOP COME IMMEDIATELY STOP PLEASE BLAIR

At home, ignoring Mrs. Shainess's protests, Blair refused to eat any supper and fell onto the bed, fully clothed, at eight o'clock.

She was awakened by the sound of someone struggling with the bedroom door.

"Lee?" she called, and there was no answer. She got up from the bed, went to the door and opened it. Leander stood there with his shirt dirty, torn, bloody. "What's happened?" she asked, instantly alert. "Who's been hurt?"

"I have," Lee said hoarsely and staggered into the room.

Blair felt her stomach fly into her throat and, for a moment, she just stood there and watched as he staggered toward the bed.

"You're going to have to help me," he said, as he started to pull off his shirt. "I don't think it's bad, but it's bleeding a lot."

Blair recovered herself in a rush. She took her medical bag from the closet floor, removed scissors and began to cut away Lee's shirt. She propped his arm on her shoulder and looked at the wounds. There were two long bloody furrows close together on his right side, tearing the skin away from his side, in one place exposing the ribs. She'd seen enough bullet wounds to recognize them as such. Since he'd bled a great deal, she didn't think there would be an infection.

Her mouth was dry when she spoke. "It needs cleaning," she said, as she began to remove instruments and disinfectant. Her hands were shaking badly.

"Blair," Lee said, and the only sign he gave that he was in pain was the sound of his ragged breathing. "You're going to have to help me more than this. I think the men who shot at me suspect who I am. I think they may come here to arrest me."

Blair was so intent on his wound that she didn't quite understand what he was saying. It was the first time she'd ever worked on someone she loved—and she hoped she'd never have to do it again. She was beginning to sweat and her hair was plastering itself to her forehead.

Lee put his hand under her chin to make her look at him. "Are you listening to me? I think there will be some men here in a few minutes, and I want them to think that I've been here all night. I don't want them to think that I've been shot at."

"And hit," she managed to rasp out, as she finished cleaning the wounds and began to bandage him. "Who are these men?"

"I . . . I'd rather not say."

She was worried and afraid because he was hurt, but part of her was becoming angry that he'd ask for her help, but not tell her what she was helping him do. "They're Pinkerton men, aren't they?"

At least, she had the satisfaction of seeing the look of total surprise on Lee's face. "You may think I don't know anything, but I know more than you think." She put the last of the bandages around his ribs. "If you move about much, it'll start bleeding again." Without another word, she went to the closet and withdrew the gown and robe that she'd worn on her wedding night, then hurriedly stripped and dressed in it. Lee sat on the bed and watched her, obviously not sure what she was going to do next.

"We'll see how much time we have," she said as she pitched him a clean shirt. "Can you get into that by yourself? I need to hang upside down."

Lee, in too much pain, too shocked at what Blair had already said to him, did not question her, but tried his best to stuff his injured body into the shirt, while Blair hung herself head down across the bed.

They both froze when the pounding on the door downstairs started.

Blair stood. "Take your time. I'll keep them occupied for as long as I can." Quickly, she glanced into the mirror and ruffled her hair in a becoming way. "How do I look?" she asked, as she turned back to him. Her face was flushed from hanging upside down, and her hair was down about her shoulders in a pretty disarray. She looked for all the world like a woman who had just been made love to.

Blair was surprisingly calm when she reached the front door to the house. When she opened it, there were three big, mean-looking men standing there and they rushed past her into the house.

"Where is he?" one of the men demanded.

"I can go with you," Blair said. "I'll just get my bag."

"We don't want you," said the second man. "We want the doctor."

Blair stood on the second step, so that she was above eye level with the men. "You will get what there is," she said angrily. "I have had about all I can take of this town. Whether you believe it or not, *I* am a doctor just as my husband is, and if you need help, I can give it. Leander is very tired and he needs his rest, and I assure you that I can sew a wound quite as well as he can. Now that that is settled, I'll get my bag." She turned to go up the stairs.

"Wait a minute, lady, we ain't here for no doctorin'. We're here to take your husband to jail."

"Whatever for?" she asked, turning back to them.

"For bein' where he ain't supposed to be, that's what."

Blair took a step down toward them. "And when was this?" she asked softly.

"About an hour ago."

Slowly, with great show, Blair began to tuck her hair into some semblance of order. Most of the time, she wasn't concerned with how she looked, but right now, she wanted to look as seductive as she could. She let the gown fall a little bit off one shoulder, and she began to smile at the men. "Sirs, one hour ago my husband was with me."

"You got any proof of that?" one of the men asked. The other two were looking at her with their mouths slightly open.

"Absolutely none." She smiled graciously. "Of course, I am giving the word of a Chandler in a town named for my father. Perhaps, if you'd like to challenge what I say . . ." She blinked innocently as the men looked up at her.

"I don't think they'd like to do that, dear," said Lee from behind her. His face was flushed and he looked tired—but then, so would a man who'd just made vigorous love to his wife. "I believe I heard you say that I was somewhere else an hour ago." He moved to stand beside Blair and, to the men below, she must have looked as if she were leaning against him, but in truth she was supporting him.

For a few moments, there was silence in the dark little house, and Blair and Lee held their breaths as the men paused, glaring up at them. Finally, the man who was the leader gave a sigh. "You may think you've tricked us, Westfield, but you haven't. We'll get you yet." He looked at Blair. "You wanta keep him alive, you better keep him at home."

Neither Blair nor Lee said a word as the men left the house, slamming the door behind them. Blair ran down the stairs to lock the door, and as she turned back, she saw that Lee was growing paler. She hurried up the stairs and helped him to bed.

Blair didn't sleep any more that night. After she got Lee to bed, she sat by him, watching his every breath as if he might stop breathing if she weren't there to protect him. Whenever she thought of how close those bullets had come to his heart, she began shaking again, and she clutched his hand harder.

He slept fitfully, a couple of times opening his eyes and smiling at her, then sleeping again.

Blair's emotions ranged from terror that he'd come so close to death, to a realization of how much she loved him, to fury that he was doing something that could possibly get him killed.

When the early morning light filtered into the room, Lee awoke at last and tried to sit up. Blair opened the curtains.

"How do you feel?" she asked.

"Stiff, sore, raw, hungry."

She tried to smile at him, but her lips wouldn't work properly. Every muscle in her body ached from having been held rigid all night. "I'll bring you some breakfast."

She gathered up the bloody rags and Lee's shirt to take downstairs with her. One good thing about a doctor's house was that no one would notice a trash barrel full of blood-soaked rags.

It was too early yet for Mrs. Shainess, so Blair fried half a dozen eggs for the two of them, cut inch-thick slices of bread and filled big mugs full of cool milk. She carried the big tray upstairs, and when she found Lee already out of bed and half dressed, she said nothing but began to set the little table by the window.

Lee painfully sat in the chair and began to eat while Blair sat across from him and moved her food about on her plate.

"All right," Lee said. "Tell me what's on your mind."

Blair took a drink of milk. "I have no idea what you mean."

He took her hand. "Look at you. You're shaking as badly today as you were yesterday."

She jerked her hand away. "I guess you're planning to go to the hospital today."

"I have to show up. I have to pretend that nothing's happened. I can't let people know where I was last night."

"Not *anyone*," she spat at him as her fist came down on the table, and the next moment she was on her feet. "Look at you, you can barely sit up, much less stand in surgery all day. And what about your patients? Can you wield a scalpel accurately? Where were you last night? What is worth risking your life for?"

"I can't tell you that," he said, as he turned back to his eggs. "I would, but I can't."

Tears began to close her throat. "Yesterday, you were furious with me because I'd risked my life. You ordered me to stop risking it, but now the tables are turned, and I'm not allowed the same rights. Same! I'm not even allowed to *know* what I may lose my husband for. I'm just to be a good girl and stay home and wait and, if he comes home bleeding, I'm to patch him. I'm allowed to flirt with Pinkerton men in the middle of the night, but I don't know why. I'm allowed to watch you suffering, but for what I don't know. Tell me, Lee, do you shoot back on these forays? Are you in a kill or be killed situation? Do you murder as many people as you repair?"

Lee kept his head down, eating deliberately and slowly. "Blair, I've told you all I can. You're going to have to trust me."

For a moment, she turned away, trying to control her tears. "That's what a good little wife would do, wouldn't she? Sit at home and wait and ask no questions. Well, I'm not a good little girl! I've always been defiant. I've always been a participator and not an observer. And right now, I want to know what I'm participating in."

"Damn it, Blair," Lee shouted, then closed his eyes against the pain at his side. He looked back at her. "Maybe for once you should be an observer. I've told you what I can. I don't want you involved any more than you are."

"So, I'm to stay innocent, is that right? At your trial, I can honestly say that I know nothing, that even when my husband came home with two bullet wounds, I remained innocent."

"Something to that effect," Lee mumbled, then put down his fork and looked at her. "You say you love me, maybe that you've loved me for years; well, now's the test. If you do love me, you'll have to trust me. For once in your life, you're going to have to put aside your defiance and your participation. I need you now, not as a colleague or an equal, but as a wife."

Blair stood looking at him for a long time. "I think you're right, Lee," she said softly. "I think that maybe until now I never realized what a wife was supposed to be." Her voice lowered. "But I'm going to try to learn. I will trust you, and I won't ask you again where you went. But if you want to tell me, I'll be here to listen."

Much of the pain began to leave Lee's face as he leaned his left hand on the table and raised himself. Blair went to help him.

"Lee," she said. "Why don't you go to the clinic today? You won't have any surgery to do, Mrs. Krebbs will be there to help you, and it will be easier. Besides, a Pinkerton man will look conspicuous amid all the women."

"That's a good idea," he said, kissing her forehead. "That's the kind of talk I like."

"Just trying to be a good wife. Here, let me help you dress."

"What about you? Shouldn't you be getting dressed?"

"To tell you the truth, I think I'm a little tired today. After the dreadful experience of yesterday morning, and then last night, not to mention today, I think I'd like to stay home and pamper myself."

"Why, yes, of course," Lee said. She made sense, but he'd never heard Blair say such a thing before. "You stay home and rest. I'll take care of the clinic."

She smiled up at him through her lashes. "You are the kindest of husbands."

Five minutes after Lee left the house, Blair was on the telephone to her sister. "Houston, where can I buy a twenty-pound box of bath salts? And where can I get a manicurist and an hourly supply of chocolates, and where can I buy silk yarns? Don't laugh at me. I'm going to become the epitome of the perfect wife by this evening. I'm going to give my dear husband what he *thinks* he wants. Now, are you going to giggle all day or answer my questions?"

Chapter 32

When Leander got home at six, he found Blair stretched out on the couch in the parlor, a box of chocolates on the floor beside a litter of magazines. Blair, seemingly unaware of his entry, was sucking on a piece of candy and avidly reading a novel. As he walked toward her, he could see the word "seduction" in the title of the book.

"This is something new," Lee said, smiling down at her.

Blair slowly moved her head to look up at him, a slight smile on her lips. "Hello, dear. Did you have a pleasant day?"

"It wasn't until now," he said, eyes alight as he bent toward her. But Blair turned away just as his mouth came near hers, and his kiss landed on her cheek.

She put the entire piece of chocolate into her mouth, and from the difficulty she was having chewing, it must have been a caramel. "Would you be a dear and go get me some more lemonade while I finish this chapter? And then, you'd better dress for dinner. Mrs. Shainess and I have arranged something special."

He stood, taking the empty glass she handed him. "Since when have you and the housekeeper done things together?"

"She's really a very good woman, if one knows how to talk to her. Now, Leander, please go. I am perishing from thirst, and you wouldn't want to keep a lady waiting, would you?"

With a puzzled look, he backed away. "Sure, I'll be right back."

When he had gone, Blair finished chewing her candy, smiling to herself as she continued reading her book. She hoped the heroine would break a chair over the "sardonic" hero's head and tell him to go drown himself.

"Why, Lee," she said when he reappeared with her lemonade, "you haven't changed for dinner yet."

"I've been too busy fetching lemonade for you so you won't perish," he snapped.

Instantly, Blair's eyes filled with tears, and she applied a lace-edged handkerchief to the corners. "I'm so sorry I imposed on you, Leander. I just thought that since you were up and I . . . Oh, Lee, I've been working so hard today and—."

Lee winced as he knelt beside her, taking her hand in his as he pushed three magazines aside to get to her. "I'm sorry I was cross. But it's nothing to cry about."

Blair sniffed delicately. "I don't know what's wrong with me lately. Everything seems to upset me."

Lee kissed her hand, stroked it. "It's probably nothing. All women get this way sometimes."

He had his head down and didn't see Blair's eyes flash fire. "You're probably right. I'm sure it's just female problems, the vapors or something."

"Probably," he said, smiling, as he stroked her forehead. "You just rest while I change. A nice dinner will make you feel better."

"You're so wise," Blair murmured. "I have the very wisest of husbands."

He stood, smiling down at her, then, with a wink, he left the room.

When Blair heard him go up the stairs, she jumped off the couch and stood with her back to the fireplace, her hands on her hips and glared toward the direction of their bedroom.

"Of all the vain, imperious—," she said aloud. " 'All women get that way sometimes'! He's worse than I thought." Her anger made her begin to pace. "I'm going to give you 'women problems,' Leander," she said. "You wait and see if I don't. I'm going to be more of what you think a woman is than you ever dreamed."

By the time Lee had bathed and dressed for dinner, Blair had managed to calm herself so that she could smile at him again. He was very solicitous, holding her chair for her, carving the meat and serving her. Blair was quiet and calm, not saying much, but smiling demurely as she cut her meat into tiny little pieces.

"Something interesting came into the clinic today," Lee was saying. "The woman thinks she's pregnant, but I think it's a cyst. I'd like you to look at her tomorrow."

"Oh, Lee, I can't. Houston made me another appointment with her dressmaker, and then Nina and I have a luncheon engagement, and in the afternoon I need to be back here to supervise the house. I really have no time at all."

"Oh, well, I guess it can wait until later in the week. So, you won't be at the Women's Infirmary again tomorrow?"

"I don't see how I can be." She looked up at him through her lashes. "It takes more time than I thought being a wife. There seem to be so many things that need to be done. And now that I'm going to be a part of Chandler again, I really do think I should help with the charity work. There's the Ladies Aid Society and the Christian Mission and—."

"The Westfield Infirmary," he added. "It seems that what you're doing there is more than enough to help the town."

"Well, of course," she said stiffly, "if you insist, I'll go to the clinic tomorrow. I'll cancel the dressmaker, and I'm sure the other wives can get along without me. They'll have to understand that you want me to work outside the home. I'm sure I can make them understand the concept of a woman having to help pay for the food on the table.''

"Pay for—!'' Lee gasped. "Since when have I made you pay for anything in this house? When did I ever fail in my duties of supporting you? You don't have to work tomorrow or ever. I thought you *wanted* to work!''

Blair looked close to tears again. "I did; I do. But I had no idea being a wife took so much time. Today, I had to plan meals, that new maid was utterly impossible, and when the ribbons for my new dress arrived, they were the wrong color! I just want to look nice for you, Lee. I want to make a nice home for you and be the best, the prettiest wife any man ever had. I want you to be proud of me, and it's so difficult when I'm at the infirmary all day. I didn't know—.''

"All right,'' Lee interrupted, throwing his napkin on the table. "I didn't mean to yell at you. I just misunderstood what you meant. You don't have to go to the infirmary tomorrow or ever.'' He caught her hand and began caressing her fingertips.

She pulled away from him and began folding her napkin. "This morning, John Silverman called and asked me to tell you that there was an important meeting tonight at your club. He didn't explain, and I didn't ask what it was about.''

"I know what it's about, and they can do without me. I really did have a couple of patients I wanted to talk to you about. There's a man at the hospital who has an infected hand. I thought you might look at him. I'd value another opinion.''

"Mine?'' Blair fluttered her lashes. "You flatter me, Lee. I haven't even finished my medical training yet. What could I tell you that you, with all your experience, don't already know?''

"But in the past—.''

"In the past, I wasn't someone's *wife*. I didn't know what my full responsibilities were. Lee, I really think you should go to your club. I'd feel dreadful if I knew I'd kept you away from your friends. Besides, I really would like to finish my novel.''

"Oh,'' Lee said bleakly. "I guess I could go.''

"Yes, dear, you should,'' she said, rising. "I wouldn't ever want it said that I interfered in your life. A wife should support her husband in whatever he does and not hinder him.''

Lee pushed his chair back and started to rise. His side ached, and he wanted to stay home and read the newspaper, but then it was true that he hadn't visited his club since he'd been married. Maybe Blair was right and he should go. He could sit down there as well as at home, and maybe he could find out what they'd heard about the shooting at the mine last night.

"All right," he said. "I'll go, but I won't stay long. Maybe we can talk when I get back."

"One of a wife's duties is to listen to her husband," Blair said, smiling. "Now, you go along, dear, to your club. I have a little sewing to do, then an early night." She kissed his forehead. "I'll see you in the morning." She swept from the room before Lee could say a word.

Upstairs, she watched him from the guest room window. He moved awkwardly, and she knew his side hurt, but she didn't feel much guilt about sending him away alone. He certainly deserved to be taught a lesson.

When the carriage was out of sight, Blair went downstairs and called Nina.

"Let's go riding tomorrow," Blair said, "or I may go crazy from lack of exercise. Do you think your father can get me into the hospital to see a patient tomorrow? In secret? Without anyone knowing I was there?"

Nina was silent a moment. "I'm sure he can, and, Blair, welcome home."

"It's good to be home," she said, smiling. "I'll meet you at nine at the fork of the Tijeras." She heard Nina hang up the phone, then said sharply, "And, Mary Catherine, if one word of this leaks out, I'll know who did it."

"I resent that, Blair-Houston," the telephone operator said. "I do not eaves—." She realized what she was saying and pulled the plug on the line.

Blair went to the kitchen, where she fixed herself a roast beef sandwich. At dinner, she'd had such a ladylike portion that now she was starving.

By the time Lee came home, she was already in bed and pretending to sleep. And when he began to caress her hip and raise her nightgown, she pleaded tiredness, told him she had a splitting headache. As he turned away, Blair had second thoughts about what she was doing. Was she hurting herself more than him?

"It's osteomyelitis," Blair said to Reed, as she carefully put the man's hand down. "Next time you hit someone in the mouth, find someone who brushes his teeth," she told the patient.

"I believe that was Lee's thought, too," Reed said. "But he wanted another opinion."

She closed her medical bag and moved toward the door. "I'm flattered he chose me to ask. But it's agreed that you won't tell him I was here?"

Reed frowned, his ugly face moving into deep round furrows. "I've agreed, but I don't like it."

"As you've agreed to help Lee with whatever he does that brings him home with bullet wounds?"

"Lee was shot?" Reed gasped.

"A few inches to the left and the bullet would have pierced his heart."

"I didn't know. He didn't tell—."

"It seems that he doesn't tell anyone much about himself. Where does he go that makes him come home bloody?"

Reed looked at his daughter-in-law, saw the fire burning in her eyes, and knew he couldn't tell her about Lee's trips into the mines. Not only did he owe respect to his son's wishes, but he didn't trust Blair's save-the-world personality. It was just like her to do something foolish—maybe as foolish as what Lee was doing. "I can't tell you," he said at last.

Blair merely nodded and left the room. Outside, a saddled horse was waiting for her, and she rode hard and fast to reach the south fork of the Tijeras River where she was to meet Nina.

Nina looked up at Blair, then at the horse, both sweaty, both panting. "My brother caused you to run like this?"

Blair dismounted. "He is the most infuriating, close-mouthed, secretive, impossible man alive."

"I agree, but what's he done specifically?"

Blair began to unsaddle her horse to let the poor animal rest. "Did you know that your father calls him, day or night, wherever he is, then Lee disappears for hours and refuses to tell anyone where he's gone? Two days ago, he came home with two bullet wounds in his side and Pinkertons chasing him all the way to the front door. *They* were the ones who shot at him. What is he *doing?*" she yelled, as she dropped the saddle to the ground.

Nina's eyes were wide. "I have no idea. Has this been going on for long?"

"I don't know. I'm considered too stupid to know. I'm just allowed to sew up his wounds, not to question where he got them. Oh, Nina, what am I supposed to do? I can't just stand by and watch him leave and not know if he'll ever come back."

"Pinkertons shot at him? Then what he's doing must be . . ."

"Illegal?" Blair asked. "At least, on the far side of the law. And you know something, part of me doesn't even *care*. All I want is his safety. I'm not sure it'd matter to me if he were robbing banks in his spare time."

"Robbing—?" Nina sat down on a rock. "Blair, I really have no idea what he's doing. Dad and Lee always protected me from any unpleasantness. And Mother and I always protected them from what unpleasantness we saw. Maybe Mother and I were too involved in what we were secretly doing to think that our men had any secrets."

With a sigh, Blair sat down by her sister-in-law. "Lee found out about my taking the pamphlets into the mine."

"I'm glad to see your head's still on your shoulders. First time you'd seen his temper?"

"And the last, I hope. I tried to tell him that I was just as upset by his disappearances as he was by mine, but he wouldn't listen to me."

"He has a head made of marble," Nina said resignedly. "Now, what are we going to do? No one else has access to the mines, and if Lee found out so easily, I'd be afraid to send the pamphlets with Houston or the other wagon drivers."

"Yesterday, I had time to think, and something Houston said gave me an idea. She said she'd always wanted to write for a ladies' magazine. What if we started a magazine and, out of a sense of charity, we gave copies to the ladies of the coal mines? We could submit preview copies to the mining board for approval, and I'm sure they'd let us distribute it, since it'd be full of utterly innocuous articles."

"On the latest hair styles?" Nina asked, eyes beginning to light up.

"Our most militant plea will be to stop the South American slaughter of hummingbirds for feathers on ladies' hats."

"And not one word about organizing a union?"

"Not one word anyone can *see*."

Nina smiled. "I think I'm going to like your explanation. Oh, Alan, please finish school so we can come home. *How* will we include our information?"

"Code. I read of a code used during the American Revolution. It was a series of numbers and letters that referred to a specific page in a specific book. The numbers referred to letters and, with a little counting, you could figure out the message. I would imagine that every house has a Bible."

Nina stood, her hands clenched in excitement. "We could put a psalm reference in the first page of the magazine and then . . . How do we disguise the numbers? Won't the mining committee be suspicious of a page of numbers in a ladies' magazine? After all, we ladies don't understand mathematics."

Blair gave her a cat-that-swallowed-the-cream smile. "Crochet patterns," she said. "We'll have pages of crochet patterns full of numbers. We'll put in a 'to make the left sleeve' now and then, but the entire thing will be in code, telling the miners what's going on across the country with the unions."

Nina closed her eyes and put her head back for a moment. "It is absolutely brilliant, Blair, and, more important, I think it'll work. You're at the clinic all the time, so I'll go to the library and study this code and—."

"I won't be at the infirmary for a few days," Blair said, unsmiling.

"But the last I heard, you had so many patients, they were waiting on the street."

Blair looked away toward the river. "I did," she said softly, then abruptly stood. "I could strangle your brother sometimes!" she said passionately. "I'm trying to teach him a lesson, but he may be too pigheaded to learn. He thinks he's my father! He gives me presents—a women's infirmary—he gives me orders, he supervises everything I do and, when I dare ask about him, he acts scandalized, as if I were a child asking her father how much money he earns. I know so little about Leander. He doesn't share one single thing about himself with me, but I can't even step out the door without his knowing about it. I don't want another father, I'm perfectly content with the one I had. But how do I teach him I'm not a little girl?''

"I never made any progress," Nina said. "It's a wonder my father doesn't still buy me dolls for my birthday. You said you were trying to teach Lee a lesson. How?"

"I, ah . . ." Blair looked away. "He keeps telling me he wants a lady, so I've been trying to be one."

Nina thought for a moment. "You mean as in bubble baths and being helpless and crying over broken dishes?"

Blair turned back with a grin. "And spending too much and eating chocolates and having headaches at night."

Nina began to laugh. "I warn you that it may take Lee ten years to realize he's being taught a lesson. You ought to exaggerate what you do. Too bad you can't faint at the sight of a hangnail."

Blair sighed. "So far, except for the headache, he's liked what I've done. He doesn't mind if I just stay home all day and give directions to Mrs. Shainess."

"But you're going crazy, right?"

"Not anymore." Blair smiled. "This afternoon, I'll start working out a code for the unionist material. At least, that'll give me something to do. If I continue staying home, my mother might start sending me baskets of berries to can."

"I have a damson plum recipe that—."

"Will make your mouth cry with joy," Blair finished. "I've heard of it," she said, as she put the saddle back on the horse. "I'm not yet reduced to collecting recipes, but if I look at another fabric swatch, I may actually faint. I'll call you tomorrow and tell you how I'm doing on our crochet patterns. I'd like to get them done before we start on the rest of the magazine, and before we let anyone know of our plans. We'll print them and show the others what we're talking about. When do you have to return to Philadelphia?"

"Another ten days. It's going to seem like an eternity before Alan finishes school."

"I want you to meet my aunt and uncle in Pennsylvania. I'll give you their address and write them about you. And I have a few friends there. You won't be entirely alone."

"Thank you. Maybe they'll help make the time pass faster. Good luck with Lee," she called, as Blair mounted and rode away.

Chapter 33

After four days of being the perfect lady, Blair didn't know whether she was going to be able to stand the strain. Concerning herself with little more than the mundane duties of running a household was making her tired and cross. And the worst part of it was trying to teach a man a lesson when he didn't even know he was in school. He'd had four days of seeing his wife as a semi-invalid, no sex, and all Blair had heard from him was a mumbled, "Guess the honeymoon's over."

During the day, she worked on the code until she was nearly blind, counting words and making notes and translating Nina's pamphlet into a bizarre combination of words and numbers.

By the morning of the fifth day, she was sure that she couldn't last much longer. She left the house with the intention of going shopping and purchasing something frivolous that she could show Lee but, instead, she ended up in Mr. Pendergast's bookstore looking for anything she could find about medicine.

She wasn't even aware of anyone near her until the man spoke.

"He's to deliver the goods on Thursday night."

Blair looked up to see the man Lee had called LeGault standing near her. She had to control a shudder that threatened to shake her. If the man were lying on a cot, bleeding, she wouldn't mind touching him, but, alive and well, she couldn't bear to stand even this close to him. With a slight, cool nod to him, she moved away.

She was looking over a copy of *She* by H. Rider Haggard when her head came up. What had he said to her?

She looked around the store until she saw him about to leave. "Sir," she called, and was aware of the curious looks she received from the store owner and the two women customers in the back. "I found the book you said you were looking for."

LeGault smiled at her. "Thank you so much," he said loudly before moving toward her.

Blair knew that now she had to think as fast as she'd ever thought in her life. She didn't want this man to know that she knew nothing about what he was referring to. And, at the same time, she wanted to find out all that she could.

"He's to deliver them the same place as last time?" she asked.

"Exactly." He was examining the book as if fascinated by it. "There'll be no problems, will there?"

"None." She hesitated. "Except that this time, I'll be making the delivery."

LeGault put the book back on the shelf. "It's not what I was looking for after all," he said loudly. "Good day to you, ma'am." He tipped his hat and left the store.

Blair waited for as long as she dared, then left behind him. Since it seemed that anything that one of the Chandler twins did was news, she could almost feel the eyes of the people in the bookstore watching her as she left. Taking her time to pull her gloves on securely, she could see, out of the corner of her eye, LeGault heading east on Second Street toward Parkers' Ladies Wear. Blair went north, behind the Denver Hotel, across Lead, behind the Raskin Building and came out again on Second—away from the prying eyes of the customers of Mr. Pendergast's bookstore.

LeGault was sauntering down the street, cane over his arm,

looking for all the world like a man window-shopping without a care in the world. Blair crossed the street and went to look in the window of the Parker store.

She didn't feel that she had time for small talk with the man. "I know all about everything."

"I thought you did, or I wouldn't have mentioned it to you in the first place." He was looking straight ahead into the window. "But it's not a place for a woman."

"I don't imagine it's a place for a man, either."

He looked at her. "Imagine? I thought you knew."

"I do. I also know that this is the last time my husband will be doing this. He hasn't recovered from his wounds last time, and so I must take his place. After that, you'll have to do what you must by yourself. Neither of us will be involved again."

He seemed to be thinking about her words. "All right then. Thursday night at ten. Meet us at the usual place."

He started to turn away.

"Where should I leave my carriage? I don't want it recognized."

He turned back. "I'm beginning to doubt the wisdom of this. Are you sure you can handle this? That you know what's involved?"

Blair thought it was better to keep her mouth shut, so she just nodded.

"We'll need your carriage, so park it behind the Aztec Saloon on Bell Lane. Wait there, and someone will meet you and give you the trunk. Don't fail me. If you don't show up, it'll be your husband that catches it."

"I understand," she whispered.

For the two days until Thursday, Blair was utterly stupid. She couldn't seem to remember anything, do whatever she was supposed to do, or think of anything besides what she was to do on Thursday night. On that night, she would find out what it was that her husband was doing in secret. She'd told Nina that she didn't care if he were a criminal or not, that she loved him just the same. But soon the moment of truth would come. She was sure that Lee was involved in something illegal, and now she was going to participate in order to keep Lee out of it. She was hoping that what she did would make him stop whatever he was doing.

On Thursday night, she dressed in her medical uniform. Lee was called to the hospital to sew up three gunslingers who had shot it out near the New Mexico border, so Blair was alone. She was frightened and nervous as she went down the stairs to the stable where her carriage awaited her.

Only once before had she been to the part of town where she was to wait for LeGault, and that was the night she'd been with Lee when he ran to save the prostitute who'd tried to commit suicide. Ignoring catcalls at the sight of a woman alone in this area, she pulled in behind the Aztec Saloon and waited.

Kane Taggert woke slowly, feeling that something was wrong but not knowing what it was. The bed was vibrating and he was cold. Startled, he turned to Houston. She was shivering violently, and although she was huddled under covers, she was very cold to touch. He gathered her in his arms and, to his consternation, she still seemed to be sleeping.

"Houston, honey," he said with gentleness but some urgency. "Wake up."

The moment Houston woke, she began to shiver even more as Kane held her.

"My sister is in danger. My sister is in danger," she repeated. "My sister—."

"All right," Kane said, getting out of bed. "You just stay here, I'll call her house and see what's goin' on."

Kane took the stairs down two at a time and ran into the library. There was no answer to the ringing at the Westfield house. The operator said she thought Leander'd been called to the hospital, that there'd been a shooting in the country and he was needed. Kane put a call through to the hospital. The nurse who answered was reluctant to summon Leander to the telephone.

"I don't care what he's doin', it ain't as important as this. Tell him his wife's life is in danger."

Leander was on the phone in under a minute. "Where's Blair?"

"I don't know. Houston's upstairs shiverin' so bad she's about to break the bed and she's colder'n a corpse. She keeps sayin' Blair's in danger. I don't know nothin' else, but I thought you should know. She wasn't like this when Blair was taken by that Frenchwoman, so maybe she's really in danger this time."

"I'll find out," Lee said and put down the receiver to break the connection, then picked it up again. "Mary Catherine," he said to the operator, "I want you to find my wife. Call whomever you have to, but find her as soon as possible. And don't let anyone know you're looking for her."

"I'm not sure I should after what she said to me last week. She accused me of *eavesdropping.*"

"You find her, Mary Catherine, and I'll see that she delivers all your children for free—and your sister's. And I'll remove those warts off your right hand."

"Give me an hour," the operator said and pulled the plug.

Lee was sure it was the longest hour of his life. He went back to surgery and was glad to see that Mrs. Krebbs had sewn the wounded gunslinger back together. She had a few things to say to him about leaving the operating room, but he didn't listen. All he could think of was that he was going to kill Blair when he got his hands around her neck. No wonder she'd been so docile lately: she'd probably been planning something that was putting her life in danger.

He went back to the big entry hall of the hospital where the telephone was and smoked one cigar after another, until some of the nurses began to complain about the smoke. He growled so fiercely at the lot of them that they retreated timidly. He paced by the telephone, and when a proud new father started to pick it up, Lee threatened his life and his descendants if he so much as touched the thing. Every two or three minutes, he picked up the receiver to ask Mary Catherine what she'd heard. After the fifth such questioning, she told him she couldn't find out anything if he kept taking her time.

He managed to stay off the phone for an entire five minutes before he reached for it again. It rang as his hand touched it. "Where is she?" he demanded.

"We should have been able to guess. Someone—and I am not at liberty to say who for fear this person's reputation would be damaged forever—said they saw her down past the railroad tracks, pulling in behind the Aztec Saloon. Not that I know where that is, because I've certainly never been there, and Blair shouldn't have been there—."

"Mary Catherine, I love you," Lee said as he dropped the telephone on the nurse's desk and ran out the door.

His Appaloosa was trained to move quickly, and the town was used to getting out of the way for Lee's carriage, but tonight, Lee outdid himself as he tore through the streets and across the Tijeras bridge to the part of town that Blair should not have been in. He kept thinking that maybe someone had come to his house wanting help, and Blair'd stupidly gone with the person, but, for some reason, Lee was sure that she was into something more than just a medical case.

At the Aztec Saloon, he left his horse to stand, untied, as it had been trained to do, and went inside. One of the benefits of being a doctor was that he was well known, and that if someone didn't owe him a favor now, they probably would very soon.

"I want to talk to you," Lee said to the big man behind the bar.

Ignoring a customer's request for more beer, the man walked out from behind the bar and nodded to Lee to follow him into a back room.

"Wait a minute!" a cowboy shouted as he was unbuckling his pants. A woman, dirty, bored-looking, lay on a filthy mattress.

"Get out," the bartender ordered. "And you, too, Bess."

Tiredly, the woman got up and started toward the door. "I thought I got lucky this time, and you was comin' to me," she said as she smiled at Lee and ran her fingertips across his jaw before leaving the room.

When they were alone, Lee turned to the bartender. "I heard my wife was waiting behind here tonight. I figure you have to know something about why."

The man ran his hand over a three-day growth of beard,

then toyed with one of his many chins. "I don't like gettin' mixed up with somethin' like this. LeGault and that woman of his—."

"What's that piece of slime got to do with this?" Lee asked.

"He was the one she was waitin' for."

Lee turned away for a moment. He had hoped that he was wrong and Blair was only repairing somebody, but if she was meeting LeGault . . . "You don't have a choice in this," he said to the fat man. "I don't want to use blackmail or bring the sheriff into this, but I mean to use any method I can to find my wife."

"The sheriff's already in this, and he's after LeGault and that woman. Course they'll look innocent, 'cause that feisty little wife of yours is doin' all their dirty work."

Lee leaned toward the man. "You'd better tell me all of it and fast."

"It's none of my business what they do. I just sell them a little whiskey and mind my own business. All right, don't get so riled up, I'll tell you. LeGault rented a room from me so he could hide a woman in it. I don't know who she was and I only saw her once. Talked funny. A foreigner."

"French?" Lee asked.

"Yeah, maybe. She was a looker, anyway."

"So, LeGault was planning something with Frankie," Lee said thoughtfully. "What else do you know?"

"I happened to overhear them sayin' somethin' about gettin' the goods out of town, and that they was lookin' for somebody nobody would suspect. They talked about this a lot."

Lee turned around and slammed his fist into the wooden wall. The pain did him good. "So they found somebody stupid enough to be suckered in. Where did they go, and what did they want taken out of town?"

"I don't know. I guess you could ask LeGault. He's sittin' in a bar down the street. I told him to get out of here, since I didn't want no ladies in here 'cause they do nothin' but cause trouble."

Lee didn't say a word before he left the room and was soon on the street again. He slammed into three bars before he found LeGault. He didn't speak to the man but walked straight toward him, grabbed him by the shirt front and hauled him out of the chair.

"You want to come with me peacefully or dripping blood?"

The cards dropped from the gambler's hands and he moved his feet to regain his balance. He gave Lee a quick nod as Lee began to shove him out the back door. No one followed them into the alley, whether because they didn't care, or because they didn't want to anger a doctor, wasn't clear.

Leander was so angry that he could barely speak. "Where is she?"

"It's too late for that now. You should have been here a couple of hours ago."

Lee grabbed the man's shirt front and slammed him against the back wall of the saloon. "I've never killed a man in my life, and I took an oath to save lives, but so help me, LeGault, if you don't answer me right now, I'll break your scrawny little neck."

"By now, she's in the hands of the sheriff, no doubt under arrest for stealing a million dollars' worth of securities."

Lee was so astonished that he released the man and took a step backward. "Where? How?" he managed to whisper.

"I told you I'd get back at you for all those years I spent in jail. She was easy. She thinks she's saving your life, but instead, she's taking stolen goods out of town, and the sheriff has been informed of what she's doing, and by now she's in his custody. I hope you like seeing her in jail."

As Lee raised his hand to strike LeGault, the man began to sneer. "I wouldn't try it if I were you. I have a pistol aimed at your belly. Now, why don't you be a good boy and go visit that pretty wife of yours in her cell? I'm sure it'll be the first of many such visits."

Lee didn't want to waste time on the man, and he didn't think he'd have the courage to shoot him, so he backed out of the alley—he didn't want to give LeGault a clear view of his back.

Lee ran down the street to where his buggy waited and, on second thought, he confiscated a big black gelding that stood tied to the hitching post, vaulted into the saddle and took off southeast out of town. The only place that could have a million dollars' worth of securities was the train station.

He came to a rise and, in the moonlight, he could see a buggy to his right and what could be a posse of men to his left. It looked as if Blair were riding into the men who meant to arrest her—and he was half a mile away.

Chapter 34

Leander kicked the horse, started yelling, fired his pistol, grabbed a rifle from the scabbard on the horse and began firing it, all at the same time. The poor horse, terrified of the strange rider and all the noise and gunpowder, bolted forward, tearing across the moonlit countryside at breakneck speed. Lee wanted to draw attention to himself, to get the posse's mind off his wife.

He succeeded.

When a few "stray" bullets landed a foot away from the lead horse of the posse, all the men halted, trying to control their horses, and giving Lee the precious minutes he needed to reach Blair before they did.

As it was, they all met at the same time. One glance at the sheriff's solemn face and Lee knew that what LeGault had said was true—they'd come to see if one of the Chandlers had indeed been involved in a robbery.

"Damn you!" Lee yelled at Blair as he pulled back on the horse's reins and dismounted, slapping the horse's rump to head it back toward the lights of town. "I can't trust you out of my sight for a minute." He climbed into the buggy, grabbed the reins from her and looked up at the sheriff. "Let a woman have her own carriage, and it's no telling how much trouble she'll get into. And this is the worst. Always doing things for other people, never taking into account her own safety."

The sheriff studied Lee for a long moment, a moment so long that Lee began to sweat.

"Boy, you oughta take care of your wife," the sheriff said solemnly. "Or somebody else might."

"Yes, sir," Lee said. "I'll have her taken care of by morning."

"Six hours, Leander. I'll give you six hours, and then I might be that somebody."

"Yes, sir," Lee said, and felt like crying, he was so grateful. "It won't take me that long, sir." He snapped the reins and moved the buggy off the road, heading it back toward the freight office.

Once they were on the road, Blair spoke for the first time. "So you did come, after all. How did you find out the delivery was tonight?"

Lee didn't look at her. "If you know what's good for you, you'll keep your mouth shut. Your silence may stop me from blistering your rear end and keeping you tied inside the house for the rest of your life."

"Me? Me!" she gasped, holding on to the side of the carriage. "I was just filling in for you. I hoped that if I took over for you once, you'd see the misery you put me through."

"Took over for *me!*" He turned toward her, and his eyes were blazing with rage. "Do you think *I* was stealing securities? That *I* was working with LeGault?"

"What else could you be doing? You don't make any money as a doctor, but you can afford all the medical equipment and the house and the expenses for me, and you come home with bullet wounds and . . ." She stopped as Lee halted the buggy fairly close to the dark freight office.

He jumped down. "Get down and let's see what LeGault planted on you."

As Blair moved, Lee opened the compartment in the back of the buggy and withdrew a small wooden chest and opened it, withdrawing large pieces of floridly engraved paper. He held them up to one of the two carriage lanterns. "Not only were you stealing, but these belong to Taggert and the Chandler National Bank. You could have bankrupted half the town."

Blair took a moment to realize what he was saying, and when it hit her, she sat down on the running board of the carriage. "Oh, Lee, I had no idea. I just thought—."

He grabbed her shoulders and pulled her up. "We don't

have time for remorse now. We have to see what LeGault did inside there. Get your bag." He unhooked a lantern from the carriage and began to run, Blair on his heels, her heavy medical bag in her hand.

There was only one entrance into the dark freight office, and as they entered, they saw the big, empty safe standing open, a body before it. Since neither the electric lines nor the telephone lines extended this far out of town, they had to keep the lantern lit.

Lee reached the man first. "It's Ted Hinkel. He's alive, but he's been hit on the head pretty hard."

Blair reached into her bag and withdrew the smelling salts. "If you weren't working with LeGault, where were you?"

Lee gave a big sigh as he took the salts. "I thought I could save you from yourself, but I guess I can't. I didn't tell you what I was doing, because I feared that you'd do some fool thing like this. The truth is, for some time now I've been sneaking unionists into the coal camps."

"Unionists?" she said blankly. "But LeGault—."

"How could you believe I'd have anything to do with a criminal like him? You yourself said that he hated me. I guess he found out about the unionists, figured I'd never tell you what I was doing and used what he knew to make you work for him. If you got the securities out of town, great; if you didn't, even better; he'd have repaid me for sending him to prison."

"But the money . . . ," Blair began as she moved the lantern closer to Ted's head. She was unable to comprehend what Lee was saying.

Lee was frowning at the inert young man as he tried to revive him. "How did somebody like me fall for somebody like you? I was raised to believe that how much money a man made was his business and his alone. My mother was from a very rich family, and I'm certainly not one of the richest men in America like Taggert, but I have more than enough. I even *told* you that."

"Yes, but the clinic cost so much."

Lee gritted his teeth and moved Ted upright. "If we ever get out of this, I'll show you my assets. I could afford twenty clinics."

"Oh," Blair said, and handed him carbolic and a cloth to clean the wound on Ted's head. "So I've just stolen . . . How much *have* I stolen?"

"One million dollars."

The bottle of carbolic dropped from her hand, but Lee caught it. "How did you know, and why was the sheriff there, and what was the talk of six hours about?"

"Houston sensed you were in danger and Mary Catherine found out where you'd last been seen. LeGault turned you in to the sheriff, and the sheriff's given me six hours to get the securities back before anyone knows they were stolen. Come on, Ted, wake up!"

Blair put her face in her hands. "Oh, Lee, I've made a mess of everything."

He barely glanced at her, as his concern was with the young man now. "That you have, sweetheart."

"Do you think I'll go to jail?"

"Not if we can get the securities back."

"And how do you plan to do that? Say, 'By the way, Ted, I found this outside'?"

"No, I . . ." His eyes lit. "He's coming to. Give me your underdrawers."

"Lee! Now's not the time—."

"I have some rope, and I'll use your drawers as a sling and lower the chest down the chimney. You have to convince Ted he saved it and the crooks never even got away with it."

Without another word, Blair stood, dropped her drawers, handed them to Lee, then sat and took Ted's head in her lap as Lee went outside.

"Ted! What happened?" she said, holding the salts under his nose.

"The station was robbed," he said, sitting up, his hand to his head. "I have to call Mr.—."

"You have to sit down," she said, helping him to stand, then almost pushing him into a chair. "I have to look at that cut."

"But I have to tell—."

"Here!" Blair put a stinging antiseptic on the cut, and the new pain weakened the young man enough that he leaned back in the chair. "Tell me what happened," she said.

"Two men came in and held a gun to my head. One of them, the little one, knew the combination to the safe."

Out of the corner of her eye, Blair could see something white appearing in the fireplace. "Turn this way toward the light. What happened then?"

"I just stood there while the little one opened the safe and took out a chest. I don't know what was in it. Then, somebody hit me on the head, and the next thing I knew, I woke up and you were here. Blair-Houston, I have to call—."

"That couldn't be *all* of the story. You must have put up a great struggle."

"But I didn't, I—."

"Ted, I want you to lie down on the floor for a minute or two. I'm worried about that cut. You've lost a lot of blood. Yes, that's right, stretch out behind that cabinet. I need to clean my instruments."

Blair ran to the fireplace, grabbed the white drawers and the rope off the chest and stuffed them into her medical case. "I think you'll be all right now, Ted. Why don't you come in here and get your gun, and I'll drive you to the sheriff's?"

Ted, with his hand to his head, walked haltingly around the cabinet, then stood staring in disbelief. "That's it."

"What do you mean?"

"The chest they stole. There it is. How long has it been here?"

"It was here when I came in. Do you mean the robbers didn't take it, after all? Gee, Ted, I know you said you put up a struggle, but you were being modest. Do you mean you prevented them from stealing the chest?"

"I . . . I don't know. I thought—."

"There's the evidence. You *must* have saved it. Ted, you're a hero."

"I'm not so sure. I seem to remember—."

"With a crack like that on your head, you're sure to be fuzzy, but the evidence is right here before us. Why don't we lock it in the safe, and I'll ride to the nearest telephone and get the sheriff out here? And the newspaper. They'll want to hear about *this*."

"I . . . I guess so." He straightened his shoulders. "Sure, why not?"

Blair put the chest in the safe, locked the door, helped Ted to a chair, then ran outside. Lee grabbed her hand and they ran to the buggy together. It was only a mile to the nearest telephone, and Lee suspected the sheriff had been waiting.

Lee put down the receiver, thanked the bartender for the use and went outside to where Blair waited for him in the buggy.

"Is it really over?" she asked, leaning back.

"The sheriff said LeGault and a very small man—who I suspect is Françoise—got on the train for Denver an hour ago. I don't think we'll see them for a while."

"And all along it was unionists," she murmured. "You know, Lee, I have some ideas about the unions in the coal mines, too. Maybe together we could—."

"Over my dead body!" he said, snapping the reins.

"What am *I* supposed to do? Stay home and darn your socks?"

"You're not bad at darning socks, and I *like* knowing where you are."

"Like you've known for the last couple of weeks?"

"Yeah, I rather like a wife who—."

"Let me tell you, doctor, if you think I'm going to read one more book about a simpering heroine or plan one more dinner, you're out of your mind. Saturday morning, I'm going back to *my* clinic and see to *my* patients."

"Saturday? What about today? Why don't I just drop you off there and you can go right to work?"

"Because I'm spending today in bed with my husband. I have a lot of lost time to make up for."

Lee gave her a quick, startled look, then grinned. "Hijah!" he yelled to the horse. "School's out and Teacher wants to play."

It was Blair's turn to look startled. "You *did* know!"

But Lee only grinned and winked at her.